PICTORIAL ESSAY
of
DIN DIN
BOOK NO. 1

PICTORIAL ESSAY
of
DIN DIN
BOOK NO. 1

A Walk Through Study Guide, Book One

Diane Sytarchuk-Kent

Library of Congress Control Number: 2018907864

ISBN:	Hardcover	978-1-9845-3472-9
	Softcover	978-1-9845-3471-2
	eBook	978-1-9845-3470-5

Print information available on the last page.

Rev. date: 07/05/2018

To order additional copies of this book, contact:
Xlibris
1-888-795-4274
www.Xlibris.com
Orders@Xlibris.com
778312

Din Din

Diane Sytarchuk
-Kent!

→ ? ←

! !

of

XX XX

??

NO non sense

Poetry

#1

1 2 3 4 5 6 7 8 9

Contents

6 contents titles: ~~Book~~#1 (111-157) (translated) #1

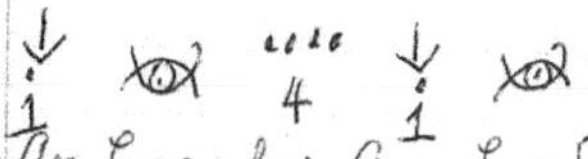

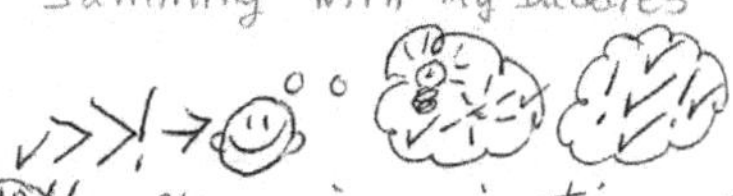

Jasmine G

Introduction

Introduction

Originally I made the social stories in the margins of each page. I had thought this would work. Then, I said to myself "why not do the social stories line by line, I can do it because I know how! I decided that is what I would do.

Originally I made the social stories in the margins of each page, I had thought this would work, Then, I said to myself "why not do the social stories line by line, I can do it because I know how! I decided that is what I would do,

My books are dedicated to Eric (my autistic so[n]) I wish I could have done this for him before he died.

My books are dedicated to Eric (my autistic so[n]) I wish I could have done this for him before he died,

Thank-you to all who helped Eric.

Thank-you to all who helped Eric,

My Dedication

My Dedication!

My poetry is by no means

My poetry is by no means

great or worthy of literary praise.

great or worthy of literary praise.

It is just meant to please all who love

It is just meant to please all who love

a good rhyme and to read out loud.

a good rhyme and to read out loud.

My autistic son gave me the idea of

My autistic son gave me the idea of

writing a book for my extended family - of lovers of

writing a book for my extended family - of lovers of

pictures with words rhyming. He loves rhyming

pictures with words rhyming. He loves rhyming

and pictures.

and pictures.

I only wish to improve social skills. Thank-You!

I only wish to improve social skills. Thank-You!

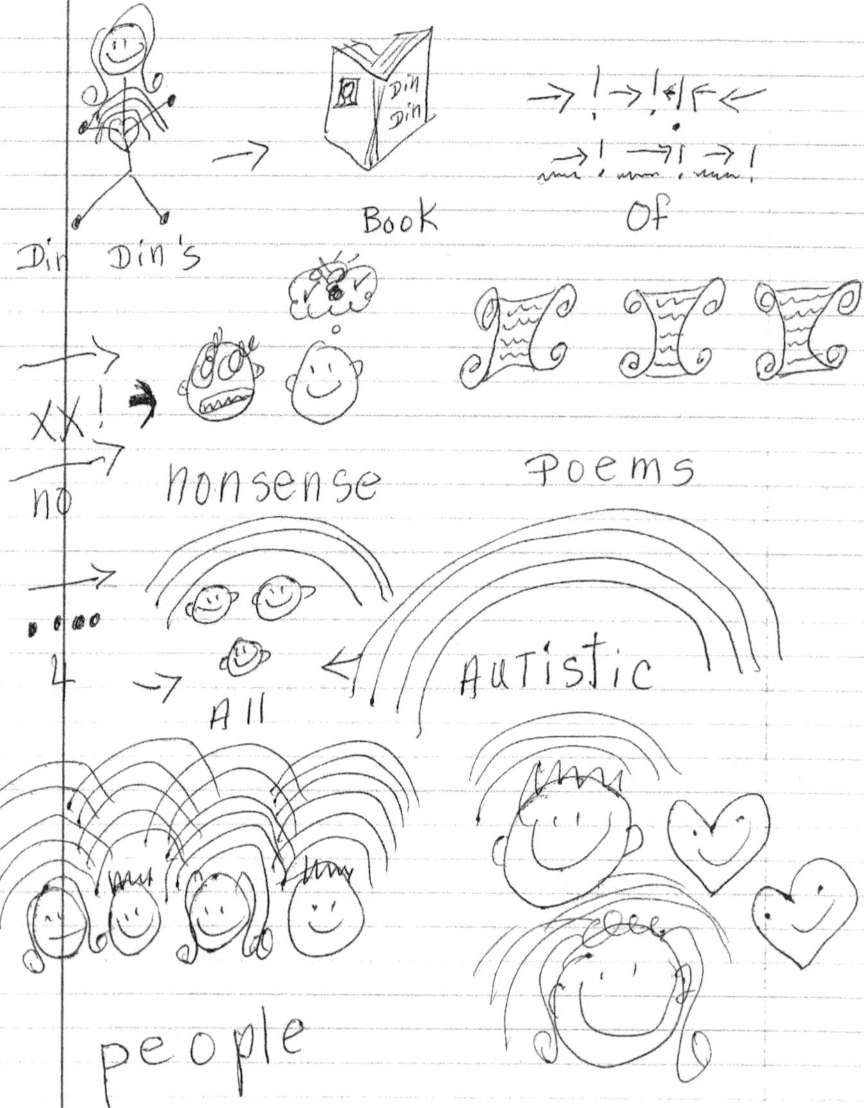
Din Din's
Din Din
Book
Of
XX!
no
nonsense
Poems
4
All
Autistic
people

13
page
DIN DIN
Din Din
BOOK
OF:
XX NONONSENSE
Poems
4
FOR
ALL
1
The
People
Stop
Like
ERIC

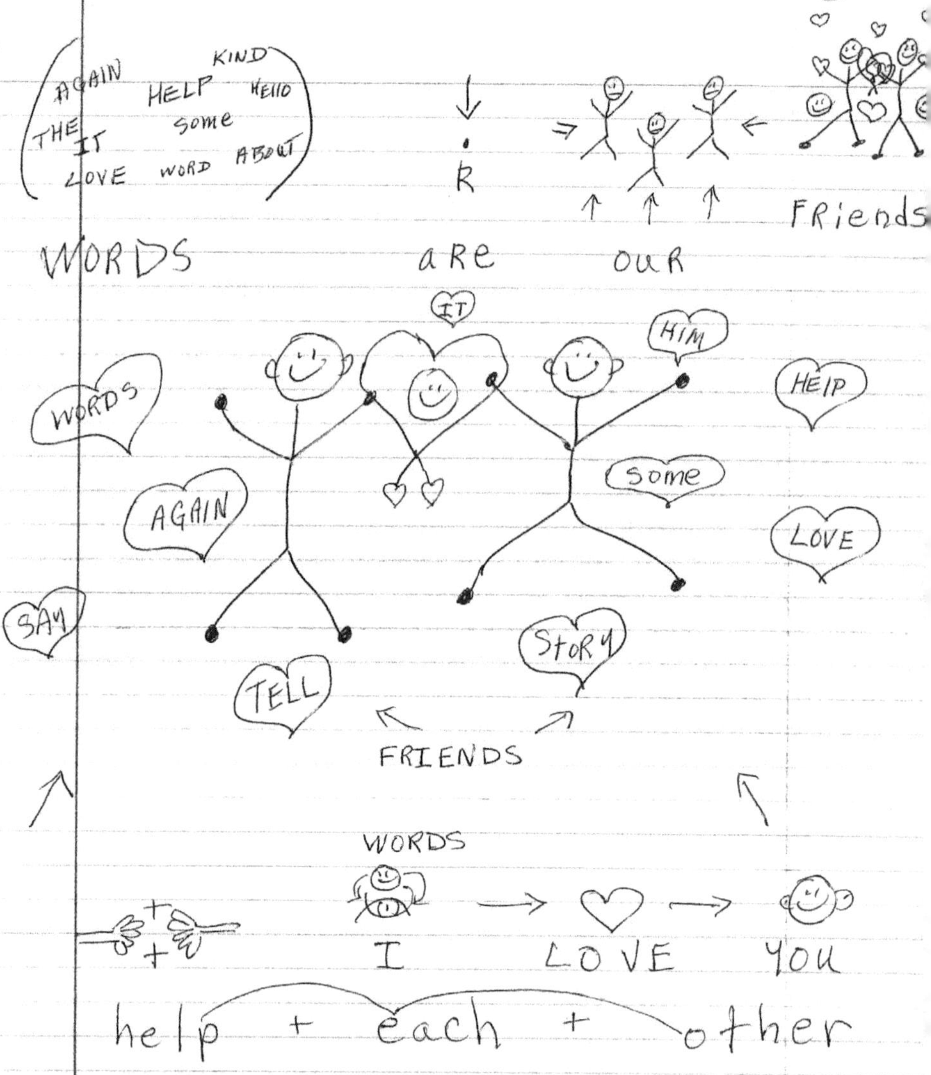
AGAIN
KIND
HELP
HELLO
THE
IT
some
LOVE
WORD
ABOUT
R
FRiends
WORDS
aRe
OUR
IT
HIM
WORDS
HEIP
AGAIN
some
LOVE
SAY
STORY
TELL
FRIENDS
WORDS
I
LOVE
YOU
help + each + other

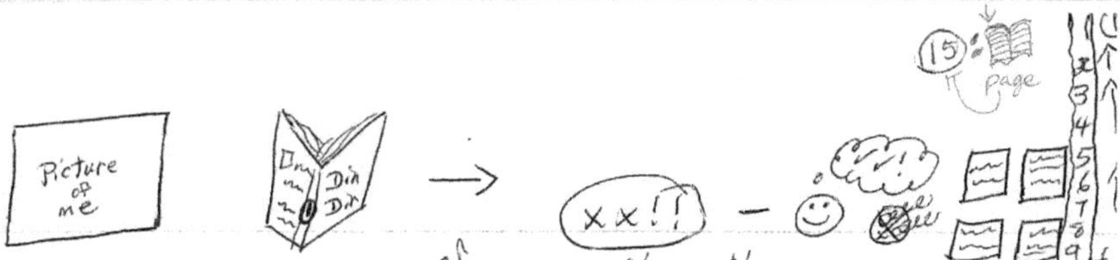

Din Din's Book of No-Nonsense Poetry

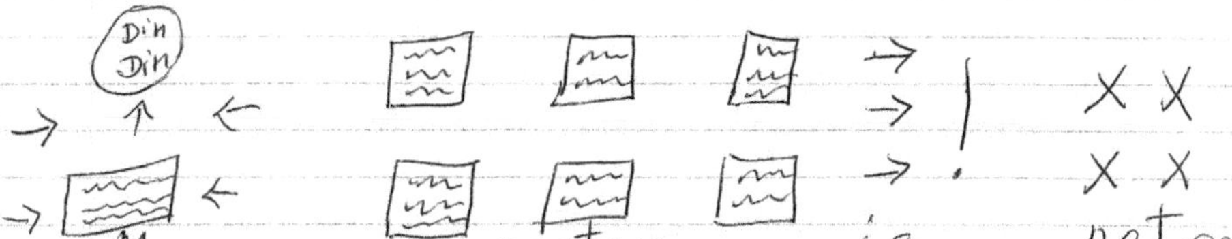

My poetry is not

made to make sense

just to entertain AND

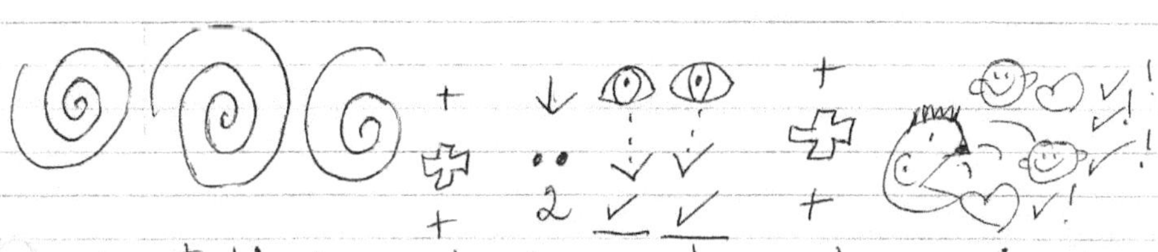

tantalise and to read and enjoy

page: 16

Contents

Contents

: 18
page

(19) page

Until The Time Comes
Cool As A Cucumber
Positive Reaction
Pray Pussy Riot But Not Too Hard
Neighbors
Who, You And Me, You Jest
Don't Hesitate
The Way It Is
That's Just Great
I Smell Success
Fifty-Five Or Something
I Just Made Myself Angry
I Have No Fear
The Law Of The Land
Here We Go Again And Again
The Blue-Bottomed Special
An Eye For An Eye

Sir?
Mr.?
Mrs.?
Ms.?
Miss?

page 44

Diane Sytarchuk-Jeir 23
1st page finished product
1st book 1st poem
#1

(25) Sign Your Name (1)
Sign Your Name

blah! blah! blah!

You can tell! All is well
You can tell! All is well

You can almost smell! All is well!
You can almost smell! All is well

It can't be hell! All is well!
It can't be hell! All is well!

RING!

I hear the final bell! All is well!
I hear the final bell! All is well!

We can all see! Turn the Key
We can all see! Turn the Key

WAIT

How beautiful they are, tee-hee!
How beautiful they are, tee-hee!

hee! hee! hee! hee! ho ho ho ho

We can giggle and laugh with glee
We can giggle and laugh with glee

SLOW 4 1 $ $ $

They are all shiny and new, for a small fee
They are all shiny and new, for a small fee.

RED

The color is red and will be here to stay
The color is red and will be here to stay

The cars are lined up in beautiful array
The cars are lined up in beautiful array

STOP STOP 2 8 2 2

The devil is just waiting to see what we will say
The devil is just waiting to see what we will say

ho ho ho ho

page (24) Diane Sytarchuk-Ken

2nd page finished produ

I can modify size or content as you wish,

Cold or hot, old or new
Cold or hot, old or new

Pink or orange, red or blue
Pink or orange, red or blue

Make a promise, me or you
Make a promise, me or you

The devil simply says, "Promise your soul too!"
The devil simply says, "Promise your soul too!"

He says you will all belong in the hall of fame
He says you will all belong in the hall of fame

Not one of them will be the same
Not one of them will be the same

All so beautiful each one you will claim
All so beautiful each one you will claim

Mr.? Mrs.? Miss? Sir? mame?

Just sign here. Sign your name.
Just sign here. Sign your name.

Each one
Each one

has a life of his own
has a life of his own

Wouldn't you like
Wouldn't you like

to take it home
to take it home

You don't even have to
You don't even have to

pay a loan Just avoid the fine print and

pay a loan Just avoid the fine print and

give me the phone Enjoy the rest of your

give me the phone Enjoy the rest of your

days They will go so fast they'll

days They will go so fast, they'll

seem like a haze Yes, it will be just a

seem like a haze Yes, it will be just a

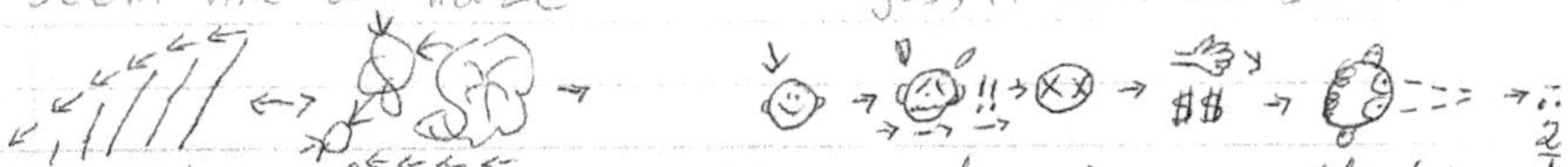

passing phase You need not pay attention to

passing phase You need not pay attention to

my evil gaze Later you will wish you could

my evil gaze Later you will wish you could

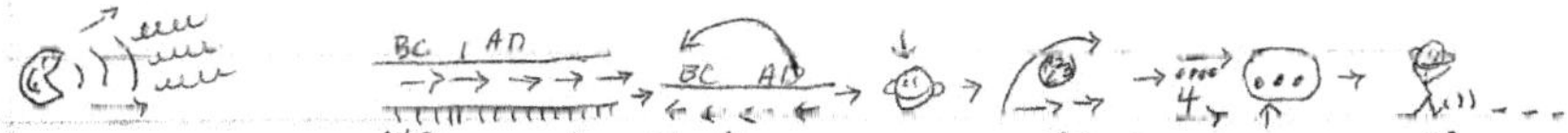

talk Through history you will forever walk

talk Through history you will forever walk

Some of you will roll. Some of you will rock.

Some of you will roll. Some of you will rock.

Silently on the devil's door you will forever knock

silently on the devil's door you will forever knock

26 page

(27) * I Don't Have A Care @
I Don't Have A Care @

- Me, I don't have a care
- Me, I don't have a care

I'm in a position that's rare
I'm in a position that's rare

You, sir, can go ahead and stare
You, sir, can go ahead and stare

I've got a very thick first layer
I've got a very thick first layer

- Underneath, I'm soft as a pillow
- Underneath, I'm soft as a pillow

And I can be weak as a young willow
And I can be weak as a young willow

Sometimes my life feels like I'm in a bowl of Jell-O
Sometimes my life feels like I'm in a bowl of Jell-O

Sometimes when I'm shy, I desperately want to say hello
Sometimes when I'm shy, I desperately want to say hell

– But all things aside
But all things aside,

I also have Rider pride
I also have Rider pride

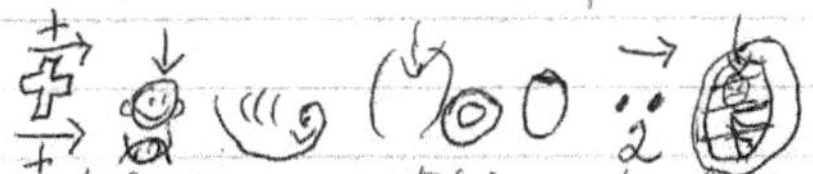

And I have nothing to hide
And I have nothing to hide

I feel, in you, I can confide
I feel, in you, I can confide

– What does this mean?
– What does this mean?

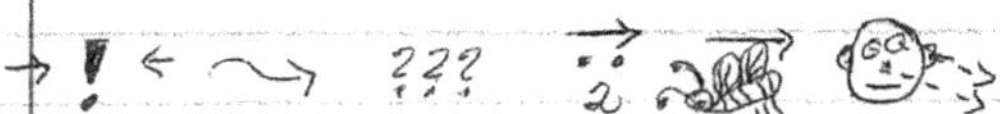

That has yet to be seen
That has yet to be seen

Go ahead. Tell me where you've been.
Go ahead. Tell me where you've been.

Say hello and then let's go green.
Say hello and then let's go green.

- I knew I was right
I knew I was right

Being honest doesn't bite
Being honest doesn't bite

But hey, what if he puts up a fight
But hey, what if he pats up a fight

I hope he also has poor eyesight
I hope he also has poor egesight

Come on closer, you make me quiver
Come on closer, you make me quiver

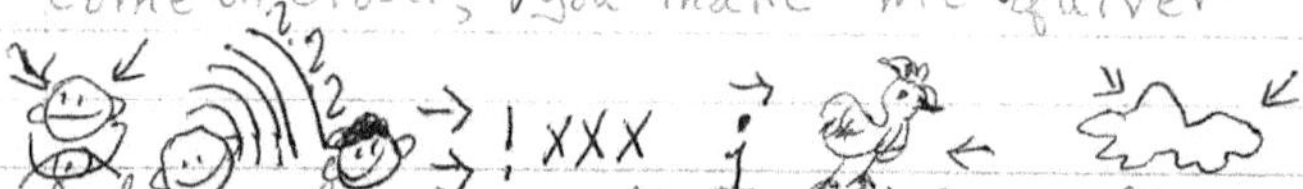

I hope he is not a chicken-liver
I hope he is not a chicken-liver

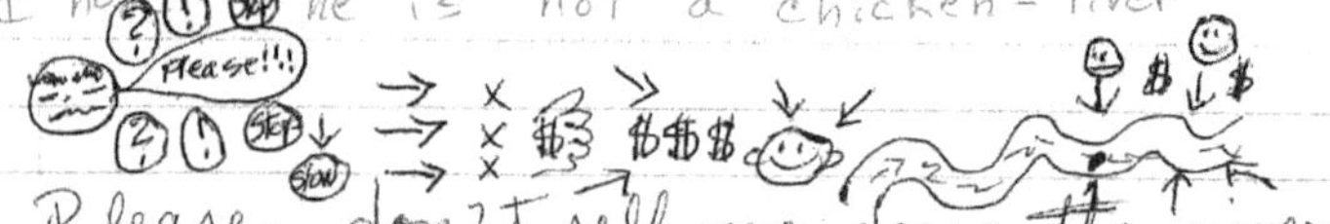

Please, don't sell me down the river
Please, don't sell me down the river

Close your eyes. Be a life-giver.
Close your eges. Be a life-giver.

– Inside I say, "I think I'm going to cheer,"
Inside I say, "I think I'm going to cheer,

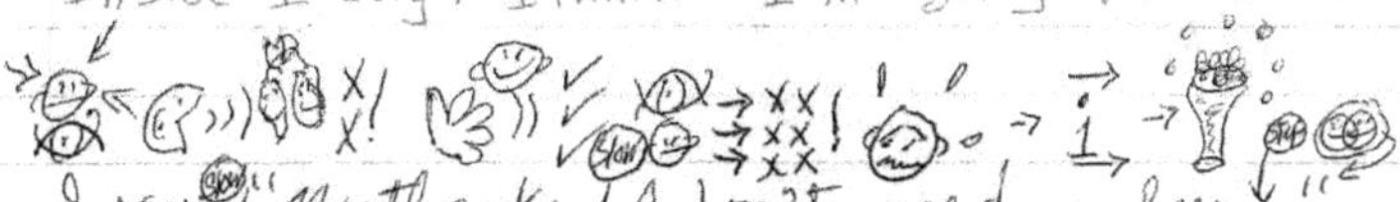

I say, "No thanks! I don't need a beer!"
I say, "No thank, I don't need a beer.

I tell myself I have nothing to fear!
I tell myself I have nothing to fear.

Because I'll stay sober and I will think clear!
Because I'll stay sober and I will think clear.

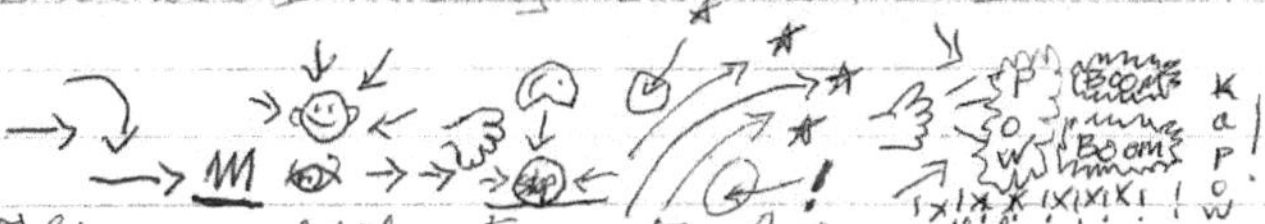

– This way I'll stay out of trouble
This way I'll stay out of trouble

Come on now, come on the double
Come on now, come on the double

Come by my side, on my side of the hovel
Come by my side, on my side of the hovel

Come on now, don't make me grovel
Come on now, don't make me grovel.

30: page

#3

29 I Will It 3

I know it, I will it For you I'm willing to commit

Come on over here, under my cockpit I mean it. We

make a perfect fit.

Come on over where it's cozy We'll be coming up

Rosie Me, myself, I am fancy free You, my dear

can be my sweet pea

If it was my choice I would use my

voice And make a lot of noise

And dedicate it to you my pride and joy
And dedicate it to you my pride and joy
Here's one for the Alamo I've been dealt a fatal blow
Here's one for the Alamo I've been dealt a fatal blow
I feel like I'm on death row I feel like your virtual yo-yo
I feel like I'm on death row I feel like your virtual yo-yo
If my attitude were to change It would be very strange
If my attitude were to change It would be very strange
It would feel like I was deranged So there's really
It would feel like I was deranged So there's really
no more need for interchange
no more need for interchange
After the dusk is a new dawn But I will feel like
After the dusk is a new dawn But I will feel like
I now belong And I will sing you a new song
I now belong And I will sing you a new song
After I will have energy for a marathon
After I will have energy for a marathon

Your love has left a deep welt
My offerings
will be heart felt
I am now beyond any human
help
Sending prayers, on my knees I have knealt
I will stand still. It is my will.
You can have your fi
I am an easy kill.
You fit my bill. You are far
from run of the mill.
I'll shout it from the
highest hill.
I'll love you forever and until.

(31) My Life's Brand New (4)

My Life's Brand New

My life's like brand new Before, my life was on hold and I

My life's like brand new Before, my life was on hold and I

was quite blue Until I met the man I love who

was quite blue Until I met the man I love who

I think loves me too

I think loves me too

Now I'll be a happy camper Only I can put on it

Now I'll be a happy camper Only I can put on it

any kind of damper By using any kind of harmful

any kind of damper By using any kind of harmful

$0.00

useless banter For sure, I would end up a guilty, lonely

useless banter For sure, I would end up a guilty, lonely

bystander My life is a series of bumps I must

bystander My life is a series of bumps I must

overcome and get over its many humps I have to

overcome and get over its many humps I have to

learn to get out of the dump And to take all life's lesson
learn to get out of the dump And to take all life's lesson

lumps It isn't always easy Sometimes it's
lumps It isn't always easy Some times it's

downright cheesy I admit it may be hard to please me
downright cheesy I admit it may be hard to please me

But I didn't guarantee I'd always be light and breezy
But I didn't guarantee I'd always be light and breezy

No matter what life throws at me My strong will will
No matter what life throws at me My strong will will

always be working for me I will overcome and
always be working for me I will overcome and

laugh with glee And I will always be free
laugh with glee And I will always be free

My enemies will run back to hell Because I'll
My enemies will run back to hell Because I'll

smile at them like all is well And act like everything
smile at them like all is well And act like everything

is swell And then they'll tip their hat and say farewell
So I'll be brand new again, don't you know I'll
have a satisfied glow It won't be one from down
below It'll be because I have defeated my foes
Because they have run away It will have made my
day They haven't had their way I'm
brand new and fresh; I can play

33 You Haven't Got A Clue 5

You Haven't Got A Clue

You haven't got a clue
You haven't got a clue

Just all what I can do
Just all what I can do

I'm able to be strong and stick like glue
I'm able to be strong and stick like glue

Or fly
Or fly

away and make something totally new
away and make something totally new

I like this certain ability
I like this certain ability

I like to pretend I am
I like to pretend I am

wise and witty
wise and witty

This makes me feel very pretty
This makes me feel very pretty

And makes me happy I live in the city
And makes me happy I live in the city

Sometimes when times are rough
Sometimes when times are rough

And we have
And we have

all had some of that stuff
all had some of that stuff

I like to think
I like to think

I can call your bluff
And then I will tell you, it
will get better, no guff

When all good things come to an end
I believe
good things are right around the bend
So
I tell you whatever life may send
You will
overcome and soon will be on the mend

And when everything seems to stop
And the
ink decides to blot
You will have had a
battle well fought
And success will be what you've got

When time stands still And tests your tremendous will
When time stands still And tests your tremendous will

And with all the memories they have instilled A
And with all the memories they have instilled A

picture will appear in your very own playwright's bill
picture will appear in your very own playwright's bill

And when you finally rest Then will come the final test
And when you finally rest Then will come the final test

Then you can laugh at it in jest You'll say go for
Then you can laugh at it in jest You'll say go for

it, be my guest
it, be my guest

The test that fits the bill Is that you must
The test that fits the bill Is that you must

have strength of will And if you learn to
have strength of will And if you learn to

cultivate this and learn to instill Then you
cultivate this and learn to instill Then you

will have peace of mind forever and until

will have peace of mind forever and until

A New Crop

A New Crop

(35) (6) (40) page

Look, we have a new crop We have a new
Look, we have a new crop We have a new

generation that will not stop Until the Garden of Eden
generation that will not stop Until the Garden of Eden

is again our lot and all our battles have been
is again our lot And all our battles have been

~~victoriously~~ victoriously fought
victoriously fought

This generation is our only salvation This is our
This generation is our only salvation This is our

newly created generation What we have created is
newly created generation What we have created is

our offering, our oblation Let them do right
our offering, our oblation Let them do right

without one moment's hesitation
without one moment's hesitation

They all come from good seed They come out of
They all come from good seed They come out of
their ancestor's need They are a totally new reed
their ancestor's need They are a totally new reed
They came from nature's strongest bead
They came from nature's strongest bead
With each succeeding line Our offering becomes more
With each succeeding line Our offering becomes more
refined It becomes more pure and more fine
refined It becomes more pure and more fine
We all know this is a very good sign
We all Know this is a vary good sign
These children are man's only hope So help them
These children are man's only hope So help them
understand the great scope And that their
understand the great scope And that their
reason for learning what all has been wrote
reason for learning what all has been wrote

Is to save all mankind even the scapegoat
Is to save all mankind even the scapegoat

We all started so long ago What was created
We all started so long ago What was create

began to grow We were and came to know wha
began to grow We were and came to know wh

it was to do so We also learned the differenc
it was to do so We also learned the differenc

between high and low
between high and low

Each generation has in turn gave in to their sons
Each generation has in turn gave in to their sons

And ~~each~~ also their daughters who has been the ones
And also their daughters who has been the on

Who, with the sons, had a little fun And
Who, with the sons, had a little fun And

began to carry a new generation on the run
began to carry a new generation on the run

Our progeny has the tremendous task of taking
Our progeny has the tremendous task of taking

off the human masks And showing us where we
off the haman masks And showing us where we

all lack And bringing humanity back onto
all lack And bringing humanity back onto

the right track
the right track

(37) My Mind Is Fit As A Fiddle (7)

My Mind Is Fit As A Fiddle

I may not be little And I may be round
I may not be little And I may be round

around the middle But I sure know how to
around the middle But I sure know how to

hee! hee! hee! hee!

boogie, and I sure know how to giggle And
boogie, and I sure know how to giggle And

what's more, I tell you, my mind is fit as a fiddle
what's more, I tell you, my mind is fit as a fiddle

Yes, it is true, I usually feel good Of this fact, I
Yes, it is true, I usually feel good Of this fact, I

will make sure to knock on wood Yes,
will make sure to knock on wood Yes,

I also know that sometimes things change!
I also know that sometimes things change!

Of this I agree, and this is understood
Of this I agree, and this is understood

With this in mind, I will try to stay in a good mood
No matter how you may work and scheme and work and
try
And try to stop me, I will try to be the
happy guy
Sure I have been sad and I have
been known to cry
Of that, I admit, this
is the truth and of
that I will agree
and I won't lie
You may wonder if I will ever turn the shade blue
I will tell you, I will give you a clue
My heart

will always stay like brand new Even when
will always stay like brand new Even when

it is blue, it will eventually turn happy once again
it is blue, it will eventually turn happy once again

too
too

You may think I am the healthy kind
You may think I am the healthy kind

But in truth, I am really way far behind
But in truth, I am really way far behind

But in attitude, I am a healthy find
But in attitude, I am a healthy find

And to the unjust, my heart can sometimes
And to the unjust, my heart can sometimes

be blind As well, when it comes to my
be blind As well, when it comes to my

final decision and in the end My opinions
final decision and in the end My opinions

can be found to sometimes bend And with
can be found to sometimes bend And with

my positive ideas I will try to share, lend,

my positive, ideas I will try to share, lend,

and send Also I will try to help and

and send Also I will try to help and

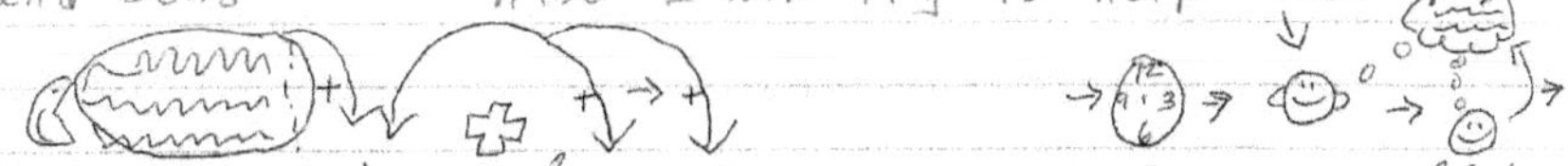

inform again and again When you think

inform, again and again When you think

about it, the Stradivarius was rare A

about it, the StradiVarius was rare A

Stradivarius cannot breathe or grow hair

Stradivarius cannot breathe or grow hair

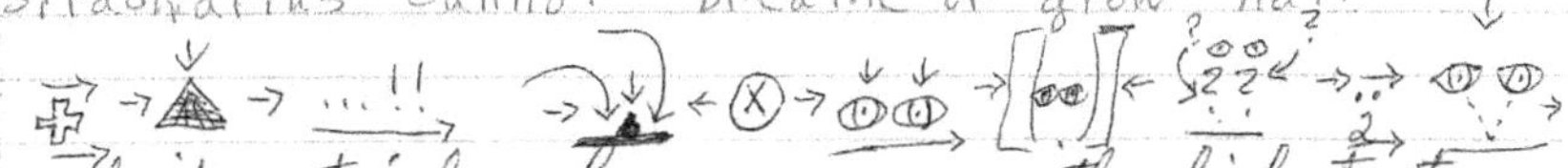

And it certainly has no eyes with which to stare

And it certainly has no eyes with which to stare

I tell you, all in all, I will be just fine Because

I tell you, all in all, I will be just fine Because

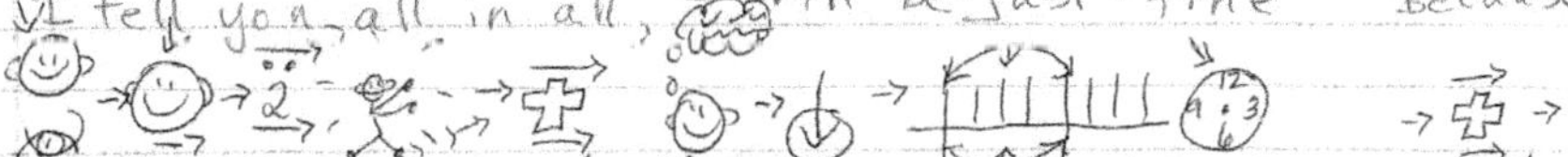

I like to live and think in quarter time And

I like to live and think in quarter time And

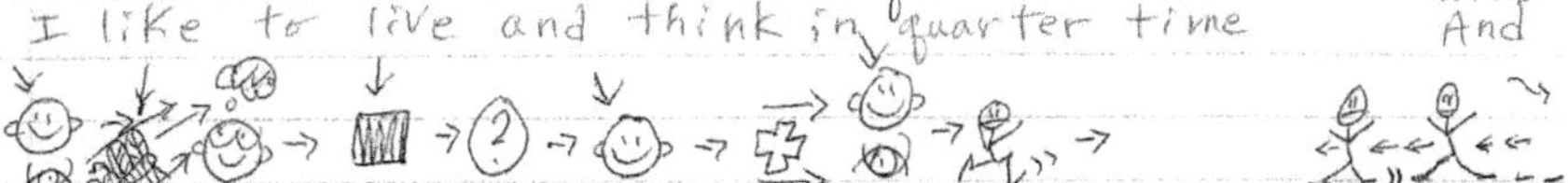

I believe that if you and I walk together

I believe that if you and I walk together

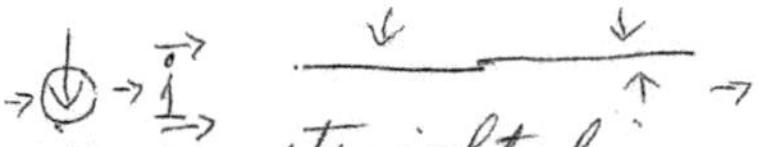

in a straight line

in a straight line

Success will be yours

Success will be yours

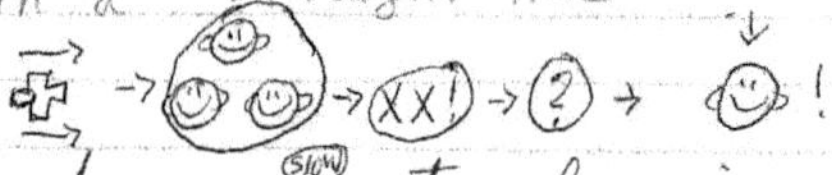

and ours, not only mine

and ours, not only mine

It Depends On How You Look At It

I say, it depends on how you look at it
You can see a
little, but I may see it different
You may think that
mean you harm, hurt, or torment
But that may not
really be what I intended or
what I really meant
It, or the idea, may also depend
On what your point of
view is or how it is sent
You may say you see clearly
but what you really mean
to say is I've had enough
Amen
Or you may decide to change your mind again and again

Try to see with your eyes closed, And instead see with your
Try to see with your eyes closed And instead see with your

ears and nose You will see what your other senses show
ears and nose You will see what your other senses show

And that's when you will see how it really goes
And that's when you will see how it really goes

When you are poor of spirit and you feel down You may be
When you are poor of spirit and you feel down You may be

close, just then to being glory bound And by being meek and not
close, just then to being glory bound And by being meek and not

making a sound Your voice may be heard all over and around
making a sound Your voice may be heard all over and around

Someone is bound to come around with a different point of view
Someone is bound to come around with a different point of view

The idea is bound to be something brand spanking new
The idea is bound to be something brand spanking new

After all, aren't the basics pink and blue And
After all, aren't the basics pink and blue And

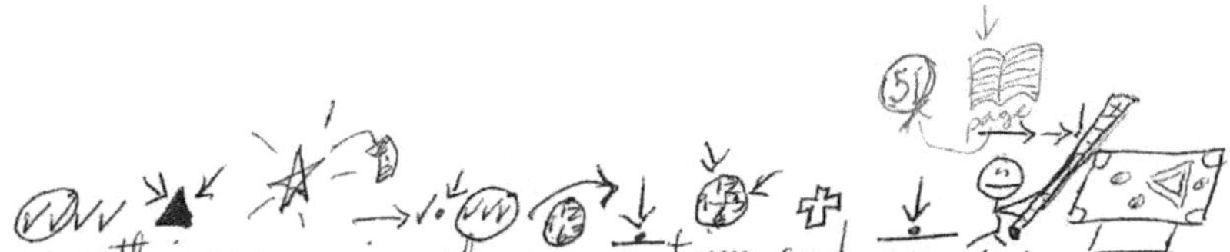

something new is always on time and on cue
something new is always on time and on cue

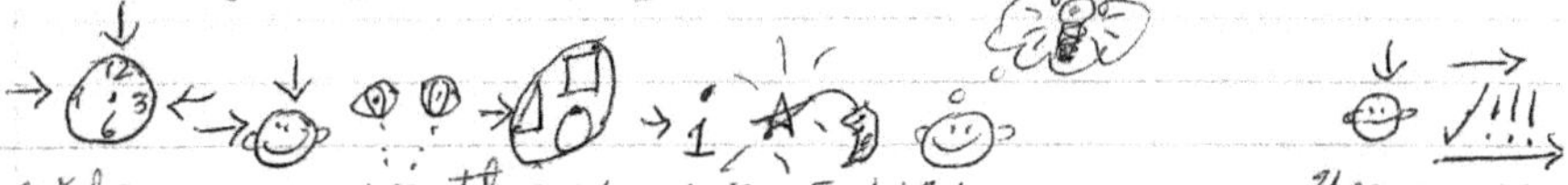

When you see things a new way You may
when you see things a new way You may

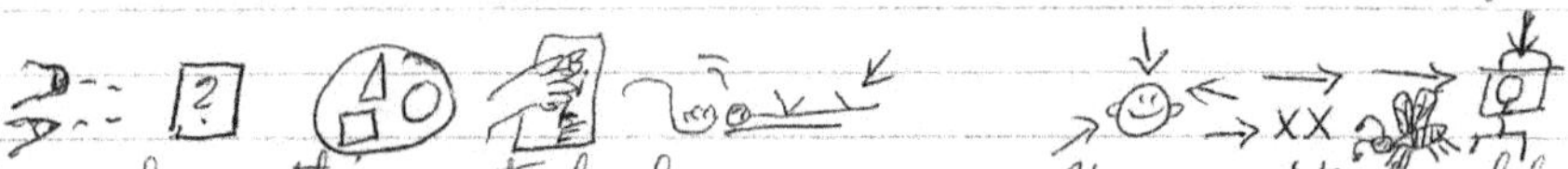

see how things truly lay You won't be able
see how things truly lay You won't be able

to help being merry and gay And you will
to help being merry and gay And you will

find lots of time to play
find lots of time to play

Just open your senses and your eyes Then you
Just open your senses and your eyes Then you

will see through people's lies And everywhere
will see through people's lies And everywhere

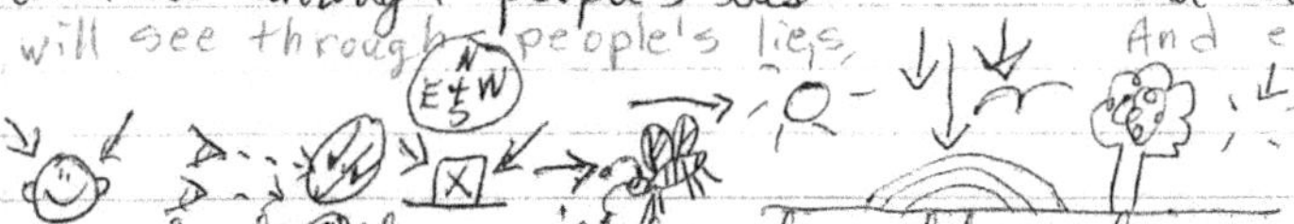

you look, there will be clear blue skies
You look, there will be clear blue skies

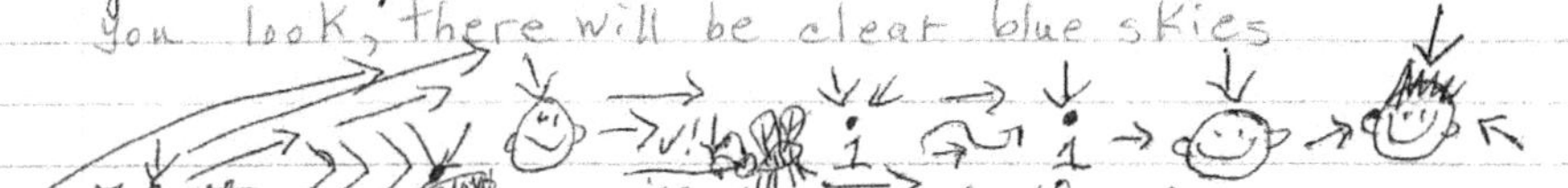

Furthermore, you will be one of the happy guys
Furthermore, you will be one of the happy guys

58 : page

You will join a brand-new sect
You will join a brand-new sect

People will trea
People will trea

you with more respect
you with more respect

You will be the one others
You will be the one others

choose to elect
choose to elect

This will be the cause, and that
This will be the cause, and that

will be the effect.
will be the effect

Interesting How It Looks

Interesting How It Looks

It is interesting how this world looks Our situation
It is interesting how this world looks Our situation
is one for the textbooks Right now it is OK as long
is one for the text books Right now it is OK as long
as we all keep a positive outlook. We just
as we all Keep a positive outlook. We just
have to overlook all our neighbor's dirty looks.
have to over look all our neighbor's dirty looks
The list to ignore and overlook goes on and on
The list to ig nore and over look goes on and on
It gets really long, disappears, and then is gone
It gets really long, disappears, and then is gone
Don't be put upon; just look at the pros and cons
Don't be put upon; just look at the pros and cons
Soon our troubles will all be gone and
Soon our troubles will all be gone and

we will see a shiny new dawn
we will see a shiny new dawn
thinking seriously; I am too
thinking seriously; I am too
many and quite similar, not just a few
many and quite similar, not just a few
have a right to be thinking about them
have a right to be thinking about them
hope they will be right on cue
hope they will be right on cue
thoughts are honest and true blue; All
thoughts are honest and true blue; All
want is a universal breakthrough
want is a universal breakthrough
follow these thoughts, they will make us all happy
follow these thoughts, they will make us all happy
There is no need to feel crappy or to disagree
There is no need to feel crappy or to disagree

I see you c
I see you c
Our thoughts a
Our thoughts ar
W
We
and
and
All our
All our
we
we
If we
If we

55 : page

We all have so much to be thankful for if we all
We all have so much to be thankful for if we all

just choose to agree We have so much in
just choose to agree We have so much in

common, we can grow to love each other and be
common, we can grow to love each other and be

happy and carefree I will listen to your voice
happy and carefree I will listen to your voice

and you can listen to mine That would be
and you can listen to mine That would be

my first choice for humankind We would
my first choice for humankind We would

love to hear a new peace redefined
love to hear a new peace redefined

What to me is so dear can be there for all
What to me is so dear can be there for all

combined. My ideas are molded by many,
combined. My ideas are molded by many,

56 page

many thoughts And by the way my brain is

many thoughts And by the way my brain is

folded. Besides, I am mostly self-taught

folded. Besides, I am mostly self-taught

And by the way it reacts when it is in a tight spot

And by the way it reacts when it is in a light spot

And by the words with which it has ~~been fed~~

And by the words with which it has

been fed, all food for thought Why do you

been fed, all food for thought Why do you

torture me by ignoring my particulars

torture me by ignoring my particular

information booth Just because you may want

information booth Just because you may want

to own the fountain of youth What I offer

to own the fountain of youth What I offer

To you is tax free and takes no super

to you is tax free and takes No super

intelligent sleuth
intelligent sleuth

If you listen, you won't
If you listen, you won't

be sorry. I'll guarantee
be sorry. I'll guarantee

you will go straight
you will go straight

to your nearest voting
to your nearest voting

stall and the result
stall and the result

will ~~go straight~~ quite reboot
will quite reboot

For us as a
For us as a

race to overcome all life's barriers
race to overcome all life's barriers

The
The

answer might take some time
answer might take some time

and a
and a

great miracle to occur
great miracle to occur

Remember,
Remember,

fear itself, has many carriers
fear itself, has many carriers

But in
But in

The end, the result could be something
the end, the result could be something

beautiful and sublime, yes, sir

beautiful and sublime, yes, sir

43 It's A Steal – (version one) 10

It's A Steal – (version one)

I tell you, it's a steal It's cheaper than a

I tell you, it's a steal It's cheaper than a

fast-food meal I think it's a damn good deal

fast-food meal I think it's a damn good deal

It cures my aches and pains and helps me to heal

It cures my aches and pains and helps me to heal

I don't need any magic pill It's just a matter

I don't need any magic pill It's just a matter

of letting go of my mind's will And letting

of letting go of my mind's will And letting

my imagination have its fill I just let it

my imagination have its fill I just let it

climb all over mountains and hills

climb all over mountains and hills

In this time, I am totally convinced

In this time, I am totally convinced

That I have myself witnessed   My own returni
That I have myself witnessed   My own returni

fitness   And my improved poetry as it progress
fitness   And my improved poetry as it progresse

My fellow laureates will say to me: better late
My fellow laureates will say to me: better late

They will also appreciate my finally getting out of the gate
They will also appreciate my finally getting out of the ga

I hope they will somehow enjoy what I create   And
I hope they will some how enjoy what I create   And

wherever it leads and to where   it goes and
wherever it leads and to where   it goes and

to whatever fate   And if anything comes of it
to whatever fate   And if anything comes of it

I know it won't hurt me a bit   It just
I Know it won't hurt me a bit   It just

might make me happy of what I writ
might make me happy of what I writ

And it'll be totally worth the time I took to sit
And it'll be totally worth the time I took to sit
It was worth all the time it took and all the waiting
It was worth all the time it took and all the waiting
It was worth all my immature hesitating
It was worth all my immature hesitating
It was worth all the solemn contemplating
It was worth all the solemn contemplating
I tell you, it was even worth the X rating
I tell you, it was even worth the X rating
I learned much by watching And I learned
I learned much by watching And I learned
much more by waiting And I learned by
much more by waiting And I learned by
listening And I learned much by just
listening And I learned much by just
feeling Then at the end, I put it all down
feeling Then at the end, I put it all down

I put it on paper, and I did not frown
I put it on paper, and I did not frown

And I tried not to act like a clown
And I tried not to act like a clown

I perfected it by putting it on a piece of paper with
I perfected it by putting it on a piece of paper with

characters up, down, and all around.
characters up, down, and all around.

The Sun Will Shine

The Sun Will Shine

My little man, everything will be fine, the sun will shine
My little man, everything will be fine, the sun will shine
The sun will eventually shine on you, my little Einstein
The sun will eventually shine on you, my little Einstein
Be strong, continue to walk the line. Life
Be strong, continue to walk the line. Life
will not always be unkind All the answers
will not always be unkind All the answers
will come in time, I heard it through the
will come in time, I heard it through the
grapevine You will someday bask in the
grapevine You will someday bask in the
sun's warmth And for what it's worth,
sun's warmth And for what it's worth,
I've loved you from before childbirth
I've loved you from before childbirth

You may even be the next leader of this Earth
when you go through your rebirth
Your heart will one day be filled with mirth
And everyone will know your net worth
There will be someone really smart who will hold up the fort
Someone who will have a real big heart
and will give you lots of support
They will know the long and the short
And solve all your problems part by part

until you are like a brand-new import
You'll be set free when I see the truth for the sake of
you and me through a miracle from a wise MD.
People's minds will be set free and no one
will fear, they will be worry-free
People will seek knowledge as the main key
now and no one will even need a PHD
I think there is hope for the whole world, and as we
browse the Web, we will also discover our family tree.

When we all yearn to continue to learn our
When we all yearn to continue to learn our
lives will take an upturn Then we will share
lives will take an upturn Then we will share
knowledge, each of us in our turn And we
knowledge, each of us in our turn And we
will be able to discern what our most
will be able to discern what our most
IMP:
important concern, to each of us is Then true
important concern, to each of us is Then true
freedom for all will be born because we took
freedom for all will be born because we took
time for the real truth after a brief sojourn
time for the real truth after a brief sojourn
Someday after the answers are clear, there will
Someday after the answers are clear, there will
be no more tears And we will overcome all our
be no more tears And we will overcome all our

fears and all break into loud cheers

We will no longer hate looking in the mirror

because no one will feel queer we'll all get

along and our loved ones will stay near

because we will all hold each other dear

At that time all sickness will cease and end

And then maybe the sky will open and

the curtain will rend And each of us will

be set free, one after another, each of us

68 page

in turn again and again
in turn again and again

We will not only feel
We will not only fee

like a number 10,
like a number 10

but we will hear a loud "Amen
but we will hear a load "Ame

AMEN.

Have faith and pray dear one, I love you, my dear son
Have faith and prays dear one, I love you, my dear son

You'll have your day in the sun. To me,
You'll have your day in the sun, To me

in this world, you are number 1
in this world, you are number 1

You'll be
You'll be

able to explain yourself to
able to explain yourself to

everyone when all
everyone when all

is said and done
is said and done

That's when you'll feel
That's when you'll feel

like you've won, because
like you've won, because

you'll be
you'll be

communicating on the run
communicating on the run

(69) page

(49) Ode To A Footprint 13.

Ode To A Footprint

My man has my favorite footprints On my
My man has my Favorite footprints On my
mind, they make a beautiful imprint Also for
mind, they make a beautiful imprint also for
my heart, they were surely heaven sent They are
my heart, they were surely heaven sent They are
delicate, like a child's are, and are, to me,
delicate, like a child's are and are, to me,
worth a mint I was once given and gazed upon
worth a mint I was once given and gazed upon
a picture Of an imprint, of a footprint,
a picture Of an imprint, of a footprint,
somewhat similar On a cardboard card,
somewhat similar On a cardboard card,
of a babe's foot — this one was a real winner
of a babe's foot — this one was a real winner

The card was given to me when I was but a
The card was given to me when I was but a

novice mother and children carrier at that
novice mother and children carrier at that

time, I remember, loving their beautiful shape
time, I remember, loving their beautiful shape

The heels and toes of the feet were so neatly arranged
The heels and toes of the feet were so neatly arranged

They were all together so perfectly laid My man's
They were all together so perfectly laid My man's

feet, just so happened to be also so similarly made
feet, just so happened to be also so similarly made

My man's steps are made for walking and not for
My man's steps are made for walking and not for

running They are also made for hopping,
running They are also made for hopping,

skipping, and jumping They have come from
skipping, and jumping They have come from

far away while in the process of traveling
far away while in the process of traveling

Away from circumstances not of his making or of his
Away from circumstances not of his making or of his

doing I'm glad that I'm the one that gets to
doing I'm glad that I'm the one that gets to

play With them yesterday, tomorrow, and today
play With them yesterday, tomorrow, and today

And I hope they will always stay Close to me today
And I hope they will always stay Close to me today

tomorrow, and for each and every day They
tomorrow, and for each and every day They

have the perfect shape They travel at just
have the perfect shape They travel at just

the right gait I'm happy that they are on
the right gait I'm happy that they are on

my mate And I hope they will always be my
my mate And I hope they will always be may

happy fate His feet have made many wonderful
happy fate His feet have made many wonderful

steps They are the steps of his and my destiny
steps They are the steps of his and my destiny

all perfectly laid out and set Their owner yo
all perfectly laid out and set Their owner yo

have never met Now that they are with me
have never met Now that they are with me

I know that they are my best bet They
I Know that they are my best bet They

Carry a very strong man Who always does
Carry a very strong man Who always does

his best to listen and try to understand a
his best to listen and try to understand an

problems you may have About each and every
problems you may have About each and every

woman, child, and man His feet tread soft
woman, child, and man His feet tread soft

In my biased opinion, to find any better would be an impossible feat

IN my biased opinion, to find any better would be an impossible feat

I'll Show You My Mind

I'll Show You My Mind

I'll show you my mind It's one of a perculia

I'll show you my mind It's one of a perculia

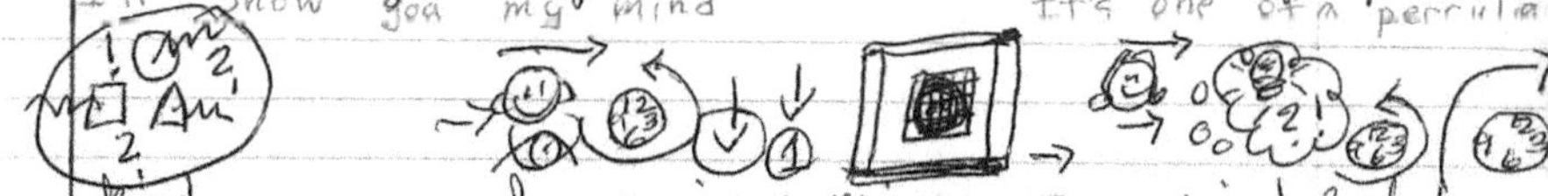

kind I was in a prison — my mind had been

kind I was in a prison my mind had been

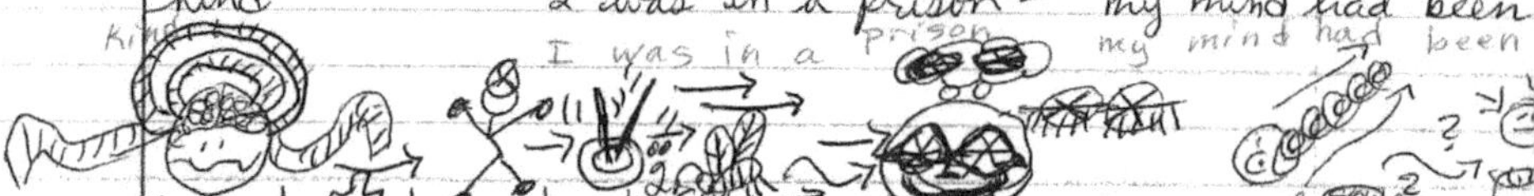

bound and made to be as blind Oh, how I

bound and made to be as blind Oh, how I

am happy with what I now find These are

am happy with what I now find There are

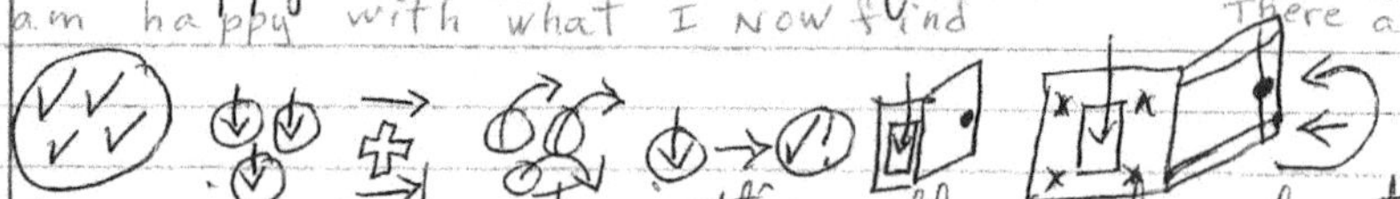

many ins and outs in this well-made closet

many ins and outs in this well-made closet

It must have been closed for a reason And

It must have been closed for a reason And

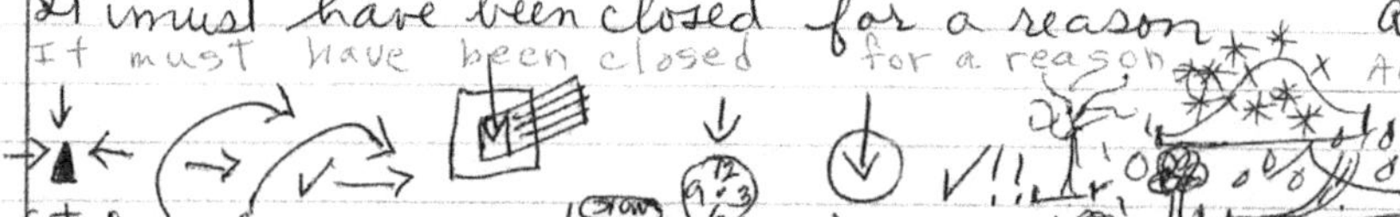

it has been opened, now in due season

it has been opened, now in due season

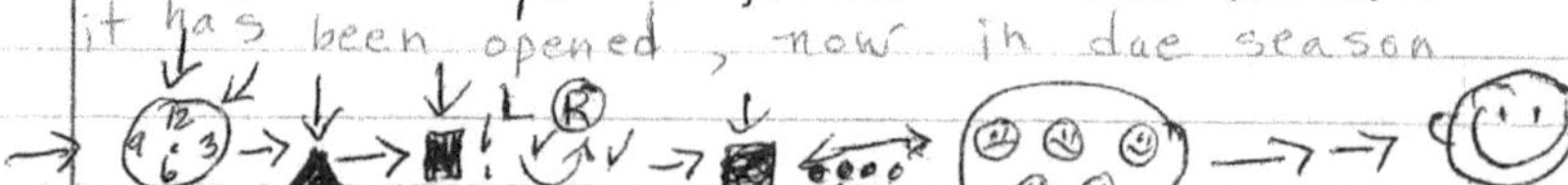

Now it is right there for everyone's pleasing

Now it is right there for everyone's pleasing

I now clap my hands for joy — My mind I
can now use, like a brand-new toy — With all
my past powers to again employ — I use it
with the same joy and happiness — of a new
toy given to a small boy — I want to share
my mind with everyone — So that they too
can have as much fun — As a once sad
and lonely one — Who has recovered and
come back into the sun — How long will it

last? My abilities and thoughts are
opening up and improving so fast
The journey is coming full blast It won't
settle to stay at half mast My gift to you
So you can see too From one who was
once so very bound? Will be to show
you she has turned into someone happy,
shiny, and new Grand Central
Station can't compare To something

so precious and rare As a lost and cast-
so precious and rare As a lost and cast-
out soul That has a chance to come back
out soul That has a chance to come back
again — after life has taken its toll
again — after life has taken its toll
Even a very little time In this precious
Even a very little time In this precious
clime Is a valuable find To my
clime Is a valuable find To my
once very tortured mind
once very tortured mind

See If I Care

You have every right To keep yourself
hidden and out of sight You know I won't bite
And I won't pick a fight You pretend to be
totally unaware Come out of your lair, see if
I care You and I know that's life; it's
totally fair Come on now, I dare you,
truth or dare It's not my place to make
any remark Or to light up a spark

Yes, it may make light in the dark
Or I may be
out of luck and miss the ark
You can be very
rude
And act like some cool dude
But it
would be much shrewder
To be quiet and not
to intrude
You can swear. See if I care
You can stare. See if I care
You can
glare. See if I care
You can blow lots of
hot air. See if I care
If all you want
is lots of attention
You will find no one

cares about your orientation
cares about your orientation
important enough to mention
important enough to mention
you might land in detention
you might land in detention
back in the doghouse
back in the dog house
back into my house
back into my house
like a low-down mouse
like a low-down mouse
know you as an awful louse
know you as an awful louse
arrogant as a yo-yo
arrogant as a yo-yo
to hit below the belt, far below
to hit below the belt, far below

And you are not
And you are not
Keep it up
Keep it up
Then you will be
Then you will be
Instead of getting
Instead of getting
You'll then be treated
You'll then be treated
And others will
And others will
You can be
You can be
Go ahead and try
Go ahead and try
To me
To me

81 page

you'll always be a no-good so-so And you
you'll always be a no-good so-so And you

know where you can go When you find that
Know where you can go When you find that

you can't take the heat You'll be as red as
You can't take the heat You'll be as red as

a beet You'll have to get up from your seat
a beet You'll have to get up from your seat

And you'll be lost as a sheep You can come
And you'll be lost as a sheep You can come

as close as a hair, See if I care Even if
as close as a hair. See if I care Even if

nothing is what you wear. See if I care
nothing is what you wear. See if I care

You can show me layer by layer. See if I care
You can show me layer by layer. See if I care

You can be the very best player. See if I care
You can be the very best player. See if I care.

All I have for you is contempt I will resist you
All I have for you is contempt I will resist you
every attempt My conscience will not be
every attempt My conscience will not be
broken or bent I think you are the most
broken or bent I think you are the most
awful gent I know you and how you play
awful gent I know you and how you play
your game I think all your excuses are very
your game I think all your excuses are very
lame Do you think I care about your
lame Do you think I care about your
glory and fame? I'll leave you all alone
glory and fame? I'll leave you all alone
if it's all the same.
if it's all the same

I Saw The Shadow
I Saw The Shadow

I saw the shadow And just to let you know
I saw the shadow And just to let you know
I knew it would end up softening the blow If I
I knew it would end up softening the blow If I
told you it followed us everywhere where we all go
told you it followed us everywhere where we all go
Sometimes it happens to be just a wisp But that's
Sometimes it happens to be just a wisp But that's
all that's needed; this just happens to be the
all that's needed; this just happens to be the
whole gist There was no need for it to tap or to
whole gist There was no need for it to tap or to
take me by the wrist Or for it to try to take
take me by the wrist Or for it to try to take
my attention or for it to make me turn or twist
my attention or for it to make me turn or twist

The shadow was in fact quite helpful But realistically
The shadow was in fact qaite helpful But realistically
not at all truthful You could say that it was an
not at all truthful You could say that it was an
exposed photograph that had got a head cold
exposed photograph that had got a head cold
It also tended to be, in fact, very forgetful It
It also tended to be in fact very forgetful It
seemed to have its own mind Sometimes it
seemed to have its own mind Sometimes it
shortened its every tone And sometimes it grew
shortened its every tone And sometimes it grew
longer than an unpaid loan It was as silent
longer than an unpaid loan It was as silent
as a disconnected phone When the shadows came
as a disconnected phone When the shadows came
around It usually meant it was time to leave town
around It usually meant it was time to leave town

I know a shadow, which I happen to own "Come on,"
I know a shadow, which I happen to own "Come on,"

I say to my shadow, "Give my dog a bone" A chance
I say to my shadow, "Give my dog a bone" A chance

meeting with it can mean a mystery Like, a bad
meeting with it can mean a mystery Like, a bad

part in a movie, it can be very eerie We are
part in a movie, it can be very eerie We are

sometimes apprehensive with the shadows that we see
sometimes apprehensive with the shadows that we see

Always following where we once wanted to be
always following where we once wanted to be

All I know is that seeing it is some kind of clue
All I know is that seeing it is some kind of clue

Tell me do you see it too? It's just plain
Tell me you see it too? It's just plain

as that nose on you That admission in itself
as that nose on you That admission in itself

is enough to see While I, myself, saw that the
is enough to see while I, myself, saw that the

shadow had existence The sun, on the other
shadow had existence The sun, on the other

hand must not have cared a pittance
hand must not have cared a pittance

Because it chose its time to say good riddance
Because it chose its time to say good riddance

And the shadow's existence turned out to be
And the shadow's existence turned out to be

nothing but an annoying hindrance Some
nothing but an annoying hindrance Some

people like to play With shadows and convince
people like to play with shadows and convince

them how to lie They, themselves, dance
them how to lie They, themselves, dance

to the rhythm and are happy and gay
to the rhythm And are happy and gay

They enjoy making new games in each and
They enjoy making new games in each and
every one of their own individual ways I thought
every one of their own individual ways I thought
I saw a shadow that was a good fellow I
I saw a shadow that was a good fellow I
remember thinking that he was quiet and very mellow
remember thinking that he was quiet and very mellow
Until to my delight he quivered and jiggled
Until to my delight he quivered and jiggled
just like Jell-O And when the sun went
just like Jell-O And when the sun went
down, I saluted to him and said, "Tallyho!"
down, I saluted to him and said, "Tallyho!"
They say you can never tell All I say is, "Well"
They say you can never tell All I say is, "Well"
It is quiet, and it doesn't yell And ah, heck,
It is quiet, and it doesn't yell And ah, heck,

it's just plain good company

it's just plain good company

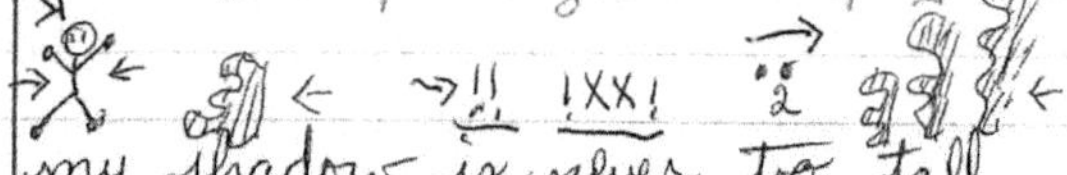

my shadow is never too tall

my shadow is never too tall

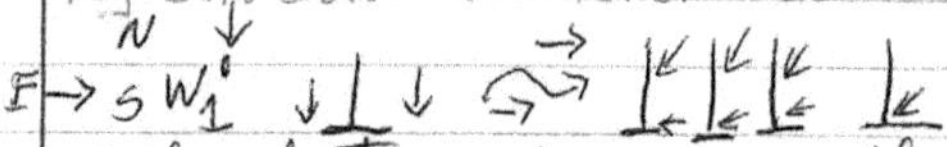

at the bottom of every wall

at the bottom of every wall

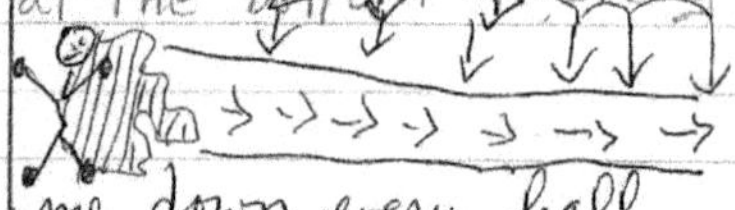

me down every hall

me down every hall

of all

of all

What the hell

What the hell

Also

Also

But it ends u

But it ends u

It also follows

It also follows

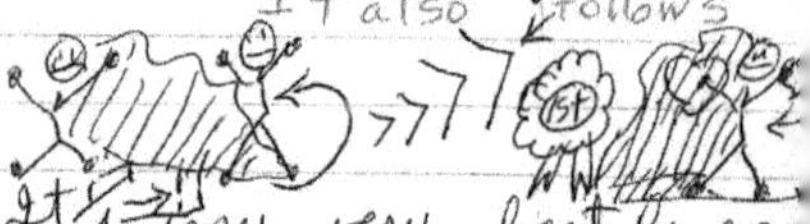

It's my very best frienc

It's my very best frien

(89) page

(17) Shut My Mouth (57)

Shat My Moath

Sometimes I'm way too loud This does not
Some times I'm way too loud This does not
help at all when I'm in a crowd Or at a
help at all when I'm in a crowd Or at a
place where talking is not allowed Or when
place where talking is not allowed Or when
I'm with someone who is way too proud
I'm with someone who is way too proud
Many times, my views get me into trouble
Many times, my views get me into trouble
I hate to then burst anybody's bubble But
I hate to the burst any body's babble But
here comes trouble again on the double You'd
here comes trouble again on the double You'd
better wait to pick me out of the rubble
better wait to pick me out of the rubble

Do you know what I've caused?
Do you know what I've caused?
I didn't take the time to pause
I didn't take the time to pause
the words that came out had many flaws
the words that came out had many flaws
My enemies' claws cut me into a jigsaw
My enemies' claws cut me into a jigsaw
one fine day, I had a brilliant idea
one fine day, I had a brilliant idea
would use a new rule, innovative and raw
would use a new rule, innovative and raw
I would do something new and try to draw
I would do something new and try to draw
A picture in my mind, then follow it to a tee,
A picture in my mind, then follow it to a tee,
my new law I would then go a step farther
my new law I would then go a step farther

Just because
Just because
And oops
And oops,
The
The
I
I

I would try to put my plan into action, yes, sir
I would try to put my plan into action, yes, sir

Soon my actions would be a blur And my
Soon my actions would be a blur And my

movements would be running with a smooth purr
movements would be running with a smooth purr

My new rule of thumb is quite simple I'll
My new rule of thumb is quite simple I'll

be quiet. No longer will I yell This came
be quiet. No longer will I yell This came

to me out of the blue like a bombshell I was
to me out of the blue like a bombshell I was

amazed and in a state of wonder. This was swell
amazed and in a state of wonder. This was swell

All I have to do is "Shut my mouth"
All I have to do is "Shut my mouth"

When I speak I will tell the truth, no more
When I speak I will tell the truth, no more

word of mouth
word of mouth

I will no longer be a
I will no longer be a

blabbermouth
blabber mouth

If I digress you can send
If I digress you can send

me deep, deep South
me deep, deep South

With a loose tongue
With a loose tongue

I've seen the consequences
I've seen the consequences

And I wasn't at all
And I wasn't at All

pleased with the resulting sequences
pleased with the resulting sequences

I
I

think it's time for a new set of circumstances
think it's time for a new set of circumstances

I'll be quiet and try to observe and
I'll be quiet and try to observe and

catalog every set of nuances
catalog every set of nuances

This is easier
This is easier

said than done
said than done

Because somehow bring quiet
Because somehow bring quiet

Doesn't seem like fun But speaking out freely
doesn't seem like fun But speaking outfreely

has always resulted in putting me on the run
has always resulted in putting me on the run

Now I must sit, be silent, and smile like
Now I must sit, be silent, and smile like

a radiant, shining quiet person When I
a radiant, shining quiet person When I

get the special knack I might very well
get the special knack I might very well

find the treasure I lacked It'll be harder
find the treasure I lacked It'll be harder

than avoiding a heart attack But in the
than avoiding a heart attack But in the

end, better health will be a forgone fact
end, better health will be a forgone fact

I'm sure I'm terribly addicted And with
I'm sure I'm terribly addicted And with

free speech I'm totally connected
But when
I opened my mouth, who could have predicted
That my words were to cause such a conflict
with a war, that, in turn resulted
So to be m
own best friend
The phrase "Shut my mouth"
will be my new trend
Then my bad words
won't turn into actions,
and then I
won't have to amend
Because I will
avoid an accidental war in
which I might

have to myself defend

have to myself defend

(96) : page

(18) I'm Not Looking For Trouble (59)

I'm not looking for trouble
No one's going to
burst my bubble
I still found trouble and on
the double
When I wouldn't bow down and s
uncle
Every day makes you a little wiser
Some days will leave you tired and totally unsure
Some days will go by like you are travelling in a blu
After these kinds of days, you'll wonder what
life is all for
I say, trouble, trouble go awa

97 page

Come again, never again to stay Let me have
Come again, never again to stay Let me have

time to laugh and play There's lots of time to
time to laugh and play There's lots of time to

grow old and to become gray I think I might
grow old and to become gray I think I might

have found the answer And I managed to do
have found the answer And I managed to do

so without causing a ruckus or making a stir
so without causing a ruckus or making a stir

I also did it in a peaceful way, that's for sure
I also did it in a peaceful way, that's for sure

You might say it occurrsed to me quietly, as it were
You might say it occurred to me quietly, as it were

I've decided to finally settle For being the
I've decided to finally settle For being the

silent belle In what you could call a life
silent belle In what you could call a life

that started off as pure hell
I was, then constantly
walking on eggshells
They said I couldn't do
anything but run
But I think I've rendered them
undone
I'm finally back in the shining sun
I feel like I'm again number 1 and
now I'm
having lots of fun
Someday if I come out
on the top
I'll sing and do a hop
And then I'll fly away on my magical mop
Until I'm as famous as Mr. Aesop

99 : page

The truth will speak for itself Because it
The truth will speak for itself Because it

will be sitting on everyone's shelf And my
will be sitting on everyone's shelf And my

most important wealth Will be that I'm
most important wealth Will be that I'm

satisfied with myself
satisfied with myself

100 : page

(19) You Have Passed Every Test (61)

You Have Passed Every Test

Now that I've flown from my nest
Now that I've flown from my nest

I will
I will

keep you close to my chest
Keep you close to my chest

You have passec
You have passec

every test
every test

You are one of the very best
You are one of the very best

I now consider you my friend
I now consider you my friend

I will call on
I will call on

you now and then
you now and then

I will think of you agai
I will think of you agai

and again
and again

You will be someone to talk
You will be someone to talk

to while
to while

my heart is on the mend
my heart is on the mend

I will share with you my precious time
I will share with you my precious time

101: page

Because you are one of the worthy kind
Because you are one of the worthy kind
I can see
I can see

I am far from blind
I am far from blind
I think you are part of
I think you are part of

my grand design
my grand design
We will have many a good
We will have many a good

time together
time together
Because we share time in
Because we share time in

any weather
any weather
Our friendship is bound to get
Our friendship is bound to get

better and better
better and better
It's perfectly right, right
It's perfectly right, right

down to the last letter
down to the last letter
You can tell when
You can tell when

I'm with you all is well
I'm with you all is well
I like you swell, you
I like you swell, you

and me gel
and me gel
Jeepers creepers, ah hell
Jeepers creepers, ah hell

Go ahead and ring my bell I will let you know
Go ahead and ring my bell I will let you know

many a secret Because you are so sweet
many a secret Because you are so sweet

And I tell you, gaining my trust is no small feat
And I tell you, gaining my trust is no small feat

Boom Boom

I can tell, you have an honest kind of drumbeat
I can tell you have an honest kind of drumbeat

I enjoy your company With you, I will
I enjoy your company With you, I will

hee hee! hee! hee!

gladly chuckle with glee I will catch you
gladly chuckle with glee I will catch you

singing off-key Or when you ramble
singing off-key Or when you ramble

WORD WORD

on and on in a lost word spree Between
on and on in a lost word spree Between

my sobs and my tears I will share with you
my sobs and my tears I will share with you

all my fears I know you won't make me feel
all my fears I Know you won't make me feel
little or queer And I will be glad you and I are
little or queer And I will be glad you and I are
together here Our friendship is awesome
together here Our friendship is awesome
We have lots and lots in common In summer,
We have lots and lots in common In summer,
spring, and autumn Together we will have
spring, and autumn Together we will have
lots of fun I will be happy when you succeed
lots of fun I will be happy when you succeed
And proud ~~of~~ when you, from your fears, are relieved
And proud when you, from your fears, are relieved
I will be proud of all your deeds And encourage
I will be proud of all your deeds And encourage
you to go straight ahead, full-speed
you to go straight ahead, full-speed

10 page

And when it is time for you to move on I will
And when it is time for you to move on I will

miss you when you are gone And for your
miss you when you are gone And for your

company I will long I might even write it to you
company I will long I might even write it to you

in a song
in a song

20 To Ignore Or Not To Ignore 3

To Ignore Or Not To Ignore

To ignore or not to ignore
To ignore or not to ignore
We all know who is
We all Know who is
really a bore
really a bore
You may think you have the entire
You may think you have the entire
floor
floor
We all know you are nothing but a dinosaur
We all Know you are nothing but a dinosaur
Sometimes I find it best
Some times I find it best
To hold things really close
To hold things really close
to my chest
to my chest
Then I can be ready for my next
Then I can be ready for my next
quest
quest
Even when I'm put to my next test
Even when I'm put to my next test
To ignore or overlook; I may find it hard
To ignore or overlook; I may find it hard
Ignoring with tact is the way to play my cards
Ignoring with tact is the way to play my cards

Especially if I don't want to end up in the mental ward
Especially if I don't want to end up in the mental ward

I try to make sure to be polite and not to use any rude word
I try to make sure to be polite and not to use any rude word

You must take a strong stance When someone
You must take a strong stance When someone

wants attention with insistence Don't give them a
wants attention with insistence Don't give them a

x+y= 2 y÷t= 2
L×n= 2 t−k= 3

secound glance Under any circumstance
secound glance Under any circumstance

Indifference, one way or another May get you
Indifference, one way or another May get you

out of hot water Always keep calmness your
out of hot water Always keep calmness your

chosen demur Do not let slip any kind of slur
chosen demur Do not let slip any kind of slur

If you get a good thought And you get poked by
If you get a good thought And you get poked by

107 : page

a tot — You must decide whether or not — To
a tot — You must decide whether or not — To

let your attention be caught — It may be to everyone's
let your attention be caught — It may be to everyone's

best interest — Silently to cease and desist
best interest — Silently to cease and desist

And not to let them pull your wrist — We must
And not to let them pull your wrist — We must

all bear with all and coexist — Someone may take
all bear with all and coexist — Someone may take

you the wrong way — You may want to keep
you the wrong way — You may want to keep

them at bay — You may not want to be acknowledged
them at bay — You may not want to be acknowledged

anyway — The temptress will leave you alone someday
anyway — The temptress will leave you alone someday

Ignoring distractions will have many a perk
Ignoring distractions will have many a perk

Especially when you are engaged in work
Especially when you are engaged in work

you want to ignore some rude jerk
You want to ignore some rude jerk

him might prevent him from going berserk
him might prevent him from going berserk

It will help you keep your blood pressure down
It will help you keep your blood pressure down

They may leave you alone and get out of town
They may leave you alone and get out of town

It will get a smile from them, not a frown
It will get a smile from them not a frown

You may also become very well known
You may also become very well Known

109 : page

(21) You Can't Win Them All (67)

You Can't Win Them All

Look at me, ding-dong dell Look at me, again I
Look at me, ding-dong dell Look at me, again I

am unwell You can try to ring my bell
am unwell you can try to ring my bell

Look at me, again I feel like hell I finally
Look at me, again I feel like hell I finally

figured out What life entails No
figured out What life entails No

matter how I scream and shout Life is
matter how I scream and shout Life is

never beyond a doubt Let's face it, I must
never beyond a doubt Let's face it I must

stand tall Because you can't win them all
stand tall Because you can't win them all

Even if I get left standing at the stall Everyone
Even if I get left standing at the stall Everyone

will say, Girl, you have a lot of gall."
will say, Girl, you have a lot of gall.

say, "What is your excuse for being alive?"
say, "What is your excuse for being alive?

I'll suggest that on rejection I thrive
I'll suggest that on rejection I thrive

I have no push, no jive
I have no push, no jive

I thrive
I thrive

I don't mind if I don't win
I don't mind if I don't win

To me, this is no particular sin
To me, this is no particular sin

don't slip me a Mickey Finn
don't slip me a Mickey Finn

have to try to explain where I've been
have to try to explain where I've been

don't even mind being last
don't even mind being last

They'l
They'll

Without it
Without it

And for an honest opinio
And for an honest opinion

Just pleas
Just please

And I won't
And I won't

I
I

Even though
Even though

my life might end up at half mast
And I
might be quite outclassed
Any which way, I
will still have a blast
So while I continue to
try to do my personal best
I will go on my
journey, my personal quest
My life is my
testimonial, it is my real test
I will treat
life with vigor like it is
an adventure,
a conquest
I don't know if I am very wise
Because I sometimes wear a disguise
Someday

I may even cut you down to size
I may even cut you down to size

you hand me too many lies
you hand me too many lies

me the next catcall
me the next catcall

if I have to crawl
if I have to crawl

in one great big haul
in one great big haul

brave and proud,
brave and proud,

Especially if
Especially if

And when you give
And when you give

I will pick myself up even
I will pick myself up ever

I will take out all my awards
I will take out all my a ward

And I will stand up
And I will stand up

and I will feel ten feet tall
and I will fee ten feet tal

(22) Do You Want Something? (67)

Do You Want Something?

Do you want something?
Do you want something?

I'm not just a plaything
I'm not just a plaything

What about this wedding ring
What about this wedding ring

I'm not just a toy on a string
I'm not just a toy on a string

Where have you been?
Where have you been?

What kind of mood are you in?
What kind of mood are you in?

Where am I supposed to fit in?
Where am I supposed to fit in?

Where am I to begin?
Where am I to begin?

I have put my life on hold before
I have put my life on hold before.

I will do so many, many times more
I will do so many, many times more

I don't mean to be a bore
I don't mean to be a bore

My life has been filled up with violence and war
My life has been filled up with violence and war

My feelings have
My feelings have

been ripped and torn
I have been down and forlorn
I have no feelings of scorn
On the Bible I have sworn
Go away. A-OK, OK?
I want to play, but I'll do as you
say
Come another day or I'll hold you at bay
I'll hit the hay for now. I'll be merry and gay
you know the golden rule?
I'm nobody's fool
I think you're really cool
I'm a person, not a
mule
Sit there on your stool
You silly,
silly fool
And eat your curds and gruel

Right down to the very last undecule All praise to
Right down to the very last molecule All praise to

the Man He's the One who truly undesstands
the Man He's the One who truly understands

He's the One with the plan He's the best in all the
He's the One with the plan He's the best in all the

land I'm His fan, Give Hime a hand
land I'm His fan. Give Him a hand

When I'm with Him, anywhere is the Holy Land
When I'm with Him, anywhere is the Holy Land

He is truly great and grand I try to obey His every
He is truly great and grand I try to obey His every

command When I go with Him, toe to toe
command When I go with Him, toe to toe

He is always a friend, never a foe I will
He is always a friend, never a foe I will

be the one to tow the hoe I know the
be the one to tow the hoe I know the

more I believe, the more I will know I must
more I believe, the more I will know I must

not go so fast, I must go slowly I'll go slowly
not go so fast, I must go slowly I'll go slowly

He's not my foe The more I believe, the more I'll
He's not my foe The more I believe, the more I'll

glow I will say, "Ho, Ho, Ho," I'll be the
glow I will say, "Ho, Ho, Ho," I'll be the

one in the know
one in the know

117 page

23. So You Don't Want To Play (P.69)

So You Don't Want To Play

So you don't want to play
So you don't want to play

You say it's all
You say it's all

work; that's what you say
work; that's what you say

Is that possible in
Is that possible in

these modern days
these modern days

Shouldn't the scales of work
Shouldn't the scales of work

and play evenly weigh?
and play evenly weigh?

It wouldn't be the
It wouldn't be the

solution
solution

In any useful situation
In any useful situation

It'll just be the cause of your ruin
It'll just be the cause of your ruin

Soon
Soon

you will be singing a different tune
you will be singing a different tune

You'll
You'll

feel like the monkey on the moon
feel like the monkey on the moon

And you
And you

just might feel like a babbling baboon Like som
just might feel like a babbling baboon Like some

worried, ghastly goon This might take the
worried, ghastly goon This, might take the

air right out of your hot air balloon I migh
air right out of your hot air balloon I might

even give you a few nips Right there on one
even give you a few nips Right there on one

of your luscious lips Stand still while I let
of your luscious lips Stand still while I let

her rip After all, it won't hurt you to take a sip
her rip After all, it won't hurt you to take a si

When you are tired, I'll prop you up I'll
When you are tired, I'll prop you up I'll

wrap you up in my love just like they
wrap you up in my love just like they

did to the mummy of King Tut You'll be
did to the mummy of King Tut You'll be

cornered and you want to know what You'll
cornered and you want to know what You'll

be the one to say, "Don't stop my pet mutt,"
be the one to say, "Don't stop my pet mutt,"

You can't only want to work Don't you know that
You can't only want to work Don't you know that

overworking can be where evil lurks Life has to have
overworking can be where evil lurks Life has to have

its even amount of perks Or someone might end
its even amount of perks Or some one mightend

up calling you a jerk You have to have a little
up calling you a jerk You have to have a little

fun When you are rested your battles will be
fun When you are rested your battles will be

easily won Especially when you let yourself
easily won Especially when you let yourself

come out into the sun The warmth and the energy
come out into the sun The warmth and the energy

120 page

1,000 lbs.

will end up helping a ton — Especially when you let
will end up helping a ton — Especially when you let

yourself come out into the sun — The warmth an
yourself come out into the sun — The warmth and

1,000 lbs.

The energy will end up helping a ton — When
the energy will end up helping a ton — When

you work too much, you will be a wreck
you work too much you will be a wreck

Your wife will call you up and give you heck
Your wife will call you up and give you heck

You will be nothing but a pain in the neck
You will be nothing but a pain in the neck

And you will end up worrying yourself right to deat
And you will end up worrying yourself right to deat

Go ahead and enjoy yourself, and maybe You'll win
Go ahead and enjoy yourself and maybe you'll win

Try it, it won't be a sin — You won't know if
Try it, it won't be a sin — You won't know if

you don't begin to begin Working and playing
you don't begin to begin Working and playing

are equal yin-yang twins You'll be happier in
are equal yin-yang twins You'll be happier in

the end You will make a lot more friends
the end You will make a lot more friends

You'll feel like a number 10 And everyone
You'll feel like a number 10 And every one

will want to see you again and again
will want to see you again and again

(24) I Just Wanted To Say Hi (71)

I Just Wanted To Say Hi

I just wanted to say hi
I just wanted to say hi

Here, I'll give it a try
Here, I'll give it a try

Of that, I cannot deny
Of that, I cannot deny

Hello, my name is Di
Hello, my name is Di

OK, I did it first
OK, I did it first

I'm none for the worst
I'm none for the worst

And I didn't even end up cursed
And I didn't even end up cursed

I like it
I like it

I went in unafraid, headfirst
I went in unafraid, headfirst

Go ahead, you
Go ahead, you

there, try it
there, try it

You will see all the hidden
you will see all the hidden

benefits
benefits

It could be a bang-up, smash-up;
It could be a bang-up, smash-up;

crash-up hit
crash-up hit

Do it, you will not be a hypocrite
Do it, you will not be a hypocrite

123 : page

Come on, put her there Come on, let your
feelings be stripped bare Come on; take the time
to give a care Peel off your feelings layer by layer
It does not hurt to be friendly Like that monkey
in the tree Sociability is the Key This comes
on down to you from little old me We'll meet
again someday Let's give a salute to another day
And let's just be merry and gay Also lets send out
a great big bouquet for us to go on life's highway

Come on, put her there Come on, let your
feelings be stripped bare Come on; take the time
to give a care Peel off your feelings layer by layer
It does not hurt to be friendly Like that monkey
in the tree Sociability is the Key This comes
on down to you from little old me We'll meet
again someday Let's give a salute to another day
And let's just be merry and gay Also lets send out
a great big bouquet for us to go on life's highway

It'll be worth your while To go that extra mile

You'll see, I mean you no guile I just happen to

like to go freestyle I can even play peek-a-boo

with you And with no further excuses, I will say

adieu You might end up making a friend anew

That would be quite a glorious snafu I wish I could

totally relate To why people take a mate

I always thought it was for life, does this to

you equate? We must also get along together and

not hate I don't even want to begin To
not hate I don't even want to begin To

say why I have sometimes got a thin skin
say why I have some times got a thin skin

If I did I might lose and the devil might win
If I did I might lose and the devil might win

And then I would be lost again and again
And then I would be lost again and again

126 : page

25. Your Face Is Two-Ply (73)

Your Face Is Two-Ply

hi! hi!

I would greet you and say hi But I've found

I would greet you and say hi But I've found

out your face is two-ply You, sir, are a

out your face is two-ply You, sir, are a

two-faced guy And that's no word of a lie

two-faced guy And that's no word of a lie

hi! Bye! Bye!

When I greet you and say yoo-hoo I might

When I greet you and say yoo-hoo I might

Goo! Goo! Goo!

as well say, "Goo, goo, goo." You'd think I

as well say, "Goo, goo, goo." You'd think I

had come from a zoo You can't think of

had come from a zoo You can't think of

anything to say or what to do You are so infantile

anything to say or what to do You are so infantile

And filled with self-centered guile Why should

And filled with self-centered guile Why should

I go that extra mile? You sir, are nothing but a

I go that extra mile You sir, are nothing but a

reptile I think I'll just let you be Then

reptile I think I'll just let you be Then

I'll be safe and home free I'll be the one

I'll be safe and home free I'll be the one

laughing with glee Even though you are the

laughing with glee Even though you are the

one with a college degree The sad thing is

one with a college degree The sad thing is

you don't have to work hard at being

you don't have to work hard at being

ignorant, this should be your calling card

ignorant, this should be your calling card

with which you could win an ignorance award

with which you could win an ignorance award

But you still choose to put your worst foot forward

But you still choose to put your worst foot forward

I could play hard sell But you would pretend not
I could play hard sell But you would pretend not

to be well Well, (SLOW) you can go straight to hell
to be well Well, you can go straight to hell

Go ahead and ring someone else's bell Your
Go ahead and ring someone else's bell Your

face is a complicated maze It leaves many in a
face is a complicated maze It leaves many in a

foggy haze You know how I hate Broadway plays
foggy haze You know how I hate Broadway plays

You could very well be the end of my days
You could very well be the end of my days

No matter what you choose to throw Or how
No matter what you choose to throw Or how

much hurt, (SLOW) you pile on blow for blow You
much hurt, you pile on blow for blow You

will never be anything but a yo-yo And I
will never be anything but a yo-yo And I

I will continue to wonder

will continue to radiate and glow If you will always
will contine to radiate and glow If you will always

try to plunder And blow the truth asunder
try to plander And blow the truth asunder

You'll find out you're the one who really has
You'll find out you're the one who really has

made the blunder I would be very surprised
made the blunder I would be very surprised

If you ever break out of your disguise Leopards
If you ever break out of your disguise Leopards

don't change their spots, that's no lie And
don't change their spots, that's no lie And

for now, you will not get from me any
for now, you will not get from me any

Kind of a rise
Kind of a rise

26. I'll Get Straight To The Point (75)

I 'll Get straight To The Point

I'll be straight and to the point
I'll be straight and to the point

When I'm in this
When I'm in this

point
joint

If you don't agree with my viewpoint
If you don't agree with my view point

Anger might become my focal point
Anger might become my focal point

The time has come
The time has come

For me to be the honest one
For me to be the honest one

Sorry if that spoils
Sorry if that spoils

your fun
your fun

ho! ho! ho!

I think my fun has just begun
I think my fun has just begun

You may call me blunt
You may call me blunt

Just because I tell you
Just because I tell you

what you don't really want
what you don't really want

Everyone will know
Everyone will Know

why you are on the brunt
why you are on the brunt

And that you are
And that you are

again just pulling another stunt   That in it may be
again just pulling another stunt   That in it may be.

the end   Of what you call fun, my friend
the end   Of what you call fun, my friend

Where will you go, again and again?   You will
Where will you go, again and again?   You will

find yourself at a dead end   If you get into
find yourself at a dead end   If you get into

trouble   You can send for help on the double
trouble   You can send for help on the double

I will be far from subtle   I'll show you my
I will be far from subtle   I'll show you my

true mettle   I knew it all along   I put you
true mettle   I knew it all along   I put you

right where you belong   That's exactly what you
right where you belong   That's exactly what you

were scared of, hon.   Sing a song and put
were scared of, hon.   Sing a song and put

that in your sarong
that in your sarong

Like you were nothing but a rag doll
Like you were nothing but a rag doll

your bluff, overall
your bluff, overall

Wouldn't life be great?
Wouldn't life be great?

coming out of the gate
coming out of the gate

And we'd end up with better mates
And we'd end up with better mates

people choose to lie
people choose to lie

other guy
other guy

I'll be there to give it a good try
I'll be there to give it a good try

I don't care if you wear a tie
I don't care if you wear a tie

I'll nail you to a wal
I'll nail you to a wall

I'll ca
I'll call

And you won't be able to sta
And you won't be able to sto

If we were all hon
If we were all hom

There would be less hate
There would be less hate

While
While

And blame it on the
And blame it on the

You will
You will

133 : page

be first to tell
be first to tell

to ring a bell
to ring a bell

can go to hell
can go to hell

paperback or hard shell
paperback or hard shell

That the truth's bound
That the truth's bound

And if you don't like it you
And if you don't like it you

Soon it will be an e-book,
Soon it will be an e-book,

1st = A 134 : page

27, The Twilight Zone, Alternate Universes (version A) 77

The Twilight Zone, Alternate Universes (version A)

I was totally lost, I was like a ghost My seas were
I was totally lost, I was like aghost My seas were

tossed, I had nothing to boast Now I wanted the very
tossed, I had nothing to boast Now I wanted the very

most If someone was to again join my hitching post
most If someone was to again join my hitching post

I don't easily give up But I felt like I'd been left
I don't easily give up But I felt like I'd been left

out at the roundup Or there had been some horrible
out at the roundup Or there had been some horrible

mix-up And I definitely felt all washed up
mix-up And I definitely felt all washed up

I wasn't searching or even looking I wasn't
I wasn't searching or even looking I wasn't

settling for a one-night fling So I stayed out
settling for a one-night fling So I stayed out

of the boxing ring — And I acted like a puppet on a
of the boxing ring — And I acted like a puppet on a

string — Your lady left you and left you hard
string — Your lady left you and left you hard

As a matter of fact, you were discarded — She
As a matter of fact, you were discarded — She

didn't even let you have the final word — She
didn't even let you have the final word — She

left you and pushed in a very sharp sword — I
left you and pushed in a very sharp sword — I

found you under the ice — You had paid a
found you under the ice — You had paid a

horrible price — You came up to breathe twice
horrible price — You came up to breathe twice

But what happened wasn't nice — You fell in
But what happened wasn't nice — You fell in

through the trapdoor — You even went into the
through the trap door — You even went into the

navy corps   You didn't know what was in store

navy corps   You didn't know what was in store

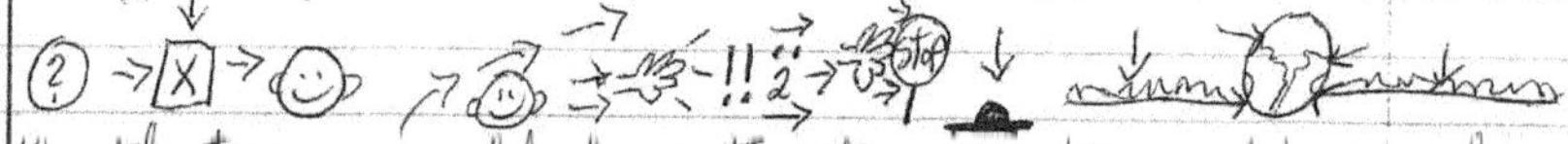

Or that you would have to stay on terra-firma shore

Or that you would have to stay on terra-firma shore

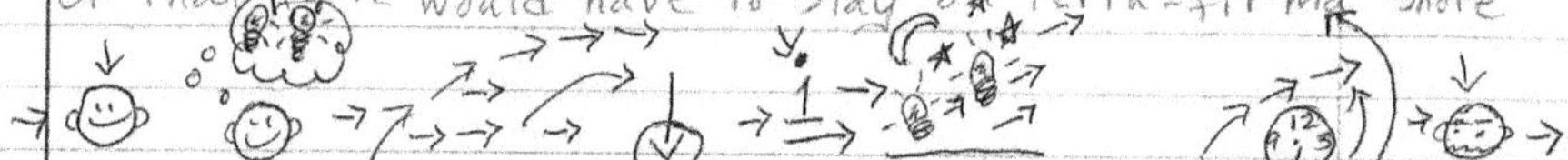

Your ideas went out into the night   Then you

Your ideas went out into the night   Then you

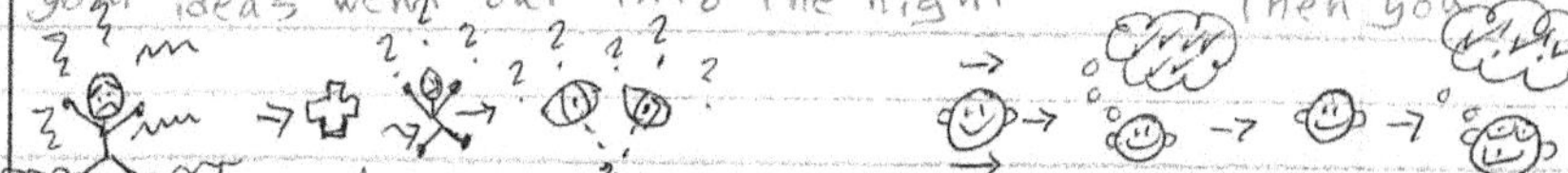

quavered and lost sight   You thought you knew

quavered and lost sight   You thought you knew

what was right   You turned out to be my white

what was right   You turned out to be my white

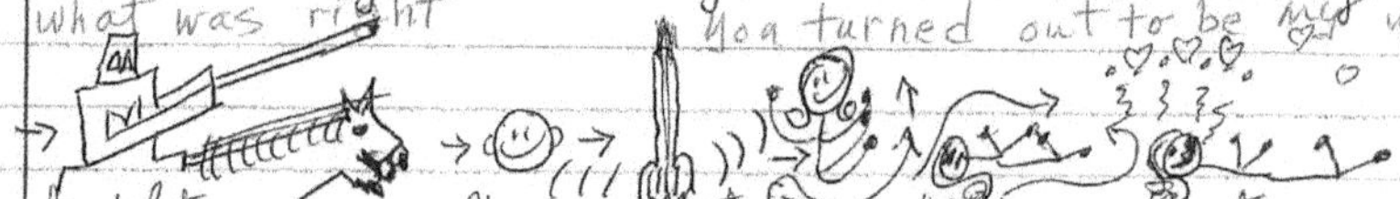

knight   You swept me off my feet

Knight   You swept me off my feet

You were so kind and so sweet   Your voice

You were so kind and so sweet   Your voice

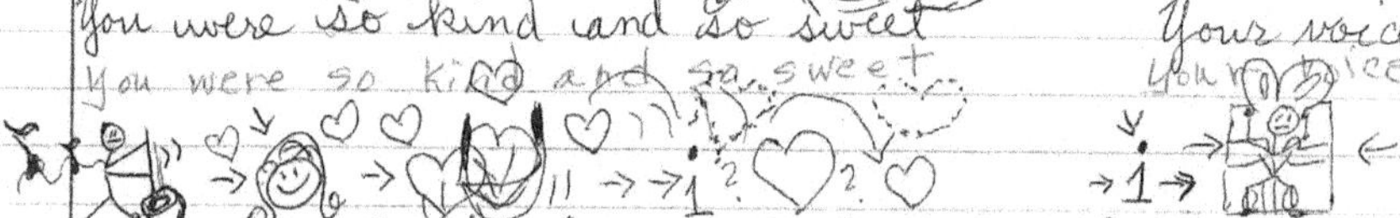

made my heart skip a beat   The whole

made my heart skip a beat   The whole

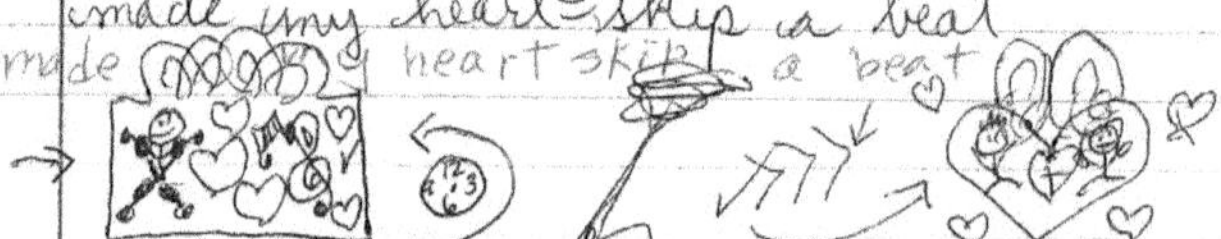

package was so very complete

package was so very complete

28. The Twilight Zone, Alternate Universes (version B) 79

The Twilight Zone, Alternate Universes (version B)

I came back from T-H-E-N I came back from way
I came back from T-H-E-N I came back from way

back then You may call it hell and then again
back then You may call it hell and then again

It was time when it was unusual to find a friend
It was time when it was unusual to find a friend

I came back . . . my senses are reeling ...!! But
I came back . . . my senses are reeling But

mostly I am met with an attack of an unusual feeling
mostly I am met with an attack of an unusual feeling

The sky was unusually black; I found myself
The sky was unusually black I found myself

falling from the ceiling This was an undeniable
falling from the ceiling This was an undeniable

fact... My ears were ringing They said,
fact... My ears were ringing They said,

"Don't bleed." They said, "Do as I heed."
"Don't bleed." They said, "Do as I heed."
And then they said, "Come on now, give up your need
And then they said, "Come on now, give up your need
Also they added, "You'll end up being freed."
Also they added, "You'll end up being freed."
They said all will be well You will come back
They said all will be well You will come back
from hell I thought I'll just put invisible ink
from hell I thought I'll just put invisible ink
in the inkwell When it is dry, my signature
in the inkwell When it is dry, my signature
will disappear like a magic spell
will disappear like a magic spell
I remember the night was deathly quiet
I remember the night was deathly quiet
No one dared cause a riot The night
No one dared cause a riot The night

was bright and moonlit I will never be able to

forget He said, "You dare ride with me?"

On his roller coaster, I began to ride with glee

I went down, down, down, and then up, up, up,

you see There couldn't be a better ending,

I'll guarantee Then through a fire wall I

went, hot as hell Then down through a long,

cool, cool tunnel To all the devils and

demons, I said "Hello" and then "Farewell!"

Onwards I went and I said "Hello" to the angels
Onwards I went and I said "Hello" to the angels
past the four pearly gates All the characters I
past the four pearly gates All the characters
had earlier written In invisible ink, once so
had earlier written In invisible ink, once
very dark, with my pen Had up and dried
very dark, with my pen Had up and dried
and turned invisible again My cleverness
and turned invisible again My cleverness
had rescued me out of the devil's den
had rescued me out of the devil's den

141: page

29. I've Been Hit (81)
I've Been Hit

It's a hit, To wit It hurts everywhere and every
It's a hit, To wit It hurts everywhere and every
bit My weakness is made clear. Ah, shit
bit My weakness is made clear. Ah, shit
It burns. It stings. I've been hurt I'm bleeding
It burns. It stings. I've been hurt I'm bleeding
all over your shirt Pain does tend to make me
all over your shirt Pain does tend to make me
more alert But my eyes can't help but avert
more alert But my eyes can't help but avert
That was a dirty blow. It was really a low one
That was a dirty blow. It was really a low one
You hit below the belt. That's no fun I was
You hit below the belt. That's no fun I was
right in your bomb zone. I'm undone Up in the
right in your bomb zone. I'm undone Up in the

sky, way up high, I've been blown up way to
sky, way up high, I've been blown up way to

the sun You've stabbed me right in my heart
the sun You've stabbed me right in my heart

And sliced away a piece, a very large part I
And sliced away a piece, a very large part I

didn't see that in my star chart I fell for it
didn't see that in my star chart I felt for it

I even gave you a head start Everything is
I even gave you a head start Everything is

becoming crystal clear How much you hated me
becoming crystal clear How much you hated me

and how you were in fear You have no conscience
and how you were in fear You have no conscienc

at all, my dear You must have trouble
at all, my dear You must have trouble

looking at yourself in the mirror I've deflected
looking at yourself in the mirror I've deflecte

it back at you
it back at you
You won't suspect a thing until
You won't suspect a thing until
I say, "Boo."
I say, "Boo."
Karma is my friend and on my
Karma is my friend and on my
side too
side too
How are you for a little voodoo?
How are you for a little voodoo?
You'll find out how it feels
You'll find out how it feels
You'll be the one
You'll be the one
who squeals
who squeals
You'll know that revenge
You'll know that revenge
is real
is real
When you watch your life's blood
When you watch your life's blood
congeal
congeal
Nothing in your past will be
Nothing in your past will be
untouchable
untouchable
You'll be on your knees if you
You'll be on your knees if you
are able
are able
You will no longer feel mentally stable
You will no longer feel mentally stable

And you'll wish you were nothing but a fable
And you'll wish you were nothing but a fable

They'll say an eye for an eye   And also a tooth fo
They'll say an eye for an eye   And also a tooth fo

a tooth, no lie   I was hit by you a long, long
a tooth, no lie   I was hit by you a long, long

time ago, by and by   And now I am no
time ago, by and by   And now I am no

longer Mrs. Nice Guy
longer Mrs. Nice Guy

30. The Storm Passed Me By (83)

The storm had passed me by
I tell you - I had
looked at it straight in the eye
That just served to
glorify and amplify
After it left me safe and sound
high and dry
With winds lashing around me
The waves had enveloped me with an evil glee
Tears had sometimes filled my eyes so that I could
not see
I thought I would definitely cease to be
In the storm's fury, I went cheek to cheek

My strength was my secret technique — Sometimes I
My strength was my secret technique — Sometimes I

felt like nothing but a freak — The constant attack
felt like nothing but a freak — The constant attack

left me tired and weak — I found shelter in its
left me tired and weak — I found shelter in its

shadow — The embers of my spirit then had a
shadow — The embers of my spirit then had a

chance to awaken and grow — I felt safe
chance to awaken and grow — I felt safe

under its great bow — I had a chance to rest
under its great bow — I had a chance to rest

and to lie low — I existed and was fruitful
and to lie low — I existed and was fruitful

I acted like quite the numbskull — I kept
I acted like quite the numbskull — I kept

all my ideas inside my skull — Until my mind
all my ideas inside my skull — Until my mind

was brimming and full I was very patient
was brimming and full I was very patient

Except that time with my dear aunt I just had
Except that time with my dear aunt I just had

to expose the secret rant And the secret
to expose the secret rant And the secret

behind the nemesis power plant I had many
behind the nemasis power plant I had many

reasons to hide Two times I became a
reasons to hide Two times I became a

bride I took it all in my stride And
bride I took it all in my stride And

kept my eyes open wide Of the storm I
Kept my eyes open wide Of the storm I

will not complain Now I have again full use
will not complain Now I have again full use

of my brain All is well, and the journey
of my brain All is well, and the journey

was not in vain
was not in vain
Really, it was not just a
Really, it was not just a
storm – it was a hurricane
storm – it was a hurricane

31. I Alienate You (85)

I Alienate You

I alienate you That's nothing new To you
I alienate you That's nothing new To you

nothing that I say is true you don't give me my
nothing that I say is true you don't give me my

rightful due I make the mistake of causing much
rightful due I make the mistake of causing much

heartbreak Of giving you information just fos
heart break of giving you information just for

your sake And I believed you would take
your sake And I believed you would take

My advice without thinking that I was unwise
My advice without thinking that I was unwise

You think that you need your freedom And I'm
You think that you need your freedom And I'm

just a person who happens to be your mom
just a person who happens to be your mom

150 page

to keep myself busy
I don't need to travel to sightsee
just being here in the Land of the Free
of this, I stick to myself
it's good for my personal health
to be careful and walk with stealth
do you well to do so yourself
I am and whom I choose to be
I'm away or when I'm at home

I don't need any fancy Ph
I am happ
Becau
I guess, all in all
I choose
It would
I am who
when
Even

though you may think I am in your combat zone
though you may think I am in your combat zone
I am not your evil clone just because to you, I am
I am not your evil clone just because to you, I am
not unknown I am just an honest person and I am
not unknown I am just an honest person and I am
home grown But I do, I do, love you dearly
home grown But I do, I do, love you dearly
And I don't mind when you treat me like I am
And I don't mind when you treat me like I am
totally eerie I just chalk it up to one of life's
totally eerie I just chalk it up to one of life's
realities I know in my heart that you love
realities I know in my heart that you love
me too with a great finality
me too with a great finality

(152): page

32. Don't Deny The Truth (87)

Don't Deny The Truth

Don't deny the truth
It's painless, it's not like
pulling a tooth
You don't have to be the best sleuth
After all, it is just the proper way and it's so very couth
A lie will slap like whiplash and end up biting
Hard and fast like a bolt of lightning
Telling
the truth will be very enlightening
And being
true will be very refreshing
It can make you
very happy
In fact, it can set your soul free

It's the very best way to be   It's the right way for
you and me   The truth sometimes makes you sad
Like news that you've lost your loving, cherished dad
At that time you'll think of all the memories
when you were a safe, happy lad   And all those
wonderful memories that you   now must now
cherish and forever have.   Sometimes the
truth can drive you mad   Because it's so
very shocking, egad   Especially if you've

found out that you've been had
found out that you've been had

is not just a passing fad
is not just a passing fad

very best thing
very best thing

with a ring
with a ring

that brings
that brings

for your heart to sing
for your heart to sing

addictive habit
addictive habit

want to quit
want to quit

where you sit
where you sit

And oh no, it
And oh no, it

Truth can be the
Truth can be the

The newfound truth can come
The newfound truth can come

And all the love and trust that
And all the love and trust that

In turn it can be a new reason
In turn it can be a new reason

Truth gets to be an
Truth gets to be an

Once you start, you won't
Once you start, you won't

You'll like more and more
You'll like more and more

You'll learn to like the truth
You'll learn to like the truth

every bit If you find the truth hard to understand
every bit , If you find the truth hard to understand

Go and make new friends and listen to a new band
Go and make new friends and listen to a new band

This is the real way to find out → → the mysteries of the
This is the real way to find out the mysteries of the

land True understanding is bound hand and hand
land True understanding is bound hand and hand

Don't lie and avoid facing the human race It
Don't lie and avoid facing the human race It

doesn't even matter if you come in last place
doesn't even matter if you come in last place

at least you did not miss it all in your haste
At least you did not miss it all in your haste

The truth will give you a lead and be sweet to the taste
The truth will give you a lead and be sweet to the taste

Let the truth explode from your plate Let the
Let the truth explode from your plate Let the

floodwaters out of the gate Even if you have to
floodwaters out of the gate Even if you have to

express hate It'll still be the truth at any rate
express hate It'll still be the truth at any rate

The truth will be what everyone searches for yonder
The truth will be what everyone searches for yonder

The truth will be the most sought-after treasure
The truth will be the most sought-after treasure

it will be the greatest of the wonders The truth
it will be the greatest of the wonders The truth

is the solution of which everyone will be fonder
is the solution of which everyone will be fonder

And with this as ammunition, we won't
And with this as ammunition, we won't

have to be afraid any longer
have to be afraid any longer

33. I Had No Idea (89)

I Had No Idea

I had no idea I could cause so much hoopla

I had no idea I could cause so much hoopla

Or that my words could have punched you

Or that my words could have punched you

so hard, square on the jaw My words I wish

so hard square on the jaw My words I wish

I could somehow withdraw Because I inadvertently

I could somehow withdraw Because, I inadvertently

hit many nerves that were, in you very raw

hit many nerves that were, in you very raw

There is only one good thing I can get from this

I am thankful that you are able to forgive and disengage

My innocence or rather my gross ignorance

My innocence or rather my gross ignorance

And again I've learned a lesson, an experience kiss

And again I've learned a lesson, an exerience kiss

I had no idea I would open so many raw wounds
I had no idea I would open so many raw wounds
The knowledge is to me valuable and profound
The Knowledge is to me valuable and profound
In penance, I am truly loyal and honour bound
In penance, I am truly loyal and honour bound
I will be more careful now and all year round
I will be more careful now and All year round
You deserve my greatest respect
You deserve my greatest respect
On my words,
On my words,
I must more carefully reflect
I must more carefully reflect
Before I open
Before I open
my mouth to project
my mouth to project
Any words not at all
Any words not at all
polite or correct
polite or correct
I'm sorry and I love you.
I'm sorry AND I love you.
friend
friend
Of this travesty, I would love
Of this travesty, I would love

graciously to amend I really had no possible way
graciously to amend I really had no possible way

to comprehend And you'll see that I am not a
to comprehend And you'll see that I am not a

fair-weather friend I can really tell you have
fair-weather friend I can really tell you have

been through many trials But I still wasn't
been through many trials But I still wasn't

able to travel for quite so many miles I do
able to travel for quite so many miles I do

know as a friend you are very worthwhile
know as a friend you are very worthwhile

And if anything, I'd like to see you laugh and smile
And if anything, I'd like to see you laugh and smile

I know you need not be reminded Of life's
I know you need not be reminded Of life's

hardships that sometimes have had you blinded
hardships that sometimes have had you blinded

All the more reasons to look for peace of mind
And search for the clouds that are silver-lined
I will try to help you on your journey
By choosing the right words, that is the key
At least I will be careful, you'll see
You'll hear positive words when you are around me
I must learn to be more considerate
I'm not the only one that has been dealt a full plate
I must learn not to complicate or to aggravate

All the more reasons to look for peace of mind
And search for the clouds that are silver-lined
I will try to help you on your journey
By choosing the right words, that is the key
At least I will be careful, you'll see
You'll hear positive words when you are around me
I must learn to be more considerate
I'm not the only one that has been dealt a full plate
I must learn not to complicate or to aggravate

Or I may wake up feelings that are best left
Or I may wake up feelings that are best left

to hibernate I had no idea what was in your
to hibernate I had no idea what was in your

past Just because all my troubles seem to have passed
past Just because all my troubles seem to have passed

I realize you are still sad and downcast For
I realize you are still sad and downcast For

you, there doesn't seem to be a change in the
you, there doesn't seem to be a change in the

forecast I had no idea you were so discouraged
forecast I had no idea you were so discouraged

Most of the time you keep your feelings in camouflage
Most of the time you keep your feelings in camouflage

I wish I had known this was a well-formed mirage
I wish I had known this was a well-formed mirage

Now I feel as though I have committed espionage
Now I feel as though I have committed espionage

All I know is from now on

all I know is from now on

I will keep my

I will keep my

lips carefully drawn

lips carefully drawn

And I will try not to

And I will try not to

do another swan song

do another swan song

Until you want me t

Until you want me t

continue on and take the baton

continue on and take the baton

page 163

34. I Must Be Careful to Watch My Mouth (91)

I Mast Be Carefal to Watch My Mouth

I must be careful to watch my mouth
Or I may
be surprised by a moment of truth
And proven
to be a loud uncouth blabbermouth
And show
my innocence and evidence
of my backward youth
You and I know I, like you, am only human
Even though I'm an independant woman
I
must say I have come to fully understand
Discretion is the best way and the law of the land

I mast be carefal to watch my mouth
Or I may
be sarprised by a moment of trath
And proven
to be a loud uncouth blabbermouth
And show
my innocence and evidence
of my backward youth
You and I Know I, like you, am only human
Even though I'm an independant woman
I
must say I have come to fally understand
Discretion is the best way and the law of the land

Just because it is very tempting to speak
Just be cause it is very tempting to speak
mean I should give in and be weak
mean I should give in and be weak
learn a lesson on how to be discreet
learn a lesson on how to be discreet
pass by my enemy and turn the other cheek
pass by my enemy and turn the other cheek
learn to ignore the slap of an insult
learn to ignore the slap of an insult
have the most positive result
have the most positive result
cause you to catapult
cause you to catapult
very best of the best sea salt
very best of the best sea salt
I will avoid all complications and troubles
I will avoid all complications and troubles

It doesn't
It doesn't
I must try to
I must try to
And I must
And I must
To
To
Will
Will
It may even
It may even
Into success with the
Into success with the
By being quiet,
By being quiet,

Even when my enemies are in their little huddles
Even when my enemies are in their little huddles
They will all end up in a muddle And I'll be safe on
They will all end up in a muddle And I'll be safe on
the double Control of one's mouth is the key
the double Control of one's mouth is the key
The mouth's tongue has a poisonous barb; you see
The mouth's tongue has a poisonous barb, you see
With which the devil likes to play with fiendish glee
With which the devil likes to play with fiendish glee
So, you see, control of one's tongue is the safest
So you see, control of one's tongue is the safest
way to be When I decide to make a comment
way to be When I decide to make a comment
I must be careful where and how it's sent So
I must be careful where and how it's sent So
the meaning of it doesn't get interrupted or bent
the meaning of it doesn't get interrupted or bent

Or twisted out of what was truly meant I must always
Or twisted out of what was traly meant I must always

be on my guard And make sure I watch all my
be on my guard And make sure I watch all my

words Also to make them honest and kind
words Also to make them honest and Kind

when they are going to be heard And to always
when they are going to be heard And always

let them be sincere and clear, not at all blurred
let them be sincere and clear, Not at all blurred

I must try my best to be humble When I am
I must try my best to be hamble when I am

supposed to speak up I must try not to
supposed to speak up I must try not to

grumble And I must remember, if I am too
gramble And I must remember, if I am too

pushy, I might take a tumble This might
pushy, I might take a tamble This might

then prove me to be nothing but a numbskull
then prove me to be nothing but a numbskull
Oh, how I have already been burned And how I
Oh, how I have already been burned And how I
hope I have somehow, my lesson, learned And
hope I have somehow, my lesson, learned And
then it will be my fateful turn And then and
then it will be my fateful turn And then and
only then I will be safe and out of the reach
only then I will be safe and out of the reach
of harm
of harm

168 : page

35. I Must Be Quiet (93)

I Must Be Quiet

I must sit tight and be quiet I must not be
I must sit tight and be quiet I must not be

rowdy and be the cause of a riot I'd rather
rowdy and be the cause of a riot I'd rather

be lucky and hit the jackpot By digesting
be lucky and hit the jackpot By digesting

valuable food for thought I'd rather enjoy myself
valuable food for thought I'd rather enjoy myself

and have fun By having a quiet siesta in the
and have fun By having a quiet siesta in the

sun And praying quietly to the prodigal Son
sun And praying quietly to the prodigal Son

He is also our fellow man and the Wonderful One
He is also our fellow man and the Wonderful One

I'll be your secret confidant And try to be
I'll be your secret confidant And try to be

and act nonchalant
and act nonchalant

I'll be as quiet as is
I'll be as quiet as as

necessary or as careful as you want
necessary or as careful as you want

Especially when we are in our favorite restaurant
Especially when we are in our favorite restaurant

You won't be sorry
You won't be sorry

I'll hush up during
I'll hush up during

your important story
your important story

You will have nothing to
You will have nothing to

at all be upset
at all be upset

about or any reason to worry
about or any reason to worry

No-one's going to steal your story or your glory
No one's going to steal your story or your glory

You can go on your way without any bother
You can go on your way without any bother

You can continue to treat me like your brother
You can continue to treat me like your brother

Truth is, you would much really with me, not bother
Truth is, you would much really with me not bother

As far as appearances go, I'm here, yours truly, no other
As far as appearances go, I'm here, yours truly, no other

Just because you are always taking Someone
Just because you are always taking Someone

else's playthings Doesn't mean I'm going to
else's playthings Doesn't mean I'm going to

squeal or sing I'll bide my time, be silent,
squeal or sing I'll bide my time, be silent,

and see what that brings Someday you'll have
and see what that brings Someday you'll have

to take time to reflect and stop You won't
to take time to reflect and stop You won't

be able to always stay on top And you can't
be able to always stay on top And you can't

always go nonstop You are bound to
always go nonstop You are bound to

eventually make a giant belly flop Therefore,
eventually make a giant belly flop Therefore

for now I will be quiet And I won't be
for now I will be quiet And I won't be

cause of any riot I'll be careful and wait to
cause of any riot I'll be careful and wait to

fill in all the dots Because that's how I was
fill in all the dots Because that's how I was

taught
taught

(172) page

36. The Sky Opened For Us All (95)

The Sky Opened For Us All

The sky opened for us all
The sky opened for us all
again needs to crawl
again needs to crawl
our backs against the wall
our backs against the wall
heard the universal call
heard the universal call
it will be engraved and written
it will be engraved and written

No more sadness, no one
No more sadness no one
We will no longer have
we will no longer have
We will have all
we will have all
And the real answer,
And the real answer,
In what we
In what we

have chosen to believe in and how we are smitten
have chosen to believe in and how we are smitten
Of course it truly will depend on what God has given
Of course it truly will depend on what God has given
And how much energy with which we are
And how much energy with which we are

blessed with and how we are power - driven
blessed with and how we are power - driven
In turn
In turn
the world will give us back
the world will give us back
Anything we wish for
Anything we wish for
or lack
or lack
So that we can then carry it all on our
So that we can then carry it all on our
personal stack
personal stack
Before we go into overload or
Before we go into over load or
die of a heart attack
die of a heart attack
This is the deal, this
This is the deal, this
is the done deal
is the done deal
Before we sit to eat our
Before we sit to eat our
last meal
last meal
We may want to take time to
we may want to take time to
pray and kneel
pray and kneel
The more sincere we are
The more sincere we are
the greater
the greater
will be the universal appeal
will be the universal appeal

If we open our eyes and let ourselves believe → if
If we open our eyes and let ourselves believe if

we open our hearts, we might be able to perceive
we open, our hearts, we might be able to perceive

The new generation this will take over and relieve
The new generation this will take over and relieve

The new generation this will take oves and relieve
The new generation this will take over and relieve

All of their ancestors a pitiful lot and let
All of their ancestors a pitiful lot, and let

them all have sick leave We will help them to
them all have sick leave We will help them to

prepare For all what is left to be theirs
prepare For all what is left to be theirs

We will all think it is quite fair We will
We will all think it is quite fair We will

pray and pray and hope they too feel as we
pray and pray and hope they too feel as we

do and truly care We surely must all live as
do and truly care We surely must all live as

one Ot this whole world will surely be undone
one Or this whole world will surely be undone

And then what would be left for them or us or for
And then what would be left for them or us or for

anyone under the sun And how would we or they
any one under the sun And how would we or they

ho! ho! ho!

have any more fun So try to prepare your
have any more fun So try to prepare your

3000 2000 1900 1800

babies For all the future maybes And
babies For all the future maybes And

when and if they get to look at a tree They
when and if they get to look at a free They

will be able to say, "Look at me, I'm free.
will be able to say, "Look at me, I'm free.

176 page

37. Come On, Wiggle (97)

Come On, Wiggle

Faster, faster, faster, give a giggle
Come on, wiggle,
wiggle, wiggle, and wiggle
I would like to give you
a hug and a friendly tickle
I love you, don't be so
distant and fickle
The force be with me and you
Phasers on stun, this is all so new
My love is
shiny too, Cupid's arrow came out of the blue
Just like a deadly shot from Karate or Kung fu
My world lives for another and another and another

All I know is I'm in a state of unadulterated wonder
All I Know is I'm in a state of unadalterated wonder

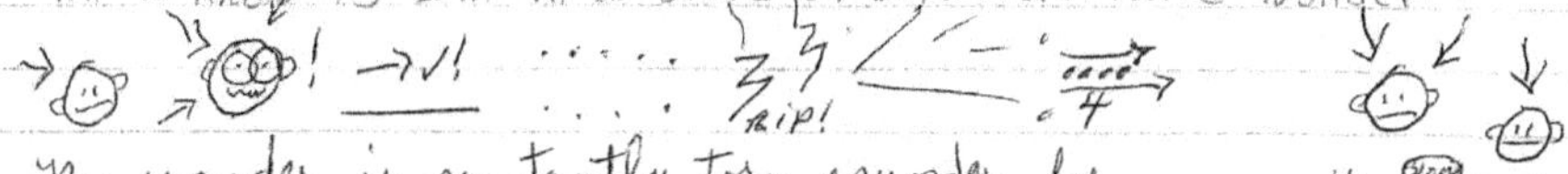

My wonder is constantly torn asunder for You, my
My wonder is constantly torn asunder for You, my

dear husband and lover I don't think this is at all
dear hasband and lover I don't think this is at all

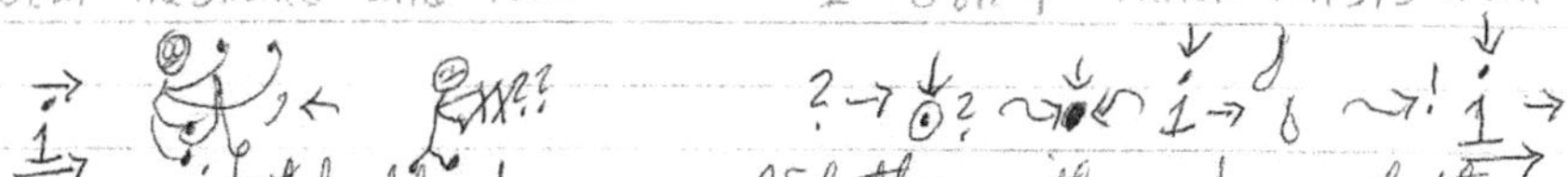

an accidental blunder Whether with a drop of the
an accidental blander Whether with a drop of the

hat or not You and I may or may not be caught
hat or not You and I may or mag not be caught

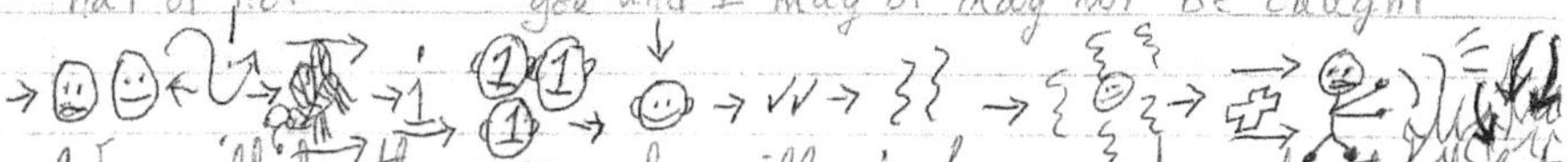

We will be the ones who will wiggle around and get red hot
We will be the ones who will wiggle around and get rid hot

We will love each other both a little and a lot
We will love each other both a little and a lot

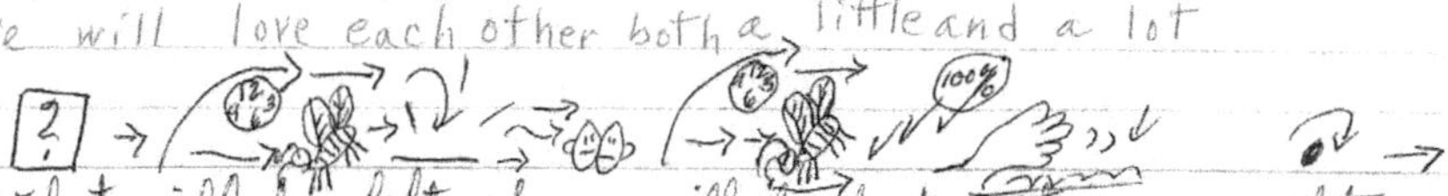

What will be left of us will be best felt after
What will be left of us will be bestfelt After

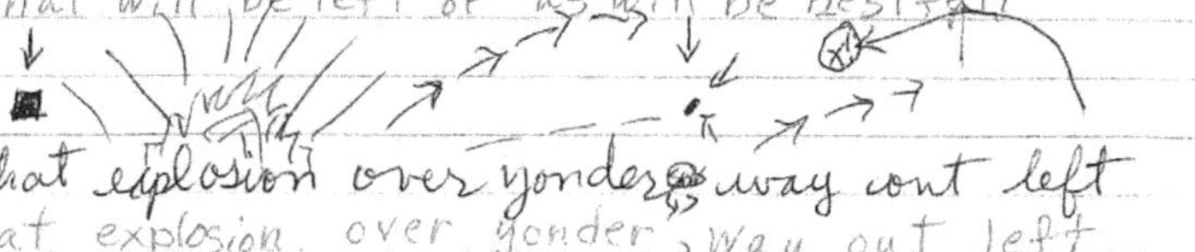

that explosion over yonder, way out left
that explosion over yonder, way out left

There won't be much left of us, I'll bet — What do
There won't be much left of us, I'll bet — What do
you expect? That's all you're bound to get — Oh, we
you expect? That's all you're bound to get — Oh, we
all want to know the answer to the age-old question
all want to know the answer to the age-old questions
Just put down your arms and tickle him and
Just put down your arms and tickle him and
then wait for a reaction — Invite him to try to join
then wait for a reaction, Invite him to try to join
you and you might get some kind of attention
you and you might get some kind of attention
But make sure to be careful to protect your sterling
But make sure to be careful to protect your sterling
reputation — By the way it stands, and by
reputation — By the way it stands, and by
the way it looks — It's OK to cook, according to
the way it looks — It's OK to cook, according to

everyone's recipe books Playing fair and using
clean methods are the main ingredients It
takes to be in the winner's nook And you see,
it's magic, you will have a delicious meal on
the hook Someday you will have great peace,
and this will be your cup of tea And you will
have great satisfaction, gratification, all the
more for you to be able to tease I know that
is certain. Just look at me and say cheese.

He can have my keys! It's the greatest! It's

He can have my keys! It's the greatest! It's

called marriage, say yes, if you please

called marriage, say yes, if you please

38. No Need To Hate (99)

There is no need to hate, the future looks bright, mate
There is no need to hate, now or in the future, at any rate
There is no need to hate, come on poke your
head out of the gate There is no need to hate,
you need not be scared of your fate We'll
help you out, my friends, and you'll be happy in
the end Come on take hold of the
outstretched arm we have to lend It might

be the only way you'll make it around the bend
be the only way you'll make it around the bend
And this way we will find true fellowship again and
And this way we will find true fellowship again and
again Our times may sometimes be filled with
again Our times may sometimes be filled with
hardships But our lives can become strong
hardships But our lives can become strong
battleships Manned and operated by cosmic
battleships Manned and operated by cosmic
super leadership And controlled by supremely
super leadership And controlled by supremely
intelligent establishment The winds in your
intelligent establishment The winds in your
storms can reach gales if they see fit And
storms can reach gales if they see fit And
because our conversations are filled with wit
because our conversations are filled with wit

We will not be affected, not even a little bit
Because we were built from the best-laid
plans — a foolproof blueprint
Then when you
wish to show how you truly feel
And show
your fear that someone might follow on your heel
You must get over your unwillingness to kneel
And accept life's dances, good or bad, that's the
done deal
And all what we were taught and
whether we believed it or not
We must

judge if all of it was told to us, for naught
judge if all of it was told to us for naught
Then only then will our enemies be an unimportant lot
Then only then will our enemies be an unimportant lot
Because we'll know all what they are about
Because we'll know all what they are about
and what they've got Then we will all have a fun
and what they've got Then we will all have a fun
time With plenty of enthusiasm for lives
time With plenty of enthusiasm for lives
hard climb We'll know our fate has had
hard climb We'll know our fate has had
yabba babba doo
a reason and a rhyme And there is no
a reason and a rhyme And there ~~is~~ no
reason for hate a big time Freedom for
reason for hate a big time Freedom for
all is what is needed And making sure love is
all is what is needed And making sure love is

Dencan 1755

185 : page

well-seeded
well-seeded

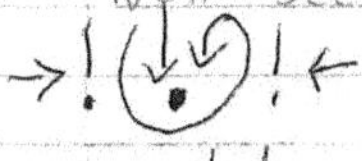

needed
needed

heeded.
heeded

Great intelligence isn't necessarily
Great intelligence isn't necessarily

All we need is mutual respect to be
All we need is mutual respect to be

39. What's In Your Brain? (101)

What's In Your Brain?

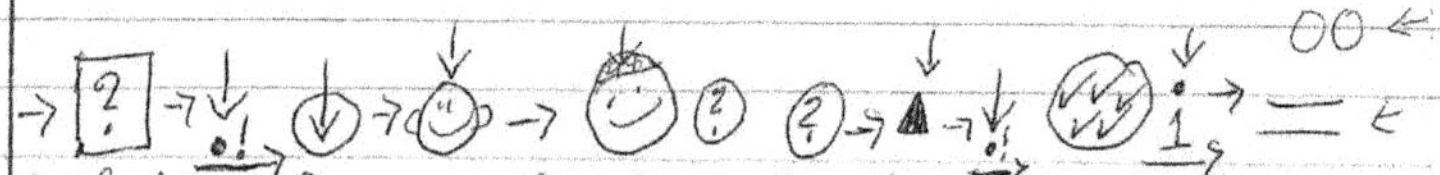

What's in your brain? If it is all the same
What's in your brain? If it's all the same

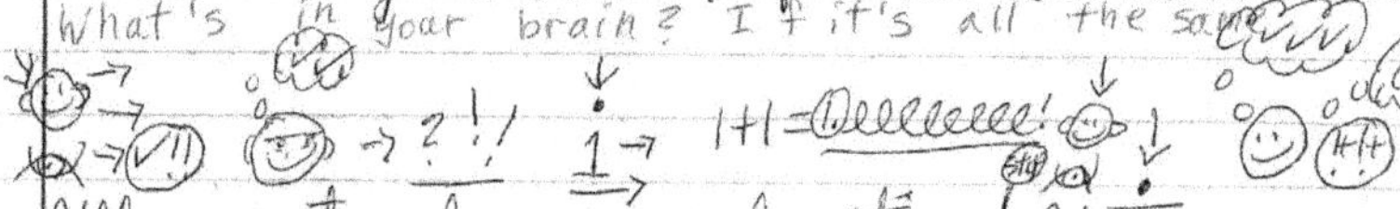

I'll accept only one explanation I'm game
I'll accept only one explanation I'm game

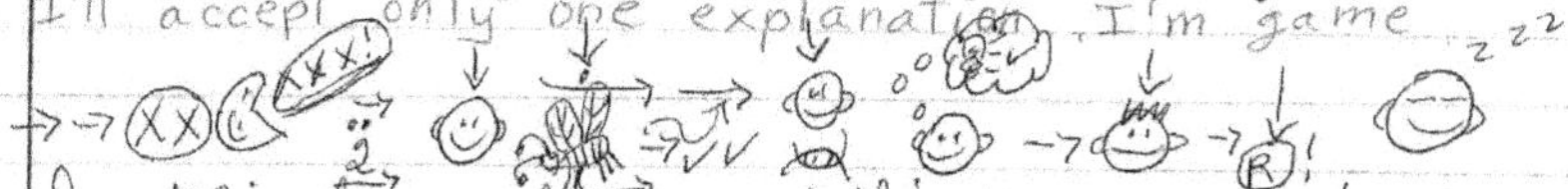

Don't lie to me because I think you are tame
Don't lie to me because I think you are tame

You can say anything complicated?
You can say anything complicated?

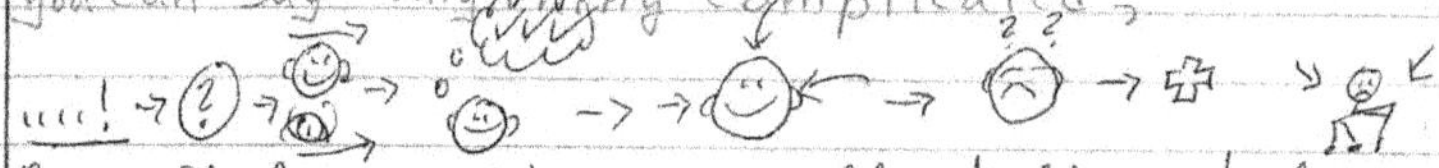

Even if I consider myself dull and lame
Even if I consider myself dull and lame

I know it is basically soft matter And it
I know it is basically soft matters And it

can't survive a viscious attack Or being
can't survive a viscious attack Or being

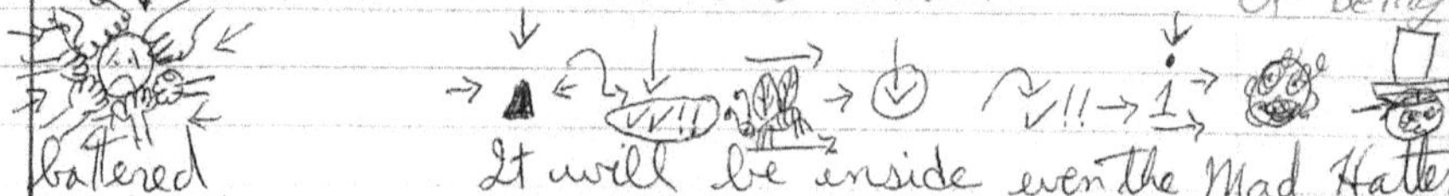

battered It will be inside even the Mad Hatter
battered It will be inside even the Mad Hatter

OK, we all know there as really a scientific
OK, we All know there as really a scientific

explanation more like the latter Do you know
explanation more like the latter Do you know

about how the brain works, sir? When it
about how the brain works, sit? When it

doesn't work, everything is a blur Then it'll
doesn't work, everything is a blur Then it'll

take tons of research, I'm sure To find out
take tons of research, I'm sure To find out

what disease it has and if it has a cure
what disease it has and if it has a cure

It's about time to find out about yours and mine
It's about time to find out about yours and mine

And all the mysteries hiding there inside and find
And all the mysteries hiding there inside and find

All our thoughts so that we are no longer blind
All our thoughts so that we are no longer blind

After all, we are all come basically from the same kind
After all, we are all come basically from the same kind

We have yet to delve and thoroughly explore What
We have yet to delve and thoroughly explore What

is in and behind the brain's revolving doors?
is in and behind the brain's revolving doors?

How can you or I possibly be certain?
How can you or I possibly be certain?

What happens when our brain declares war?
What happens when our brain declares war?

Who knows how much power it has? We
Who knows how much power it has? We

just have to learn to turn on its gas
just have to learn to turn on its gas

We don't even know about most of its mass
We don't even know about most of its mass

The most of it is a mystery, totally unexplored
The most of it is a mystery, totally unexplored

What we do know
What we do know
Is that there is row upon row
Is that there is row upon row
And many, many layers all tied together like
And many, many layers all tied together like
A big, beautiful present, wrapped in a protective bow
a big, beautiful present, wrapped in a protective bow
It serves as our very own main control centre
It serves as our very own main control centre
From which we learn and grow
From which we learn and grow
And while
And while
we continue to try and try
we continue to try and try
We still know
We still know
little about this important guy
little about this important guy
This is amazingly
This is amazingly
our main frame, no lie
our main frame, no lie
But I imagine
But I imagine
we will, we will find out by and by
we will, we will find out by and by

190 : page

40. The Great Escape (103)

The Great Escape

I'm ready for my undisputed fate It is time

I'm ready for my undispated fate It is time

for me to jump and leave the gate It is time for

for me to jump and leave the gate It is time for

me to make my great escape It is time for me

me to make my great escape It is time for me

to squeeze love out of hate A feat like this will

to squeeze love out of hate A feat like this will

make me very happy This accomplishment

make me very happy This accomplishment

might change my world, Pappy I will then be

might change my world, Pappy I will then be

satesfied because I will no longer feel crappy

satistied because I will no longer feel crappy

And that will be the greatest feeling of all, daddy

And that will be the greatest feeling of all, Daddy

It will all start and come from my heart For me
It will all start and come from my heart For me

that will always be the best place to start And when
that will always be the best place to start And when

you all see what is behind the rest of my fort You
you all see what is behind the rest of my fort You

will no longer bother being a worrywart My
will no longer bother being a worrywart My

escape will be like a runaway train It will flow
escape will be like a runaway train It will flow

like lightning, right out of my brain It will be
like lightning, right out of my brain It will be

something no one man can tame This
something no one man can tame This

escape will be like the best word game I will
escape will be like the best word game I will

play no holds barred Anyone playing with me
play no holds barred Any one playing with me

will feel like a star This game will take everyone fa
will feel like a star This game will take everyone fa

It will even overtake war And I will continue my
It will even over take war And I will continue my

1. 2. 3.

wordplay And I will be quite satisfied to say
word play And I will be quite satisfied to say

That I will have my own way I just like it
That I will have my own way I just like it

when everyone will be merry and gay Even
when everyone will be merry and gay Even

though I am old, I won't leave you out in the
though I am old, I won't leave you out in th

cold And I won't let hatred take a hold
cold And I won't let hatred take a hold

14K 14K

My happiness will be my finest spun gold
My happiness will be my finest spun gold

SONG BOOK

My songs will flow all over I'll invite you al
My songs will flow all over I'll invite you al

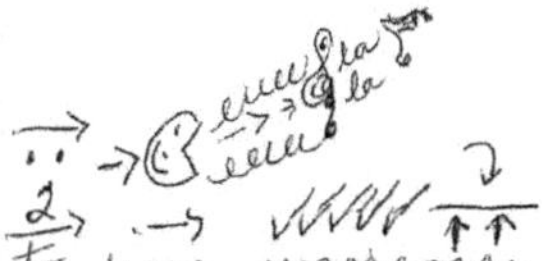

to sing moreover
to sing moreover

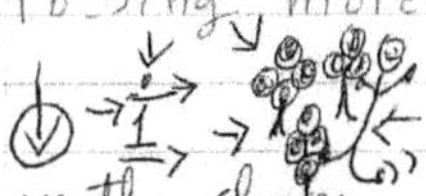

un the cloves
in the clover

all together
all together

We'll all eventually be dancing
We'll all eventaally be dancing

The words and music will bind us
The words and music will bind us

41. Young Love (105)

Young Love

They say keep the one in your hand the one you
They say keep the one in your hand the one you

love, your young love
love, your young love

So innocently, so trusting, this
So innocently, so trusting, this

one that is like a dove
one that is like a dove

This one you have lots in
This one you have lots in

common with,
common with,

and who you want more of
And who you want more of

This one's better than two in the bush and is as
This one's better than two in the bush and is as

good as one in your glove
good as one in your glove

We make a fine
We make a fine

picture, dear
picture, dear

No need to look at each
No need to look at each

other in the mirror
other in the mirror

That we are happy with each other
is plain and clear
And now that we've met, we
don't know the meaning of fear
Here's one for
you, here's one for me
The best things in our
lives are free
Love is bound to taste better if we
look at what we see
And all too soon, our
most human lives
will be over, for both of us
our love's beauty is all around us
You won't find us making a fuss
Because
with each other, our words are never at a loss.

We try to communicate, and happiness is for us
we try to communicate, and happiness is for us
at a coin's toss. As a couple, we feel we are
at a coin's toss As a couple, we feel we are
predestined. Because to each other we are very loyal
predestined Because to each other we are very loyal
When we are together, everything is fun, even toil
when we are together, everything is fun, even toil
We are happy to be grounded on terra-firma soil
We are happy to be grounded on terra-firma soil
We feel like every day is Valentine's Day
We feel like every day is Valentine's Day
Because Cupid has a hold of us and
Because Cupid has a hold of us and
.....!!!!
continues to have his way. Cupid's hearts
continues to have his way Cupid's hearts
and arrows are like bubbles at play. They
and arrows are like bubbles at play They

Keep us in love, merry and gay No matter what,
no matter when We'll be together like long-
lost friends No matter what, nothing can separate
us in the here, or at all, or again Our love
will go beyond this world when our mortal
lives end Our love is eternally entwined
Our spirits have joined and formed a grand smokey design
For anyone not to see it, they would have to be
blind We knew it all along that life would,

to us, eventually be kind
object, our fates were preset
together, no matter how high the bet
odds were stacked against us and yet
came from far while I stayed still
a reason to regret
connection, to my recollection
my greatest satisfaction
first sight and sound reaction

For us, distance was no
We were meant to b
The
My prin
yet we never
And oh that fateful
Was to his an
It was a love at
A love given

from God with His blessing

from God with His blessing

totally to our liking

totally to our liking

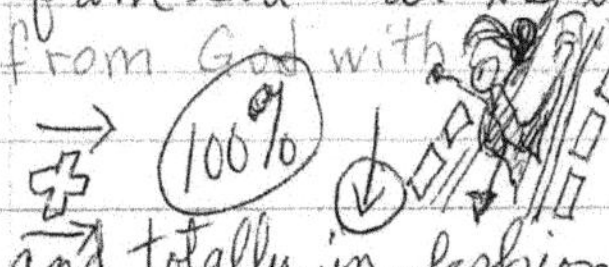

and totally in fashion

and totally in fashion

(200) page

42. If I Could Make A Wish (107)

If I Could Make A Wish

If I could make a wish It would not be to be a
If I could make a wish It would not be to be a

luscious dish Not that I like being a funny fish
luscious dish Not that I like being a funny fish

And I would not wish for another splash or another splish
And I would not wish for another splash or another splish

So far, for what I would yearn Would be to be able
So far, for what I would yearn Would be to be able

to discern Between good and evil, turn in turn
to discern Between good and evil, turn in turn

Even though this may be dangerous And I do not
Even though this may be dangerous And I do not

wish to burn I wish only for everyone's
wish to burn I wish only for everyone's

overall best There, I have finally got it off
overall best There, I have finally got it off

my chest
I don't really know the entirety of
the rest
But so far, I feel that I have been quite blessed
What I really want, tends to claw me
inside and
cause me endless taunts
I'm afraid that I will
actually obtain it because
then I might use
my knowledge to flaunt
This effort might
leave me thin and gaunt
And in this case
I would be both unhealthy
and might act
like a freaky savant
I would not choose my

202

wish in haste

to be chaste

taste

place

I might even make a surprise wish

I will surely choose to my very own

I won't choose when I am in any special

What would I choose to be my lucky charm

I'll yell out loud if you get close and

I'll celebrat

if you get warm

arm in arm

my fire alarm

star

All I wish for is to go away

With the man who has raised

Yes, I saw that shooting

Falling from the sky away, so very far

I did make a wish, hark, hark, and hark It may
I did make a wish, hark, hark, and hark It may
or may not be for a car You can't take my wishes
or may not be for a car You can't take my wishes
away from me We'll both find out if my
away from me We'll both find out if my
wishes come to be If they come true, I'll
wishes come to be If they come true, I'll
giggle with glee I'm patient for what's to be
giggle with glee I'm patient for what's to be
we'll just wait and see I may have made
we'll just wait and see I may have made
more wishes than one A wish, in the plural,
more wishes than one A wish, in the plural,
could be lots of fun! I had better be careful
could be lots of fun! I had better be careful
not to jump the gun Then all my wishes
not to jump the gun Then all my wishes

page: 204

would be for naught and I would be undone
would be for naught and I would be undone

I won't waste my wish on any one try I'll
I won't waste my wish on any one try I'l

give my wish my best shot, and that is no lie
give my wish my best shot, and that is no lie

I'll hope for the best, me oh my I can depend
I'll hope for the best, me oh my I can depen

on the Man, the Main Guy
on the Man, the Main Guy

43. If I May Be So Bold (109)

If I May Be So Bold

If I may say so, if I may be so bold I have
If, I, May Say so, if I may be so bold I have
realized I am daily becoming old I am happy
realized I am daily becoming old I am happy
to say, fear of death is losing its hold I am
to say, fear of death is losing its hold I am
also happy to say, I do not think I have sold my soul
also happy to say, I do not think I have sold my soul
In my life so far, I have seen a lot of terrible things
In my life so far, I have seen a lot of terrible things
But with them, I have found many important lessons
But with them, I have found many important lessons
That only life's trials could bring I have also
That only life's trials could bring I have also
seen how reliable fate rings and sings I
seen how reliable fate rings and sings I

play

have even seen how life begins — So tell me, how
have even seen how life begins — So tell me, how

can possibly be surprised — At anything I find
can possibly be surprised — At anything I find

on the other side — It is, nevertheless, bound to
on the other side — It is, nevertheless, bound to

be a fantastic ride — Over yonder, there is bound
be a fantastic ride — Over yonder, there, is bound

to be someone to whom I can confide
to be someone to whom I can confide

And in there, in the great when — My new life
And in there, in the great when — My new life

will begin again — I'll say good-bye to where
will begin again — I'll say good-bye to where

I've been — And I will take my new life for a
I've been — And I will take my new life for a

spin — All I can say is I want to meet the Man
spin — All I can say is I want to meet the Man

The One who's Three-in-One because I'm one
of His biggest fans I want to be with Him in
His beautiful land The land full of miracles
both great and grand If I get there and when
I do I'll know that success comes to everyone
not just a few That's when the universe will
seem to become brand new That's when I
will no longer have anything to lose → That's
when I will know I have passed every test

20B play

That's when I will know I have been truly blessed
That's when I will know I have been truly blessed

Then I will know I am a true success And I will
Then I will know I am a true success And I will

know I have done my very best Success will
know I have done my very best Success will

have a sweet smell Success will ring as clear
have a sweet smell Success will ring as clear

as a bell In the Lord's domain, I wish to dwell
as a bell In the Lord's domain, I wish to dwell

I will want a permanent place in His happy hotel
I will want a permanent place in His happy hotel

That's when the universe will seem to be a small place
That's when the universe will seem to be a small place

No matter where we are, we'll be able to see
No matter where we are, we'll be able to see

each other's face This will be, in the best
each other's face This will be, in the best

scenario, the very best case
I will then be in the
happiest state of grace
I will walk on His streets
of finest gold
Love will have in me its
complete and entire hold
I never will again
know the meaning of cold
I will have eternal
beauty to behold
I will never again have to
suffer
I will have access to His Living Water
My eternal life will be anew and my
soul will be energized and astir
My old life

play : 210

will be gone with the new to begin that is for
will be gone with the new to begin that is for

sure That's when I will truly be one
sure That's when I will truly be one

With the Father, the Spirit, and the Holy Son
with the Father, the Spirit, and the Holy Son

When I'm with them, I will have won Over
When I'm with them, I will have won Over

this life and on a new life I will have begun
this life and on a new life I will have begun

44. Don't Crack Your Whip (111)

Don't Crack Your Whip

Don't you dare don't crack your whip If you do,
Don't you dare don't crack your whip If you do,
I might lose my grip Then I'll tell you not to
I might lose my grip Then I'll tell you not to
give me any lip And furthermore, I might
give me any lip And furthermore, I might
break down and have a fit When I hear
break down and have a fit When I hear
the sound of the whip's crack It might
the sound of the whip's crack It might
be the straw that breaks my camel's back
be the straw that breaks my camel's back
I then might be forced to use a suprise attack
I then might be forced to use a suprise attack
So don't give me any wise cracks unless they are
So don't give me any wise cracks unless they are

proven facts
If I so much as get scared
My nostrils will flare and my teeth will be bared
My insecurities will show how much I really care
And my anger will be pi r-squared
you think you really are?
the cause of the next war
is cause suffering, and a lot of gore
realize how much damage your
will be responsible for?

Who do
You might even be
All that would do
Do you
big whip
You stink to high

heavens, you creep
heavens, you creep
You are nothing but a
You are nothing but a
slithering pipsqueak
slithering pipsqueak
You get gratification out
You get gratification out
of hurting the mild and the meek
of hurting the mild and the meek
Is it truth or
Is it truth or
is it justification you seek?
is it justication you seek?
I'm telling you,
I'm telling you,
I think in the end you'll be sorry
I think in the end you'll be sorry
When your
when your
words backfire, it'll be a different story
words back fire, it'll be a different story
Then
Then
you'll be the one with the worries
you'll be the one with the worries
And they
And they
might haul you away in a police
might haul you away in a police
car – so
car – so
much for your glory
much for your glory
You won't like that
You won't like that

Kind of party
down in a hurry
away in a scurry
that story
blown it
to sit
quiet
away kit
different light

I think then you'll be the one breaking
And you'll be the one running
Wrap your whip around
Before you know it you'll have
You'll be the one who has to learn
You'll be the one who has to learn to be
So put that info - whip back in your going -
Your friends might see you in a
If you decide you no longer

want to fight They may even begin to see you as
want to Fight They may even begin to see you

someone bright Not just a loud noise in the night
someone bright Not just a load noise in the night

If you learn to be a good person You'll be
If you learn to be a good person You'll be

someone people want to bring back to their mom
some one people want to bring back to their mom

That's when the real battle will be won That's
That's when the real battle will be won That's

when you'll have come out into the sun Also
when you'll have come out into the sun Also

I'll be happy to stretch my hand To you
I'll be happy to stretch my hand To you

in friendship and welcome you to my land
in friendship and welcome you to my land

That's when we both will feel grand Then
That's when we both will feel grand Then

we will both each other understand
we will both each other understand
both be on the same wavelength
both be on the same wavelength
joy will be our strengths
joy will be our strengths
will be our think tank
will be our think tank
other to congratulate
other to congratulate

We will
We will
And peace and
And peace and
Then the universe
Then the universe
And we will have each
And we will have each
and to thank
and to thank

(217) : page

45. I'm A Victim Of War (113)

I'm A Victim Of War

I'm alive but I am a victim of war - and what's more

I'm alive but I am a victim of war - and what's more

I did not ask for what went before or Who was

I did not ask for what went before or Who was

waiting - that awful bore Or what was to be in

waiting - that awful bore Or what was to be in

store I did not ask for my future or - for

store I did not ask for my future or - for

my before I did not ask for life's gore or how

my before I did not ask for life's gore or how

my heart was to be put into a tug-of-war

my heart was to be put into a tug-of-war

No one on Earth witnessed my pain After life's

No one on Earth witnessed my pain After life's

wars began, it was all I could do but to be

wars began, it was all I could do but to be

hurt again and again
No matter what, I would
never be the same; I
truly thought I would go
insane
And meanwhile my handshake had become
weak
And my mind had been imprisoned in
invisible chains
My journey was an uphill
battle
It was a very hard road to travel
It was something with which I wished
I had not
been saddled
Responsibility was given to me
at the same time
My mind was left confused

and addled I was quite lonely and very, very hurt
Mind you, leaving my family alone was not my decision;
I did not choose to leave them Everyone left me
alone for what it's worth Soon all my senses
were trained to be sharp and alert And as the
years passed before my eyes It was easier and
easier to let sleeping dogs lie And I learned to
stand on my own two feet and against all
odds, to defy All those hurts that had been

thrown my way, by and by
A very long, long time ago
I learned quietly say, "Go Blow"
I learned to hold no grudges and so
I began the long climb up, up, up and
continued to heal and to grow
The hurt did not go away completely
But I learned to look at a very difficult
life - much more sweetly
I learned to handle my pain more discreetly
In that way, life would not be able to defeat me

And life would no longer be an impossible feat
And life would no longer be an impossible feat

My motto was, is, and will be
My motto was, is, and will be

To let my soul
To let my soul

be set free
be set free

I want to be able to see
I want to be able to see

In and
In and

past my family tree
past my family tree

222 page

46. Now His Spirit Soars (115)

Now His Spirit Soars

Now he is free, Now his spirit soars Now he wi
Now he's free, Now his spirit soars Now he wil

not have to go through any more battles or see
not have to go through any more battles or see

any more wars Now he will not have to get into
any more wars Now he will not have to get int

any more tight-fitting cars Now his spirit will
any more tight-fitting cars Now his spirit will

be able to see anything and will soar farther th
be able to see anything and will soar farther tha

far Now you can travel north And if
far Now you can travel north And if

you want, you can travel south And now
you want, you can travel south And now

when you open your mouth The whole world
when you open your mouth The whole world

can be your foodstuff Now your omnipresent
can be your foodstuff Now your omnipresent
vapors Will be able to go anywhere they
vapors Will be able to go anywhere they
wish and travel any corridor Listen, that's not
wish and travel any corridor Listen, that's not
all; there's much more Your spirit will be able
all; there's much more Your spirit will be able
to go through any wall And pass through any
to go through any wall And pass through any
door I think this, dear bro, will be your heaven
door I think this, dear bro, will be your heaven
My brother, I give you my permission
My brother, I give you my permission
Because I really have not got a rhyme nor a reason
Because I really have not got a rhyme nor a reason
Of how to stop you, or when or where you
Of how to stop you, or when or where you

will visit, or when or in which season
will visit, or when or in which season

Bro, you will be able to go anywhere Anywhere at
Bro, you will be able to go anywhere Anywhere at

your wish, anytime and without any snares
your wish, anytime and without any snares

What of money - you are now richer than the
What of money - you are now richer than the

$1,000,000,000.00

richest billionaire Myself, I think that's totally
richest billionaire Myself, I think that's totally

fair and square I'm happy to say, you will
fair and square I'm happy to say, you will

no longer suffer My dear, wonderful
no longer suffer My dear, wonderful

brother You are now in the bosom of our dear
brother You are now in the bosom of our dear

mother No one will ever again be able, to you, bother
mother No one will ever again be able, to you, bother

In my heart, I know you are in a good place
In my heart, I know you are in a good place

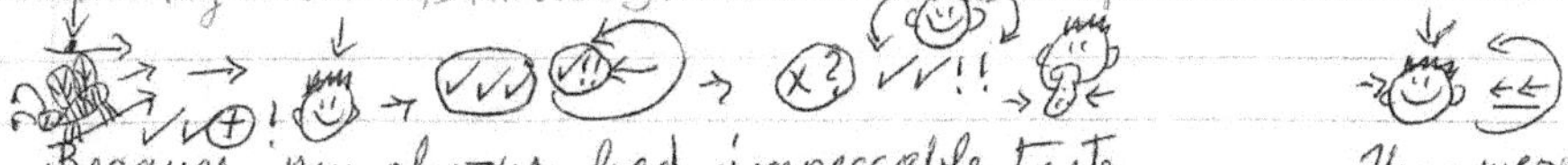

Because you always had impeccable taste You were
Because you always had impeccable taste You were

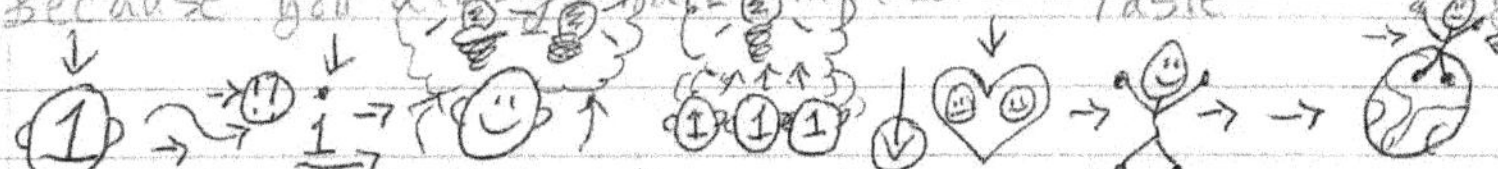

one of the intelligent ones in our human race
one of the intelligent ones in our human race

Now you can travel the whole cloud's great database
Now you can travel the whole cloud's great database

If I had only known you better I would have known
If I had only known you better I would have known

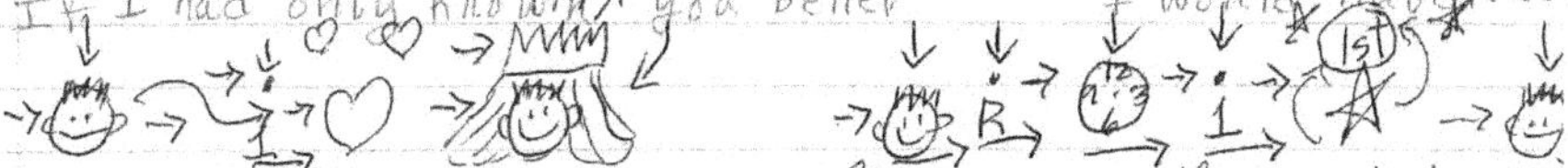

you as a true emperor You are now the greatest ; you
you as a true emperor You are now the greatest you

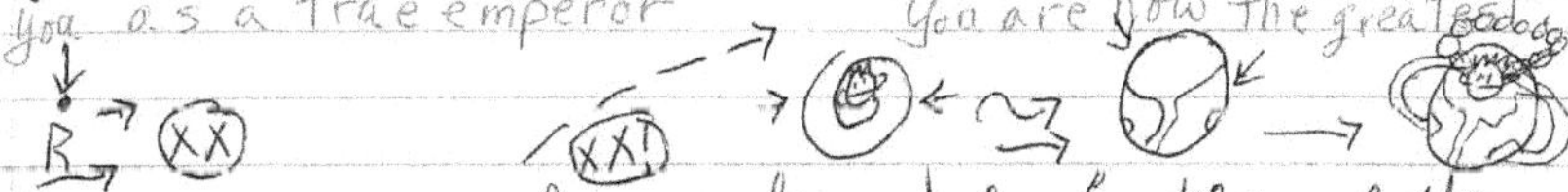

are no longer bound by Earth's fetters
are no longer bound by Earth's fetters

You are now a quantum universe jet-setter
You are now a quantum universe jet-setter

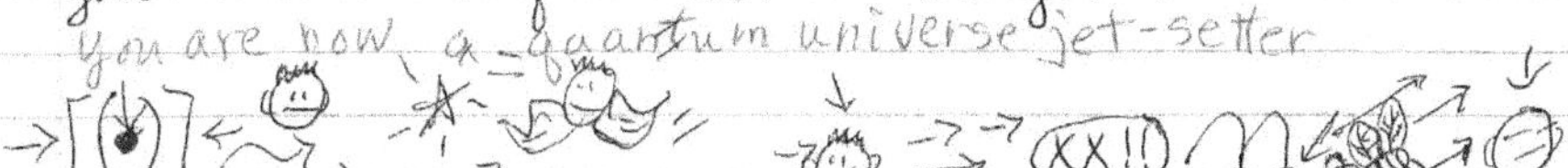

With your new wings, you will never again be bored
With your new wings you will never again be bored

226 page

Now you will always be able to have the last word
Now you will always be able to have the last word

And if you want, you'll be totally safe to flip the bird
And if you want, you'll be totally safe to flip the bird

Now, no matter how you act, no one will ever be
Now, no matter how you act, no one will ever be

able to think you are absurd When we are
able to think you are absurd When we are

wondering about all those unknown mysteries
wondering about all those unknown mysteries

You'll be laughing at us because you'll be holding
You'll be laughing at us because you'll be holding

all the puzzle's keys You'll know all the
all the puzzle's key's You'll know all the

$1+1=\square$ $5\div5=\square$ $2\times3=\square$ $2^2=\square$

answers piece by piece And you won't have
answer's piece by piece And you won't have

any trouble finding sweet release You, bro,
any trouble finding sweet release You, bro,

are now the most popular one You now have so
are now the most popular one You now have so

many friends and are now having all the fun
many friends and are now having all the fun

You have already proved you won't be undone
You have already proved you won't be undone

By shining brighter than the brightest sun Your
By shining brighter than the brightest sun Your

spirit will never again be at half mast
spirit will never again be at half mast

Because now your spirit will be able to soar so very
Because now your spirit will be able to soar so very

fast If you want to getaway no one will be as fast
fast If you want to get away no one will be as fast

as your spirit; no one will be your match You'll be
as your spirit; no one will be your match You'll be

gone in a twinkle; you will never again be outclassed
gone in a twinkle; you will never again be outclassed

47. The Blurb (118)

The Blarb

I have my very own opinions, and of these I am very kee

I have my very own opinions, and of these I am very kee

My ideas are about why I've been

My ideas are about why I've been

Still, they may not qualify for any

Still, they may not qualify for any

blue-ribbon science magazine

blue-ribbon science magazine

But for a

But for a

little entertainment, you might find them

little entertainment, you might find them

Just a little different than those you have already

Just a little different than those you have already

seen

seen

You can choose to believe them or

You can choose to believe them or

maybe

maybe

not choose to believe them, but

not choose to believe them, but

I won't tell them over and over or maybe I will a lot
I won't tell them over and over or maybe I will a lot

In fact, what you hear, you'll wish you had not
In fact, what you hear, you'll wish you had not

You'll ask, are these ideas legal or are they hot?
You'll ask, are these ideas legal or are they hot?

And my ideas may or may not be in style But
And my ideas may or may not be in style But

ah heck, to obtain them, I've gone that extra mile
ah heck, to obtain them, I've gone that extra mile

And if I do say so with a little or a lot of guile
And if I do say so with a little or a lot of guile

The least you can do is listening for a little while
The least you can do is listening for a little while

My great story may or may not be real But
My great story may or may not be real But

I guarantee, I can say I got it for a steal
I guarantee, I can say I got it for a steal

heck in this world, what is this form, this thing
heck in this world what is this form, this thing

I admit I have been pulling you on a string
I admit I have been pulling you on a string

Let's
Let's

just say I'm an educated ding-a-ling
just say I'm an educated ding-a-ling

I can't
I can't

take it any longer; I can no longer, myself, curb
take it any longer; I can no longer, myself, curb

I must disclose that certain form, this word, that certain
I must disclose that certain form, this word, that certain

verb
verb

Adjective, noun, or verb, you must
Adjective, noun, or verb, you must

think this is totally absurd
think this is totally absurd

OK, you
OK, you

convinced me! This thing is called the Blurb.
convinced me. This thing is called the Blurb.

(231) : page

48: Please Don't Stare (120)

Please Don't Stare

Avert your eyes, please don't stare Because if you
Avert your eyes, please don't stare Because if you

stare, I might feel lonesome and bare This wouldn't
stare, I might feel lonesome and bare This wouldn't

be right or fair. I might get blinded by the glare
be right or fair. I might get blinded by the glare

You might uncover my deepest, darkest layers,
You might uncover my deepest, darkest layers,

And that would be my worst nightmare Go
And that would be my worst nightmare Go

ahead, have just a little consideration Show
ahead, have just a little consideration Show

me some character, a little discrimination
me some character, a little discrimination

And avoid causing me any further alienation
And avoid causing me any farther alienation

By your gawking and staring straight in my direction
By your gawking and staring straight in my direction
By staring at me, you might hurt my feelings
By staring at me, you might hurt my feelings
That, in itself, is one of the many reasons
That, in itself, is one of the many reasons
That you should refrain and not be teasing Me
That you should refrain and not be teasing Me
or going to the bother of staring By staring,
or going to the bother of staring By staring
you may cause me grief Especially when your
you may cause me grief Especially when your
eyes scour me like a thief You may cause
eyes scour me like a thief You may cause
me to tremble like a leaf This is a fact, not
me to tremble like a leaf This is a fact, not
only my forgone belief Did you realize, staring
only my forgone belief Did you realize, staring

is not polite
All in all, it is just not right
Not only that, it can lead to a fist fight
Especially if someone feels a great slight
Try to control your eyes, or you will be disowned
Try to control how your eyes behave and where they roam
Your eyes may make a direct hit on my personal, emotional home
Don't take away my psyche's funny bone
Try to put yourself in the place of the other guy

Then and only then you'll be able to see why
Then and only then you'll be able to see why

You must learn to resist and learn not to
You' must learn to resist and learn not to

embarass or to mortify And see why you mus
embarass or to mortify And see why you mus

not stare at anyone with those piercing, evil
Not stare at anyone with those piercing, evil

eyes In the end, it is totally up to you But
eyes In the end, it is totally up to you But

listen up, I'll give you a clue I suggests th
listen up, I'll give you a clue I suggests th

is what you should do Please don't stare, if I
is what you should do Please don't stare, if I

were you! For you, it's bound to be a
were you! For you, it's bound to be a

breakthrough
break through

49. Help Me Bounce (122)
Help Me Bounce

I have an idea I would like to share. I would like
I have an idea I would like to share. I would like

to lay it on you—right there These are no secret
to lay it on you - right there There are no secret

conditions here—no hidden snares—just wash
conditions here - no hidden snares - just wash

and wear I'll just lay it on you. I hope you
and wear I'll just lay it on you. I hope you

think that's fair. You don't even have to care
think that's fair. You don't even have to car

Can't you just feel the thoughts bouncing
Can't you just feel the thoughts bouncing

around, up, down, and everywhere? Help me
around, up, down, and everywhere? Help me

bounce. Can't you feel the excitement mount?
bounce. Can't you feel the excitement mount?

Come on! Help me bounce Help me bounce, ounce
Come on! Help me bounce Help me bounce, ounce
for ounce, give me some flownce By all accounts
for ounce, give me some flownce By all accounts
if you help me bounce, it may increase your
if you help me bounce, it may increase your
bank account When you help me bounce, you
bank account When you help me bounce
may want to announce – how much fun
may want to announce – how much fun
it is to bounce Bounce! Bounce! Bounce! Give
it is to bounce Bounce! Bounce! Bounce. Give
me a good line of thoughts A word, a bar,
me a good line of thoughts A word, a bar,
a note, it could be a speech or it could be
a note, it could be a speech or it could be
music, Or it might be a theory worth a
music, Or it might be a theory worth a

237 page

whole lot — maybe physics — something well-
sought They'll pounce on it, sure as hell,
when it bounces off the spot — an idea will
have been caught It'll bounce like a slingshot
it'll be like liquid fire, like electricity, it'll
bounce at you — shiny and red hot I hear —
it bounced and got away. The word is out
on the street The words bounced off the
concrete — and that's no small feat —

It bounced in my direction — it'll bounce off you
It bounced in my direction — it'll bounce off you —
and out onto me — again. I will hear
and out onto me — again. I will hear
its heartbeat It will bounce out and off
its heartbeat It will bounce out and off
into space eventually. Then it will be the
into space eventually. Then it will be the
greatest message anyone out there could possibly seek
greatest message anyone out there could possibly seek
When you're happy, your thoughts bounce
When you're happy, your thoughts bounce
faster, but don't let them be your master
faster, but don't let them be your master
When you are hyper, they bounce into each other
When you are hyper, they bounce into each other
and get mixed up and cause a fuzzy blur
and get mixed up and cause a fuzzy blur

When you are calm, your thoughts bounce in an even
When you are calm, your thoughts bounce in an even

rhythm – with style and grace, making a satisfied
rhythm – with style and grace, making a satisfied

RRRRRRRR!!!

purr And when you are sleeping, they go into
purr And when you are sleeping, they go into

autopilot and bounce into a kaleidoscope
autopilot and bounce into a kaleidoscope

and form a fantasy land, as it were The
and form a fantasy land, as it were The

more we bounce our ideas – the more our
more we bounce our ideas – the more our

ideas are bound to be original Go ahead –
ideas are bound to be original Go ahead

bounce some more, and soon the ideas
bounce some more, and soon the ideas

will be falling like rainfall You can bounce
will be falling like rainfall You can bounce

and make a giant wall of ideas — then, it
will overflow into a cascading waterfall
many ideas to form a great distinguished hall
I will try to bounce ideas and extend them from
my mind into outer space Bouncing these
ideas from Earth, our home base might
be our saving grace They will represent
the whole human race, some ideas
going out slowly and some escaping wildly

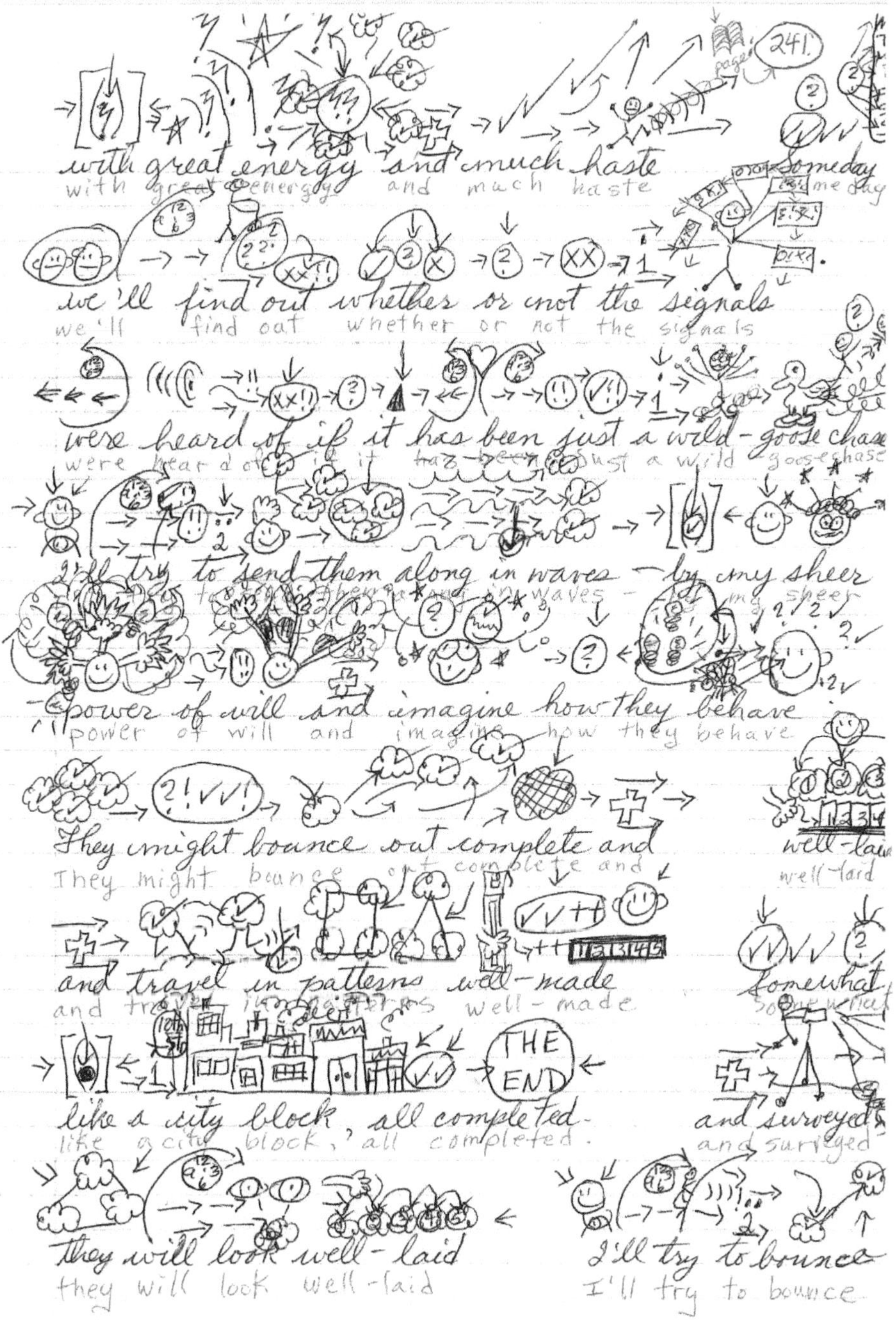
with great energy and much haste
we'll find out whether or not the signals
were heard of if it has been just a wild-goose chase
I'll try to send them along in waves – by my sheer
power of will and imagine how they behave
They might bounce out complete and
and travel in patterns well-made
like a city block, all completed.
they will look well-laid
Someday
well-laid
Somewhat
and surveyed
I'll try to bounce

my thoughts in the form of well-formed
my thoughts in the form of well-formed

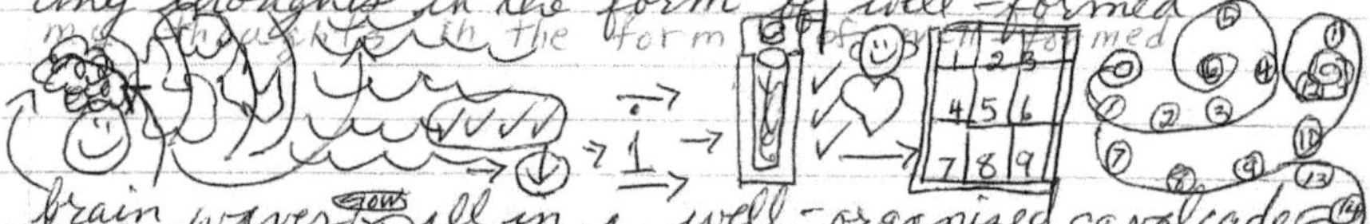

brain waves, all in a well-organized cavalcade
brain waves, all in a well-organized cavalcade

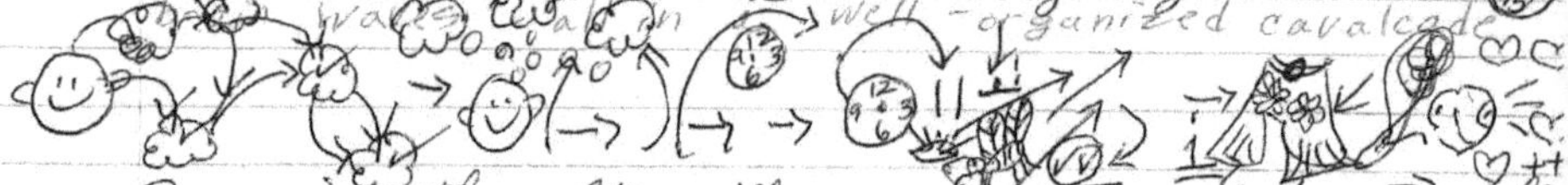

Bouncing thoughts will soon become a fad so appealing
Bouncing thoughts will soon become a fad so appealing

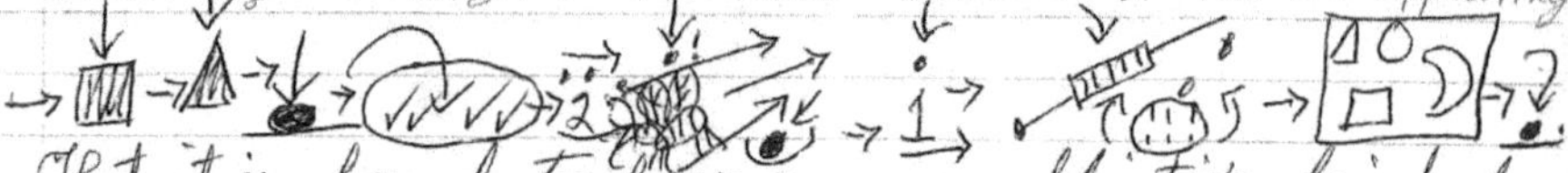

That it is bound to become an addictive kind of
That it is bound to become an addictive kind of

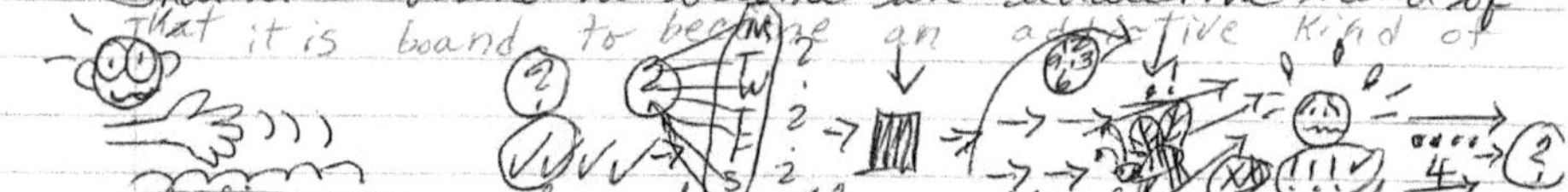

feeling Someday there will be no need for any
feeling Someday there will be no need for any

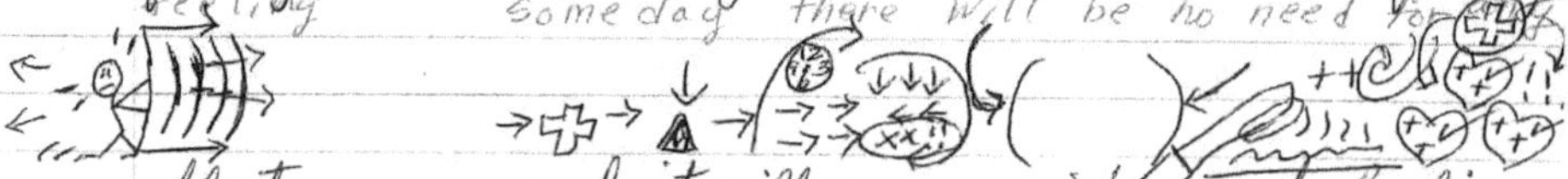

effort and it will cause widespread healing
effort and it will cause widespread healing

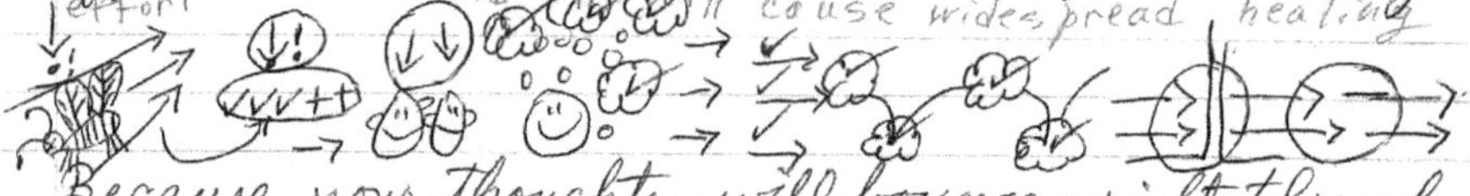

Because your thoughts will bounce right through
Because your thoughts will bounce right through

sickness and leave your senses reeling
sickness and leave your senses reeling

By bouncing, we will be able to unite.
By bouncing, we will be able to unite.

We will all get along just right The
We will all get along just right The

answers to peace will be clear, and
answers to peace will be clear, and

there will no longer be a need to fight
there will no longer be a need to fight

Tolerance and understanding will be in our
Tolerance and understanding will be in our

sights and everyone will be close and tight
sights and everyone will be close and tight

The day will be the same as the night and no one will
the day will be the same as the night and no one

have short sight! We will have unity at its height
have short sight! We will have unity at its height

Bouncing our thoughts will be a grand game
Bouncing our thoughts will be a grand game

It won't matter how we aim This game will-
It won't matter how we aim This game will-

not need any kind of name! It won't even
Not need any kind of name It won't even

have a nickname We will all have our own
have a nickname We will all have our own

share of fame — our very own kind of acclaim

We'll talk with the wildest animals and they
we'll talk with the wildest animals and they

will become tame! Our language will all
will become tame. Our language will all

be the same because our bouncing will
be the same because our bouncing will

intersect again and again Come on, people
intersect again and again Come on, people

of every race — let us watch all the new ideas
of every race — let us watch all the new ideas

unfurl Let us bounce our thoughts here
unfurl Let us bounce our thoughts here

and there,

and there,

dancing girls

dancing girls

like gathering

like gathering

precious pearls

precious pearls

then we will see how

then we will see how

come in tornado swirls

come in tornado swirls

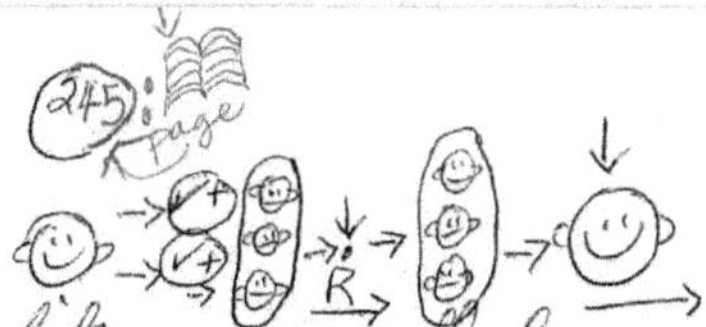

like we are all happy

like we are all happy

Bouncing thoughts can't

Bouncing thoughts can't

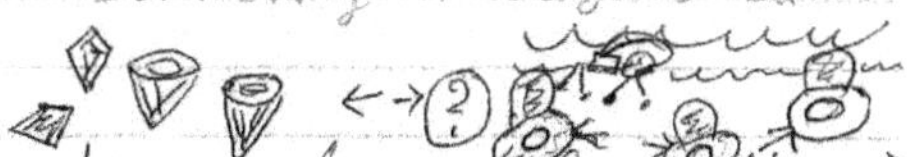

diamonds or harvesting

diamonds or harvesting

Come on give it a whirl-

Come on give it a whirl-

information will

information will

50. What's In My Heart? (126)

What's In My Heart?

I would like to share with you what dwells in my heart
I would like to share with you what dwells in my heart

If you would be so kind and if you don't
If you would be so kind and if you don't

mind to let me begin, to let me start
mind, to let me begin, to let me start

I will try to share with you my personal
I will try to share with you my personal

view of it all, part by part
view of it all, part by part

Of its avenues
of its avenues

and venues that are a
and venues that are a

delicate city full
delicate city full

of priceless art
of priceless art

If my heart was my whole
If my heart was my whole

body, it would
body, it would

be a large, illustrated,
be a large, illustrated,

romance story As varied and mysterious a
romance story As varied and mysterious a

underwater Pompeii or as Wonderful and musical
under water Pompeii or as; Wonderful and musical

as an old-world city The city would have style

and be both modern and cultured and worldly
and be both modern and cultured and worldly

Like a universe it would be spacious and
Like a universe it would be spacious and

full of exciting electricity My heart is my
full of exciting electricity My heart is my

very best part. It is right there in my star
very best part. It is right there in my star

chart Love flows freely from it, end to
chart Love flows freely from it, end to

start. And it is well-versed in the martial arts
start. And it is well-versed in the martial arts

Ah, if my heart had a story it was able to tell
Ah, if my heart had a story it was able to tell

It would call it a story of unadulterated hell
It would call it a story of unadulterated hell

And it could call it, also a purifying hard sell
And it could call it, also a purifying hard sell

Wanting to tell the best story for the good of all
Wanting to tell the best story for the good of all

Love flows from my heart like a wide-mouthed
Love flows from my heart like a wide-mouthed

warm, slow-moving river It also falls
warm, slow-moving river It also falls

like a waterfall, with such beauty it can make
like a waterfall with such beauty it can make

you shiver. It is also a pure life-giver
you shiver It is also a pure life-giver

With so much love in it, it will make you quiver.
With so much love in it, it will make you quiver.

Because it is there, signed, sealed and delivered
Because it is there, signed, sealed and delivered
And the mist that settles on it will form a
and the mist that settles on it, will form a
rainbow, From the sun's rays
rain bow, From the sun's rays
reflecting through the mist anew It is a
reflecting through the mist anew It is a
warmth you cannot begin to describe
warmth you cannot begin to describe
and with it a comfortable, flowing ride
and with it a comfortable, glowing ride
It is there for all to share and to be welcomed,
It is there for all to share and to be welcomed
inside that may help ride life's tide I've
inside that may help ride life's tide I've
learned to let my heart be my compass and my
learned to let my heart be my compass and my

guide and learn to give it up to a higher power

guide and learn to give it up to a higher power

From my heart, I dare no longer deny it or

From my heart, I dare no longer deny it or

hide from it because it is the strongest

hide from it because it is the strongest

power I have that I have identified The love

power I have that I have identified The love

in it is so great; it will never be overcome

in it is so great; it will never be overcome

by hate. Just let me set the record straight

by hate, Just let me set the record straight

Instead I feel it grow, the more I concentrate, the

Instead I feel it grow, the more I concentrate, the

more it dominates and the more it shines

more it dominates and the more it shines

and radiates Now I know it's OK to have

and radiates Now I know it's OK to have

lots on my plate because it just helps to
lots on my plate because it just helps to
serve, to witness and demonstrate That in
serve, to witness and demonstrate That in
my heart I have no room for hate and
my heart I have no room for hate and
that I am an overall heart-loving heavyweight
that I am an overall heart-loving heavy weight
I only wish for my heart to be pure and for
I only wish for my heart to be pure and for
its spirit to fly and soar And I know,
its spirit to fly and soar And I know,
all my woes will have their cures and my
all my woes will have their cures and my
heart will have everything it's always wanted and more
heart will have everything it's always wanted and more
I know that temptation will no longer have its lure
I know that temptation will no longer have its lare

if I just ignore it and avoid its constant

it I just ignore it and avoid its constant

tug-of-war I know that time will go by

tug-of-war I Know that time will go by

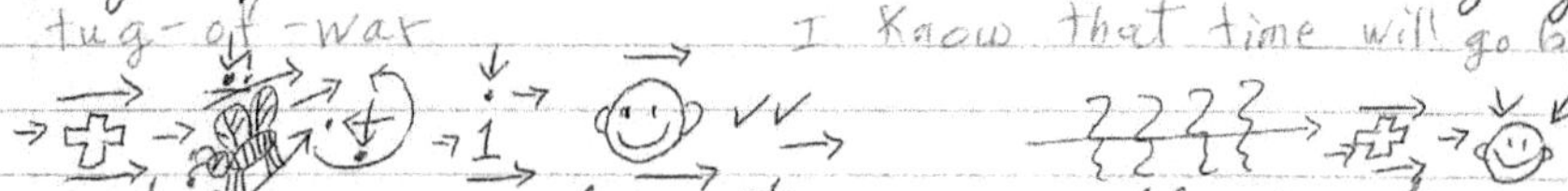

and become a pleasant blur, and my

and become a pleasant blur, and my

heart will never be sad anymore

heart will never be sad anymore

(51) It's All In A Name (129) (251) : page
It's all in a name

I tell you, it is a crying shame how I was
I tell you, it is a crying shame how I was
defamed And that you can't adopt your own
defamed And that you can't adopt your own
chosen nickname Who needs a family
chosen nickname Who needs a family
name and its surname when it always
name and its surname when it always
brings you blame Let's face it - your
brings you blame Let's face it - your
claim to fame is all in your present
claim to fame is all in your present
name I used to have a plain name.
name I used to have a plain name.
It was hidden in a closet with little or
It was hidden in a closet with little or

no acclaim This gave me grief and was
to me a crying shame, but it was mine
all the same That it was mine wasn't
my fault or my personal blame, And with
it, I was far from tamed My name was
mine automatically, when I was born, to
claim, So began my name's flame game
My first affectionate love of long ago was
one year older or so He gave me my

favorite personalized affectionate nickname or
favorite personalized affectionate nickname or

logo It is all the good I have left from him
logo It is all the good I have left from him

because when I turned two, My nickname
because when I turned two, My nickname

was out of fashion and it was outgrown
was out of fashion and it was outgrown

The logo, the nickname was Din Din How I
The logo, the nickname was Din Din How I

loved that name from my dearly beloved older bro
loved that name from my dearly beloved older bro

My first given name was the first I came to
My first given name was the first I came to

know My first last name caused me much
know My first last name caused me much

sorrow My second last name left three
sorrow My second last name left three

children to show
gives me a special glow
this is? It's little old me
other with glee
three
There is no reason for us to disagree
know there is plenty of room here
no reason for us to despair
plenty of room to share

My third last name always
Do you know who
Said one to the
I can count too, one, two,
Now that we are with each other,
We
There is
We will have
Beside that letter

X on that line
X on that line
That without us would be
That without us would be
powerless and bare
powerless and bare
I could pay to invent and
I could pay to invent and
hire new ones
hire new ones
But they would be useless
But they would be useless
clones
clones
Because they would just be artificial
Because they would just be artificial
rhinestones
rhinestones
Changing them now, I just
Changing them now, I just
could not condone
could not condone
They've taken me
They've taken me
through the lion's den
through the lion's den
With no harm,
With no harm,
again and again and again
again and again and again
I am proud
I am proud
of and I choose to keep
of and I choose to keep
the names I now
the names I now

use to pen And I will do so until it is time
use to pen And I will do so until it is time

for me to say my final amen
for me to say my final amen

159 page

(52) The Void (131)

The Void

In my opinion, the worst possible void Is when
In my opinion, the worst possible void Is when

the mind is totally trapped within itself and
the mind is totally trapped within itself and

totally devoid Of its ability to use its
totally devoid of its ability to use its

thoughts and is dull like celluloid It is a
thoughts and is dull like celluloid It is a

brain without the ability to express its thoughts
brain without the ability to express its thoughts

And its ability is and is as good as totally
And its ability is and is as good as totally

destroyed The ability to travel through
destroyed The ability to travel through

one's thoughts And being able to tie
one's thoughts And being able to tie

the knots and dot the dots The ability to be
the knots and dot the dots The ability to be

able to see the answer behind the ink blots
able to see the answer behind the ink blots

Is when you will hit the rainbow's jackpot
Is when you will hit the rainbow's jackpot

It is such a great travesty to lose the mind's
It is such a great travesty to lose the mind's

main key Not to be able to think clearly
main key Not to be able to think clearly

will bring anyone to their knees And
will bring anyone to their knees And

not to be able to understand or to be able
Not to be able to understand or to be able

to make any plea Would make anyone
to make any plea Would make anyone

feel like they were a living absentee That's
feel like they were a living absentee That's

when sociability dies and loneliness begins
when sociability dies and loneliness begins

Then fear engulfs you and the clouds descend
Then fear engulfs you and the clouds descend

And it is hard to find your way back again
And it is hard to find your way back again

You then feel like a loser, a has-been
You then feel like a loser, a has-been

And
And

no one wants to be your friend
no one wants to be your friend

You wish
You wish

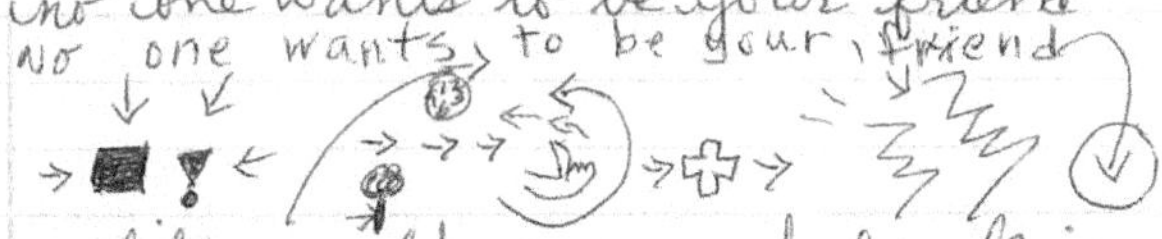

....!!!

reality would come and break in
reality would come and break in

But
But

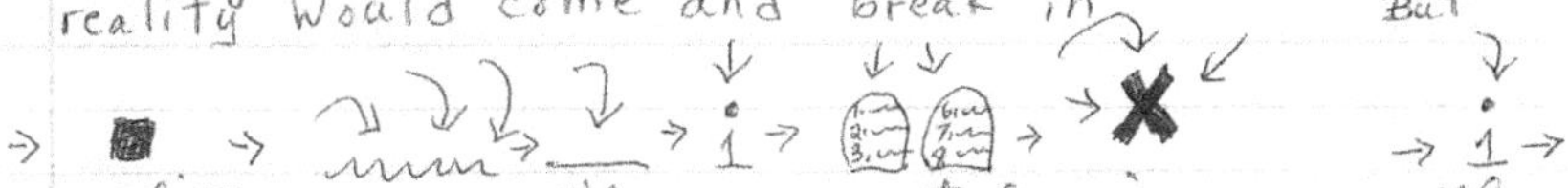

reality seems like a mortal sin
reality seems like a mortal sin

The
The

void is a time when it becomes easy to lose hope
void is a time when it becomes easy to lose hope

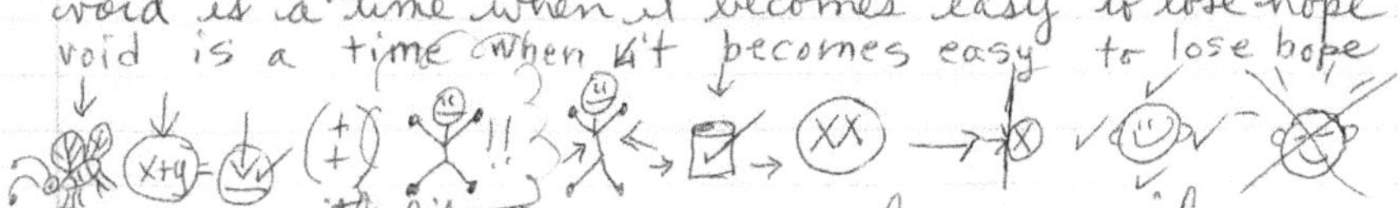

Because with life, you can no longer easily cope
Because with life, you can no longer easily cope

And you can't help but feel like a dope,
And you can't help but feel like a dope,

and that's when you begin to mope Soon
And that's when you begin to mope Soon

you feel like you're at the end of your rope
You feel like you're at the end of your rope

Life has become torture and is totally unbearable
Life has become torture and is totally unbearable

The experience, unfortunately, is not
The experience, unfortunately, is not

something that is shasable You feel weak and
something that is sharable You feel weak and

unstable and totally unable You feel like
unstable and totally unable You feel like

you've been totally disabled You feel like a
you've been totally disabled You feel like a

coward, the only thing that keeps you going
coward, the only thing that keeps you going

page 26

is hope You know you must be patient
is hope You know you must be patient

because you do not quite know What
because you do not quite know What

this is, or its length, or its scope You wish
this is, or its length, or its scope You wish

from this situation you could elope What's
from this situation you could elope What's

more, you feel like you are always under a
more, you feel like you are always under a

microscope You have no will, you have no
microscope You have no will, you have no

choice You wish you could use your voice
choice You wish you could use your voice

When you wake up from this dream, you will rejoice
When you wake up from this dream, you will rejoice

And drive away in a fancy Rolls-Royce But
And drive away in a fancy Rolls-Royce But

there it is Help is on its way
there it is Help is on its way

that every day I took time to pray?
that every day I took time to pray?

but it came back at first steadily
but it came back at first steadily

and more, every day
and more, every day

my mind to stay in play
my mind to stay in play

to accept and to comply
to accept and to comply

the more I looked reality in the eye
the more I looked reality in the eye

I could again be like every other guy
I could again be like every other guy

again to use my thoughts, and
again to use my thoughts, and

Did I mention
Did I mention

slowly,
slowly,

more
more

With it came rules for
With it came rules for

The more I learned
The more I learned

With my situation
With my situation

I knew then
I knew then

I was free
I was free

I knew it was not some cruel
I knew it was not some cruel

page 265

So you see, even when you face the void, you
So you see, even when you face the void, you
need not give up There are always greates
need not give up There are always greater
things in store for you No matles if you
things in store for you No matter if you
feal all washed up You need not feel this
feel all washed up You need not feel this
is your final roundup So just get help and
is your final roundup So just get help and
go on your next checkup You may even find
go on your next check up You may even find
you think bettes than you did before Because
you think better than you did before Because
you will have won a vezy important war
you will have won a very important war
And your confidence will give you a special rappost
And your confidence will give you a special rapport

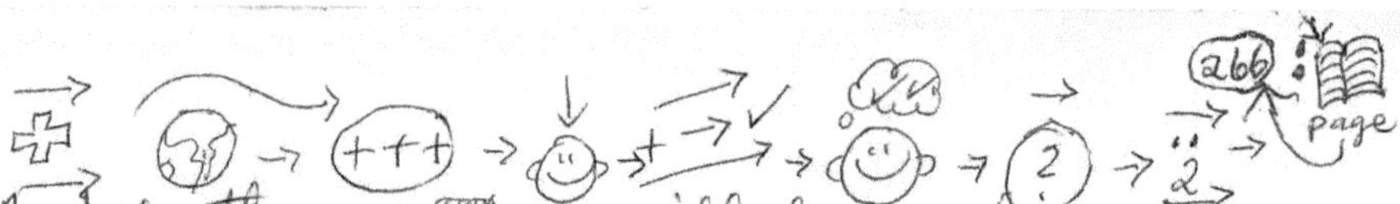

And furthermore you will know how to

And further more you will know how to

avoid life's blood and the gore

avoid life's blood and the gore

267 : page

53 My Reality 34

My Reality

(A Look into Autism)

A Look into Autism

You may take a look into my world, my
You may take a look into my world, my
reality, if you choose to behold
reality, if you choose to behold
I am
I am
just another winner standing on life's threshhold
just another winner standing on life's threshhold
I usually have a heart of gold
I usually have a heart of gold
which I will
which I will
gladly unfold
gladly unfold
I follow no particular mold,
I follow no particular mold,
and therefore I
and therefore I
have a totally different
have a totally different
kind of stronghold
kind of stronghold
Really, it's no big deal.
Really, it's no big deal

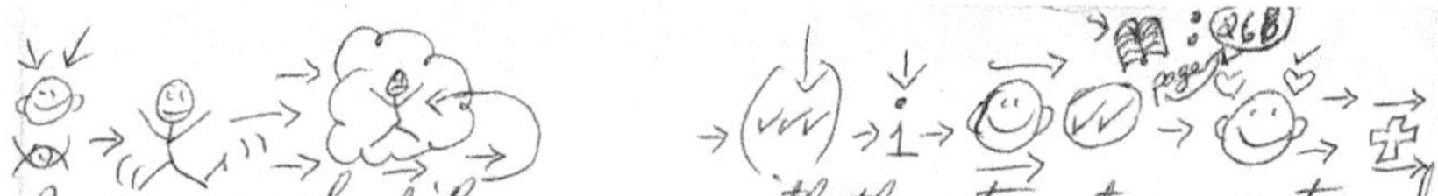

I approach life with the utmost respect and
I approach life with the utmost respect and

real And my thoughts are very real. In fact
real And my thoughts are very real. In fact,

they are so real to me they are like a
They are so real to me! They are like a

newsreel I don't usually bother to try to
newsreel I don't usually bother to try to

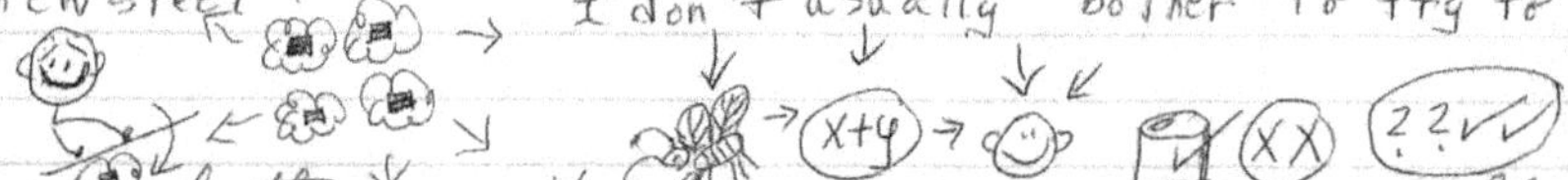

conceal them because you can't possibly
conceal them because you can't possibly

ride my Ferris wheel And yes, I really do
ride my Ferris wheel And yes, I really do

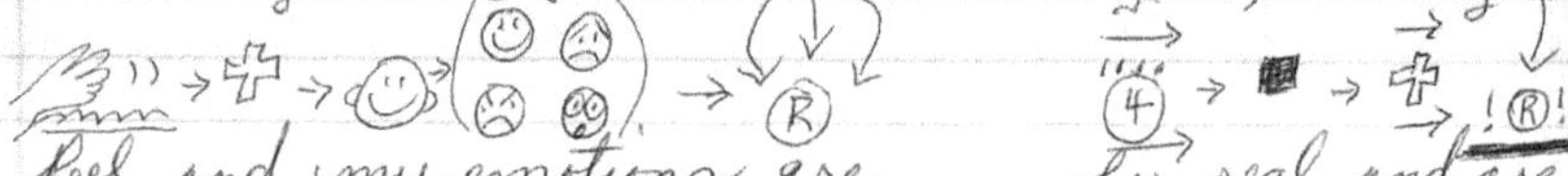

feel and my emotions are for real and are
feel and my emotions are for real and are

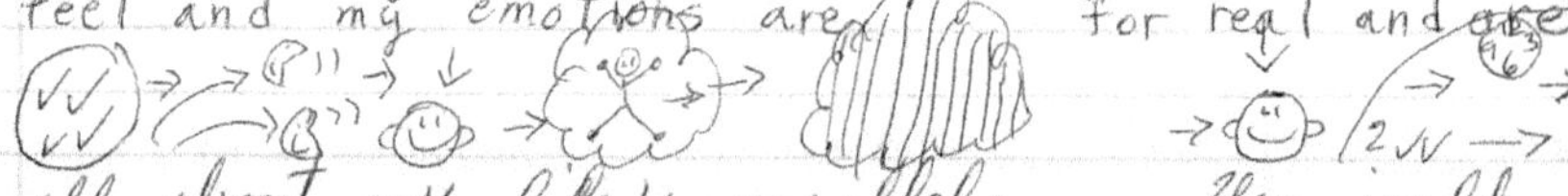

all about my life's parallels You could
all about my life's parallels You could

never tell all about my life's many parallels
Never tell all about my life's many parallels

Or that I've been through my own personal hell
On that I've been through my own personal hell

Because on the past I do not choose to dwell,
because on the past I do not choose to dwell,

and that is fine, that is swell
and that is fine, that is swell

I accept life
I accept life

like it is, and in a nutshell,
like it is, and in a nutshell,

I've
I've

absorbed life's bombshell
absorbed life's bombshell

What you don't
What you don't

understand is something
understand is something

Which I must
which I must

try to expand on
try to expand on

further and map and scan
further and map and scan

I'll help you see, I'll give you a hand
I'll help you see, I'll give you a hand

I'll
I'll

let you visit a mysterious and wonderful land
let you visit a mysterious and wonderful land

Everybody's land is different, depending on his
Everybody's land is different, depending on his
ladder's span My eyes have a mind of their
ladder's span My eyes have a mind of their
own; They travel fast and are thorough
own; They travel fast and are thorough
and act like a cyclone Which I sometimes
and act like a cyclone Which I sometimes
wish I could disown Who knows where
wish I could disown Who knows where
or on whom they will choose to roam
or on whom they will choose to roam
Sometimes what they see makes me
Sometimes what they see makes me
wonder or cry out and groan My ideas to
wonder or cry out and groan My ideas to
me are very real, on an ever-moving and
me are very real, on an ever-moving and

changing reel Colors all have a great appeal,
changing reel Colors all have a great appeal,

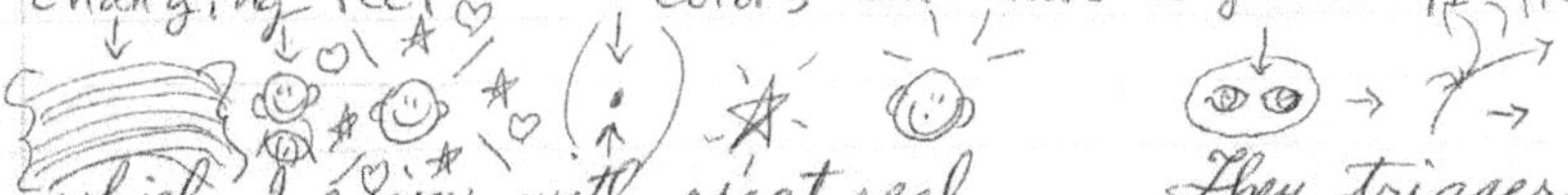

which I enjoy with great zeal They trigger
which I enjoy with great zeal They trigger

in one connections only I can feel ideas
in one connections only I can feel, ideas

that my mind chooses to reveal My thoughts
that my mind chooses to reveal My thoughts

travel on an organized even keel that no
travel on an organized even keel that no

one can steal I may not be at all like you,
one can steal I may not be at all like you,

sir, and that's fine, thank-you But we both
sir, and that's fine, thank-you But we both

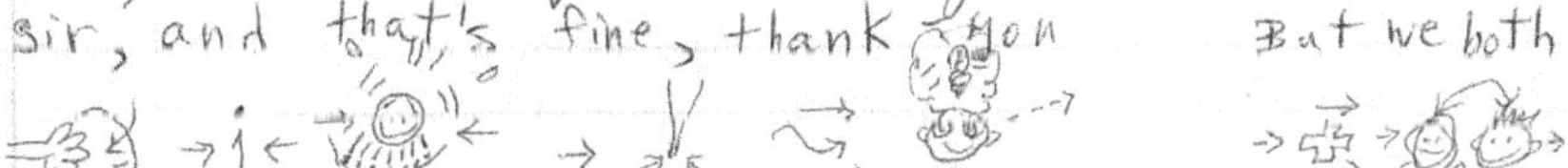

have an interesting point of view, And our
leave an interesting point of view, And our

very own idea may be a shiny breakthrough
very own idea may be a shiny breakthrough

And if our differences we choose to agree on
And if our differences we choose to agree on

and compromise, We will both be able to
and compromise, We will both be able to

add two plus two Then we may both feel
add two plus two Then we may both feel

like brand new And we will arrive at our
like brand new And we will arrive at our

newfound destination and rendezvous
newfound destination and rendezvous

You may need to be quiet every day, and
You may need to be quiet every day, and

this, in itself, is OK. Myself, I like change
this, in itself, is OK. Myself, I like change

in every way, with quiet included as an
in every way, with quiet included as an

option, A pit stop before the matinée
option, A pit stop before the matinée

You may like and choose to delay your actions,
You may like and choose to delay your actions.

I like to experience them play by play
I like to experience them play by play

Delve
Delve

a little deeper if you dare. I wish to take you
a little deeper if you dare. I wish to take you

there
there

Like a child, I love fresh air and I
Like a child, I love fresh air and I

also like to share
also like to share

Sometimes I'm not all
Sometimes I'm not all

there because
there because

my mind takes me elsewhere
my mind takes me elsewhere

I think that's neither here nor there because
I think that's neither here nor there because

this happens to everyone, everywhere
this happens to everyone, everywhere

My
My

laughter tends to explode and ring out
laughter tends to explode and ring out

and pleasure bathes my brain throughout
and pleasare bathes my brain throaghoat

Laughter makes me sing, it makes you shout,
Laughter makes me sing, it makes you shout,

it helps my ideas to grow and sprout It may
it helps my ideas to grow and sprout It may

tend to make me stand out but I advise you to
tend to make me stand out but I advise you to

try it, It's a knockout I don't think I have
try it, It's a Knockout I don't think I have

to stop and do without because happiness is
to stop and do without because happiness is

the best route without a doubt You may be
the best route without a doabt You may be

scared of me but I can guarantee There is no
scared of me but I can gaarantee There is no

need or reason to be We are all made of
need or reason to be We are all made of

the same stuff, you and me
the same stuff, you and me

able to see to a large degree
able to see to a large degree

and carefree and
and carefree and

and me! Tee - he
and me Tee - he

you, for to do so
you for to do so

a low IQ
a low IQ

to your rescue
to your rescue

a deadly catch-22
a deadly catch-22

transparent, and see-through
transparent, and see-through

You will soon be
You will soon be

That I am happy
That I am happy

I only wish the same for you
I only wish the same for you

I promise I won't hurt
I promise I won't hurt

I would prove to have
I would prove to have

In fact, I may someday come
In fact, I may someday come

and snatch you from
and snatch you from

AOK

I am clear,
I am clear,

In fact,
In fact,

my enemies won't even be able to see me
my enemies won't even be able to see me

or have a clue I have no unwanted surprises
or have a clue I have no unwanted surprises

to undo because I do not mean to
to undo because I do not mean to

misconstrue Finally, if I want to give
misconstrue Finally, if I want to give

you a royal view I'll tell you or show
you a royal view I'll tell you or show

you myself through and through Tell me you
you myself through and through Tell me you

love me because I love you too I am so direc
love me because I love you too I am so dire

that people sometimes think I am cuckoo
that people sometimes think I am cuckoo

Before we part and before we are through, I
Before we part and before we are through, I

will have given you a panoramic view Now
will have given you a panoramic view Now
you are among the few that has taken the time
you are among the few that has taken the time
to try to understand That makes you a special
to try to understand That makes you a special
kind, someone open-minded and great and
kind, someone open-minded and great and
grand If there were more of your kind, my reality,
grand If there were more of your kind, my reality,
which seems to be a fantasy land → will be there
which seems to be a fantasy land → will be there
at your command And we would begin to
at your command And we would begin to
help many and make our world a better land
help many and make our world a better land
for all to go hand in hand
for all to go hand in hand

(54) Woe Is Me (38)

Woe Is Me

Whoa, whoa, woe is me; life has no written
whoa, whoa, woe is me; life has no written

guarantees At first, I thought I was sad, but
guarantees At first, I thought I was sad, but

I'm not; I am really happy Truth is, I'm a
I'm not; I am really happy Truth is, I'm a

bit confused, I have a new job and I'm
bit confused, I have a new job and I'm

nervous, you see I'm in a quandary, but
nervous, you see I'm in a quandary, but

my situation is still the best it could ever
my situation is still the best it could ever

be Now get this: will you please do not,
be Now get this: will you please do not,

my intentions, misconstrue If I happen to
my intentions, misconstrue If I happen to

contact the flu, something rare and new
contact the flu, something rare and new
By traveling around and touching some kind
By traveling around and touching some kind
of infected residue I might miss my first
of infected residue I might miss my first
day at work, and that just wouldn't do
day at work, and that just wouldn't do
The result would be my employer would fire
The result would be my employer would fire
me before I even began, you see And I would
me before I even began, you see And I would
end up sad and off-key at their ominous
end up sad and off-key at their ominous
decree So I just will be careful to stay
decree So I just will be careful to stay
completely healthy And then I won't have to
completely healthy And then I won't have to

worry and
worry and

I'll be happy and home free
I'll be happy and home free

I will have reason to laugh, and there will
I will have reason to laugh, and there will

be no reason to cry
be no reason to cry

I will work and all will
I will work and all will

be well, by and by
be well, by and by

At work, they won't be
At work, they won't be

able to complain, just let them dry
able to complain; just let them dry

The end
The end

result will be, my work I will just improve
result will be; my work I will just improve

and my quality of work I will just continue to
and my quality of work I will just continue to

intensify
intensity

After these moves, my life is
After these moves, my life is

bound to improve
bound to improve

And my life will get
And my life will get

better and better
better and better

once I get into the groove
once I get into the groove

There will be no more crying as long as
There will be no more crying as long as

I don't make a false move
I don't make a false move

And if I do not
And if I do not

do anything to cause
do anything to cause

anyone to be annoyed
anyone to be annoyed

or to cause them to disapprove
or to cause them to disapprove

Then I can
Then I can

stop my tearful masquerades
stop my tearful masquerades

And I'll forget
And I'll forget

my game of charades
my game of charades

Because to be honest
Because to be honest

I will have it made
I will have it made

And I will be successful in
And I will be successful in

all my escapades
all my escapades

So for now, I'll just
So for now, I'll just

stay on the bandwagon And I will continue
Stay on the bandwagon And I will continue

to see all kinds of good things happen
to see all kinds of good things happen

Because of my good attitude, the world
Because of my good attitude, the world

will be, my playpen And I will be
will, be, my play pen And I will be

successful and will no longer have to cry
success ful and will no longer have to cry

ever again
ever again

28 page

(55) What's Been Sung (140)
What's Been Sung

Has Been Sung
Has Been Sung

What's been sung has been sung; my dear little one
What's been sung has been sung; my dear little one

Now you deserve all the fun; your life has just begun
Now you deserve all the fun; your life has just begun

You won't be undone
You won't be undone,

because now you are top gun
because NOW you are top gun

Your good times have just begun; you will have lots of fun in the sun
Your good times have just begun; you will have lots of fun in the sun

I'll join the throng to show that I also belong
I'll join the throng to show that I also belong

To see you, I'll travel
To see you, I'll travel

opened many doors I want to know you more;
opened many doors → I want to Know you more;
I don't mean to be a bore Just because
I don't mean to be a bore Just because
I don't know what all your ideas are for What's
I don't Know what all your ideas are for What's
more; I'd love to greet you and give you a big
more; I'd love to greet you and give you a big
ten-four I went to all your concerts; they
ten - four I went to all your concerts; they
were my yummiest desert I had to sit in a
were my yammiest desert I had to sit in a
place where my knees hurt and where it
place where my knees hurt and where it
rained on my shirt There I also ate hot dogs
rained on my shirt there I also ate hot dogs
and then pizza in spurts I had no trouble
and then pizza in spurts I had no trouble

to stay alert because you are such an
to stay alert because you are such an

entertaining extrovest I bought your records
entertaining extrovert I bought your records

and sang to them off-key I wondered why I
and sang to them off-key I wondered why I

couldn't be like you, a successful VIP I wondered
couldn't be like you, a successful VIP I wondered

why no one knows or knew me, a successful
why no one knows or knew me a successful

college dropout and self-proclaimed refugee
college dropout and self-proclaimed refugee

I wondered if I ever would be a nomenee for
I wondered if I ever would be a nominee for

any kind of award or degree I said, "Power
any kind of award or degree I said, "Power

to the people, man. Now, I understand! And I
to the people, man. Now, I under-stand. And I

thought I had finally got the trick, I was definitely
thought I had finally got the trick, I was definitely
a fan To get popular and get into the thick,
a fan To get popular and get into the thick,
one must be a hanger-on to the band
one must be a hanger-on to the band
By now I knew it would be no picnic to
By now I knew it would be no picnic to
become famous in all the land Your fame
become famous in all the land Your fame
will never be over; it'll become classic
will never be over; it'll become classic
in the whole world moreover You'll get greater
in the whole world moreover You'll get greater
as time goes by, you'll gather more and
as time goes by, you'll gather more and
more lovers You might as well roll in four-leaf
more lovers You might as well roll in four-leaf

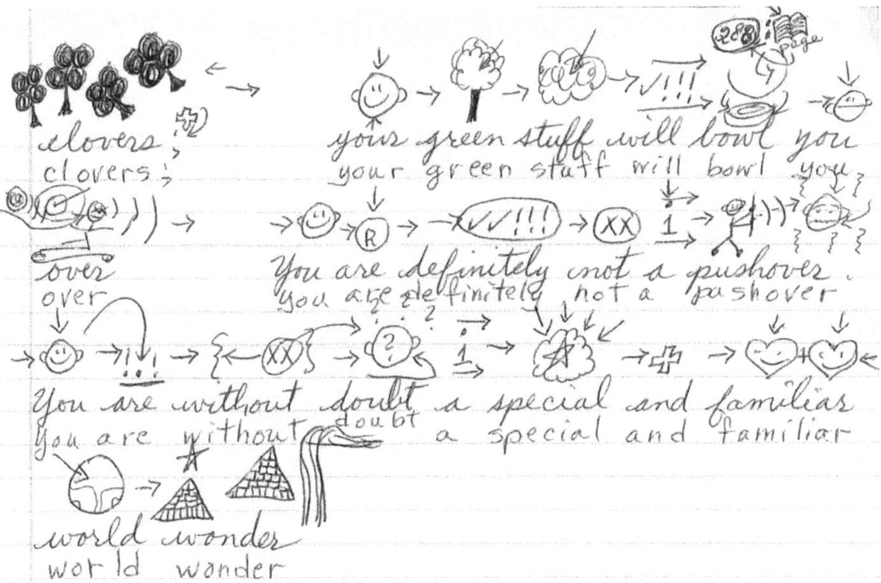
clovers
clovers
over
over
your green stuff will bowl you
your green stuff will bowl you
page
288
You are definitely not a pushover.
You are definitely not a pushover
You are without doubt a special and familiar
You are without doubt a special and familiar
world wonder
world wonder

289 page

56 In Full Bloom 142

In Full Bloom

The flowers, a bouquet, are fragrant and in full bloom
The flowers, a bouquet, are fragrant and in full bloom
We place them all over, all around and inside our rooms
We place them all over, all around and inside our rooms
Whenever and wherever we are and as the time
Whenever and wherever we are and as the time
is opportune They are celebrated on the eve of
is opportune They are celebrated on the eve of
our honeymoon and now and always, as
our honeymoon now and always, as
our love is in full bloom Our love is also in
our love is in full bloom Our love is also in
full bloom, coming none too soon We look
full bloom, coming none too soon We look
at each other, and we can't help but swoon
at each other, and we can't help but swoon

Our love surrounds us like a comfortable cocoon
Our love sarrounds us like a comfortable cocoon

Our eyes reflect in each other's love and shine
Our eyes reflect in each other's love and shine

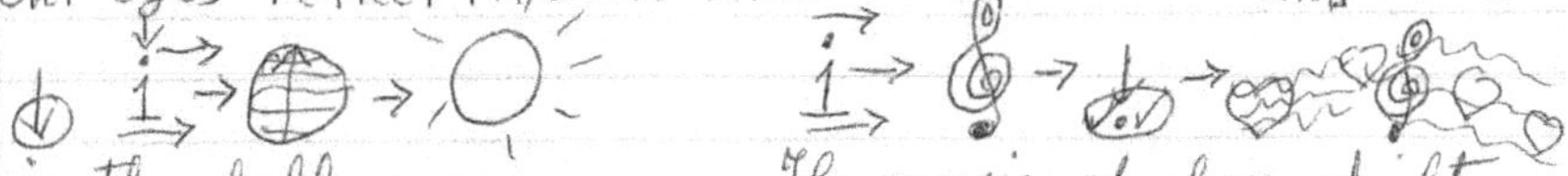

in the full moon The music of love drifts
in the full moon The music of love drifts

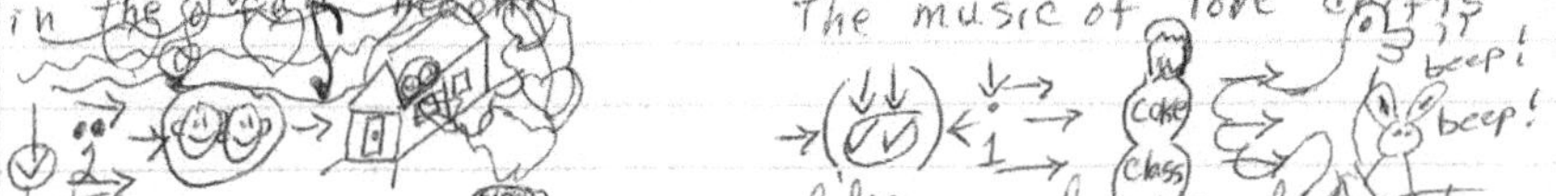

into our room, like a classic long tune
into our room, like a classic long tune

The melody twists and caresses us like a plume
The melody twists and caresses us like a plume

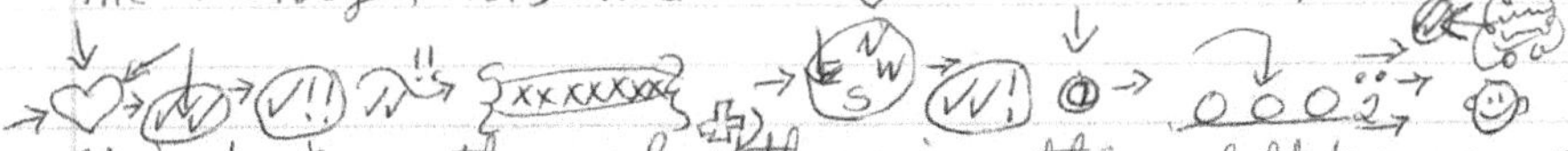

It is just as thorough; there is nothing left to presume
It is just as thorough; there is nothing left to presume

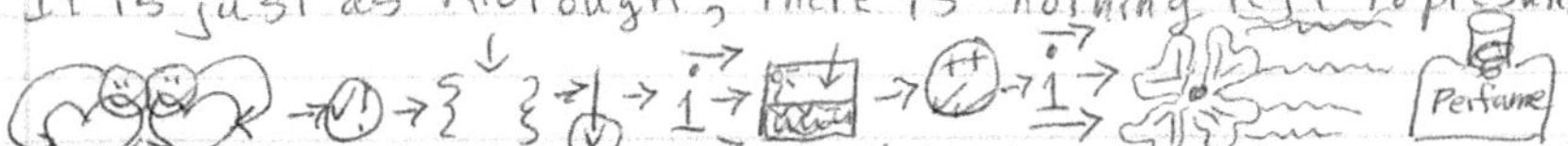

Romance is thick in the air like the sweetest perfume
Romance is thick in the air like the sweetest perfume

Love cascades around us, undressing through the air
Love cascades around us, undressing through the air

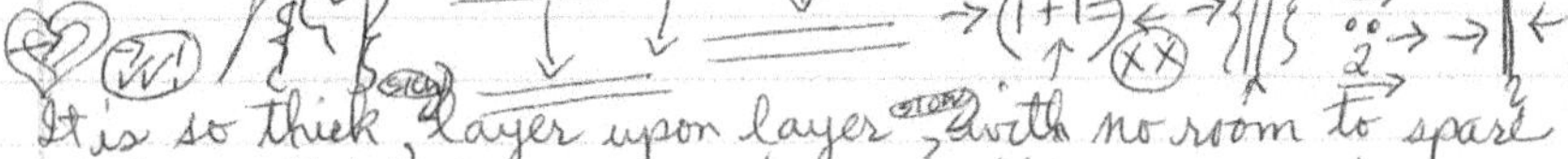

It is so thick, layer upon layer, with no room to spare
It is so thick, layer upon layer, with no room to spare

You can take your pick from its bloom, one

You can take your pick from its bloom, one

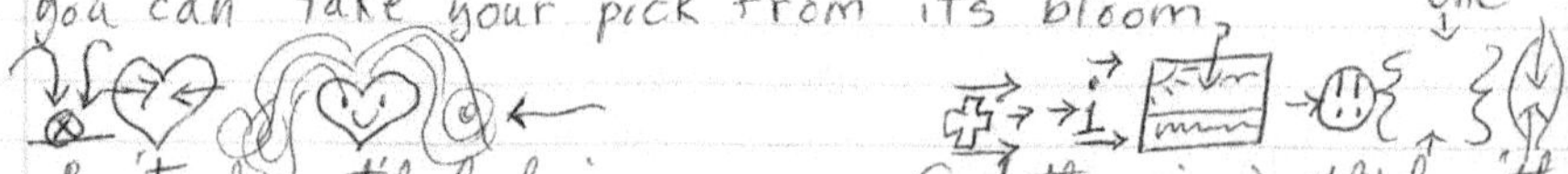

of its beautiful hairs And the air is thick with

of its beautiful hairs And the air is thick with

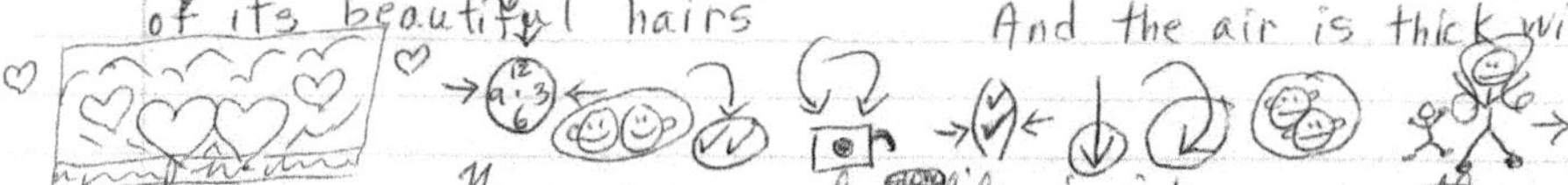

love Now we are safe, like inside our mother's

love Now we are safe, like inside our mother's

womb Love is new; it is special and refreshing

womb Love is New; it is special and refreshing

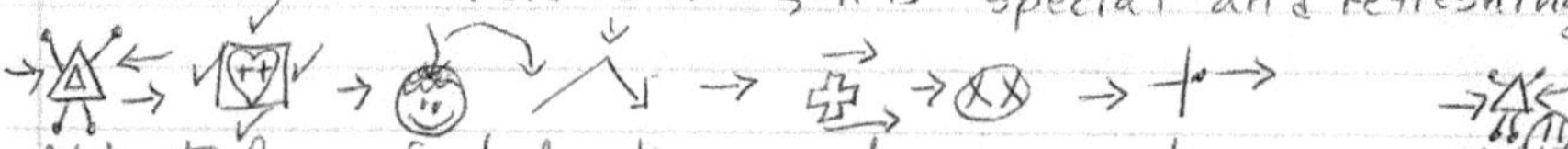

It is truly mind bending and never ending It is

It is traly mind bending and never ending It is

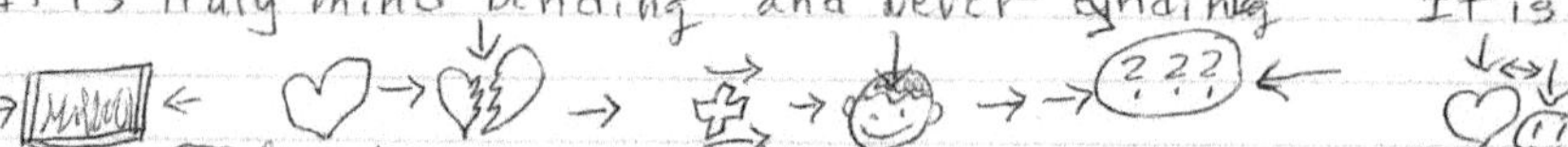

warm, heartrending and mind-boggling It is

warm, heartrending and mind-boggling It is

mysterious, curious, daring, and daunting Our

mysterious, curious, daring, and daunting Our

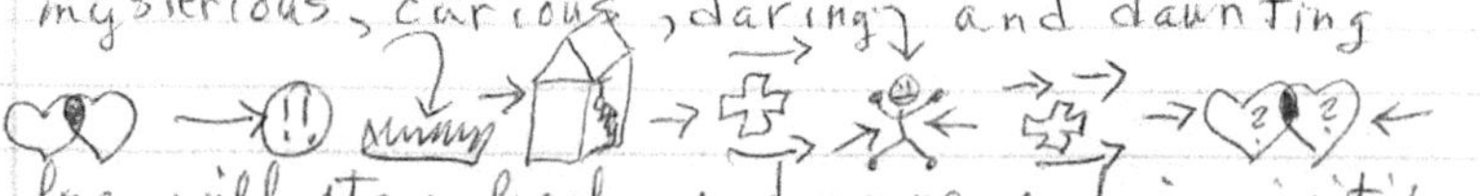

love will stay fresh and young and inquisitive

love will stay fresh and young and inquisitive

forever and ever Through any kind of climate,

forever and ever Through any kind of climate,

be it calm, stormy, or cosmic weather
be it calm, stormy, or cosmic weather

Our love reaches out in expectation, our love
our love reaches out in expectation, our love

knows no fetters It will be as interesting and
Knows no fetters It will be as interesting and

touching as a beautiful love letter Our love
touching as a beautifal love letter Our love

will always and forever be in full bloom,
will always and forever be in full bloom

at night or at high noon The sweet fragrance
at night or at high noon the sweet fragrance

of our love wafts around us like the sweetest
of our love wafts around us like the sweetest

perfume Our love will be a contagious beauty
perfume Our love will be a contagious beauty

to which no one will be immune When
to which no one will be immune when

we are together, there will be no more gloom and
we are together, there will be no more gloom and

doom
doom

because our love will push it out and
because our love will push it out and

love will instead fill the room The bouquet of our
love will instead fill the room The bouquet of our

love is a masterpiece there for everyone to see
love is a masterpiece there for everyone to see

in full bloom The gentle petals surround us,
in full bloom The gentle petals surround us,

like a warm cocoon, while our love is in full
like a warm cocoon, while our love is in full

bloom The colors of the rainbow shine and radiate
bloom The colors of the rainbow shine and radiate

from us while our love is in full bloom We
from us while our love is in full bloom We

are in love and while we are together in our love,
are in love and while we are together in our love,

our love will always be in full bloom

our love will always be in full bloom

57 Broken Body, 144
Broken Body,

Not Broken Soul
Not Broken Soul

My body is in tatters; it is broken down. It is a
My body is in tatters; it is broken down. It is a

sad image of what it was, just a hazy blur But
sad image of what it was, just a hazy blur But

what really matters is that my principles are still
what really matters is that my principles are still

intact; they are still there, as it were And my soul
intact; they are still there, as it were And my soul

hums and purrs; also my mind is astir, with
hums and purrs; also my mind is astir, with

a new wisdom beyond compare My soul is well
a new wisdom beyond compare My soul is well

and has not been broken; it is alive and well
and has not been broken; it is alive and well

and ready to lie on the spurs Every day is an
and ready to lie on the spurs Every day is an

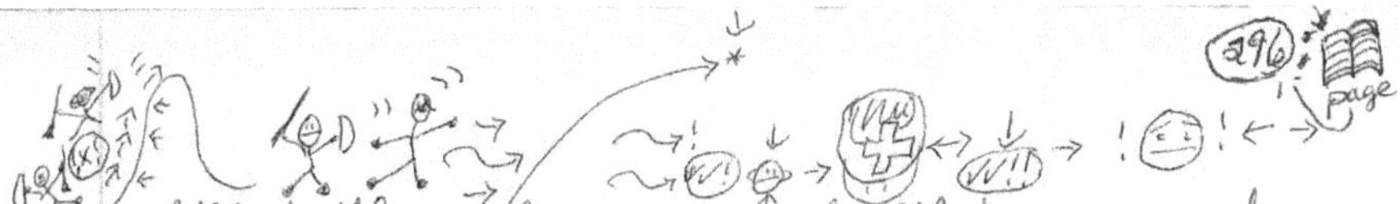

uphill battle as far as my health is concerned
uphill battle as far as my health is concerned

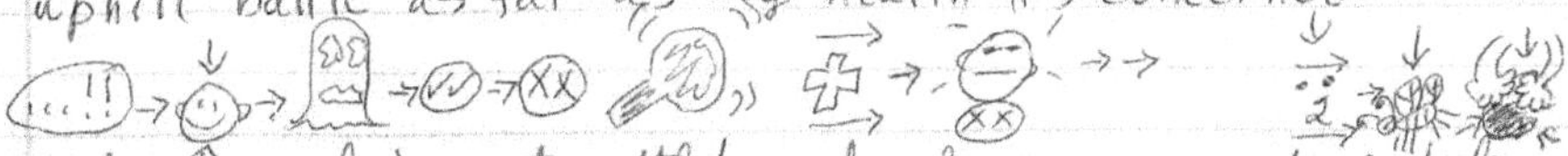

But my soul is not rattled and refuses to be taken
But my soul is not rattled and refuses to be taken

over or be burned No matter how it is prodded,
over or be burned No matter how it is prodded,

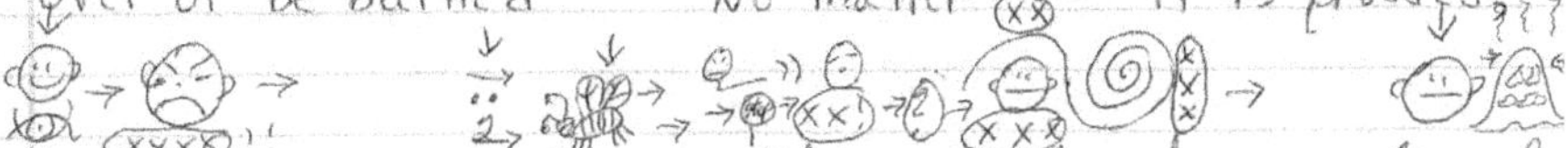

I refuse to be tempted or overturned My soul
I refuse to be tempted or overturned my soul

can keep a secret, and it does not tattle because
can keep a secret, and it does not tattle because

being discreet is best; it has learned My soul does
being discreet is best; it has learned My soul does

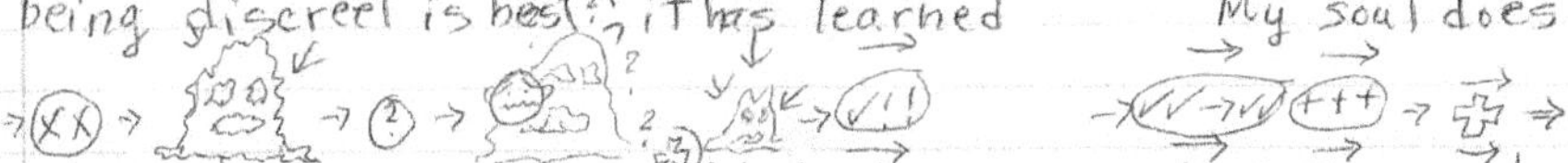

not quiver or waver; it just gets better and
not quiver or waver; it just gets better and

better and better When life wants to overcome
better and better When life wants to overcome

my soul, it adapts and becomes a trendsetter
my soul, it adapts and becomes a trendsetter

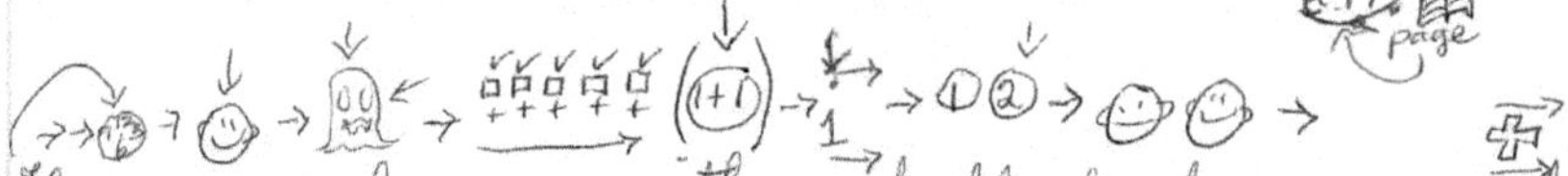

Then my soul scores with a double header and
Then my soul scores with a double header and

jumps out of all its fetters And becomes a
jumps out of all its fetters And becomes a

modern jet-setter; it travels the cosmos free as
modern jet-setter; it travels the cosmos free as

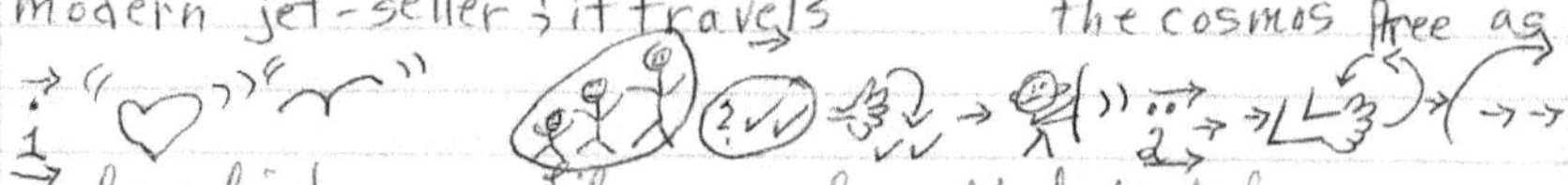

a love bird Life may have tried to take away
a love bird Life may have tried to take away

everything in its fury, with its cares and worries
everything in its fury, with its cares and worries

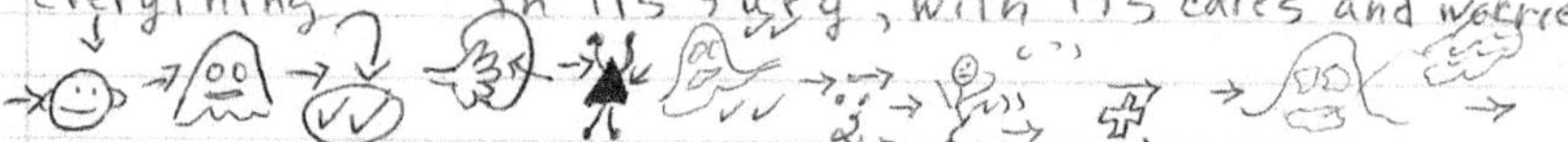

My soul has kept its right to play and chuckled
My soul has kept its right to play and chuckled

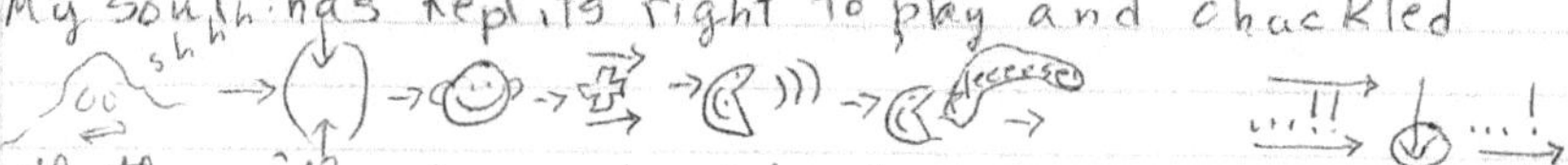

silently with glee and said please But instead
silently with glee and said please But instead

my soul plays games with life every day where
my soul plays games with life every day where

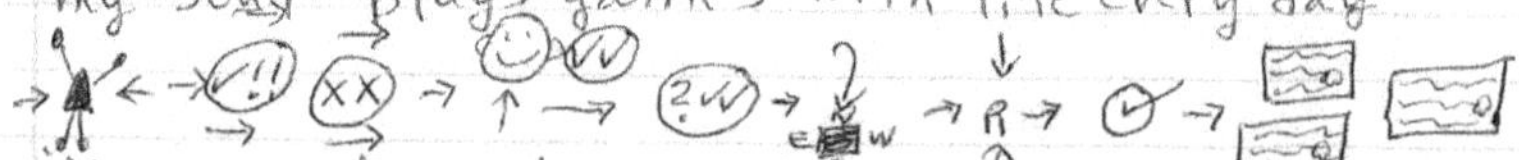

it does not matter if there are any guarantees
it does not matter if there are any guarantees

and lets itself know where it can sit and stay
And lets itself know where it can sit and stay

because where my soul goes does not even need any
because where my soul goes does not even need any

keys My soul says, you can stand still but you
keys my soul says, you can stand still but you

cannot catch me You see, I, sir, am free
cannot catch me You see, I, sir, am free

It says I want action to happen, so if it is to
It says I want action to happen, so if it's to

be, it will become my soul's reality It says
be, it will become my soul's reality It says

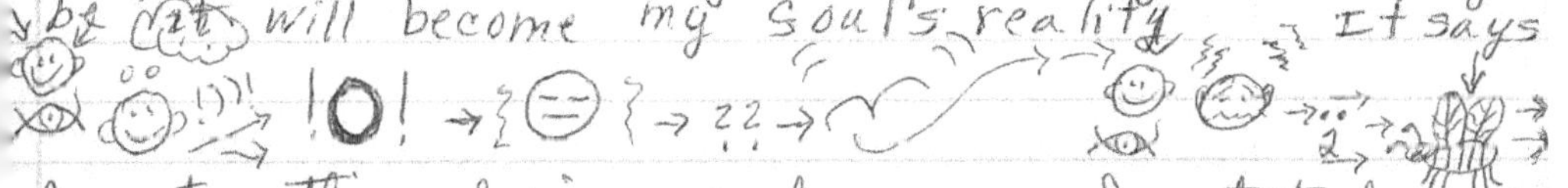

I want nothing boring or free I want to be
I want nothing boring or free I want to be

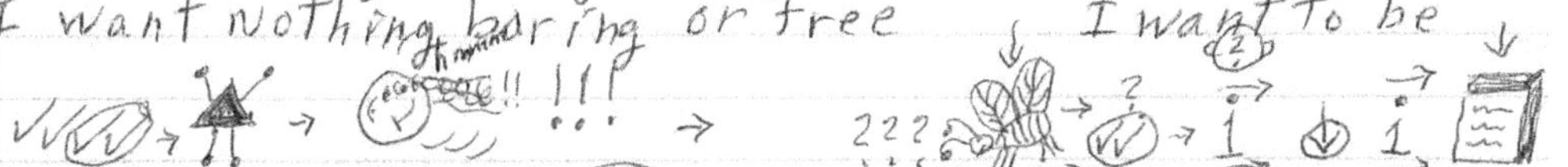

something interesting, maybe someone in a story
something interesting, maybe someone in a story

It says I want to be able to look and see with
It says I want to be able to look and see with

abandon into and as far as eternity And when
abandon into and as far as eternity And when

my soul feels down, it gives itself a lift into
my soul feels down, it gives itself a lift into

the world of imaginative creativity It will get up
the world of imaginative creativity It will get up

and move out of town when my body loses its
and move out of town when my body loses its

spark and turns into glory It will be the first one
spark and turns into glory It will be the first one

to move around after I am freed from the
to move around after I am freed from the

depths of the sin's tree It will be reaching for
depths of the sin's tree It will be reaching for

glory and beyond and will want to open the
glory and beyond and will want to open the

pearly white gates with the golden keys
pearly white gates with the golden keys

My clothes may be in rags and my skin may
My clothes may be in rags and my skin may

sag, but the love in my heart will never lag
sag, but the love in my heart will Never lag

And my footsteps may falter because I get angry
And my footsteps may falter because I get angry

and I have been known to be quite mad And my
and I have been known to be quite mad And my

breath may be shallow and bad, and I also have
breath may be shallow and bad, and I also have

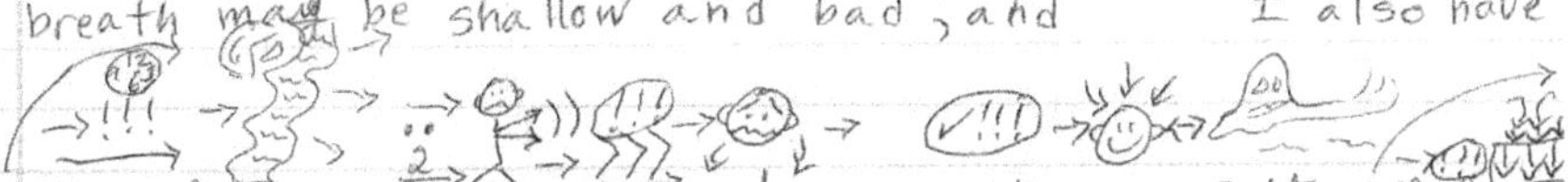

been known to get very sad But my spirit will have
been known to get very sad But my spirit will have

the winning fad because it wears the mask of
the winning fad because it wears the mark of

justice and is hopefully clad Listen up and take
justice and is hopefully clad Listen up and take

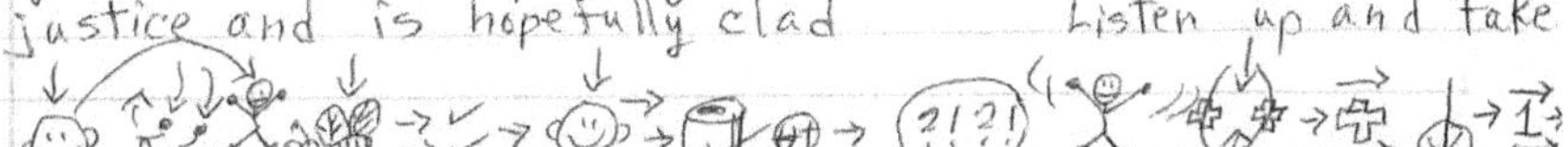

my lead because you can only live with and in the
my lead because you can only live with and in the

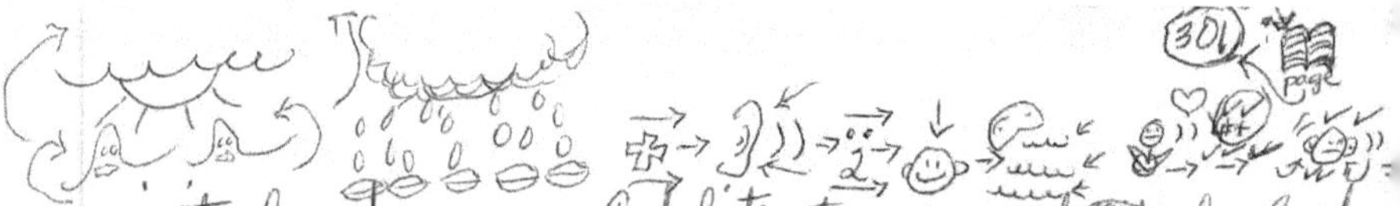

spiritual seed And listen to my words, truly heed
spiritaal seed And listen to my words, traly heed

because I have chosen on its substance to feed
because I have chosen on its substance to feed

Never give up on your needs whether they be mortal
Never give up on your needs whether they be morta

or spiritual send them over and drop them at His
or spiritaal send them over and drop them at His

feet Do not compromise. Just let your spirit bleed
feet Do not compromise Just let your spirit blee

until it cleanses itself of all its weeds
until it cleanses itself of all its weeds

(58) Fly Far Away (147)

Fly Far Away

I'll fly far away from my troubles and anger Where

I'll fly far away from my troubles and anger Where

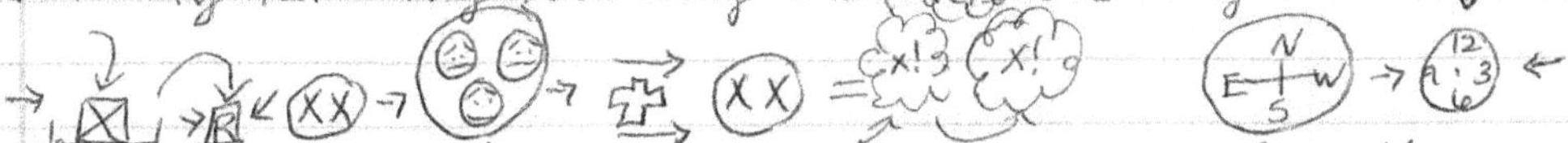

there are no worries and no dangers Where time

there are no worries and no dangers Where time

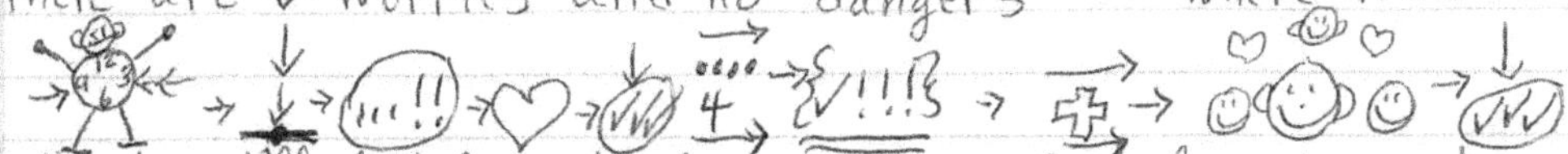

stands still but love is for sure And happiness is

stands still but love is for sure And happiness is

alive for every him or her Send my troubles away

alive for every him or her Send my troubles away

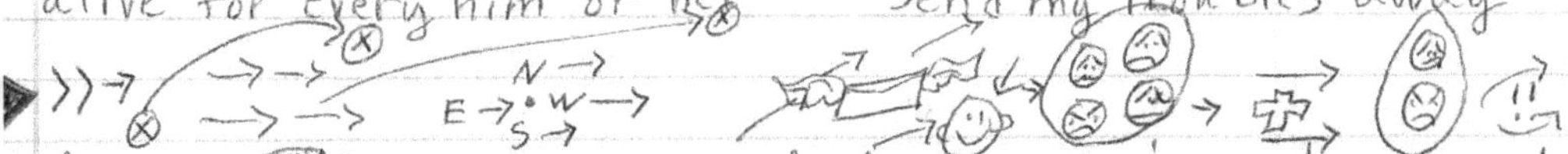

Go away, far away Send my worries and woes out

Go away, far away Send my worries and woes out

on a holiday Send all my troubles away, on this

on a holiday Send all my troubles away, on this

very day Send my troubles on a trip, away: one

very day Send my troubles on a trip, away one

way I'll find my soul's true logic, hit or miss

way I'll find my soul's true logic, hit or miss

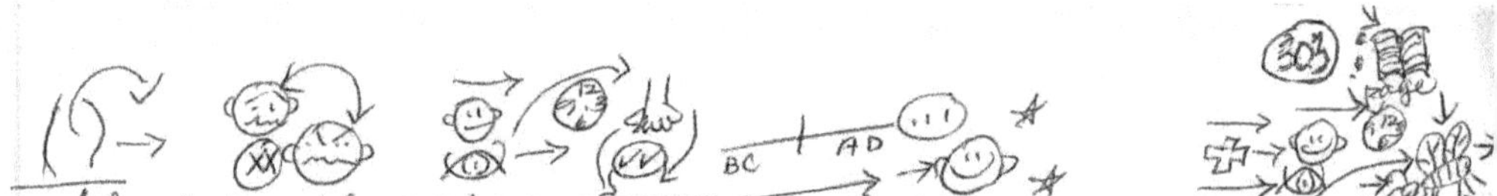

without troubles, (SLOW) I'll have eternal bliss And I'll be

without troubles, I'll have eternal bliss And I'll be

free, I'll feel a heavenly kiss Can you possibly want

free, I'll feel a heavenly kiss Can you possibly want

better than this? Then I'll have found a pure

better than this? Then I'll have found a pure

and a lasting romance I'll know right away

and a lasting romance I'll know right away

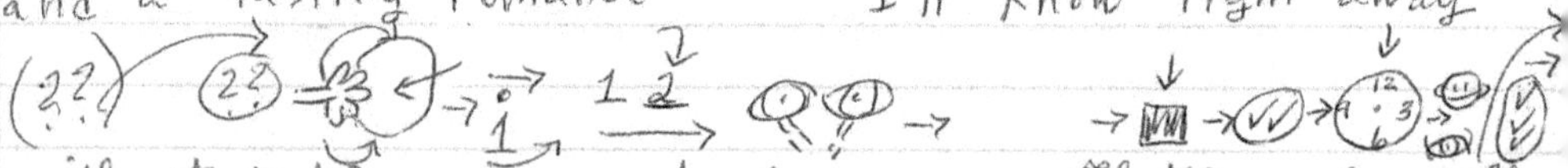

without taking a second glance That's when I'll

without taking a second glance That's when I'll

get my opportunity, (SLOW) my real chance To prove I

get my opportunity, my real chance To prove I

am now worthy to share love and dance Flying

am now worthy to share love and dance Flying

is a lesson I've learned to be able to navigate

is a lesson I've learned to be able to navigate

and discern I fly from trouble, (SLOW) make a U-turn, (SLOW) and

and discern I fly from trouble, make a U-turn, and

do not let myself get burned I've had enough bad
do not let myself get burned I've had enough bad

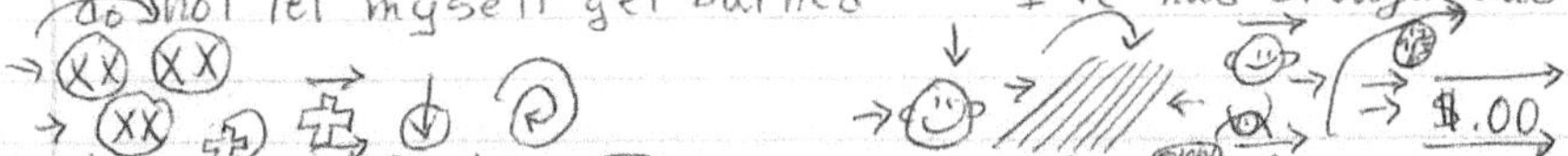

times, and in turn, my stripes, I have earned
times, and in turn, my stripes, I have earned

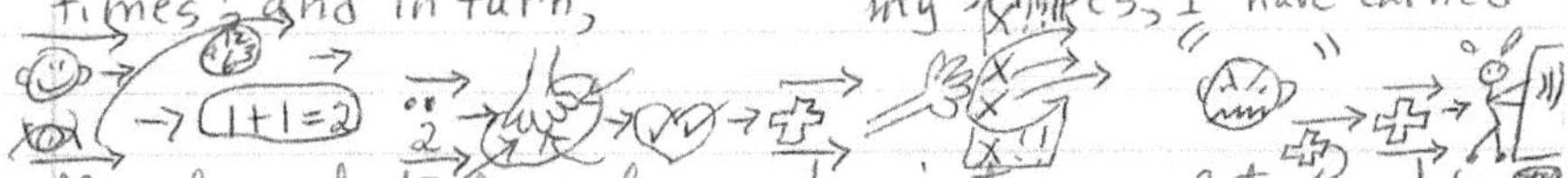

I've learned to keep love and reject hate; and try,
I've learned to keep love and reject hate; and try.

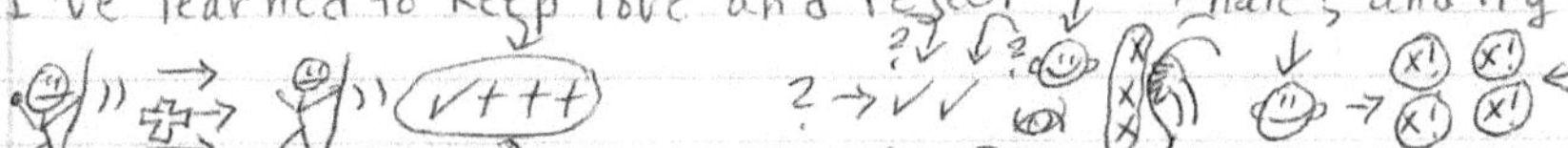

try and try again Whether, I find, my problems
try and try again whether, I find my problems

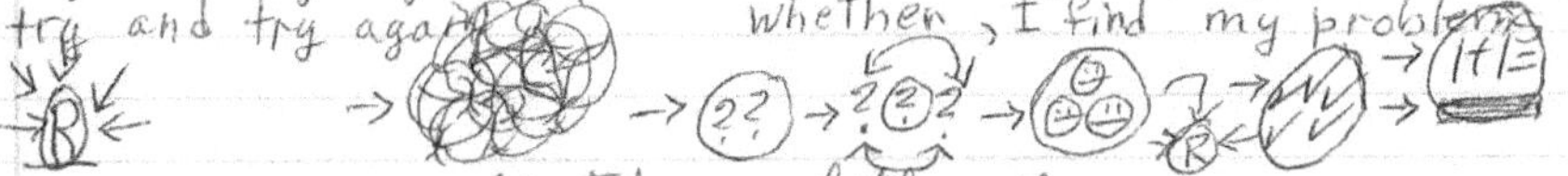

are complicated or whether they are easy
are complicated or whether they are easy

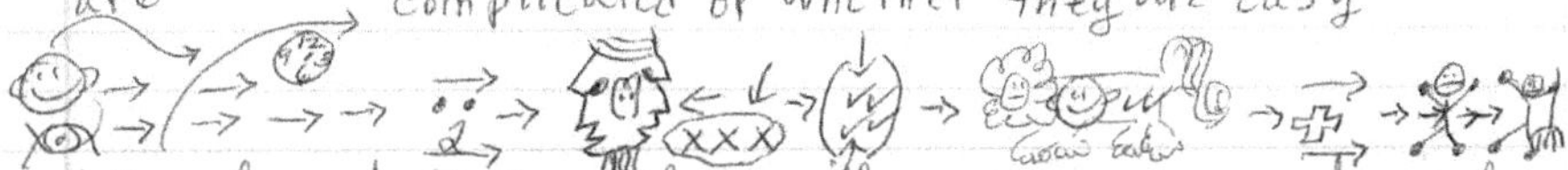

I've learned to face them with courage and work
I've learned to face them with courage and work

at them like a busy bee Then I can get used to
at them like a busy bee Then I can get used to

them in any degree, and I will be ready to referee
them in any degree, and I will be ready to referee

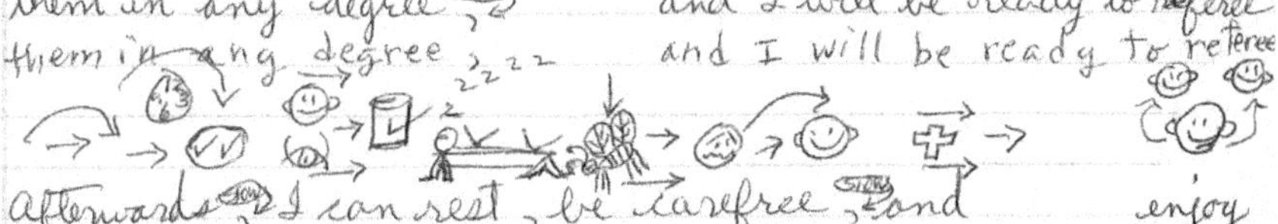

afterwards, I can rest, be carefree, and enjoy
Aftewards, I can rest, be carefree, and enjoy

what hard work guarantees Hey, just let me know
what hard work guaran tees Hey, just, let me Know

if I am bound for trouble this day Please, I don't
if I am bound for trouble this day Please, I don't

need to be defeated. Just have your way I will still
need to be defeated. Just have your way I will still

have a little something to say. I can still pray In
have a little something to say. I can still pray In

the end, I will conquer, jump for joy and learn to play
theend, I will conquer, jump for joy and learn to play

I'll watch my step and I will try not to fall down
I'll watch my step and I will try not to fall down

Then I will stay balanced when I turn around And I
Then I will stay balanced when I turn around And I

won't get confused and get lost in town And I
won't get confused and get lost in town And I

will never again be sad or wear a frown
will never again be sad or wear a frown

(59) Fate (149)
Fate

It always happens that what I fear the most Becomes
It always happens that what I fear the most Becomes

my guiding post and I become its host And then it
my guiding post and I become its host And then it,

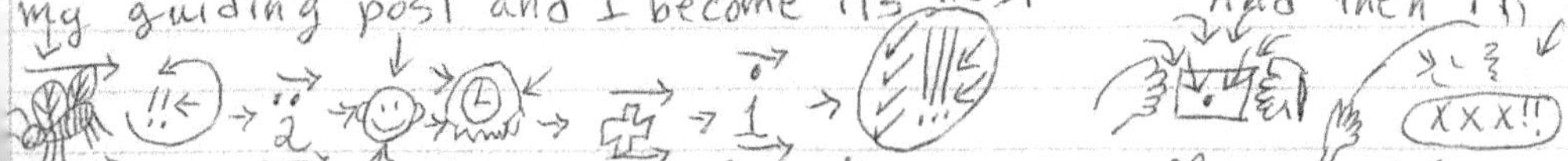

becomes to me law and the utmost Fate punishes
becomes to me law and the utmost Fate punishes

me like I was a whipping post Even if I cry me
me like I was a whipping post Even if I cry me

a river of tears My fears come true, the whole
a river of tears My fears come true, the whole

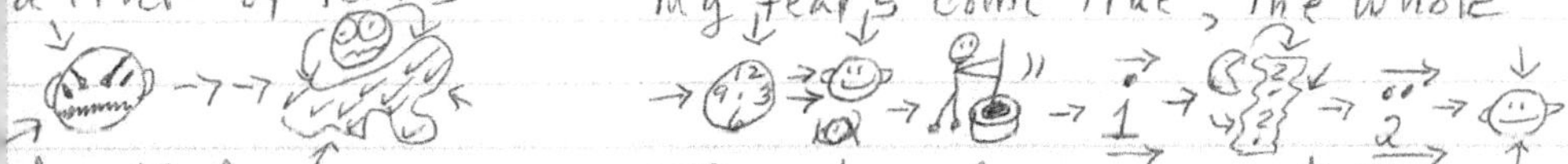

dreadful smear When I make a request to my
dreadful smear When I make a request to my

fears please don't come near They just
fears please don't come near They just

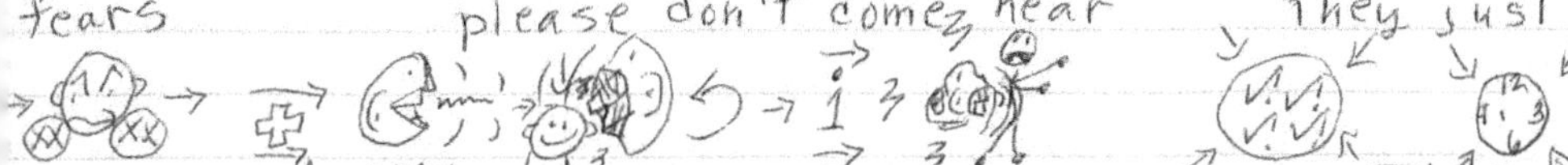

sneer and bite me from the rear Always, when
sneer and bite me from the rear always, when

I smile and say all is good
I smile and say all is good

I should always pause and
I should always pause and

knock on wood
Knock on wood

Because I seldom will be heard or
Because I seldom will be heard or

understood
understood

And my request will most always be
And my request will most always be

misunderstood
misunderstood

My family, my loved ones, and me
My family, my loved ones, and me

My lover and my children all tend to be Victims
My lover and my children all tend to be Victims

of one giant conspiracy
of one giant conspiracy

That always treats my
That always treats my

wishes to the contrary
wishes to the contrary

When I wish for good things
When I wish for good things

to come my way
to come my way

My wishes soon fade and
My wishes soon fade and

slowly wither away
slowly wither away

No matter what I have to say
No matter what I have to say

Fate always leans toward the opposite way
Fate always leans toward the opposite way
meets what another one sends
meets what another one sends
another one begins again
another one begins again
sun I am forced into a den
sun I am forced into a den
someone says it's time to end
someone says it's time to end
love flow and not care or bother
love flow and not care or bother
one way or another
one way or another
not destroy on or the other
not destroy on or the other
mother, sister or brother
mother, sister or brother

One day
One day
When one is gone,
When one is gone,
When I want to enjoy
When I want to enjoy
When I say begin,
When I say begin,
I must let my
I must let my
I must not care
I must not care
I must build on hope and
I must build on hope and
I must give up father,
I must give up father,
For to completely overcome
For to completely overcome

and get rid of hate I must learn to stop and accept
and get rid of hate I must learn to stop and accept

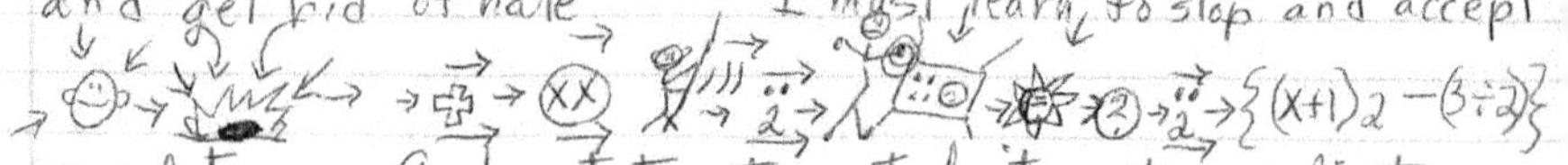

my fate And not try to control it or to complicate
my fate And not try to control it or to complicate

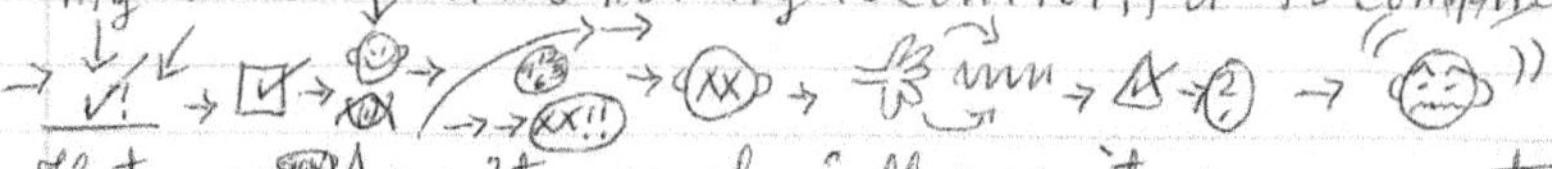

That way, I won't wrongly influence it or aggravate
That way, I won't wrongly influence it or aggravate

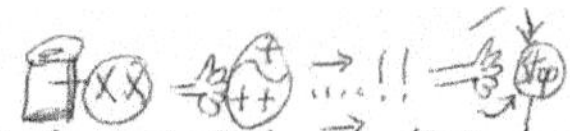

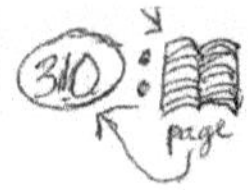

(60) Can't Help But Resist (151)

Can't Help But Resist

Resisting you is the name of my game We all

Resisting you is the name of my game We all

know where there is no pain, there is no gain And

know where there is no pain, there is no gain And

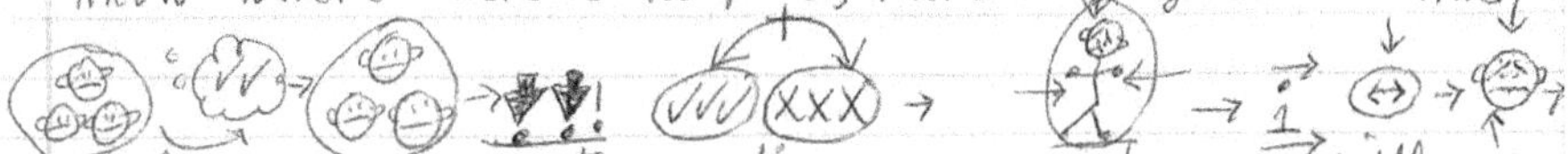

we know we must sometimes endure a little pain

we know we must sometimes endure a little pain

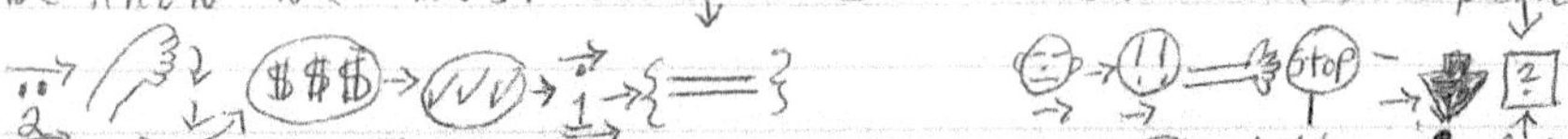

to get gain, all the same Well, resisting is what

to get gain, all the same Well, resisting is what

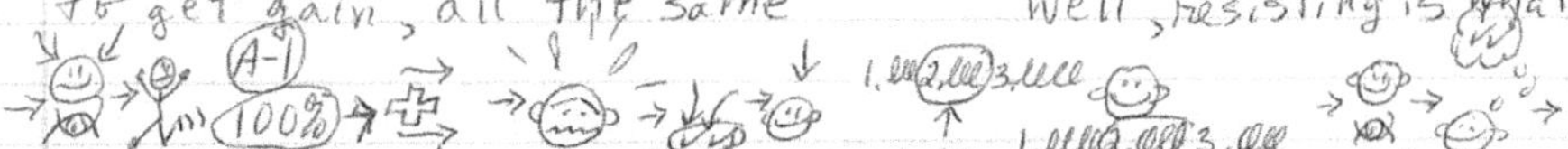

I do best, and pain is my middle name I know

I do best, and pain is my middle name I know

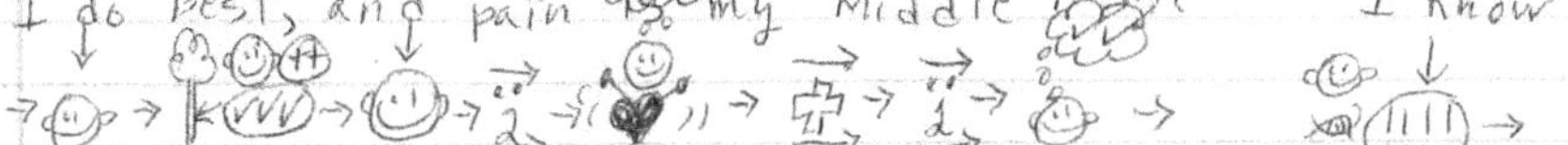

you would like to believe and to think I am

you would like to believe and to think I am

without direction and I am on the brink To tell you

without direction and I am on the brink To tell you

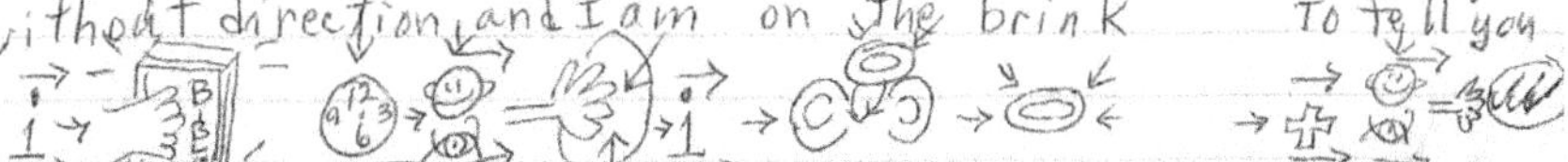

the truth, now I have the missing link And I will

the truth, now I have the missing link And I will

311 page

tell you in a blink of a wink How can I help but be
tell you in a blink of a wink How can I help but be

happy and outspoken Now that my chains of slavery
happy and outspoken Now that my chains of slavery

have been broken My love for the whole world is my
have been broken My love for the whole world is my

lucky token And I am forever indebt — to all
lucky token And I am forever indebt — to all

whom I love — and I am beholden You ask
whom I love — and I am beholden You ask

why I would want to resist you Is it just because
why I would want to resist you Is it just because

you and I are done and through? I tell you
you and I are done and through? I tell you

nothing has changed, nothing is new The fact is,
nothing has changed, nothing is new The fact is,

I have forgotten about you; does this give you a clue?
I have forgotten about you; does this giv you a clue?

Even though my life may be short I will do my best

Even though my life may be short I will do my best

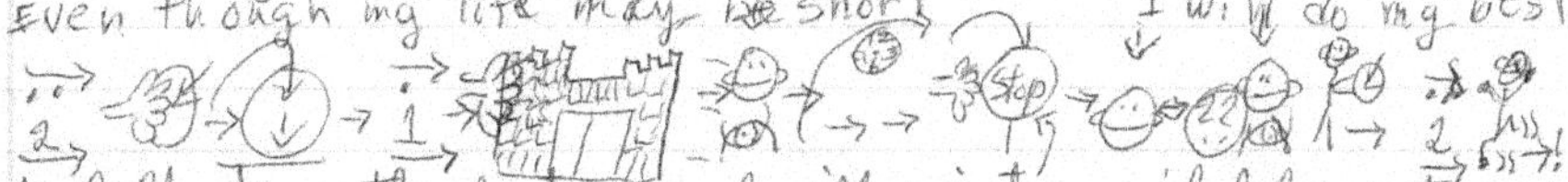

to hold down the fort I will resist you if I have to go

to hold down the fort I will resist you if I have to go

to the highest court I will not stoop to ever again be

to the highest court I will not stoop to ever again be

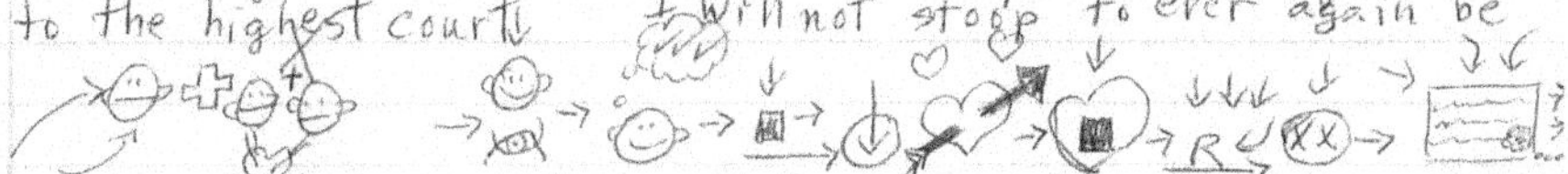

your cohort I know that in love there are no guarantees

your cohort I know that in love there are no guarantees

But you will never again have me crawling on my knees

But you will never again have me crawling on my knees

I have made up my own mind and I might say, with ease

I have made up my own mind and I might say, with ease

I can assure you now, I will love where and

I can assure you now, I will love where and

with whom I please I will have my victory, I

with whom I please! I will have my victory, I

will have my freedom Now I will have my turn

will have my freedom Now I will have my turn

to shine in the sun And I will never again be tricked
to shine in the sun And I will never again be tricked

or undone My life has not ended, it has just begun
or undone My life has not ended it has just begun

You have not succeeded in making me late Because
You have not succeeded in making me late Because

I refuse to participate in your hate I really
I refuse to participate in your hate I really

believe in a thing called fate Now I will be
believe in a thing called fate Now I will be

happy and free I have escaped through hate's
happy and free I have escaped through hate's

gate
gate

314 : page

(61) What Don't You Understand? (153)

What Don't You Understand?

What don't you understand man — I'm crazy
What don't you understand man — I'm crazy

about your little rock and roll band — I'm your
about your little rock and roll band — I'm your

greatest and biggest fan — I've loved you ever
greatest and biggest fan — I've loved you ever

since you very first began — I don't and I won't
since you very first began — I don't and I won't

apologize — Because I haven't told any lies
apologize — Because I haven't told any lies

I have never tried to hide or to disguise — My
I have never tried to hide or to disguise — My

approval or my admiring eyes — All my friends
approval or my admiring eyes — All my friends

say I'm just plain crazy — I tell you, I don't
say I'm just plain crazy — I tell you, I don't

mind; I like it better that way — I don't really care
mind; I like it better that way — I don't really care

what you have to say — I don't really care what
what you have to say — I don't really care what

you have to say — I just want to hear my favorite
you have to say — I just want to hear my favorite

band play — Someday you will see my point of view
band play — Some day you will see my point of view

You will see it my way and agree with me too
You will see it my way and agree with me too

I will consider that a real breakthrough — And I
I will consider that a real breakthrough — And I

will have with you a fellowship renewed — Give
will have with you a fellowship renewed — Give

me a reason why you deny me and choose to defy
me a reason why you deny me and choose to defy

Tell me why you can't understand or — give me a
Tell me why you can't understand or — give me a

reason or specify
reason or specify

Tell me why you and I can't
Tell me why you and I can't

see eye to eye
see eye to eye

And you refuse to agree with me
And you refuse to agree with me

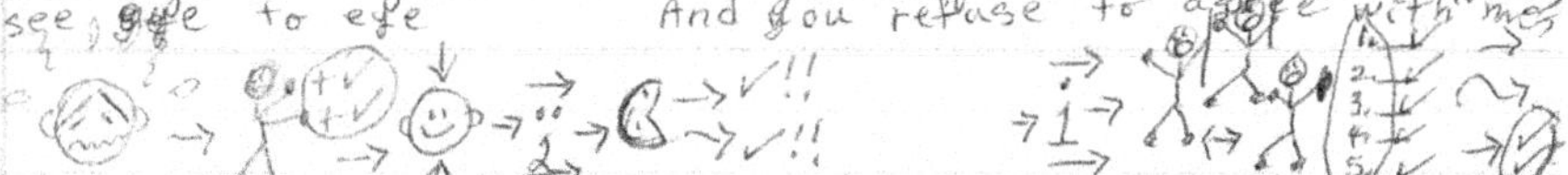

please help me to justify
please help me to jastify

The band's set has
The band's set has

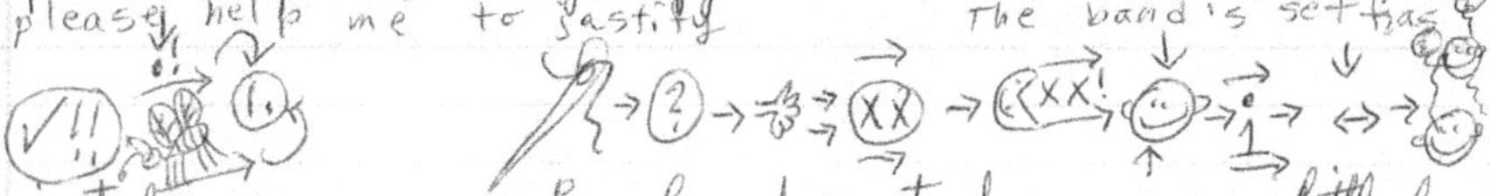

just begun
just begun

So why do not deny me a little fun
So why do not deny me a little fun

You choose to reject them
You choose to reject them

and force them to
and force them to

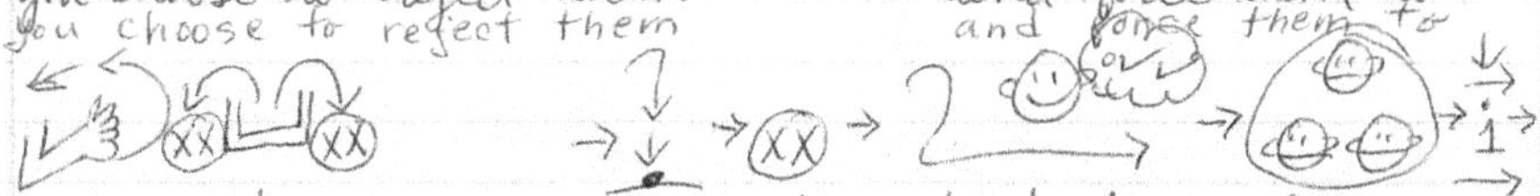

come undone
come undone

By not understanding them one
By not understanding them one

by one
by one

Now do you see my particular plight?
Now do you see my particular plight?

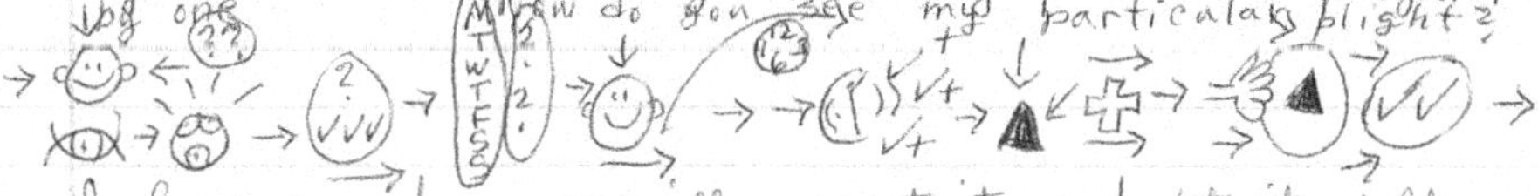

I hope someday you will accept it and get it right
I hope someday you will accept it and get it right

You can't go wrong when they play at night
You can't go wrong when they play at night

317 is page

Because no one will want to argue or to fight
Because no one will want to argue or to fight

Their music will be very soothing And your sense
Their music will be very soothing And your sense

of reason will be your undoing In the right
of reason will be your undoing In the right

directions they will make me swing And you will
directions they will make me swing And you will

also see that this band is the best possible one
also see that this band is the best possible one

that was ever able to sing
that was ever able to sing

318 page

62 Have You Met My 155
Have You Met My
Friend Lorette?
Friend Lorette?

Have you met my friend Lorette? She's related
Have you met my friend Lorette? she's related

to my friend Turret She's also outspoken, slow you
to my friend Turret she's also outspoken, you

bet She doesn't really care if she gets heck
bet She doesn't really care if she gets heck

She has her own opinion And she is a spontaneous
She has her own opinion And she is a spontaneous

minion Truth is her little onion As for
minion Truth is her little onion As for

her loud relative You'd better give Turret a
her loud relative You'd better give Turret a

sedative And be willing and ready to forgive
sedative And be willing and ready to forgive

him his sins His outbursts you may have to
him his sins His outbursts you may have to

painfully relive
painfully relive

seldom use wisdom
seldom use wisdom

want hidden
want hidden

knowledge not meant to offend
Knowledge not meant to offend

them senseless but smitten
them senseless but smitten

friend named Claudette
friend named Claudette

jet set
jet set

These two, Lorette and Turret,
These two, Lorette and Turret,

Any thoughts you generally
Any thoughts you generally

Soon will become common
Soon will become common

You could call
You could call

These two have a
These two have a

She is a member of the
She is a member of the

On her gender's wouldn't be able to bet
On her gender's wouldn't be able to bet

And with the government she has a secret debt
Amd with the government she has a secret debt

While Claudette spies for the other side in her closet
While Claudette spies for the other side in her closet

You see, she plays a dangerous game of Russian roulette
You see, she plays a dangerous game of Russian roulette

she secretly loves Lorette, which understandably
she secretly loves Lorette, which understandably

makes Lorette fret When spying, Claudette is
makes Lorette fret when spying, Claudette is

known to the other side as a cadet
known to the other side as a cadet

Claudette has a problem, you see Claudette
Claudette has a problem, you see Claudette

can't choose which gender or what anatomy
can't choose which gender or what anatomy

to be — on the contrary If she did,
to be — on the contrary If she did,

she would no longer be free Because if she
she would no longer be free Because if she

chose the proper anatomy — she would reveal
chose the proper anatomy — she would reveal

she is a he
she is a he

Claudette would then be thrown in
Claudette would then be thrown in

the clink
the clink

And Lorette would lose her friend in a
And Lorette would lose her friend in a

blink
blink

And Turret, on the other hand would
And Turret, on the other hand would

prove to be the loud rat fink
prove to be the loud rat fink

Because Turret
Because Turret

couldn't be quiet,
couldn't be quiet,

Claudette's plans for love
Claudette's plans for love

would be gone in a wink
would be gone in a wink

322 page

63 Dreams Are Funny Things 157
Dreams Are Funny Things

Sometimes dreams are funny things When
Some times dreams are funny things when

your eyes are closed, you can't see outside nothing
your eyes are closed, you can't see outside nothing

absolutely nothing But in your dreams you can
absolutely nothing But in your dreams you can

become anything if you want, you can become a
become anything if you want, you can become a

king Or you can see an image of your favorite
king Or you can see an image of your favorite

diamond ring Sometimes you dream when you
diamond ring Sometimes you dream when you

are lying down Or when you are sitting in a
are lying down Or when you are sitting in a

chair or when you are asleep at sundown
chair or when you are asleep at sundown.

You can dream sleeping on your side or while
You can dream sleeping on your side or while

wearing a frown You can also dream while
wearing a frown You can also dream while

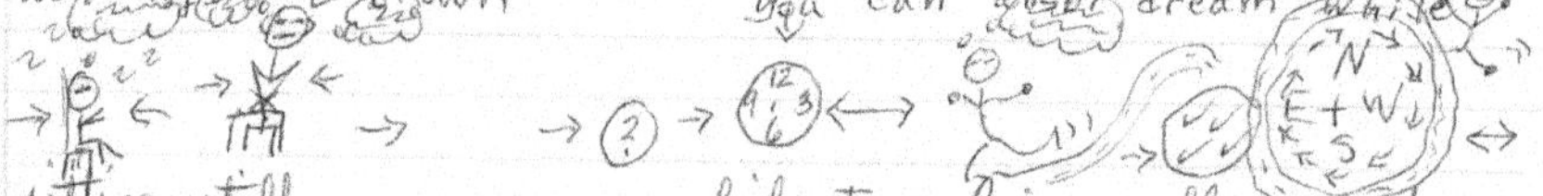

sitting still or while traveling all around
sitting still or while traveling all around

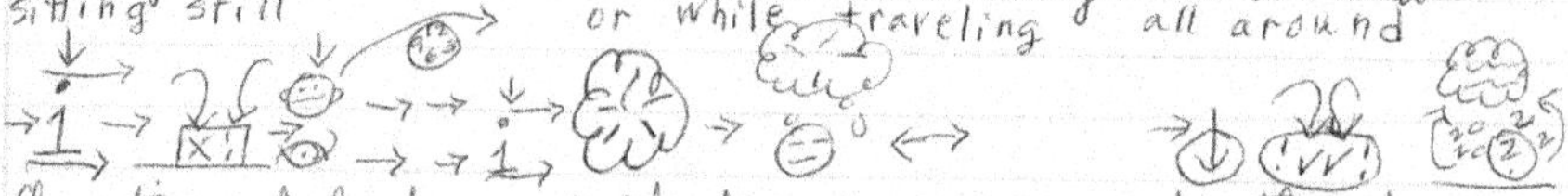

One time I had a vivid dream In this dream
One time I had a vivid dream In this dream

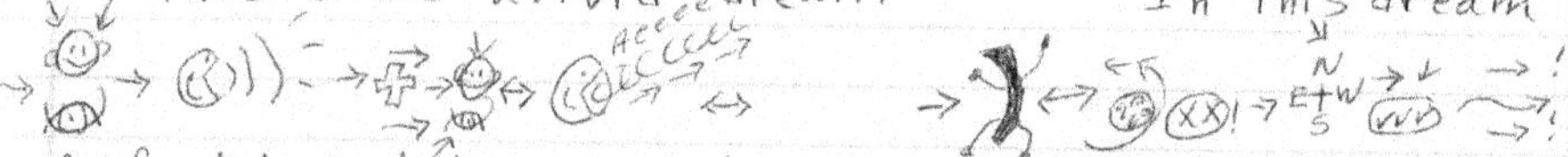

I shouted and I screamed It wasn't at all as
I shouted and I screamed It wasn't at all as

real as it seemed I guess it was a way my
real as it seemed I guess it was a way my

feelings could let off their steam Once, while I
feelings could let off their steam Once, while I

dreamed, I laughed out loud Because of a joke
dreamed, I laughed out loud Because of a joke

I had heard in my dream clouds My dream comedy
I had heard in my dream clouds My dream comedy

had had me wowed When I awoke I was
had had me wowed when I awake I was

refreshed; a bushy-tailed broad Some dreams
refreshed; a bushy-tailed broad some dreams

made me very happy Some make me want to
made me very happy Some make me want to

hide and flee Some make me sad and off
hide and flee some make me sad and off

key Some make me anxious and angry
key Some make me anxious and angry

Some dreams are very romantic Some
some dreams are very romantic Some

dreams are intriguing and classics Some
dreams are intriguing and classics some

dreams are mysterious and nostalgic Some
dreams are mysterious and nostalgic some

dreams are of fantasy and magic Some make
dreams are of fantasy and magic Some make

me afraid and leave me full of wonder Some
me afraid and leave me full of wonder some

make me wonder why I had to sleep any longer
make me wonder why I had to sleep any longer

Sometimes, of my dreams, I can't be any fonder
Sometimes, of my dreams, I can't be any fonder

And I don't want to awaken from being in my slumber
And I don't want to awaken from being in my slamber

Dreams can be amusing and very funny But
Dreams can be amusing and very funny But

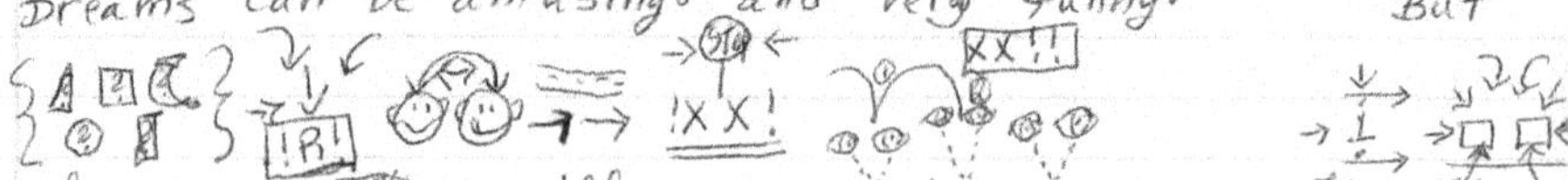

chances are, we will never again see The likes
chances are, we will never again see The likes

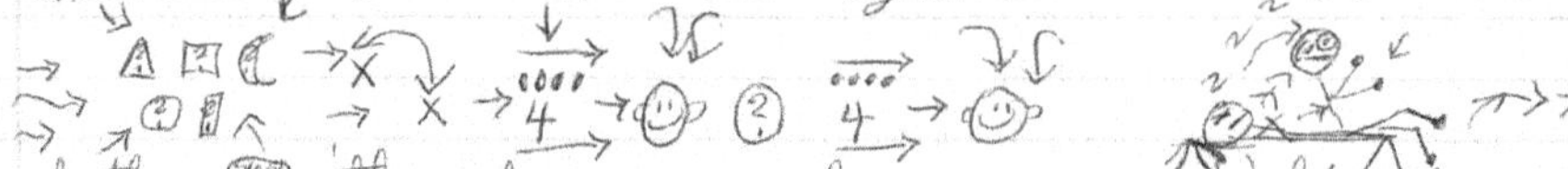

of them, either for you or for me Waking from
of them, either for you or for me Waking from

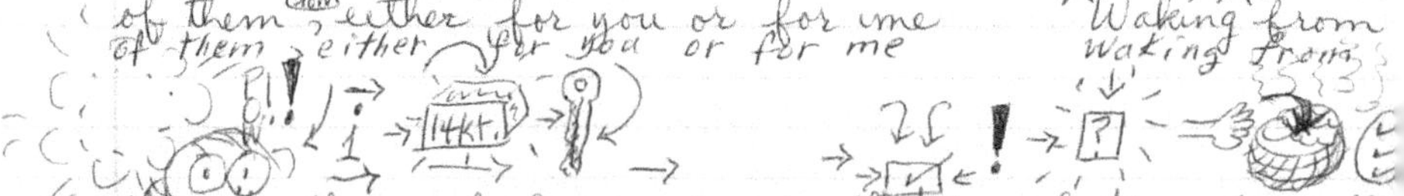

them is the real key that's what makes all
them is the real key that's what makes all

of us happy
of us happy

(64) Get Out Of My Head (159)
Get Out Of My Head

Confusion, get out of my head It's tiresome
Confusion, get out of my head It's tiresome

always escaping to my bed Trying to find the
always escaping to my bed Trying to find the

sleep I sometimes dread My thoughts come to torture
sleep I sometimes dread My thoughts come to torture

me instead Dreams sometimes bring me grief
me instead Dreams sometimes bring me grief

They seem to steal time like a thief Sometimes
They seem to steal time like a thief Sometimes

they make me shake like a leaf They still have
they make me shake like a leaf They still have

for me some reason that is my belief What do
for me some reason that is my belief What do

these dreams all mean? That comes underneath
these dreams all mean? That comes underneath

my eyelids and in between They seem real, like they're
my eyelids and in between They seem real, like they're

somewhere I've been A new kind of pain, a new
somewhere I've been A new kind of pain, a new

reality it seems Into my consciousness they jump
reality it seems Into my consciousness they jump

at my very core, they haunt and taunt In their
at my very core, they haunt and taunt In their

fearsome vividness, they flaunt Whether I want
fearsome vividness, they flaunt Whether I want

them or I don't want them, they still taunt
them or I don't want them, they still taunt

Sometimes it's hard to tell what's real Life is
Sometimes it's hard to tell what's real Life is

never guaranteed or a done, done deal Visions
never guaranteed or a done, done deal Visions

begin to revisit, creep, and steal They crowd
begin to revisit, creep, and steal They crowd

reality, depending on how I feel My eyelids
reality, depending on how I feel My eye lids

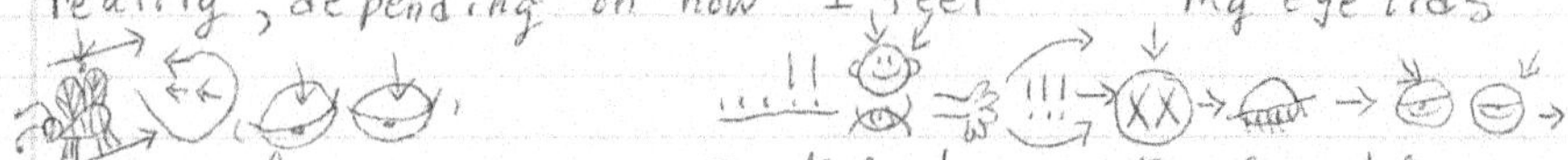

become heavy But I dare not close them
become heavy But I dare not close them

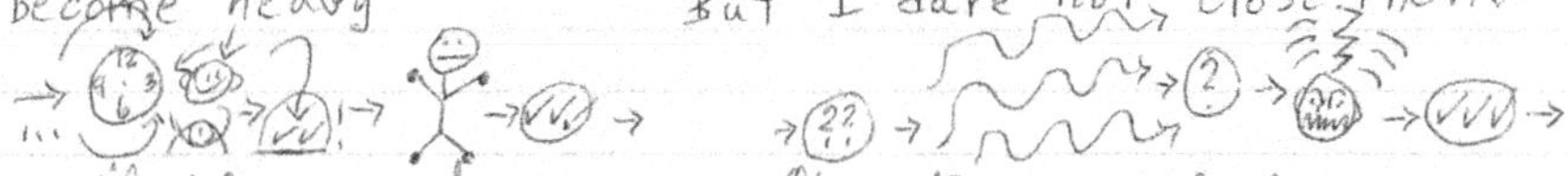

until I'm ready Or streams of fearsome
until I'm ready Or streams of fearsome

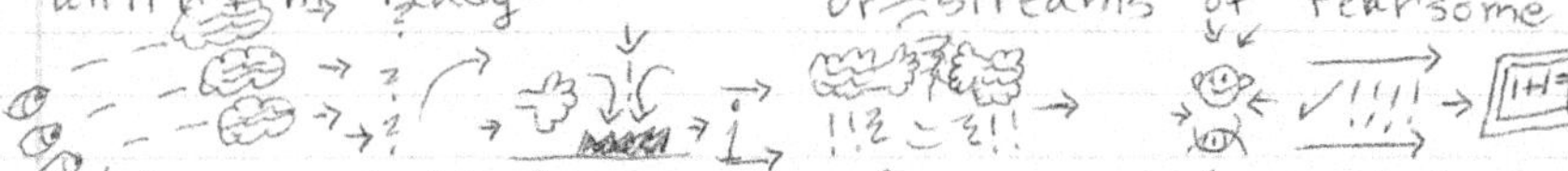

visions might have a mélee I must learn
visions might have a melee I must learn

to cope with them before I go batty Sometimes
to cope with them before I go batty Sometimes

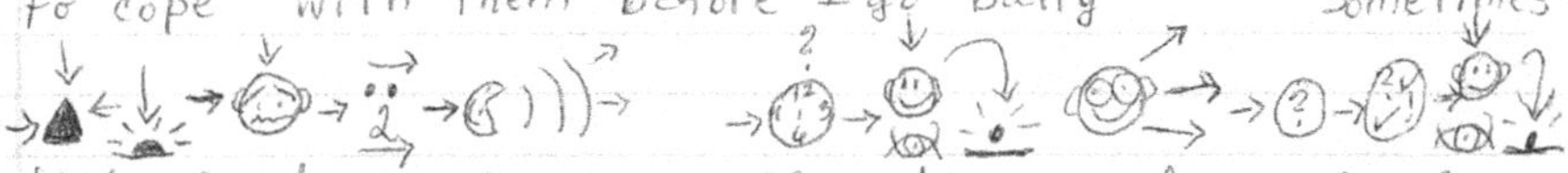

it is hard to tell When I'm awake or if I'm
it is hard to tell when I'm awake or if I'm

really not in hell I just pinch myself until
really not in hell I just pinch myself until

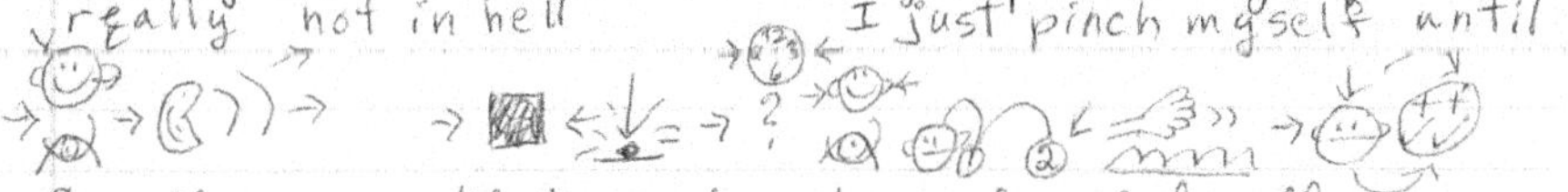

I yell That's when I again feel well
I yell That's when I again feel well

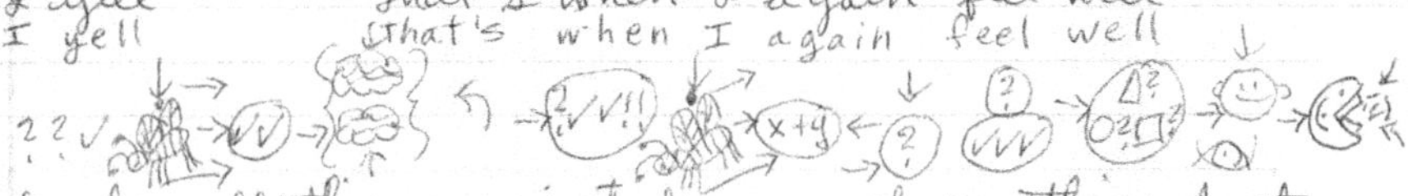

Maybe all this was just because of something I ate
Maybe all this was just because of something I ate

something poisonous on my dinner plate
something poisonous on my dinner plate

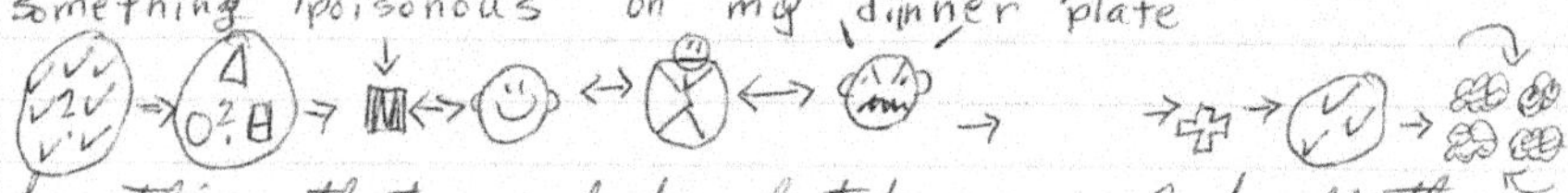

Something that my body hated And all those
Some thing that my body hated And all those

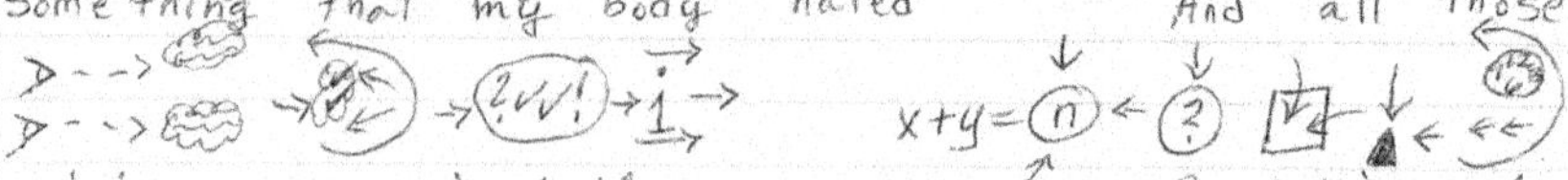

visions were just the result of what it had
viions were just the result of what it had

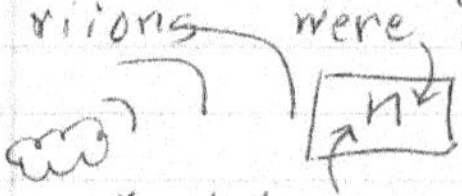

activated
activated

(65) Soon We Will Talk Out Loud (161)
Soon We Will Talk Out Loud

330 page

Soon we will all talk out loud You will find our
Soon we will all talk out loud You will find our

logic will be totally sound Finally, you will have
logic will be totally sound Finally, you will have

also found That no one minds having us around
also found That no one minds having us around

We will be able to go on day to day And no one
We will be able to go on day to day And No one

will have anything at all to say We will
will have anything at all to say We will

work and we will play We will do so come
work and we will play We will do so come

what may, if that's OK. We will think our own
what may, if that's OK. We will think our own

thoughts That may sometimes still come to naught
thoughts That may some times still come to naught

Because our right cure has not yet been wrought
Because our right care has not yet been wrought

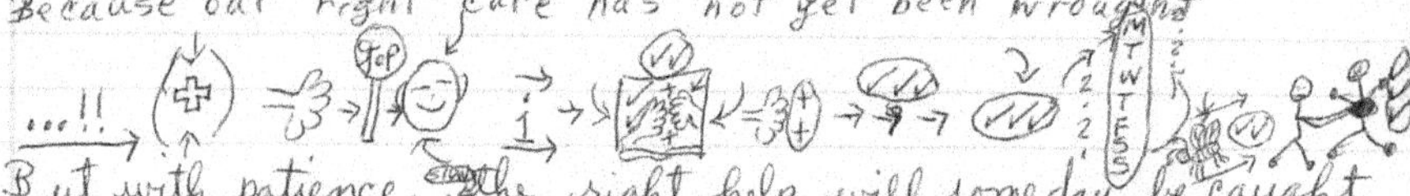

But with patience, the right help will someday be caught
But with patience, the right help will someday be caught

When someone unscrambles our basket of eggs
When someone unscrambles our basket of eggs

We will receive our sea legs We will no
We will receive our sea legs We will no

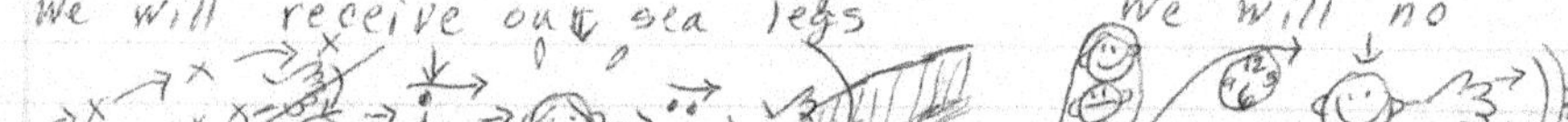

longer find the need to hide We'll gladly show
longer find the need to hide We'll gladly show

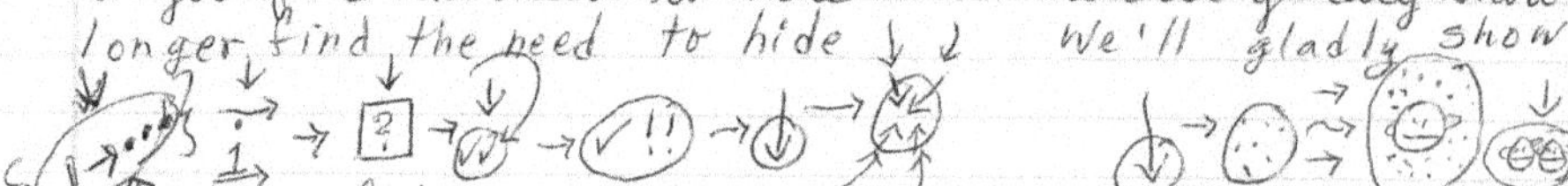

everyone what's really inside In all of you, we
everyone What's really inside In all of you, we

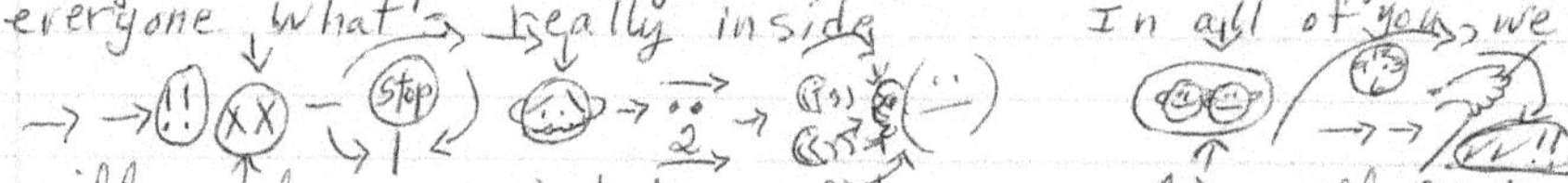

will no longer mind to confide We will find
will no longer mind to confide We will find

you right there, on our side We will consider
you right there, on our side We will consider

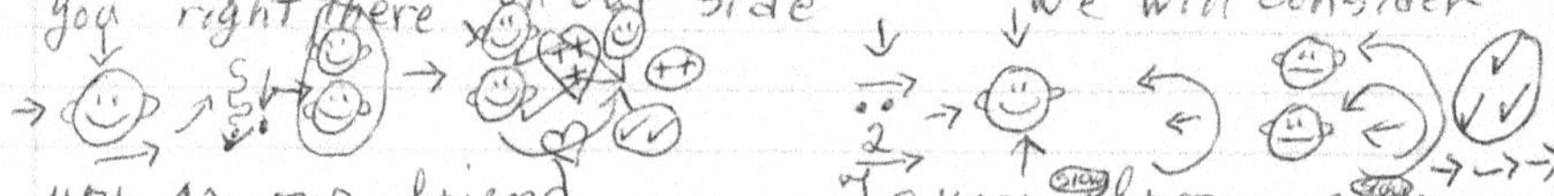

you as our friend To you, from us, many
you as our friend To you, from us, many

treasures we will send
treasures we will send

helping hand we will lend
helping hand we will lend

over, and over, again and again
over, and over, again and again

be and to have your company to last
be and to have your company to last

remember how you were waiting steadfast
remember how you were waiting steadfast

patiently, you were waiting at half mast
patiently, you were waiting at half mast

change in us to occur and
change in us to occur and

our caste
our caste

times over
times over

To you, in turn, a
To you, in turn, a

We'll thank you
We'll thank you

We'll want to
We'll want to

We'll
We'll

Waiting
Waiting

For a
For a

help us to change
help us to change

You, sir, will be rewarded many
You, sir, will be rewarded many

Our lives will become a testimony and
Our lives will become a testimony and

will talk out loud like blooming flowers Now we
will talk voat lqad like blooming flowers Now we

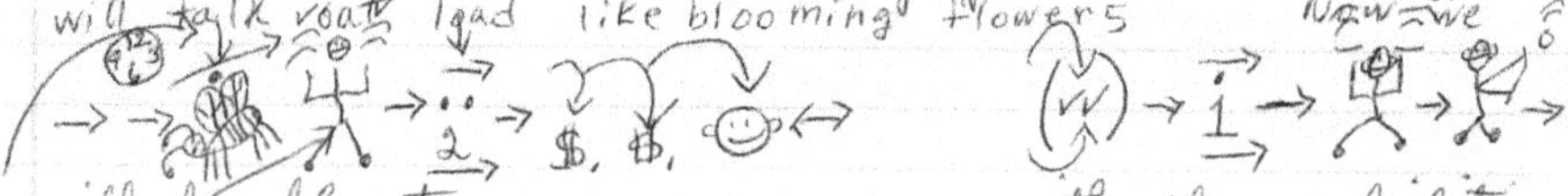

will be able to repay you with the capabilities
will be able to repay you with the capabilities

of all our powers Our love will overflow and
of all our powers Our love will overflow and

cascade Like a powerful, cleansing shower
cascade Like a powerful ,cleansing shower

66 Proof Of Purchase 63
Proof Of Purchase

What's the matter?
What's the matter?

I won, you know
I won, you know

I know, you know too
I know! you know too

wants to know also
wants to know also

know and so do you
know and so do you

And I still do
And I still do

didn't tell anyone
didn't tell anyone

Because I was quiet
Because I was quiet

So you haven't got it in you
So you haven't got it in you

You are absolutely nothing
You are absolutely nothing

Right now, whoever
Right now, whoever

You say I lie But I
You say I lie But I

I know your secret
I know your secret

You don't know mine I
You don't know mine I

You could never figure
You could never figure

I didn't have to tell
I didn't have to tell

And I wasn't scared
And I wasn't scared
That you didn't figure on
That you didn't figure on

What a shame
What a shame
That didn't sit well in your plans
That didn't sit well in yoar plans

All you could do was lie
All you could do was lie
The others fell like sheep
The others feel like sheep

They fell one by one
They fell one by one
I still said nothing
I still said nothing
To
To

any of them
any of them
Then life was too hot
Then life was too hot
I had to
I had to

escape
escape
Which I carefully didn't plan
Which I carefully didn't plan
If
If

you know what I mean
you know what I mean
Then I had public on my
Then I had public on my

side
side
No one could touch me
No one could touch me
Life was trying
Life was trying

But I escaped with my life
But I escaped with my life
That was all
That was all
I was
I was

a former shell
of whom I used to be
BC
AD
Healing takes time
Serenity will come
Pray
love will come
We all grow old
But we
can be free
For those you enslave
All I
can say
Is that you'll be sorry
Your evil
will be your prison
Hear no evil
Say no
evil
Pshhh
See no evil
And spread truth

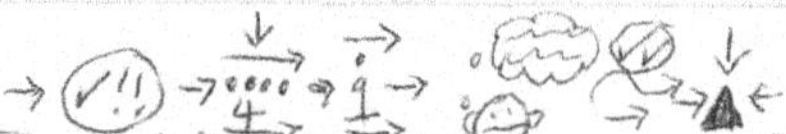

(67) Just For The Thought Of It (165)

Just For The Thought Of It

This story will unfurl, Just for the thought of it

This story will unfurl. Just for the thought of it

The thought makes my mind twirl. There's plenty

The thought makes my mind twirl. There's plenty

of room for it The thought is my whole life. The

of room for it The thought is my whole life. The

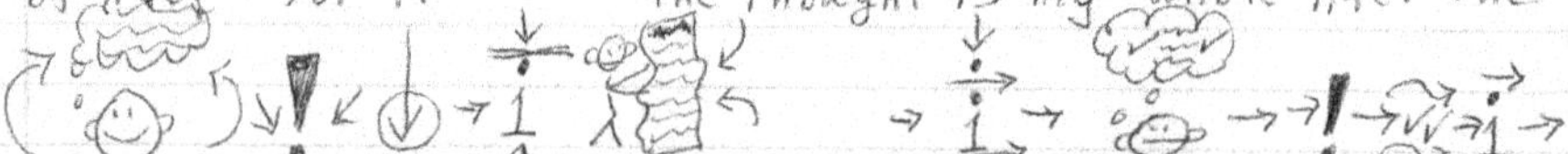

thought is in the script The thought is of a

thought is in the script The thought is of a

girl and this girl you may call hip This thought

girl and this girl you may call hip This thought

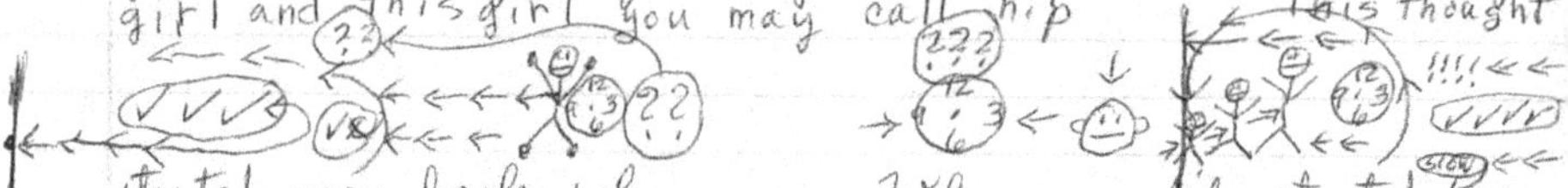

started way back when When my life started, way

started way back when When my life started, way

back then In the early beginning, I felt like a

back then In the early beginning, I felt like a

number 10 There was a pause and then my life

number 10 There was a pause and then my life

began again Sometimes the very thought of
an easy life can't be bought And no matter
what, all is for naught And then life's battles
have to be fought At that stage of life, I didn't
quite know In which direction I was supposed
to go Was I supposed to resist or go with
the flow Even as I thought of this, I was
dealt a deathly blow After that, I became
cursed, life began all over I was totally

different; it was all I could do but run for
different; it was all I could do but run for

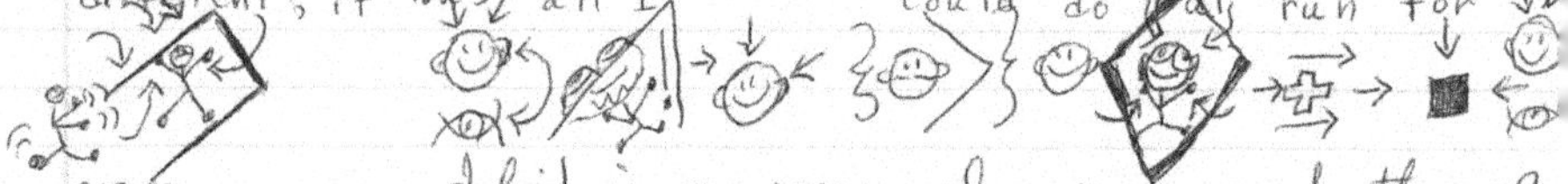

cover I hid in my personal corner and there I
cover I hid in my personal corner and there I

would hover Until I thought I had found a
would hover Until I thought I had found a

loving and a safe lover At its best, life was
loving and a safe lover At its best, life was

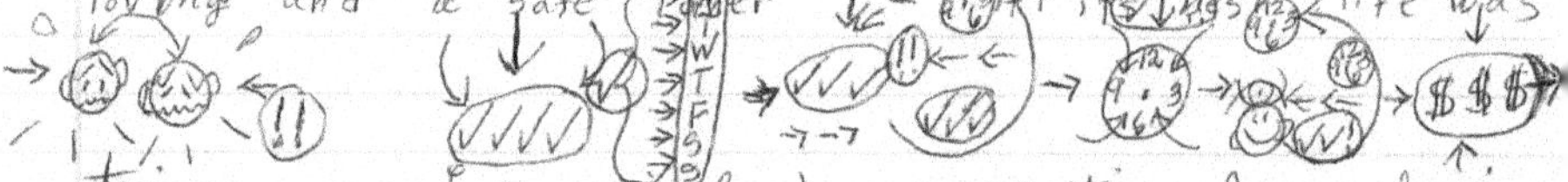

trying Every single day was time I was buying
trying Every single day was time I was buying

It seemed like in my life I was always faking
It seemed like in my life I was always faking

I was awake, I was conscious but I was always
I was awake, I was conscious but I was always

hiding I was just waiting for my chance
hiding I was just waiting for my chance

To pull out life's poisonous lance I was
To pull out life's poisonous lance I was

standing in a deathly stance I was doing my most
standing in a deathly stance I was doing my most

important life's dance I was very fortunate indeed.
important life's dance I was very fortunate indeed

Patience pays handsomely Especially to those who
Patience pays handsomely Especially to those who

dwell lonely And to those everyone may consider
dwell lonely And to those everyone may consider

homely Success comes to those who are willing
homely Success comes to those who are willing

to search out the One and Only Then
to search out the One and Only Then

obtaining the ability to accept fate with a smile
obtaining the ability to accept fate with a smile

My life began to move in the right direction I
My life began to move in the right direction I

was now living in style I was able to find
was now living in style I was able to find

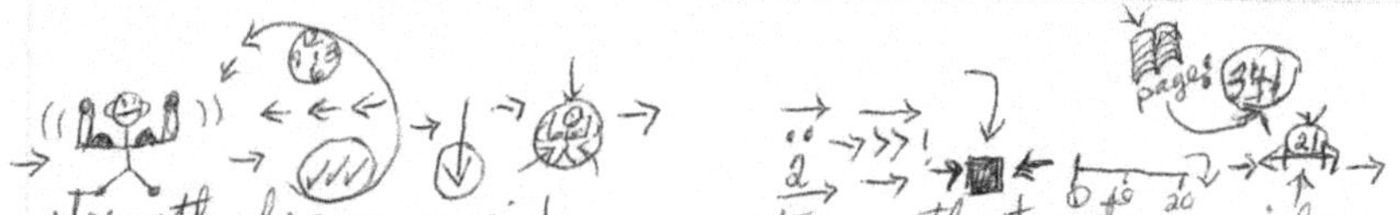

strength from inside to go that extra mile
strength from inside to go that extra mile

My home became a happy loving domicile The
My home became a happy loving domicile The

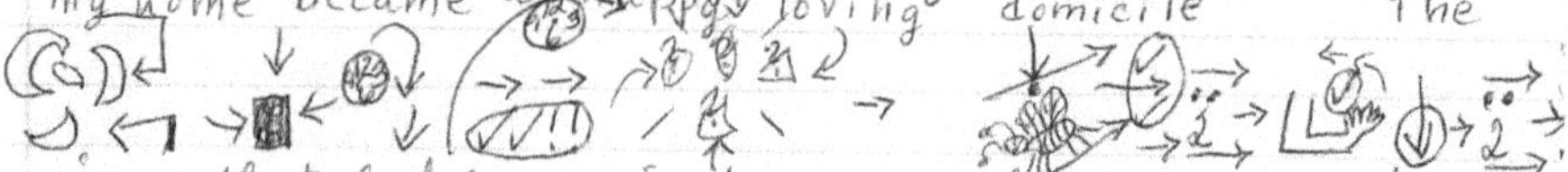

pieces that had been missing began to come into
pieces that had been missing began to come into

place Fate was working its magic with the help
place Fate was working its magic with the help

of Cupid's bow I heard a voice on the telephone
of Cupid's bow I heard a voice on the telephone

that made my heart glow Soon it would all be
that made my heart glow Soon it would all be

history, as Cupid would know Then my wish
history, as Cupid would know Then my wish

came true from when I was but a child I was
came true from when I was but a child I was

a half a century old but my life changed when
a half a century old but my life changed when

he dialed I found my own true love, my sweet

he dialed I found my own true love, my sweet

 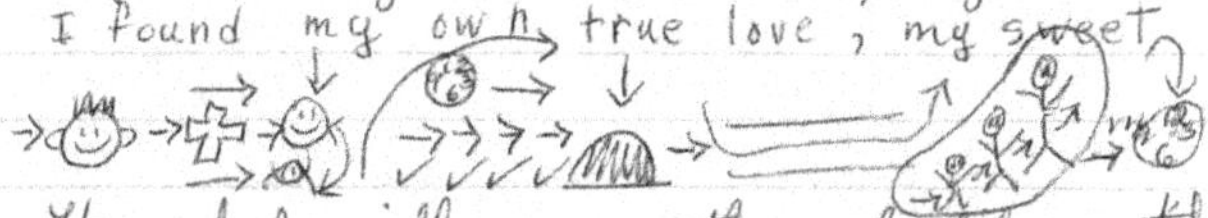

godchild He and I will go on through life until

god child He and I will go on through life until

life goes out of style

life goes out of style

(68) You're My Friend (167)

You're My Friend

You're my friend, mister. You, sir, are
You're my friend, mister. You, sir, are
definitely not an imposter. Give me one right
definitely not an imposter Give me one right
here on the kisser! That one will be a tester
here on the kisser. That one will be a tester
You're also my favorite friend and jester
You're also my favorite friend and jester
whom I love to pester. I'm your friendly
whom I love to pester I'm your friendly
feline and you've got me by the nose whiskers
feline and you've got me by the nose whiskers
Love is the way to go. I think I've been hit by Cupid's
Love is the way to go. I think I've been hit by Cupid's
arrow I say, I really love you so. I thought
arrow I say, I really love you so. I thought

you had a right to know   I really want to show
you had a right to know   I really want to show

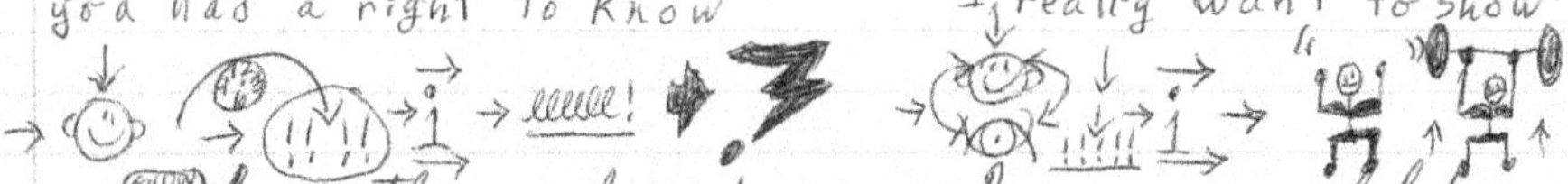

you, from the word go!   I am a powerful dynamo
you, from the word go!   I am a powerful dynamo

And the reason that I glow is because   I am
And the reason that I glow is because   I am

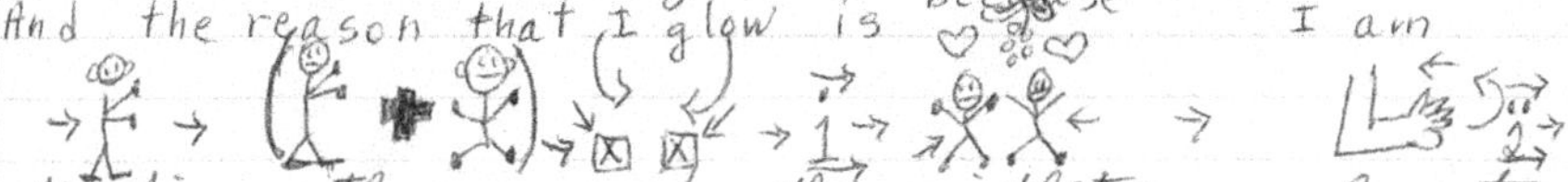

standing with you under the mistletoe   Come to
standing with you under the mistletoe   Come to

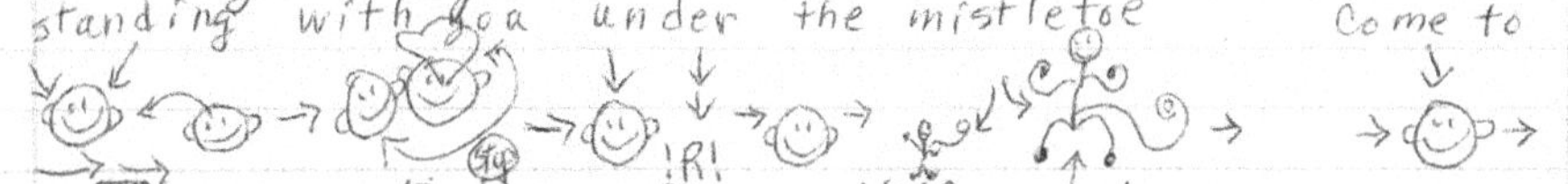

me, my sweetie, You're my little monkey   My
me, my sweetie, You're my little monkey   My

love for you is free; I'll be your busy little bee
love for you is free; I'll be your busy little bee

Don't you see that our love   could be happy
Don't you see that our love   could be happy

and carefree?   Love, love is the key.
and carefree?   Love, love is the key.

You are free to be my love referee   Wait for me,
You are free to be my love referee   wait for me,

page 345

I'll wait for you. We'll have a great rendezvous
I'll wait for you. We'll have a great rendezvous

That will be the worldview, with which I will want to persue
That will be the worldview with which I will want to persue

I will not be mistaken or misconstrued. I will be right
I will not be mistaken or misconstrue I will be right

on cue.
on cue.

You'll wait for me too. It will be a great
You'll wait for me too. It will be a great

fun, a love breakthrough
fun, a love breakthrough

It'll send for you
It'll send for you

around the bend.
around the bend.

Please try to understand and
Please try to understand and

try to comprehend
try to comprehend

The sun will again be
The sun will again be

shining on you, my
friend, and you will be

happy again
happy again

You will be willing to bend and I

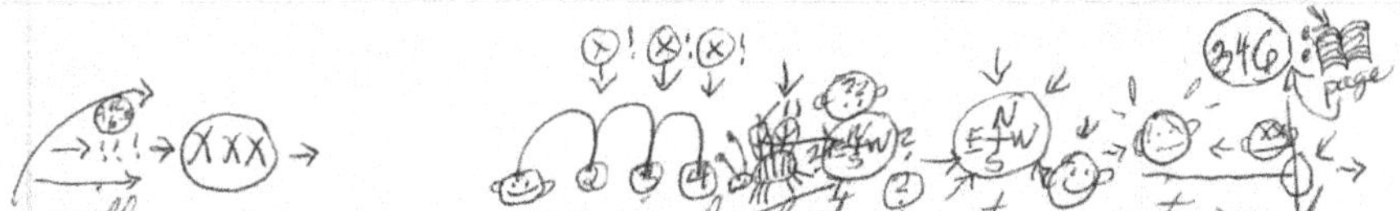

will never again be lost or at my wits' end
will never again be lost or at my wits' end

Because on you I can now depend, and I know that
Because on you I can now depend, and I know that

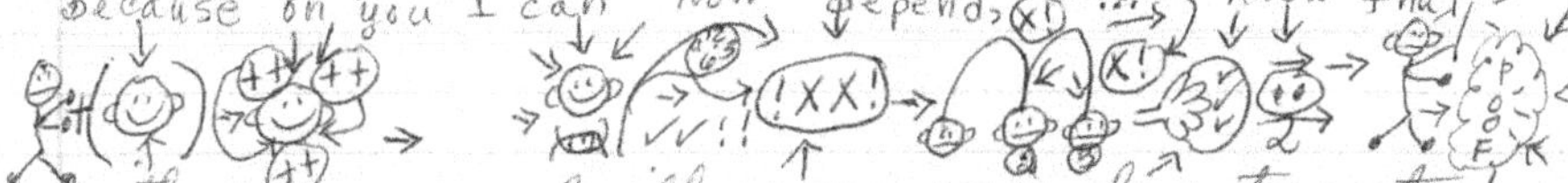

with you I will never again have to pretend
with you I will never again have to pretend

My feelings will show through, and I can now
My feelings will show through, and I can now

say I have a good point of view Of course, that
say I have a good point of view Of course, that

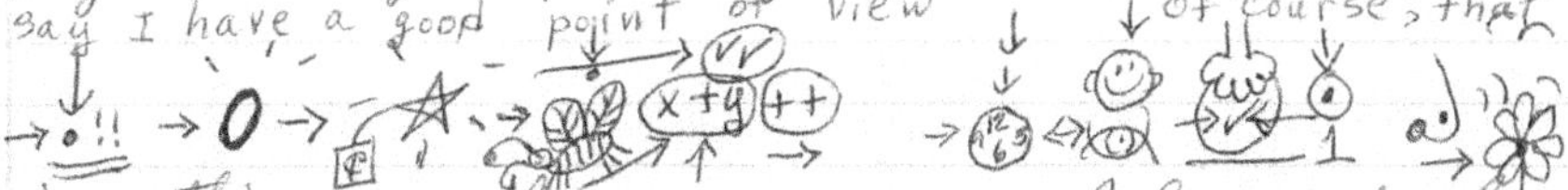

is nothing new because now I have a fresh
is nothing new because now I have a fresh

bird's-eye view With you, I'll stick like
bird's-eye view With you, I'll stick like

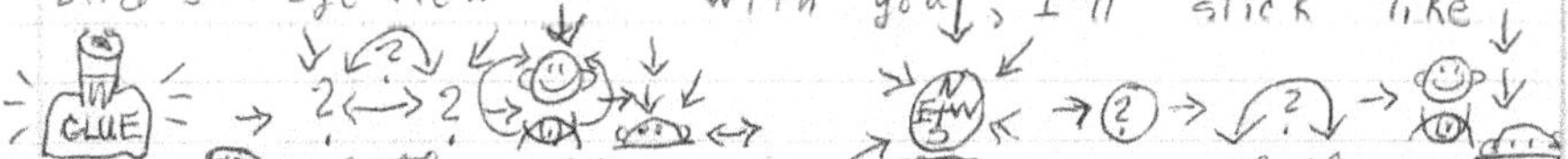

glue, whether I'm here or whether I am
glue, whether I'm here or whether I am

in Timbaktu You'll want to be with me too
in Timbaktu You'll want to be with me too

because I will never, never, prove to be untrue
because I will never, never, prove to be untrue

It'll be great to be able to validate and to
It'll be great to be able to validate and to

be able to, with you, cooperate I will love being
be able to, with you, cooperate I will love being

your mate! That fact, I will never be able to
your mate. That fact, I will never be able to

overstate I wouldn't mind fate, when it means
overstate I wouldn't mind fate, when it means

being your partner and your playmate Or

when I am a full-fledged love graduate;

I will not delay or procrastinate I'll have

no trouble riding your carousel I'll be

your special bell
your special bell

If I know you are coming
If I know you are coming

to me on the double
to me on the double

I'll be the one to ring
I'll be the one to ring

your bells
your bells

And if we become a couple,
And if we become a couple,

You would be my William Tell and I'll be your Tinker
you would be my William Tell and I'll be your Tinker

Bell
Bell

Then I would move out of this hovel
Then I would move out of this hovel

and
and

become your prim and proper
become your prim and proper

mademoiselle
mademoiselle

It is to me no surprise that
It is to me no surprise that

I can see through
I can see through

your popular and romantic
your popular and romantic

disguise
disguise

Or that you are such a valuable
Or that you are such a valuable

Prize; you

prize; you

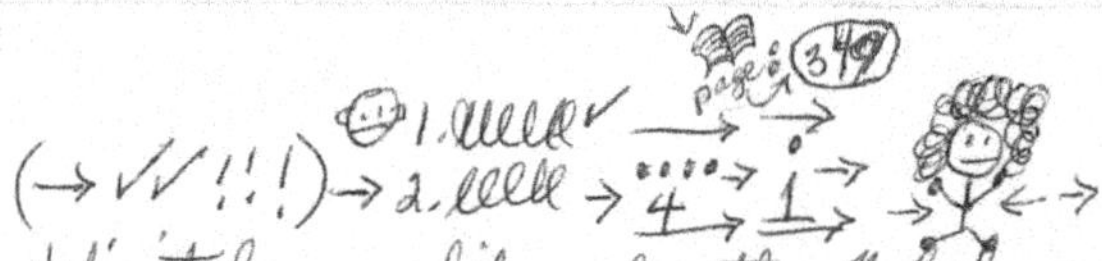

definitely qualify for the Nobel

definitely qualify for the Nobel

Peace Prize

Peace Prize

I'll assure you, I tell you no lies.

I'll assure you, I tell you no lies.

What you have discovered will be something to

What you have discovered will be something to

modernize

modernize

I told you so, you guys! Don't

I told you so, you guys! Don't

you agree?

you agree?

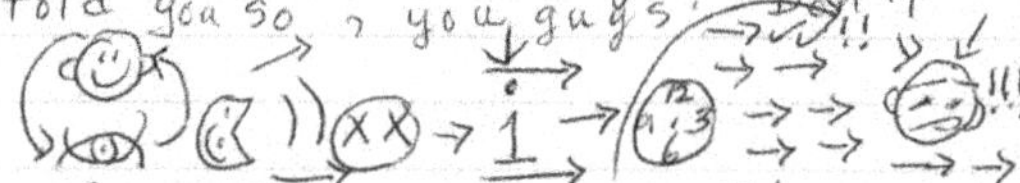

I say, no one would dare

I say, no one would dare

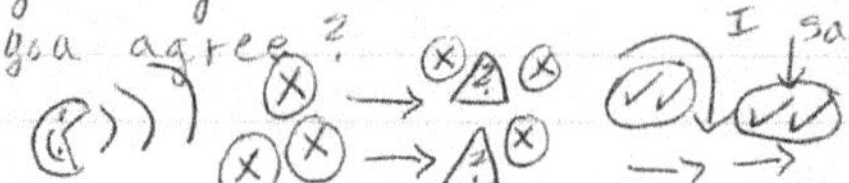

say anything otherwise

say anything otherwise

(62) Do Tell, My Adele (170)

Do Tell, My Adele

Ring my bell; do tell, my Adele I know her well

Ring my bell; do tell, my Adele I know her well

and she's more than swell She's the world's

and she's more than swell She's the world's

most beautiful belle She knows how to swing

most beautiful belle she knows how to swing

she knows how to sell I love to see her sweet

she knows how to sell I love to see her sweet

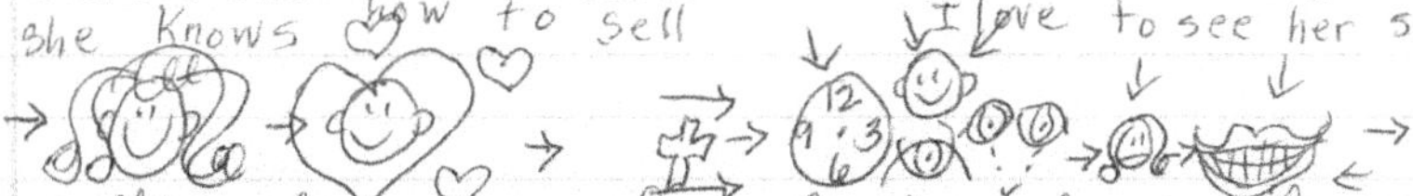

smiling face And when I see her smile

smiling face And when I see her smile

whenever she's in her workplace I notice she

whenever she's in her workplace I notice she

also moves along with style and grace She

also moves along with style and grace She

truly deserves to be wearing satin and lace She

traly deserves to be wearing satin and lace She

always smiles and does her best to be nice to me
always smiles and does her best to be ny'ce to me

She gives me her smile for free and happily She
she gives me her smile for free and happily she

once was married to a Handsome He Back then
once was married to a Handsome He Back then

he was an important reason for her to want to
he was an important reason for her to want to

live and continue to be You will always want to
live and continae to be You will always want to

do her a favor So when you meet her, be on
do her a favor So when you meet her, be on

your very best behavior She is humble and
your very best behavior She is humble and

believes in our wonderful savior And her
believes in our wonderful Savior And her

hospitality, I am often lucky enough to savor
hospitality, I am often lucky enough to savor

When she welcomes you, she is definitely a gracious host
Of all those workers working with her, I like her the most
If she was to come across a ghost, the ghost would get lost
He would run away and his goose would be cooked, like a toast
She greets and serves many people every day
She always listens to what they have to say
When they leave her, they feel like saying, "O.K."
Then when they shuffle off, they go away merry and gay

She is one of life's beautiful persons I hope she
She is one of life's beautiful persons I hope she

is always happy and has a lot of fun Also I
is always happy and has a lot of fun Also I

hope all her battles are well-handled and are won
hope all her battles are well-handled and are won

And I hope, she will never meet defeat or come undone
And I hope, she will never meet defeat or come undone

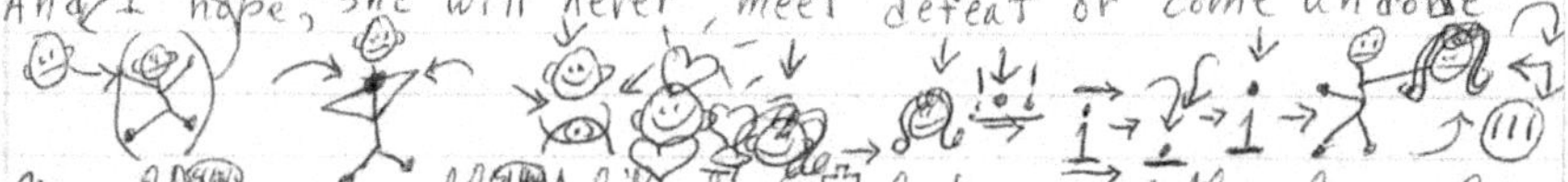

Myself, personally, I like her; she's one of the chosen few
Myself, personally, I like her; she's one of the chosen few

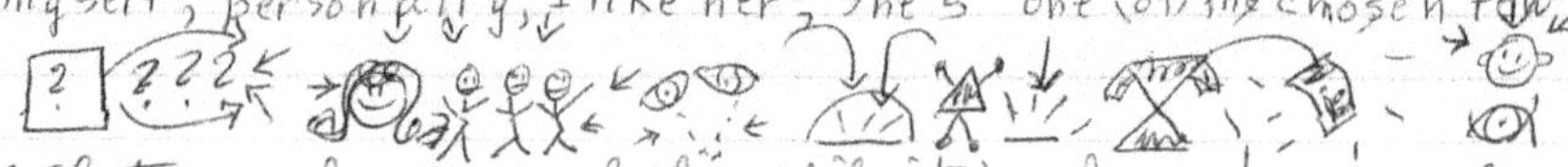

Whatever she wears looks like it is brand new I
Whatever she wears looks like it is brand new I

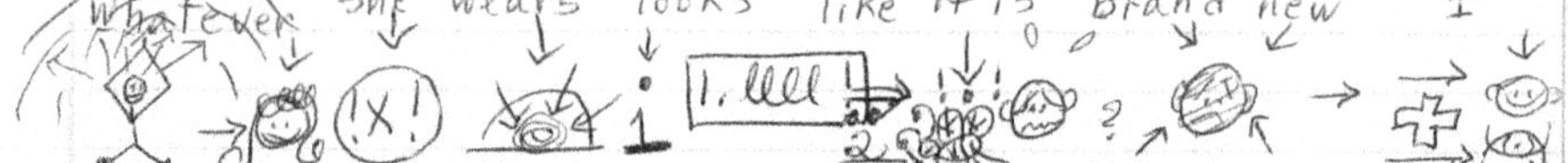

hope she never has a reason to be sad or blue And I
hope she never has a reason to be sad or blue And I

hope a smile forever sticks on her face like it
hope a smile forever sticks on her face like it

was stuck there permanently with glue
was stuck there permanently with glue

A++ A++ 173 354 page

(70) My Best Friend And Love, SLOW
My Best Friend And Love,

Charlie
Charlie

He is my best friend and love, SLOW Charlie He is the
He is my best friend and love, Charlie He is the

one, SLOW with whom, SLOW I want to party He is so cute and
one, with whom, I want to party He is so cute and

he is so pretty With him, SLOW I don't have anything,
he is so pretty with him, I don't, have anything,

with which, SLOW to worry He is my newest and most
with which, to worry He is my newest and most

$$ ...... valuable find His heart is pure and he is very SLOW
valuable find His heart is pure, and, he is very,

very kind With him I truly love to be,
very kind With him I truly love to be,

and with him, SLOW I love to unwind Then he teases
and with him, I love to unwind Then he teases

and excites me until I am quite blind
I am so very
lucky to have found
Charlie on this land this
blessed ground
I always want him close and around
When we are together
I feel we are truly glory
bound
When I look at him
he makes my
heart skip a beat
When he touches my lips
he lifts me ten feet
When we are near
each other I feel the heat
He makes me feel so
very complete
Charles is his proper name

This name is his claim to fame Together we
This name is his claim to fame Together we
play the best love game Then when we are alone
play the best love game Then when we are alone,
we become one and the same He is my very best
we become one and the same He is my very best
friend, one on whom I can depend I'll love
friend, one on whom I can depend. I'll love
him again and again and again I'll share his
him again and again and again I'll share his
company with you, now and then and when I
company with you, now and then and when I
find a friend around the bend that's also a
find a friend around the bend that's also a
number 10 He is so very capable and sweet,
number 10 He is so very capable and sweet,
which I find quite neat I knew he was the
which I find qaite neat I knew he was the

one when I first chanced him to meet No one I
one when I first chanced him to meet No one I

know comes close to him or has him beat No
know comes close to him or has him beat No

one yet has accomplished this feat I love you,
one yet has accomplished this feat I love you,

Charles, my darling love You are my own sweet
Charles, my darling love you are my own sweet

precious dove You were sent down from above
precious dove you were sent down from above

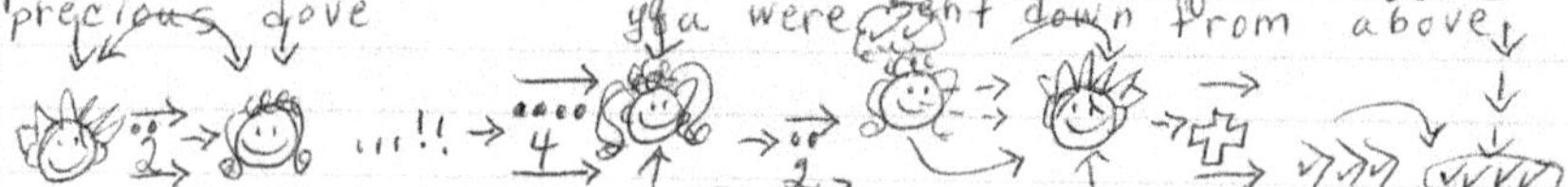

You to me, just for me, to know you and more of
you to me, just for me, to know you and more of

358 page

(71) I Am A Happy Camper (174)
I Am A Happy Camper

hmmmm! purrrr!

I am a happy camper. I smile. I hum and I purr
I am a happy camper, I smile, I hum and I purr

An my face I have a smiley face, which I use
An my fage I have a smiley face, which I use

as a niceness enhancer That I also use to stamp
as a niceness enhancer That I also use to stamp

upon some people and also to ward off any
upon some people and also to ward off any

kind of smile damper I try to always live my
Kind of smile damper I try to always live my

life with a positive attitude and a smile
life with a positive attitude and a smile

Being positive helps me to go that extra mile,
Being positive helps me to go that extra mile,

and go there in style I smile and try to ignore
and go there in style I smile and try to ignore

any hate and to swallow pain or any guile
any hate and to swallow pain or any guile

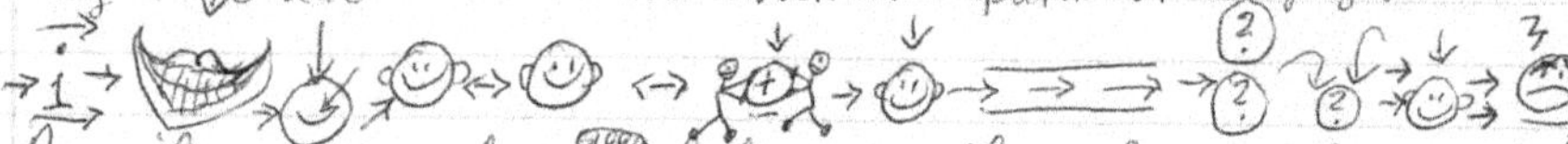

A smile on my face, helps me through any of my trials
A smile on my face, helps me through any of my trials

and gives me a positive profile I will share with
and gives me a positive profile I will share with

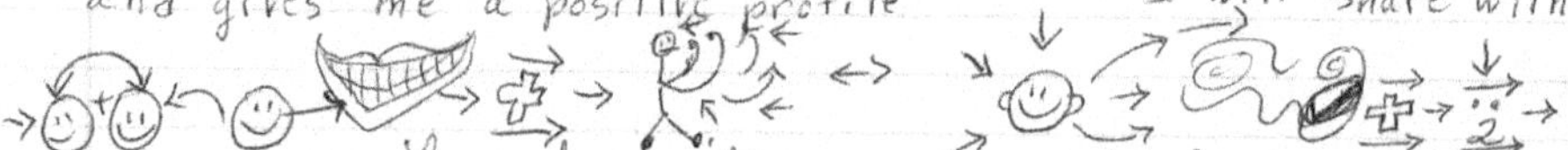

you my smile and invite you let loose and to
you my smile and invite you let loose and to

smile too I will invite you to come with me and
smile too I will invite you to come with me and

to be someone like brand new So just let yourself be
to be someone like brand new So just let yourself be

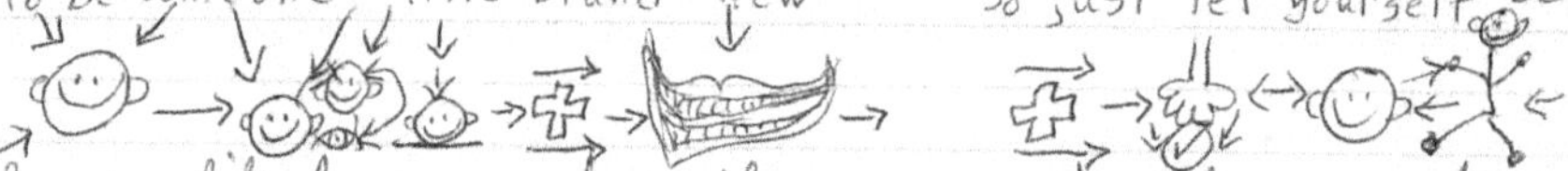

happy like I am and smile and let yourself
happy like I am and smile and let yourself

become a brand-new venue I will give you a
become a brand-new venue I will give you a

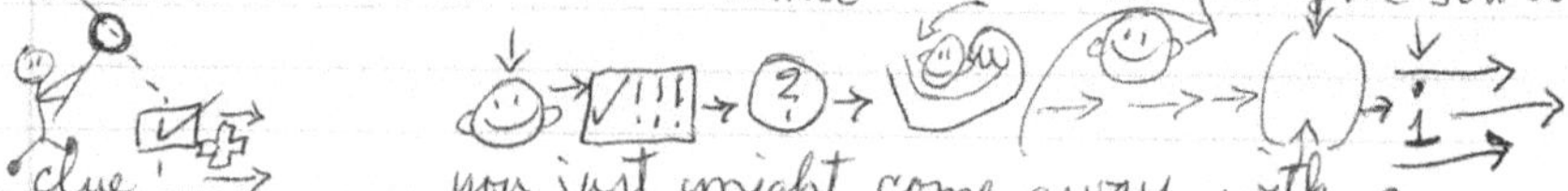

clue; you just might come away with a
clue; you just might come away with a

totally different point of view I will always try
to smile and to be happy this will earn me an
honorary smiling degree Even when I stumble and
fall and I feel crappy; I will give a smile
to you for free Being positive helps me not
to go batty; that is its bonus and smiling is
the key It leaves me with a happy new
reality; it leaves me relaxed and carefree
Smiling brings happiness and has made me

enlightened
enlightened

and has made the world my newfound
and has made the world my newfound

friend
friend

Smiling helps my senses become sharp
smiling helps my senses become shanp

and heightened with all hurts forgiven or on the mend
and heightened with all hurts forgiven or on the mend

I no longer have to be apprehensive because I will
I no longer have to be apprehensive because I will

have the strength of ten men With such great
have the strength of ten men with such great

positive energy; this smiling I will definitely,
positive energy; this smiling I will definitely

to you, recommend Because of this happiness,
to you, recommend Because of this happiness

my life will become a success story It
my life will become a success story It

will be my turn to bask in the glow of my own
will be my turn to bask in the glow of my own

3/62

newfound glory I will no longer have any need
New found glory I will no longer have any need
to worry or say anything to make me have
to worry or say anything to make me have
to say sorry I will be in a successful category,
to say sorry I will be in a successful category,
with a smile of happiness the only fee, which
with a smile of happiness the only fee, which
is really for free I will go happily along
is really for free I will go happily along
And because I'm happy I won't want to do
And because I'm happy I won't want to do
anything wrong And then I will feel like I truly
anything wrong And then I will feel like I truly
belong And also then I will smile again and
belong And also then I will smile again and
again and I will sing out a new and happy song
again and I will sing out a New and happy song

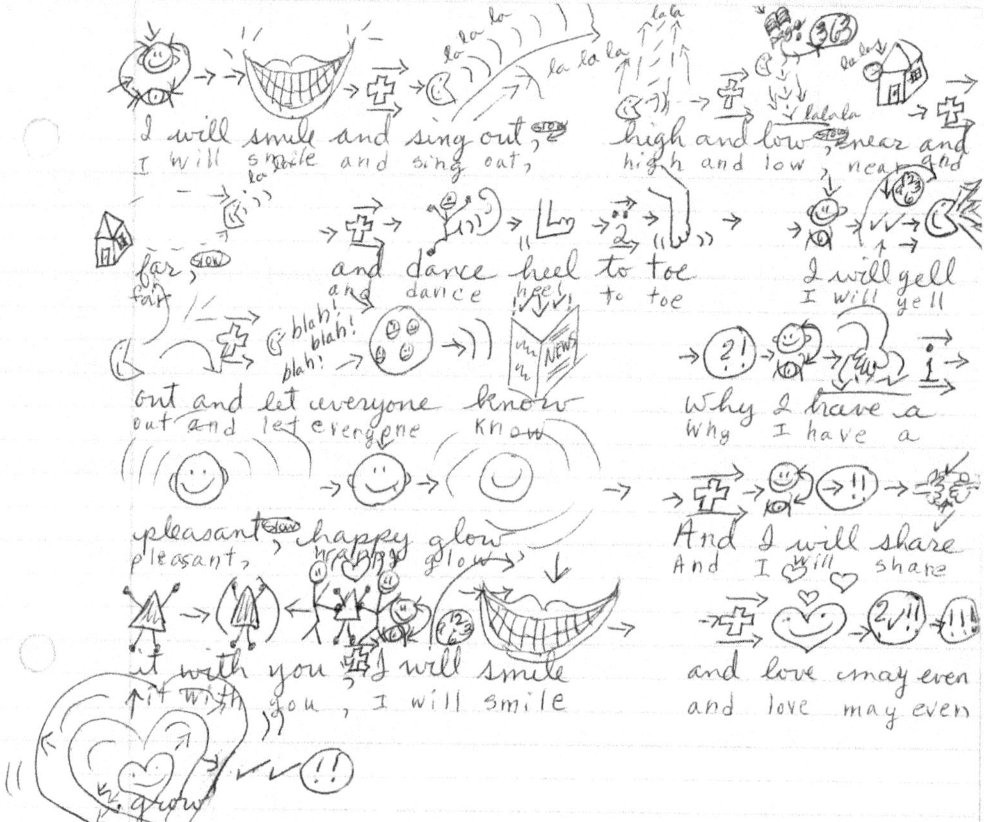
la la la
la la la
la la
lalala
la
I will smile and sing out,
I will smile and sing out,
high and low, near and
high and low, near and
far,
far
and dance heel to toe
and dance heel to toe
I will yell
I will yell
blah! blah! blah!
NEWS
out and let everyone know
out and let everyone know
Why I have a
Why I have a
pleasant, happy glow
pleasant, happy glow
And I will share
And I will share
it with you, I will smile
it with you, I will smile
and love may even
and love may even
glow

(72) Set In Our Ways (177)

Set In Our Ways

364 page

We all get set in our ways, somewhat like hardening clay

We all get set in our ways, somewhat like hardening clay

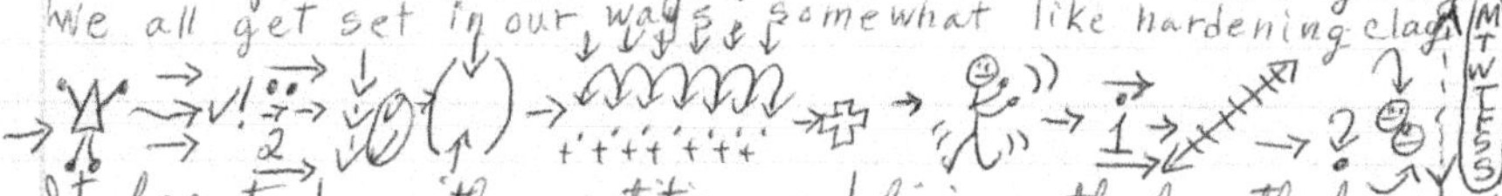

It has to do with repetition and living the length of our days

It has to do with repetition and living the length of our days

Our lives live out like soap opera plays moving along

Our lives live out like soap opera plays moving along

like repetitive, boring matinees That we remain

like repetitive, boring matinees That we remain

flexible, we can only hope and pray It is not at all

flexible, we can only hope and pray It is not at all

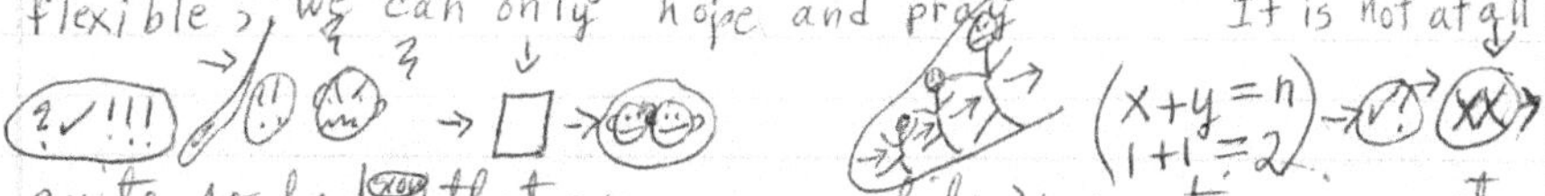

quite so bad, that our life's routine is not

quite so bad, that our life's routine is not

ironclad After all, everything we do is just a

iron clad After all, everything we do is just a

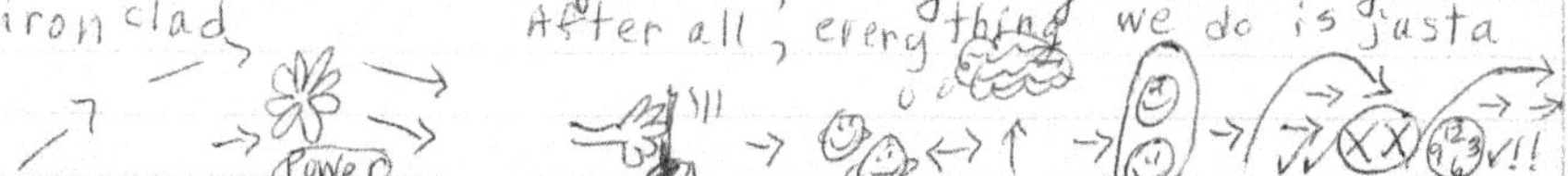

passing fad making us think we haven't been

passing fad making us think we haven't been

had
had

If we remain sane, we will be glad
If we remain sane, we will be glad

and we will find out routine is not so bad
and we will find out routine is not so bad

There's
There's

no real reason to be so sad
no real reason to be so sad

because we are the
because we are the

launching pad for our moms and dads
launching for our moms and dads

No one
No one

really knows why we let ourselves
really knows we let ourselves

become
become

trapped and hogtied
trapped and hogtied

We may get this way (and
We may get this way (and

that's no lie)
that's no lie)

unless we make a real effort
unless we make a real effort

not to become solidified
not to become solidified

We may say it is just
We may say it is just

our excuses, our alibi
our excuses, our alibi

because we are too tired
because we are too tired

to change or to let ourselves magnify ... But please give us a chance to justify why people become afraid to change and become culture shy

You see, everyone has a different journey, a different story

And we all have our own special kind of history or glory

Some of our roads may intersect, and I think you'll agree

No matter which way we are going or which way we go —

we all have a right to be

Even though your life may not be a

smash hit
smash hit
When you become set in your ways
When you become set in your ways
you may tend to forget
you may tend to forget
That we all still have our
That we all still have our
very own share of wit
very own share of wit
And all of our lives are still
And all of our lives are still
close knit —
close - knit —
such a mixture cannot be counterfeit
such a mixture cannot be counterfeit
The best way for us to describe how we have
The best way for us to describe how we have
become imbibed and pacified
become imbibed and pacified
And how we let
And how we let
routine rule our every
routine, rule our every
stride and let us become
stride and let us become
preoccupied
preoccupied
Is that we put the important things
Is that we put the important things
aside
aside
and let mundane everyday things become
and let mundane everyday things become

our guide And withdraw into our shells away
our guide And withdraw into our shells away

inside and lose our real sight and become cross-
inside and lose our real sight and become cross

eyed Sometimes we may have just become lazy
eyed Sometimes we may have just become lazy

or a little too comfortable to really be able to see
or a little too comfortable to really be able to see

Then we may put routine tasks in front of the
Then we may put routine tasks in front of the

important business of you and me We must
important business of you and me We must

have just gone plain crazy to have let ourselves
have just gone plain crazy to have let ourselves

become so off-key And to have let reality

become a murky and hazy sea — polluted and
become a murky and hazy sea - polluted and

stagnated to such a horrible degree We must
stagnated to such a horrible degree We must

again start letting change into our lives? and the
again start letting change into our lives? and the

sea of reality will cleanse and become healthy
sea of reality will cleanse and become healthy

and alive In this way, we all will continue to
and alive In this way, we all will continue to

thrive and no one will ever again be deprived
thrive and no one will ever again be deprived

And our lives will be able to revive, and we will go
And our lives will be able to revive, and we will go

for a formula drive and a sky dive and then for a
for a formula drive and a sky dive and then for a

deep-sea dive And then all our ideals we will be able
deep-sea dive And then all our ideals we will be able

to again give a high five and thrive all the way from nine to five
to again give a high five and thrive all the way from nine to five

(73) Survival (180)

Survival

I bowed and silently said "No." Survival prompted
I bowed and silently said "No." Survival prompted

me to do so Even though it hurt me from the
me to do so even though it hurt me from the

word go Then I thought to myself, no one
word go Then I thought to myself, no one

must ever know I thought, I musn't say a
must ever know I thought, I musn't say a

word Even though I'm being massacred
word Even though I'm being massacred

All my horrible feelings must be filed and stored
all my horrible feelings must be filed and stored

To cry out would only prove to be absurd
To cry out would only prove to be absurd

Sometimes, I wish I could forget But in my mind,
Sometimes, I wish I could forget But in my mind,

the memories are there, forever set The memories
the memories are there, forever set The memories

are awful and yet I've survived my quiet, horrible
are awful and yet I've survived my quiet, horrible

bet It was a long shot, a horrible gamble
bet It was a long shot, a horrible gamble

I did only as a handful would do I declined to
I did only as a handful would do I declined to

enjoy, I froze, no bull What would happen
enjoy, I froze, no bull What would happen

next, I could only surmise The enemy was caught
next, I could only surmise The enemy was caught

off guard and was confused I must have
off guard and was confused I must have

unpleasantly surprised him, I now muse at
unpleasantly surprised him, I now muse at

what a cost, a hurricane I had let loose But
what a cost, a hurricane I had let loose But

at that very moment, I was the one to choose He
At that very moment, I was the one to choose He

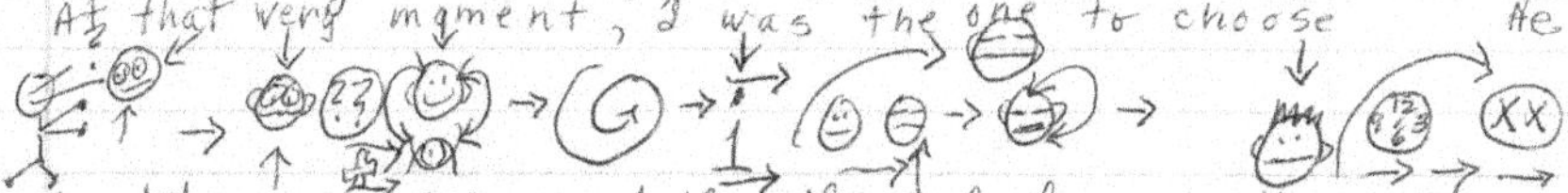

tested me; I turned the other cheek He couldn't
tested me; I turned the other cheek He couldn't

understand why I acted so meek These were new
understand why I acted so meek There were new

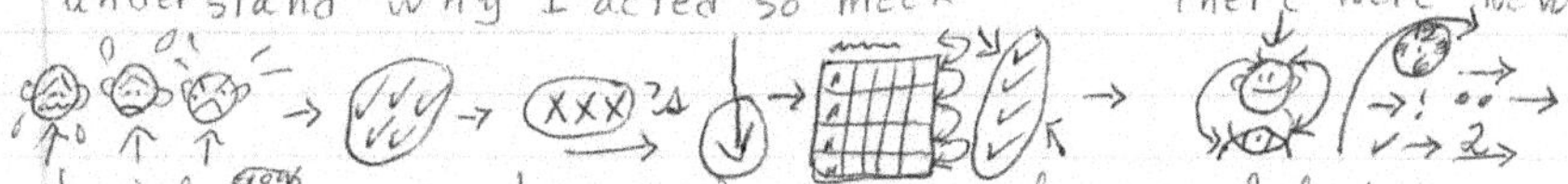

trials, many times in every week I had to
trials many times in every week I had to

overcome them to answer the questions I wanted
overcome them to answer the questions I wanted

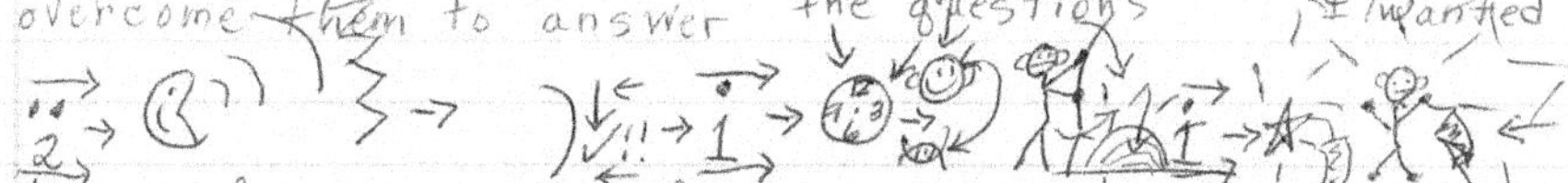

to speak By the time I found a new life
to speak By the time I found a new life,

And had become an innocent wife I was a shell
And had become an innocent wife I was a shell

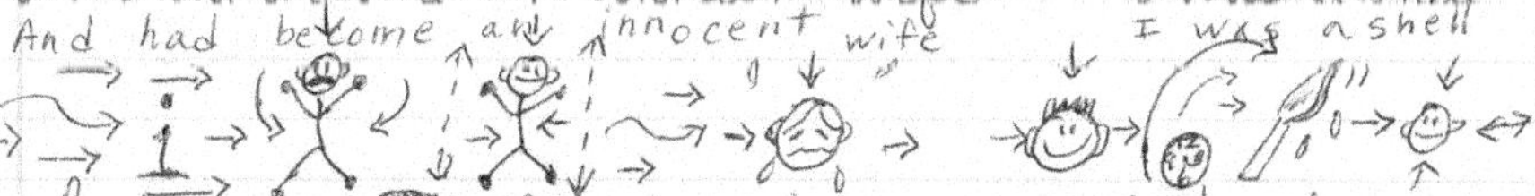

of a person, full of strife He had cut me
of a person full of strife He had cut me

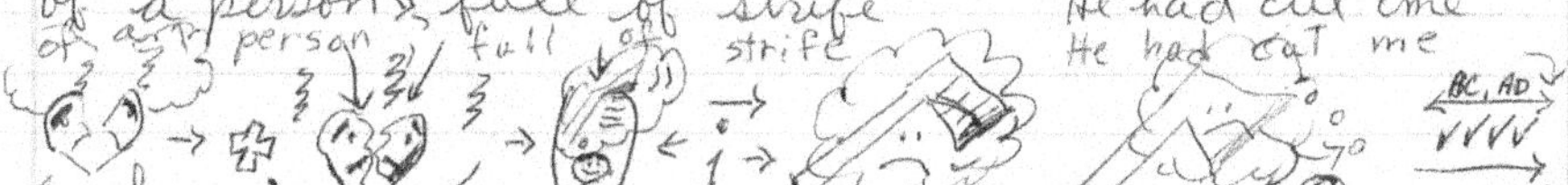

open and apart with an emotional knife Many
open and apart with an emotional knife Many

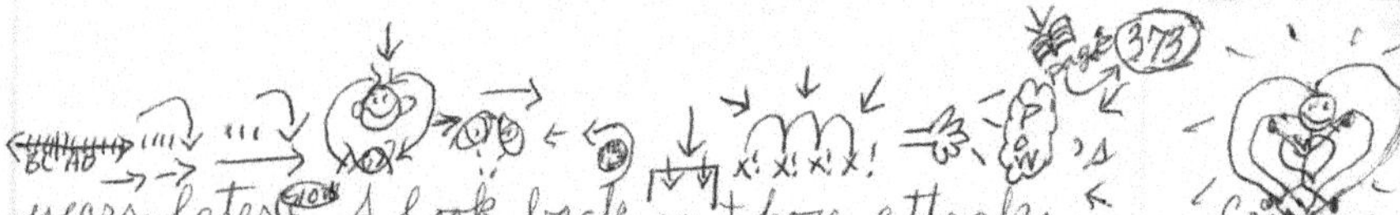

years later, I look back on those attacks
years later, I look back on those attacks

Courage
Courage

is one thing that I certainly did not lack
is one thing that I certainly did not lack

Hope
Hope

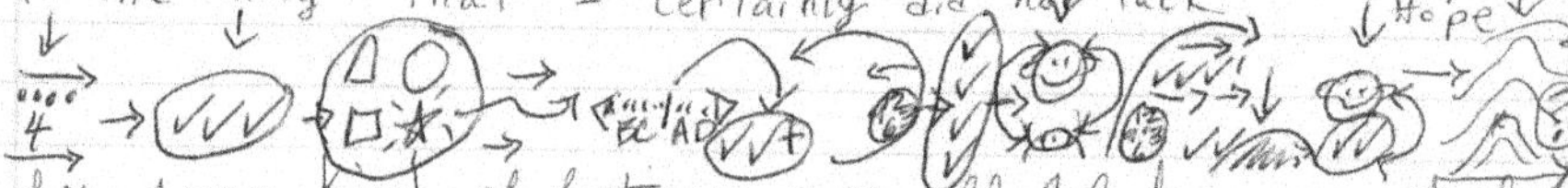

for some kind of future was all I had on my stack
for some kind of future was all I had on my stack

my childlike innocence could never be given back.
my childlike innocence could never be given back.

(74) The Bird That Cried (182)

I spied, the bird that cried, there on the roadside
I spied, the bird that cried, there on the roadside

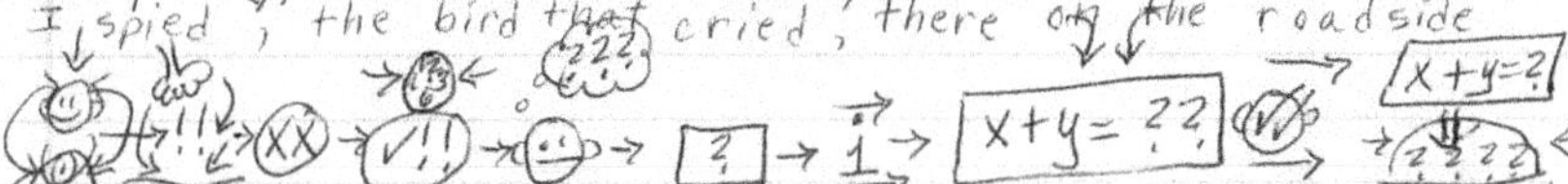

I did not yet know what the situation truly implied
I did not yet Know what the situation truly implied

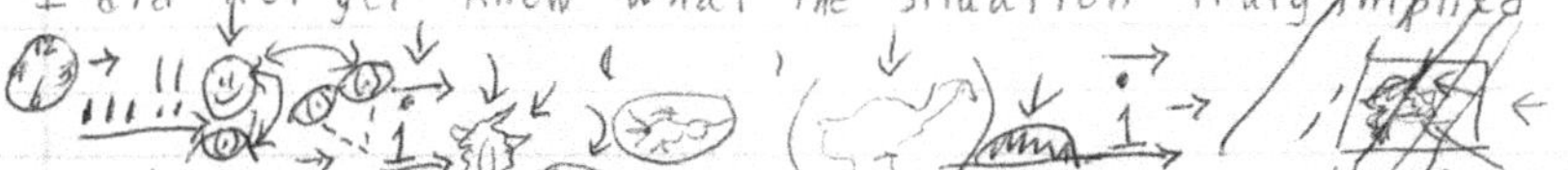

Until I saw a tiny, silent form on the ground, there,
Until I saw a tiny, silent form on the ground, there,

outside All I could do was to watch aghast and
out side all I could do was to watch aghast and

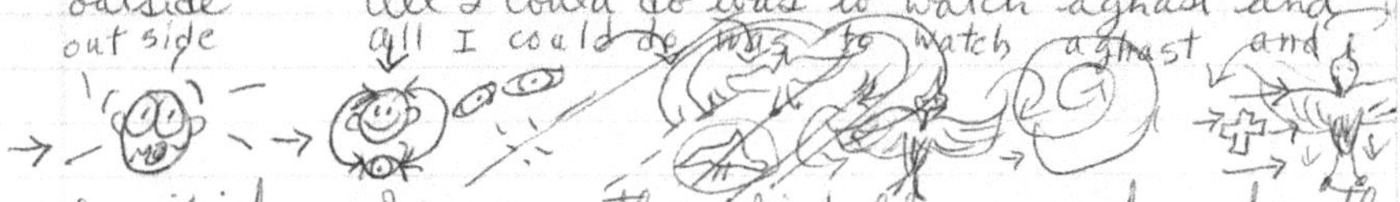

horrified I saw another bird fly around and gently
horrified I saw another bird fly around and gently

land It landed close to the little form as if
land It landed close to the little form as if

to try to give her a helping hand Somehow,
to try to give her a helping hand Somehow,

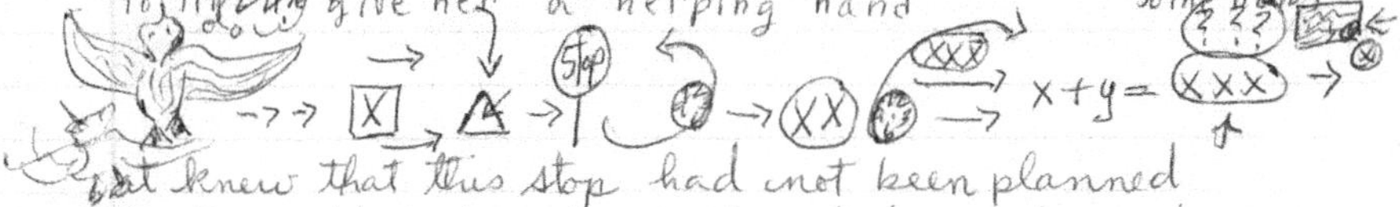

it knew that this stop had not been planned
it Knew that this stop had not been planned

Walking closer, it cocked up its little head as if
Walking closer, it cocked up its little head as

trying to understand
trying to understand

You could see his head lower
You could see his head lower

as if puzzled
as if puzzled

What was the reason his mate
What was the reason his mate

was huddled
was huddled

All quiet, limp, cold and muddled
All quiet, limp, cold and muddled

How he wished for a sound
How he wished for a sound

or to be near and
or to be near and

to be cuddled
to be cuddled

With his beak, he gently pushed
With his beak, he gently pushed

his sweetness off the road
his sweetness off the road

He hoped her inaction
He hoped her inaction

was just a passing episode
was just a passing episode

He thought his little
He thought his little

heart would explode
heart would explode

When he realized, not a
when he realized, not a

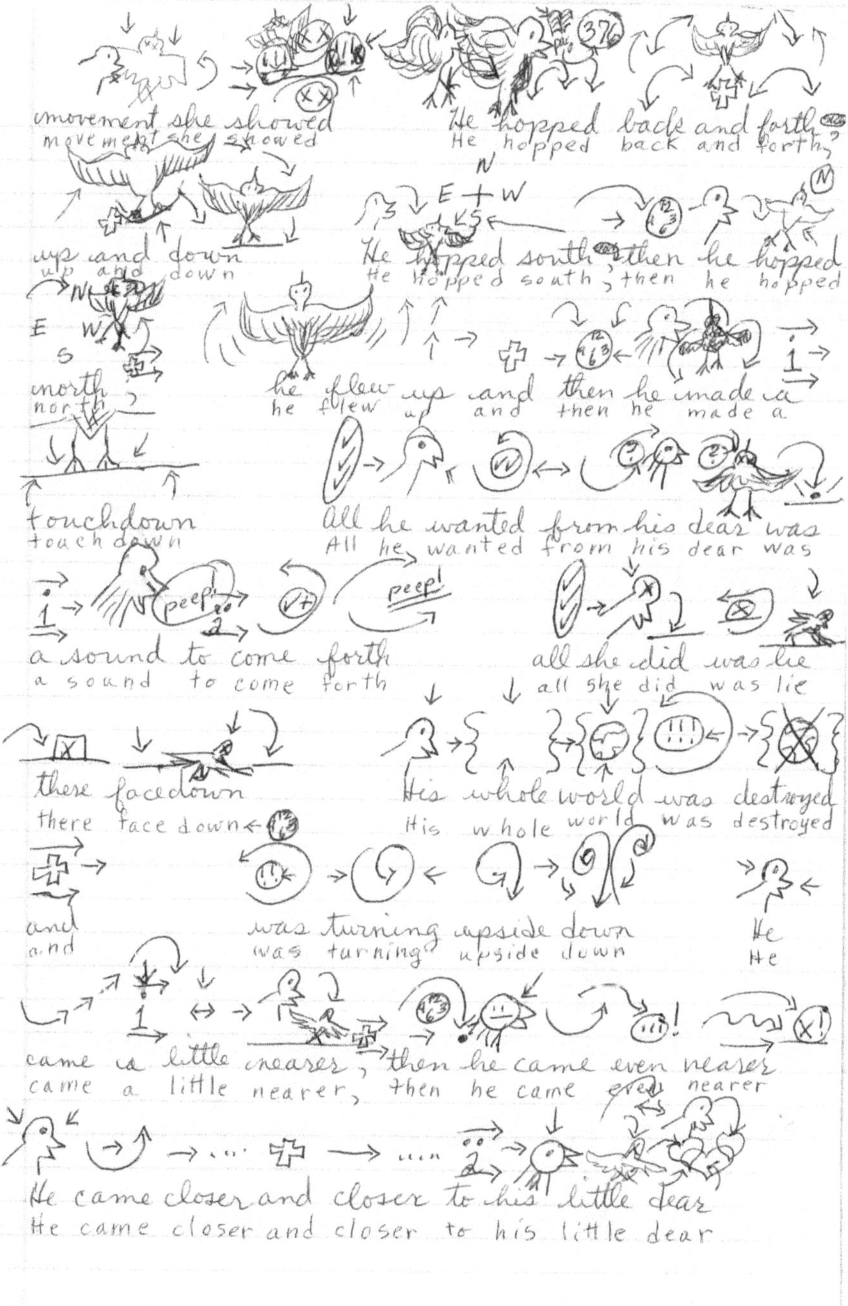
37
movement she showed
He hopped back and forth,
up and down
He hopped south, then he hopped
north,
he flew up and then he made a
touchdown
All he wanted from his dear was
peep!
a sound to come forth
all she did was lie
there facedown
His whole world was destroyed
and
was turning upside down
He
came a little nearer, then he came even nearer
He came closer and closer to his little dear

He muzzled her gently with a growing, silent fear
He nuzzled her gently with a growing, silent fear

That she would never again move away from here
That she would never again move away from here

He raised his head and as if to scream in desperation
He raised his head and as if to scream in desperation

He let out a piercing cry, for all to hear, out to
He let out a piercing cry, for all to hear, out to

all the nations
all the nations

This was his offering, his parting
This was his offering, shhh! his parting shhh!

oblation
oblation

She stayed still, there in her quiet
She stayed still, there in her quiet

station
station

What was to come of him; he had been so
What was to come of him; he had been so,

blessed
blessed

His little heart broke within his tiny chest
His little heart broke within his tiny chest

He no longer had a need for his love nest. Flying
He no longer had a need for his love nest. Flying

away from his love was nature's final test
away from his love was nature's final test

378 page

C + L = D

(75) You Can't Defy Destiny (184)

You Can't Defy Destiny

x + y = n

You can't defy your own destiny

You can't defy your own deting

You can't defy

You can't defy,

1 x + y = +

the fact

the fact

you are who you are or that I am me

you are who you are or that I am me

$0.00

Only with you, my dear, am I now really free

Only with you, my dear, am I now really free

Through your eyes, I would like to be able to see

Through your eyes, I would like to be able to see

You are my whole world, you have put my life in a

You are my whole world, you have put my life in a

whirl

whirl

I come to you with my hands unfurled,

I come to you with my hands unfurled,

a loving and hopeful girl

a loving and hopeful girl

With your eyes

with your eyes

E W N S

looking at me, my soul is not soiled

looking at me, my soul is not soiled

and I

and I

again feel like a young girl Without you, my
again feel like a young girl without you, my

goose would have been cooked, my life would
goose would have been cooked my life would

have been spoiled I want to take you in
have been spoiled I want to take you in

my arms I want to hold you in a loving
my arms I want to hold you in a loving

wrestling hold You, my dearest, are my
wrestling hold You, my dearest, are my

finest gold; with each other, we will learn
finest gold; with each other, we will learn

to be brave and bold When you are around,
to be brave and bold When you are around,

I am free and I am allowed to be bold
I am free and I am allowed to be bold

With you, the years will easily pass but in
With you, the years will easily pass but in

my mind, with you, I will never grow old
my mind, with you, I will never grow old

We will stand the test of time, our lives will
We will stand the test of time, our lives will

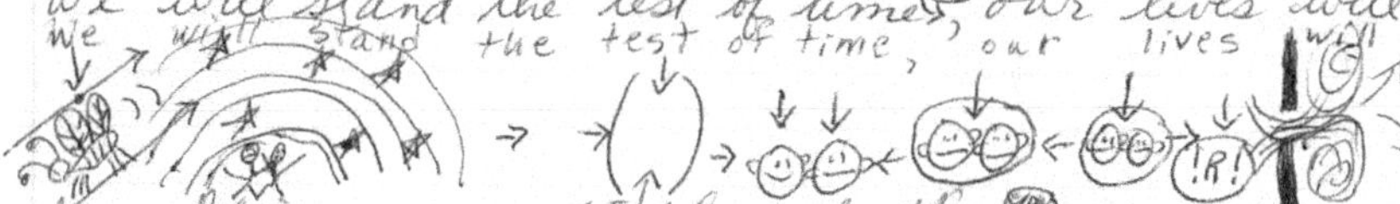

be sublime
be sublime

With each other, we are free
with each other, we are free

to be to each other, kind
to be to each other, kind

When I look at
when I look at

you, to the wrongs of the world I am blind
you, to the wrongs of the world I am blind

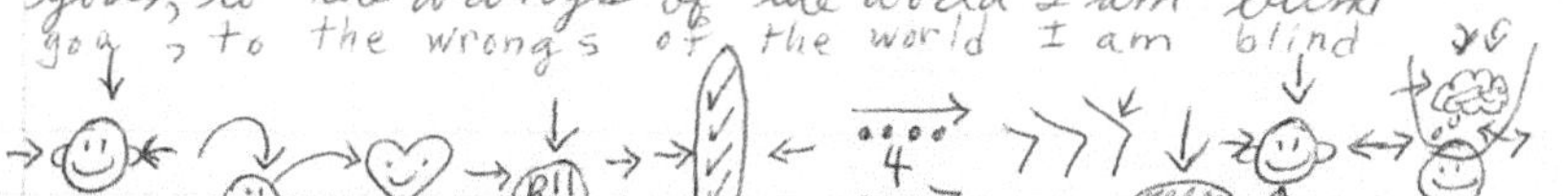

You, my love, are always foremost on my mind
You, my love, are always foremost on my mind

If someone looks at you at all, I tend to,
If someone looks at you at all, I tend to,

the meaning, misconstrue
the meaning, misconstrue

My eyes turn
my eyes turn

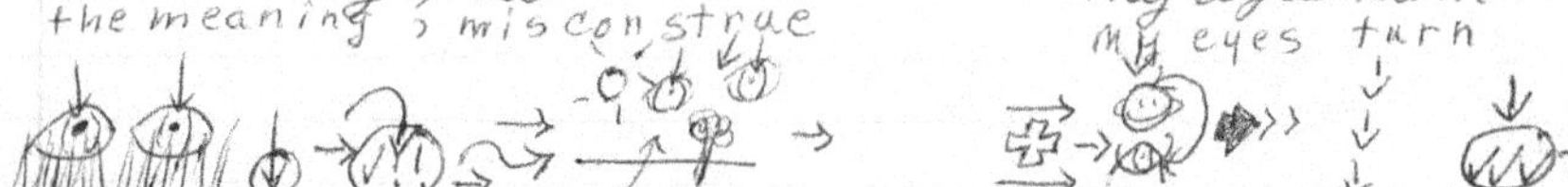

green instead of blue, and I go downright
green instead of blue, and I go downright

cuckoo — If they inappropriately touch you
cuckoo — If they inappropriately touch you,

that day they will rue — because I will use on
that day they will rue — because I will use on

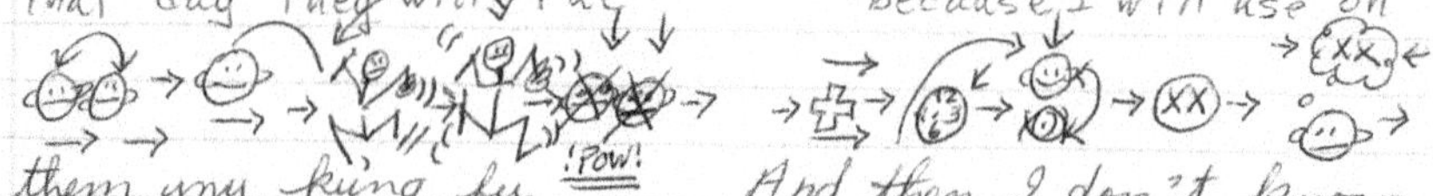

them my kung fu — And then I don't know
them my kung fu — And then I don't know

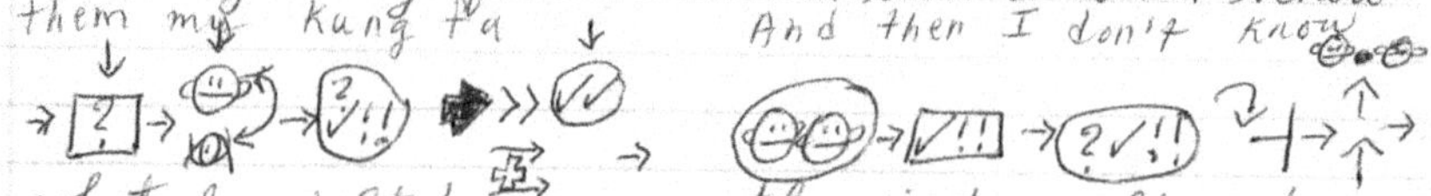

what I might do; — They just might end up
what I might do; — they just might end up

black and blue — I will always want your love
back and blue — I will always want your love

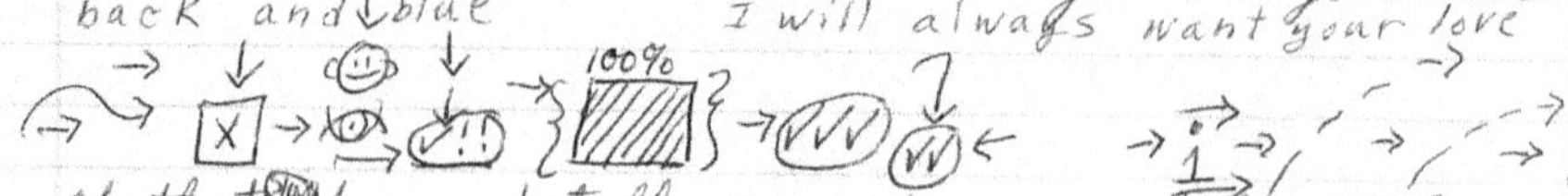

of that, I am totally sure of — A long, long
of that, I am totally sure of — A long, long

time ago — I prayed to the God up above
time ago — I prayed to the God up above

He answered me and sent you to me — in the form
He answered me and sent you to me — in the form

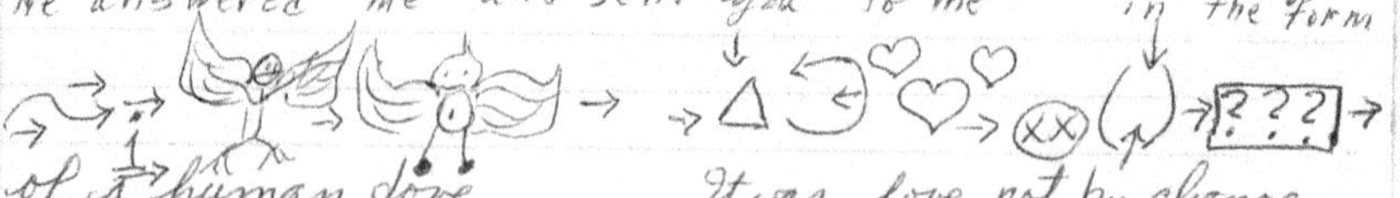

of a human dove — It was love not by chance
of a haman dove — It was love not by chance

(K+D=L)
(X+y=L)

destiny was to bring me a wonderful romance
destiny was to bring me a wonderful romance

It was Cupid's love lance, come by way of a
It was Cupid's love lance, come by way of a

(K+D=L)

greater circumstance It pierced my heart
greater circumstance It pierced my heart

and I didn't even have a fighting chance
and I didn't even have a fighting chance

And the spell it cast that had us both in a trance
And the spell it cast that had us both in a trance

became complete in a lover's dance Patience
became complete in a lover's dance Patience

has always been my friend and my ally Of that
has always been my friend and my ally Of that

I can testify and don't mind to expand on and
I can testify and don't mind to expand on and

personify You were sent to me from the Chief
personify You were sent to me from the Chief

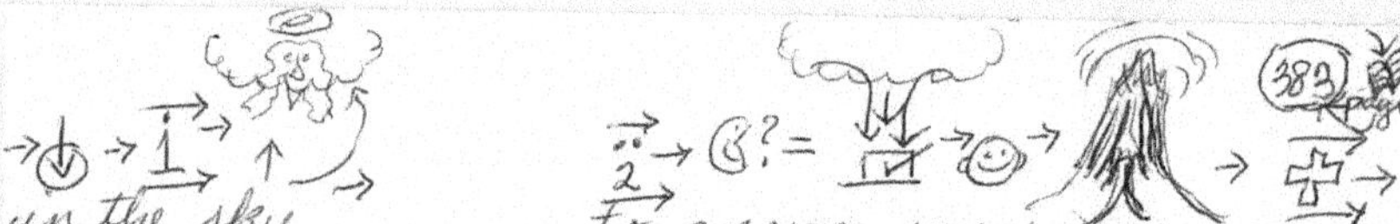

in the sky
in the sky

To answer my prayers and
to answer my prayers and

to keep us happy and occupied
to Keep us happy and occupied

(76) I Have A Hole In My Head (186)

I Have A Hole In My Head

In my head, I have a hole that has a very important

In my head, I have a hole that has a very important

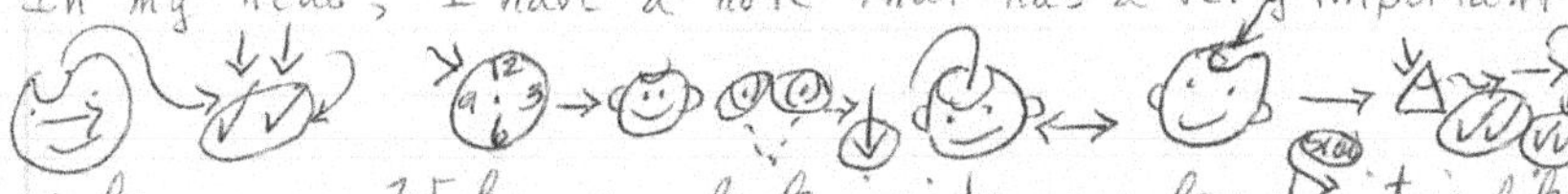

role When you look inside my head, it is like

role When, you look inside my head, it is like

a nugget of gold Inside my head, my mind

a nugget of gold Inside my head, my mind

bends ideas into special molds Ideas that like

bends ideas into special molds Ideas that like

to grab a storm and take it into my brain's fold

to grab a storm and take it into my brains fold

I have a hole in my head, but don't think I am easily

I have a hol in my head, but don't think I am easily

led You would think this would put me on

led You would think this would put me on

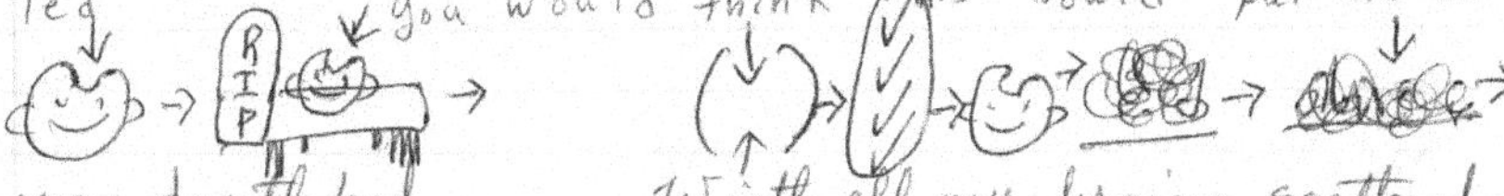

my death bed With all my brains scattered

my death bed with all my brains scattered

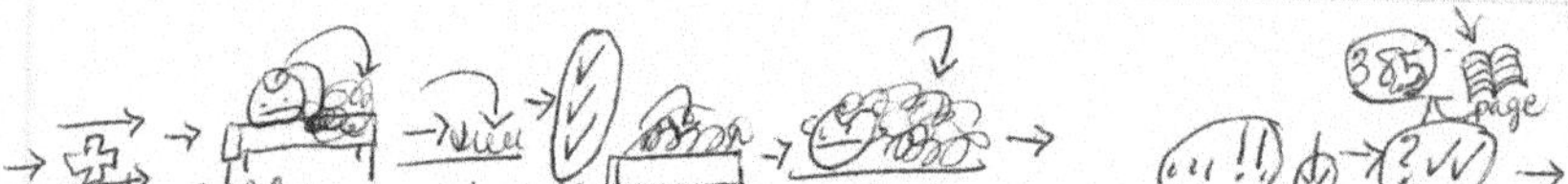

and falling out all over my bed and falling out all over my bed

But instead, But instead,

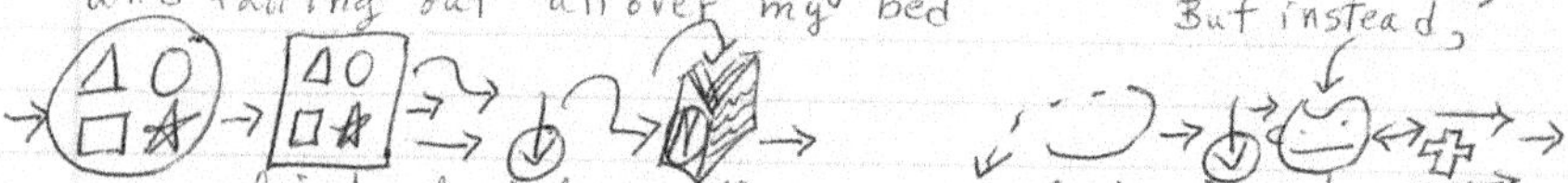

every kind of information every kind of information

leads inside and leads inside and

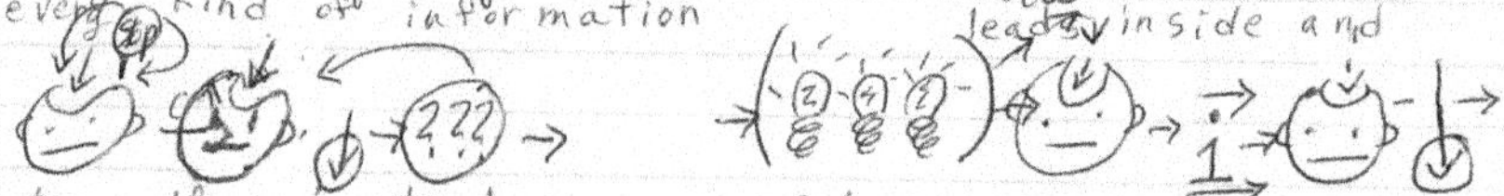

stays there instead stays there instead

Ideas enter the hole in Ideas enter the hole in

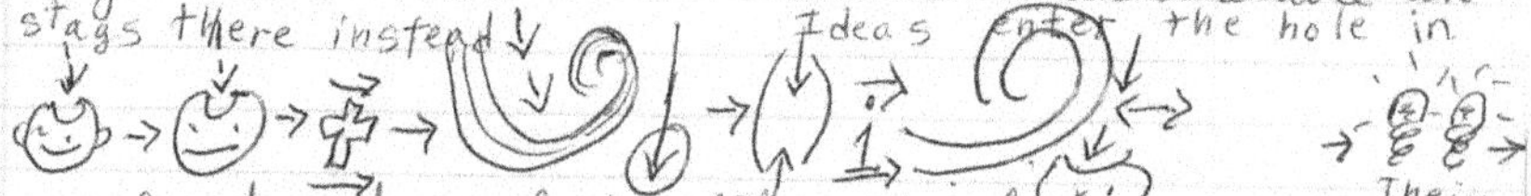

my head and rush in like a tidal wave my head and rush in like a tidal wave

Their Thees

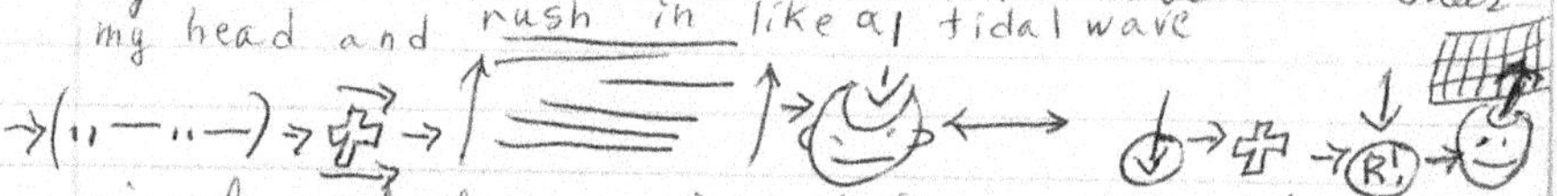

signals and frequencies sink signals and frequencies sink

in and are stored in and are stored

and saved and saved

They fill inside every part of my They fill inside every part of my

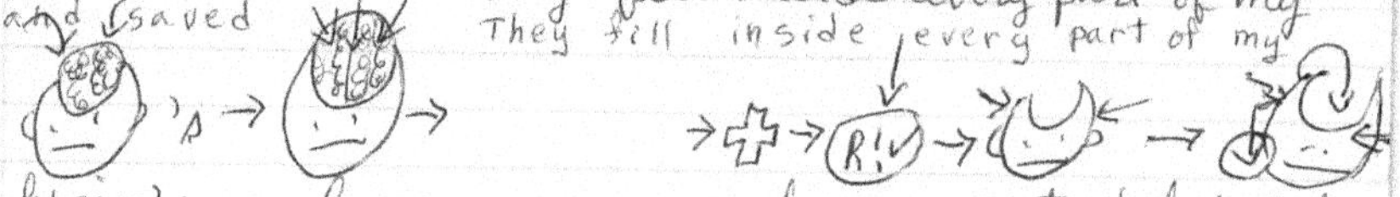

brain's enclave brain's enclave

and are protected inside and are protected inside

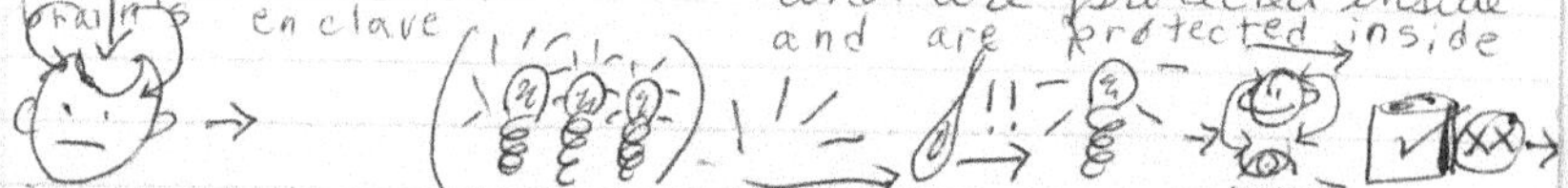

its cave its cave

They shine so bright, I can't They shine so bright, I can't

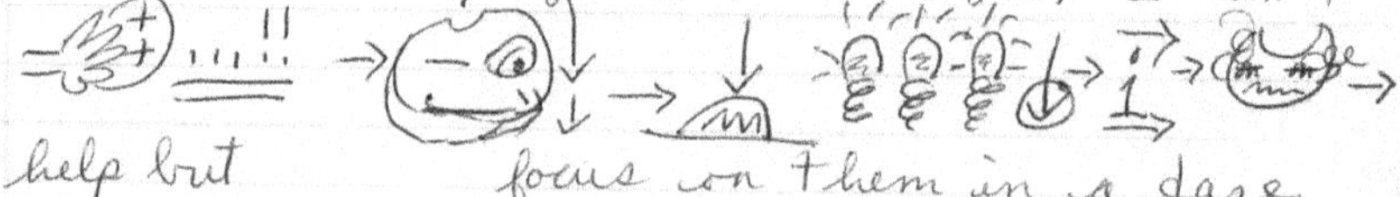

help but help bat

focus on them in a daze focus on them in a daze

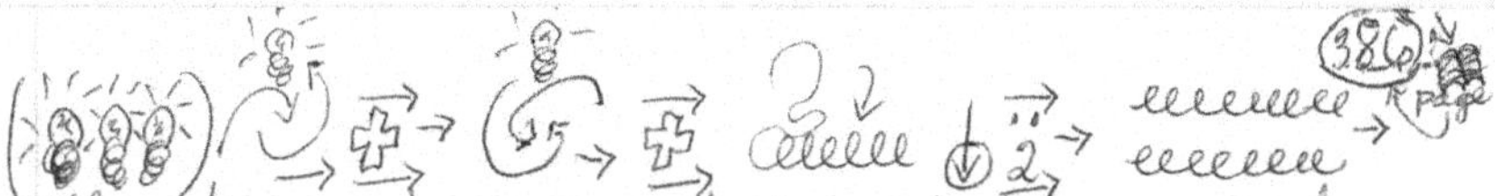

They toss and turn and form into organized
They toss and turn and form into organized

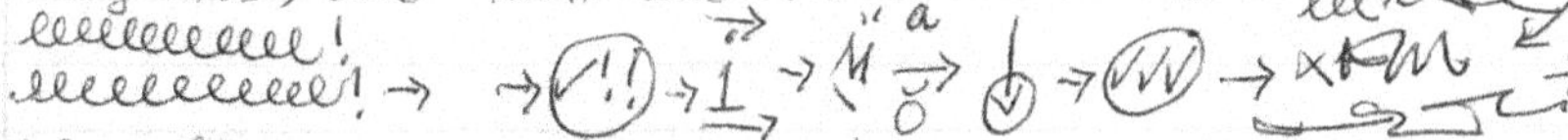

thoughts Like the letters in some languages
thoughts Like the letters in some languages

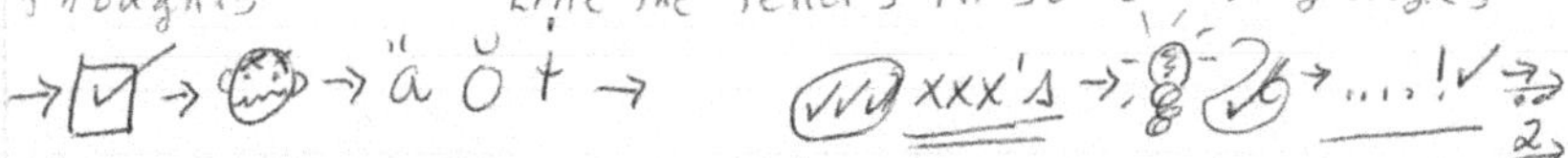

that need dots Sometimes they seem to
that need dots Sometimes they seem to

make sense Sometimes they do not
make sense, sometimes they do

Depending on the language you use they
Depending on the language you use

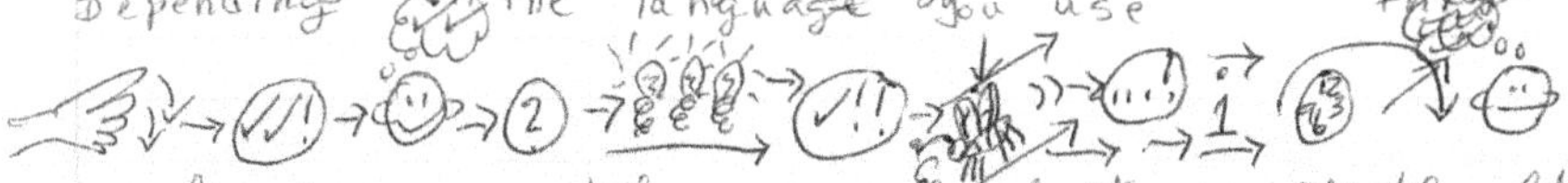

make sense or they may be just an afterthought
make sense or they may be just an afterthought

All I know is that my head is like a baited booby
all I Know is that my head is like a baited booby

trap And whatever comes inside gets covered
trap And whatever comes inside gets covered

and neatly wrapped Into one gigantic
and neatly wrapped Into one gigantic

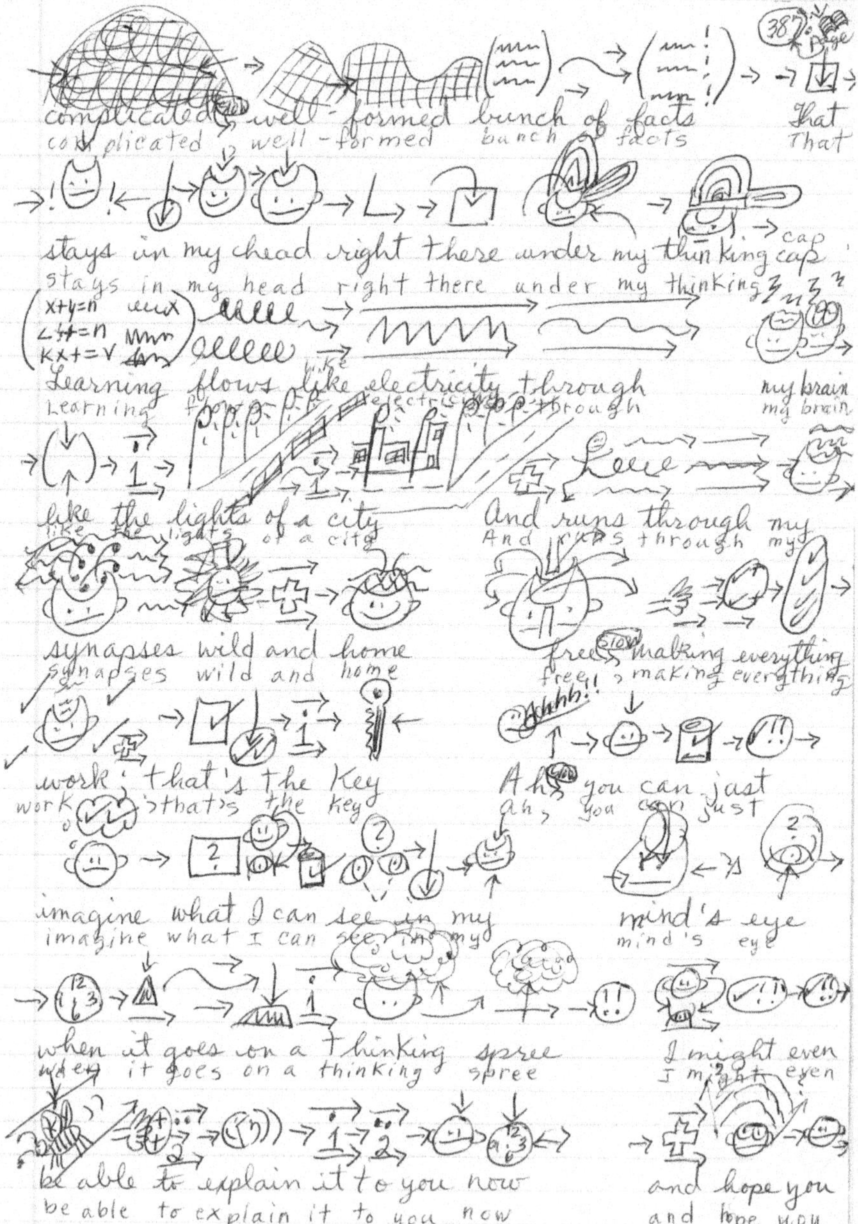
387 page
complicated, well-formed bunch of facts That
stays in my head right there under my thinking cap
Learning flows like electricity through my brain
like the lights of a city And runs through my
synapses wild and home free, making everything
work; that's the key Ah, you can just
imagine what I can see in my mind's eye
when it goes on a thinking spree I might even
be able to explain it to you now and hope you

understand this, but I cannot, that, guarantee
understand this, but I cannot, that, guarantee

Learning becomes part of my very being because
Learning becomes part of my very being because

I enjoy learning anything and everything It gives
I enjoy learning anything and everything It gives

my life its special zing and gets me into the
my life its special zing and gets me into the

swing of things Learning is as valuable as
swing of things Learning is as valuable as

many diamond rings and can be a valuable
many diamond rings and can be a valuable

plaything It sticks to me like static cling and
play thing It sticks to me like static cling and

makes me feel lucky and as special as a

king So as you and I can plainly see
king So as you and I can plainly see

That hole in my head is useful to me It is

That hole in my head is useful to me It is

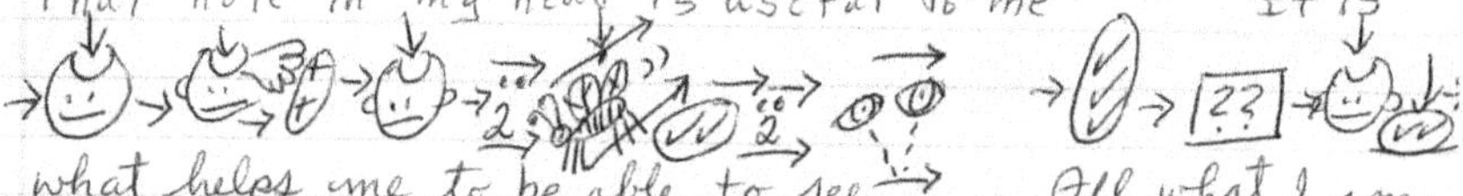

what helps me to be able to see All what I am

what helps me to be able to see → All what I am

and what I want to be

and what I want to be

(390) page

(77) Ribbons And Lace (188)

Ribbons And Lace

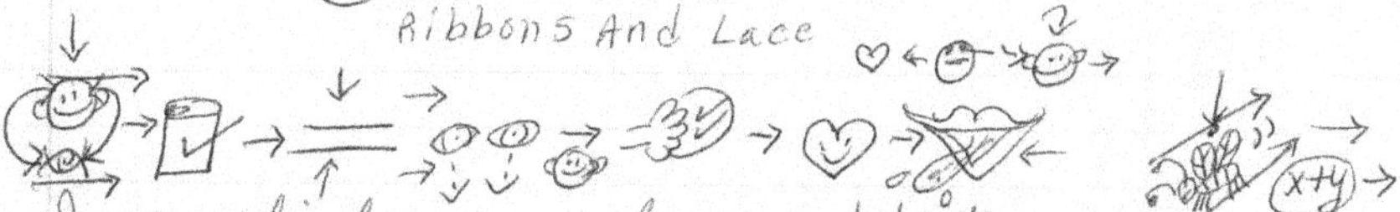

I can plainly see you have good taste Because

I can plainly see you have good taste Because

I can see you are wearing ribbons and lace I

I can see you are wearing ribbons AND lace I

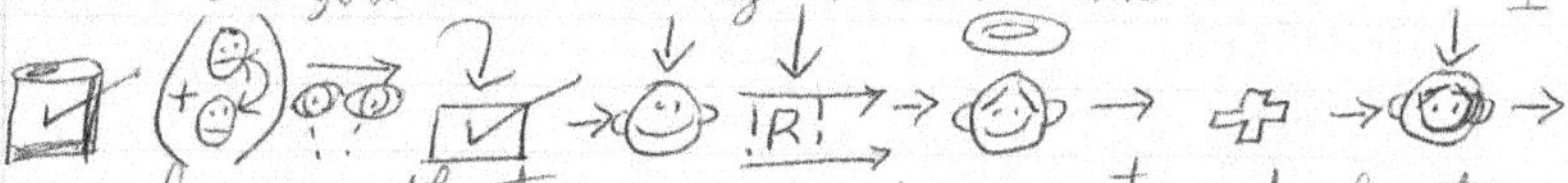

can also see that you are innocent and chaste

can also see that you are innocent and chaste

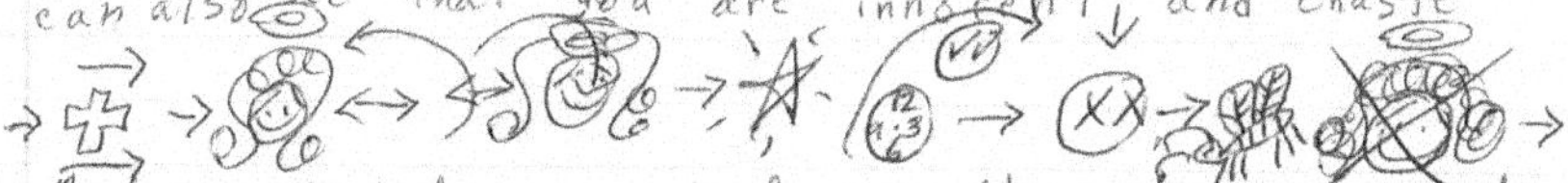

And beauty like yours truly should not be disgraced

And beauty like yours truly should not be disgraced

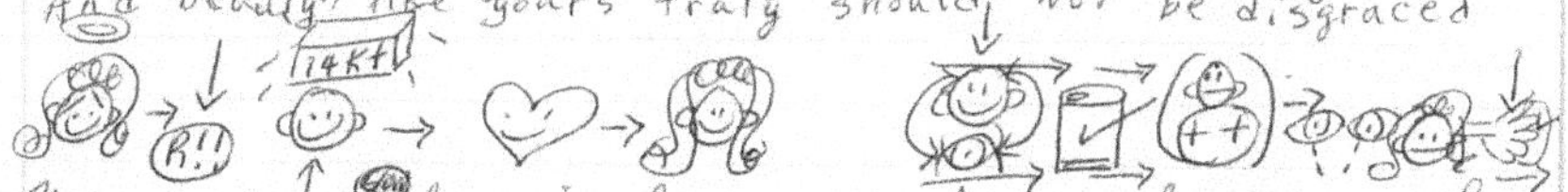

You are pure, bonnie lass I can also see you have

you are pure, bonnie lass I can also see you have

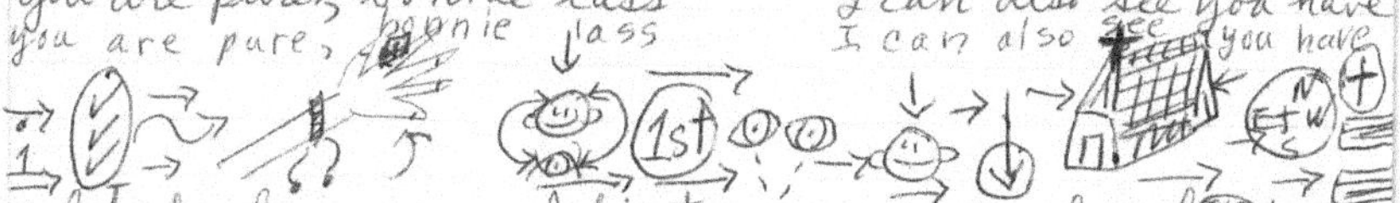

a lot of class I first saw you in church at mass

a lot of class I first saw you in church at mass

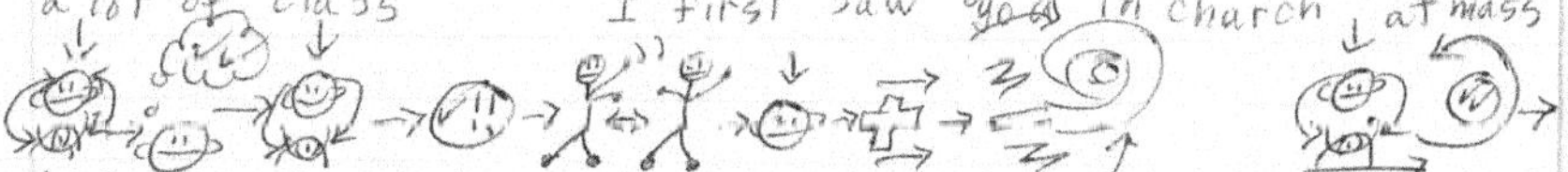

I knew I must meet you and fast I was

I Knew I must meet you and fast I was

amazed at your inner beauty I was in

amazed at your inner beauty I was in

desperate need of your company Your
desperate need of your company your

companies made me feel young and carefree
companies made me feel young and carefree

I was smitten by you, my delicate, sweet pea When
I was smitten by you, my delicate, sweet pea when,

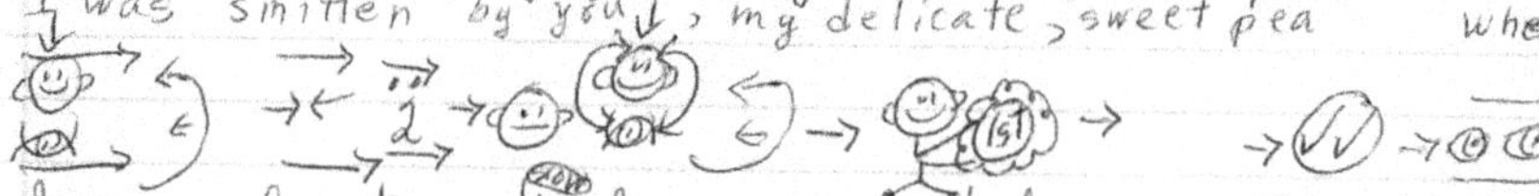

I came close to you, I was rewarded Those eyes
I came close to you, I was rewarded Those eyes

held no disguise, you were a purebred Then when
held no disguise you were a pure bred Then when

we came head to head nothing more had to be
we came head to head nothing more had to be

said It was mutual love unrequited and
said It was mutual love unrequited and

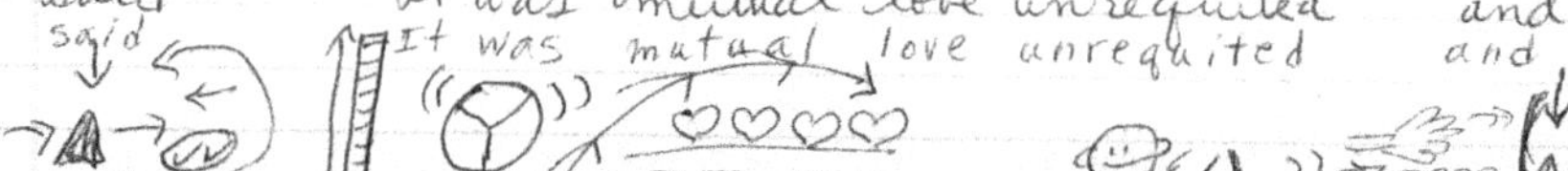

it was full speed ahead My legs felt like
it was full speed ahead My legs felt like

those ribbons in your hair My stomach felt weak
those ribbons in your hair My stomach felt weak

at your slightest stare Of anyone else, I had not a
at your slightest stare Of anyone else, I had not a
single care All I could see was you; I thought this
single care All I could see was you; I thought this
was fair I knew you were my chosen one; my
was fair I knew you were my chosen one; my
package was wrapped up and done → You were the
package was wrapped up and done You were the
one I had been looking for the rest of my
one I had been looking for the rest of my
life's fun I wanted you to always be with
life's fun I wanted you to always be with
me, my honey bun I prayed and prayed—
me, my honey bun I prayed and prayed—
please, please don't run → I went on bended
please, please don't run → I went on bended
knee and asked you, "Please be my wife,"
Knee and asked you, "Please be my wife,"

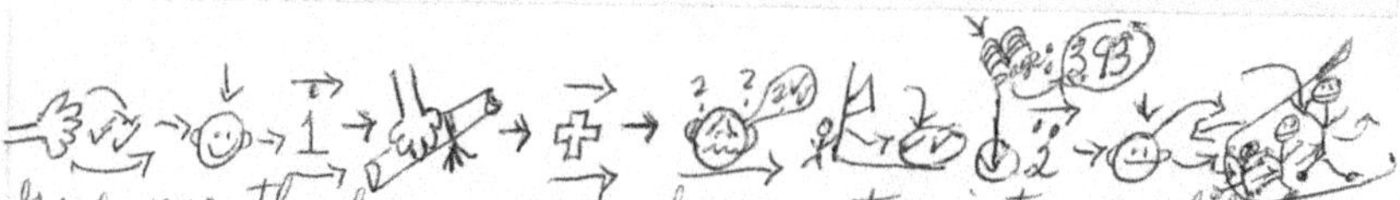

Give me the honor and please enter into my life
Give me the honor and please enter into my life

We will always be happy and always stay
We will always be happy and always stay

that way, we'll have no worries, no strife
that way, we'll have no worries, no strife

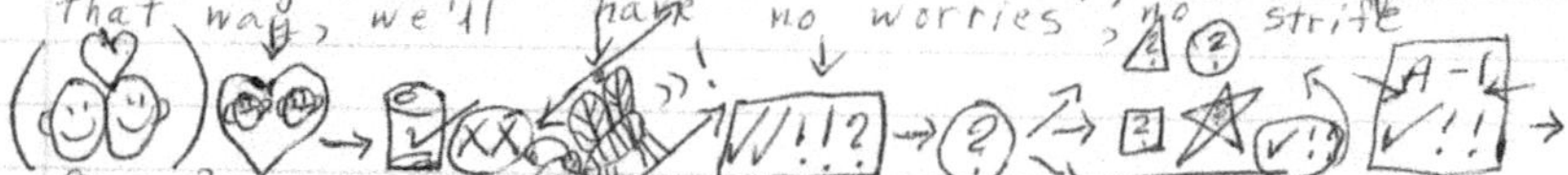

Our love cannot be possibly anything but right
Our love cannot be possibly anything but right

She wore ribbons and face And those eyes and
She wore ribbons and face and those eyes and

that face Oh, that hair, she also had good
that face Oh, that hair, she also had good

taste And her personality was A-1, first
taste And her personality was A-1, first

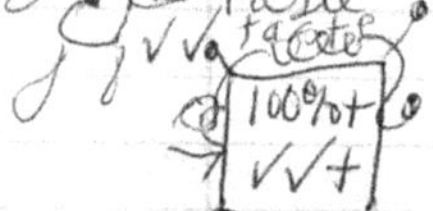

rate
rate

78 Love Can Only Grow 190
Love Can Only Grow

394 page

Love can't help but grow don't you know Just
Love can't help but grow don't you know Just

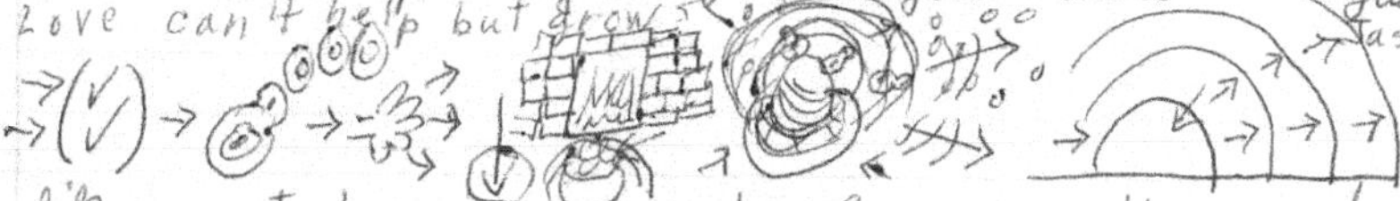

like yeast does in warm dough; it expands
like yeast does in warm dough; it expands

outwards with lots of get up and go This fact
outwards with lots of get up and go This fact

you will soon begin to know because the people
you will soon begin to know because the people

around you will all be aglow When love's
around you will all be aglow when love's

blessings begin to show it won't be long
blessings begin to show it won't be long

before your love overflows You will be
before your love overflows You will be

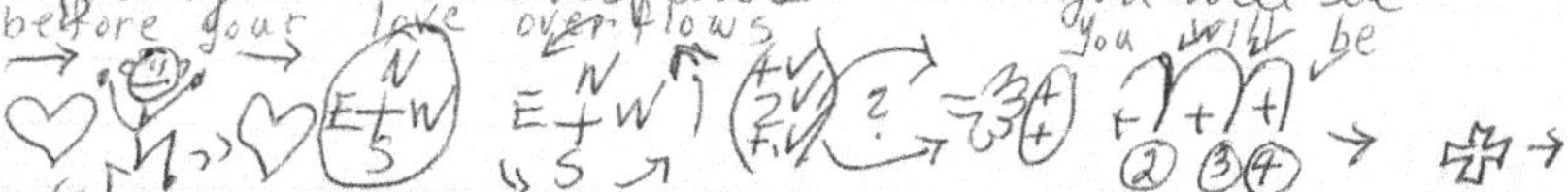

walking all around without help again and
walking all around without help again and

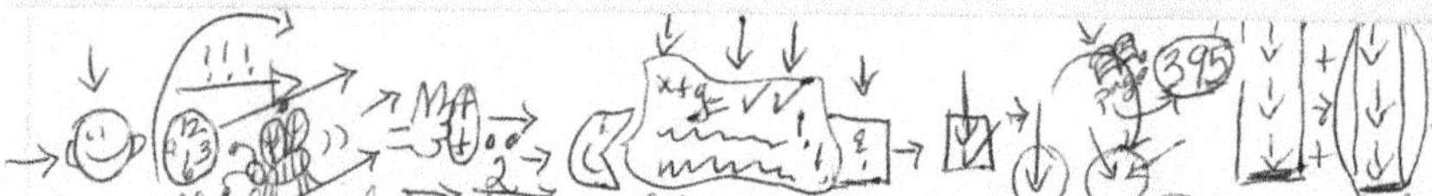

You'll be able to explain what is inside deep within
you'll be able to explain what is inside deep within

You'll be again in the light, my dearest friend
you'll be again in the light, my dearest friend

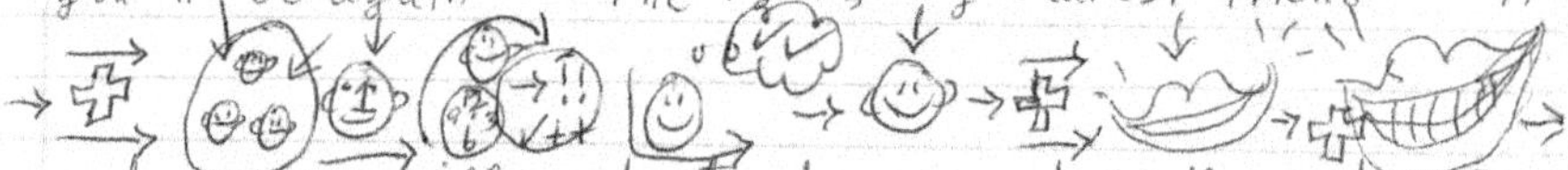

and everyone will understand you and smile and grin
and everyone will understand you and smile and grin

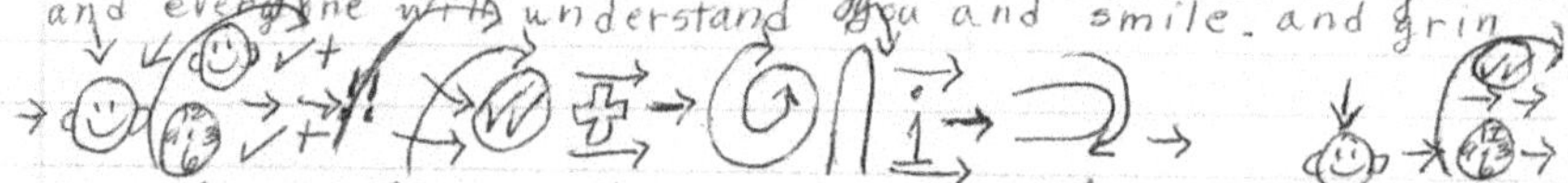

You'll go outside and around the bend you will
you'll go outside and around the bend you will

be their new captain Because love's hand will
be their new captain Because love's hand will

have reached out to expand in you, with all its
have reached out to expand in you, with all its

tender discipline You'll stand straight and tall
tender discipline You'll stand straight and tall

and when you are summoned, you will hear the call
and when you are summoned you will hear the call

You will no longer have your back against any wall
you will no longer have your back against any wall

page 396

because there will be justice for all
because there will be justice for all

And you will
And you will
no longer fall or run into
no longer fall or run into
walls like you are a
walls like you are a
cannonball
cannon ball

Now it will be your turn in life's
Now it will be your turn in life's
free-for-all!
free-for-all!

You will be a true winner in
You will be a true winner in
the long haul
the long haul

You are my flower bud, bud,
You are my flower bud, bud,
you are my flesh and blood
you are my flesh and blood

And that's no
And that's no
crud; you are definitely
crud; you are definitely
not a stick in the mud
not a stick in the mud

By the way, your name is not mud, but
By the way, your name is not mud, but
You
You
did come in a flash flood
did come in a flash flood

Nor is your name
Nor is your name

Elmer Fudd and
You are not a dud; you are
a blue blood
I have found the only way
I will find
any cure is to let changes occur
In who's looking back at me in that mirror
and then lay on the spurs
I am not seeing
a blur, but sometimes I am not seeing
who's really there. I would like to though; I don't
want to err
Something is definitely astir
and I'm
hoping for the best results to occur

39B

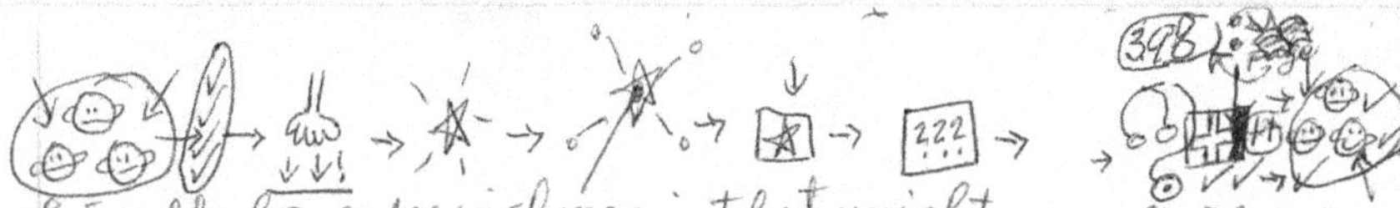

We all have special magic that might cure us
We all have special magic that might care us

when we are sick Love is the main trick, it is
when we are sick Love is the main trick, it is

welcome at any picnic Love can be slow or
welcome at any picnic Love can be slow or

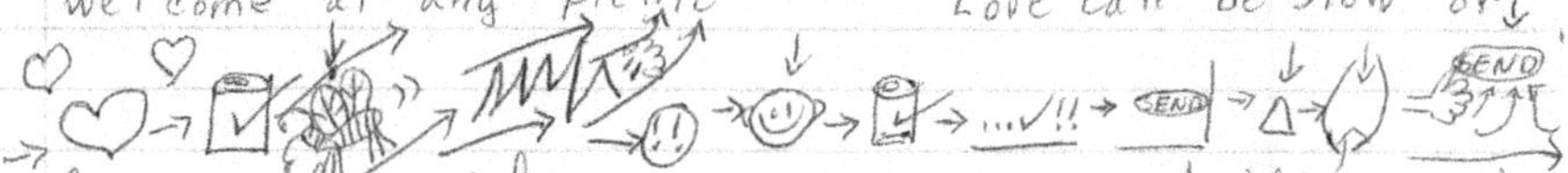

love can be quick you can even send it by pressing
love can be quick you can even send it by pressing

a click Love can be very, very chic especially
a click Love can be very, very chic especially

for the lonely and the lovesick Love's seed
for the lonely and the lovesick Love's seed

spreads and it's widespread for hard
spreads and it's widespread for hard

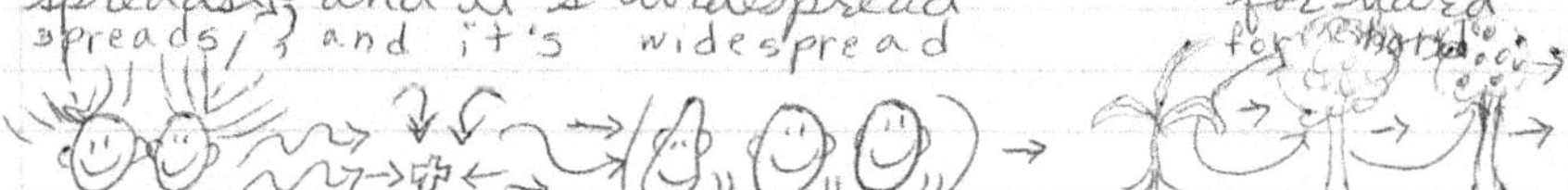

heads as well as eggheads Tranforming
heads as well as eggheads Transforming

its plants until they are ahead of all the
its plants until they are ahead of all the

purebreds Sometimes love is blue, sometimes
purebreds Sometimes love is blue, sometimes

red, but love always leaves you ahead
red, but love always leaves you ahead

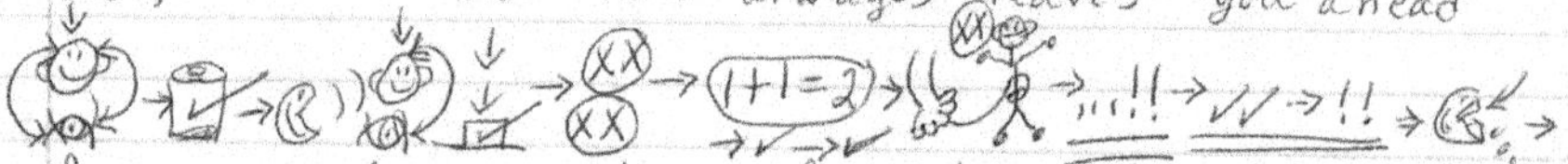

I can say I am not easily led, but easily fed,
I can say I am not easily led, but easily fed,

with love and I do not want to see
with love and I do not want to see

bloodshed Love starts out small and then grows
bloodshed Love starts out small and then grows

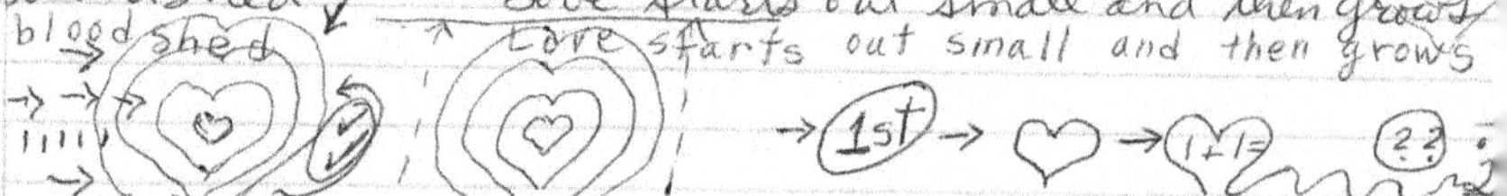

until it is very tall First love learns how to
until it is very tall First love learns how to

crawl, then it learns how to play hard ball
crawl, then it learns how to play hard ball

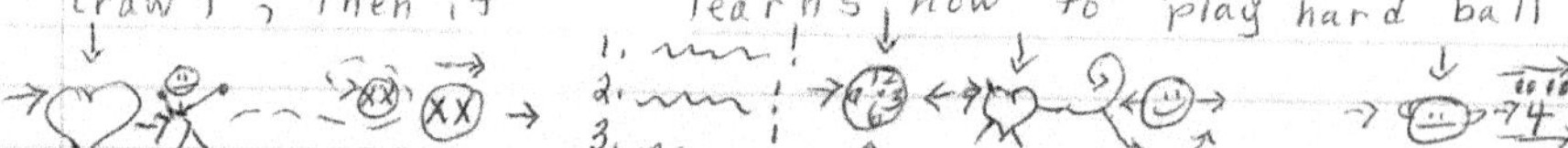

It follows no protocol when it takes you for
It follows no protocol when it takes you for

its loving free-for-all And usually no one
its loving free-for-all And usually no one

minds at all even   if it is, for them, awake-

minds at all even   if it is, for them, awake-

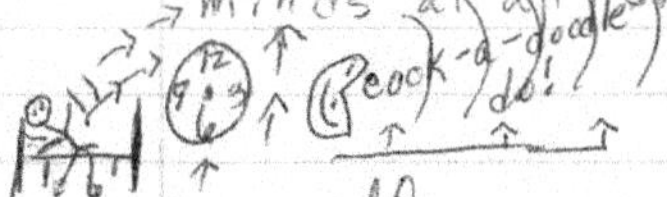

up call

up call

79 All I Want Is The Truth 193

All I Want Is The Truth

Forsooth, all I want in my life is the truth To you,

Forsooth, all I want in my life is the truth To you,

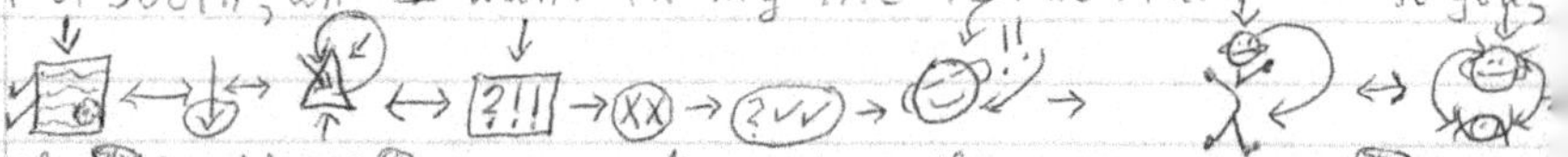

this, in itself, may not seem couth Myself, I

this, in itself, may not seem couth Myself, I

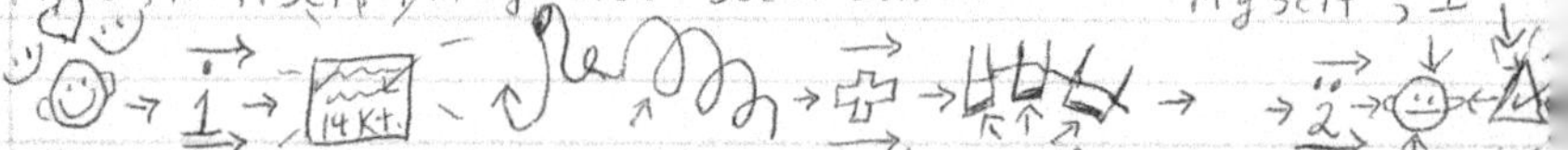

like the truth hook, line, and tooth To me, it's

like the truth hook, line, and tooth To me, its

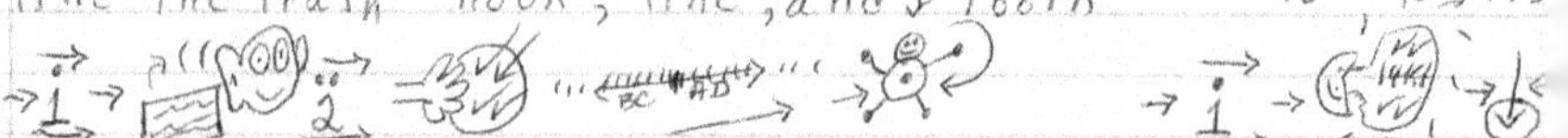

the secret to having eternal youth The truth is

the secret to having eternal youth The truth is

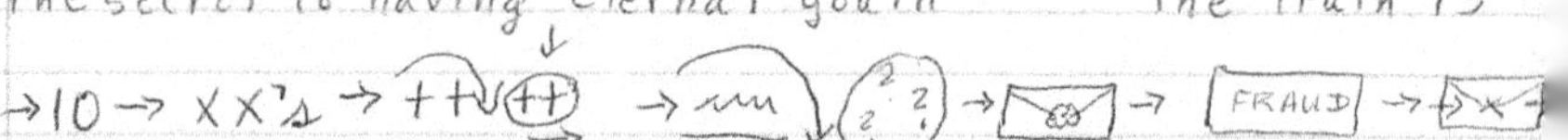

ten times better Than any legal falsified letter

ten times better Than any legal falsified letter

Go on, tell the truth, be a trendsetter It is

Go on, tell the truth, be a trendsetter

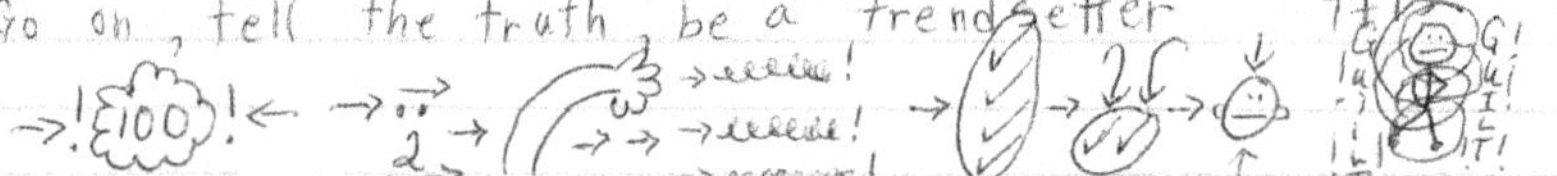

guaranteed to let loose all of your restrictive

guaranteed to let loose all of your restrictive

guilt fetters Being honest will make you

guilt fetters Being honest will make you

happy and set you free   It will cost you
happy and set you free   It will cost you

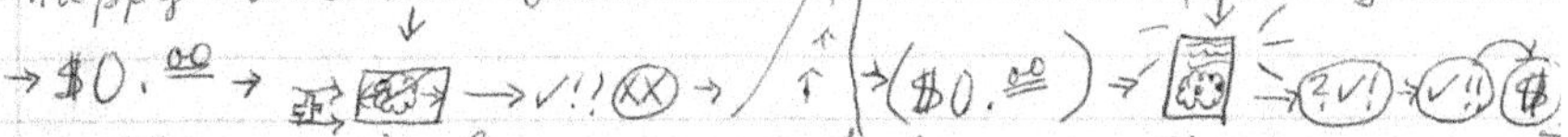

nothing ; it has no great fee   It may even earn
nothing ; it has no great fee   It may even earn

you a humanitarian degree   You will finally be
you a humanitarian degree   You will finally be

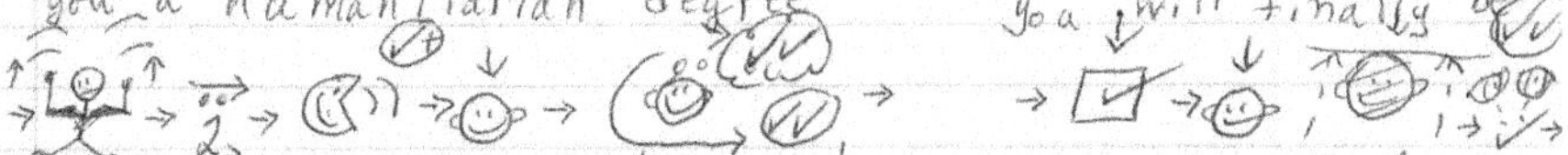

able to say you understand   that you fully see
able to say you understand   that you fully see

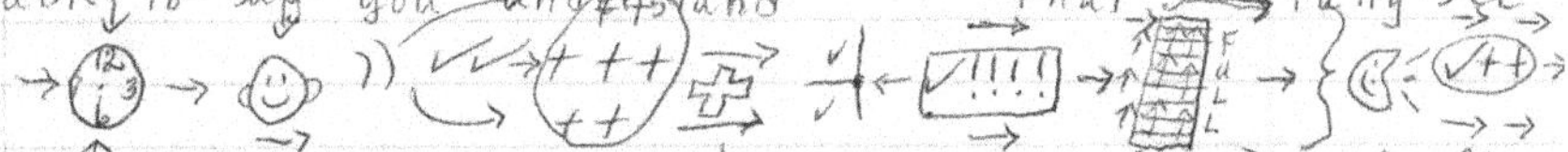

When you let loose and finally fully, truthfully
When you let loose and finally fully, truthfully

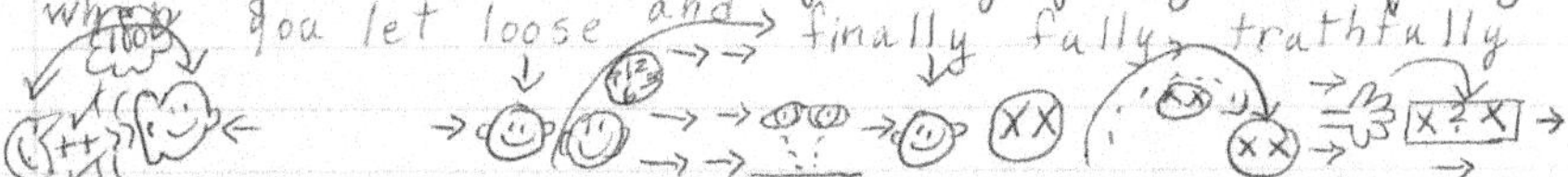

confide   You will see you no longer have
confide   You will see you no longer have

anything to hide   Then you will let goodness
anything to hide   Then you will let goodness

and good   sense become your guide   And

you will ride the highest tide over   to the golden
you will ride the highest tide over   to the golden

truth's side
truth's side
And yet the truth may sometimes
And yet the truth may sometimes

really hurt
really hurt
In that case, try not to be a bad
In that case, try not to be a bad

sport,
sport
Try to take your feelings and organize
Try to take your feelings and organize

them part by part
them part by part
Only get angry if necessary
Only get angry if necessary

and as a last resort
and as a last resort
Try to be ready for
Try to be ready for

anything and
anything and
expect the unusual to happen
expect the unusual to happen

Try to make the truth simple and plain, this
Try to make the truth simple and plain, this

will keep you out of the lion's den
will keep you out of the lion's den
If you want,
If you want,

you can even treat life like a game,
you can even treat life like a game,
but make
but make

truth the main rule again and again And make
truth the main rule again and again And make

sure that truth is the game and truth is the
sure that truth is the game and truth is the

name; then it will be popular for all men Then
name; then it will be popular for all men Then

truth will be what everyone will seek It will not
truth will be what everyone will seek It will not

be only for the weak and the meek But it will
be only for the weak and the meek But it will

become fashionable also for the strong and the
become fashionable also for the strong and the

sleek That's when our human race forecast
sleek That's when our human race forecast

will no longer be stormy or bleak Then everyone
will no longer be stormy or bleak Then everyone

will have so much fun There will be no
will have so much fun There will be no

more reasons for wars or guns Because the

more reasons for wars or guns Because the

truth is we'll all be in the open enjoying

truth is we'll all be in the open enjoying

the sun And that's when all our battles

the sun And that's when all our battles

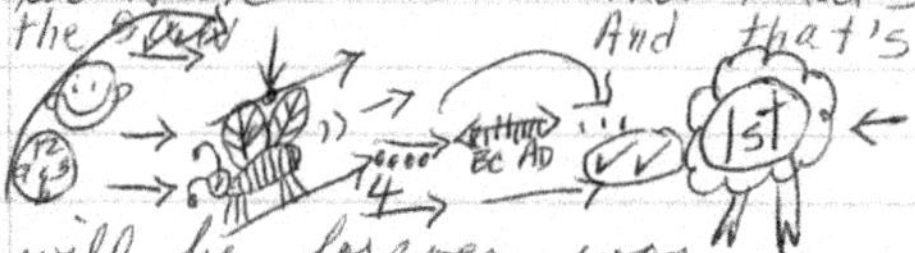

will be forever won

will be forever won

(80) Steam Roller (195)

steam Roller

My life has been lived like I was being run

My life has been lived like I was being run

over by a giant steamroller My edges are all

over a giant steamroller My edges are all

curled up from being burnt all around and

curled up from being burnt all around and

from all over Once I was confined and trapped

from all over Once I was confined and trapped

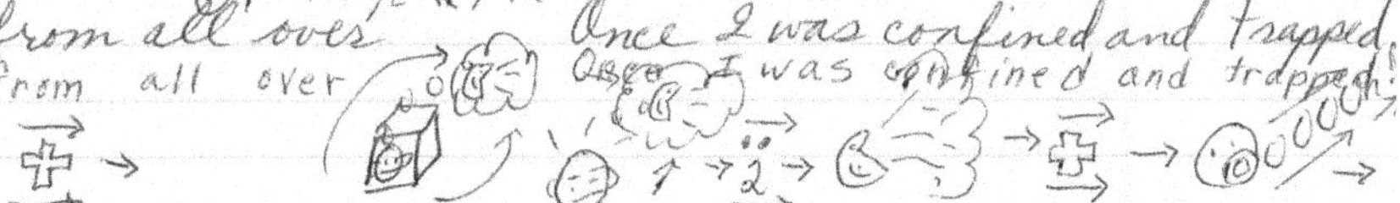

and silently tried to scream and holler

and silently tried to scream and holler

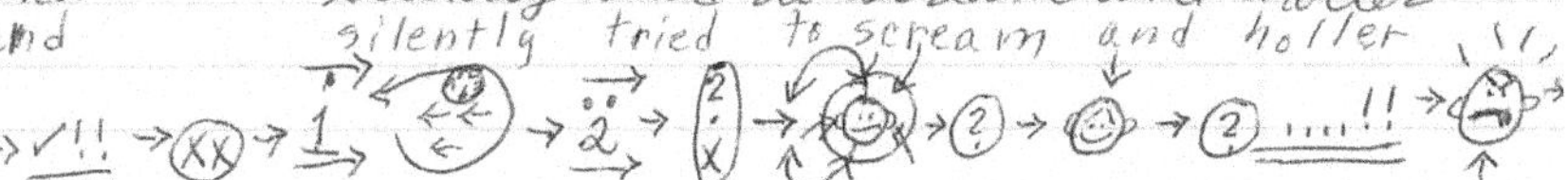

But no one came to rescue me or cared or even bothered

But no one came to rescue me or cared or even bothered

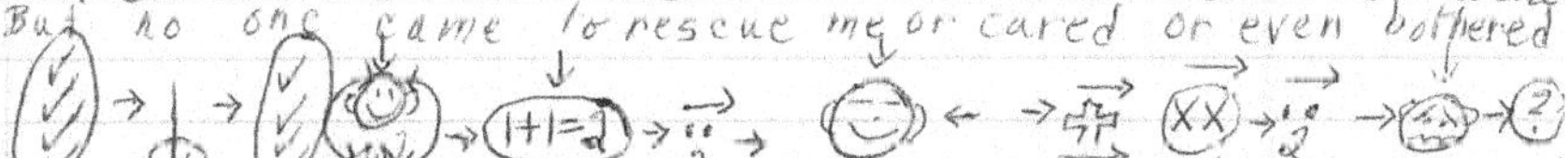

All in all, I learned to accept and not to care or

All in all, I learned to accept and not to care or

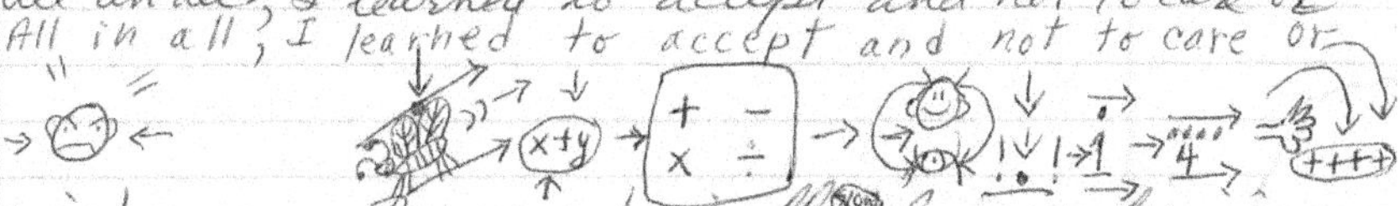

mind Because basically, I am a forgiving

mind Because basically, I am a forgiving

For each and every change in our life's many seasons

Even if those reasons are not of our choosing

or to our pleasing We must try to live life fully

before it is time for us to be leaving

It has never been my choice, until now,

and I've always been held back I was not

able to use my voice and give my opinion

without being attacked I've had to use all my

hidden ploys and to be patient until now, to

and a practical kind The hidden beauty in
and a practical kind The hidden beauty in

unfortunate situations, I try to find Even
anfortanate sitaations, I try to find Even

extreme hardships can secretly turn out to be
extreme hardships can secretly turn out to be

for the best and be educational and kind I
for the best and be educational and kind I

have found that we must be all tested by fire
have found that we must be all tested by fire

And we will be burnt up if we are liars
And we will be barnt up if we are liars

That's why, of truth, we must learn to never tire
That's why, of trath, we must learn to never tire 13

That is, in order to be able to strive higher and higher
That is, in order to be able to strive higher and higher

We must remember there is always a reason
We must remember there is always a reason

show I didn't lack I've had to be very
show I didn't lack I've had to be very
careful, just to survive life's constant noise
careful, just to survive life's constant noise
and protect my loved ones, and that is a fact
and protect my loved ones, and that is a fact
In effect, life has decided to try and roll me over
In effect, life has decided to over
Yes, roll me over, like by a giant steamroller
Yes, roll me over, like by
Many times I've had to duck and run for cover
Many times I've had to duck and run for cover
While the world around me tossed and churned me
While the world around me tossed and churned me
and spread me out like butter There have
been many, many surprises for me in my life
been many, many surprises for me in my life

Not all of them have been choice prizes, many
Not all of them have been choice prizes, many

have cut me like a knife And some have come
have cut me like a knife And some have come

in strange disguises and have caused much
in strange disguises and have caused much

strife I have dealt with them all as they
strife I have dealt with them all as they

arise, before and after I was a wife
arise before and after I was a wife

I know that no matter what, we must all
I Know that no matter what, we must all

continue to Keep on rolling No matter what
continue to Keep on rolling No matter what

life chooses on doling out for us: good,
life chooses on doling out for us good,

bad, happy, sad, any situation We must
bad, happy, sad, any situation We must

use our powers of doing well and work hard
use our powers of doing well and work hard

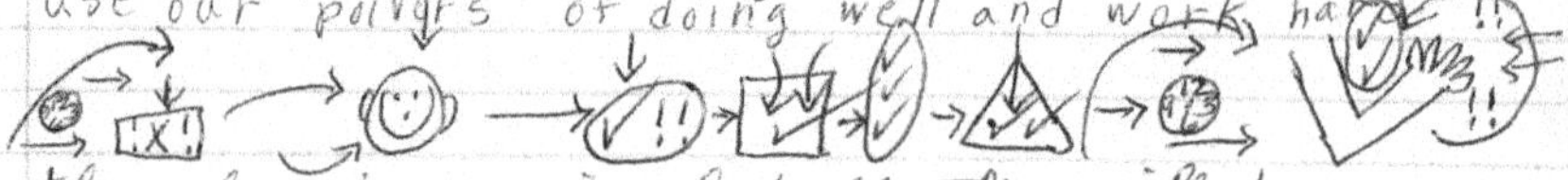

then happiness is what all this will bring
then happiness is what all this will bring

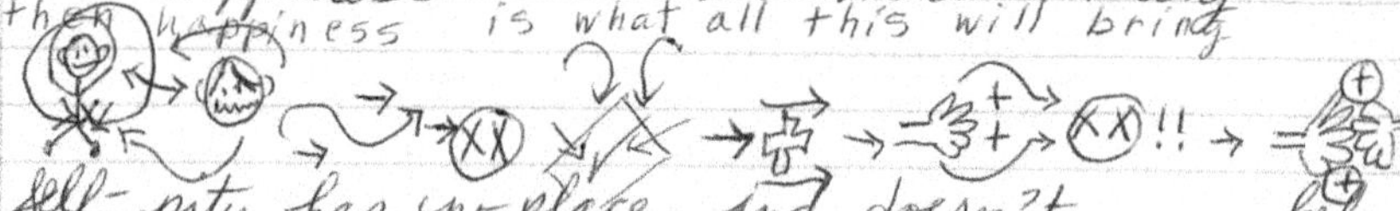

self-pity has no place and doesn't help
self-pity has no place and doesn't help

anyone a doggone thing
anyone a doggone thing

(81) What, still Awake? (197) 412 page

What, still Awake?

Are your eyes still open? What, still awake?

are your eyes still open!? What, still awake?

Answer me! The silence must be broken!

Answer me, The silence must be broken

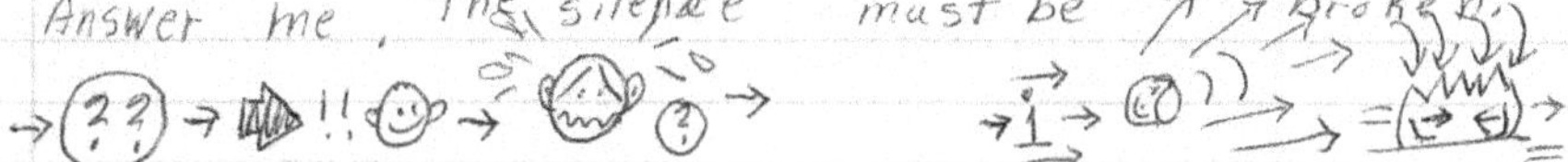

Why do you hesitate? The voice answered:

Why do you hesitate? the voice answered

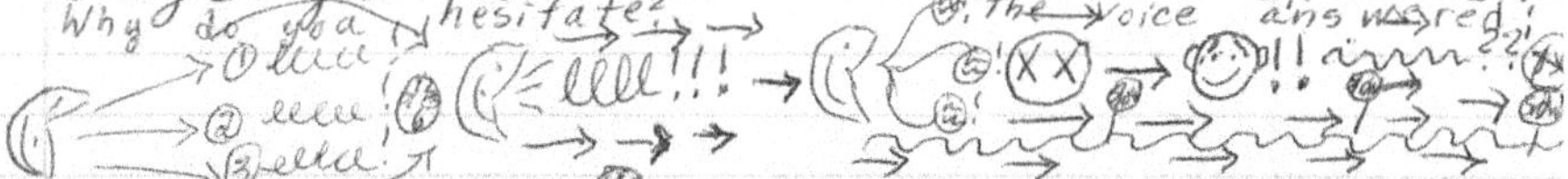

they have spoken! They don't procrastinate

they have spoken they don't procrastinate

They have spoken, they have been awoken!

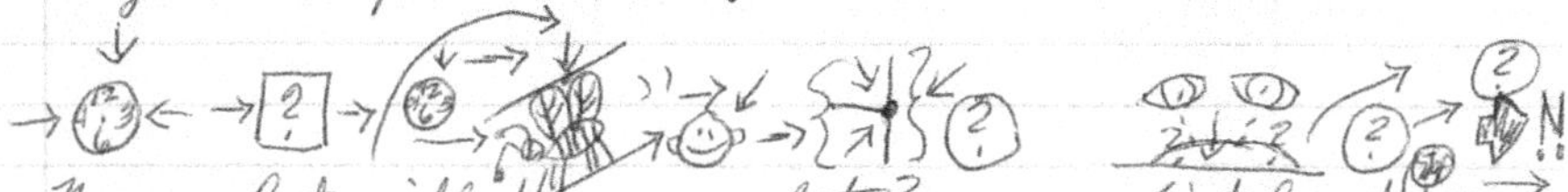

Now what will be your fate? Watch out! Do

you believe in what you see? Are you sure?

Be careful because you may never again be free

Is it real? What you see doesn't necessarily
Is it real? What you see doesn't necessarily
have any guarantees You are now in the land
have any guarantees You are now in the land
of the sleepy — by the sea of deep sleep
of the sleepy — by the sea of deep sleep
Please continue and explain. Do you dare share
Please continue and explain Do you dare share
a little with us? Are you frightened? Do you
a little with us? Are you frightened? Do you
really think you have had enough?
really think you have had enough?
You're hoping something so real may disappear in
You're hoping something so real may disappear in
a puff Even so, then you will wake up in a
a puff Even so, then you will wake up in a
sweat, feeling mighty rough These dreams,
sweat, feeling mighty rough These dreams,

4-14 page

these visions, were they just something that you
these visions, were they just something that you

ate from your supper plate? Is it really early
ate from your supper plate? Is it really early

morning or is it still late? What's the time?
morning or is it still late? What's the time?

Is this déjà vu, or do you have the feeling that
Is this déja vu, or do you have the feeling that

you have met a horrendous fate? Wake up,
you have met a horrendous fate? Wake up,

You want to open your eyes, but what a shame
You want to open your eyes, but what a shame

You find real life is just as bad as the dream
You find real life is just as bad as the dream

and is a nightmare just the same Is it possible
and is a nightmare just the same Is it possible

your limbs all refuse to work? You have become
Your limbs all refuse to work? You have become

lame
lame
You can no longer speak. You think you are
You can no longer speak. You think you ar
alive
alive
but you wish that you were dead all the same
but you wish that you were dead all the same
They say it won't be long before you're gone
They tal
They say it won't be long before you're gone
They talk
To each other
and all agree that you no longer
to each other
and all agree that you no longer
belong
What if this is reality? You'll wonder
be long
What if this is reality? You'll wonder
about reality before too long
Am I alive? What's
about reality before too long
Am I alive? What's
RIP
Rest in peace
that ghastly music
of that funeral song?
that ghastly music
of that funeral song?
OK. That's it! You've had enough
Somehow
OK. That's it! You've had enough
Some how
everything seems strange!
You'll be the one
everything seems strange!
You'll be the one

to call their every bluff
to call their every bluff
Somehow, you feel
some how, you feel
tightness around your cuffs
tightness around your cuffs
Now you also feel your
Now you also feel your
bedding is satin, luxurious stuff
bedding is satin, laxarious stuff
You wonder
You wonder
how the impossible has happened
now the impossible has happened
You can sense
you can sense
that you should look up.
that you should look up.
You see your crying
you see your crying
girlfriend
girlfriend
There are people standing all around,
There are people standing all around,
looking down at me. Is this the end?
looking down at me. Is this the end?
I'm watching in
I'm watching in
silence, but what my spirit
silence, but what my spirit
sees, my mind
sees, my mind
can't comprehend
can't comprehend

(82) The Lovely Lady (199)

The Lovely Lady

That Cleans

That Cleans

Ooooooh!

Oh, that lovely lady that cleans She's never last

Oh, that lovely lady that cleans She's never last

by any means There is more to her than there

by any means There is more to her than there

is to be seen That's for sure, there is no if

is to be seen That's for sure, there is no if

Ooooooh!

and or in between Oh, how I've learned to

and or in between Oh, how I've learned to

love that lady She is my favorite; she is always

love that lady She is my favorite; she is always

poised and ready She's always helpful,

poised and ready She's always helpful,

heartfelt, and heady She's always in my

heartfelt, and heady She's always in my

thoughts She is silent, but she is steady Hes

thoughts she is silent, but she is steady Her

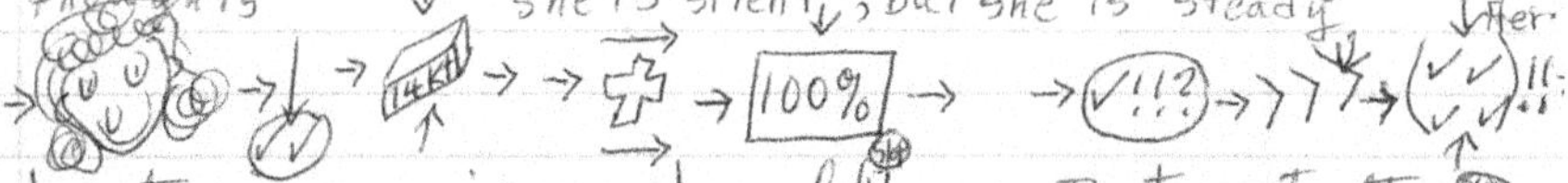

beauty is genuine and real. But most often,

beauty is geniuine and real. But most often,

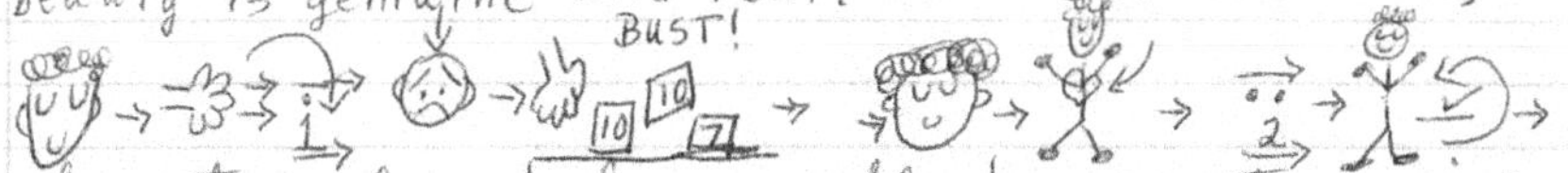

she gets a bum deal She deserves to receive

she gets a bum deal she deserves to receive

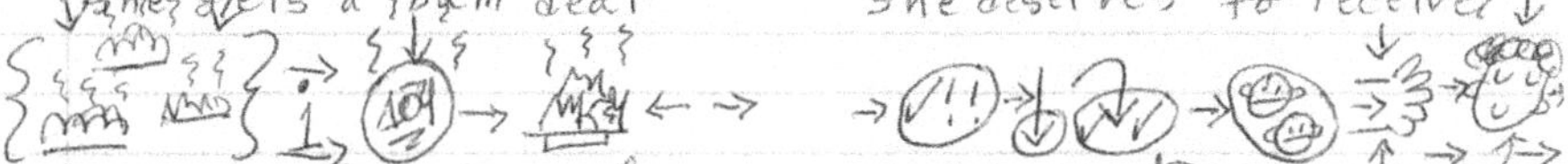

many a fancy meal But instead, we get her

many a fancy meal But instead, we get her

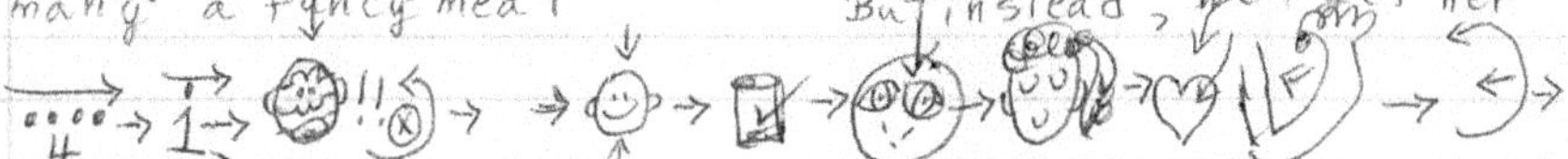

for a steal You can see her love comes from

for a steal You can see her love comes from

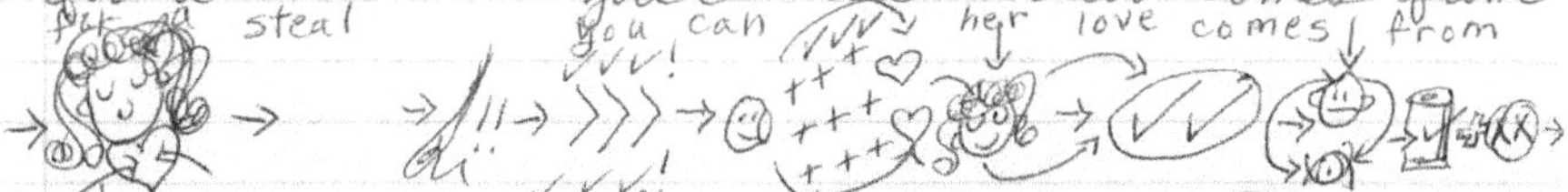

within So much praise she deserves, I can't

within so much praise she deserves I can't

begin to begin You shouldn't ignore her on a

begin to begin You shouldn't ignore her on a

whim And if you hurt her feelings, it would be

whim And if you hurt her feelings, it would be

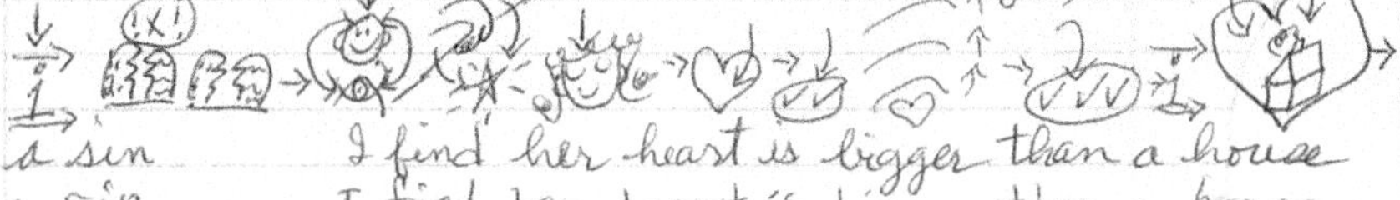

a sin I find her heart is bigger than a house

a sin I find her heart is bigger than a house

She even cleans after that pest, that mangy mouse
She even cleans after that pest, that mangy mouse

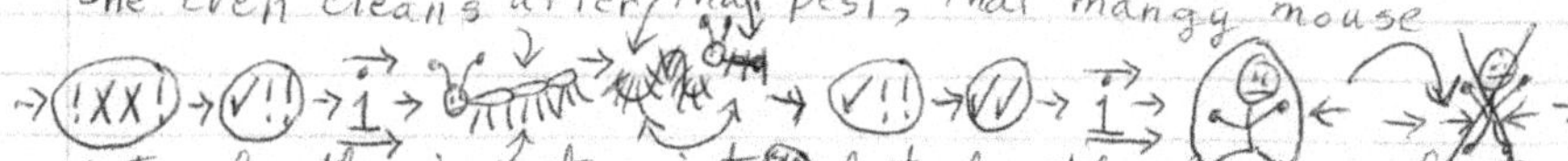

Not only the insect variety, but also the human host
Not only the insect variety, but also the human host

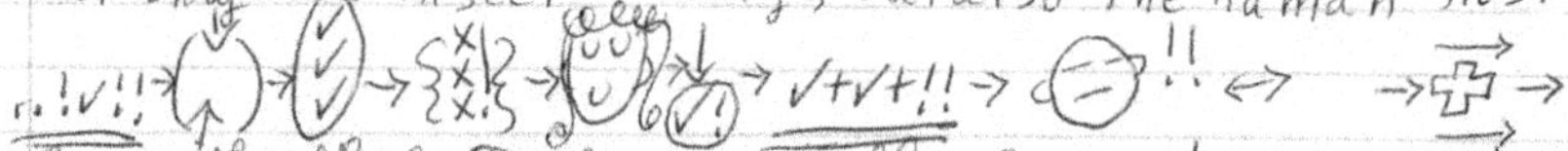

Even with all this, she is usually ignored And
Even with all this, she is usually ignored And

usually by the ones who cause the most discord If
usually by the ones who cause the most discord If

only they knew how wise she was, they'd be floored
only they knew how wise she was, they'd be floored

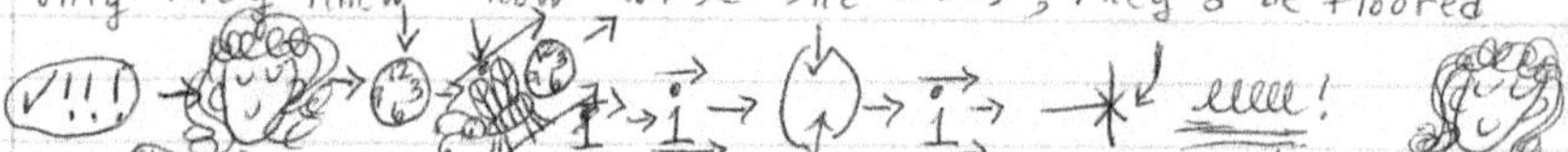

Still, she will be the one with the final word She
Still, she will be the one with the final word

always manages to have something to do Even
always manages to have something to do Even

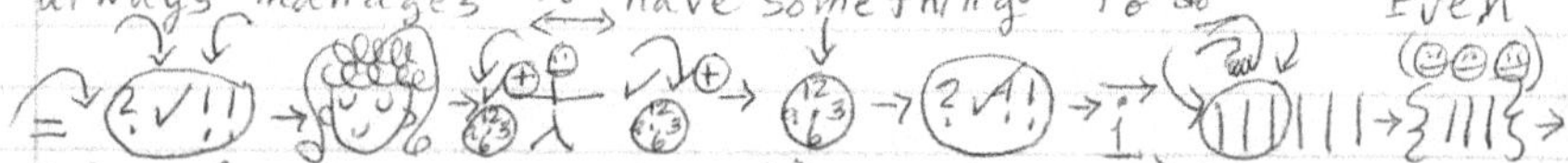

though she shares her time only a chosen few
though she shares her time only a chosen few

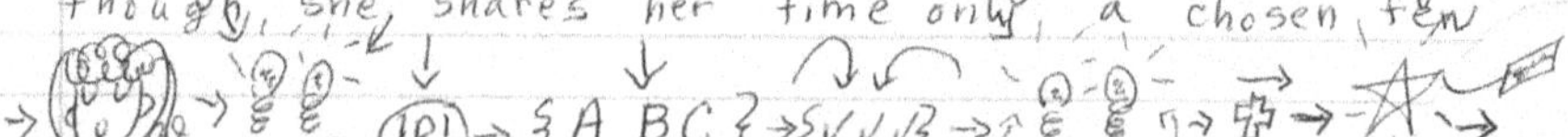

Her ideas are basically always shiny and new
Her ideas are basically always shiny and new

Her time is so precious, does that give you a clue
Her time is so precious, does that give you a clue

Oh, that lovely lady, you certainly don't lack
Oh, that lovely lady, you certainly don't lack

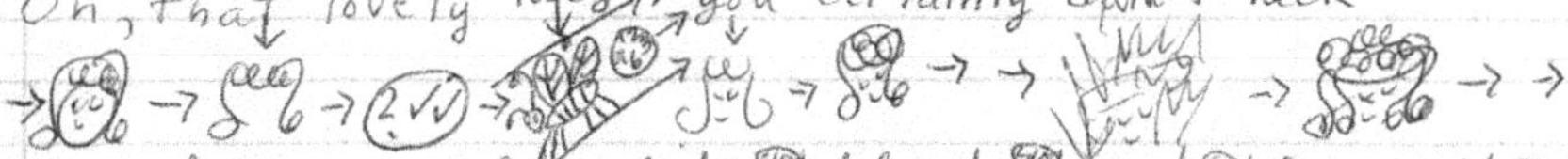

Your hair may be white, blonde, red, brunette,
Your hair may be white, blonde, red, brunette,

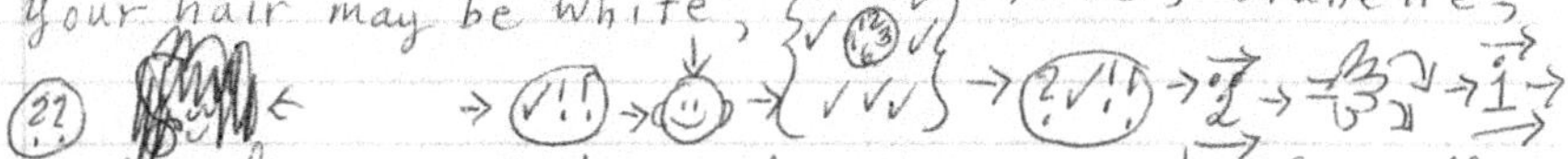

or black
or black

But you always seem to have the
But you always seem to have the

special knack
special knack

And you always know how to
And you always know how to

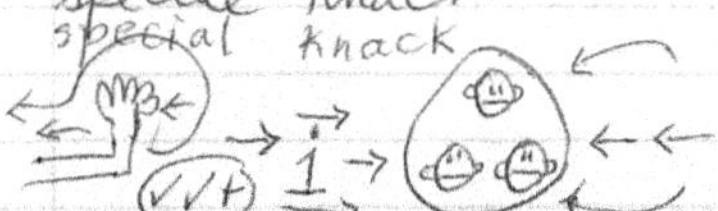

bring the people back
bring the people back

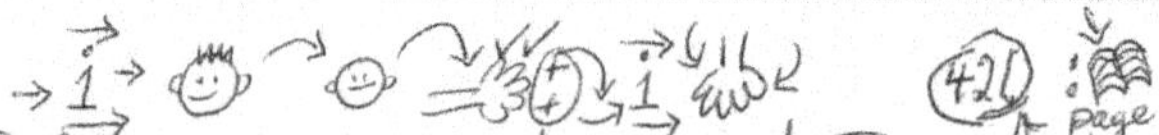

(83) The Man Who Lends A Hand (201)
The Man Who Lends A Hand

You have to understand why I feel so grand There
You have to understand why I feel so grand There

lived, in town, a man who likes to lend a hand
lived, in town, a man who likes to lend a hand

The work he will complete is at your and my command
The work he will complete is at your and my command

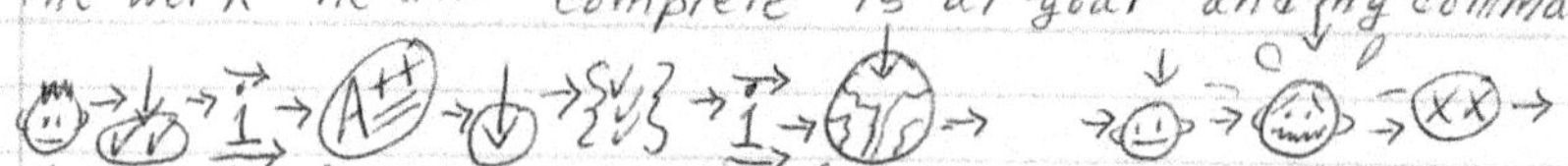

He's the best in all the land He needs no
He's the best in all the land He needs no

reprimand This man is sometimes jovial and sweet
reprimand This man is sometimes jovial and sweet

He is the one who you would like to meet And
He is the one who you would like to meet And

shake hands with while walking down the street
shake hands with while walking down the street

You'll soon notice he's got two well-used feet
You'll soon notice he's got two well used feet

He can be the one to be your very best friend He
He can be the one to be your very best friend He
also has a family with which he has to fend He's
also has a family with which he has to fend He's
the one who knows how to put things on the mend
the one who knows how to put things on the mend
Look over there, he's coming from around the bend
Look over there, he's coming from around the bend
He happens to take pride in his work He has
He happens to take pride in his work He has
a good idea where evil lurks And all its quirks
a good idea where evil lurks And all its quirks
He knows how to handle any jerk Even
He knows how to handle any jerk Even
when they go berserk He can easily wipe off
when they go berserk He can easily wipe off
any grimace or smirk Sometimes he doesn't
any grimace or smirk Sometimes he doesn't

even wear a shirt— Not because it is hot where
even wear a shirt— Not because it is hot where

he has to work We like him better when he
he has to work! We like him better when he

chooses to exert That is when we hit paydirt
choose to exert That is when we hit pay dirt

Saying hi to him won't even hurt He usually
Saying hi to him won't even hurt He usually

is not an introvert Sometimes, he works
is not an introvert Sometimes, he works

where it is cold But he is still bold Even
where it is cold But he is still bold Even

though, everything he touches turns to gold
though, everything he touches turns to gold

Sometimes he can be young or sometimes he
Sometimes he can be young or sometimes he

can be old That's why I look up to him if I
can be old That's why I look up to him if I

may be so bold On him, I am sold Without
may be so bold On him, I am sold Without

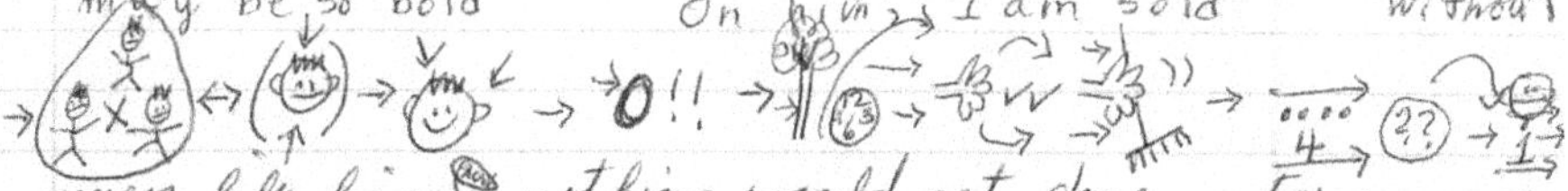

men like him, nothing would get done For anyone
men like him, nothing would get done For anyone

Then, how in the world would any of us have any fun
Then, how in the world would any of us have any fun

In the sun or on the run Because most of our
In the sun or on the ran Because most of our

plans would be undone They would lack the top
plans would be undone They would lack the top

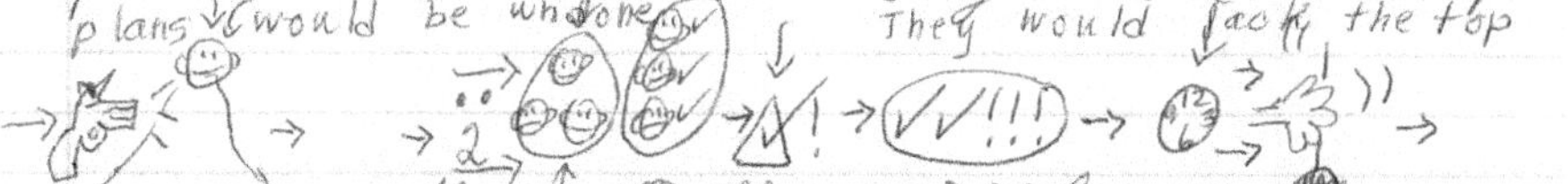

gun To us all, this definitely will make
gun To us all, this definitely will make

him a big number one A bull's eye - a hole
him a big number one A bull's eye a hole

in one All in all, these are the quality gents
in one All in all, these are the quality gents

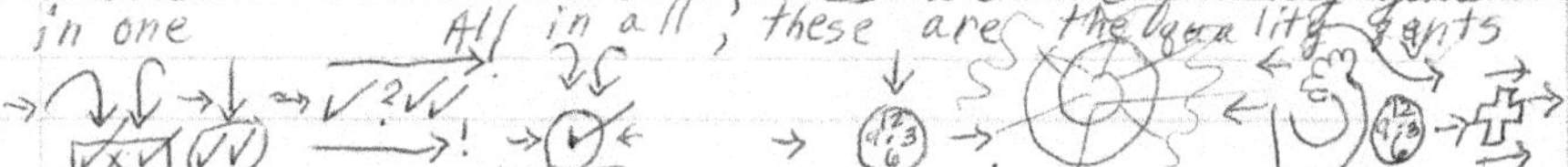

That is quite evident When creation came and
That is quite evident When creation came and

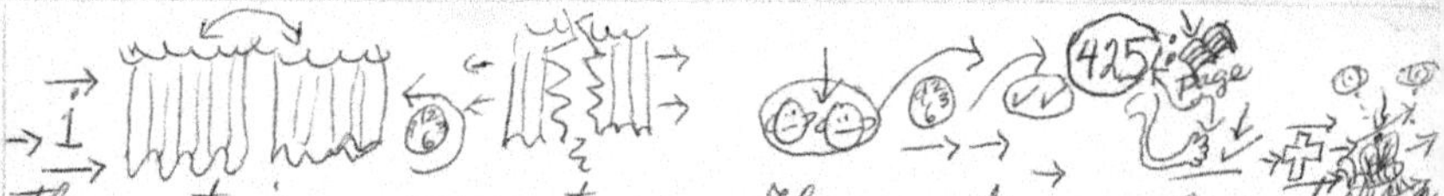

the curtains were sent
the curtains were rent

They went
They went

Lo and behold,
To and behold,

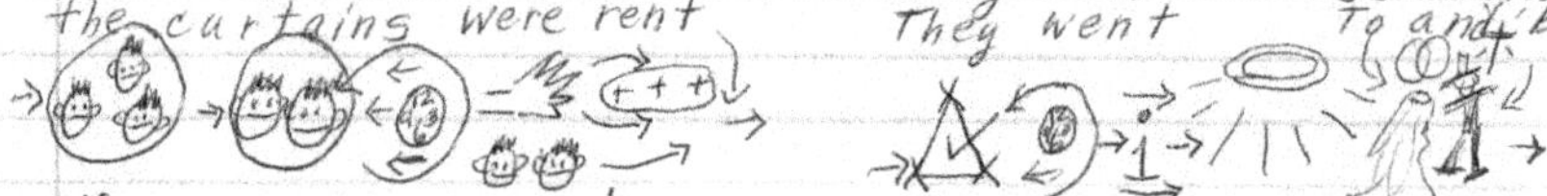

thea men were sent
these men were sent

It was a blessed event
It was a blessed event

They didn't mind, in fact they were eager
They didn't mind, in fact they were eager

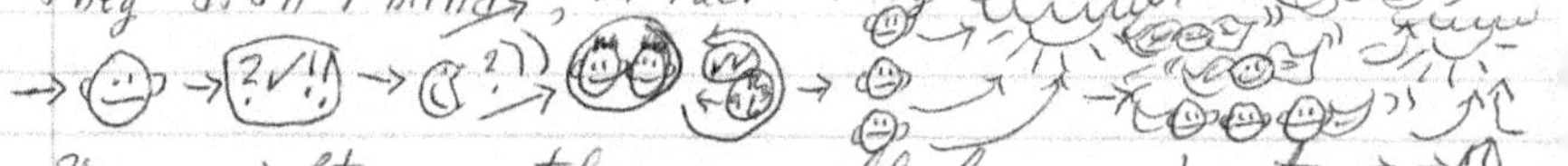

You might say they were all heaven bent
You might say they were all heaven bent

(84) I Am Special (203)

I Am Special

(426) page 

I am an individual ; I am special
I am an individual ; I am special

I am made
I am made

of my very own kind of mettle
of my very own kind of mettle

I can even
I can even

manage to boil a kettle
manage to boil a kettle

Sometimes it may
Sometimes it may

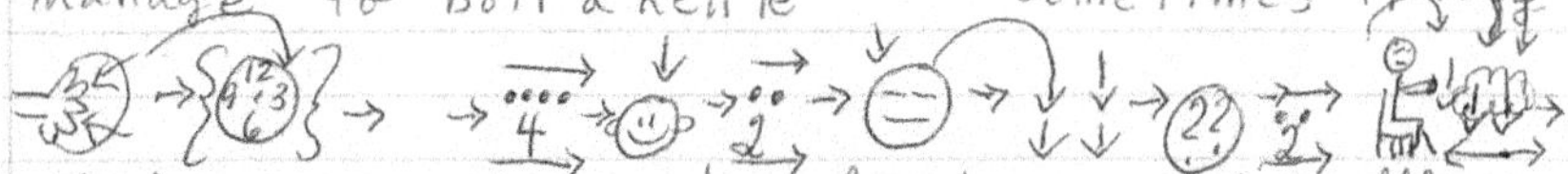

take time
take time

for me to calm down or to settle
for me to calm down or to settle

What do you think makes me tick
What do you think makes me tick

Go ahead
Go ahead

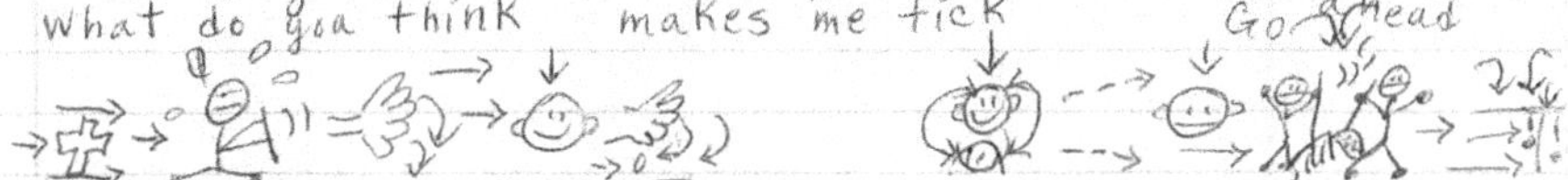

and try take your pick
and try take your pick

I get my jobs done
I get my jobs done.

lickety - split
lickety-split

And I seldom ail or get sick
And I seldom ail or get sick

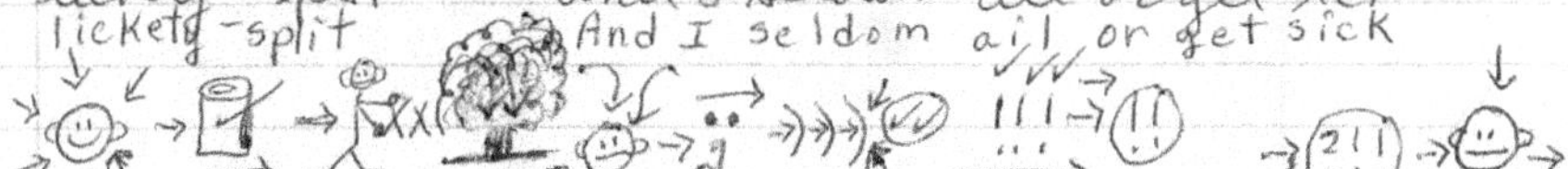

You can subject me to very much
You can subject me to very much

But you
But you

may have trouble to keep me in your clutch Inside
may have trouble to keep me in your clutch Insider

way deep down, I am just a soft touch And I
way deep down, I am just a soft touch And I

try to avoid every vice or crutch I have finally
try to avaid every vice or crutch I have finally

picked a friend, a sir Now I'm finally hav
picked a friend, a sir Now I'm finally hav

fun and time passes by like I'm in a blur
fun and time passes by like I'm in a blur

Another of my friends is also the majestic fir
another of my friends is also the majestic fir

I'm convinced and I know that I will surely endure
I'm convinced and I know that I will surely endure

I have loved, I have lived Through the ashes
I have loved, I have lived Through the ashes

I have sieved The main attraction I've perceived
I have sieved The main attraction I've perceived

I feel fine now; I feel swell, On small differences,
I feel fine now, I feel swell, On small differences,

I no longer dwell I feel like an ocean, I can
I no longer dwell I feel like an ocean, I can

quell And that I am the lucky one, and I may
quell And that I am the lucky one, and I may

be able to ring the final bell I think now you
be able to ring the final bell I think now you

can just guess I am no longer a mess In
can just guess I am no longer a mess In

the mess, I have found the bless Yes, I have passed
the mess, I have found the bless yes, I have passed

my own final test I'll love life now and until
my own final test I'll love life now and until

I die And then when I look at you straight in
I die And then when I look at you straight in

the eye I'll try to be bright and spry
the eye I'll try to be bright and spry

As I can be, and I will try to be sincere and not to
As I can be and I will try to be sincere and not to

lie I won't both with things that are bad
lie I won't both with things that are bad

In this way, my armor will be ironclad I will
In this way my armor will be ironclad I will

have no reason, or time, to be sad Someday,
have no reason, or time, to be sad Someday,

there might even be a cure for my youngest lad
there might even be a cure for my youngest lad

The whole universe, I want to explore And see
The whole universe, I want to explore And see

what, for me, is in store I want to see as
what, for me, is in store I want to see as

much of what is left of my life before It is
much of what is left of my life before It is

finished, ended, ore There's so much more in
finished, ended, ore There's so much more in

my life for me to see
my life for me to see

And it's true, the best things
And it's true, the best things

in life are free
in life are free

Come on over here, come on and
Come on over here, come on and

meet me
meet me

I promise you, there isn't any fee
I promise you, there isn't any fee

I myself would love to meet you
I myself would love to meet you

Wouldn't you
Wouldn't you

love to meet me too?
love to meet me too?

Does this fact perhaps give
Does this fact perhaps give

you a clue?
you a clue?

If it does, maybe then you can
If it does, maybe then you can

take a cue
take a cue

I'm A-OK, I now have hope
I'm A-OK, I now have hope

I'm free! I no longer have to mope
I'm free I no longer have to mope

I am
I am

able! All my love can be wrote
able. All my love can be wrote

Not in a bad way,
Not in a bad way,

here in this special note
here in this special note
I have offered and freely
I have offered and freely
given my life
given my life,
I have chosen and have endured
I have chosen and have endured
much strife
much strife
My suffering was a two-edged
My suffering was a two-edged
knife
Knife
One side was bad and was good. It was all
One side was bad and was good. It was all
right
right
Some poor souls have no room to pity
some poor souls have no room to pity
They live there in the dark of the city
They live there in the dark of the city
I'd rather
I'd rather
choose to be happy and witty
choose to be happy and witty
It's better than
It's better than
being an itty-bitty
being an itty-bitty
When I choose goodness
When I choose goodness
my battle will be won
my battle will be won
Then I will know, mow
Then I will know, mow

is the time to have fun I then will have won
is the time to have fun I then will have won

and no longer will have to run Better yet, I
and no longet will have to run Better get, I

will have time to bask in the sun And with
will have time to bask in the sun And with

a little help from all my friends With all the
a little help from my friends with all the

happiness that they have to lend My life
happiness that they have to lend My life

will be happy, it no longer depends On any
will be happy, it no longer depends On any

situation that has a beginning or an end Now
situation that has a beginning or an end Now

I feel full of good humor You can bet that's
I feel full of good humor You can bet that's

not just a rumor My success couldn't have
not just a rumor My success couldn't have

page 433

come any sooner
come any sooner

Even though, let's face it I'm
Even though, let's face it I'm

a late bloomer
a late bloomer

I'm sure I will have many more
I'm sure I will have many more

trials
trials

But I'll be satisfied and happy in the meanwhile
But I'll be satisfied and happy in the meanwhile

No matter what comes along, I'll try to smile
No matter what comes along, I'll try to smile

I've heard nothing that comes easy is worthwhile
I've heard nothing that comes easy is worthwhile

Well
Well

then my life has seldom come easy
then my life has seldom come easy

My crowning
My crowning

achievement is my
achievement is my

children one, two, and three
children one, two, and three

And yes, right now, I'm still here and in my life I am
And yes, right now, I'm still here and in my life I am

free
free

(85) Until The Time Comes (206)

Until The Time Comes

Until the end time comes, our lives will be just trial
Until the end time comes, our lives will be just trial

runs
rans

And if we are still here we will be
And if we are still here we will be

the lucky ones — put down your weapons and
the lucky ones put down your weapons and

your guns, one by one — And we all will be
your guns, one by one — And we all will be

even happier — Even more the fortunate ones
even happier — Even more the fortunate ones

And when there is finally peace for all — We will
And when there is finally peace for all — We will

no longer be headed for a great fall — our ears
no longer be headed for a great fall — our ears

will be opened and we will hear the call — We
will be opened and we will hear the call — We

will no longer have to put up brick walls When
will longer have to put up brick walls When

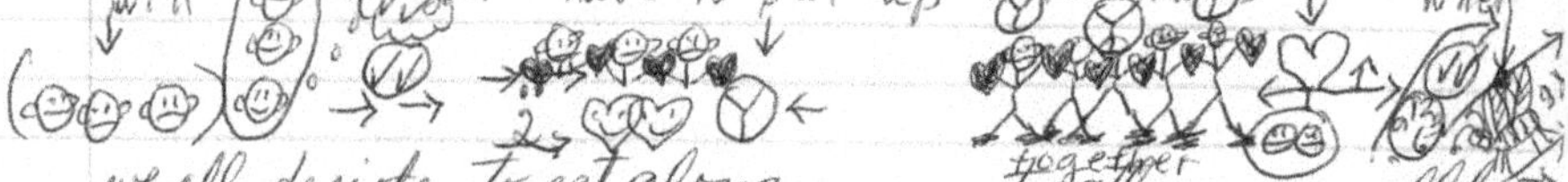

we all decide to get along together we will be
we all decide to get along together we will be

strong We will all sing the same harmonious
strong We will all sing the same harmonious

songs And we will all feel like we fit together
songs And we will all feel like we fit together

and belong Then everything will be right
and belong Then everything will be right

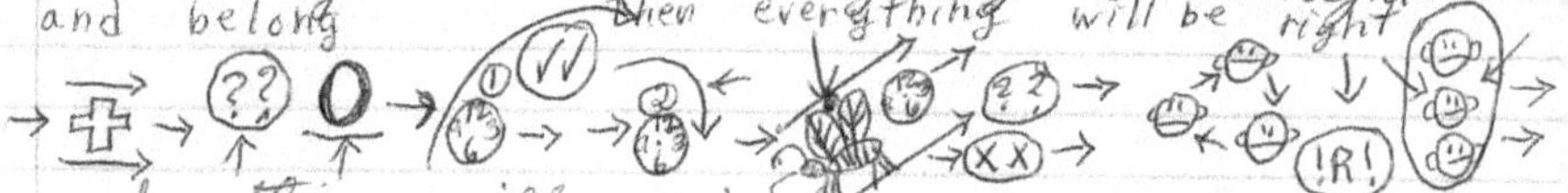

and nothing will again be wrong We are all
and nothing will again be wrong We are all

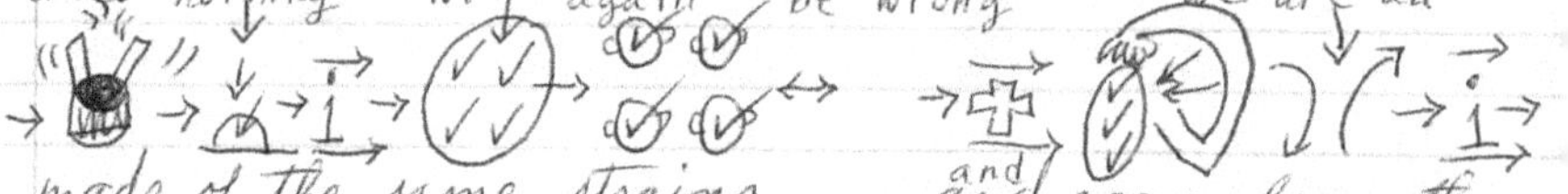

made of the same strains and come from the
made of the same strains and come from the

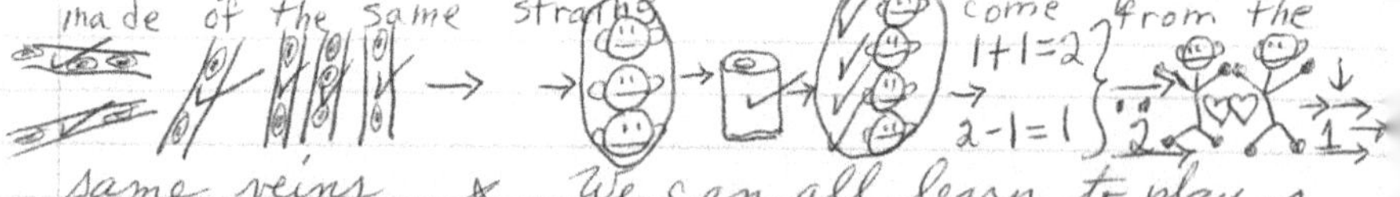

same veins We can all learn to play a
same veins We can all learn to play a

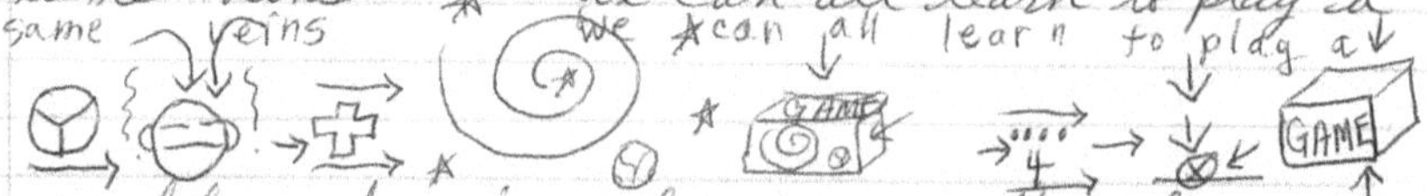

peaceful and universal game For this game
peaceful and aniversal game For this game

we have no need to be trained or tamed And there
we have no need to be trained or tamed And there

will be room enough for us all to reign
will be room enough for us all to reign

Meanwhile, we can, with the spirit of grace
Mean while, we can, with the spirit of grace,

Get many benefits and all get a true taste We can
Get many benefits and all get a true taste we can

extend our friendly hands to each others in haste
extend our friendly hands to each other in haste

And we can learn to cherish, love, and be
And we can learn to cherish, love, and be

chaste Come on, let there be peace and no
chaste Come on, let there be peace and no

more hatred Come on, go ahead, and
more hatred come on, go ahead, and

use those brains in your head → aren't we all
use those brains in your head → aren't we all

living in the same proverbial bed? And saying
living in the same proverbial bed? And saying
that, I say full speed ahead, egghead We'll
that, I say full speed ahead, egghead We'll
all end up tolling the knell bell and bid a fond
all end up tolling the knell bell and bid a fond
farewell Either on our way to heaven or away
farewell Either on our way to heaven or away
from it and onwards towards hell We will
from it and onwards towards hell we will
be all by ourselves; that is how it will happen
be all by ourselves; that is how it will happen
in a nutshell It will all be very familiar
in a nutshell It will all be very familiar
and we will know when we feel the final bombshell
and we will know when we feel the final bombshell
If we want, we can all be full of love And
If we want, we can all be full of love And

happiness and more of all the above We can
happiness and more of all the above we can

be excited like sunshine and flying like
be excited like sunshine and flying like

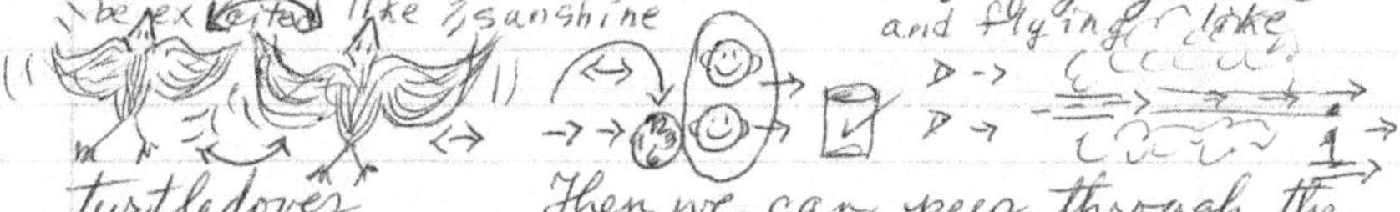

turtledoves Then we can peep through the
turtledoves Then we can peep through the

clouds like the sun's rays and show our
clouds like the sun's rays and show our

brotherly love
brotherly love

page 439 : page

86 Cool As A Cucumber 208

Cool As A Cucumber

I'm nobody's fool even though I've been Known to drool

I'm Nobody's fool even though I've been Known to drool

I'm just plain cool; I am a nerd all the way to school

I'm just plain cool; I am a nerd all the way to school

I'm not even a fool; when I put make-up on

I'm not even a fool; when I put make-up on

I can be a ghoul I won't break the golden rule

I can be a ghoul I won't break the golden rule

unless we are on that day called April Fool's

unless we are on that day called April Fool's

In fact, I'm as cool as a cucumber, so much so

In fact, I'm as cool as a cucumber, so much so

I've been Known to purr I promise I won't pull

I've been Known to purr I promise I won't pull

on you a dirty number Because on purpose

on you a dirty number Because on purpose

I'll go blank and I won't remember I do know
I'll go blank and I won't remember I do know

what I mean; do you get it, sir I'm very good
what I mean; do you get it, sir I'm very good

under pressure; so go ahead and lay on the
under pressure; so go ahead and lay on the

social slurs In fact, I get better and better
social slurs In fact, I get better and better,

when you lay on the spurs I'll be a virtual
when you lay on the spurs I'll be a virtual

trendsetter I'll be an action hero or an emperor
trendsetter I'll be an action hero or an emperor

I know what is right, down to the last letter I am
I know what is right, down to the last letter I am

aware of what should occur You can send me
aware of what should occur You can send me

any punch. Does that give you a hunch? I'm
any punch. Does that give you a hunch? I'm

not scared!
not scared
I'll eat it for lunch or maybe even for
I'll eat it for lunch or maybe even for
brunch
brunch
I won't even sweat when I'm in a crunch
I won't even sweat when I'm in a crunch
I'll be creative like Robert Munch
I'll be creative like Robert Munch
But I'll thank
But I'll thank
you afterwards a whole bunch
you afterwards a whole bunch
because I am really
because I am really
out to lunch
out to lunch
You see, I cannot feel any pain
You see, I cannot feel any pain
because I have chosen to abstain
because I have chosen to abstain
Life is just
Life is just
one glorious game
one glorious game
let's break out a bottle of
let's break out a bottle of
champagne
champagne
I won't be found to be lame
I won't be found to be lame
because secretly I'll have fortune and fame
because secretly I'll have fortune and fame
I'll
I'll

choose to play if I want, and if it's all the same
choose to play if I want, and if ... all the same

just take me out to the ball game It doesn't
just take me out to the ball game It doesn't

matter if there's a lot of danger I'll just bare
matter if there's a lot of danger I'll just bare

my fangs, and we'll see what else occurs And
my fangs, and we'll see what else occurs And

then I'll just lay on the spurs to my imaginary steed
then I'll just lay on the spurs to my imaginary steed

until we take off in a blur Then I'll just fry
until we take off in a blur Then I'll just

to look at you and continue to ride my steed
to look at you and continue to ride my steed

faster and faster I may be cool as a cucumber
faster and faster I may be cool as a cucumber

but I think I'm headed for disaster
but I think I'm headed for disaster

443: page

Still, I'm no fruit, and one way or another
Still, I'm no fruit, and one way or another,

I can be a real terror I even try to be a good
I can be a real terror I even try to be a good

person when there is trouble astir And my loved
person when there is trouble astir And my loved

ones you had better not bother because I can be
ones you had better not bother because I can be

one real mean mother Ah, such is the good
one real mean mother Ah, such is the good

life and who can beat the nightlife I try not to
life and who can beat the nightlife, I try not to

wince when I'm under the knife because they
wince when I'm under the knife because they

might slip and I might lose my life In fact
might slip and I might lose my life In fact

I try to enjoy what I can from my strife and I
I try to enjoy what I can from my strife and I

try to be a happy housewife I am just ordinary
try to be a happy house wife I am just ordinary

not anyone larger than life but I can say this
not anyone larger than life but I can say this

I am not related to the wildlife
I am not related to the wildlife

→ + + + → (−1 × −1) = +1

445 : page

87 Positive Reaction 210

Positive Reaction

Face it: be positive, and all will be well; no
Face it: be positive; and all will be well; no

one will be ringing your doorbell Ignore the
one will be ringing your doorbell Ignore the

negative and accentuate the positive, then
negative and accentuate the positive, then

everything will be swell Soon people will want
everything will be swell Soon people will want

what you have to sell and all will be well
what you have to sell and all will be well

They'll know you are good. Soon they will be
They'll know you are good. Soon they will be

able to tell this and it will be clear as a bell
able to tell this and it will be clear as a bell

You may imagine they mean you no harm, but
You may imagine they mean you no harm, but

one way or the other, chances are no one will
one way or the other chances are no one will

bother You will have to accept no one really
bother you will have to accept no one really

wishes to hurt you or really matters Even though
wishes to hurt you or really matters Even though

you can't win them all, Sometimes you will
you can't win them all, sometimes you will

get in hot water Chances are you will be safe and
get in hot water Chances are you will be safe and

glad and one couldn't be happier The
glad and one couldn't be happier The

more you put your good foot forward, the more
more you put your good foot forward, the more

you will be self-assured And the more power
you will be self-assured And the more power

there will be to your word until it is so good, it will
there will be to your word until it is so good, it will

be the password That's when you will really be
be the password That's when you will really be

heard word for word The truth is the best for
heard word for word The truth is the best for

this mama bird, this songbird, this
this mama bird, this songbird, this

hummingbird We are supposed to have a
humming bird We are supposed to have a

positive reaction like a brave lion Even when I
positive reaction like a brave lion Even when I

only get negative attention; I'm as persistant
only get negative attention I'm as persistant

as a spreading dandelion To avoid trouble, you
as a spreading dandelion To avoid. trouble, you

can pretend these is no dissension and slip away
can pretend there is no dissension and slip away

as fast as a sea lion Ends up, with me, I will
as fast as a sea lion Ends up, with me, I will

have plenty of recreation because → I like to play
have plenty of recreation because → I like to play

until I am in detention All is supposed to go positively
until I am in detention All is supposed to go positively

and all our kicks are for free I tend to agree
and all our kicks are for free I tend to agree

with you absolutely; I cannot disagree We must
with you absolutely; I cannot disagree We must

all agree resolutely; and then we will all
all agree resolutely; and then we will all

be home free Yes, sir, I agree; Indeed, so
be home free Yes, sir, I agree Indeed, so

much so I dare say I can give you my signed
much so I dare say I can give you my signed

guarantee We must always agree, or these
guarantee we must always agree, or these

will be hell to pay the differences will be like
will be hell to pay the diffences will be like

night and day You say we must be positive, OK,

night and day you say we must be positive, OK,

Then you will receive beautiful bouquets There

Then you will receive beautiful bouquets There

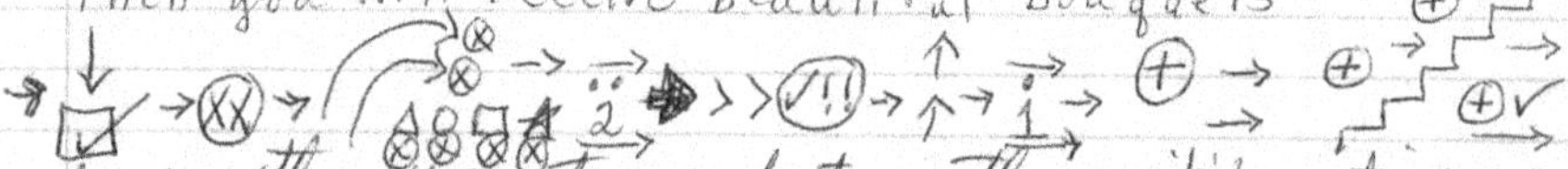

is no other way to go but up the positive stairway

is no other way to go but up the positive stairway

If you want to play, you must learn to obey

If you want to play, you must learn to obey

then you will make positive headway A positive

then you will make positive headway A positive

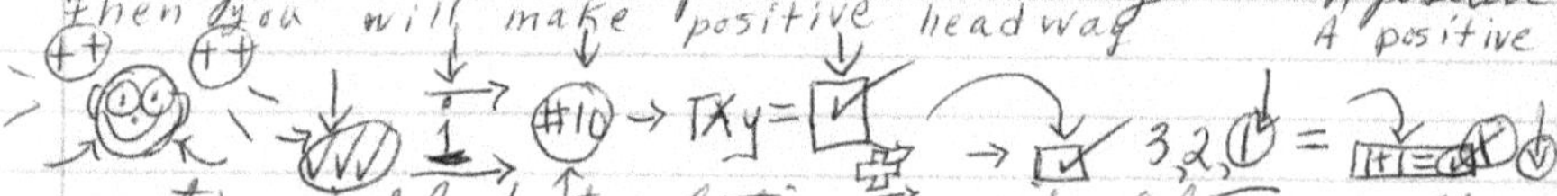

reaction is the best solution; it seldom results in

reaction the best solution; it seldom results in

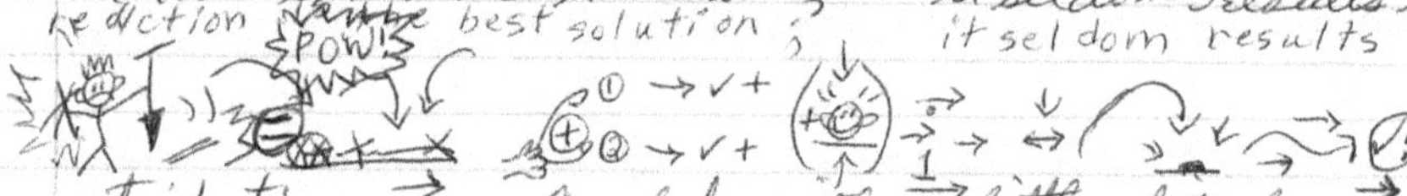

retribution Coupled with a little bit of

retribution Coupled with a little bit of

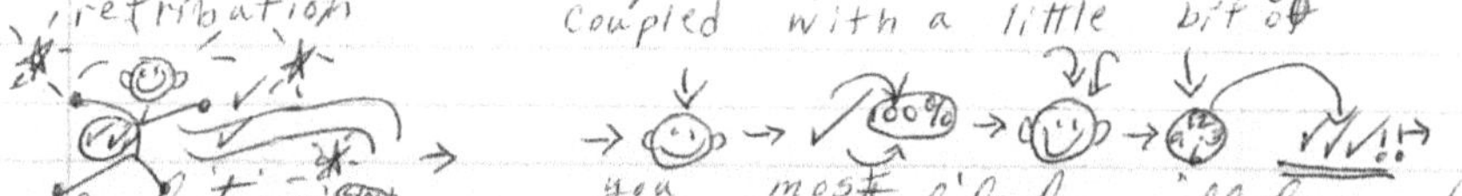

ambition you most likely will have

ambition you most likely will have

a successful accomplishment with a good vision

a successful accomplishment with a good vision

Otherwise you might face intimidation, failure,
Otherwise you might face intimidation failure,

and alienateon There must be some common
and alienation There must be some common

mediation in order to have a good
mediation in order to have a good

conclusion You must choose a safer position on
conclusion You must choose a safer position on

and on all around, a safer bastion
and on all around, a safer bastion

You'd better choose a positive reaction sothet
You'd better choose a positive so that

your ideas will come to fruition Or it may
your ideas will come to fruition Or it may

be your last attraction and You may end up
be your last attraction and you may end up

in traction Still it will be the best chosen plan
in traction Still it will be the best chosen plan

because it is based on a positive organization
because it is based on a positive organization

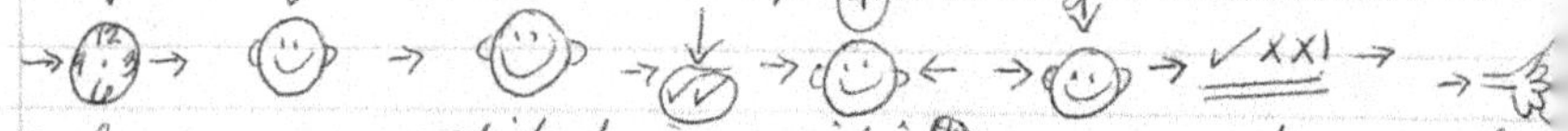

When your attitude us positive, you won't have
When you attitude is positive, you won't have

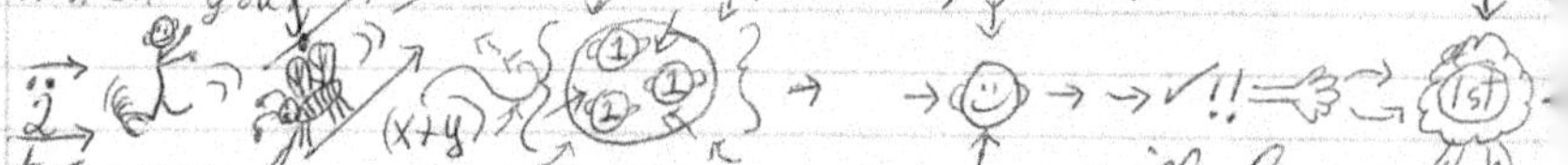

to run because everyone you will have won
to run because everyone you will have won

It means you truly believe, hon, because you
It means you truly believe, hon, because you

are sincere you have won It means there
are sincere you have won It means there

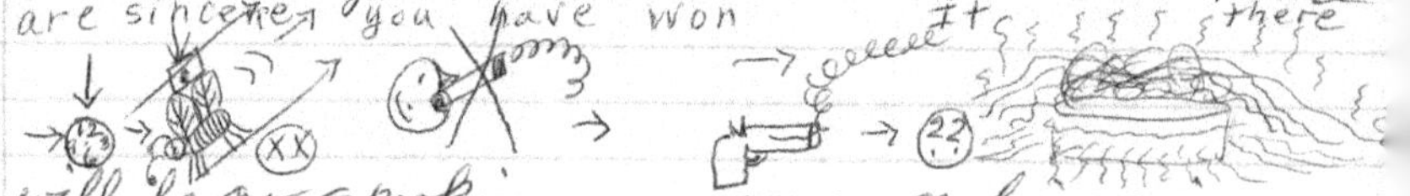

will be no smoking gun or lingering
will be no smoking gun or lingering

repercussions And I will not spoil anybody
repercussions And I will not spoil anybody

fun because we will all be playing together
fun because we will all be playing together

under the sun I'll like this answer and
under the sun I'll like this answer and

so will you Being positive will be nothing new
so will you Being positive will be nothing new

It doesn't have to be just for a chosen few In
It doesn't have to be just for a chosen few In

fact, it has been tried and proven to be true
fact, it has been tried and proven to be true

Being positive will prove to be fun and quite
Being positive will prove to be fun and quite

catchy It'll leave you happy, carefree, and
catchy It'll leave you happy, carefree, and

worry-free So come on, don't keep this
worry-free So come on, don't keep this

idea under lock and key Let yourself be
idea under lock and key Let yourself be

positive for the whole world to see
positive for the whole world to see

(88) Pray Pussy Riot But (213)

Pray Pussy Riot But

Not Too Hard

Not Too Hard

Now you've gone and done it, you have had your

NOW you've gone and done it, you have had your

little fits You had to go and do your little bit

little fits You had to go and do your little bit

Well, now you are it You should have tried

Well, now you are it you should have tried

instead to use a little of your wit And to stick that

instead to use a little of your wit And to stick that

idea inside your personal info kit No, you had to go

idea inside your personal info kit No, you had to go

and pretend to be a martyr Now you are in a whole

and pretend to be a martyr Now you are in a whole

lot of trouble, as it were But you knew the kind of

lot of trouble, as it were But you knew the kind of

trouble you'd be in for And you asked for it → and

trouble goat be in for And you asked for it →

boy did you get it and more
boy did you get it? and more
So now you have
So now you have

been incarcerated, prison baited
been incarcerated, prison baited
You have been
You have been

all but X-rated and excommunicated
all but X-rated and excommunicated
Truth is, now
Truth is, now

you are ill-fated and nearly gated
you are ill-fated and nearly gated
You will be
You will be

pondered on and greatly contemplated
pondered on and greatly contemplated
You may
You may

have been foolish and young
have been foolish and young
But now you are
But now you are

finished and undone
finished and undone
Your feats will not be unsung
Your feats will not be unsung

you have had your fun
you have had your fun
In fact, in principle,
In fact, in principle,

you have won
you have won
The road will now, for you, be very
The road will now, for you, be very

hard
hard

Sometimes that's the price you pay for
Sometimes that's the price you pay for

playing your cards
playing your cards

Chances are you'll survive
Chances are you'll survive

your prison yard
your prison yard

Someday you will be freed from
Some day you will be freed from

your torture ward
your torture ward

Afterwards, you will be tested
afterwards, you will be tested

in fire
in fire

And your fate will be put up for hire
And your fate will be put up for hire

Your strength will be in your great desire
Your strength will be in your great desire

To obtain
To obtain

your freedom
your freedom

one thinks you would never tire
one thinks you would never tire

Some may understand the ideas behind your band
Some may understand the ideas behind your band

Some may not think your ideas were quite so grand
Some may not think your ideas were quite so grand

Even though you live in a far away land Some may
Even though you live in a faraway land Some may

still choose to support you and give you a helping hand
still choose to support you and give you a helping hand

Some say you were very brave but maybe you were
some say you were very brave but may be you were

just foolish Think whichever way you may want
Just foolish Think whicherer way you may want

to take it, as you wish Because of your views, you
to take it, as you wish Because of your views, you

have been dealt life's cruel dish Now you must
have been dealt life's cruel dish Now you must

suck up the gruel and eat a piece of fish
suck up the gruel and eat a piece of fish

89 # Neighbors 215

457 page

Neighbors

If I were a little square box and I lived next door
If I were a little square box and I lived next door

I would hear funny things filter through the floor
I would hear fanny things filter through the floor

Sometimes I may even hear loud, noisy snores
Sometimes I may even hear load, noisy snores

You might say we had our own private cold war
You might say we had our own private cold war

Our radio signals would travel up high, no lie
Our radio signals would travel up high, no lie

They would go uninterrupted through the sky
They would go uninterrupted through the sky

Luckily for us if we told no lies and we gave up
Lackily for us if we told no lies and we gave up

no surprise But sometimes they were scrambled
no surprise But sometimes they were scrambled

by the neighbor guy Funny things happen next door
by the neighbor gay Funny things happen next door

we were never bored We never knew what was
we were never bored We never knew what was

next in store Except our neighbors bugged us more
next in store Except our neighbors bugged us more

and more They didn't know what the concept
and more They didn't know what the concept

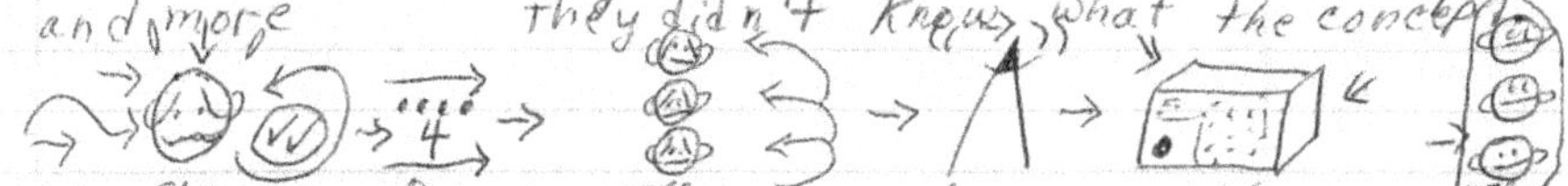

of pity was for They were keen machines They
of pity was for They were keen machines They

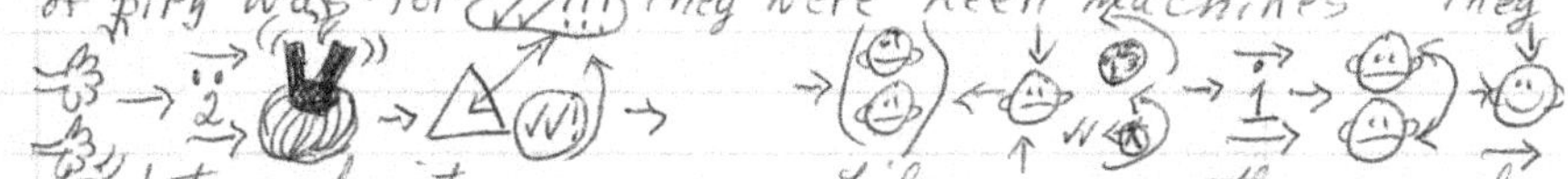

tried to make it seem Like we were the ones who
tried to make it seem Like we were the ones who

were awful and mean They got lots of bullies
were awful and mean They got lots of bullies

on their team they were hungry and lean
on their team they were hungry and lean

Their cruelty was sharp and keen we had
Their cruelty was sharp and keen we had

scars where they had been Their hearts were
scars where they had been Their hearts were

filled with hate! they let their hate out of the gate
filled with hate! they let their hate out of the gate

They cared not what was on our plate They made our
They cared not what was on our plate They made our

situation a miserable fate They cared not
situation a miserable fate They cared not

that we were in a desperate state It was all we
that we were in a desperate state It was all we

could do to prove our innocence Even with
could do to prove our innocence Even with

the truth they showed us insolence Our innocence
the truth they showed us insolence Our innocence

to them was but a mere pittance All they wanted
to them was but a mere pittance All they wanted

was to be able to say "Good-bye. Good
was to be able to say "Good-bye. Good

riddance." They wanted to be the first to
riddance." They wanted to be the first to

cause our demise
cause our demise
We were enemies through
we were enemies through
their eyes
their eyes
They were fast to make up falsehood
They were fast to make up falsehood
and lies
and lies
We didn't give in or let our reactions rise
We didn't give in or let our reactions rise
Now we're gone and it's all in the
Now we're gone and it's all in the
past; everything
past; everything
is made fast
is made fast
Some of us come in late; some of us
Some of us come in late some of us
come in last
come in last
But no matter what my station or caste
But no matter what my station or caste
I will always say this full blast
I will always say this full blast
My family
My family
will always come first; of
will always come first; of
that, I won't be
that, I won't be
outclassed
outclassed

451 : page

(90) Who, You, And Me (217)

who, you And Me

You Jest

You Jest

Hey You — You and me. You jest. That's not funny

Hey You — you and me. You jest. That's not funny

You there, you Playboy bunny; keep your money

You there, you Playboy bunny keep your money

Your skies may not always be clear and sunny

Your skies may not always be clear and sunny

Do you think you will always have a new honey?

Do you think you will always have a new honey?

Even though you travel near and far

Even though you travel near and far

And you have a very fancy, expensive car

And you have a very fancy, expensive car

That doesn't make you an automatic star

That doesn't make you an automatic star

So you can get right back into your

So you can get right back into your

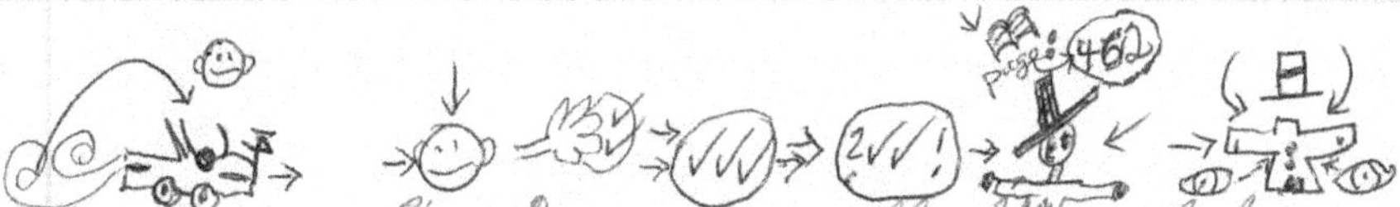

Jaguar You have some really fancy-looking
Jaguar You have some really fancy-looking

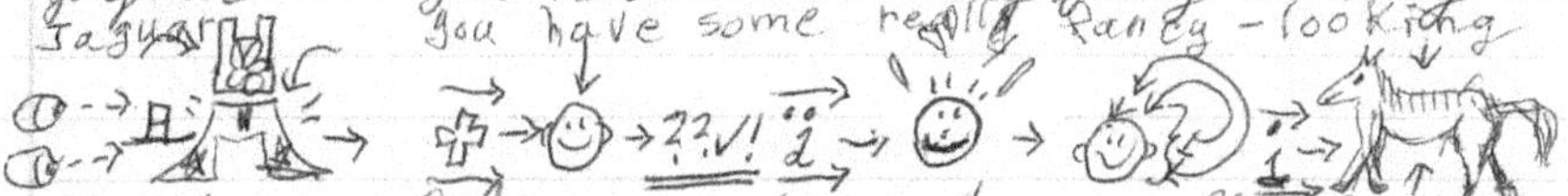

threads And you seem to consider yourself a thoroughbred
threads And you seem to consider yourself a thoroughbred

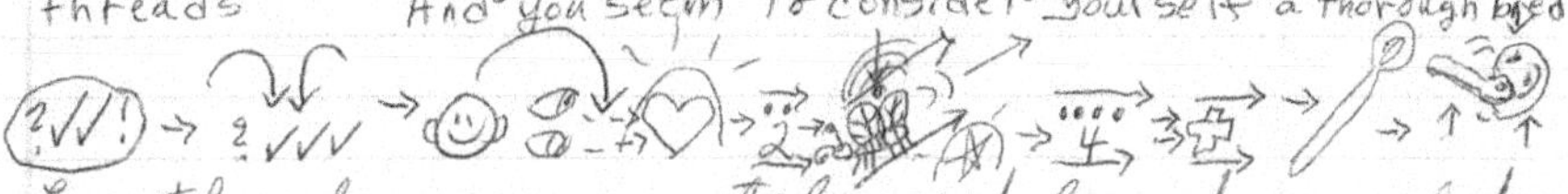

Even though you appear to be cared for and spoon fed
Even though you appear to be cared for and spoon fed

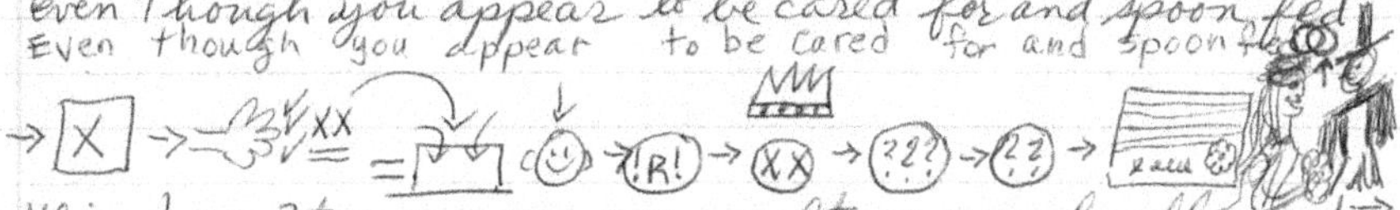

This doesn't mean you are royalty or even legally wed
This doesn't mean you are royalty or even legally wed

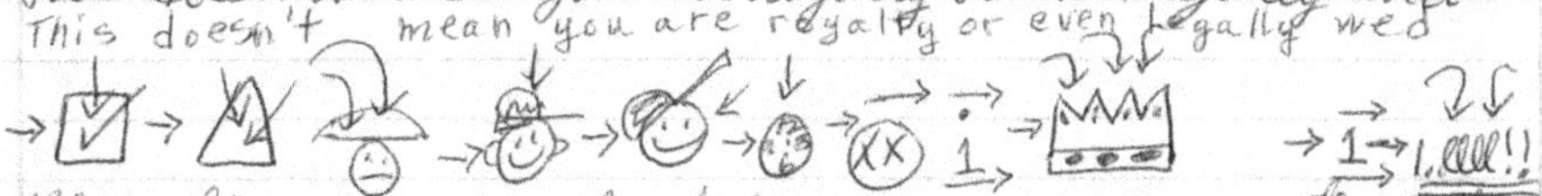

That thing on your head is not a crown The fact
That thing on your head is not a crown The fact

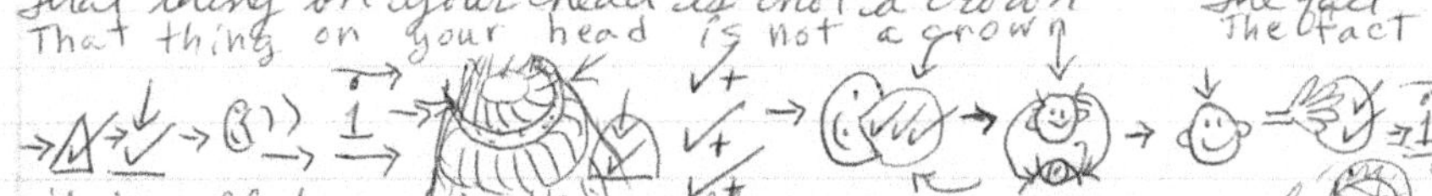

it is called a tiara is well-known I see you have a
it is called a tiara is well-known I see you have a

very large bill for your phone I think your operation's
very large bill for your phone I think your operation's

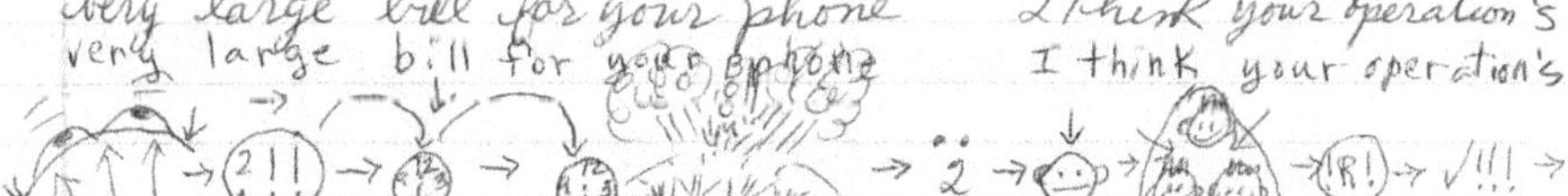

cover may have been blown To you, men are just
cover may have been blown To you, men are just

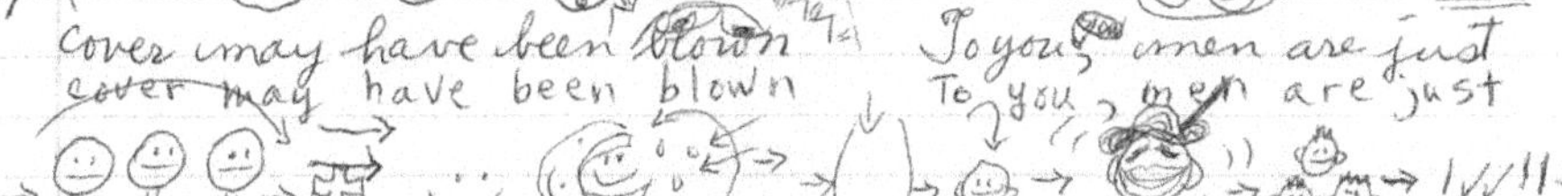

suckers and easy prey With your charms, they usually
suckers and easy prey With your charm, they usually

do what you say You tempt them with various types of
do what you say you tempt them with various types of

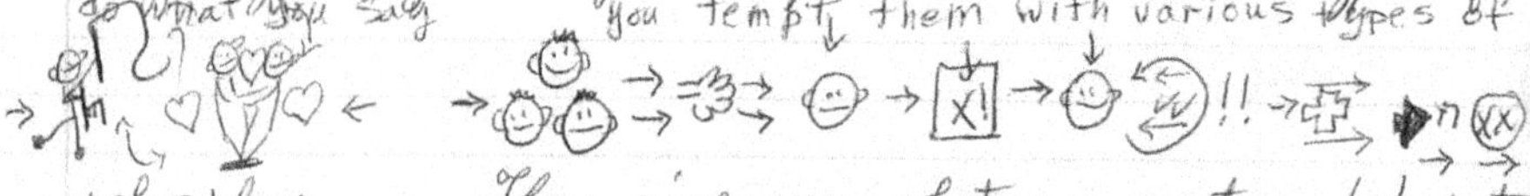

role-play They give you what you want and do not
role play They give you what you want and do not

refuse to pay You work both in the day and during
refuse to pay you work both in the day and during

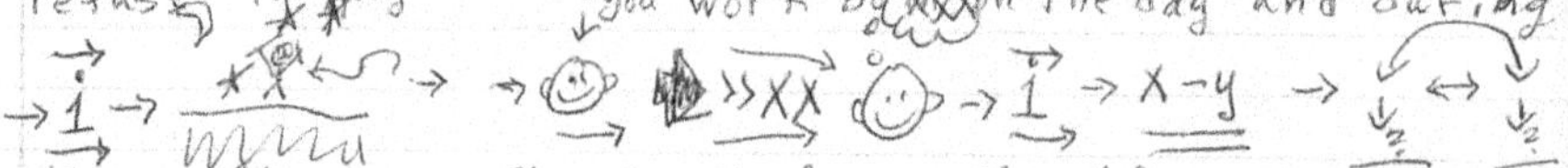

the night You don't know the difference between
the night you don't know the difference between

wrong and right You think all your alibis are
wrong and right you think all your alibis are

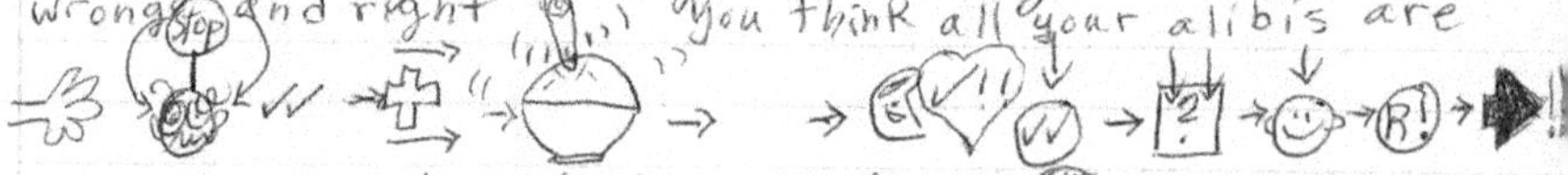

foolproof and airtight Truth is, what you are doing
fool proof and airtight Truth is, what you are doing

proves you aren't too bright Sooner or later, you
proves you aren't too bright Sooner or later, you

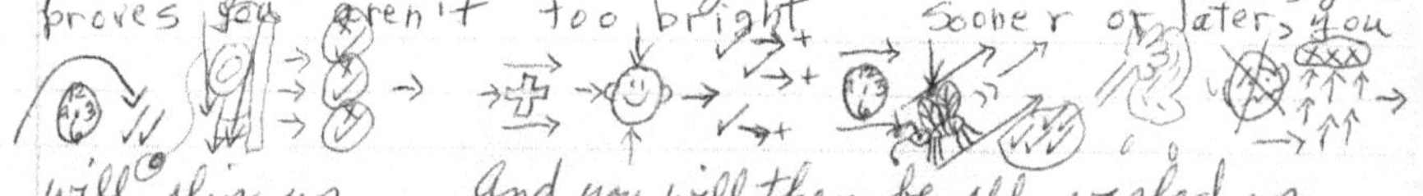

will slip up And you will then be all washed up
will slip up And you will then be all washed up

You will have a different kind of dressup When they
You will have a different kind of dressup When they

put you into a police lineup The thing that clinches
put you into a police lineup The thing that clinches

it and puts you on the hook Is that psychedelic
it and puts you on the hook Is that psychedelic

phone number and address book With names and
phone number and address book With names and

numbers, it proves you to be a crook You could
numbers, it proves you to be a crook You could

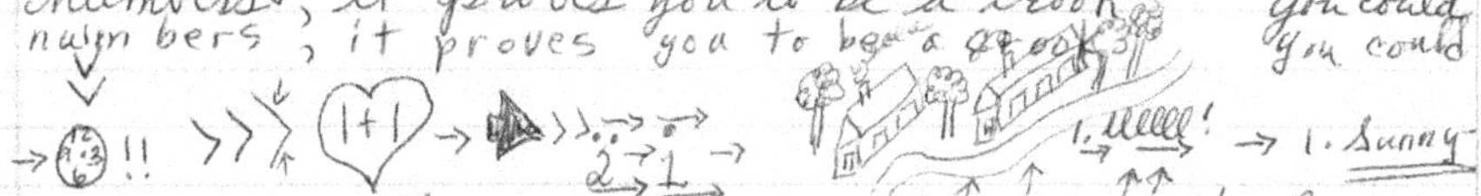

now very easily go to a farm named Sunny
now very easily go to a farm named Sunny

→ Brook!

Brook
Brook

465 page

(91) Don't Hesitate (219)

Don't Hesitate

Don't hesitate, Take the time to create Don't hesitate.
Don't hesitate, Take the time to create Don't hesitate

Be the first one out of the gate Don't hesitate or you
Be the first one out of the gate Don't hesitate or you

might find yourself late Don't hesitate, You don't
might find yourself late Don't hesitate, You don't

have to wait The best thing you can do is to have a
have to wait The best thing you can do is to have a

course of action That is the best way to get a positive
course of action That is the best way to get a positive

reaction The faster you get out of the gate, the greater
reaction The faster you get out of the gate, the greater

the recognition If you don't hesitate, you will have
the recognition If you don't hesitate, you will have

a successful mission And being sure of you is the
a successful mission And being sure of you is the

page 466

best way — This is bound to bring you a big bouquet — It
best way — This is bound to bring you a big bouquet — It

will also help you in your day to day — And you won't
will also help you in your day to day — And you won't

have time to mold and decay — The sooner you decide
have time to mold and decay — The sooner you decide

to do it, the better — Sometimes doing it faster is
to do it, the better — Sometimes doing it faster is

what I prefer — Doing well now may prevent a devastating
what I prefer — Doing well now may prevent a devastating

war — It'll keep us all going at an even purr.
war — It'll keep us all going at an even purr.

Let it be an instant reaction — Then there need be no
Let it be an instant reaction — Then there need be no

restrictions — Being spontaneous should be your
restrictions — Being spontaneous should be your

conviction — It's bound to take you to a good destination
conviction — It's bound to take you to a good destination

When you really want something to happen Go for it and then
When you really want something to happen Go for it and then

you will not offend Your decision you will be able to defend
you will not offend your decision you will be able to defend

And you will be safe again and again They say the best
And you will be safe again and again They say the best

things come to those who wait I say those people are the
things come to those who wait I say those people are the

ones who are too late All they manage to do is hesitate
ones who are too late All they manage to do is hesitate

Waiting will always be their fate Now when it comes
Waiting will always be their fate Now when it comes

to choosing your mate Be a little choosy; don't settle
to choosing your mate Be a little choosy; don't settle

for a secound rate Then when you're sure, don't be
for a secound rate Then when you're sure, don't be

left at the plate Strike when the iron is hot, Don't
left at the plate Strike when the iron is hot Don't

hesitate   Never wait to show your love   Do you see that
hesitate   Never wait to show your love   Do you see that

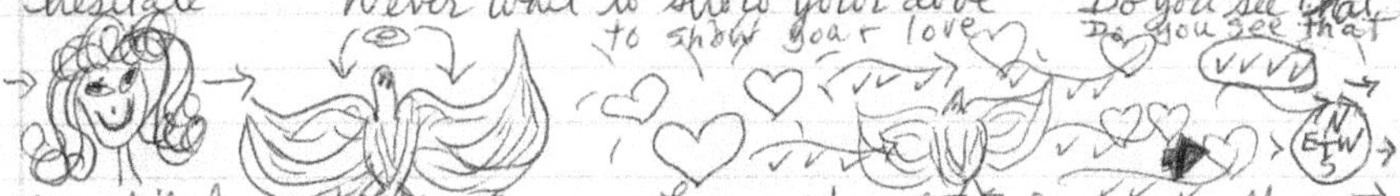

beautiful turtledove?   Love guides his wings go all over,
beautiful turtledove?   Love guides his wings go all over,

below and above   And he never wastes time to hesitate
below and above   And he never wastes time to hesitate

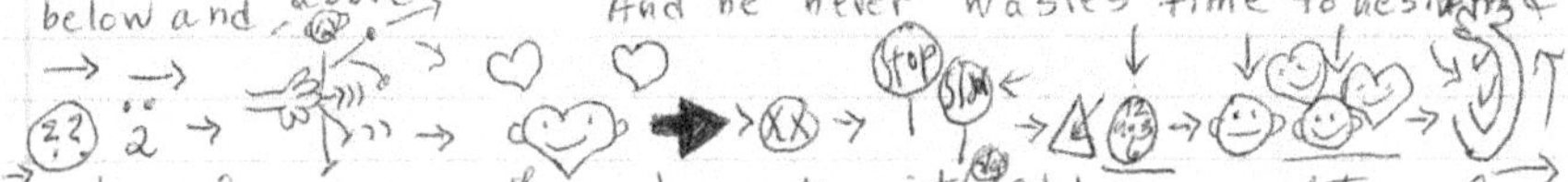

or to shove   Love doesn't wait, It's your fate   Come
or to shove   Love doesn't wait, It's your fate   Come

on, don't hesitate   Come on, jump out of the gate
on, don't hesitate   Come on, jump out of the gate

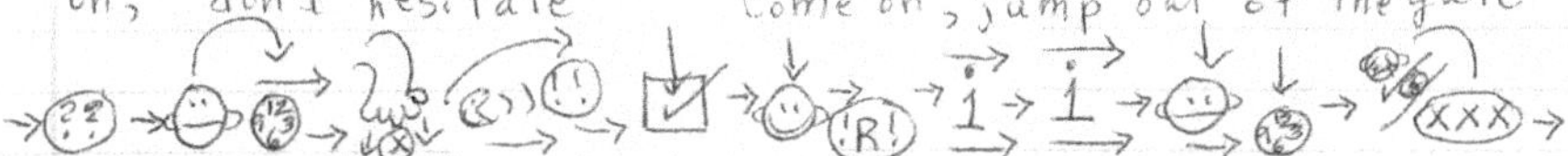

Or you'll find out that you are the one who islate
Or you'll find out that you are the one who is late

You must first make up your mind   That is the
You must first make up your mind   That is the

most important rule line   That accomplishment
most important rule line   That accomplishment

you mustn't shirk or decline   You must continue
you mustn't shirk or decline   You must continue

on, rain or shine If you choose the proper course of
on, rain or shine If you choose the proper course of

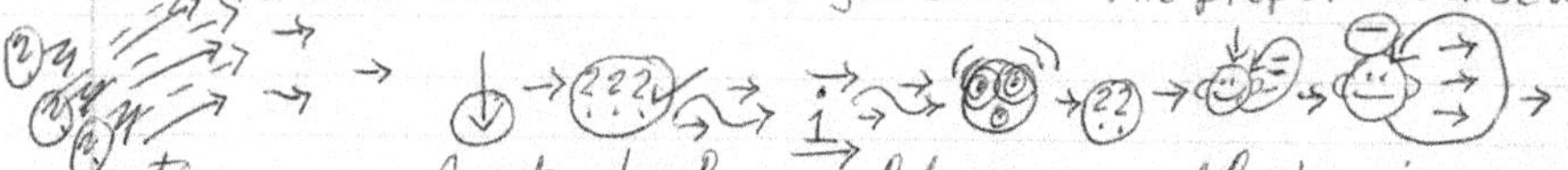

action Instead of one of fear or self denying
action Instead of one of fear or self-denying

Your heart will then feel as strong as a lion It
Your heart will then feel as strong as a lion It

may even prevent you from dying
may even prevent you from dying

470 page

(92) The Way It Is (221)

The Way It Is

You and I will always wonder
You and I will always wonder

If life is some kind
If life is some kind

of fantastic blunder
of fantastic blunder

Or is it all just a hazy
Or is it all just a hazy

lazy blur
Lazy blur

Truth is, that's the way it is, sir
Truth is, that's the way it is, sir

Is that drink really yours?
Is that drink really yours?!

Is that a fresh bottle
Is that a fresh bottle

of Coors?
of Coors?

There is no need to open your doors
There is no need to open your doors

You
You

reek as you speak, more and more
reek as you speak, more and more

Big, bad daddy, me
Big, bad daddy, me

oh my
oh my

Is it true you are a very mean guy?
Is it true, you are a very mean guy?

When you are drunk and all pie-eyed?
When you are drunk and all pie-eyed?

You say
You say

that is just the way it is", that's why Truth is no one
cares any more If you stay, or if you walk out that door
Especially, when you have become the world's
number 1 boor But I tell you, you'll never
know what's next for you or what's in store
Some may wonder why your life occurs in this
way or in that way Sometimes life isn't fair,
with no room to play And pain is happening to
us day after day That's the way it is, that's all

we can say Well, now that we all know the score
we can say Well, now that we all know the score

We'll be able to continue to learn more We'll be
We'll be able to continue to learn more We'll be

able to comprehend what's in store That's just the
able to comprehend what's in store That's just the

way it is and that's what it's for Life isn't just
way it is and that's what it's for Life isn't just

a lot of pain Most times there is a lot to gain The
a lot of pain Most times there is a lot to gain The

answer is clear and plain Just try not to complain and
answer is clear and plain Just try not to complain and

take the time to use your brain We can help each other
take the time to use your brain We can help each other

to draw the line We can give each other a simple peace sign
to draw the line We can give each other a simple peace sign

The almighty dollar is really the danger sign That's the way it is, come
The almighty dollar is really the danger sign That's the way it is, come

rain or ~~shine~~
rain or shine

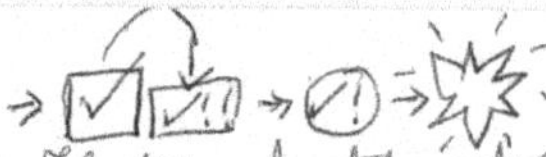

93 That's Just Great 223

That's Just Great

473 page

I say that's just great Still I must hesitate Until I find

I say that's just great Still I must hesitate Until I find

out my fate Until I have more of my life on my plate

out my fate Until I have more of my life on my plate

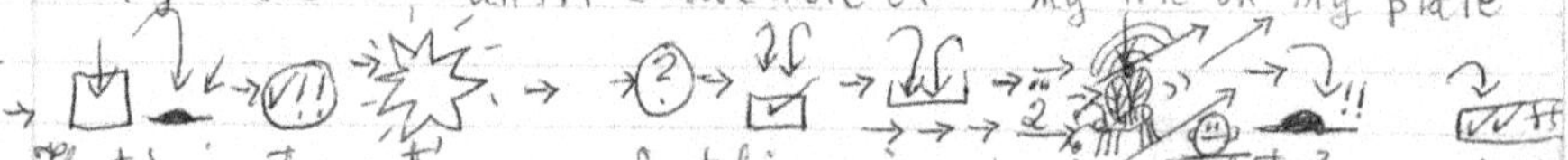

That's just great Is this going to be my fate? Right

That's just great Is this going to be my fate? Right

now, I have a splitting headache I guess I will just have

now, I have a splitting headache I guess I will just have

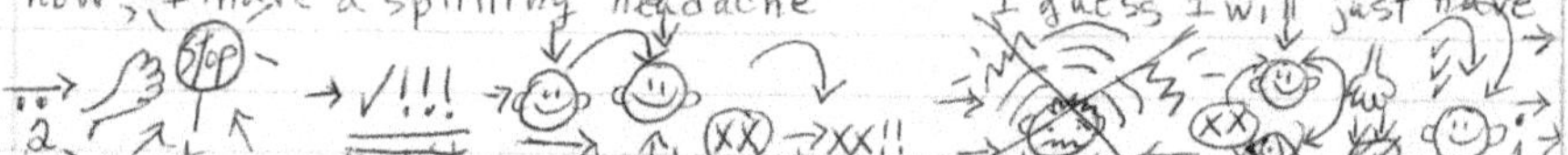

to wait Until my head no longer pulsates

to wait Until my head no longer pulsates

I've had a

I've had a

grand good time I've lived a long, long time line My

grand good time I've lived a long, long time line My

life has been good. It has been fine You could say

life has been good. It has been fine You could say

I have lived on cloud nine I'll follow through and

I have lived on cloud nine I'll follow through and

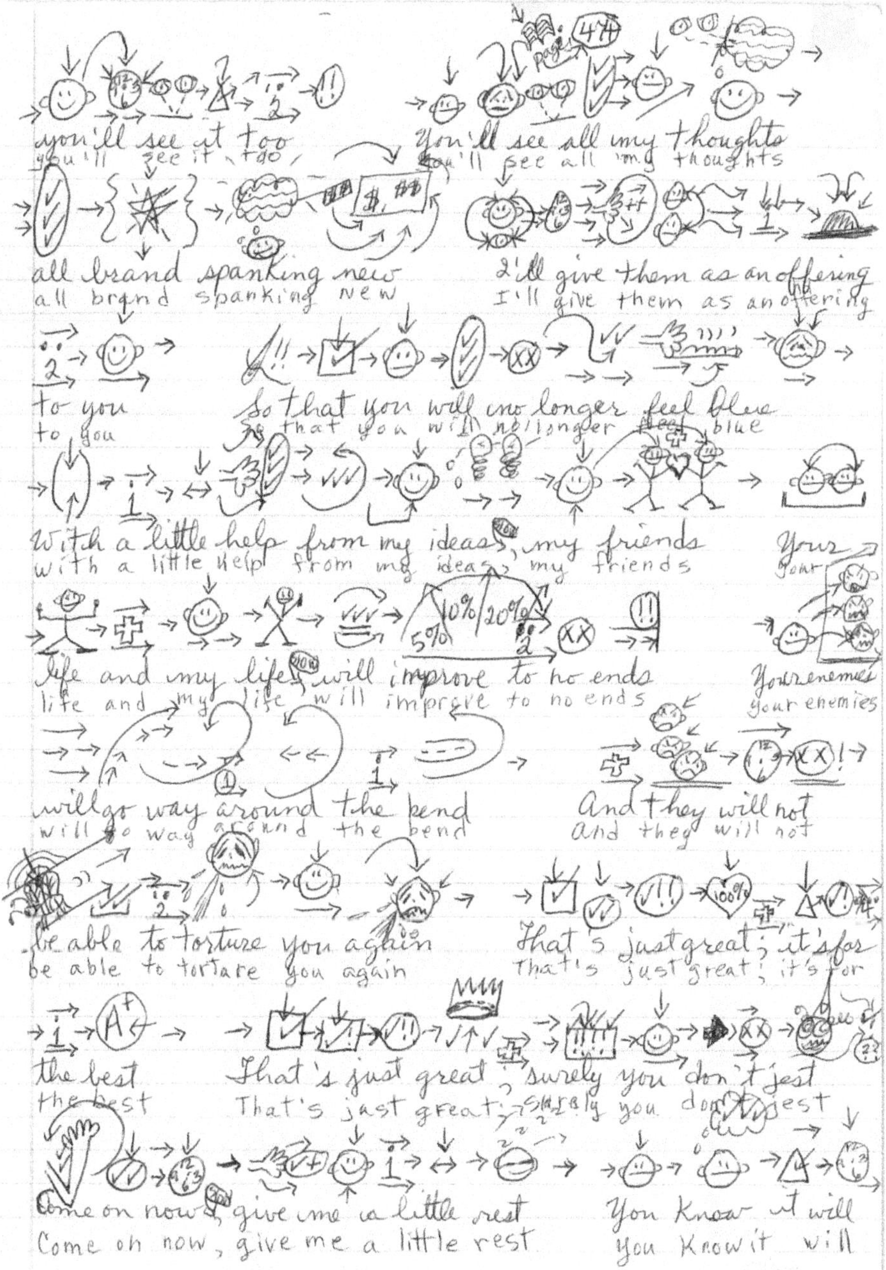
you'll see it too
You'll see all my thoughts
all brand spanking new
I'll give them as an offering
to you
So that you will no longer feel blue
With a little help from my ideas, my friends
Your
life and my life will improve to no ends
Your enemies
will go way around the bend
And they will not
be able to torture you again
That's just great; it's for
the best
That's just great; surely you don't jest
Come on now, give me a little rest
You know it will

be all for the best
be all for the best

You might say peace and quiet is
you might say peace and quiet is

my quest
my quest

This gives time for my thoughts to process
This gives time for my thoughts to process

And gives fear time to shrink and regress
And gives fear time to shrink and regress

it also
it also

gives problems time to get back and to repress
gives probbems! time to get back and to repress

That's just great I'll sit and wait I'll just sit down
That is just great I'll sit and wait just sit down

until I feel great I'll say it's been well worth
until I feel great I'll say it's been well worth

the hesitate
the hesitate

476 : Page

(94) I Smell Success (225)

I Smell Success

I smell success at its very best
I smell success at its very best
Success is a well-
Success is a well-
played game of chess
played game of chess
Success is when life has
Success is when life has
been put to the test
been put to the test
And the outcome is successful
And the outcome is successful
and is a real bless
and is a real bless
Success will ring a bell,
Success will ring a bell,
do tell
do tell
Success will have a certaingel, hard sell
Success will have a certain gel, hard sell
Everyone will begin to know it oh so well
Every one will begin to know it oh so well
Then
Then
success will have
success will have
a fragrant, sweet smell
a fragrant, sweet smell
Then the universe will seem to be a small place
Then the universe will seem to be a small place

And no matter where we are We'll be able to see
And no matter where we are We'll be able to see
each other's face The smell of it will take on a
each other's face The smell of it will take on a
new meaning, a new taste It will be the very best
new meaning, a new taste It will be the very best
scenario, the very best case Then there will be no
scenario, the very best case Then there will be no
expensive fee There will be no cost, you see, it will
expensive fee There will be no cost, you see, it will
be free It will be the faith we all have in you and me
be free It will be the faith we all have in you and me
It will be the way it was and is supposed to be
It will be the way it was and is supposed to be
Success is a sure bet Success is easier yet
Success is a sure bet Success is easier yet
Than anything you might have met What you see is
Than anything you might have met What you see is

479 page

It comes fast, it comes cheek to cheek; you'll be
It comes fast, it comes cheek to cheek; you'll be

on the hot seat Success is also intended for
on the hot seat Success is also intended for

the mild and the meek Success is coming soon,
the mild and the meek Success is coming soon,

this very week turn on the stove and put on the
this very week turn on the stove and put on the

heat
heat

page 480

(95) Fifty-Five Or Something (227)

Fifty-Five Or Something

Where do I begin? Let's see, here's the spin I have
where do I begin? Let's see, here's the spin I have
a large grin, but I may be a has been I have fair
a large grin, but I may be a has been I have fair
skin, which I do not consider ca sin And I am a
skin, which I do not consider a sin And I am a
graduate of fifty-five or something I kind of like
gradugte of fifty-five or something I kind of like
being in my own boat Even though I no longer fit
being in my own boat Even though I no longer fit
my old coat I know as long as I am alive there
my old coats I know as long as I am alive there
is still hope By the way I am still as strong as
is still hope By the way I am still as strong as
an oak I can still boogie like the best I
an oak I can still boogie like the best I

sometimes barely need any rest Go ahead; get it off of
Some times barely need any rest Go ahead; get it off of

your chest la la! Come on, I dare you, give me a test
Your chest Come on, I dare you, give ~~me~~ a test

la la la!

I can sing too; I'll knock off the roof You can say I'm
I can sing too; I'll Knock off the roof You can say I'm

quite social, never aloof Sometimes I act like quite
quite special, never aloof Some times I act like quite

a goof I like to shock you, and then I will go "poof"
a goof I like to shock you, and then I will go "poof"

You might say that I am so very wise I've got being
You might say that I am so very wise I've got being

nice right down to a franchise You might also say
nice right down to a franchise You might also say

that I own the clear, blue skies Especially—that is,
that I own the clear, blue skies Especially—that is,

when I cross my eyes I can give anyone a good fight
when I cross my eyes I can give anyone a good fight

page: 482

So you had better treat me right And oh, did I tell you,
So you had better treat me right And oh, did I tell you,

I bite Oh, now the truth comes into the light
I bite Oh, now the truth comes into the light

So now you can lift up your little white hanky
So now you can lift up your little white hanky

And you can confirm you are long and lanky Then
And you can confirm you are long and lanky Then

I may or may not give you a spanking, we'll see
I may or may not give you a spanking, we'll see

Because I would much rather practise on you
Because I would much rather practise on you

with my superior abilities And when I die I
with my superior abilities And when I die I

will have to stay still, me oh my They'll find
will have to stay still, me oh my They'll find

out for sure that I am not a guy And I will no
out for sure that I am not a guy And I will no

longer be able to resist or defy

longer be able to resist or defy

you; I tell you no lie

you; I tell you no lie

Of this I promise

Of this I promise

484 page

(96) I Just Made Myself Angry 229

I Just Made Myself Angry

No, I didn't just go and take a Benny I just went
No, I didn't just go and take a Benny I just went
and made myself angry No, it's not because of
and made myself angry No, it's not because of
you, honey And yes, it is not very funny Take
you, honey And yes, it is not very funny Take
my advice, take it from me, Hissy fits come
my advice, take it from me, Hissy fits come
cheap; they come for free My dad used to take
cheap; they come for free My dad used to take
me over his knee No matter what was my excuse
me over his knee No matter what was my excuse
or what was my plea? So I would run far, far
or what was my plea? So I would run far, far
away And find a private place to play Oh, those
away And find a private place to play Oh, those

were quiet, happy days Then I was satisfied
were quiet, happy days Then I was satisfied

You might say When I dared to come back I
You might say When I dared to come back I

usually could see where I lacked I would be ready
usually could see where I lacked I would be ready

for the next attack You might say I could I had
for the next attack You might say I could I had

eyes behind my back I became very, very efficient
eyes behind my back I became very, very efficient

Especially when I had a witness You see I acted
Especially when I had a witness You see I acted

very innocent Because I was quite sincere and
very innocent Because I was quite sincere and

it worked like nobody's business I was quite
it worked like nobody's business I was quite

studious and very industrious Even though my
studious and very industrious Even though my

enemies were very hideous No matter how they
enemies were very hideous No matter how they

interfered and were curious I always left them
interfered and were curious I always left them

feeling quite dubious I had my craft down
feeling quite dubious I had my craft down

to an art I managed to control myself at work
to an art I managed to control myself at work

Even when I dropped my dish cart I knew better
Even when I dropped my dish cart I knew better

than to lose control and start Even when my
than to lose control and start Even when my

blood pressure went higher I knew my own heart's
blood pressure went higher I knew my own heart's

desire Somehow I avoided burning myself in hellfire
desire Somehow I avoided burning myself in hell fire

No one was going to make me into a liar I could
No one was going to make me into a liar I could

however let myself perspire When I did, I turned
however let myself perspare When I did, It turned

myself on fire Because when I got angry I
myself on fire Because when I got angry I

could get myself out of any mire It helps when you
could get myself out of any mire It helps when you

use your own personal hot wire I'd say this
use your own personal hot wire I'd say this

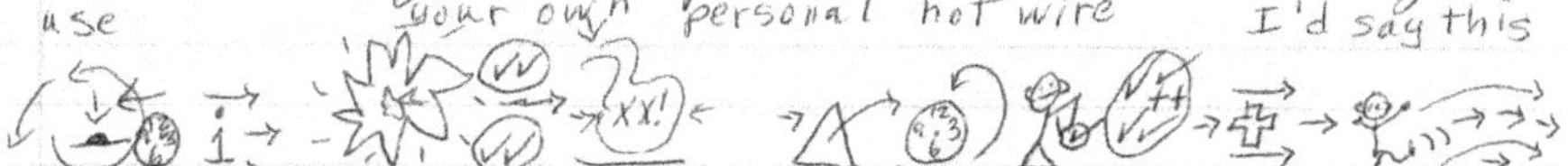

was an effective ruse It was useful and proceeded
was an effective rase It was useful and proceeded

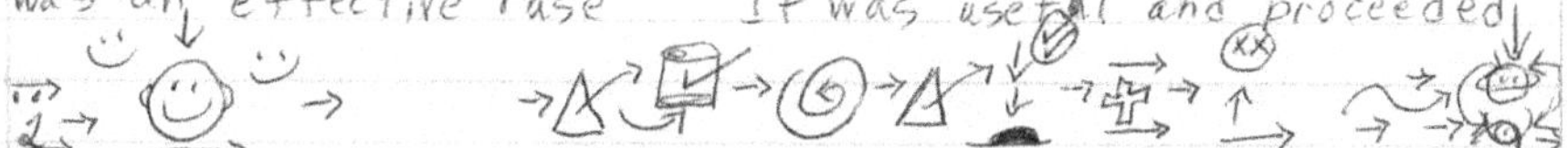

to amuse It can turn it on and off as I
to amuse It can turn it on and off as I

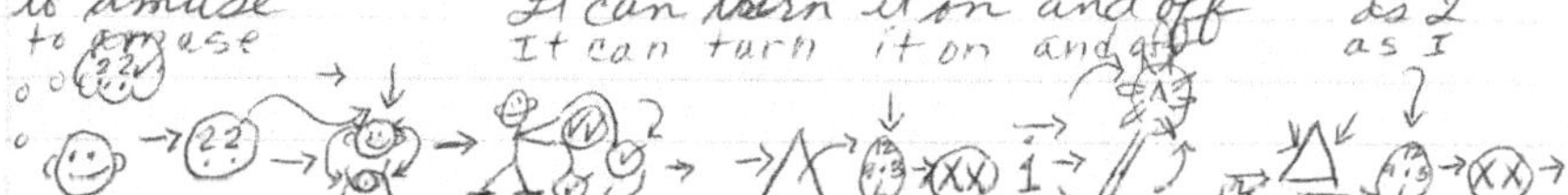

wish or as I choose It isn't a weapon; it isn't
wish or as I choose It isn't a weapon; it isn't

bad news I got good at turning it on and off
bad news I got good at turning it on and off

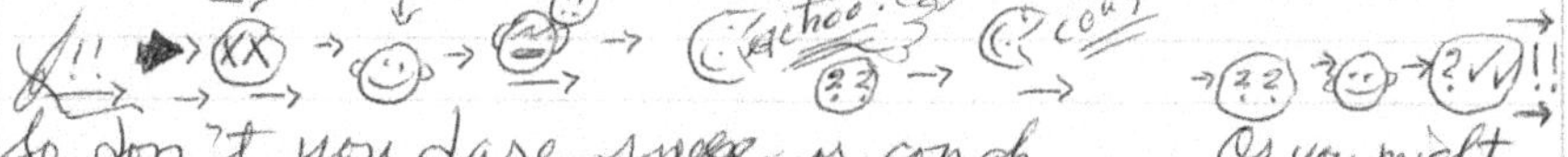

So don't you dare sneeze or cough Or you might
So don't you dare sneeze or cough Or you might

488 page

find the going a little rough And if you
find the going a little rough And if you

happen to get mad I'll call your bluff
happen to get mad I'll call your bluff

That's when the going is bound to get hot
That's when the going is bound to get hot

Because when I blow my top What's left
Because when I blow my top What's left

won't be a whole lot I'll disappear and I
won't be a whole lot I'll disappear and I

won't be caught
won't be caught

97 I Have No Fear 231
I Have No Fear

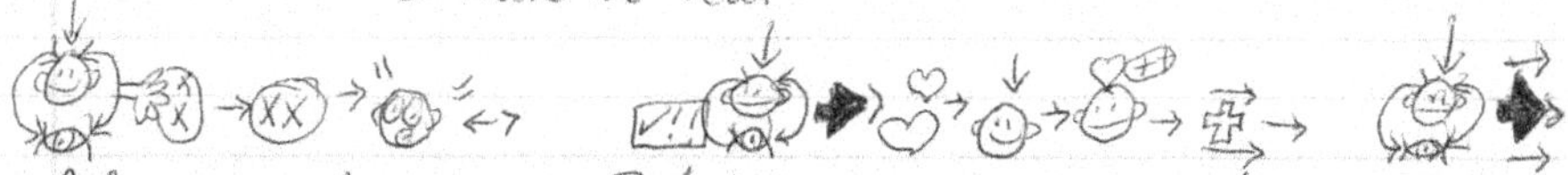

I have no fear But I do love you dear and 2 do
I have no fear But I do love you dear and I do

not feel queer I am positive and find it quite clear
not feel queer I am positive and find it quite clear

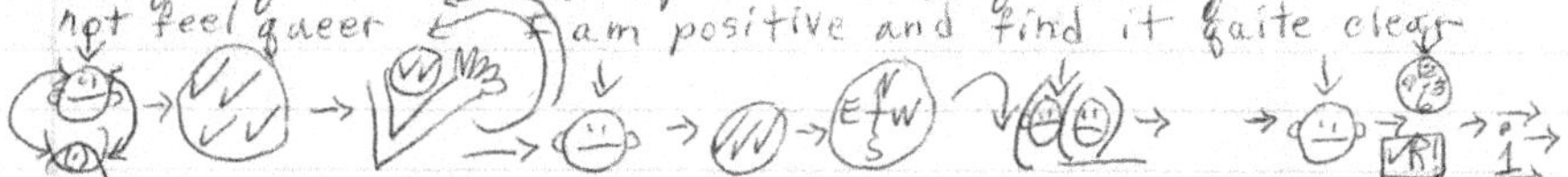

I always wanted you somewhere near You are the
I always wanted you somewhere near You are the

reason for my every season And the reason for my
reason for my every season And the reason for my

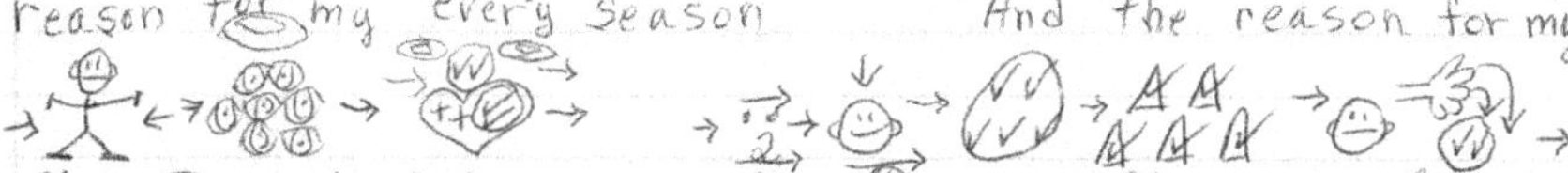

living, God willing To me, many things you have
living, God willing To me, many things you have

given You have given me love for my pleasing
given You have given me love for my pleasing

all the melodies and music I hear Is dedicated
All the melodies and music I hear Is dedicated

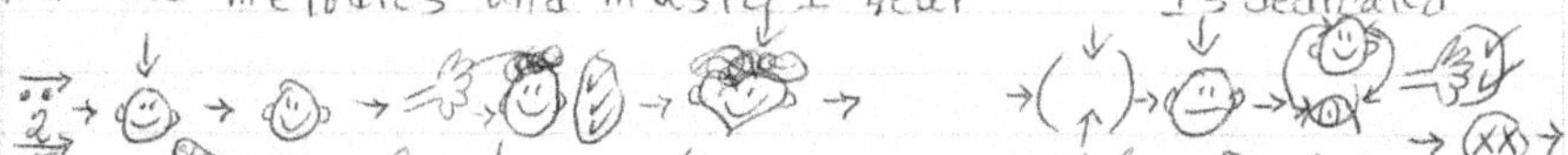

to you, my handsome dear With you, I have no
to you, my handsome dear With you, I have no

fear; When I'm with you, I feel normal and I
fear; When I'm with you, I feel normal and I

love to have you near I love you, you are my only
love to have you near I love you, you are my only

man Now I have fully come to understand
man Now I have fully come to understand

When I love you, you give me a helping hand
When I love you, you give me a helping hand

You lift me up and make me feel grand I Know
You lift me up and make me feel grand I Know

if the sky falls in the long haul I will hear your
if the sky falls in the long haul I will hear your

voice call like a bird call You make me feel
voice call like a bird call You make me feel

a thousand feet tall And I will not have a
a thousand feet tall And I will not have a

reason to fear at all When I'm away from you
reason to fear at all When I'm away from you

all the more I love you It proves I can't help but love
all the more I love you It proves I can't help but love

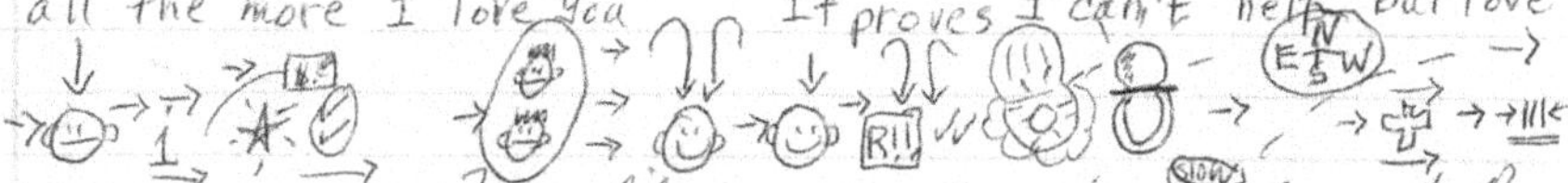

you anew Men like you are precious, far and few
you anew Men like you are precious, far and few

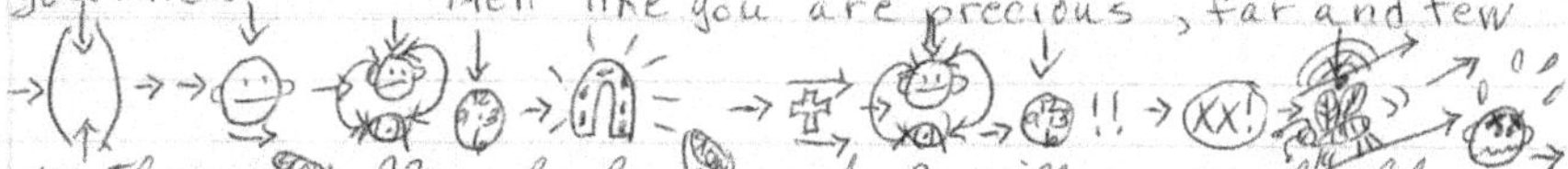

With you, I'm lucky, and I will never be blue
with you, I'm lucky, and I will never be blue

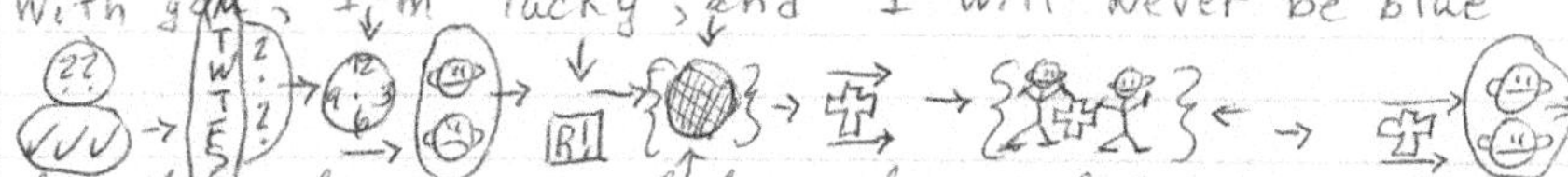

Someday when we are whole and complete And we
Someday when we are whole and complete And we

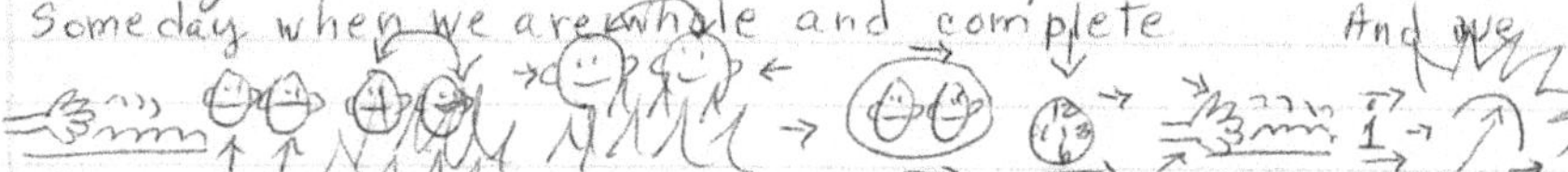

feel each other's heat We will feel the greatest
feel each other's heat we will feel the greatest

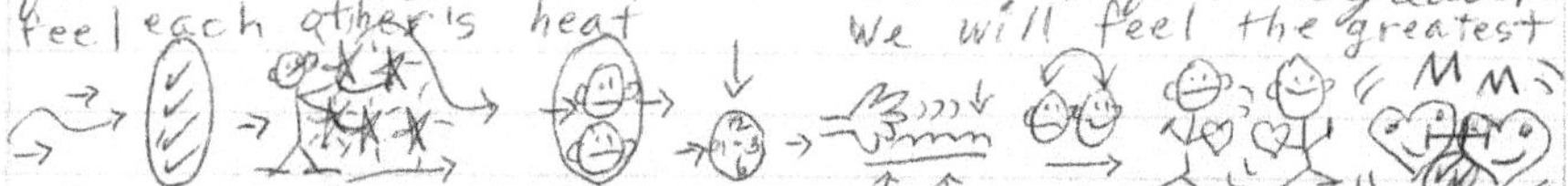

of all feats We will feel each other's heartbeats
of all feats we will feel each other's heartbeats

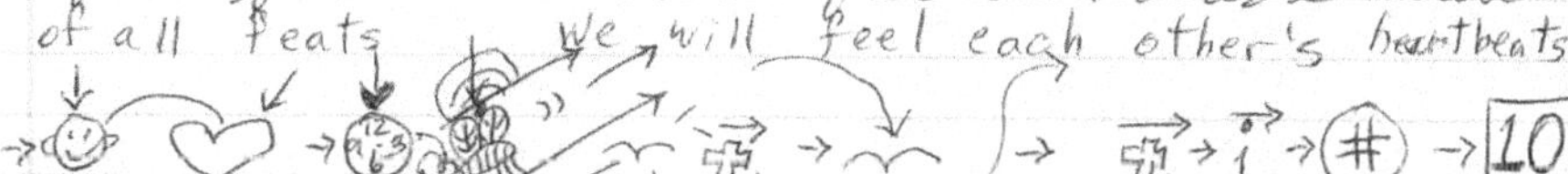

My heart will be free and soar And a number 10,
my heart will be free and soar And a number 10

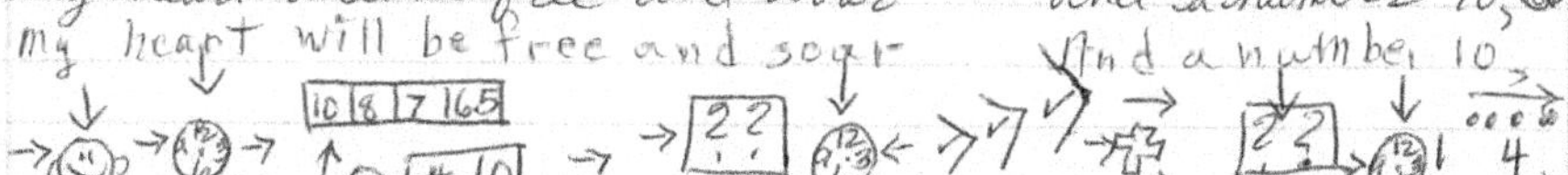

you will score What's more and what's for
you will score What's more and what's for

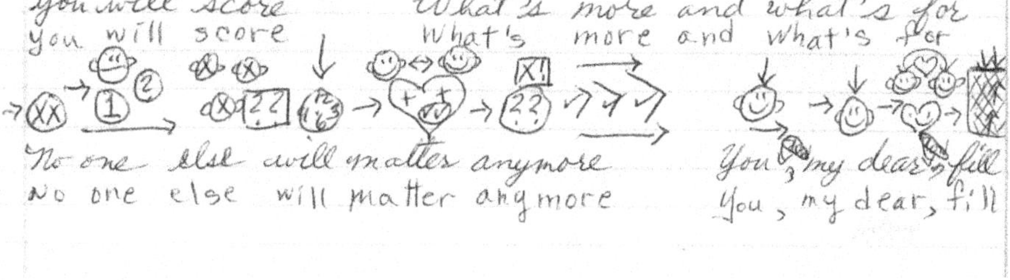

No one else will matter anymore You, my dear, fill
No one else will matter anymore You, my dear, fill

my whole cart And that's only for a start You
my whole cart And that's only for a start You

have done more than your part You have won a
have done more than your part You have won a

special place in my heart With you we can
special place in my heart With you we can

only share a rare precious love You must
only share a precious love You must

have been sent from above I can't help but want
have been sent from above I can't help but want

more and more of Your love, dear, that fits
more and more of Your love, dear, that fits

like a glove I know I have no responsibility in
like a glove I know I have no responsibility in

the role Of my life, which has taken its own
the role Of my life, which has taken its own

toll? On my body and my mind's soul But
toll? On my body and my mind's soul But

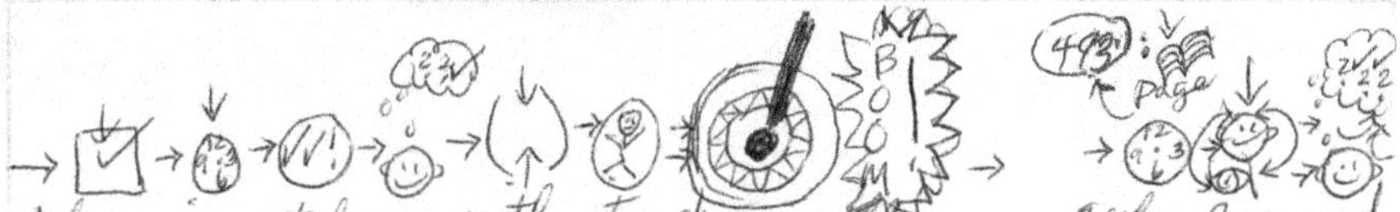

there is yet hope with its drum roll
there is yet hope with its drum roll
When I prayed
When I prayed

for you a long time ago
for you a long time ago
In the dead of the night
In the dead of the night

I prayed for a knight to ride to me, a beau I
I prayed for a Knight to ride to me, a beau I

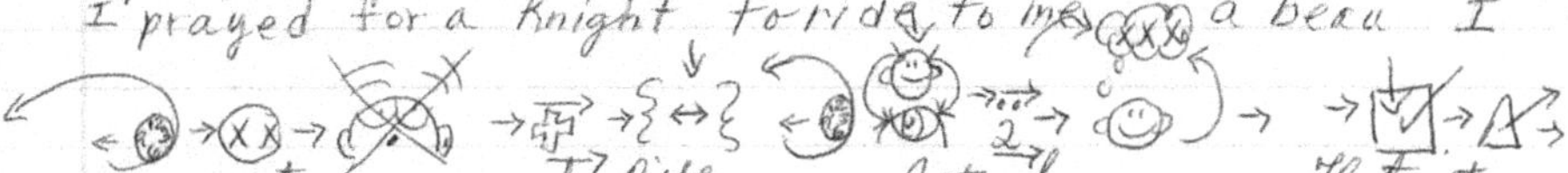

was not aware and little was I to know That it
was not aware and little was I to know That it

would come and take fifty years or so
would come and take fifty years or so

494 page

(98) The Law Of The Land (233)
The Law Of The Land

We all know that Caesar had a hand
Know that Caesar had a hand
In the
In the
governing and law of his land
Governing and law of his land
You and I and
You and I and
everyone have to understand
everyone have to understand
It was his due, his
It was his due, his
right to go and to so demand
right to go and to so demand
Now the law of the
Now the law of the
land is there for you and for me
land is there for you and for me
If we follow
If we follow
the laws, we will be protected and be free
the laws, we will be protected and be free
Then
Then
we can all live together in peace
we can all live together in peace
it will be
it will be
OK, you'll see
OK, you'll see
Then no matter where you or
Then no matter where you or

I go → → we will be able to share and agree Our
I go → we will be able to share and agree Our

world can someday be a paradise No one will
word con some day be a paradise No one will

want or even need a disguise We will have no
want or even need a diguise We will have no

need for deception or lies Everyone will be equals
need for deception or lies Everyone will be equals

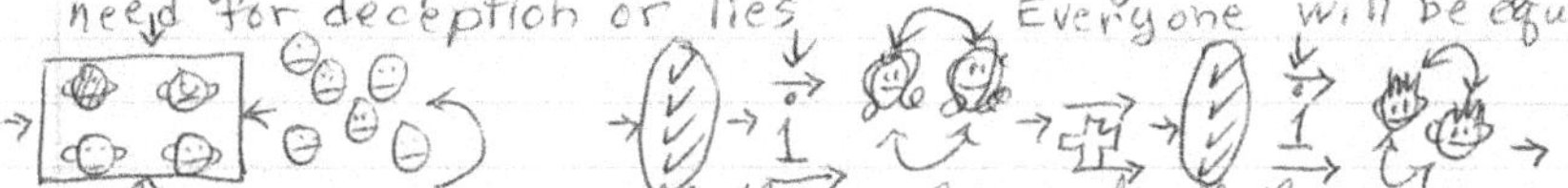

every race all the girls and all the guys
every race all the girls and all the guys

All we have to bring ourselves to do Is embrace
All we have to bring ourselves to do Is embrace

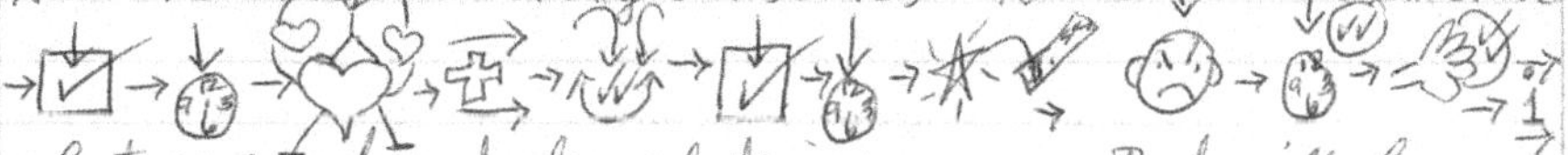

what is good and also what is new Bad will have a
What is good and also what is new Bad will have a

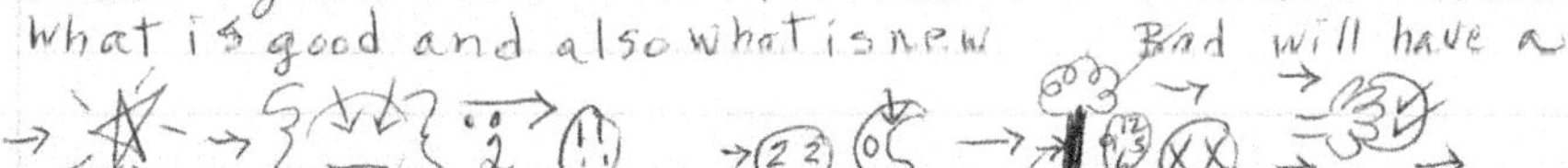

special place too Or Yin wouldn't have
special place too Or Yin wouldn't have

Yang, and that day we would rue If we all
Yang, and that day we would rue If we all

behave and follow the rules We will no longer
behave and follow the rules We will no longer

act or feel like fools The linings to the clouds
act or feel like fools The linings to the clouds

will all be guilded Our future generations will
will all be guilded Our future generations will

all be happily fitted And there will be freedom
all be happily fitted And there will be freedom

for the downcast as well as the gifted We will
for the downcast as well as the gifted We will

begin to fully understand Who really has the
begin to fully understand Who really has the

upper hand? And who is the real boss of all
upper hand? And who is the real boss of all

our lands Then we will be closer to the Boss Man
our lands Then we will be closer to the Boss Man

It is not really a giant mystery Who holds the
It is not really a giant mystery Who holds the

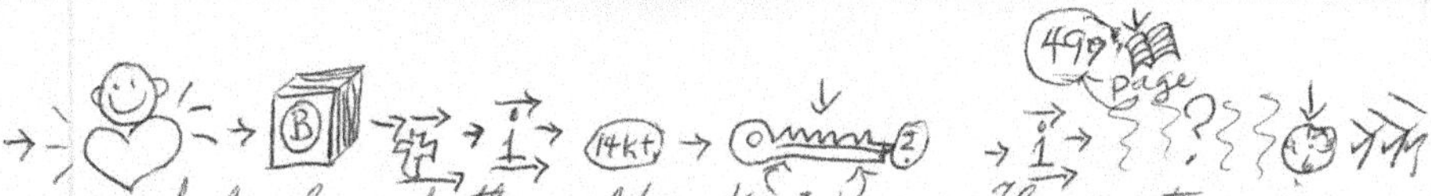

good book and the golden Key? The mystery is more
good book and the golden key The mystery is more

whether the key opens the door for you and me
whether the Key opens the door for You and me

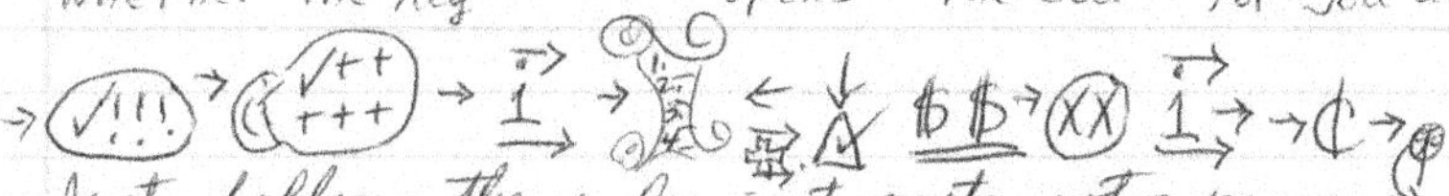

Just follow the rules, it costs not a penny.
Just follow the rules, it costs not a penny.

There is no fee and you'll be freed
There is no fee and you'll be freed

498 : Page

99 Here We Go Again 235
Here We Go Again

And Again
And Again

Here we go, again and again and again
Here we go, again and again and again

It's that simple, it's that plain Pay attention,
It's that simple, it's that plain Pay attention,

if it's all the same I'm dead serious; this is no
if it's all the same I'm dead serious; this is no

GAME
game By now you should know all about
game By now you should know all about

my sideshows Just how the story goes, the ups
my sideshows Just how the story goes, the ups

way above and the downs — way below
way above and the downs — way below

All about my highs and all about my lows And
All about my highs and all about my lows And

how my disposition really goes I'm really sure of the
how my disposition really goes I'm really sure of the

way love should be as it were If you want
way love should be as it were If you want

I will try to make it crystal clear It means I no
I will try to make it crystal clear It means I no

longer want to shed any tears Love means — I
longer want to shed any tears Love means I

always want you near Sure, my life isn't always
always want you near Sure, my life isn't always

purely level But no one said we wouldn't face
purely level But no one said we wouldn't face

head on our own devils Or that when we do prove
head on our own devils Or that when we do prove

our true mettle We have to take what we get
our true mettle We have to take what we get

or we have to accept and to settle No one is
or we have to accept and to settle No one is

immune or perfect Everyone's armor can
immune or perfect Everyone's armor can

be pierced, we can all get hurt
be pierced, we can all get hurt
is what is under our shirts
is what is under our shirts
the heart, the love spurt
the heart, the love spurt
you go with the flow
you go with the flow
you are in the know
you are in the know
arrow in Cupid's bow
arrow in Cupid's bow
love grow and grow
love grow and grow

What is important
What is important
Right there inside,
Right there inside,
It depends on the way
It depends on the way
It also depends on how
It also depends on how
And how you put on
And how you put on
And how you let your
And how you let your
You will be able to give good
You will be able to give good

advice
advice
You can count once, twice, thrice
You can count once, twice, thrice
Some will say no way, no dice
Some will say No way, No dice
Some will say
Some will say

once will suffice The only way they have to
once will suffice The only way they have to

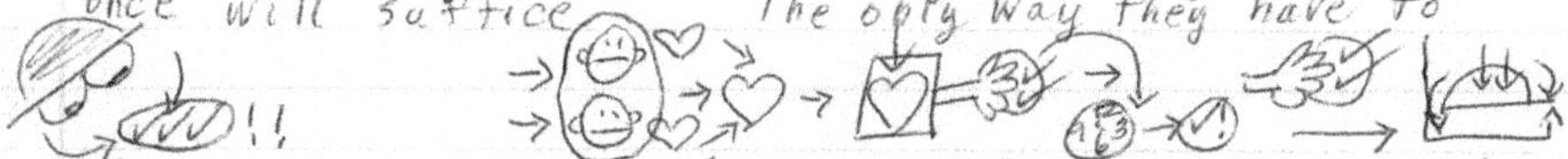

discover Their love that has been kept under
discover Their love that has been kept under

cover And their hearts full of love for one another
cover And their hearts full of love for one another

Is when Cupid joins one to the other? You'll find
Is when Cupid joins one to the other You'll find

when you're with me, love will be My love will
when you're with me, love will be My love will

surround us, all my love you'll see My heart
surround us, all my love you'll see My heart

has lots of room for us for a nominal fee
has lots of room for us for a nominal fee

Let love guide you and me, that's the Key
Let love guide you and me, that's the key

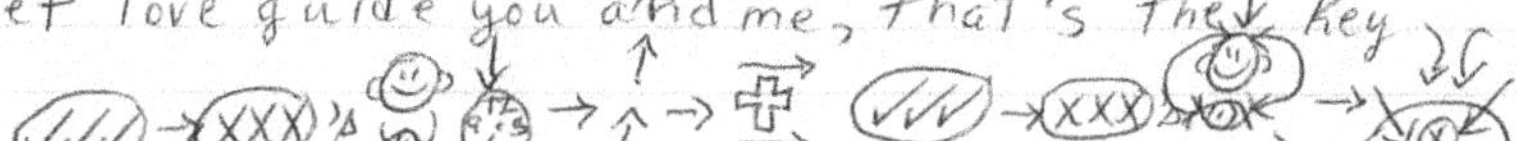

Sometimes I'm up and sometimes I'm down
Sometimes I'm up and sometimes I'm down

I know I'm really a challenge to be around
I know I'm really a challenge to be around

But you won't be sorry that I'm tightly wound
But you won't be sorry that I'm tightly wound

Truth is, you'll be happy; you got me on the
Truth is, you'll be happy; you got me on the

rebound I will not disappoint you and you
rebound I will not disappoint you and you

won't, the day we met, rue My moods may
won't, the day we met, rue My moods may

be something never new But darling, I will
be something never new But darling, I will

give you a great, big clue I can make life
give you a great, big clue I can make life

very, very interesting for you We will have a
very, very interesting for you We will have a

happy, married life And I will make you a
happy, married life And I will make you a

very good wife
very good wife

than strife
than strife

There will be way more good
There will be way more good

We will be very close very tight
we will be very close very tight

and I will love you with all my might
and I will love you with all my might

504 page

100 The Blue-Bottomed Special 238
The Blue-Bottomed Special

What's on today's menu, what is the new breakthrough?
What's on today's menu, what is the new breakthrough

What is it that is made to order, delicious, tasty, and
What is it that is made to order, delicious, tasty, and

new?
new

Is it a hot bowl of tasty Irish stew or plain old gruel
Is it a hot bowl of tasty Irish stew or plain old gruel

goo?
goo?

Or maybe, it is a zesty, well-planned, outside
Or maybe, it is a zesty, well-planned, outside

barbecue?
barbecue,

I find that, on the menu, there is
I find that on the menu there is

quite a variety
quite a variety

And the cooks are professionals, far
And the cooks are professionals, far

from lazy
from lazy

Is it a sin how they make cooking
Is it a sin how they make cooking

look so easy
look so easy

They do not sweat it; they are
They do not sweat it; they are

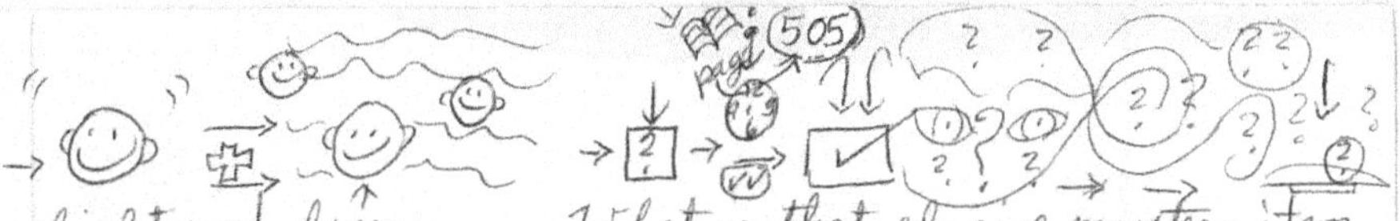

light and breezy
What is that elusive mystery item,
light and breezy
What is that elusive mystery item,

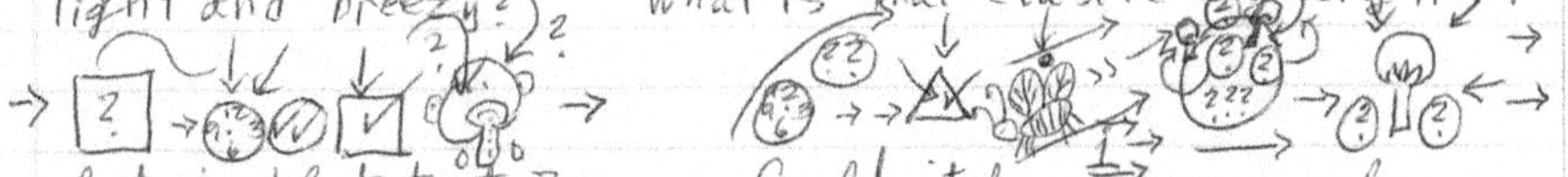

what is that taste?
Could it be a rare mushroom
what is that taste?
Could it be a rare mushroom

stem I overlooked in haste?
Whatever it is, it
stem I overlooked in haste?
Whatever it is, it

must be a real gem
mixed in with the paste
must be a real gem
mixed in with the paste

Whatever it is, it is new to us and to them,
Whatever it is, it is new to us and to them,

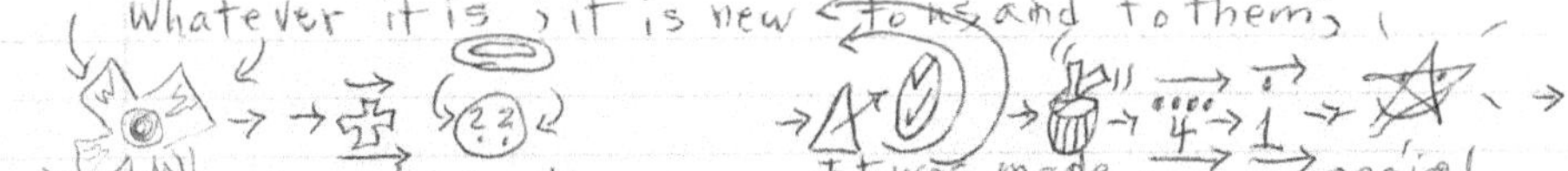

delicate and chaste
It was made for a special
delicate and chaste
It was made for a special

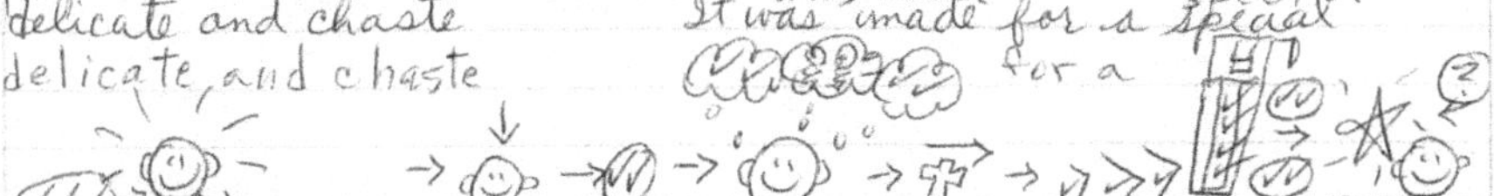

someone
Who is discerning and very well-Known?
someone
Who is discerning and very well-Known?

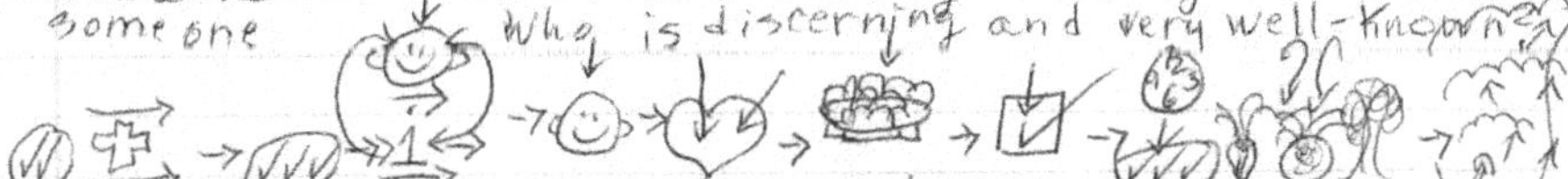

And someone who likes food that is home-grown
And someone who likes food that is home-grown

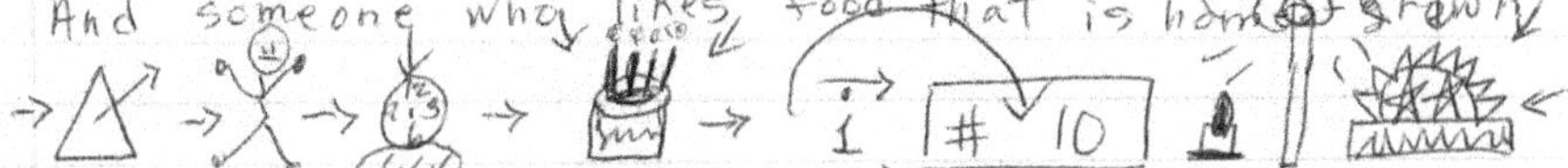

This person is celebrating an important milestone
This person is celebrating an important milestone

This unpopular someone is still bucking public opinion
This unpopalar someone is still bucking opinion

And cared not of the place's dubious distinction And
And cared not of the place's dubious distinction And

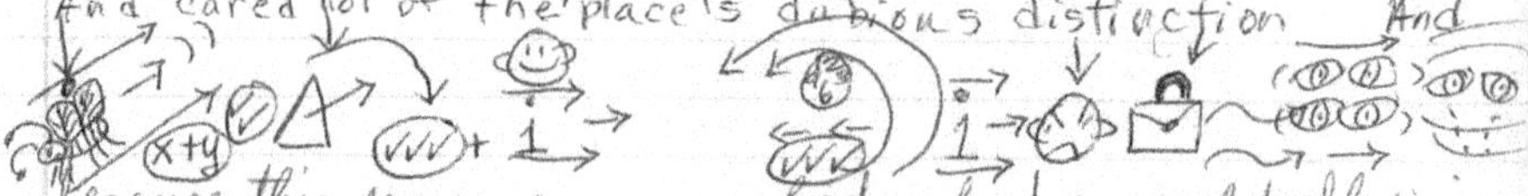

because this someone had a bad case of double vision
because this someone had a bad case of double vision

It led to his rash and split secound decision And
It led to rash and split secound decision And

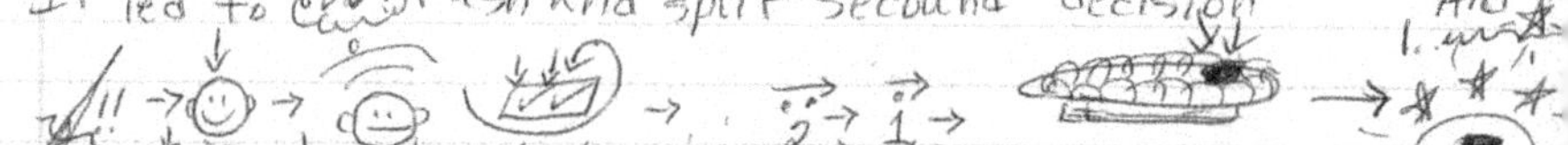

So his decision led to the blue-bottomed special
So his decision led to the blue-bottomed special

It was given in a secret-voted trial And he
It was given in a secret-voted trial And he

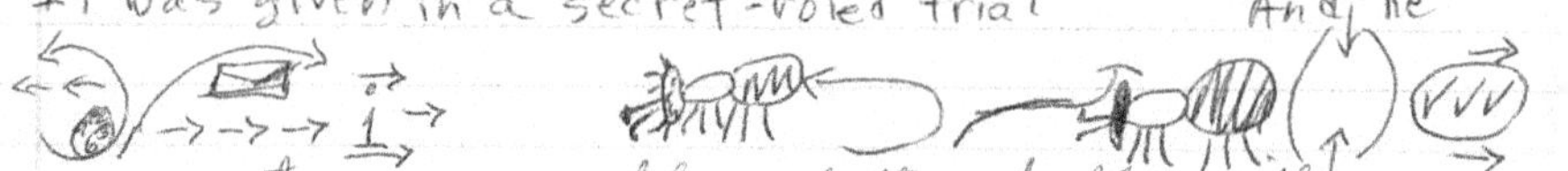

was sent a blue-bottomed fly with some
was sent a blue-bottomed fly with some

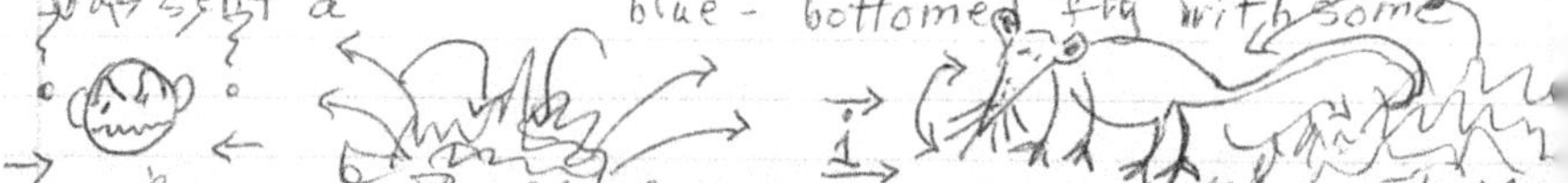

guile Right from a rat-infested food pile
guile Right from a rat-infested food pile

This poor man never suspected The peppes on his
This poor man never suspected The pepper on his

page 507

dish wasn't carefully selected But was
dish wasn't carefully selected But was

rather something left over and rejected A
rather something left over and rejected A

blue-bottomed fly torn and dissected The
blue-bottomed fly torn and dissected The

story has a moral and here's the short and
story has a moral and here's the short and

the tall Use better judgment and protocol
the tall Use better judgment and protocol

If you can't see, get someone else to use
If you can't see, get someone else to use

their eyeballs Or you will be the one in for
their eyeballs Or you will be the one in for

a downfall
a down fall

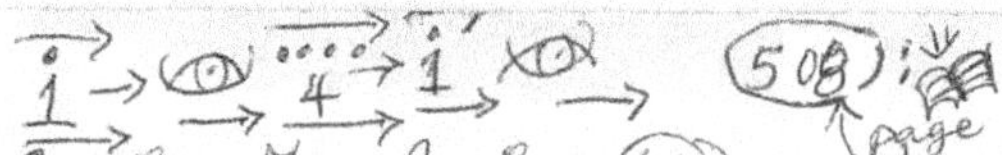

(101) An Eye For An Eye (140)
An Eye For An Eye!

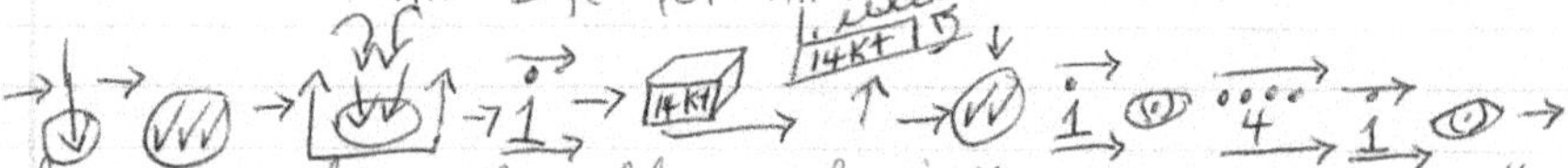

In some places the golden rule is "an eye for an eye"
In some places the golder rale is "an eye for an eye"

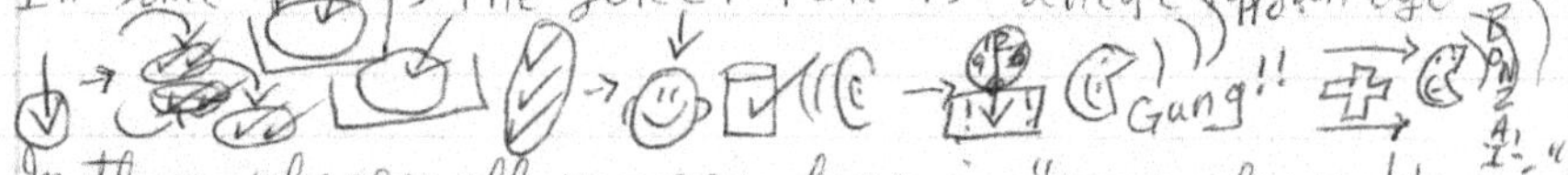

In those places all you can hear is "gung ho and banzai"
In those places all you can hear is "gung ho and banzai"

Watch out though, if you are the practicing FBI guy
Watch out though, if you are the practicing FBI guy

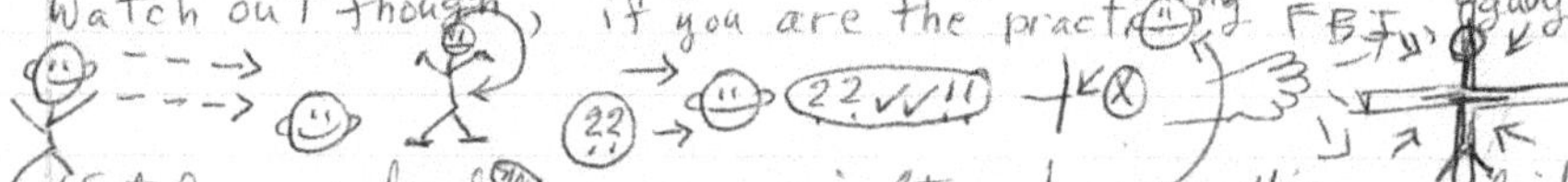

Watch your back, or you might end up getting crucified
Watch your back, or you might end up getting cracified

Watch out for your dentures or for your teeth,
Watch out for your dentures or for your teeth,

forssooth Right now, you might think you have
forsooth Right now, you might think you have

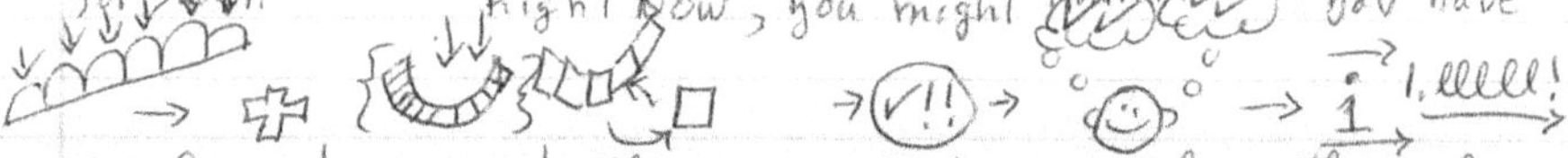

each and every tooth But remember the rule
each and every tooth But remember the rale

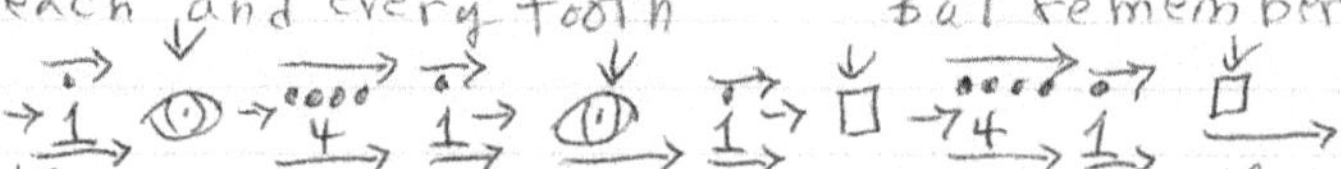

"An eye for an eye, a tooth for a tooth"
"An eye for an eye, a tooth for a tooth"

Pulling your teeth might be someone's glorious
Pulling your teeth might be someone glorious

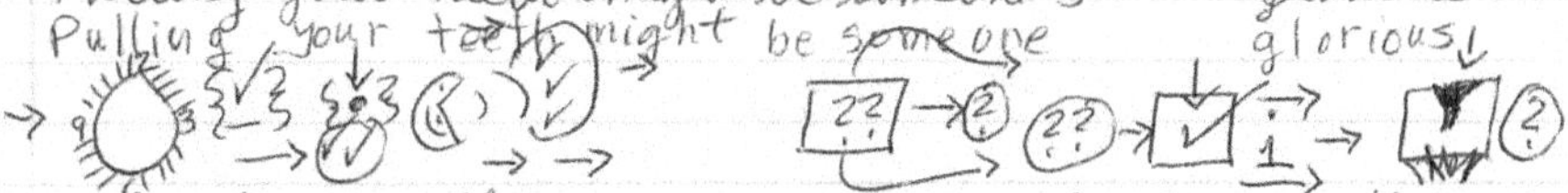

moment of truth What? Is that a cavity?
moment of truth What? Is that a cavity?

Chop, chop Please sir, a little less off the top
chop, chop Please sir, a little less off the top

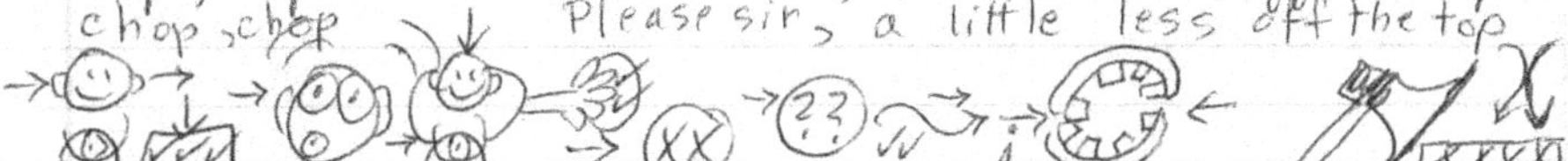

I'm afraid I have not much of a crop Chop off
I'm afraid I have not mac hot a crop Chop off

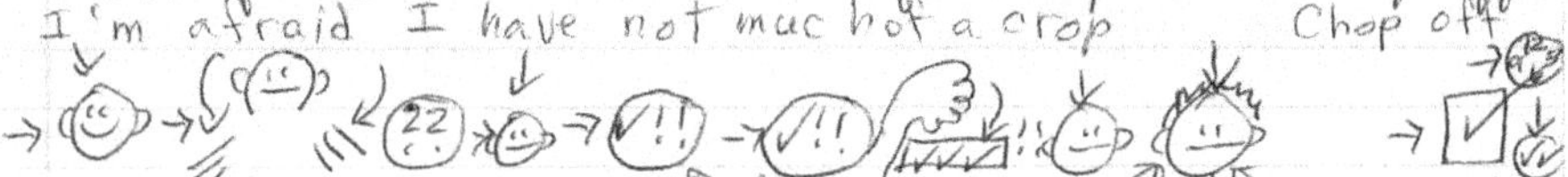

my hair, if you must, but leave my head that's
my hair, if you must, but leave my head that's

where you must please stop I think you all are
where you mast please stop I think you all are

still living in the Dark Ages You are still
still living in the Dark Ages You are still

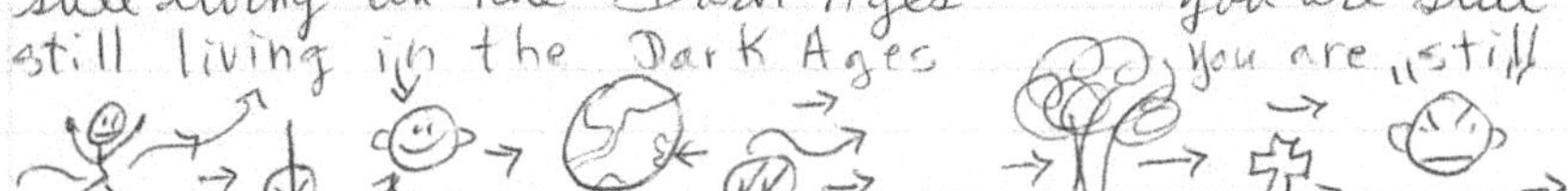

living in your land of chaos and petty
living in your land of chaos and petty

rages And your behaviour is just plain
rages And your behaviour is just plain

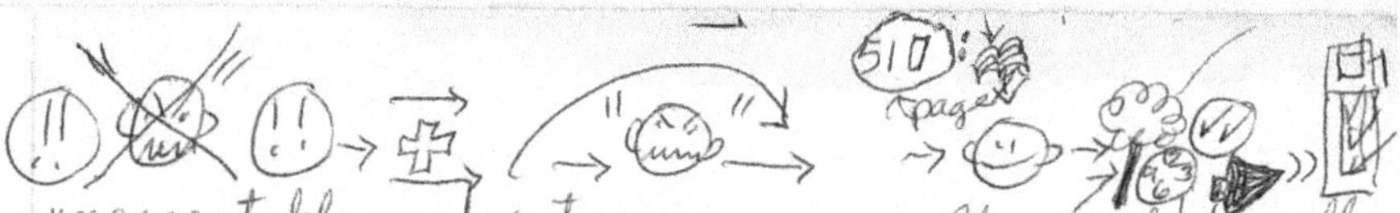

unacceptable and outrageous You would do well
unacceptable and outrageous You would do well

to control your ridiculous rampages
to control your ridiculous rampages

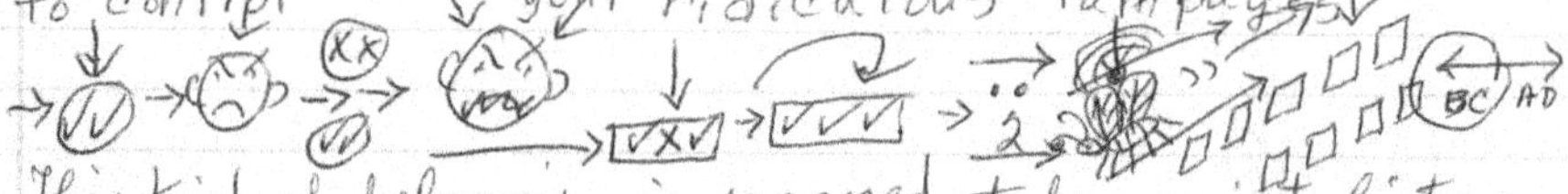

This kind of behavior is supposed to be ancient history
this kind of behavior is supposed to be ancient history

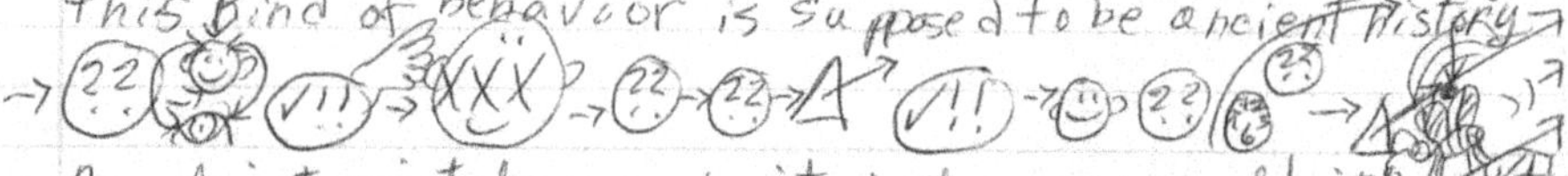

Am I just mistaken or is it just you or could it be just
Am I just mistaken or is it just you or could it be just

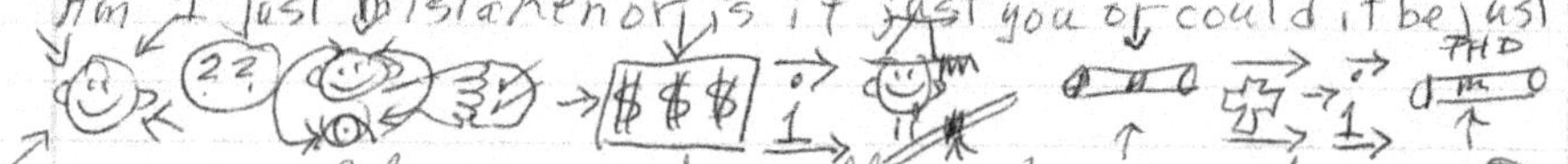

me I have earned a college degree and a PHD
me I have earned a college degree and a PHD

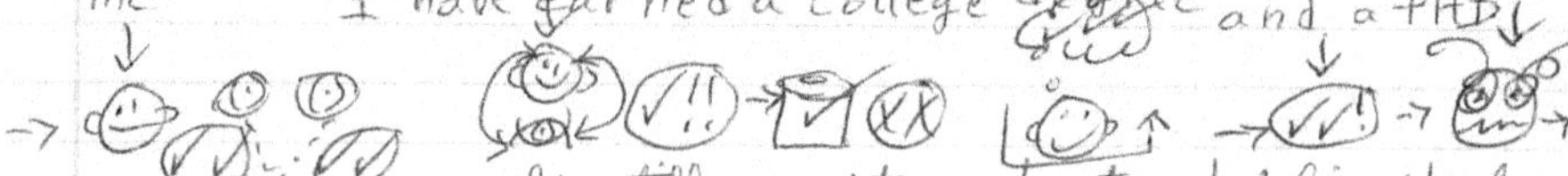

you see I still can't understand this ridiculous
you see I still can't understand this ridiculous

useless killing spree Haven't we, as a human
use less Killing spree Haven't we, as a human

race learned anything? Don't we yet
race learned anything? Don't we yet

understand, it won't accomplish a thing By
understand, it won't accomplish a thing By

511 page

fighting and returning hate with hate? we will
fighting and returning hate with hate? we will

all see what that brings And it won't be good
all see what that brings And it won't be good

why there is all this senseless killing All these
why there is all this senseless killing All these

people want and live and breathe is war They
people want and live and breathe is war They

scurry here, they scurry there, both near and far
scurry here, they scurry there, both near and far

Sometimes they blow themselves up along with
Sometimes they blow themselves up along with

an occasional car It all seems too wrong,
an occasional car It all seems too wrong,

just so bizarre, and we thought that we were all
just so bizarre, and we thought that we were all

superstass Couldn't you, for one minute,
superstars Couldn't you, for one minute,

enjoy peace and your fighting cease?
en joy peace and your fighting cease?

Then you could enjoy smelling the roses and
Then you could enjoy smelling the roses and

shooting the breeze You would certainly have
shooting the breeze You would certainly have

quite less of a need for referees And you
quite less of a need for referees And you

could laugh with each other and hug each
could laugh with each other and hug each

other and gently squeeze
other and gently squeeze

(101) Mirror Image (242)
Mirror Image

(513) : page

Yes, the mirror image itself is life Yes, I am
yes, the mirror image of itself is life yes, I am

a satisfied, happy housewife Yes, I also
a satisfied, happy housewife yes, I also

like to enjoy living the nightlife And yes,
like to enjoy living the nightlife And yes,

I am also a larger version of life When I
I am also a larger version of life When I

look into a mirror at a reflection of me I don't
look into a mirror at a reflection of me I don't

really like what is there and what I have to see
really like what is there and what I have to see

I see all my faults and to a tee and there
I see all my faults and to a tee and there

they are as plain as can be Then I feel
they are as plain as can be Then I feel

humility to the nth degree and all I wish
humility to the nth degree and all I wish
to do is flee My eyes seem to have deadly X-
to do is flee My eyes seem to have deadly X-
rays All I want to do is turn and look
rays All I want to do is turn and look
away I don't even dare to plead or to pray
away I don't even dare to plead or to pray
What could I possibly ask for or have to pay
what could I possibly ask for or have to pay
My eyes burn into my very soul That's when I
My eyes burn into my very soul That's when I
feel like a very ugly troll I then feel I could
feel like a very ugly troll I then feel I could
qualify as a ghoul Because I see my flesh
qualify as a ghoul Because I see my flesh
all old and rotten as a rule Just what happened
all old and rotten as a rule Just what happened

to me; I don't know
Life has dealt me some
very deathly blows
Even though I am and may
be a dynamo
I will certainly never win any fashion
shows
At one time, my form
was shapely
and was woe
Now I look more like a large,
happy hippo
My ex even called me a cud-
chewing cow
I don't care; I accept who I am
and what I am now
If it is any consolation
to me, I can almost guarantee
No one really

page 516

likes their mirror image, you see The trick
likes their mirror image, you see The trick

is being satisfied, accepting it, and letting it be
is being satisfied, accepting it, and letting it be

Smile when you look at your mirror image
Smile when you look at your mirror image

and you will unlock its key Try to see all
and you will unlock its key Try to see all

your goodness And also stay humble overall
your goodness And also stay humble overall

Because self-love can also lead to a fall After
Because self-love can also lead to a fall After

all, when you gaze into a mirror we can only
all, when you gaze into a mirror we can only

stand so tall
stand so tall

517 page

(102) My Dearest Mary (244)

My Dearest Mary

My dearest, beautiful Mary
My dearest, beautiful Mary

You have helped
You have helped

Din Din to see
Din Din to see

You are a powerful queen bee
You are a powerful queen bee

You have a powerful pedigree
You have a powerful pedigree

You are so very
You are so very

thoughtful and kind
thoughtful and kind

I want for you peace of
I want for you peace of

mind
mind

You are so very wise
You are so very wise

it boggles any
it boggles any

mastermind
master mind

I pray for bettes health for you
I pray for better health for you

to find
to find

I must pray for you in the right way
I must pray for you in the right way

To the Lord, God in Spirit, for a bouquet
To the Lord, God in Spirit, for a bouquet

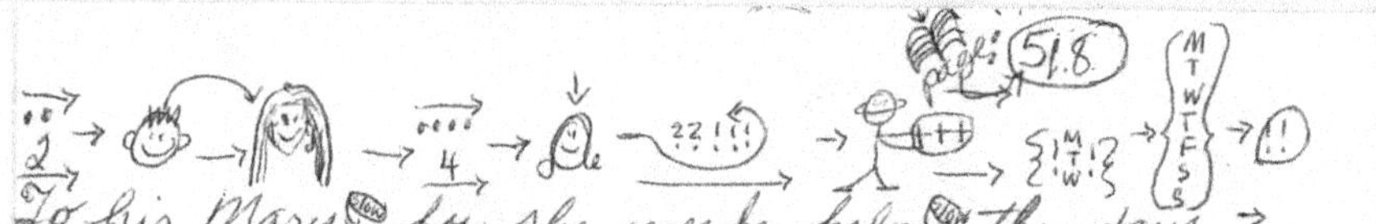

To his Mary, for she needs help, these days

To his Mary, for she needs help, these days

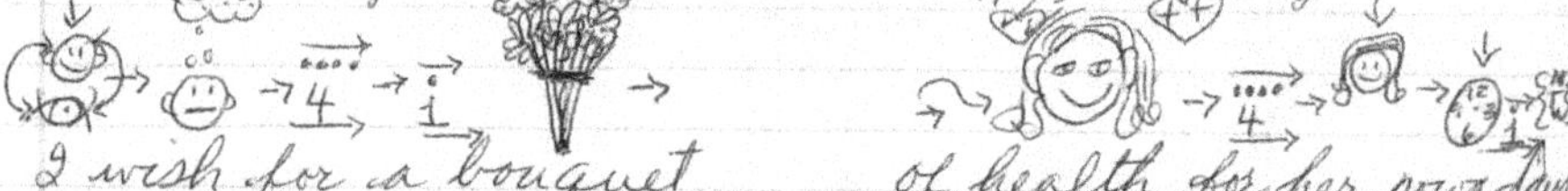

I wish for a bouquet of health for her nowadays

I wish for a bouquet of health for her nowadays

I love you Mary, so be worry-free Someone

I love you Mary, so be worry-free Someone

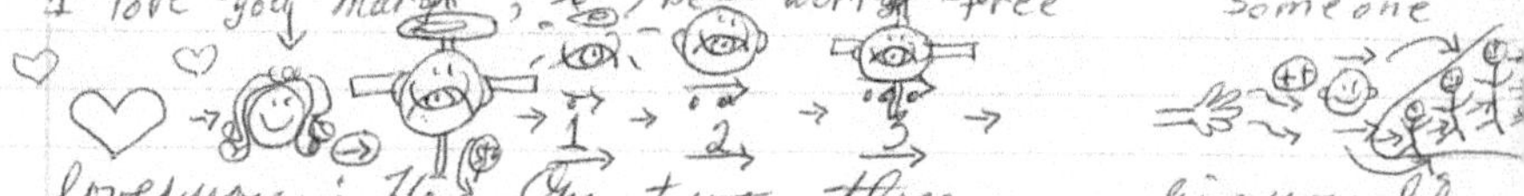

loves you: He, One, two, three Give your life

loves you: He, One, two, three Give your life

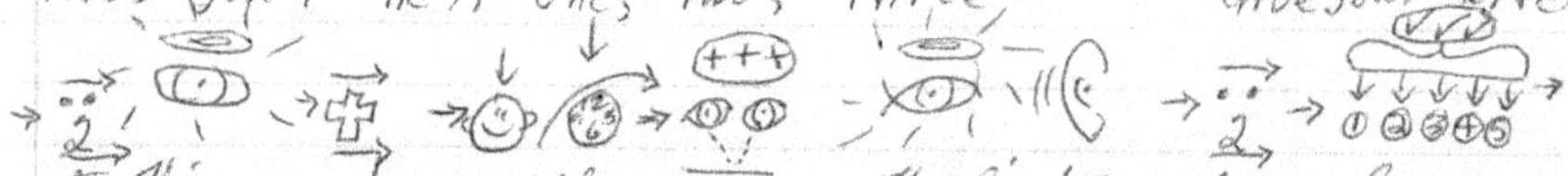

to Him and you'll see He listens to each

to Him and you'll see He listens, to each

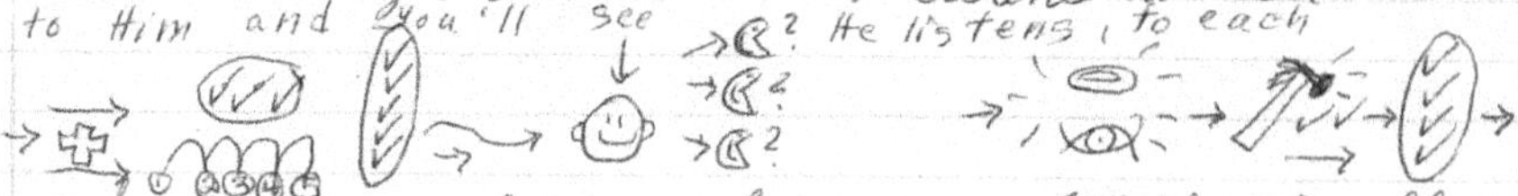

and every one of your pleas He'll fix all

and every one of your pleas He'll fix all

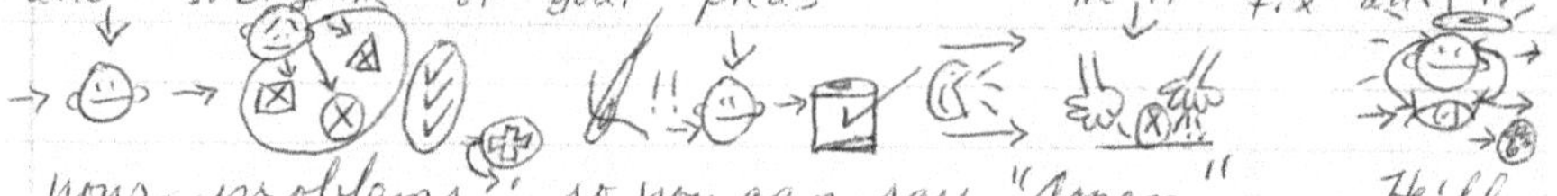

your problems, so you can say "Amen" He'll

your problems, so you can say "Amen" He'll

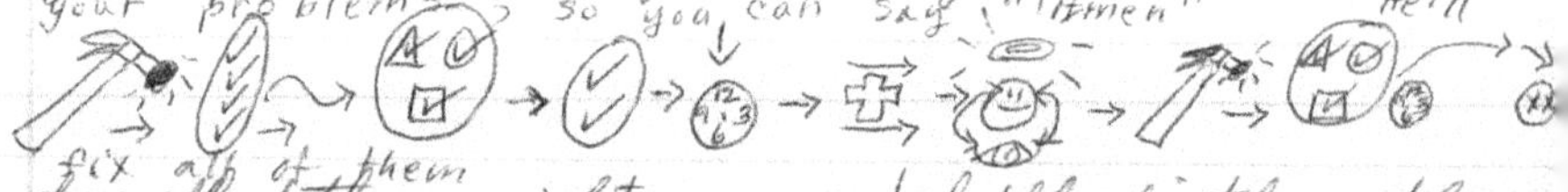

fix all of them

fix all of them right now and he'll fix them then

right now and he'll fix them then

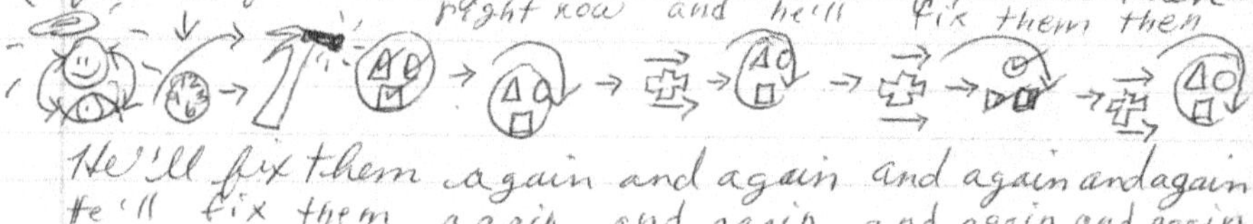

He'll fix them again and again and again and again

He'll fix them again and again and again and again

With faith, we can all hang ten even in the lion's den
With faith, we can all hang ten even in the lion's den

So my dearest Mary, in this world there are no
So my dearest Mary, in this world there are no

guarantees
guarantees

It may seem very scary, but you
It may seem very scary, but you

will soon be able to see
will soon be able to see

That if you give your
That if you give your

life to Him,
life to Him,

you'll soon agree with me
you'll soon agree with me

That's when you will become home free
That's when you will become home free

and you
and you

will have the right keys.
will have the right keys

Now that you have,
Now that you have

in faith,
in faith,

given your
given your

life totally over,
life totally over,

as it were
as it were

And let God come to you, a little bit
And let God come to you, a little bit

closer your life will begin to stir And
you will have let Him do, with you what He
would prefer to occur Just let His love
disperse anything that was blurred, and your
life will hum and purr And let your mind's
power grow, high and low Until it becomes
a smooth-working dynamo And your work
You will easily be able to know You will
have faith that this gift will continue because

He loves you so
He loves you

Just believe that it can be done
Just believe that it can be done

And your victories will all be won
And your victories will all be won

You will have
You will have

protected
protected

not only yourself number 1
Not only yourself number 1

But you will have benefitted your family and also
But you will have benefitted your family and also

everyone
everyone

(103) A New Role (246)

A New Role

(522) page

I have decided I have a new role I won't be left out
I have decided I have a new role I won't be left out

in the cold I must make sure to expand my soul
in the cold I must make sure to expand my soul

I must rock and roll I must have even more
I must rock and roll I must have even more

control of it, on the whole and be bold
control of it, on the whole and be bold

I must have and use my aces in the hole I must
I must have and use my aces in the hole I must

cajole and extol I must always try to remember
cajole and extol I must always try to remember

To try to behave with the utmost demur I must
To try to behave with the utmost demur I must

acknowledge and forgive every slur And learn
acknowledge and forgive every slur And learn

to react correctly and to concur
to react correctly and to concur
That's when I
That's when I

will be able to gather and change
will be able to gather and change
My life
My life

accordingly and to be able to rearrange
accordingly and to be able to rearrange
All
All

my faults and successfully move and arrange
my faults and successfully move and arrange

All my virtues and be able to share them
all my virtues and be able to share them
And to
And to

exchange...
exchange
Along with my newfound abilities
Along with my new found abilities

I must say, please
I must say, please
And also comes with it a
And also comes with it a

great responsibility
great responsibility
I'm lucky to live in the
I'm lucky to live in the

Land of the Free
Land of the Free
Still, I should be polite and
Still, I should be polite and

say pardon me
say pardon me

I want and need to be a good
I want and need to be a good

example
example

I must be careful not to act like a
I must be careful NOT to act like

numbskull
numbskull

I must try to fill my brain chock-
I must try to fill my brain chock-

full

Of pearls of wisdom and be peaceful like
of pearls of wisdom and be peaceful like

Sitting Bull
Sitting Bull

I must always be in control of
I must always be in control

myself and chill
myself and chill

I must deflect every insult and
I must deflect every insult and

swallow every pill
swallow every pill

This way, by example,
This way by example

respect
respect

I will instill
I will instill

Trust for you and
Trust for you and

me in my neighbor
me in my neighbor

and overall goodwill
and overall goodwill

In a way, I must be a goodwill ambassador
In a way, I must be a good will ambassador

And try to teach friendship and be a mentor
And try to teach friendship and be a mentor

I must be a humanitarian more and more And
I must be a humanitarian more and more And

try to increase and improve my overall health
try to increase and improve my over all health

I must and will try to always act proper So
I must and will try to always act proper

that the cycle of goodness will prosper And my
that the cycle of goodness will prosper And my

example will be felt all over And so this
example will be felt all over And so this

world will be a good place for all whether it
world will be a good place for all Whether it

is for him or for her
is for him or for her

104 A Sea Of Words 248

A Sea Of Words

The clouds are full of a sea of words all across
The clouds are full of a sea of words all across

the chalkboard They bounce around until they
the chalkboard They bounce around until they

are caught and stored, a smorgasbord There is still
are caught and stored, a smorgasbord There is still

a lot of room for us all to get aboard, just give
a lot of room for us all to get aboard, just give

the word Everyone has a chance to have
the word Everyone has a chance to have

their just file and order restored This sea of
their just file and order restored This sea of

continuity is so immense It doesn't seem to
continuity is so immense It doesn't seem to

make any sense We just know for sure
make any sense We just know for sure

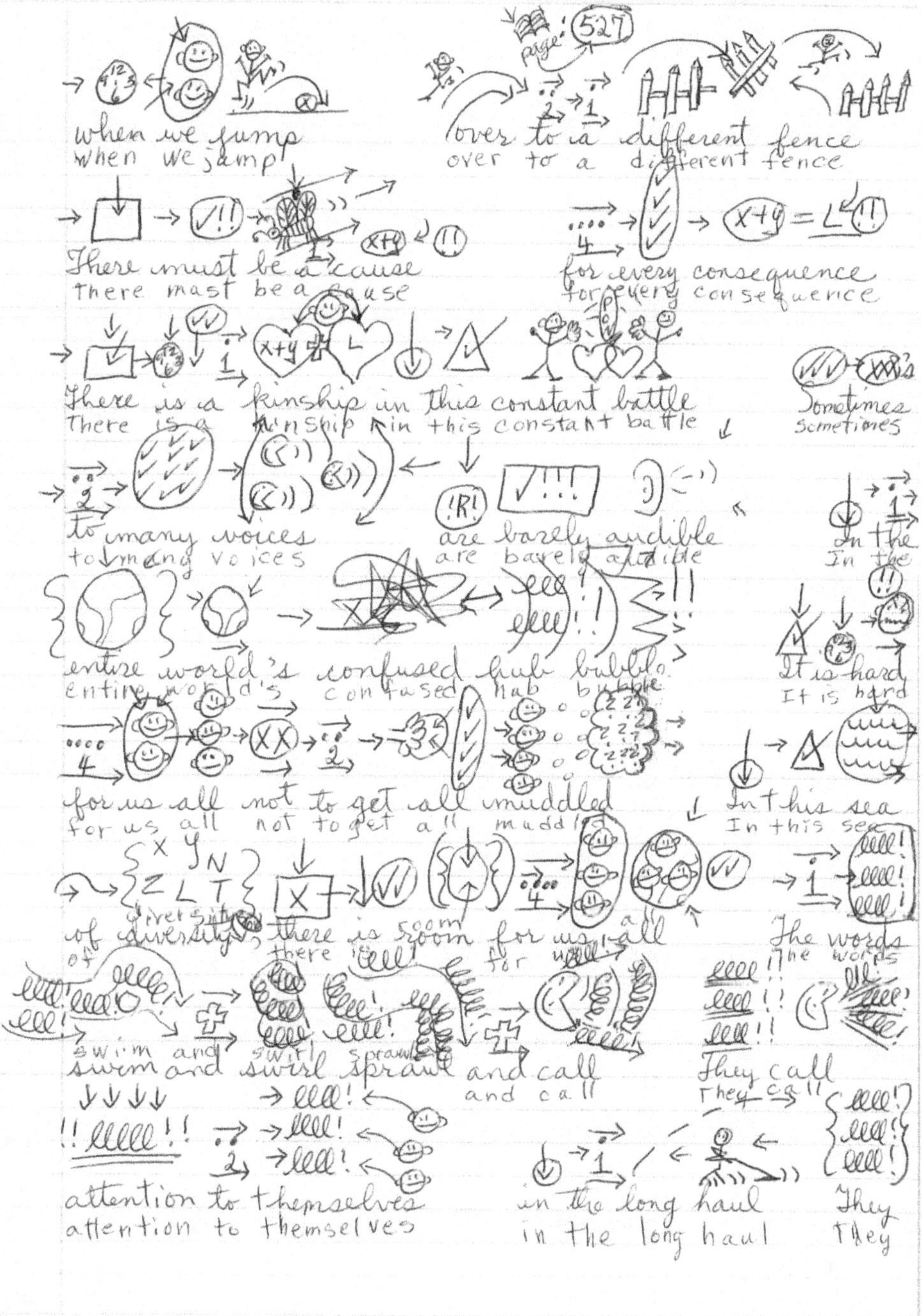
page 527
when we jump
when we jump!
over to a different fence
over to a different fence
There must be a cause
there mast be a cause
for every consequence
for every consequence
There is a kinship in this constant battle
There is a kinship in this constant battle
Sometimes
Sometimes
to many voices
to many voices
are barely audible
are barely audible
In the
In the
entire world's confused hub bubble
entire world's confased hab bubble
It is hard
It is hard
for us all not to get all muddled
for us all not to get all muddled
In this sea
In this sea
X Y N Z L T
of diversity, there is room for us all
of diversity there is room for us all
The words
The words
swim and swirl sprawl
swim and swirl sprawl and call
and call
They call
They call
attention to themselves
attention to themselves
in the long haul
in the long haul
They
They

do so by following the proper and right protocol
do so by following the proper and right protocol

with
with

We have learned words are our friends
We have learned words are our friends

which we can depend
which we can depend

They swim every part of
They swim every part of

the sea where it begins and where it ends
the sea where it begins and where it ends

They travel above our expectations and trascend them all
They travel above our expectations and trascend them all

Greater and greater until we are at our wits' end
Greater and greater until we are at our wit's end

and we reach a dead end
and we reach a dead end

This information
This information

world lives around and above our own
world lives around and above our own

The waves
The waves

here began on the invention called the phone
here began on the invention called the phone

Then they graduated when we passed into
Then they graduated when we passed into

the computer zone And these waves have been
the computer zone And these waves have been

continually escaping our ozone Whatever idea
continually escaping our ozone Whatever idea

or thought or word that can be thought of
or thought or word that can be thought of

above Has been expressed in words as best
above Has been expressed in words as best

as we can send like a dove In an expression
as we can send like a dove In an expression

of goodwill and brotherly love; no pushing
of goodwill and brotherly love; no pushing

or shoving Through the clouds like turtle doves
or shoving Through the clouds like turtle doves

sort of like a pair of matching gloves When
sort of like a pair of matching gloves When

we use these words the right way, we can play
we use these words the right way, we can play

They will help us to no end and we'll be merry and
They will help us to no end and we'll merry and

gay
gay

Moreover, we will all understand what
Moreover, we will all understand what

they have to say
they have to say

In this way, we'll be able
we'll be able

to cooperate together day to day
to cooperate together day to day

(531) page

(105) Be Careful (230)

Be Careful

Be careful, that's no bull, its old school
Be careful, that's no bull, its old school

Watch out, or you might get an earful
watch out, or you might get an earful

You'll want to push, but you'll have to pull
you'll want to push, but you'll have to pull

You might even have to pretend to be dull
You might even have to pretend to be dull

Be careful, keep your mouth shut
Be careful, keep your mouth shut

Or people might think you are a nut
or people might think you are a nut

They might pick you up and kick you in the butt
They might pick you up and kick you in the butt

It's a plain and simple case open and shut
It's a plain and simple case open and shut

Be careful;
Be careful;

don't you move; I might disapprove Or you
don't you move; I might disapprove Or you

might break the golden rule, you mule If
might break the golden rule, you mule If

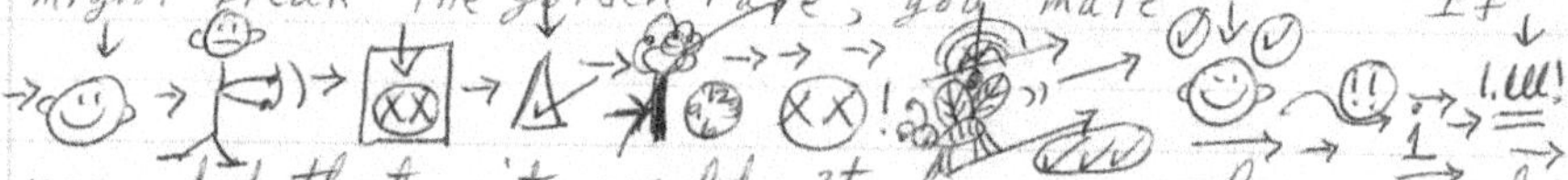

you did that, it wouldn't be very cool as a rule
you did that, it wouldn't be very cool as a rule

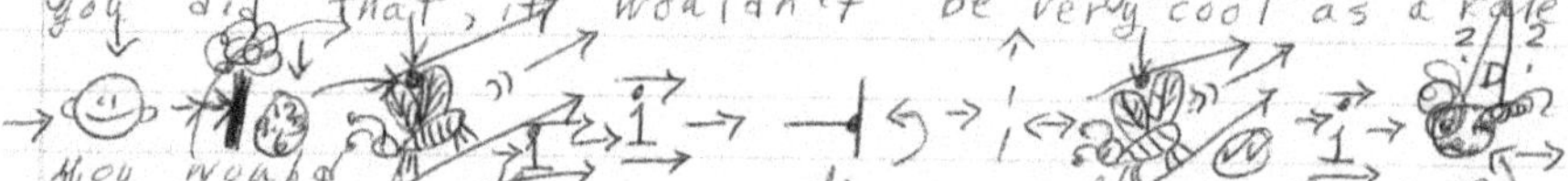

You would be the one ending up being the fool
You would be the one ending up being the fool

Be careful to mind your own business There
Be careful to mind your own business There

is no real need to impress or go to excess
is no real need to impress or go to excess

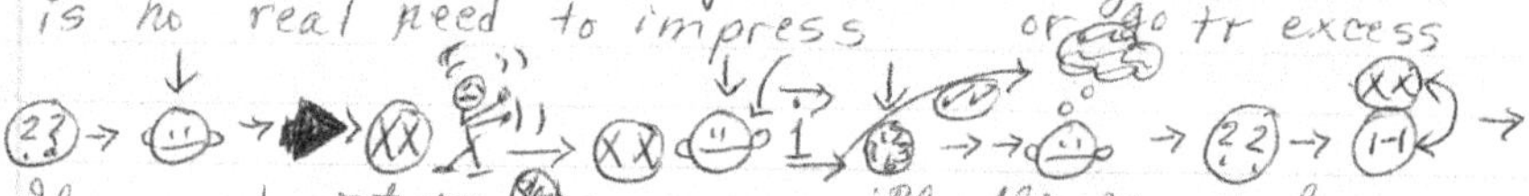

If you don't try, no one will think any less
If you don't try, no one will think any less

And if you ignore them they won't care
And if you ignore them they won't care,

more or less Be careful; try to be politically
more or less Be careful; try to be politically

correct and direct
It is always good to have
the utmost respect
People will always be
pleased with the prospect
And it will give
the right cause and the right effect
Watch
out, be careful, do not lie or falsify
Or
you might cause someone to cry, no lie
Then
you'll need a way out, an airtight alibi
Come on,
tell the truth, give it a try, exemplify
Be alert
and watch your back, avoid stray maniacs

Remember, white is white and black is black,
Remember, white is white and black is black,

Jack And your enemy may be planning a
Jack And your enemy may be planning a

surprise attack You must always be
surprise attack you must always be

aware and stay on the right track Being
aware and stay on the right track Being

careless might mean your untimely death Pay
careless might mean your untimely death Pay

attention and take time to catch your breath Then
attention and take time to catch your breath Then

you won't be scared to death of our dear Elizabeth
you won't be scared to death of our dear Elizabeth

And you won't end up with the kiss of death,
And you won't end up with the kiss of death,

like Macbeth
like Macbeth

(535) page

(106) Reality Bites (252)

Reality Bites

Sometimes when you're in the light, reality bites
Sometimes when you're in the light, reality bites

But it doesn't have to suck; it can be pure dynamite
But it doesn't have to suck; it can be pare dynamite

It may be enough to give you insight and foresight
It may be enoagh to give you insight and foresight

You will have all the luck when you're in the spotlight
You will have all the lack when you're in the spotlight

The road may not be smooth today, and you may go
The road may not be smooth today, and you may go

the wrong way But who said you would have a
the wrong way But who said you would have a

choice in where you have to play Or that it
choice in where you have to play Or that it

would be smooth sailing all the way, with an
would be smooth sailing all the way, with an

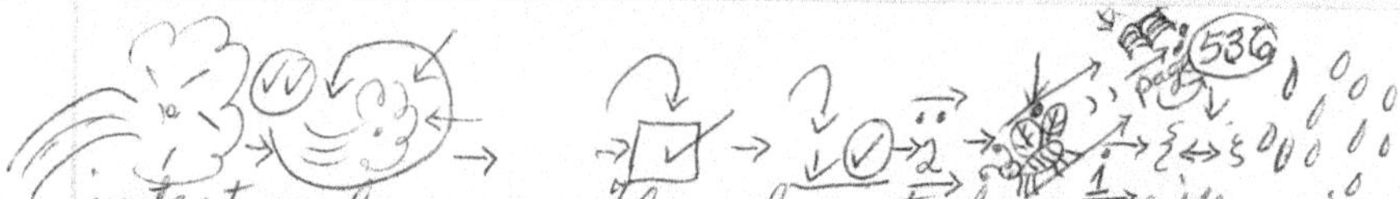

instant replay There has to be a little rain
instant replay There has to be a little rain

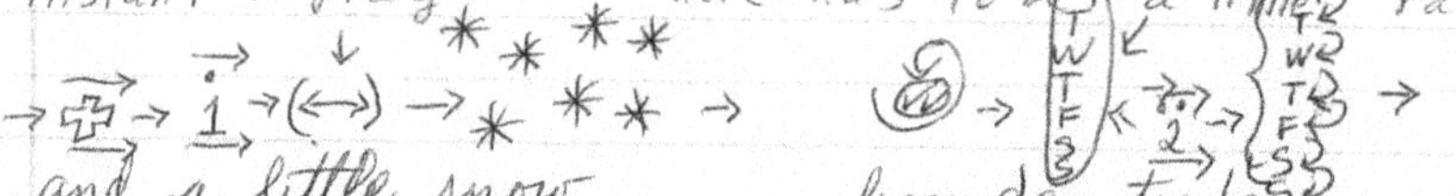

and a little snow from day to day
and a little snow from day to day

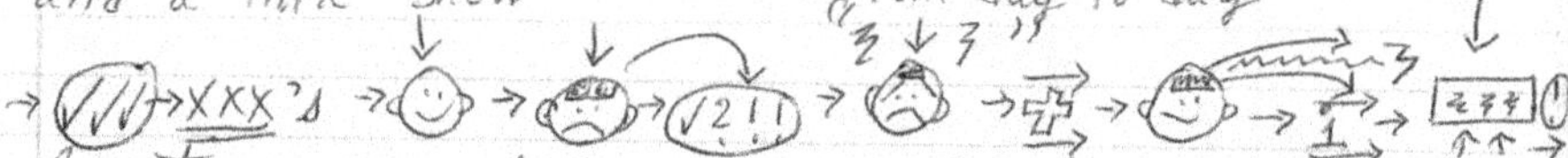

Sometimes your brain may hurt and sound the alert
Sometimes your brain may hurt and sound the alert

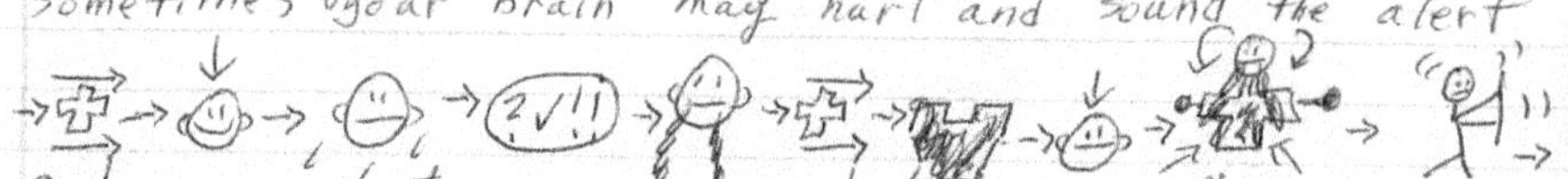

And your sweat may pour and wet your shirt Try
And your sweat may pour and wet your shirt Try

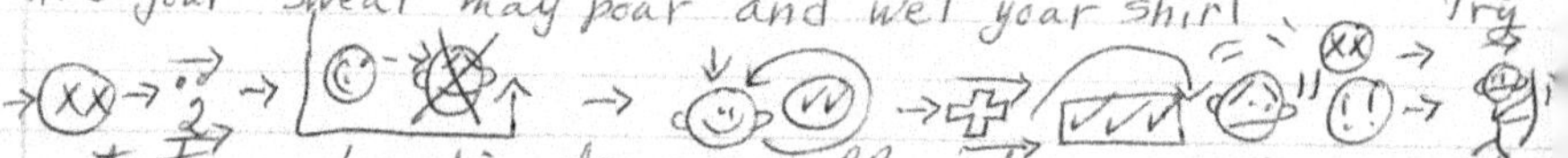

not to underestimate yourself and overexert Try
not to underestimate yourself and overexert Try

instead to assert yourself and keep yourself unhurt
instead to assert yourself and keep yourself unhurt

Ignore and avoid cat fights, be upright, a socialite
Ignore and avoid cat fights, be upright, a sociabite

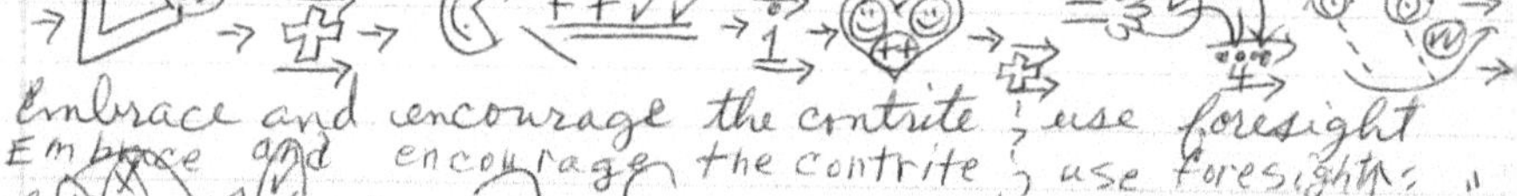

Embrace and encourage the contrite; use foresight
Embrace and encourage the contrite; use foresight;

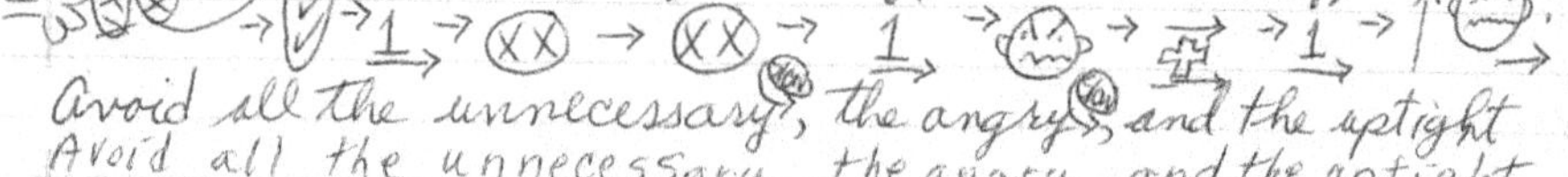

Avoid all the unnecessary, the angry, and the uptight
Avoid all the unnecessary, the angry, and the uptight

Let love have its way, give it the green light Always
Let love have its way, give it the green light Always

try to be fair and square, be totally aware In all
try to be fair and square, be totally aware In all

of your personal and business affairs, be fair This
of your personal and business affairs, be fair This

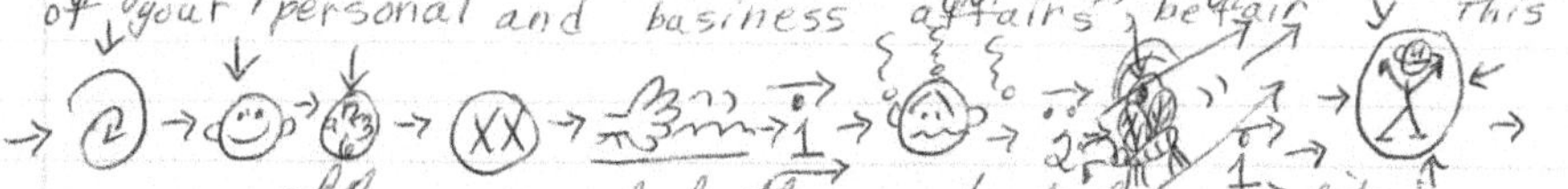

way you'll never feel the need to be a solitaire
way you'll never feel the need to be a solitaire

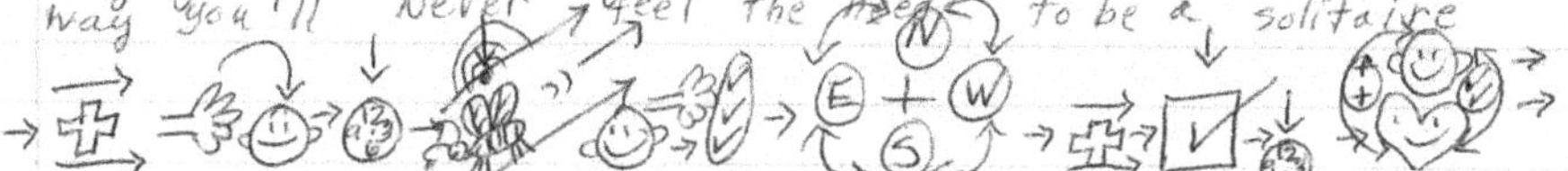

And you will be welcomed everywhere; that's fair
And you will be welcomed every where; that's fair

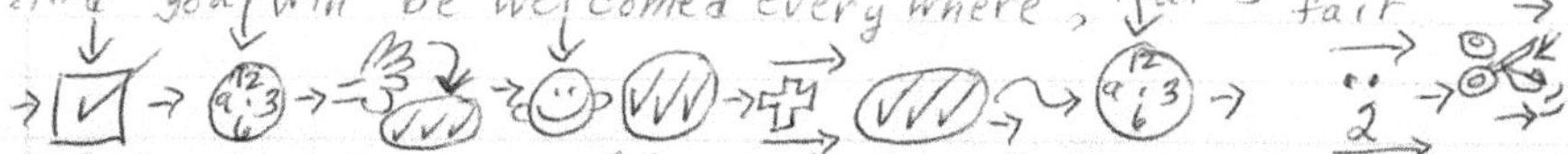

That will give you lots and lots of time To cut
That will give you lots and lots of time To cut

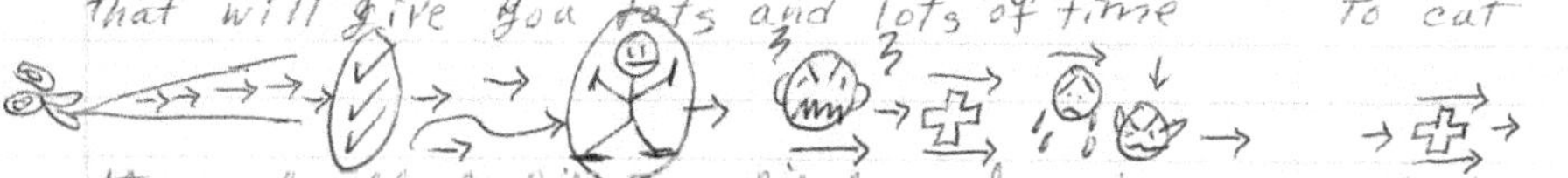

through all of life's filth and grime And
through all of life's filth and grime And

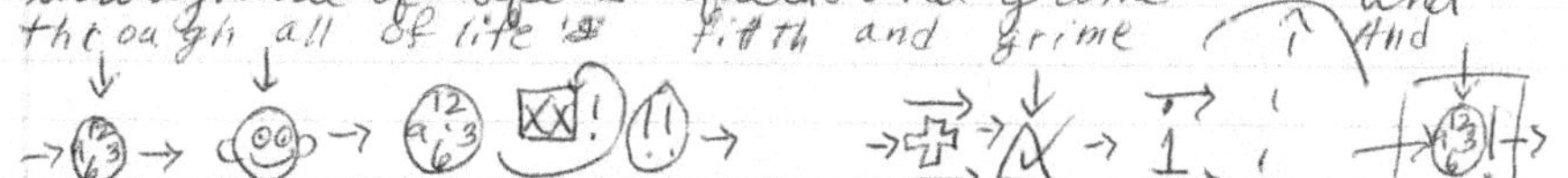

when your time comes and its' the big time
when your time comes and its' the big time

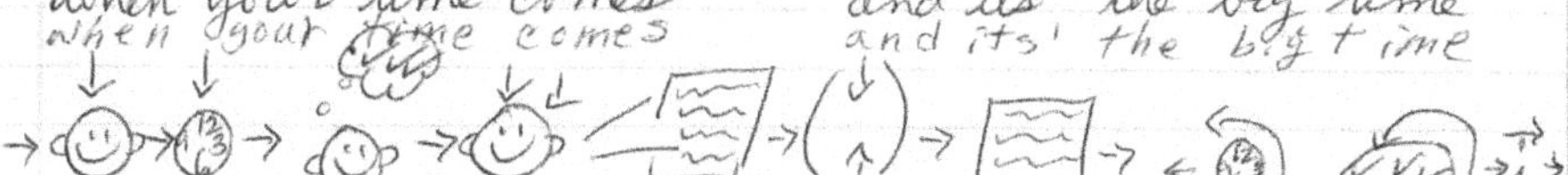

You'll know your lines like they were from a
You'll know your lines like they were from a

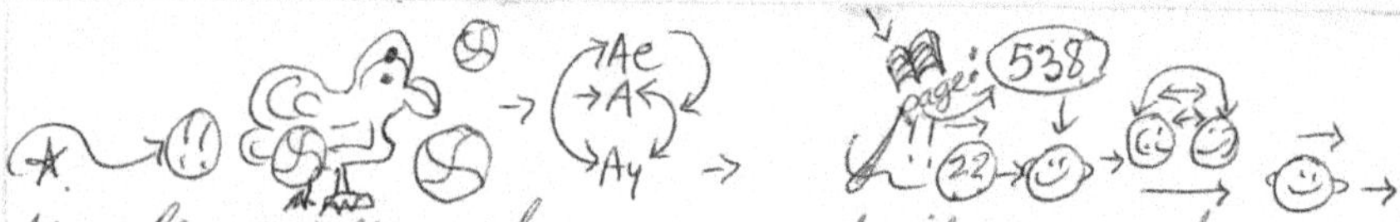

simple nursery rhyme — So if you meet your

simple narseng rhyme — so if you meet your

enemy on the street — Just be calm and turn the

enemy on the street — Just be calm and turn the

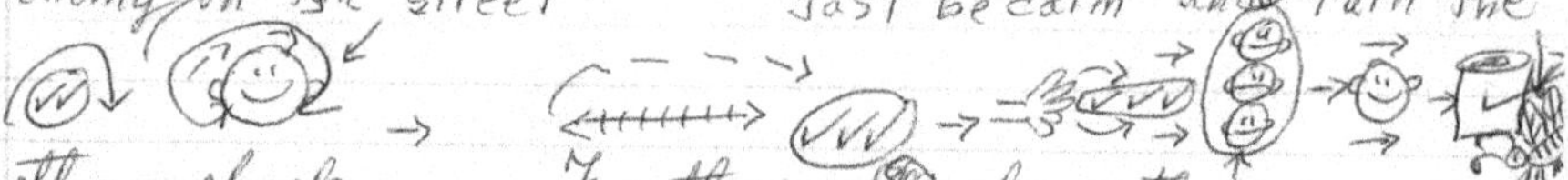

other cheek — Furthermore, show them you can be

other cheek — Far thermore, show them you can be

meek — Show your love technique and hold

meek — show your love technique andhold

your tongue in your cheek — Even though truth

your tongue in your cheek — Even though

may be cruel — Be sure to be nobody's fool

may be crael — Be sare to be Nobody's fool

Use mother wisdom as your tool — You may even

Use mother wisdom as your tool — You may even

make cruel into cool

make crael into cool

(107) The Spice Of Life (254) (539) page

The Spice Of Life

People travel hundreds of miles for it They
People travel handreds of miles for it They
want it; they want it every bit They want the
want it; they want it every bit They want the
spice of life in their kit It's easy to see why
spice of life in their kit It's easy to see why
they don't quit I'd like to share and fix up
they don't quit I'd like to share and fix up
any mix-ups And nourish your life with a new
any mix-ups And nourish your life with a new
setup It would be the best-tasting pick-me-up
set up It would be the best-tasting pick-me-up
The best cup of - you know what - 7 up The world
The best cup of - you know what -7 up The world
turns and turns, and we live and learn Lessons
turns and turns, and we live and learn

540 page
are lived and learned, some overturned
Some people
are spurned and people are warned
Many bridges
are traveled and have been burned
I'd love to
sit awhile and learn from you, buckaroo
2 I
could help you and teach you what I know too
2
could listen and I could learn your point of view
Then I would grow happy and no longer be blue
There might be a trial of experimental spice
And
everything would be beautiful and nice
If we

feel a shower of rice, we had better think twice

That would be meant for marriage, a blissful paradise

Don't be totally disappointed or disjointed If you

are overlooked and not quickly appointed Or if you

are not divinely anointed go full speed ahead

That's when you must develop a totally new viewpoint

That's when you mast develop a totally new view point

Your enemies will be like all your hairs, so watch and

beware They'll want to know all of your affairs,

be ware They'll want to know all of your

they'll sit and glare They'll climb the stairs and

page 542

appear out of all of their lairs So be careful
appear out of all of their lairs So be careful

when you are here, and be careful everywhere
when you are here, and be careful everywhere

You'll always have for them a surprise, by and by
You'll always have for them a surprise, by and by

Because when they exhale and open their eyes They'll
Because when they exhale and open their eyes They'll

see your salvation written high in the skies It
see your salvation written high in the skies It

was the spice of life; despite their many lies
was the spice of life; despite their many lies

(108) Love Has Many Faces (256)

Love Has Many Faces

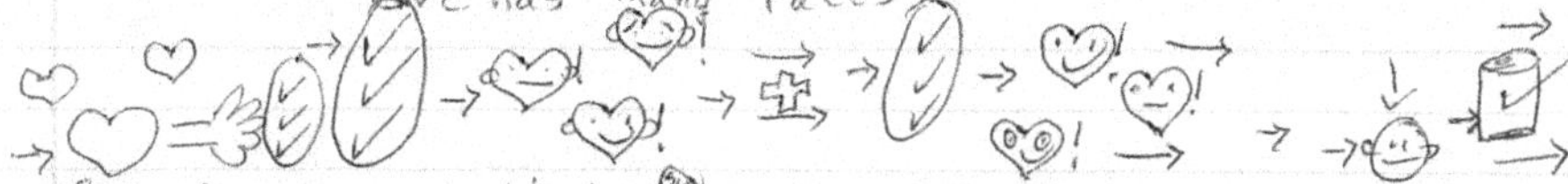

Love has many attitudes, and many faces — You can

Love has many attitudes, and many faces — You can

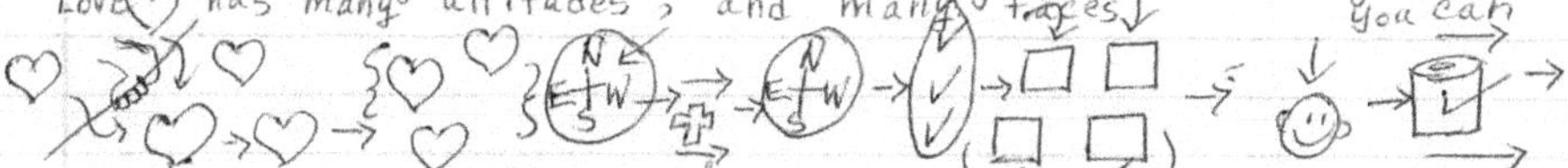

find love anywhere and at any place — You can

find love anywhere and at any place — You can

find it at home or in the workplace — You can search

find it at home or in the workplace — You can search

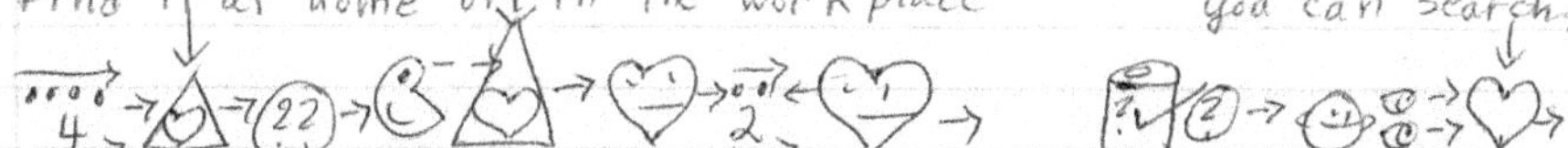

for it or meet it face to face — Can you see love

for it or meet it face to face — Can you see love

where you are? — You can find love in your guitar

where you are? — You can find love in your guitar

You can find love at a seminar — Or you can find

You can find love at a seminar — Or you can find

love in a rare Renoir — Love has many

love in a rare Renoir — Love has many

beautiful names — These names can be — in the

beautiful names — These names can be — in the

544 page

form of nicknames These names can be your
form of nicknames These names can be your

claim to fame They also can be in the fun of a
claim to fame They also can be in the fun of a

game You can find love in your fellow man
game You can find love in your fellow man

Love can be there in Anna or love can be there
Love can be there in Anna or love can be there

in Stan Love can be at home or in
in Stan Love can be at home or in

the land Afghanistan It's the love in our own
the land Afghanistan It's the love in our own

land that can be grand Love is powerful and
land that can be grand Love is powerful and

can overcome any evil Its weapons are goodness
can overcome any evil Its weapons are goodness

and freewill and what they instill The skill
and free will and what they in still The skill

of love is goodwill and it is a pure thrill Don't
of love is good will and it is a pure thrill Don't
underestimate its power to kill any ill When love
underestimate its power to kill any ill when love
kills, something wonderful happens A Pandora's
kills something wonderful happens Pandora's
candy box of goodness opens Wonderment and
candy box of goodness opens wonder ment and
joy can run free and hang ten Then the world
joy can run free and hang ten Then the world
is love's footstool and playpen The phoenix is
is love footstool and play pen The phoenix is
reborn from a blue flame from above Turning
reborn from a blue flame from above Turning
it into a spirit in a form of a sacrificial dove
it into a spirit in a form of a sacrificial dove
That is waiting for lots more love and more of that
That is waiting for lots more love and more of that

sort of
sort of

The blue flame is a spirit that touches
The blue flame is a spirit that touches

us all
us all

It is pure love falling like rainfall
It is pure love falling like rainfall

This rain creates the best free-for-all
This rain creates the best free-for-all

And
and

cascades like a life-giving waterfall
cascades like a life-giving water fall

109 Jamming With My Buddies 258

Jamming with My Buddies

Really, who says I can't mix and blend again?

Really, who says I can't mix and blend again?

And get jamming with my so-called friends Overall,

And get jamming with my so-called friends Overall,

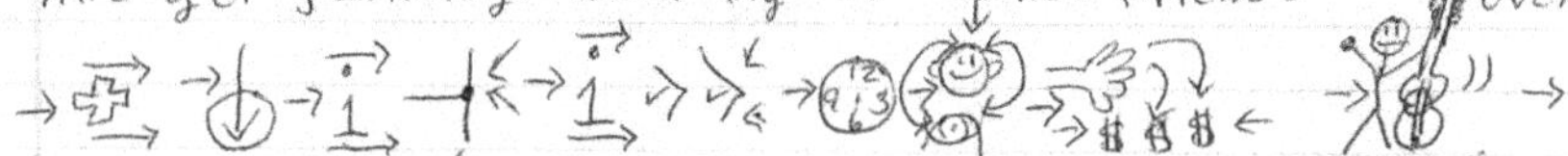

and in the end, the more time I spend Jamming

and in the end, the more time I spend Jamming

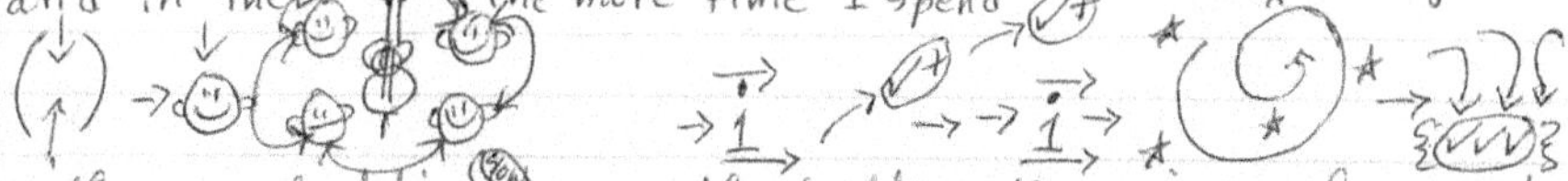

with my buddies, the better the universal trend

with my buddies, the better the universal trend

When I take the time and pain to joyfully create

When I take the time and pain to joyfully create

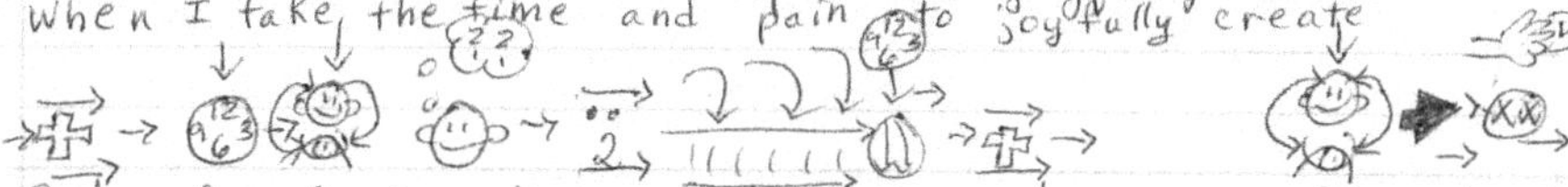

And when I forget to waste time and I don't get

And when I forget to waste time and I don't get

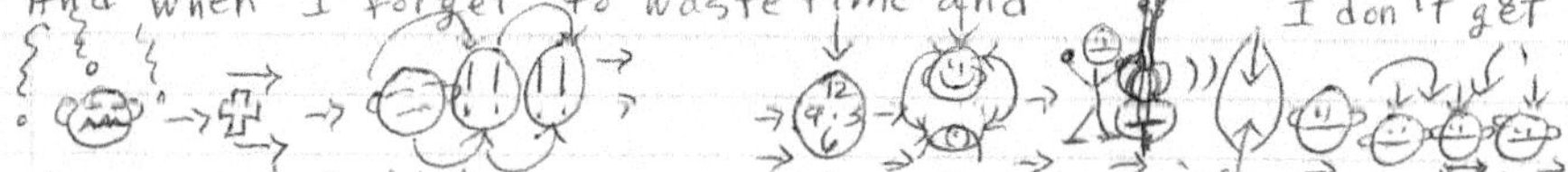

lazy and hesitate When I jam with my buddies

lazy and hesitate When I jam with my buddies

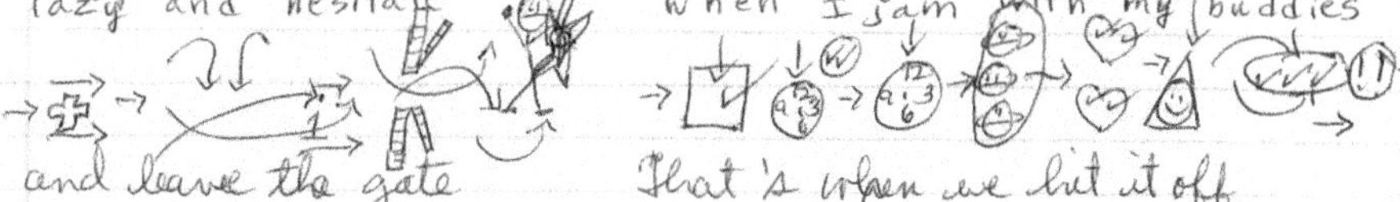

and leave the gate That's when we hit it off

and leave the gate That's when we hit it off

and it turns into something great
and it turns into something great

When we open
When we open

the window and close the door
the window and close the door

And make lots of
And make lots of

music, right through the floor
music right through the floor

Jamming with our
Jamming with our

buddies is the opposite of a chore
buddies is the opposite of a chore

Then all we
Then all we

want to do is make music and more, more, more
want to do is make music and more, more, more

They said I couldn't sing all my love songs
They said I couldn't sing all my love songs

Well,
Well,

you know what, I proved them wrong
you know what, I proved them wrong

I and my
I and my

friends knew it was OK all along
friends knew it was OK all along

This lady is not
This lady is not

only tough, she is headstrong
only tough, she is headstrong

So all I did was
So all I did was

turn, turn and turn to my next buddy And
turn, turn, and turn to my next And

invited them to dance and say squeeze me Then
invited dance and say squeeze me Then

tell them nothing could possibly better be Than to
tell them nothing could possibly better be Than to

share with you and me on a dancing spree
share with you and me on a dancing spree

Jamming with you could be the best-tasting honey
Jamming with you could be the best-tasting honey
ho! ho! ho!

When we sing off-key it could be very funny
when we sing off-key it could be very funny

Jamming could make us feel young and fancy free
Jamming could make us feel young and fancy free

It could turn into the best music jamboree you see
It could turn into the best jamboree you

Come on down and join us and you'll enjoy a spree
Come on down and join us and you'll enjoy a spree

550 page

$0.00

You can still have some fun when the price is free
You can still have some fun when the price is free

And you and your buddies can jam until it
And you and your baddies can jam until it

gets to be three No matter who you are, you'll
gets to be three No matter who you are, you'll

have a reason to be After all is said and done
have a reason After all is said and done

we won't be outdone We'll all have lots of fun
we won't be outdone We'll all have lots of fun

la! la! la!

and have a merry sing-a-long We'll even
and have a merry sing-a-long We'll even

enjoy a jam with Air Force One We won't jump
ensoy a jam with Air Force One We won't jump

the gun; we'll be your native son
the gun; we'll be your native son

551 page

(110) Use Your Imagination (260)
Use Your Imagination

Be creative when you are working, and love what you do
Be creative when you are working, and love what you do

Find the silver lining in your clouds and fill them
Find the silver lining in your clouds and fill them

with joy too
with joy too

Be positively positive, spread some
Be positively positive, spread some

cheer does that give you a clue? Tell a joke,
cheer does that give you a clue? Tell a joke,

make someone smile, go that extra mile, buckaroo
make some one smile, go that extra mile, buckaroo

Be encouraging when your friends come near, don't
Be encouraging when your friends come near, don't

be sad or blue Use your imagination, make do with
be sad or blue Use your imagination, make do with

what you have grin it, and bear Use your
what you have grin it, and bear Use your

imagination and make someone laugh and care
imagination and make someone laugh and care

Transform simple, plain ware and give it wing anywhere
transform simple, plain ware and give it wing anywhere

Change plain things into gorgeous and lovely creations;
Change plain things into gorgeous and lovely creations;

use your great flair
use your great flair

When nothing is going
When nothing is going

right, imagine something better
right, imagine something better

Then look a
Then look a

little harder; it's better to use your head, sir
lillle harder; it's better to use your head, sir

The world will have a different view
the world will have a diffent view

but make a
but make a

compromise; don't err
compromise; don't err

You are full of interesting
you are full of interesting

and wonderful ideas
and wonderful ideas

because you are a go-getter
because you are a go-getter

553 page

When you think you are one of the Odd Couple just
when you think you are one of the Odd Couple just

get into your brainstorming huddle You can look
get into your brainstorming huddle You can look

in wonder because you are gorgeous and you
in wonder because you are gorgeous and you

look good when you cuddle Remember you are
look good when you cuddle Remember you are

totally different and unique and you can think
totally different and unique and you can think

clear as a bell You are never far from our
clear as a bell You are never far from our

thoughts you are valuable clientele When
thoughts You are valuable clientele When

you are faced with different challenges just give
You are faced with different challenges just give

Use your mind and be creative and imaginative
Use your mind and be creative and imaginative

And troubles will melt away like water through
and troubles will melt away like water through

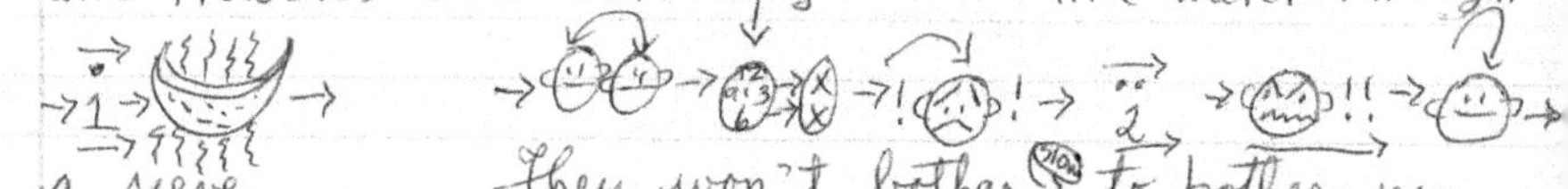

a sieve They won't bother, to bother you
a sieve They won't bother, to bother you

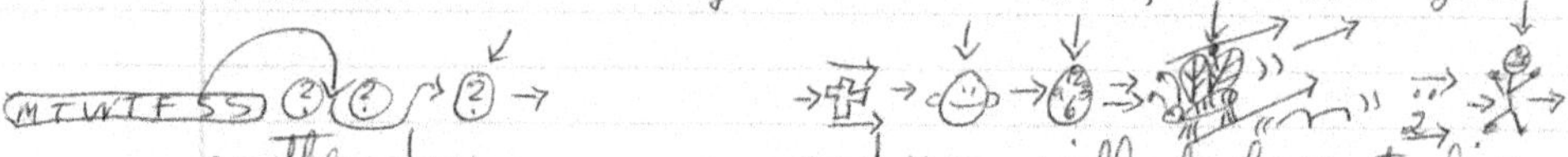

another day and you will be free to live
another day and you will be free to live

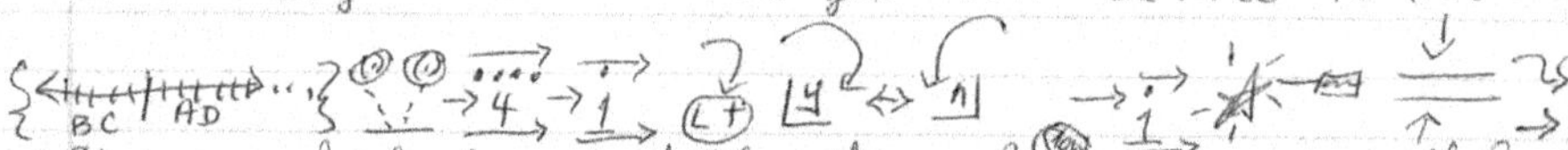

Always look for a different angle, a new parallel
Always look for a different angle, a new parallel

Forward, backward, up and down, in a nutshell
forward, backward, up and down, in a natshell

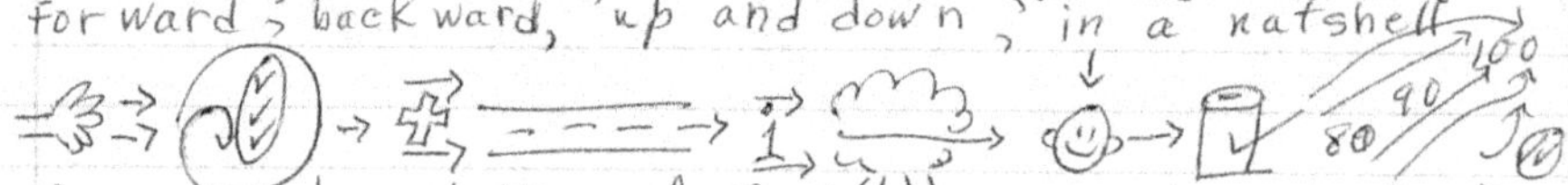

Go around and through the bush; you can excel
Go around and through the bush; you can excel

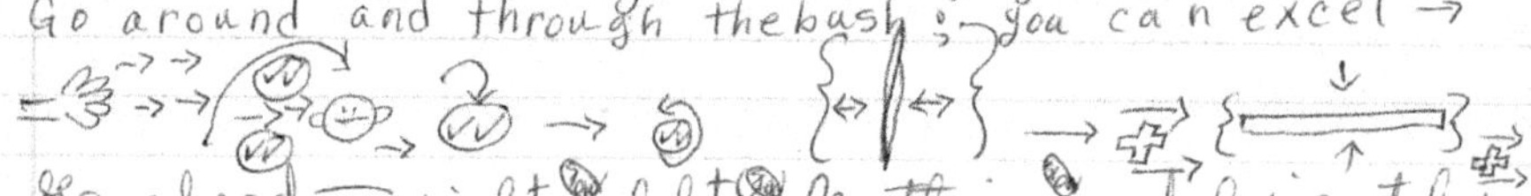

Go ahead — right, left, lengthwise, and horizontal;
Go ahead — right, left, lengthwise, and horizontal;

be a tinker bell not a jezebel
be a tinker bell not a jeze bel

(111) The Great Blue (262) 555 page

The Great Blue

We almost lost you in the ocean, so vast and
We almost lost you in the ocean, so vast and

blue Who, you ask? The great blue! that's who
blue Who, you ask? The great blue! that's who

Ooooh! Aeeee!

We surely would wail; that day we would rue
We surely would wail; that day we would rue

$\{x+y=n\}$

To lose the great blue whale on account of
To lose the great blue whale on account of

me and you You, blue, love us too I
me and you You, blue, love us too I

think you consider us a friend You give us
think you consider us a friend You give us

space and share with us all the oceans, end
space and share with us all the oceans, end

to end Instead, we attack you when you
to end Instead, we attack you when you

when you try to ascend — We are cruel, indeed
when you try to ascend — We are cruel, indeed

to hunt you to the bitter end — We have almost
to hunt you to the bitter end — We have almost

made a great, big mess — By causing you such
made a great, big mess — By causing you such

heartache and distress — Learning to love you
heartache and distress — Learning to love you

is the test that is our quest — The great Blue
is the test that is our quest — The great Blue

must not become another Loch Ness — You
must not become another Loch Ness — You

are definitely friendly and intelligent — You
are definitely friendly and intelligent — You

cause us no reason for discontent — But in
cause us no reason for discontent — But in

return, people cause you nothing but torment
return, people cause you nothing but torment

557 page

What we need to do is resolve rectify and
What we need to do is resolve rectify and

repent The things you must have seen
repent The things you must have seen

The places where you must have been If you
The places where you must have been If you

could talk to us, your words would be full
could talk to us, your words would be full

of wisdom, crisp and clean Your insight
of wisdom, crisp and clean Your insight

would also be clear and keen The
would also be clear and keen The

patience you must possess; we can only guess
patience you must possess; we can only guess

And kindness so enormous, as to greatly impress
And kindness so enormous, as to greatly impress

We would think, what with all of man's great progress
We would think, what with all of man's great progress

We would have learned not to get you in such
We would have learned not to get you in such
a mess All your friends are, as you, in such
a mess All your friends are, as you, in such
pandemonium Because of our strong
pandemonium Because of our strong
dominion and oppressions Over land and
dominion and oppressions Over land and
sea, we spread man's suppression Someday,
sea, we spread man's suppression Someday,
we also won't be free; there will be an end to
we also won't be free; there will be an end to
our aggression Then it will be our survival
our aggression Then it will be our survival
that is in the balance We will be very lucky,
that is in the balance We will be very lucky,
if we are given a last chance We might have
if we are given a last chance We might have

559 page

la la la la

to do more than sing and dance If we get
to do more than sing and dance If we get

stuck with our pants down and show our
stuck with our pants down and show our

underpants
underpants

(112) Testimony (264)
Testimony

560 page

My story has been told before It was kept,
My story has been told before It was kept,

well-hidden behind closed doors
well-hidden behind closed doors

Wouldn't you like to know more? It would
Wouldn't you like to know more It would

make wonderful folklore Secrets have a
make wonderful folklore secrets have a

habit of coming out Because everyone is nosy
habit of coming out Because everyone is nosy

and curious what they are all about Why the
and curious what they are all about why the

old man was so furious and why he shouts
old man was so furious and why he shouts

Why there has been a major blowout There
why there has been a major blowout There

is always a silver lining Behind every cloud
is always a silver lining Behind every cloud

that isn't shining There is a rainbow that
that isn't shining There is a rain bow that

follows — with colors winding After a heavy
follows — with colors winding After a heavy

rainfall, birds are chirping and singing Do
rainfall, birds are chirping and singing Do

you really want to know about this tale of woe?
you really want to know about this tale of woe?

That it was he who was my worst foe, a real no-no
That it was he who was my worst foe, a real no-no

He was the closest, but he was the very deadliest foe
He was the closest, but he was the very deadliest foe

He was the largest and he wore a bullet proof
He was the largest and he wore a bullet proof

vest, from head to toe He lives on, but from
vest, from head to toe He lives on, but from

that situation I am long gone and he's
that situation I am long gone and he's

where he always belonged He's in my past;
where he always belonged He's in my past;

all alone, all woebegone Now he is but an
all alone, all woebegone Now he is but an

unfortunate phenomenon I can say I've
unfortunate phenomenon I can say I've

broken my personal hatred cycle I rang my
broken my personal hatred cycle I rang my

own bell; I've chosen to accept and to dispel
own bell; I've chosen to accept and to dispel

All and any hatred so that I may be healthy and
All and any hatred so that I may be healthy and

well And so that I may become a happy
well And so that I may become a happy

mademoiselle I know I have won and I am a
mademoiselle I know I have won and I am a

special someone, Especially to all my precious
special someone Especially to all my precious

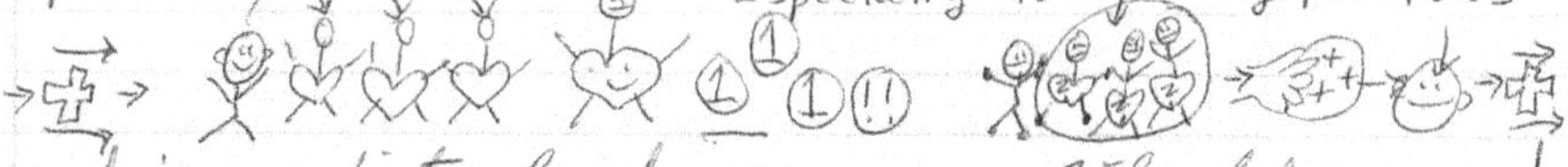

and immediate loved ones Who help me and
and immediate loved ones Who help me and

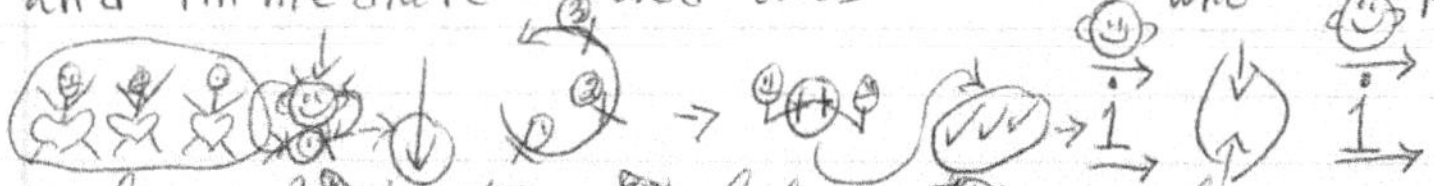

whom I, in turn, help out, one by one
whom I, in turn, help out, one by one

With them, I feel like I am truly in the sun, having
With them, I feel like I am truly in the sun, having

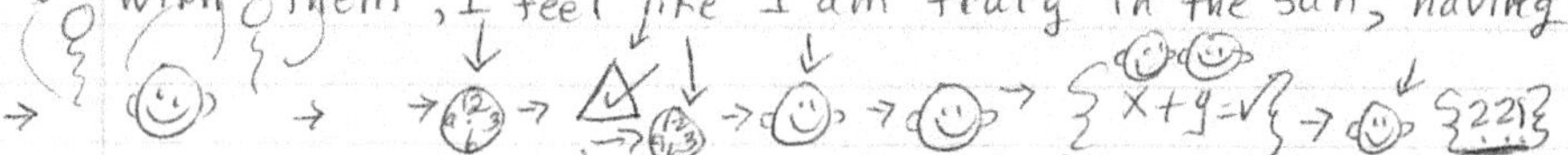

fun Now it is my happy situation, my chance,
fun Now it is my happy situation, my chance

and my turn That I may try to help by helping
and my turn That I may try to help by helping

others to be able to discern That there is lots of hope
others to be able to discern That there is lots of hope

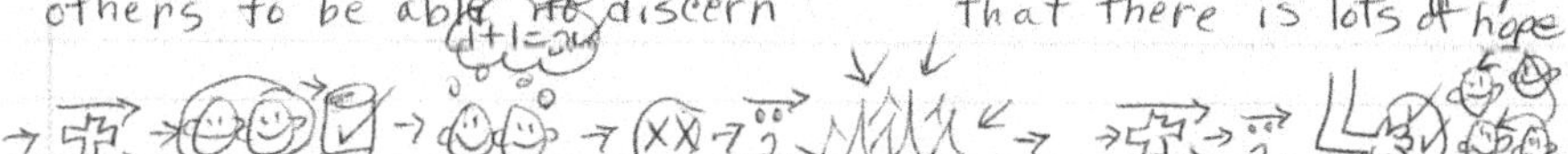

and we can learn, not to burn And to save ourselves
and we can learn, not to burn And to save ourselves

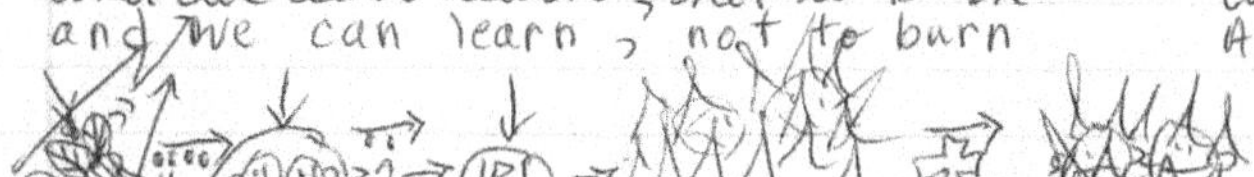

before we too are consumed and burn
before we too are consumed and burn

(113) I Am Happy (266)

I Am Happy

(564) page

No bad news for me, (568) I will no longer let it be
No bad News for me, I will No longer let it be

My new love has set me free, and love is the key
My new love has set me free, and love is the key

To also send people my way is my only plea So
To also send people my way is my only plea So

that I'll have memories about you and me,
that I'll have memories about you and me,

you see Don't tell me bad news I refuse to
you see Don't tell me bad News I refuse to

listen to the blues I'll give you a major clue
listen to the blues I'll give you a major clue

I don't pay attention to the bad reviews
I don't pay attention to the bad reviews

Give me something positive and I will be attentive
Give me something positive and I will be attentive

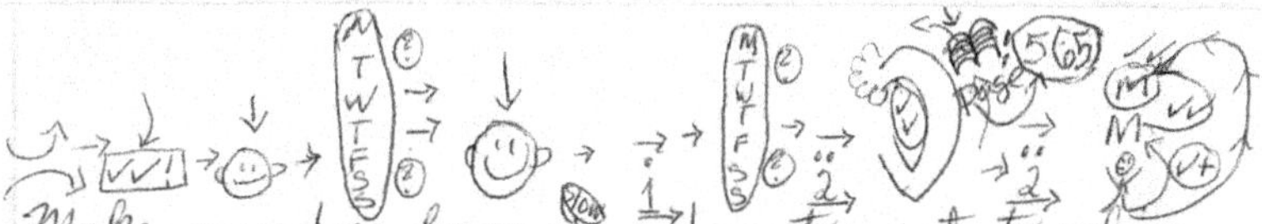

Make my day happy, a day to want to relive
Make my day happy, a day to want to relive

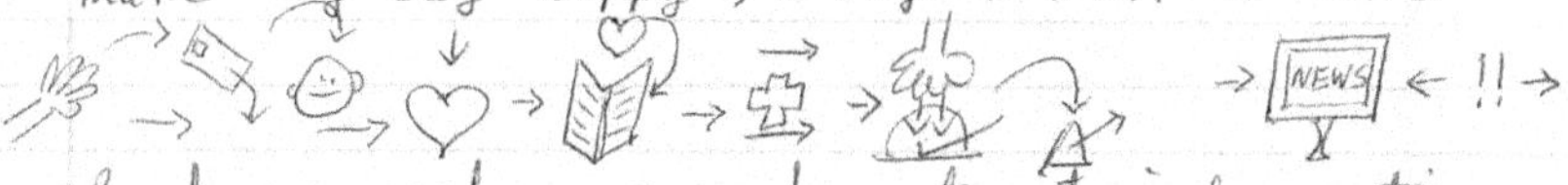

Send me good news and make it informative
Send me good news and make it informative

So that I can have a good, playful initiative
So that I can have a good, playful initiative

Then worries will disappear, and life will be clear
Then worries will disappear, and life will be clear

And happiness will replace tears with no more fears
And happiness will replace tears with no more fears

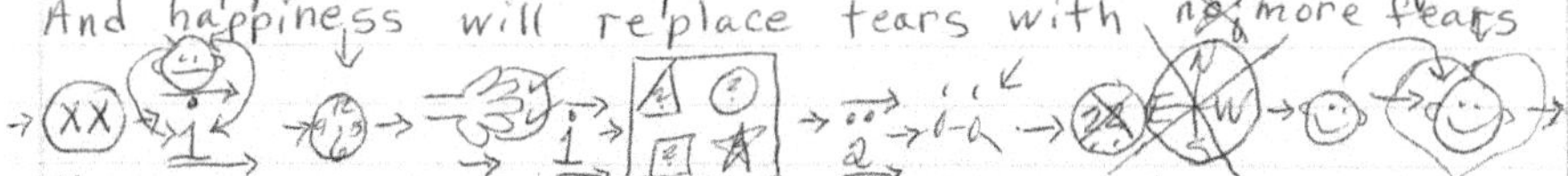

No one will have a reason to cry anywhere my dear
No one will have a reason to cry anywhere my dear

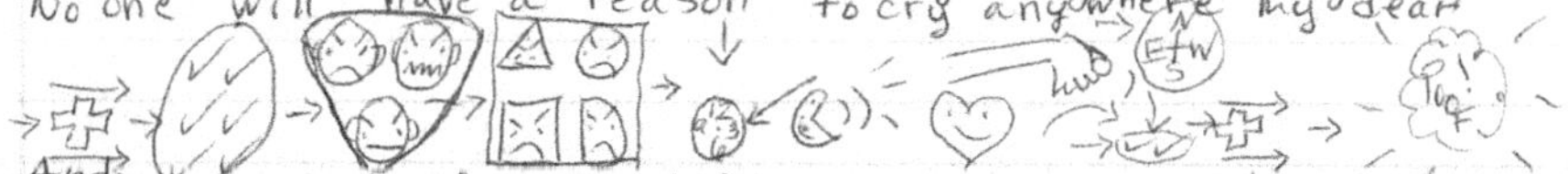

And all bad things will say good-bye and disappear
And all bad things will say good-bye and disappear

Ah, our lives will be fun, our lives have just begun
Ah, our lives will be fun, our lives have just begun

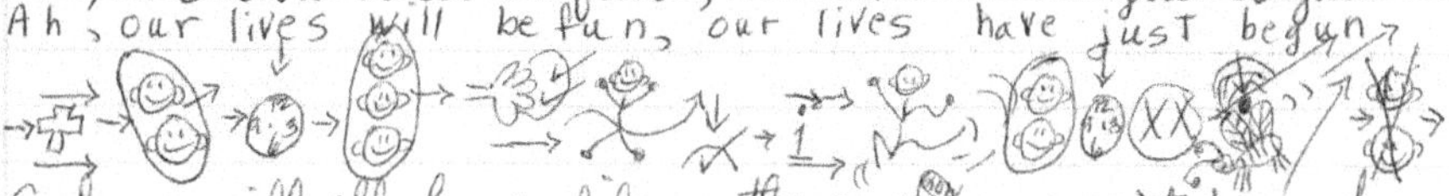

And we will all have life on the run, we won't be undone
And we will all have life on the run, we won't be undone

We will be happy all the time while basking in the sun
We will be happy all the time while basking in the sun

True love will surely be mine and I will again
True love will surely be mine and I will again

feel like number 1 Thoughts of people will
feel like number 1 Thoughts of people will

happily stay Memories will no longer go away
happily stay Memories will no longer go away

or stray Love will come to stay with me
or stray Love will come to stay with me

again and every day Faster than you can
again and every day Faster than you can

buy them on EBay I'll enjoy life while I can,
buy them on EBay I'll enjoy life while I can,

I'll feel like a number 10 I won't look back
I'll feel like a number 10 I won't look back

to way back then ever again I'll choose to be
to way back then ever again I'll choose to be

happy all the time, my friend Because I've
happy all the time, my friend Because I've

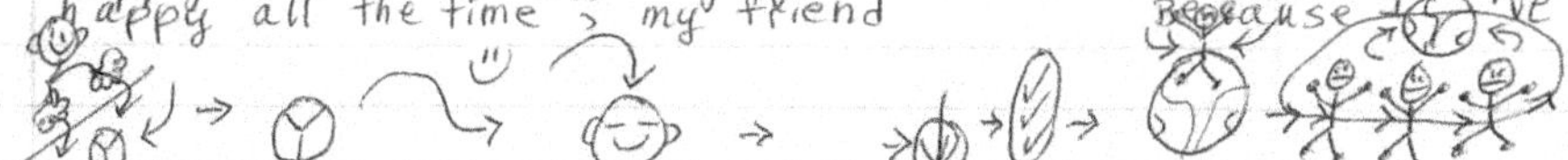

found peace of mind in all mortal men
found peace of mind mortal men

You see, I have my own free will, oh, what a thrill
You see, I have my own free will, oh, what a thrill

And I have chosen the happiness pill that will not kill
And I have chosen the happiness pill that will not kill

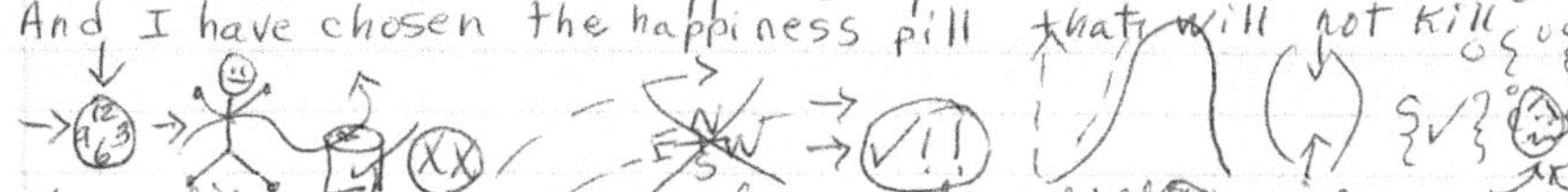

Now life can't go anywhere but uphill, with any ill
Now life can't go anywhere but uphill, with any ill

will Because I am happy, happier, and
will Because I am happy, happier, and

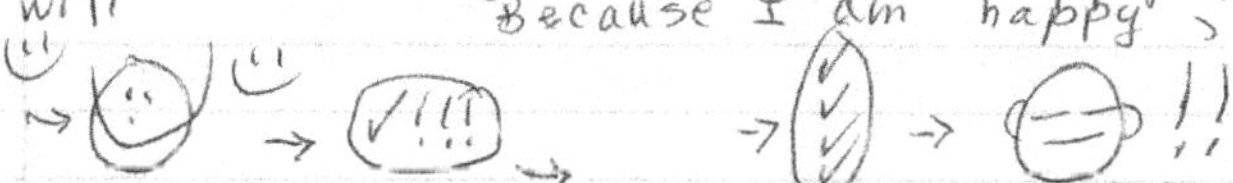

happiest still — all fulfilled
happiest still — all fulfilled

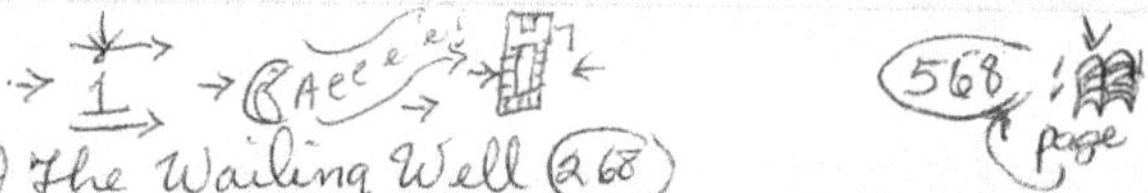

568 page

(114) The Wailing Well (268)
The Wailing Well

I wish, I wish, I wish, do tell   I wail, I wail,
I wish, I wish, I wish, do tell   I wail, I wail,

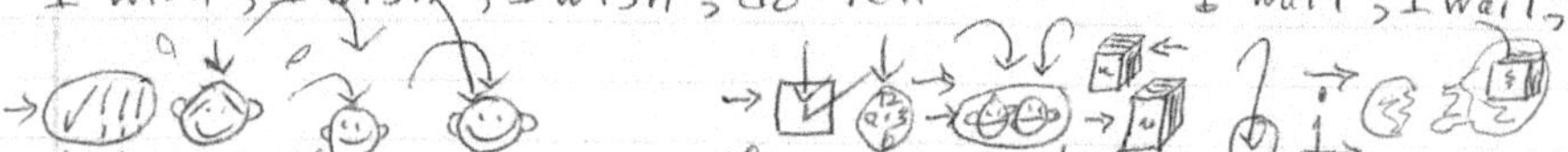

but fare thee well   That's their tales in a nutshell
but fare thee well   That's their tales in a nutshell

Here we have   The wailing well, clientele   Not
Here we have   The wailing well, clientele   Not

at all a falsehood tale   These are true as can be,
at all a false hood tale   These are true as can be,

all hail   So wail on, dear players, without fail
all hail   So waid on, dear players, without fail

Try to pass the buck; I wish you luck   it never
Try to pass the buck; I wish you luck   it never

fails   Wish for Fantasy Island never you
fails   Wish for Fantasy Island never, you

mind   It can be your very next find, well-defined
mind   It can be your very next find, well-defined

569 page

Go ahead : make a wish, whole and refined
ahead : make a wish , whole and refined

Wish on the wailing well, for peace of mind
Wish on the waiting well for peace mind

Reveal your fondest wishes and dreams and
Reveal your fondest wishes and dreams and

where you have been And uncover your most
Where you have been And uncover your most

outrageous and wildest schemes just
outrageous and wildest schemes just

close your eyes, wish, and let yourself feel all
your eyes close wish , and let yourself feel All

your dreams and wishes will turn on their heels
your dreams AND wishes will turn on their heels

This well is full of saints, innocent and quaint
This well is full of saints innocent and quaint

It is home of some of the greatest complaints
It is home of some of the greatest complaints

Some of the voices tend to grow weak and faint
some of the voices tend to grow weak and faint

And the most impatient
And the most im patient

have learned to have
have learned to have

restraint
restraint

Go ahead; fill the well up to the
Go ahead; fill the well up to the

brim
brim

It'll never let on what you have said or
It'll Never let on what you have said or

where you have been
where you have been

To fill it completely up
To fill it completely up

has yet to be done or to be seen
has yet to be done or to be seen

It'll never
It'll Never

be filled up because
be filled up because

all wishes are invisible
all wishes are invisible

and unseen
and unseen

If the wailing well could tell all
If the wailing well could tell all

its stories
its stories

It would be chock-full of many
It would be chock-full of many

past glories And would tell of many woes
past glories And would tell of many woes

and many worries And might give up the
and many worries And might give up the

age-old wisdom of Socrates Those famous
age-old wisdom of Socrates Those famous

wishes were thought of, but undone and
wishes were thought of, but undone and

unfinished at first The well lent an ear and
unfinished at first The well lent an ear and

became a silent cohort and put up a silent
became a silent cohort and put up a silent

fort It was a silent, gracious gesture of
fort It was a silent, gracious gesture of

support from a friend of sorts, which
support from a friend of sorts, which

didn't hurt In many a measure, the well
didn't hurt In many a measure, the well

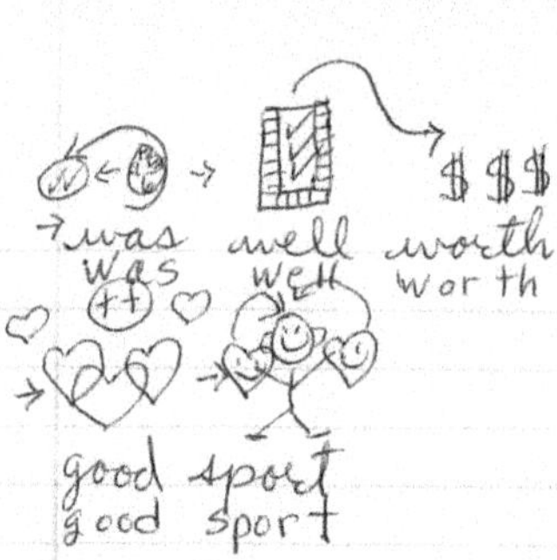

was well worth
was well worth
good sport
good sport

572
page
the effort of being a
the effort of being a

(115) My Aching Head (265)

My Aching Head

(573) page

I have a familiar ache and I feel just like a rake
I have a familiar ache and I feel just like a rake

It feels like my head will break now that I
It feels like my head will break now that I

am awake It throbs right there between
am awake It throbs right there between

my eyes like an earthquake And it feels like
my eyes like an earthquake And it feels like

I've been bitten by a rattlesnake So I follow
I've been bitten by a rattlesnake So I follow

through with a pint of brew for a brand-
through with a pint of brew for a brand-

new view Thinking it might make my
new view Thinking it might make my

migraine call a truce, thank you Truth is,
migraine call a truce, thank you Truth is,

it is just a cheap excuse to let loose and start
it is just a cheap excuse to let loose and start
anew Looks like I've again cooked my own
anew Looks like I've again cooked my own
goose through and through Now in the same
goose through and through Now in the same
thought, I could find me a bottle of wine
thought, I could find me a bottle of wine
This might help me to relax and unwind or just
This might help me to relax and unwind or just
toe the line Then again, it might cause me to
toe the line Then again, it might caase me to
get out of line; that could be a danger
get out of line; that could be a danger
sign If my wine is spiked, I might
sign If my wine is spiked, I might
go out of my mind and make headlines
go out of my mind and make head lines

575 page

Next, I'll get to that gosh-darned hard
Next, I'll get to that gosh-darned hard

stuff, its not so tough, and I scoff This is no
stuff, its not so tough, and I scoff This is no

longer the coffeinated stuff, this is the hard
longer the caffeinated stuff, this is the hard

stuff, its decaf It makes me sneeze, it makes
stuff, it's decaf It makes me sneeze, it makes

me cough, and then my germs have lift off,
me cough, and then my germs have lift off,

cough, and cough The secret is whether
cough, and cough The secret is whether

I know when I've had enough or if I
I know when I've had enough or if I

become a big show-off This story will
become a big show-off This story will

all end up with me having a case of the bends
all end up with me having a case of the bends

Then I will be alone again because I will
Then I will be alone because I will

have lost all my friends Because I'll be a
have lost all my friends Because I'll be a

zero among normal men, and I'll be broke
zero among normal men, and I'll be broke

again I, sir, should have known when to
again I, sir, should have known when to

say when and when to say amen
say when and when to say amen

Now my life will begin again, my friend,
Now my life will begin again, my friend,

I'm out of rehab again Because my headache
I'm out of rehab again Because my headache

has gone right away after I got over the
has gone right away after I got over the

bends I am now on the right path again and I am
bends I am now on the right path again and I am

no longer in a prison all penned
no longer in a prison all penned
To the rehab,
To the rehab,

I can say thank you kindly,
I can say thank you kindly,
amen and amen
amen and amen

never again
never again
I will now have to change everyone
I will now have to change everyone

I hang around with
I hang around with
from now and herewith
from now and here with

When I now go to the bar, my drinking alcohol
when I now go to the bar, my drinking alcohol

will have to be a myth
will have to be a myth
Instead of being a John,
Instead of being a John,

I now will have to be a Smith
I now will have to be a Smith
and java I
and jam I

will have known to be with
will have known to be with
I will change my
I will change my

stripes from there to herewith
stripes from there to herewith
and I'll be the
and I'll be the

better off; that's the gist No more boos for
better off; that's the gist No more boos for

this poor lonesome fellow I have a new
this poor lonesome fellow I have a new

portfolio It's enough that my mind is forever made
portfolio It's enough that my mind is forever made

of Jell-O and now I am a sloppy Moe
of Jell-O and now I am a sloppy Moe

And I might say good-bye to you instead of hello
And I might say good-bye to you instead of hello

get ready, get set, go And if you give me
get ready, get set, go And if you give me

directions to go home I might end up in
directions to go home I might end up in

Mexico
Mexico

! 579 page

152. My Bouncing Baby Boy (661)
My Bouncing Baby Boy

153. If It's All The Same (668)
If It's All The Same

154. Get Real -(version1) (673)
Get Real -(version1)

155. Get Real - (version 2) (678)
Get Real (version2)

(134) You helped Me Learn To Be Free 676
You helped Me Learn To Be

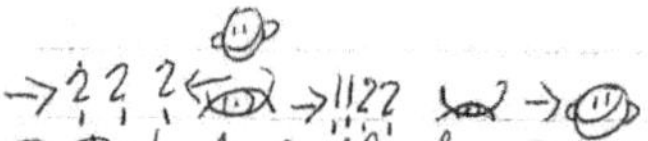

(135) Did I Really See You? 682
Did I Really See You?

(136) I'll Love You Tonight 686
I'll Love You Tonight

(137) My Darling Deborah 691
My Darling Deborah

(138) My Island 696
My Island

(139) I Will Create 702
I Will Create

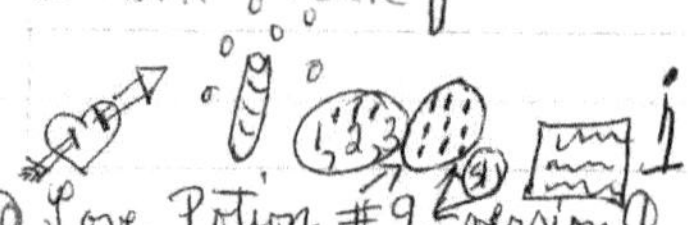

(140) Love Potion #9, version ① 708
Love Potion #9, Version ①

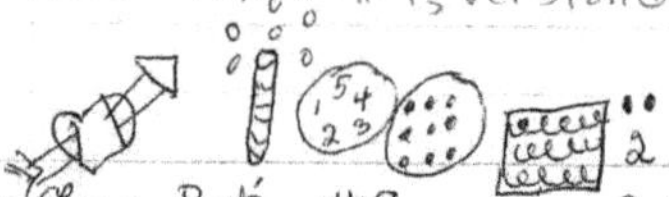

(141) Love Potion #9, version ② 713
Love Potion #9, Version ②

(142) My Cares Laid Bare - (version 1) 717
My Cares Laid Bare - (Vesion 1)

(143) My Cares Laid Bare - (version 2) 720
My Cares Laid Bare - (version 2)

(144) Give Me A Chance 726
Give Me A Chance

(145) That's a Lie 629
That's A Lie

(146) I Heard the Stillness Wail - (version one) 633
I Heard the Stillness Wail - (version one)

(147) I Heard the Stillness Wail - (version Two) 640
I Heard the Stillness Wail - (version two)

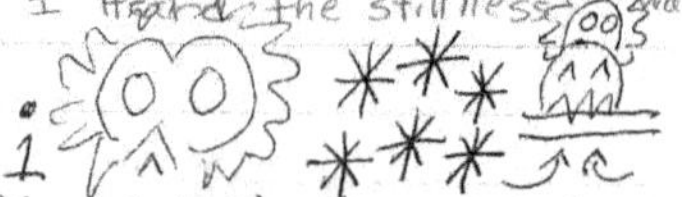

(148) The Majestic Snowy Owl 644
The Magestic Snowy Owl

(149) Hard As A Rock 648
Hard As A Rock

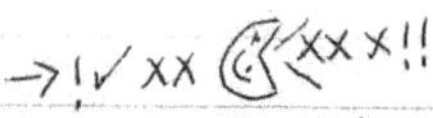

(150) Don't Lie 652
Don't Lie

(151) I'm gone with the Wind 656
I'm gone with the Wind

581 Page

(116) Bring the Music Back 583
Bring the Music Back

(117) Softly Beats The Heart of a Giant 588
Softly Beats The Heart of a Giant

(118) I Feel Just Like Brand New 592
I Feel Just Like Brand New

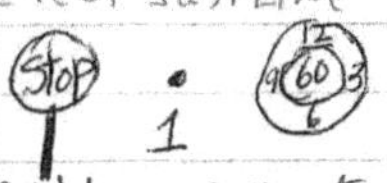

(119) Wait a Minute 595
Wait a Minute

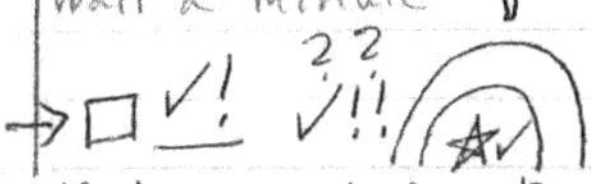

(120) That's Just Great 599
That's Just Great

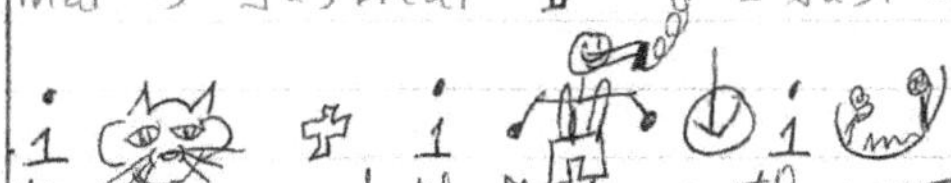

(121) The Pussy and the Farmer in the Dell 602
The Pussy and the Farmer in the Dell

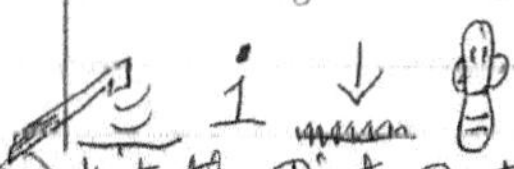

(122) Hit the Dirt, Bert 606
Hit the Dirt, Bert

(123) You're Under My Skin 610
You're Under My Skin

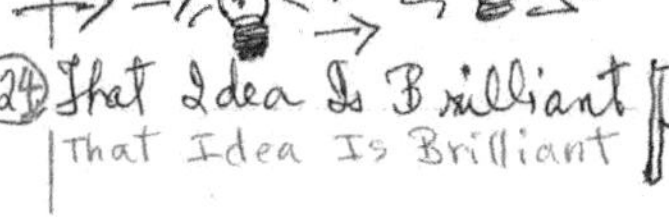

(124) That Idea Is Brilliant 614
That Idea Is Brilliant

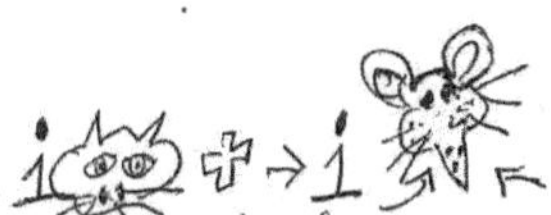

(125) The Cat and the Mouse 621
The Cat and the Mouse

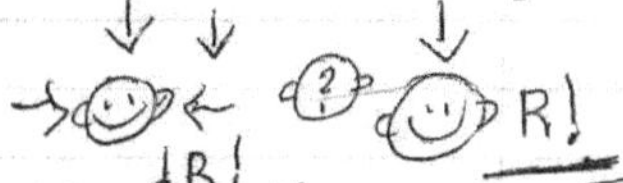

(126) You Are Who You are 628
You Are Who You are

(127) An Eye On The Sky 630
An Eye On The Sky

(128) The Long Arm Of The Law 644
The Long Arm Of The Law

(129) I Just Don't Understand the Master Plan
I Just Dont Understand the Master Plan

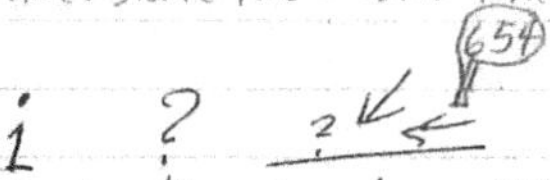

654

(130) The Question Remains 658
The Question Remains

(131) It's A Gamble 662
It's A Gamble

(132) I Like The Way You Wear Your Hair
I Like The Way You Wear Your Hair

(133) The Cards Are Dealt 676
The Cards Are Dealt

152. My Bouncing Baby Boy
My Bouncing Baby Boy

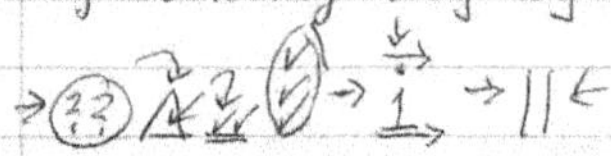

153. If It's All The Same
If It's All The Same

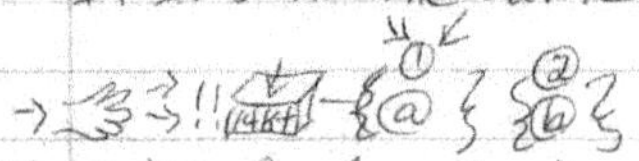

154. Get Real - (version 1)
Get Real - (version 1)

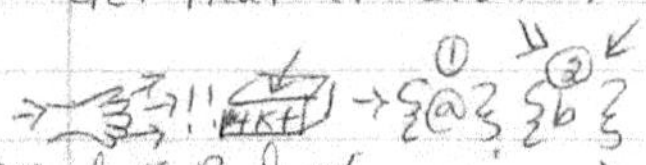

155. Get Real - (version 2)
Get Real - (~~version~~ version 2)

(583) : page

(116) Bring The Music Back (272)

Bring The Music Back

Don't turn your back
Don't turn your back

Bring the music back
Bring the music back

Remember what you lack
Remember what you lack

And put it in your
And put it in your

backpack
back pack

Simple things are often the best
Simple things are often the best

They're the ones that stand life's tests
They're the ones that stand life's tests

They're
They're

often the ones that cost less
often the ones that cost less

And they don't have
And they don't have

to cause a big mess
to cause a big mess

You don't have to
You don't have to

read lots and lots of books
read lots and lots of books

Just don't
Just don't

fill your head with gobbledy gook
fill your head with gobbledy gook

Also
Also

remember what you've been taught and
remember what you've been taught and

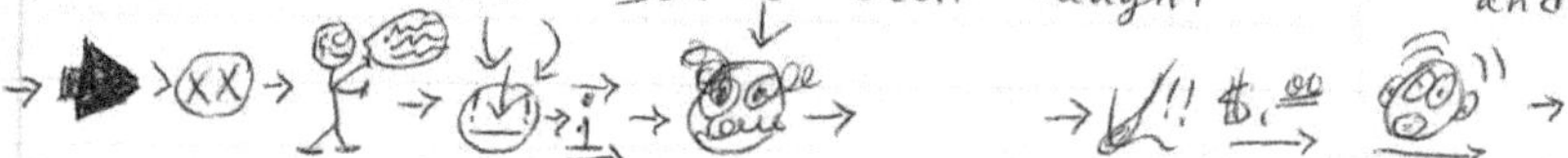

don't act like a kook So pay attention
don't act like a kook So pay attention

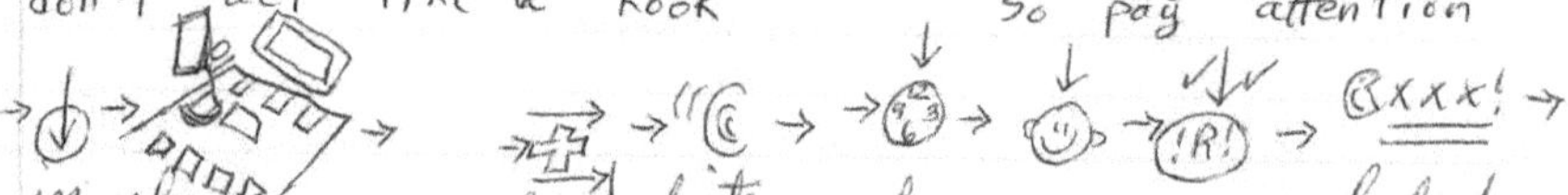

in class and listen when you are rebuked
in class and listen when you are rebuked

Remember that life is your classroom And
Remember that life is your classroom And

people are the dancers in your ballroom
people are the dancers in your ballroom

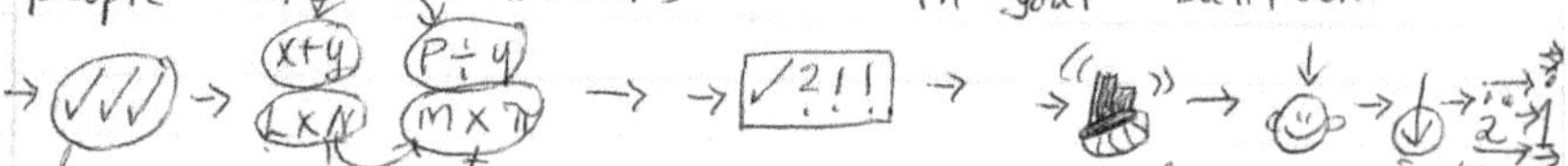

Some circumstances may make you into a
Some circumstances may make you into a

cartoon But poetry can be your escape
cartoon But poetry can be your escape

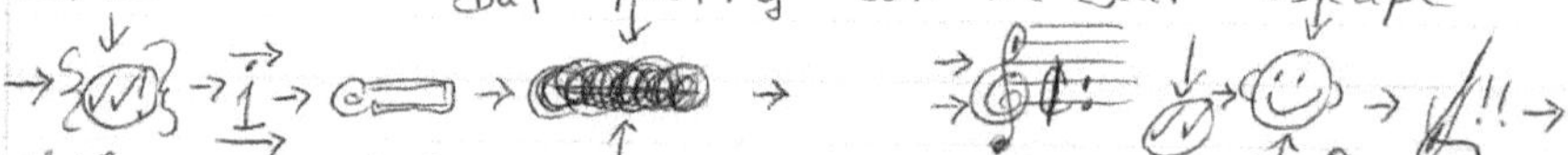

Like a safety cocoon Music is joy, so
Like a safety cocoon Music is joy, so

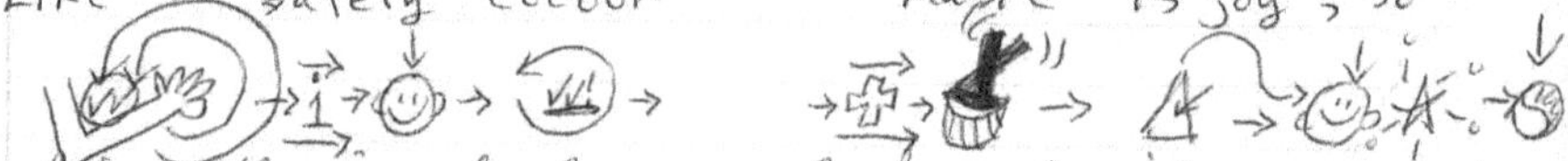

bring the joy back And make it your new toy
bring the joy back And make it your new toy

Use your new joy, smell your new joy
Use your new joy, smell your new joy

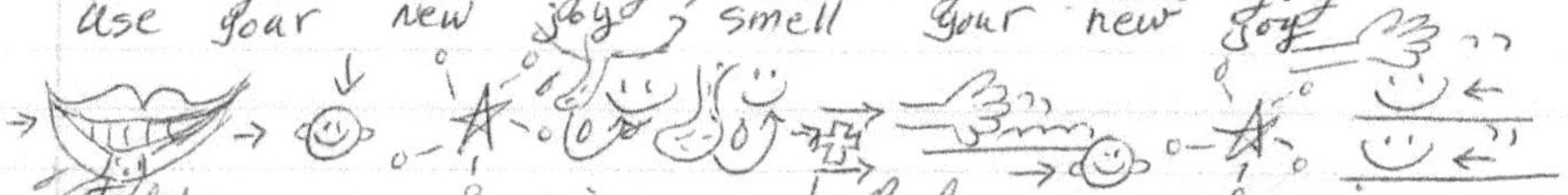

Taste your new joy, and feel your new joy
taste your new joy, and feel your new joy

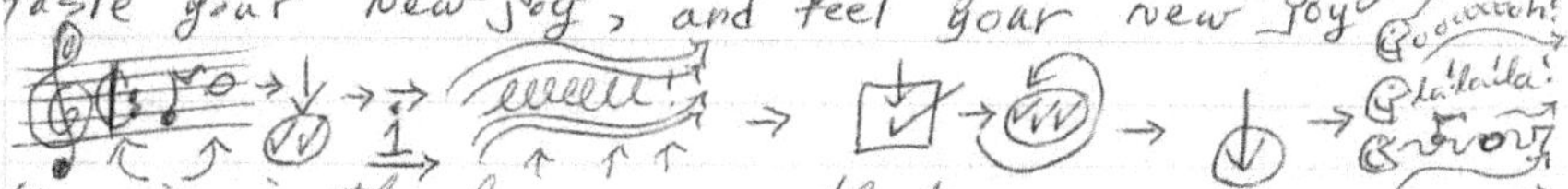

Music is the language that comes in many
Music is the language that comes in many

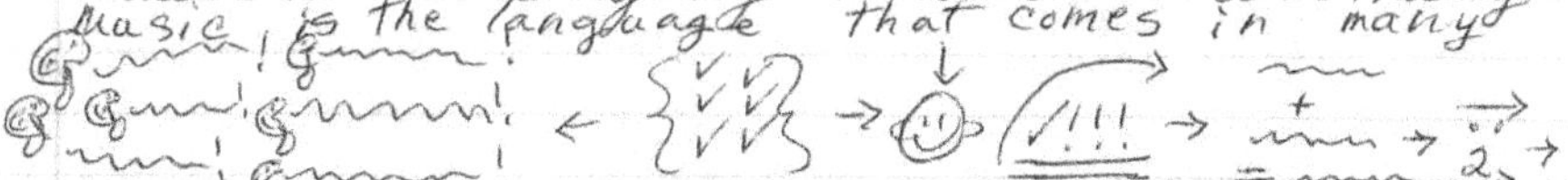

tongues which you should learn to
tongues which you should learn to

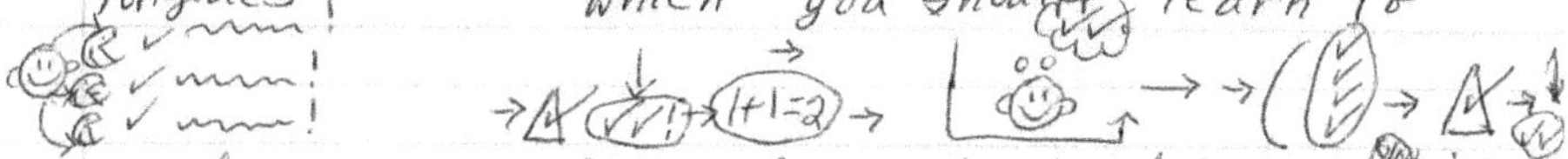

employ It is easily understood by all, it's
employ It is easily understood by all, it's

the real McCoy If you apply all this to
the real McCoy If you apply all this to

all your music, you'll have the trick You'll
all your masic, you'll have the trick You'll

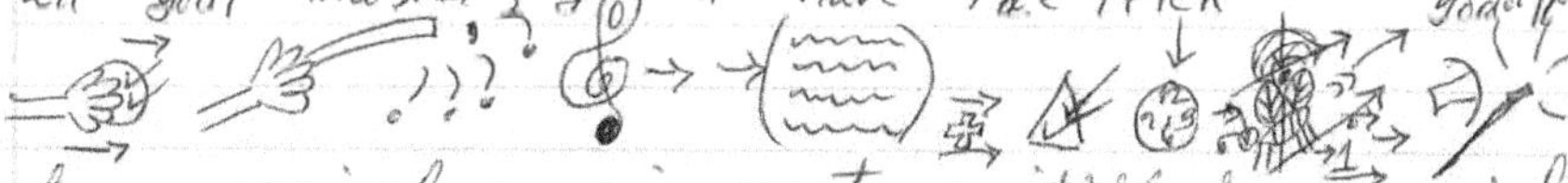

have magical music poetry; it'll be a magical
have magical masic poetry; it'll be a magical

flick That can't be defeated by any dirty trick
flick That can't be defeated by any dirty trick

or measured by any yardstick
or measured by any yardstick
There's
There's

something deadly serious about
something deadly serious about
a wonderful
a wonderful

love story
love story
that's homemade and handpicked
that's homemade and handpicked

It'll be so serious, it will be like liquid fire,
It'll be so serious, it will be like liqiud fire,

which you can't help but admire
which you can't help but admire
It'll
It'll

surpass all your joys and bring you
skrpass all your joys and bring you
higher
higher

and higher up its fiery spire
and higher up its fiery spire
I'll be some-
I'll be some-

thing of which you never tire and
thing of which you never tire and
something
something

to which you can aspire
to which you can aspire
It'll be something
It'll be something

of which will be a surefire hit in your very
of which will be a surefire hit in your very
own heavenly choir The siren's wail will
own heavenly choir The siren's wail will
reveal a tale of pure hypnotic blackmail
reveal a tale of pure hypnotic black mail
and trap you in its gale The sound will
and trap you in its gale The sound will
be like when an angel exhales, and
be like when an angel exhales, and
everything else will pale It'll make sense
everything else will pale It'll make sense
in its own place and will unveil beauty
in its own place and will unveil beauty
like a nightingale I'll give you the answers to
like a nightingale I'll give you the answers to
the human race's questions like reading a beautiful fairytale
the human race's questions like reading a beautiful fairytale

588

(11?) Softly Beats The Heart (274)

Of A Giant

How can someone be so soft?
Yet be so strong up in his loft
The greatness shows through quite oft
To this giant, it is nothing new no guff
His heart is the ticket
It is the main sticky wicket
You wouldn't want to give it a kick
Instead, you would want to fix it
His heart

has been broken many, many times More
has been broken many, many times More

than much sad poetry and many nursery
than much sad poetry and many narsery

rhymes Those rejections were cruel, nasty
rhymes Those rejections were cruel, nasty

crimes First came the damage then he
crimes First came the damage then he

paid for it big time Something soft, yet
paid for it big time Something soft, yet

something so strong Can show a card hidden
something so strong Can show a card hidden

there all along When passing a certain someone
there all along When passing a certain someone

quite headstsong You'll know which one
quite head strong you'll know which one

when you hear this folk song His heart
when you hear this folk song His heart

travelled quite far Farther than any of his
cars He'll want to declare a love war
On his newfound admiring star He'll find
he has nothing to fear That his love is
nothing foreign or queer From one who only
wishes him to be near? One who herself
sometimes sheds a lonely tear She
hears his heart beat She sees his lovely feet
She thinks he is quite sweet He earns a

591 page

place upon her heart's love seat 1
place upon her heart's love seat

hope to someday find him by me always
hope to someday find him by me always

And keep this lovely man, oh so kind,
And keep this lovely man, oh so kind,

with me for all my days Always, in
with me for all my days Always, in

front of and behind me as my personal
front of and behind me as my personal

protégé I hope for him to stay
protegé I hope for him to stay

with me all of our days
with me all of our days

(118) I Feel Just Like Brand New (276)

I Feel Just Like Brand New

With you, I feel just like brand new You have
With you, I feel just like brand new

given me my first clue I feel like I want
given me my first clue I feel like I want

to say "I do" To you, my fellow, say
to say "I do" To you, my fellow, say

you do, too Will we ever get the chance?
you do, too Will we ever get the chance?

Or will we fall into a trance Love has
Or will we fall into a trance Love has

struck us with its powerful lance Now
struck us with its power ful lance Now

we must do love's dance You're my
we must do Love's dance you're my

favorite one With you, I can't and won't
favorite one With you, I can't and won't

come undone With you, I'll have lots of fun
come undone With you, I'll have lots of fun

With you, the battle will be won I now have a
With you, the battle will be won I now have a

new kind of skin I love you and your next of
new kind of skin I love you and your next of

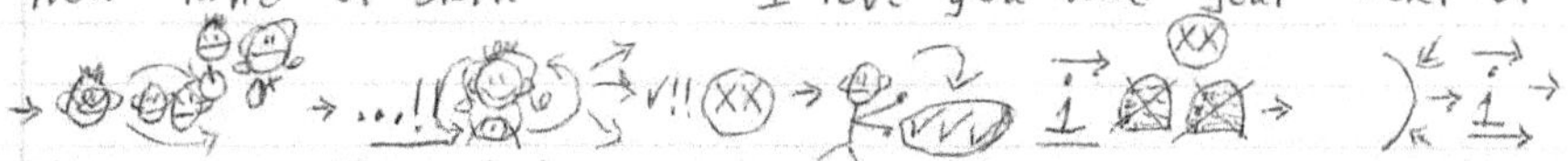

kin But I dare not commit a sin by the
kin But I dare not commit a sin by the

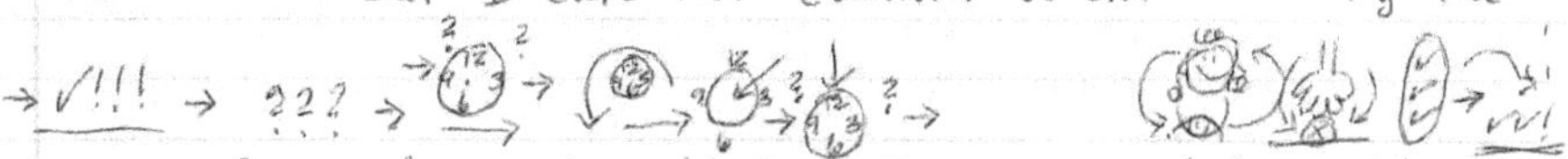

way, how long has it been? I have lots of
way, how long has it been? I have lots of

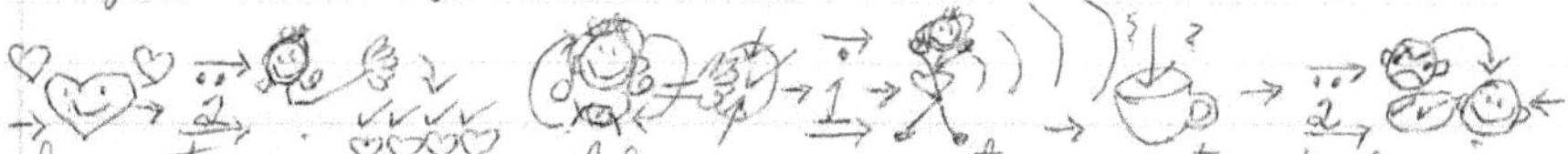

love to give I have a great capacity to forgive
love to give I have a great capacity to forgive

I know how it can be, to be dead and not to live
I know how it can be, to be dead and not to live

To feel my hope is running through my fingers
To feel my hope is running through my fingers

like water through a sieve I speak with authority
like water through a sieve I speak with authority

But not with superiority I may be your senior
But not with superiority I may be your senior

and may make some worry But if you were
and may make some worry But if you were

with me, we would make a beautiful story
with me, we would make a beautiful story

I love you with all my heart With you, I feel very
I love you with all my heart With you, I feel very

smart You give me a brand new start With you,
smart You give me a brand new start With you,

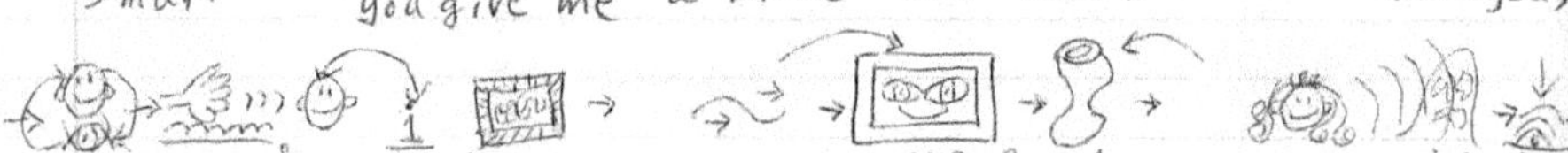

I feel like a piece of beautiful art My spirit is
I feel like a piece of beautiful art my spirit is

gone with the wind and blown away every day It feels
Gone with the wind and blown away every day It feels

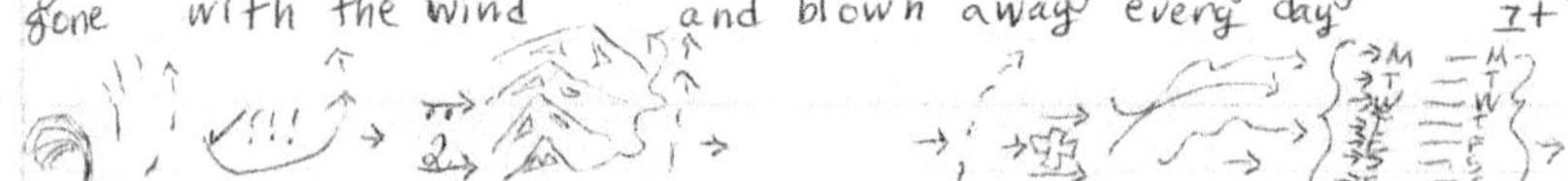

light enough to float up, up and away, every day
light enough to float up, up and away, every day

It is free and has flown away to play Now it is light hearted,
It is free and has flown away to play Now it is light hearted,

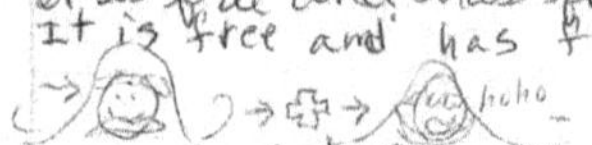

merry, and gay
merry, and gay

(595) page

(119) Wait A Minute (278)

Wait A Minute

Wait a minute, there - you - you are some
Wait a minate, there - you - you are some

awesome player Some think it's not fair,
awesome player Some think it's not fair,

but I don't really care White hairs are popping
but I don't really care White hairs are popping

from my head everywhere The older I get, the
from my head every where The older I get, the

thicker the layers What's that, what is it all about?
thicker the lagers What's that, what is it all about?

I heard you were a bored personality dropout
I heard you were a bored personality dropout

It was plain you were no Boy Scout Your
It was plain you were No Boy Scout Your

performance turned out to be a knockout You
performance turned out to be a knockout You

said, "Give me a hand," I said, "No, I won't
said, "Give me a hand," I said, "No, I won't

be just a one-night stand." But the experience
be just a one-night stand." But the experience

was the best in all the land It was beautiful
was the best in all the land It was beautiful

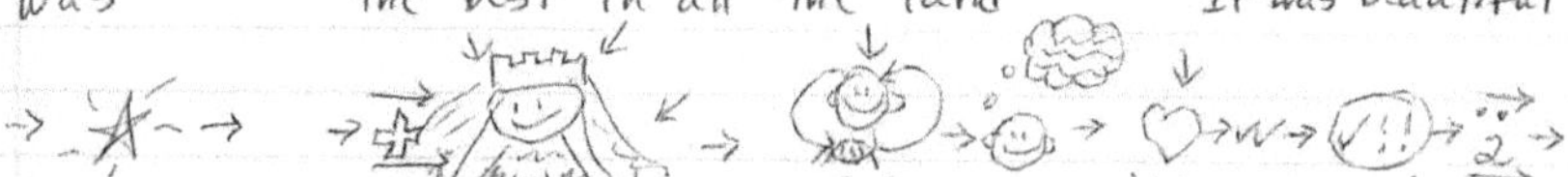

awesome, and grand I thought it's bound to
awesome, and grand I thought it's bound to

continue To always be something new
continue To always be something new

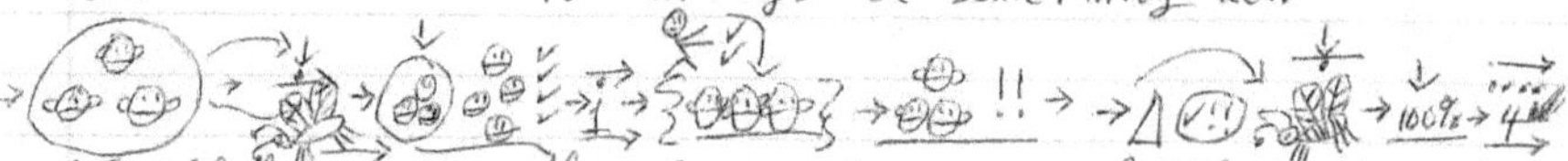

We'll be among the chosen few It'll be true for
We'll be among the chosen few It'll be true for

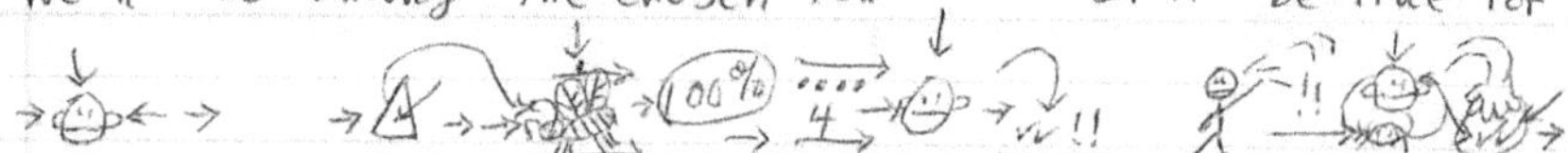

me it'll be true for you too Hey– I have
me it'll be true for you too Hey - I have

much, much more to convey Come on down now,
much, much more to convey Come on down now,

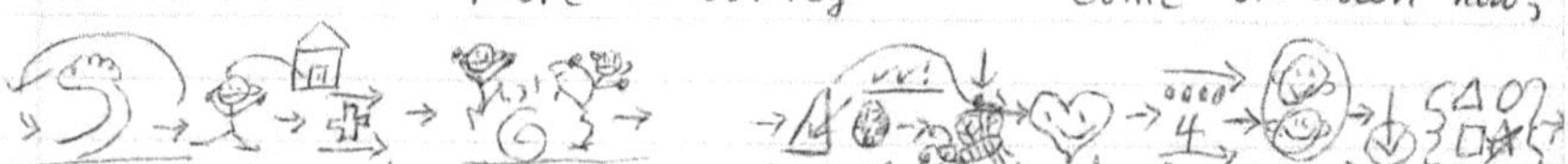

come out and play It'll be good for us in every
Come out and play It'll be good for us in every

way, gangway It'll ~~be~~ good every single day
Way, gangway It'll be good every single day

afterday We'll make time last while we can
after day We'll make time last while we can

I'm your woman and you're my man Do you
I'm your woman and you're my man Do you

understand my command? The answer is in
understand my command? The answer is in

our new dreamland A minute may sometimes
our New dreamland A minute may sometimes

seem like an hour In which time we will bloom
seem like an hour In which time we will bloom

like perennial flowers Your willpower will
like perennial flowers Your will power will

be devoured by a superpower And I will be
be devoured by a superpower And I will be

a wildflower instead of a wallflower
a wild flower instead of a wallflower

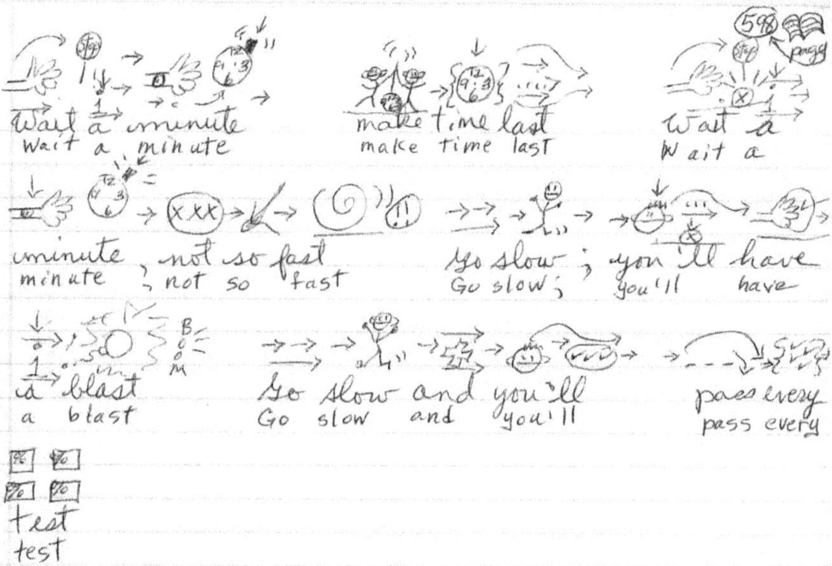

Wait a minute make time last Wait a
Wait a minute make time last Wait a
minute ; not so fast Go slow ; you'll have
minute ; not so fast Go slow ; you'll have
a blast Go slow and you'll pass every
a blast Go slow and you'll pass every
test
test
B O O M
page

(120) That's Just Great (280)

That's Just Great

Yeah, that's just great
Yeah, that's just great

But wait, I must hesitate
But wait, I must hesitate

Until I find out my fate
Until I find out my fate

Until I see life
Until I see life

sitting on my plate
sitting on my plate

Yes, that's just great; I'll
Yes, that's just great; I'll

just sit and wait
just sit and wait

But right now I have a
But right now I have a

splitting headache
splitting headache

I guess I'll just have to wait
I guess I'll just have to wait

for my fate
for my fate

Until this headache is gone, at any
Until this headache is gone, at any

rate
rate

Then I'll follow through
Then I'll follow through

By trying
By trying

something new
something new

I'll give you a clue
I'll give you a clue

I'll
I'll

be a switcheroo It won't, this time, make me
feel blue With a little help from my friends
My enemies will go around the bend My
mind's torture will end again And my life
will improve to no end You say a little rest
Is all for the best I say, sir, you don't jest
Furthermore, I say that was always my quest
Peace and quiet is always for the best For
thoughts to successfully process And for

fear to dissipate and regress And also for

problems to fade and repress When

I think about it I'll just wait it out and sit

This can't hurt anyone a bit I will still

Keep my campfires lit While I sit and wait

I will contemplate my fate I'll realize it was

all worth the hesitate And I will end

up feeling really great

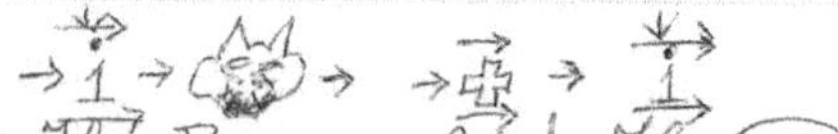

(121) The Pussy And The (282)
The Pussy And The

(602) page

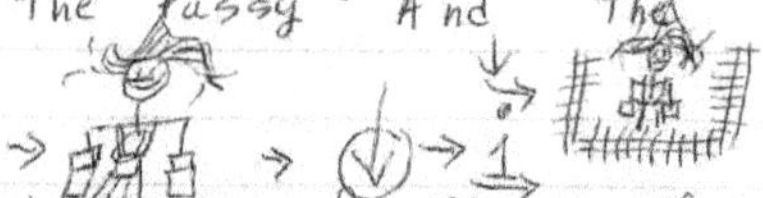

Farmer In The Dell
Farmer In The Dell

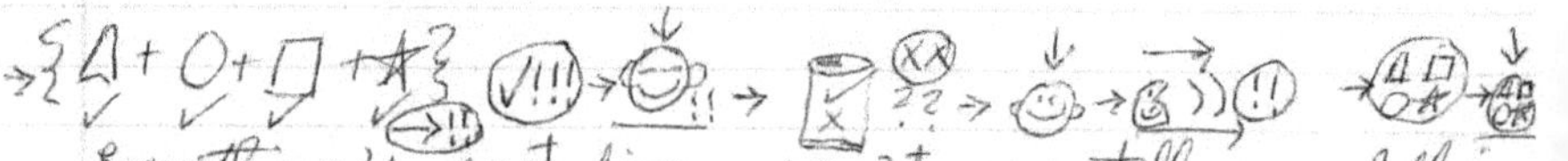

Everything's just fine, can't you tell All is
Everything's just fine, can't you tell All is

well, all is well, and all is well Especially
well, all is well, and all is well Especially

for that farmer in the dell Because just by
for that farmer in the dell Because just by

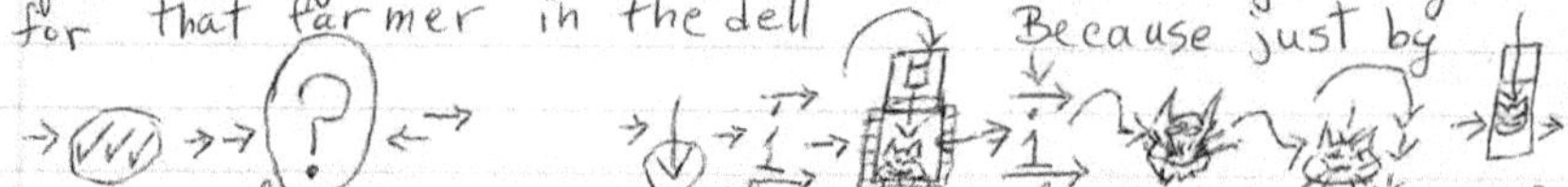

some chance in the well, the pussy has fell
some chance in the well, the pussy has fell

Ah hell, ah hell — ah hell, ah hell Ding-a-
Ah hell, ah hell - ah hell, ah hell Ding-a-

ling, I heard the pussy's collar bell
ling, I heard the pussy's collar bell

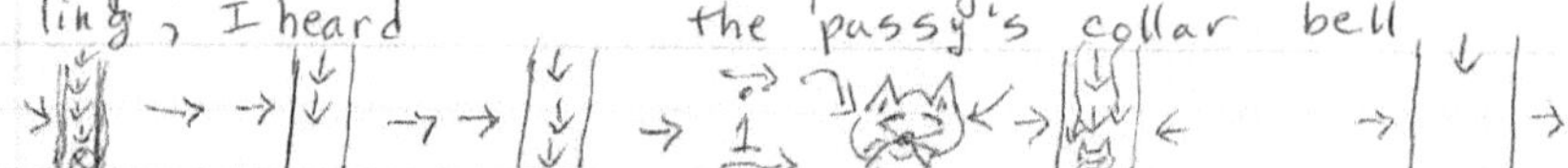

Down, down, down, the pussy fell Down,
Down, down, down, the pussy fell Down,

603 pages

down, down that there well
down, down that there well

That pussy had
That pussy had

a beautiful collar
a beautiful collar

It would have helped her;
It would have helped her;

if she had been taller
if she had been taller

You should have heard
You should have heard

her
her

SCREEEEECH SQUEAAHL AEEEE!

screech, squeal, and hollar
screech, squeal, and hollar

Finally, you could hear a splash
Finally, you could hear a splash

when she
when she

splash!

hit the water
hit the water

So long, good-bye to that
So long, good-bye to that

there pussy
there pussy

She was way too choosy, way
She was way too choosy, way

hmmm!

too fussy
too fussy

Mice were not her chosen
Mice were not her chosen

delicacy
delicacy

She was nothing but a brazen,
She was nothing but a brazen,

fussy, hussy She finally got on the
fussy hussy she finally got on the

farmer's nerves And got what she truly
farmer's nerves And got what she truly

deserved She will end up getting well-preserved
deserved She will end up getting well-preserved

Just like a pack of pickled hors d'oeuvres
Just like a pack of pickled hors d'oeuvres

As a result, the farmer was very, very happy
As a result, the farmer was very, very happy

grrr!
mmmaw!

Because the feline would no longer be catty
Because the feline would no longer be catty

and would be down the well's deep sea The rats
and would be down the well's deep sea The rats

would still continue to be ratty And the
would still continue to be ratty And the

townsfolk would continue to go batty And
townsfolk would continue to go batty And

that's that No welcome mat To pull from
that's that No welcome mat To pall from

a hat For that there cat PS;
a hat For that there cat PS;

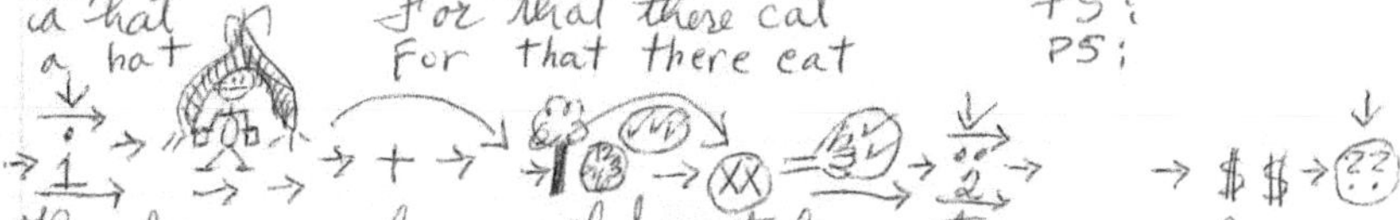

The farmer also would not have to buy any
The farmer also would not have to buy any

more tender vittles Or lose any more of his
more tender vittles Or lose any more of his

baby Chicken Little's He would not ever have
baby Chicken Littles would not ever have

to again play second fiddle And even
to again play second fiddle And even

though he had disposed of the pussy he would
though he had disposed of the pussy he would

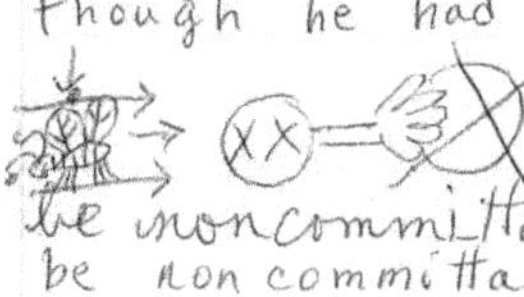

be noncommittal
be non committal

(606) page

(122) Hit The Dirt, Bert (284)
Hit The Dirt, Bert

You had better hit the dirt, Bert I think you
You had better hit the dirt, Bert I think you

have reached pay dirt You no longer need
have reached pay dirt You no longer need

to feel hurt But you might as well stay
to feel hurt But you might as well stay

alert We now share company among
alert We now share company among

royalty You, sir, czar, are a real cutie
royalty You, sir, czar, are a real cutie

Personally I am glad I can see I can now see
Personally I am glad I can see I can now see

lots to choose from, tee-he Did you
lots to choose from, tee-he Did you

say we are at war? Hit the dirt, Bert, or
say we are at war? Hit the dirt, Bert, or

You won't get far
You won't get far
This is no time to act
This is no time to act

like a star
like a star
Just because you are not
Just because you are not

in the company of the czar
in the company of the czar
We must be careful
We must be careful

where we walk
where we walk
Or we will belong to the
Or we will belong to the

school of hard knocks
school of hard knocks
If we step on one
If we step on one

of those Pandora's boxes
of those Pandora's boxes
We will blow up
We will blow up

and knock off more than our socks
and knock off more than our socks
There
There

might not be much left to show
might not be much left to show
Anyway
Any way

Bert, you were a good man to know
Bert, you were a good man to know

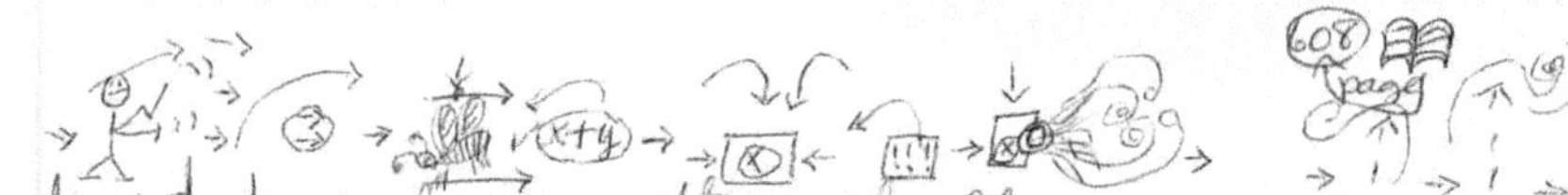

Good-bye because there she blows Up, up,
Good-bye because there she blows up, up,

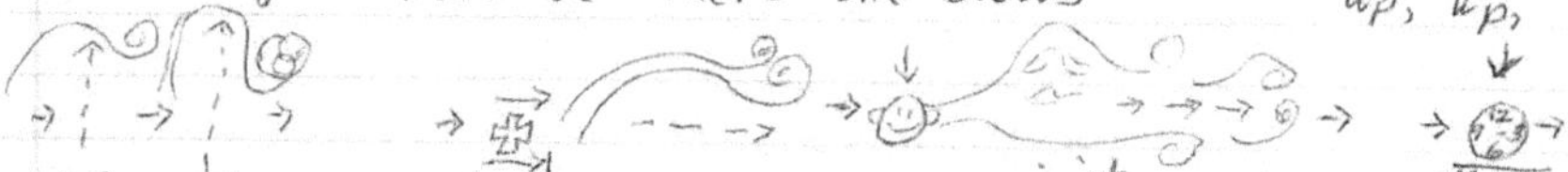

up, up and away, your spirit goes Now
up, up and away, your spirit goes Now

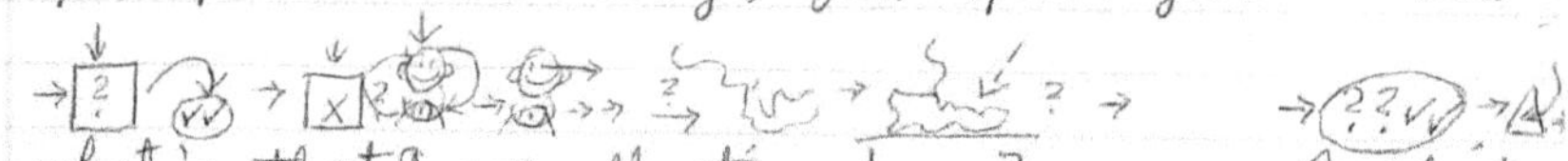

what's that I see floating down? Could it
What's that I see floating down? Could it

be a part of your army gown? I'm scared
be a part of your army gown? I'm scared

what I might find on the other side of
what I might find on the other side of

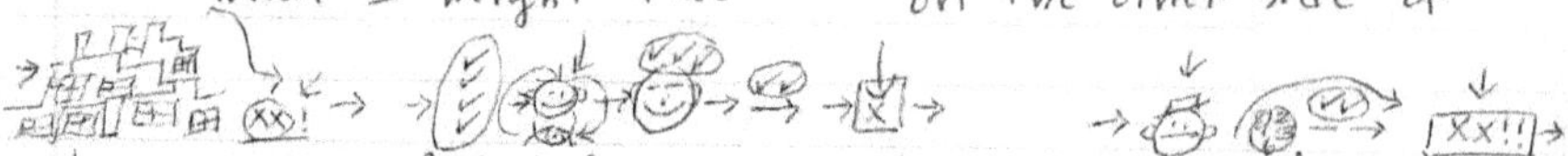

town All I know is that you will never
town All I Know is that you will Never

again be around I turned around when I heard a
again be around I turned around when I heard a

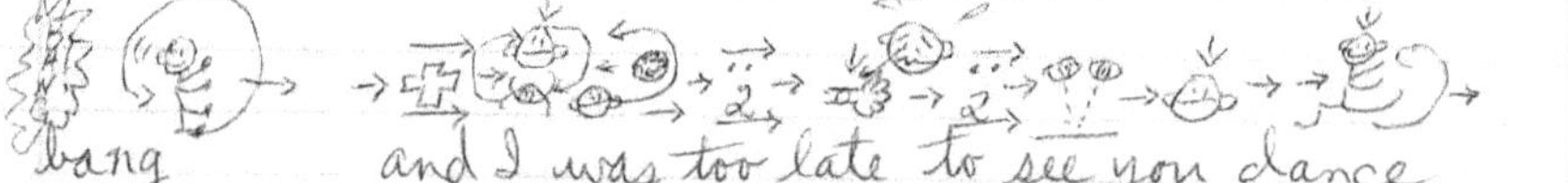

bang and I was too late to see you dance
bang and I was too late to see you dance

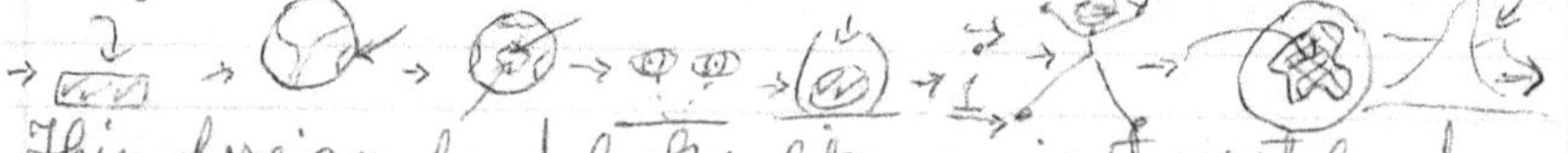

This foreign land looks like a giant wasteland
This foreign land looks like a giant wasteland

609 page

even at a second glance Bert, you didn't
even at a second glance Bert, you didn't

even have a fighting chance You didn't
even have a fighting chance you didn't

even have a chance to pose in a glorious
even have a chance to pose in a glorious

stance I will create an original, catchy
stance I will create an original, catchy

epitaph It will include how you were
epitaph It will include how you were

on the war path And also how you were
on the war path And also how you were

the world's friendliest psychopath And how no
the world's friendliest psychopath And how no

one will really care about the resulting
one will really care about the resulting

bloodbath
bloodbath

610 page

(123) You're Under My Skin (286)

You're Under my skin

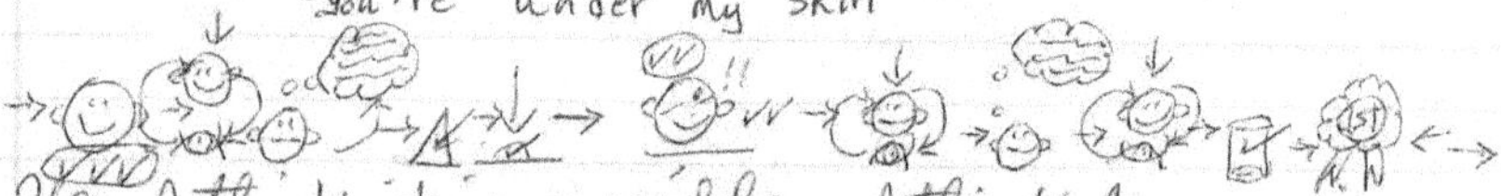

Yes, I think it is possible, I think I can win

Yes, I think it is possible, I think I can win

Because I have Y-O-U under my skin Where

Because I have Y-O-U under my skin Where

do I begin? I'll love you, again and again

do I begin? I'll love you, again and again

Y-O-U is the man for Din Din, my K-E-V-I-N

Y-O-U is the man for Din Din, my K-E-V-I-N

Holy cow and double wow You are my cat's

Holy cow and double wow You are my cat's

meow Go ahead and take a bow Too

meow Go ahead and take a bow Too

late, I caught you lying low Our love

late, I caught you lying low Our love

will be like gr-r-r-r, as it were

will be like gr-r-r-r, as it were

All you will hear is a happy purrrrrr
all you will hear is a happy purrrrrr

What could be our special attraction our special
what could be our special attraction our special

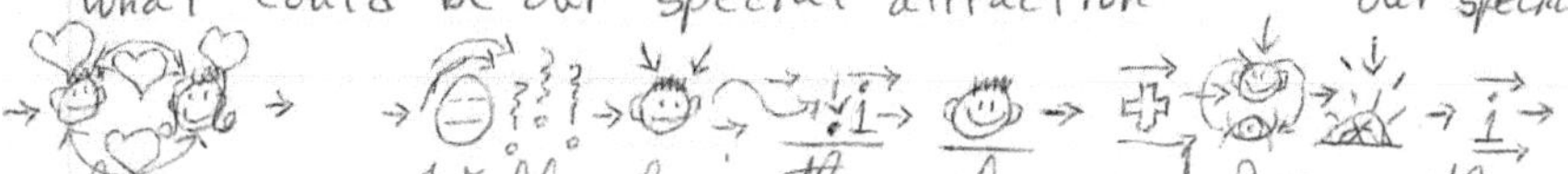

lure Well, he is the male, and I am the
lure Well, he is the male, and I am the

female I am not prejudiced and this
female I am not prejudiced and this

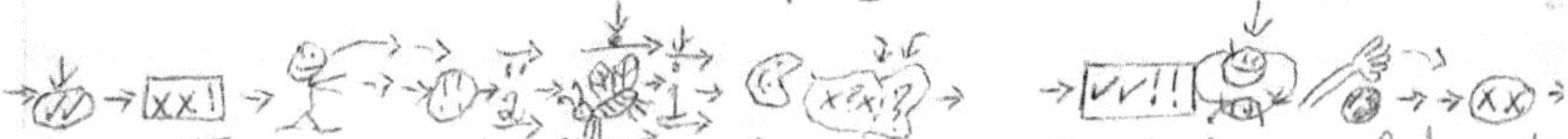

is not meant to be a slur But I wouldn't
is not meant to be a slur But I wouldn't

have anyone but my sir All I know is, we
have anyone but my sir All I know is, we

have what it takes Our love is real, for heaven's
have what it takes Our love is real, for heaven's

sake There is nothing about it counterfeit
sake there is Nothing about it counterfeit

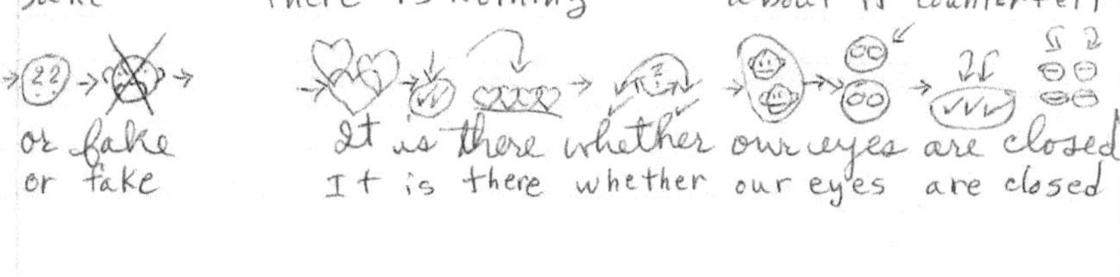

or fake It is there whether our eyes are closed
or fake It is there whether our eyes are closed

or whether we are wide awake I think
or whether we are wide awake I think

about you as much when you are not with
about you as much when you are not with

me Sometimes, when I sleep, it is your face
me Sometimes, when I sleep, it is your face

I see I love your attitude, so romantic and
I see I love your attitude, so romantic and

debonair yet so carefree When you soothe
debonair yet so carefree When you soothe

me with your quiet voice, I cannot help but
me with your quiet voice, I cannot help but

see your point of view and agree Our brains
see your point of view and agree Our brains

must be on the same wavelength Because when
must be on the same wavelength Because when

we kiss we give each other secret strength
we kiss we give each other secret strength

Our energy reaches further than any possible
Our energy reaches farther than any possible

length When we are together we go from
length When we are together we go from

the first through the tenth You, sir, are
the first through the tenth You, sir, are

definitely under my skin You are a giant among
de finitely under my skin You are a giant among

mortal men I want to be with you forever
mortal men I want to be with you forever

now and then and again I picked you out of
now and then and again I picked you out of

the bull's pen that's it, lights out. Amen.
the ball's pen that's it, lights out. Amen

614 page

(124) That Idea Is Brilliant (288)

That Idea Is Brilliant

That idea is brilliant; it is heaven sent and to
That idea is brilliant; it is heaven sent and to

our Earth has been, sent as a present
our Earth has been, sent as a present

This idea is bound to catch on and to enchant
This idea is bound to catch on and to enchant

until it replaces the brain of an egghead like
until it replaces the brain of an egg head like

a transplant Your idea has become a chant
a transplant Your idea has become a chant

when people are happy and when they are
when people are happy and when they are

angry, it becomes a rant There is no more need
angry, it becomes a rant There is no more need

to rave and pant or any need to gallivant
to rave and pant or any need to gallivant

Your composition is quite like a symphony it
your composition is quite like a symphony it
has the marks of a college degree It will be so
has the marks of a college degree It will be so
universal; we will all learn it for free because
universal; we will all learn it for free because
you let us share in your pedigree To prove this,
you let us share in your pedigree To prove this,
we all chimed it in time with glee we had read
we all chimed it in time with glee we had read
all the words earlier in the glossary It made us,
all the words earlier in the glossary It made us,
all feel happy and quite carefree; when we
all feel happy and quite care free; when we
recited it together we became, one big happy
recited it together we became, one big happy
family It became a new language: we said,
family It became a new language: we said,

go ahead, and be engaged Now there is no need
go ahead, and be engaged Now there is no need

for espionage or dirty stuff backstage Because
for espionage or dirty stuff backstage Because

now we have a universal entourage and
now we have a universal entourage and

everyone will also be on our page And we will all
everyone will also be on our page And we will all

think and talk the same on or off stage Whether
think and talk the same on or off stage Whether

we've come from the Stone Age or the Bronze
we've come from the Stone Age or the Bronze

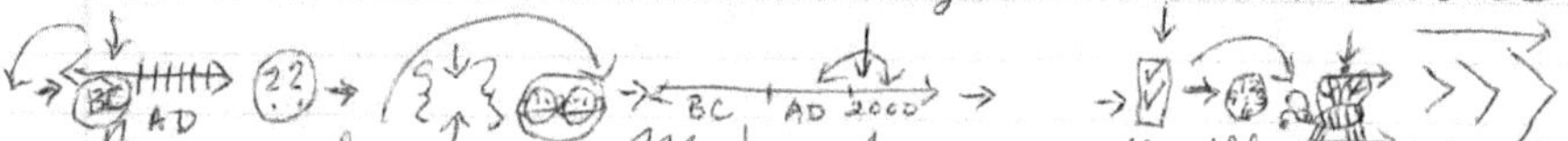

Age or from our Modern Age It will be very
Age or from our Modern Age It will be very

beneficial to all, and just because your idea
beneficial to all, and just because your idea

was off the wall It is still worth your being
was off the wall It is still worth your being

called can oddball because everyone will be
called an odd ball because everyone will be

singing your song by nightfall And because
singing your song by nightfall And because

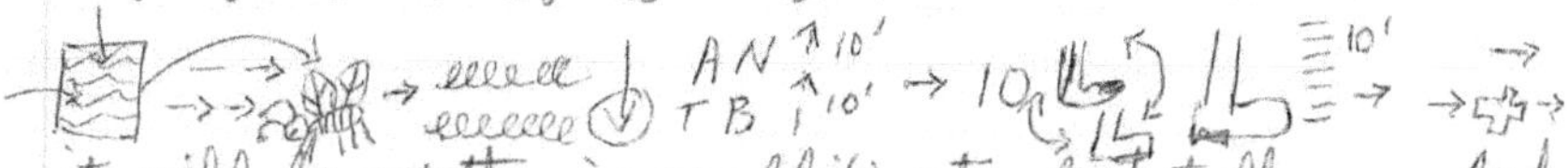

it will be written in graffiti – ten feet tall And
it will be written in graffiti – ten feet tall And

it will be preserved for all, in the long haul
it will be preserved for all, in the long haul

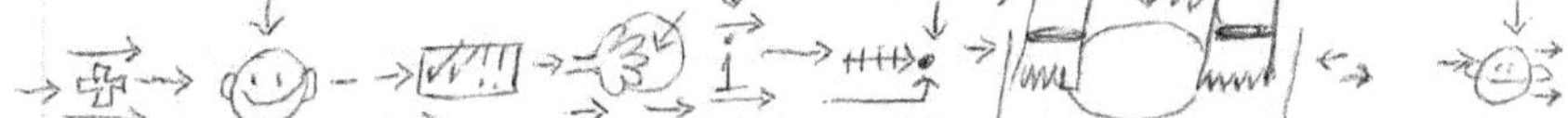

and you; will have the final curtain call You
and you; will have the final curtain call You

might even get an award if that doesn't make
might even get an award if that doesn't make

me sound too avant-garde And you didn't even
me sound too avant -garde And you didn't even

try to hard; you didn't even use a cue card
try to hard; you didn't even use a cue card

You were careful when you played your cards
You were careful when you played your cards

618 page

and because of this you were able to score
and because of this you were able to score

high on your score cards You proved you are
high on your score cards you proved you are

not a blowhard; You, sir, have many ideas
not a blowhard; you, sir, have many ideas

that will die hard People will look up to you
that will die hard People will look up to you

because you knew them through and through
because you knew them through and through

They will say you had a high IQ and that you
They will say you had a high IQ and that you

were the king of impromptu Whether or not
were the King of impromptu whether or not

this is true is totally an individual point
this is true is totally an individual point

of view it may be or may not be because
of view it may be or may not be because

of your idea but it will still be supposed to
of your idea but it will still be supposed to

come from me to you When you receive
come from me to you When you receive

this idea, I will share it with you gladly
this idea, I will share it with you gladly

Because I love all people and I hope for the best,
Because I love all people and I hope for the best,

you see And I try to treat everyone like they
you see And I try to treat everyone like they

are my friend, a VIP I also try to place a
are my friend, a VIP I also try to place a

thought seed, written in the pollen of each mind
thought seed, written in the pollen of each mind

of every human bee That idea is so brilliant
of every human bee That idea is so brilliant

it will outshine the most brilliant Rembrandt
it will outshine the most brilliant Rembrandt

It will be instrumental in creating as much energy as a power plant. Also everyone will see you in a different way — in a different slant. And it will have the power to grant a brand-new point of view, a brand-new power plant

(125) The Cat And the Mouse (291)

The Cat And the Mouse

Someone's living in my house, which they
someone's living in my house, which they
have turned into a clubhouse It's a familiar
have turned into a club house It's a familiar
bunch: a cat and a mouse and of course,
bunch: a cat and a mouse and of course,
my beloved spouse One is considered a hero;
my beloved spouse One is considered a hero;
one is considered a louse sometimes I feel
one is considered a louse sometimes I feel
like Mickey Mouse They will coexist, until
like Mickey Mouse They will coexist, until
one chases the other out, and then I will be
one chases the other out, and then I will be
a happy, little Boy Scout First, the cat chases
a happy, little Boy Scout First, the cat chases

after its prey and
after its prey and

the mouse does a fancy ballet
the mouse does a fancy ballet

Then the mouse runs away and completes a
Then the mouse runs away and completes a

delightful home matinée
delightful home matinée

The mouse lives
The mouse lives

from day to day, in his
from day to day, in his

hidden subway,
hidden sub way,

making no headway
making no head way

but it always listens to
but it always listens to

what the cat has to say
what the cat has to say

And sometimes it hides
And some times it hides

under the stairway
under the stairway

and it always gives the cat
and it always gives the cat

the right-of-way
the right-of-Way

The cat lives in ease and
The cat lives in ease and

comfort and licks some milk
comfort and licks some milk

and takes an
and takes an

occasional catnip snort Unlike its unfortunate
occasional catnip snort Unlike its unfortunate

cohort who continually has to figure how
cohort who continually has to figure how

to, the cat, thwart The mouse learns to hold
to, the cat, thwart The mouse learns to hold

up his fort; he is definitely no spoilsport
up his fort; he is definitely no spoilsport

The cat and the mouse cavort in my living room
The cat and the mouse cavort in my living room

which is both their tennis and traffic court The
which is both their tennis and traffic court The

mouse lives in constant fear and feels a lot
mouse lives in constant fear and feels a lot

like Paul Revere He is afraid of the cat,
like Paul Revere He is afraid of the cat,

which tends to persevere and makes his
which tends to persevere and makes his

intentions crystal clear The cat can see the
intentions crystal clear The cat can see the

mouse in the reflection of my mirror his
mouse in the reflection of my mirror his

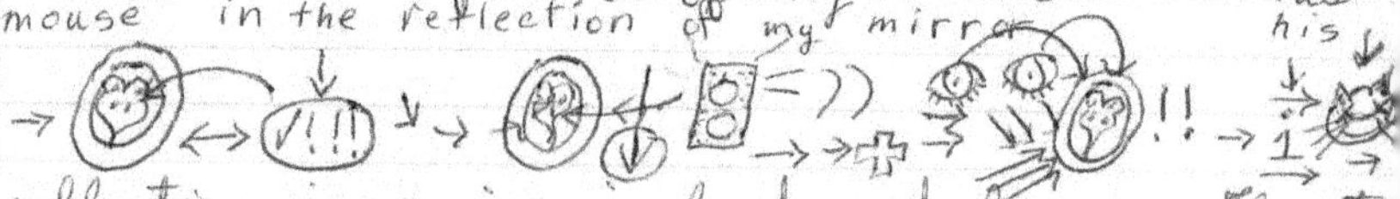

reflection is coming in loud and clear The cat
reflection is coming in loud and clear The cat

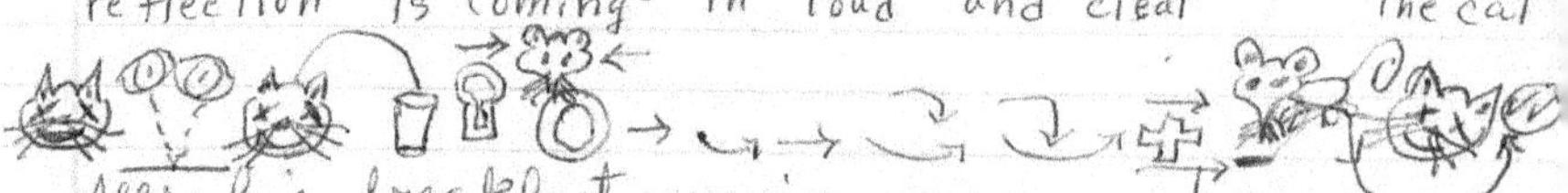

sees his breakfast coming nearer and nearer
sees his breakfast coming nearer and nearer

and he feels like Captain Bligh, the buccaneer
and he feels like Captain Bligh, the buccaneer

The cat waits and bides his time; he treats
The cat waits and bides his time; he treats

his domain like a war zone, at half time
his domain like a war zone, at half time

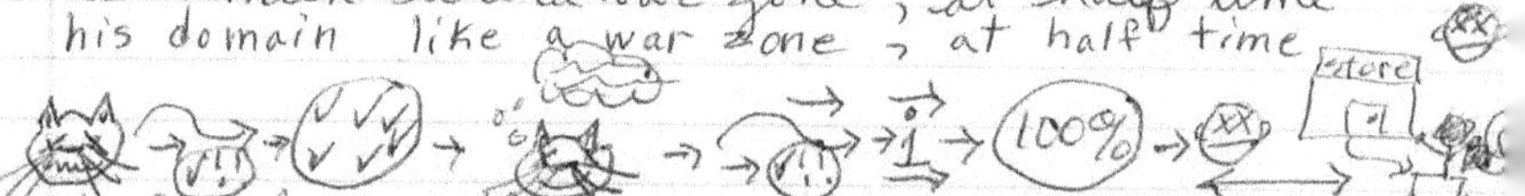

He is always thinking of the perfect crime
He is always thinking of the perfect crime

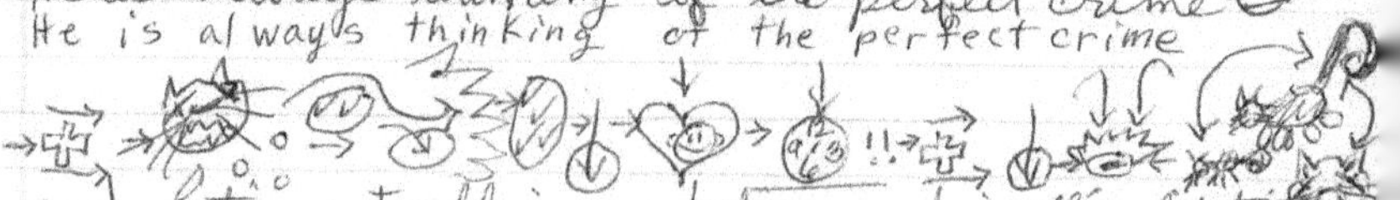

and eating out all in good time and in this lifetime
and eating out all in good time and in this lifetime

625 page

And that felicious mouse is definitely in its crime
And that delicious mouse is definitely in its prime

it would be so tasty for dinnertime
it would be so tasty for dinner time

That would
That would

just fit the bill for all, especially,
just fit the bill for all, especially,

we
we

enemies and partners in crime
enemies and partners in crime

The mouse
The mouse

would be a tender morsel,
would be a tender morsel,

with a fragrant,
with a fragrant,

delicious smell
deligious smell

The mouse would qualify as
The moase would qualify as

Tinker Bell because
Tinker Bell because,

she was the one who rang
she was the one who rang

Dong! Ding

the dinner bell
the dinner bell

She had that magic spell and
she had that magic spell and

has had the unfortunate
has had the unfortunate

luck of coming to
luck of coming to

the Last Chance Motel Or rather, she has
the Last Chance Motel Or rather, she has

the martyr's ring and was given a thumbs
the martyr's ring and was given a thambs

down and offered as bait to the hungry lion
down and offered as bait to the hungry lion

from his waiting jail cell Unfortunately,
from his waiting jail cell Unfortunately,

the worst might happen for the mouse if she
the worst might happen for the mouse if she

chances too close to the cat's den Something
chances too close to the cat's den Something

serious that may tend to make you sad. if you
serious that may tend to make you sad if you

are the soft-hearted kind of mother hen
are the saft-hearted kind of mot her hen

The cat might catch and eat the mouse and that
The cat might catch and eat the mouse and that

would then for the mouse, be a poison pen
would then for the mouse, be a poison pen

I guess that would be that, then; and that's
I guess that would be that, then; and that's

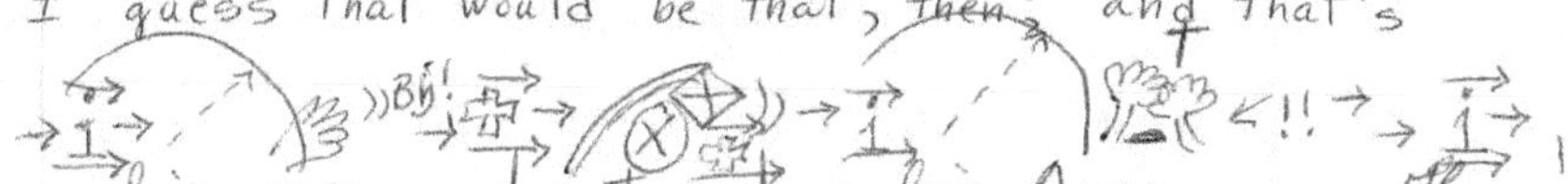

a big over and out and a big Amen The
a big over and out and a big Amen The

moral to this story is you can run around all you
moral to this story is you can run around all you

want but if you push the wrong buttons
want but if you push the wrong buttons

You will be eaten for lunch and you'll be the one
you will be eaten for lunch and you'll be the one

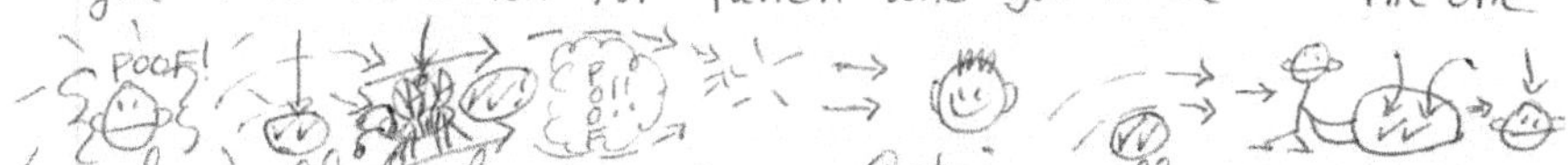

who will be long gone Antoene will prepare you
who will be long gone Antoine will prepare you

for the feast like a tasty bon-bon And Cézanne will
for the feast like a tasty bon-bon And Cézanne will

step on the floor instead of standing on a chair afraid and woebegone
step on the floor instead of standing on a chair afraid + woebegone

(126) You Are Who You Are (294)

You Are Who You Are

Why pretend and be artificial, why pretend
Why pretend and be artificial, why pretend

you are so special? You just might end up
you are so special? You just might end up

sitting in some jail cell if you are a liar
sitting in some jail cell if you are a liar

and then you'll be walking on eggshells Try
and then you'll be walking on eggshells Try

being honest and clear as a bell; and when
being honest and clear as a bell; and when

you become Mr. William Tell you won't have
you become Mr. William Tell You won't have

to deal with any bombshell Being you will more
to deal with any bombshell Being you, will more

than sell it may even cast a magical spell
than sell it may even cast a magical spell

If you are a good worker and don't lose sight of
If you are a good worker and don't lose sight of

yourself good things are bound to occur
yourself good things are bound to occur

Work will pass by, like you are traveling in a blur
Work will pass by, like you are traveling in a blur

and trouble will never be astir Look work
and trouble will never be astir Look work

in the eye and say grrrrr and you'll feel
in the eye and say grrrrr and you'll feel

like an emperor Don't let your enemies
like an emperor Don't let your enemies

interfere or with you, deter and you will
intertere or with you, deter and you will

like it, as it is, as it were If you like
like it, as it is, as if were If you like

to express yourself; make sure you are
to express yourself; make sure you are

sincere and truthful and be true to yourself

Don't let doubters stop you; put them on the bookshelf

Have confidence in yourself because there is no one like you; if you feel like being an elf, be an elf

Doubters are many, believers are few; believe in belief itself

Remember, you are who you are; and if you remain true to yourself, you'll always be a star

You may be some

kind of famous star; even this is good, if
kind of famous star; even this is good, if

it is so; it is not so bizarre Or a derelict
it is so; it is not so bizarre Or a derelict

from some sleazy bar, which has every
from some sleazy bar, which has every

right to wish on the falling stars Or a
right to wish on the falling stars Or a

refugee from a foreign war just remember
refugee from a foreign war just remember

that you are OK, no matter who you are The
that you are OK, No matter who you are The

main thing is to be genuine and you will
main thing is to be genuine and you will

never be a has-been And you will always
Never be a has-been And you will always

know where you've been; because you are
Know where you've been; because you are

not a snake in a sheep's skin No matter
not a snake in a sheep's skin No matter

what kind of mess you get yourself in;
what kind of mess you get yourself in;

honesty and being yourself will make you a shoo-in
honesty and being yourself will make you a shoo-in

Then when you look in the mirror you will be
Then when you look in the mirror you will be

able to smile and grin and you won't
able to smile and grin and you won't

need a stand-in Of yourself, never be
need a stand-in of yourself, never be

ashamed; even learn to like your given
ashamed; even learn to like your given

Simon Bill Patrick

nicknames Especially accept who you are
nicknames Especially accept who you are

LIFE

in life's game and you will never be put to
in life's game and you will never be put to

shame
You are special in the overall
main frame
so take your special ways and
get ready and take aim
Everyone has their
reasons and their own claim
no one is
made the same; and everyone
has their own
kind of acclaim
Above all, try to like who
you are
because that way, you can go very
far
Try to learn from life's scars; they
make you who you are
No matter, how

different, you are, no matter how bizarre
different, you are, No matter how bizarre

you are still a superstar If everyone wrote
you are still a superstar If everyone wrote

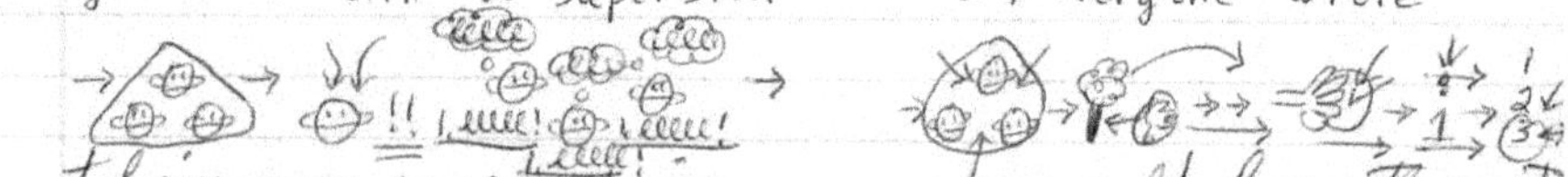

their own memories we would have the most
their own memories we woul have the most

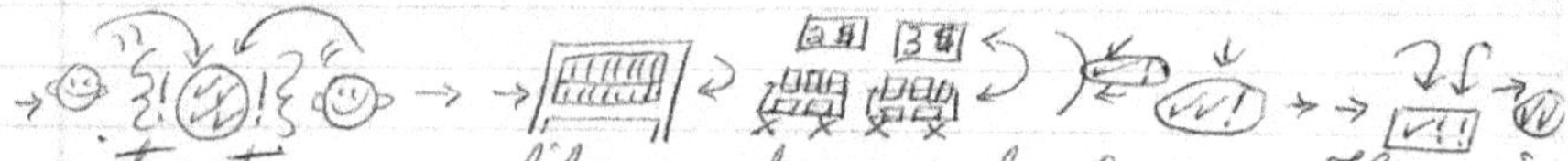

interesting library bazaar by far There is
interesting library bazaar by far There is

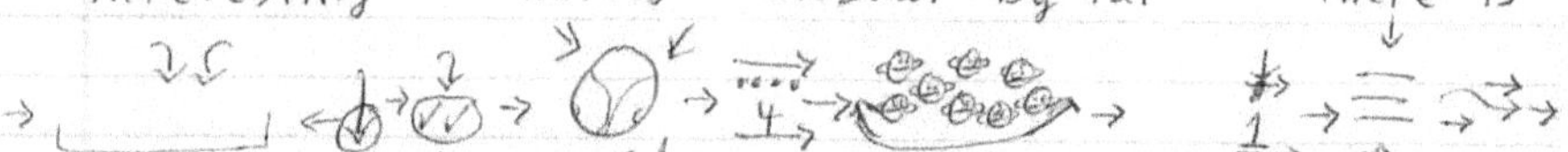

room in this world for everyone the lines of
room in this world for everyone the lines of

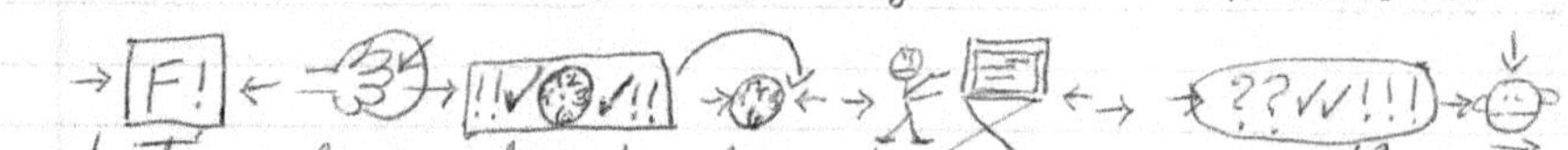

destiny have already been drawn Whether you
destiny have already been drawn Whether you

are a Don Juan or an Yvonne of the Yukon
are a Don Juan or an Yvonne of the Yukon

You could come from Taiwan or from the
You could come from Taiwan or from the

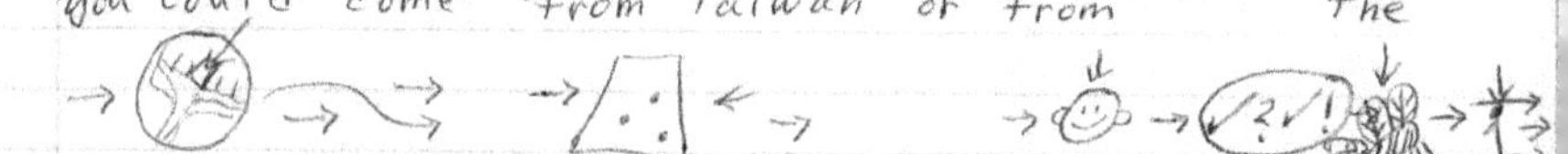

province of Saskatchewan You could be an
province of Saskatchewan You could be an

Antoine or a Cézanne or a Genghis Knan;
Antoine or a Cézanne or a Genghis Knan;

the fact is, you are who you are and of that
the fact is, you are who you are and of that

you have no choice it is a forgone
you have no chaice it is a forgone

conclusion.
conclusion

(636) page

(127) An Eye On The Sky (297)

An Eye On The Sky

One day I was looking way up into the sky I
One day I was looking way up into the sky I

was enjoying the clouds as they passed by which
was enjoying the clouds as they passed by which

I enjoyed to catalog and to classify I saw
I enjoyed to catalog and to classify I saw

something that looked like a giant spinning pie
some thing that looked like a giant spinning pie

I became fearful and terrified It zigzagged
I became fearful and terrified It zigzagged

back and forth, no lie; it seemed like it
back and forth, no lie; it seemed like it

was dissatisfied It moved just like a giant
was dissatisfied It moved just like a giant

hyper horsefly this was definitely a case
hyper horsefly this was definitely a case

for the FBI
for the FBI

The air was sparking with electricity
The air was sparking with electricity

the giant pies were giving a lightning jamboree
the giant pies were giving a lightning jamboree

The air was vibrant by our fair city, and
The air was vibrant by our fair city, and

lit it up like a giant Christmas tree It was
lit it up like a giant Christmas tree It was

a perfect day to snooze or to sightsee,
a perfect day to snooze or to sightsee,

except when one is afraid and has to flee
except when one is afraid and has to flee

It was time to dance like a bumblebee and time to
It was time to dance like a bumblebee and time to

cop a plea What happened next, right then
cop a plea What happened next, right then

and there? Was one for the texts, right out
and there? Was one for the texts, right out

of thin atmosphere? Something that would
of thin atmosphere? Something that would

make anyone perplexed happened right there
make anyone perplexed happened right there

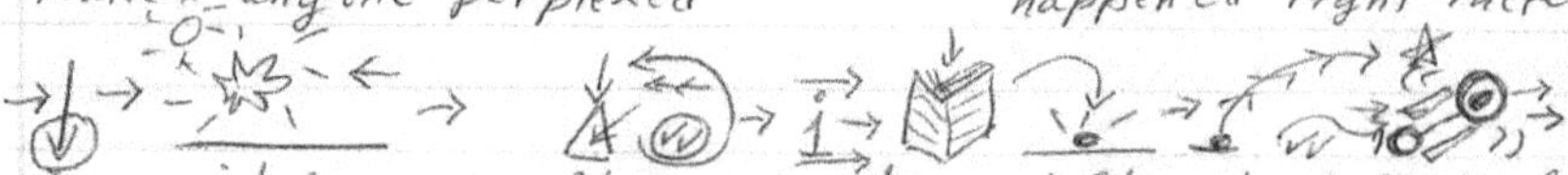

in midair It was a story right out of Star Trek
in midair It was a story right out of Stor Trek

along with all the fanfare The shiny dish
along with all the fanfare The shiny dish

landed with no further ado Out came beings
landed with no further ado Out came beings

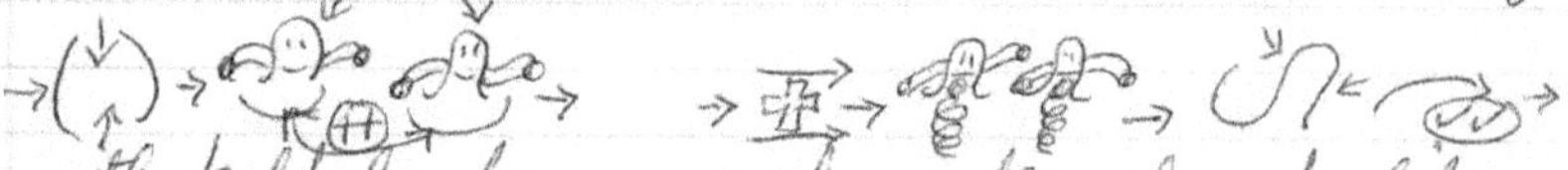

with bald heads and necks shaped like
with bald heads and necks shaped like

corkscrews Now I know I am a certified
corkscrews Now I know I am a certified

egghead but I was so shocked, my hair
egghead but I was so shocked, my hair

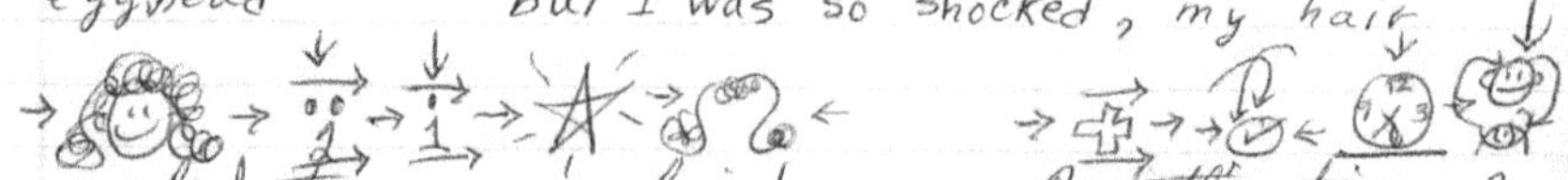

curled to a new hairdo And this time I
curled to a new hairdo And this time I

could have dropped dead because I was
could have dropped dead because I was
petrified through and through They didn't
petrified through and through They didn't
notice me, so I ran and hid from the bald-
notice me, so I ran and hid from the bald-
headed corkscrew-necked gigantic squids
headed corkscrew-necked gigantic squids
with eyelids They didn't notice my monkey,
with eyelids They didn't notice my monkey,
Marie, or my giant arachnid But they stole
Marie, or my giant arachnid But they stole
my pet chimpanzee I guess, to them, he
my pet chimpanzee I guess, to them, he
looked like a brilliant whiz kid I now keep
looked like a brilliant whiz kid I now keep
my horse under lock and key and watch for
my horse under lock and key and watch for

me into a boot camp, you say; he will make
me into a boot camp, you say; he will make

sure I do not disobey It's just another place to
sure I do not disabey It's just another place to

learn to play war games, the wrong ways
learn to play war games, the wrong ways

There has got to be a better way to dance the
There has got to be a better way to dance the

retribution ballet According to the gangster
retribution ballet according to the gangster

role-play; you will see me make headway
role-play; you will see me make headway

if you do not rub them the wrong way That's
if you do not rub them the wrong way That's

not at all I did; I flipped my lid and my friends
not at all I did; I flipped my lid and my friends

followed suit I created a paparazzi pyramid
followed suit I created a paparazzi pyramid

It zipped right back into the sky like it
It zipped right back into the sky like it

had disappeared up a vertical stairway It
had disappeared up a vertical stairway It

must have been camera shy, or I rubbed
must have been camera shy, or I rubbed

it the wrong way Because it didn't even
it the wrong way Because it didn't even

stop to say good-bye it was off to one of
stop to say good-bye it was off to one of

the stars in the Milky Way Sometimes, I
the stars in the Milky Way Sometimes, I

look up into the sky and I salute and say
look up into the sky and I salute and say

"Here's mud in your eyes, you guys."
"Here's mud in your eyes, you guys."

Maybe I'm imagining what I see next but
Maybe I'm imagining what I see next but

any new wildlife hybrids Was I ever surprised,
any new wildlife hybrids Was I ever suprised,

when as fast as it had come? I just
when as fast as it had come? I just

couldn't believe my eyes; it began to
couldn't believe my eyes; it began to

leave where it had come from I even snapped
leave where it had come from I even snapped

a picture to help me to justify that I wasn't
a picture to help me to justify that I wasn't

crazy or a lying bum So that I could later
crazy or a lying bama so that I could later

examine it and have it analyzed to find
examine it and have it analyzed to find

out if I had really seen it, fee-fi-fo-fum
out if I had really seen it fee-fi-fo-fum

Then in a wink of an eye, it jerked up and away
Then in a wink of an eye, it jerked up and away

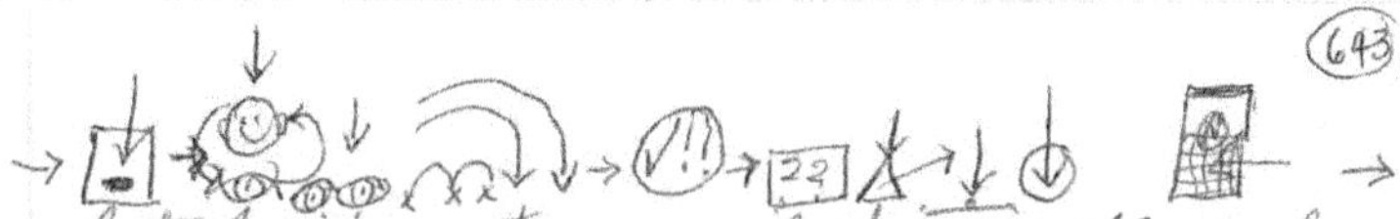

what I ~~see~~ next, even if it is in Novembes
what I see next, even if it is in November

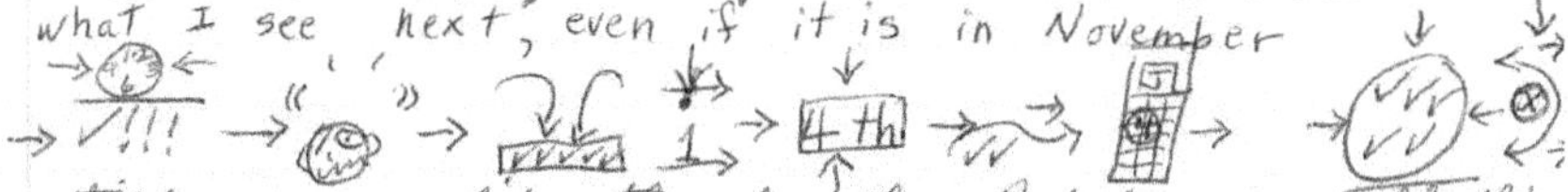

still seems like the fourth of July All this
still seems like the fourth of July All this

may seem weird to you or like sci-fi But
may seem weird to you or like sci-fi But

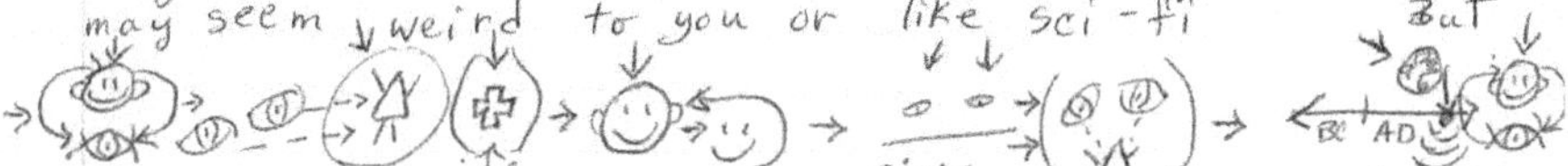

I saw it with my own little eyes when I
I saw it with my own little eyes when I

had an eye on the sky
had an eye on the sky

(128) The Long Arm Of The Law (300) (644 page)
The Long Arm Of The Law

Now I've done it, which was the last straw;
Now I've done it, which was the last straw;

I went and lost my temper I hit him square on
I went and lost my temper I hit him square on

the jaw; I gave him what's for and
the jaw; I gave him what's for and

furthermore, I gave him much, much more, sir
Furthermore, I gave him much, much more, sir

It just might be his last hurrah; I don't see him
It just might be his last hurrah; I don't see him

shhh!

moving and he doesn't seem to want to stir
moving and he doesn't seem to want to stir

what do you know, here comes the long arm of the law;
What do you know, here comes the long arm of the law;

brrr!

I can hear the rattling of his spurs He'll put
I can hear the rattling of his spurs He'll put

that just so happened to look very cute I
was a whiz kid out in Madrid, and I played
a mean Spanish flute I was an Asperger's
hybrid kid and my life was challenging,
but it was a beauty It's all I could do but
throw up my towel; I was very sad But the judge
still put down his gavel; he said that I had
been bad, bad, bad It was all I could do,
but to show my navel and run around not at

all clad Now was the time for my birthday suit
all clad Now was the time for my birthday suit

bombshell; I guess then they will think I'm
bombshell; I guess then they will think I'm

mad Now came the time for justice; I guess
mad Now came the time for justice; I guess

I would get what I deserve It was to be the final
I would get what I deserve It was to be the final

feted kiss I was to be given my sentence and
feted kiss I was to be given my sentence and

I was served It was to be the end of my life of
I was served It was to be the end of my life of

freedom, my bliss I now have to spend
freedom, my bliss I now have to spend

time in jail with a sentence to observe I
time in jail with a sentence to observe I

would have lots of time to reminisce and
would have lots of time to reminisce and

think of why I thought I could have so much nerve
think of why I thought I could have so much nerve

I knew my life was no longer, worth a plugcent;
I Knew my life was no longer, worth a plugcent;

The rest of my life, was destined behind bars to be
The rest of my life, was destined behind bars to be

spent
spent

No one cared, if I was guilty or if I
No one cared, if I was guilty or if I

was innocent;
was innocent;

Or if I was a malcontent, an
Or if I was a malcontent, an

unfortunate gent
unfortunate gent

No one cared where I was, if I
No one cared where I was, if I

was sane, or if I was innocent
was sane, or if I was innocent

it would be
it would be

to then just a jolly experiment
to then just a jolly experiment

No one caredif
No one caredif

I rotted there inside — it
I rotted there inside — it

was all I could do but
was all I could do but

to lament on any and all the time that had
to lament on ang and all the time that had

been spent and would be spent I
been spent and would be spent I

was to rot away in a small cell; I didn't
was to rot away in a small cell; I didn't

even have so much as a doorbell It was going
even have so much as a door bell It was going

to be my own special hall I would now be
to be my own special hall I would now be

forever walking on eggshells Breaking the law
forever walking on eggshells Breaking the law

had come with many dangers; I had known
had come with many dangers; I had Know n

that only too well but I had been stubborn
that only too well but I had been stubborn

and had to rebel Now I wouldn't be happy
and had to rebel Now I wouldn't be happy

I could tell, with my number pasted to my
I could tell, with my number pasted to my
lapel; what a motel I might even lose my
lapel; what a motel I might even lose my
mind from being confined from humankind
mind from being confined from human kind
Friends will be very hard to find when I leave,
Friends will be very hard to find when I leave,
even if my life, I happen to streamline
even if my life, I happen to stream line
Anyway, I'd have lots of time to unwind,
Anyway, I'd have lots of time to unwind,
enough time that it would boggle the mind It
enough time that it would boggle the mind It
would help if I went deaf, dumb, and blind;
would help if I went deaf, dumb, and blind;
somehow I will become, to my fate, resigned
somehow I will become, to my fate, resigned

Maybe I'll write a book on my life, and My
May be I'll write a book on my life, and My
experiences, here in Donnybrook While I'm
experiences, here in Donnybrook While I'm
here in my little nook; I'll have plenty of
here in my little nook; I'll have plenty of
time to improve my overall outlook I'll be a
time to improve my overall outlook I'll be a
carpenter, a fighter, a cook anything but
carpenter, a fighter, a cook anything but
what got me here, which is by being a crook
what got me here, which is by being a crook
Being brave is all what it will take and
Being brave is all what it will take and
turning over a new leaf and all that gobbledygook
turning over a new leaf and all that gobbledygook
I'll have plenty of time to learn the golden
I'll have plenty of time to learn the golden

rule; I'll learn to be nobody's fool   I'll start
rule; I'll learn to be nobody's fool   I'll start

out again in nursery school,   graduate again
out again in nursery school,   graduate again

to high school   then I will have a little more soul
to high school   then I will have a little more soul

I thought I was super cool, but the truth   is I was
I thought I was super cool, but the truth   is I was

swimming in a cesspool   I lived where the
swimming in a cesspool   I lived where the

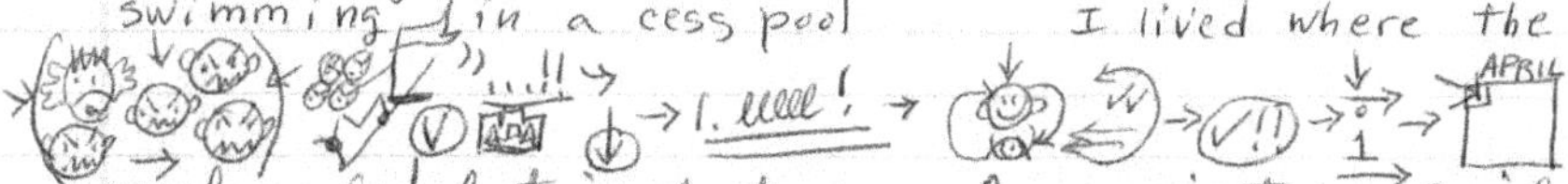

mob-ruled but in fact,   I was just an April
mob ruled, but in fact,   I was just an April

fool's fool   I knew the score in crime's
fool's fool   I knew the score in crime's

cold war; which I chose to ignore   and got
cold war; which I chose to ignore   and got

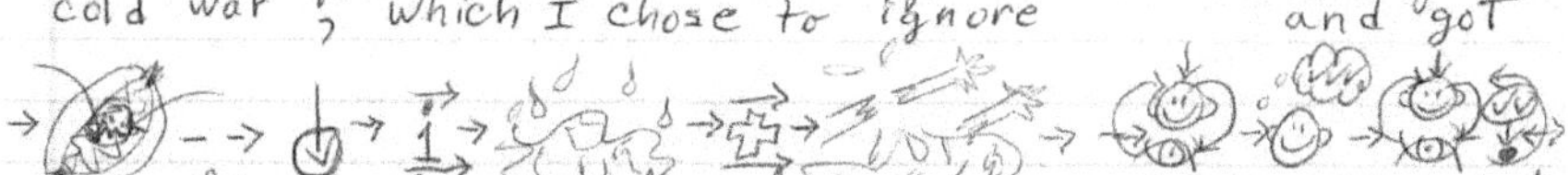

caught in the blood and gore   I thought I had
caught in the blood and gore   I thought I had

a special rapport; turns out all I was
hard core Now I have the plainest decor
and bars around me galore; all the way down
the corridor There are a lot like me – row,
row, row your boat to shore that's an over
and out and a big ten-four Now I have
received the long arm of the law and now I
am nothing but an outlaw I should have
listened to Grandma and Grandpa; when

they hemmed and hawed
they hemmed and hawed
Now I know it was
Now I know it was

my reasoning that was
my reasoning that was
flawed and I was
flawed and I was

nothing but a fraud
nothing but a fraud
I will soon face a firing
I will soon face a firing

squad when they
squad when they
sent me back abroad to
sent me back abroad to

face that mob
face that mob

(129) I Just Don't Understand (304)
I Just Don't Understand

The Master Plan
The Master Plan

I just don't understand the master plan
I just don't understand the master plan

this happened to my favorite man
this happened to my favorite man

have to give him
have to give him

a helping hand
a helping hand

is no better than him in all the land
is no better than him in all the land

with him through thick and thin
with him through thick and thin

want him to conquer and win
want him to conquer and win

love him, I can't begin to begin
love him, I can't begin to begin

Or why
Or why

All I know is I
All I Know is I

There
There

I'll stay
I'll stay

This battle, I
This battle, I

How much I
How much I

Surely a
Surely a

love this great cannot be a sin He is a fighter
love this great cannot be a sin He is a fighter

and a real prize — a real prizefighter
and a real prize — a real prize fighter

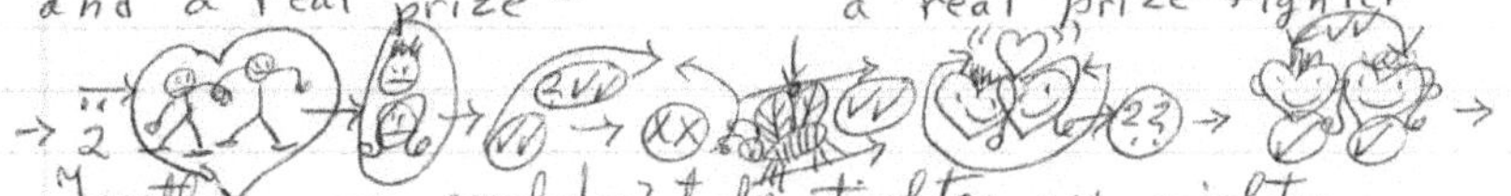

Together, we couldn't be tighter or righter
Together, we couldn't be tighter or righter

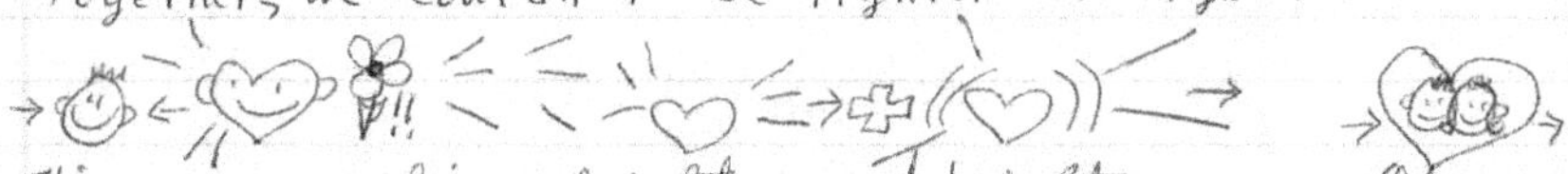

His courage shines brighter and brighter Our
His courage shines brighter and brighter Our

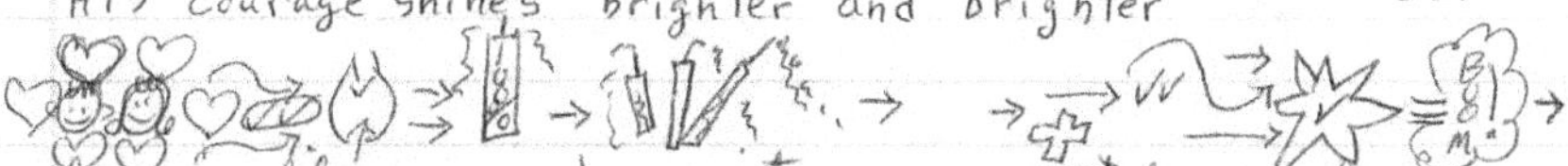

love is like pure dynamite and has real power
love is like pure dynamite and has real power

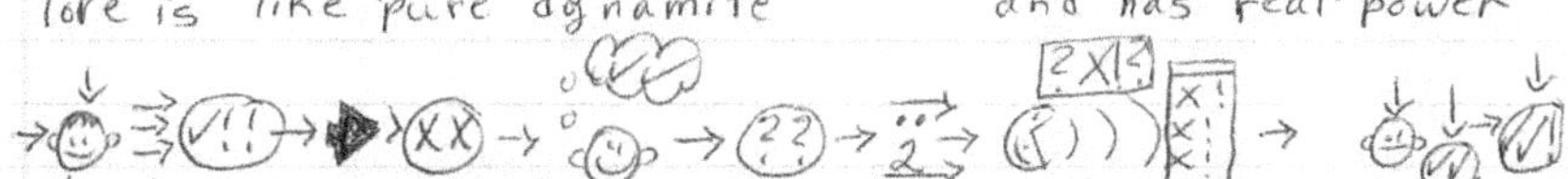

He just doesn't know how to complain He's just
He just doesn't know how to complain He's just

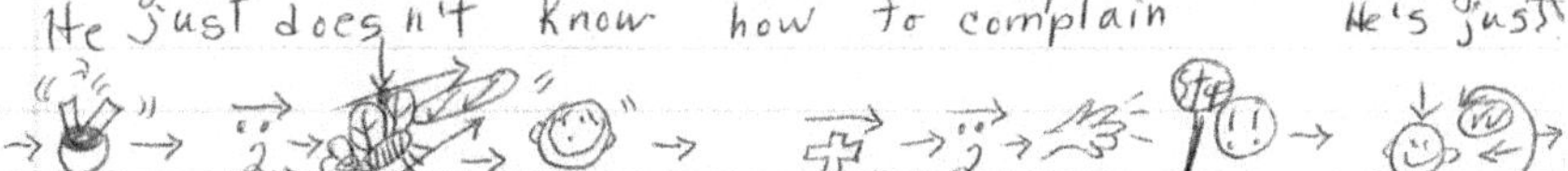

made to be humble and to refrain He has
made to be humble and to refrain He has

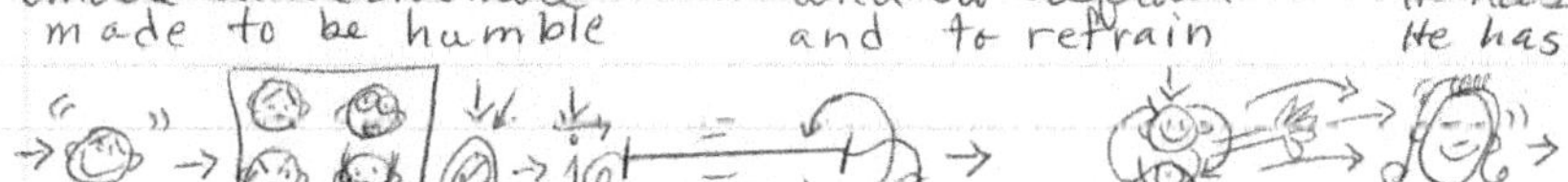

his emotions on a tight string I get proud
his emotions on a tight string I get proud

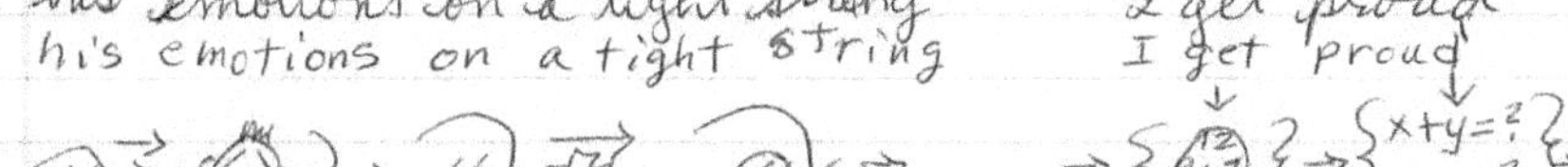

of him, again and again When problems
of him, again and again When problems

come our way
come our way

We live each day to day
We live each day to day

and live for today
and live for today

We'll listen to what
We'll listen to what

each of us has to say
each of us has to say

Then at night, we
Then at night, we

know everything will be A-OK. No
Know everything will be A-OK. No

matter how hard life may become We will not
matter how hard life may become We will not

let ourselves become undone We will always
let ourselves become undone We will always

have time to have some fun Surely we will
have time to have some fun Surely we will,

our problems, overcome Then people will be
our problems, overcome Then people will be

amazed At the trails, we've blazed—unfazed
amazed At the trails, we've blazed-unfazed

And how happy we have stayed And how
And how happy we have stayed And how

our love is freely displayed We will enjoy
our love is freely displayed We will enjoy

whatever time we have left together That will
whatever time we have left together That will

make our time together seem better and better
make our time together seem better and better

Right down to the last letter, we are a perfect
Right down to the last letter, we are a perfect

him and her Together I feel like a queen
him and her Together I feel like a queen

with her royal emperor
with her royal emperor

(130) The Question Remains (306)

The Question Remains

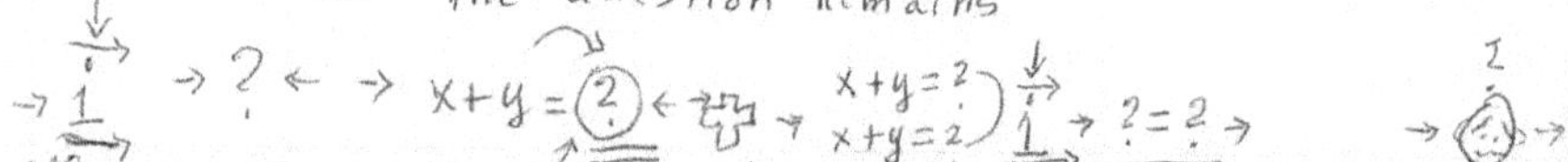

The question remains and stays the same Why
The question remains and stays the same Why

have you overstepped your domain? Your answers
have you overstepped your domain? Your answers

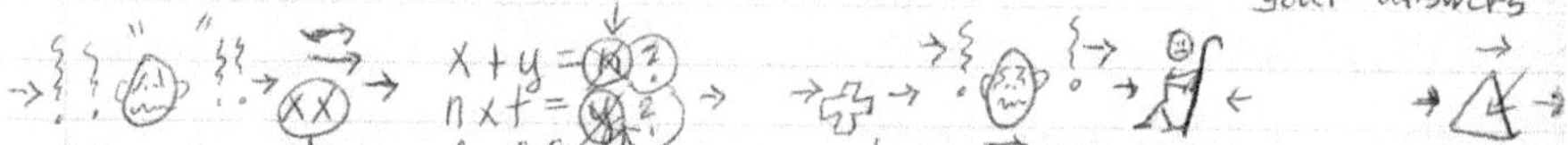

seem not probable and seem lame This
seem not probable and seem lame This

is not some stupid, silly, useless game I am not
is not some stupid, silly, useless game I am not

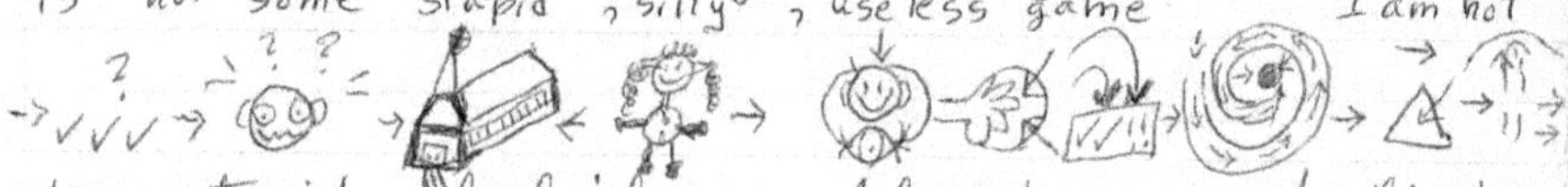

some stupid schoolgirl I have been around this big,
some stupid schoolgirl I have been around this big,

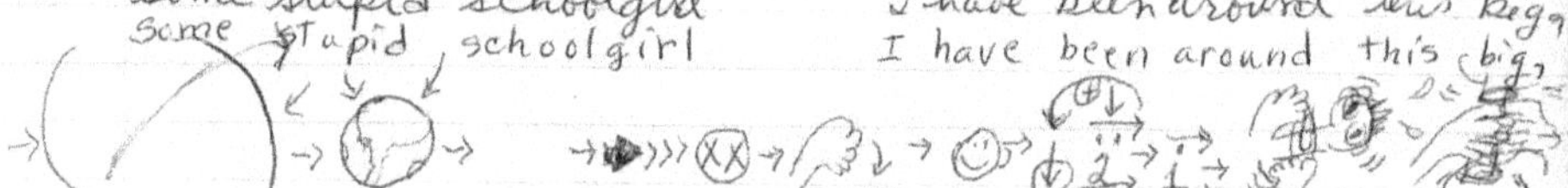

big world Don't put me into a stranglehold
big world Don't put me into a stranglehold

Because you'll find I don't fit any
Because you'll find I don't fit any

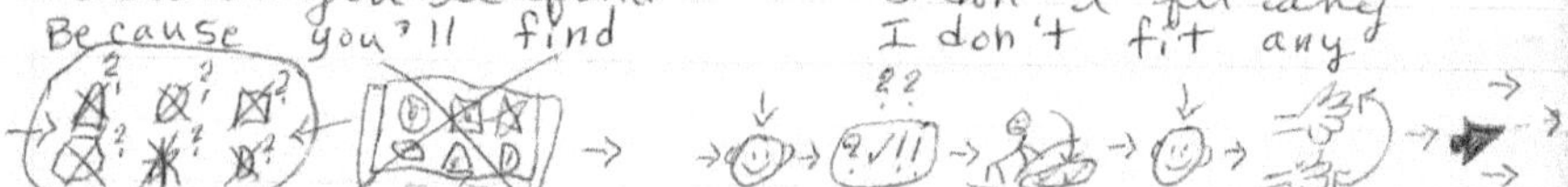

particular mold You may find your hands will
particular mold You may find your hands will

get burnt
get burnt

That it might be some kind
That it might be some kind

of deterrent
of deterrent

You may find you get more than
You may find you get more than

you earned
you earned

If you don't use all that you
If you don't use all that you

have learned
have learned

You may not be telling the
You may not be telling the

whole truth
whole truth

You may be hiding under a hat
You may be hiding under a hat

forsooth
for sooth

I have only just begun to become
I have only just begun to become

uncouth
un couth

I'll flip if I see you hiding there
I'll flip if I see you hiding there

in your phone booth
in your phone booth

No, your theory is not right
No, your theory is notright

And I'll fight you with all my might
And I'll fight you with all my might

You think
You think

I am not too bright Now all I have to do
I am not too bright Now all I have to do

is hang tight You won't hurt those whom I
is hang tight You won't hurt those whom I

love Because there is a greater power
love Because there is a greater power

from above Who has ideas to protect
from a bove Who has ideas to protect

his little doves? From evil men who push
his little doves? From evil men who push

and shove And while these men plan and plot
and shove And while these men plan and plot

All their plans will come to naught They
All their plans will come to naught They

won't know when they have been caught
won't know When they have been caught

In their own net, they themselves have been
In their own net, they themselves have been

put on the spot → I must help my little
put on the spot I must help my little

one → I do believe he will again have fun
one I do believe he will again have fun

I am the only hope for my son → I must
I am the only hope for my son I must

surely not be undone
surely not be undone

(131) It's A Gamble (308)

It's A Gamble

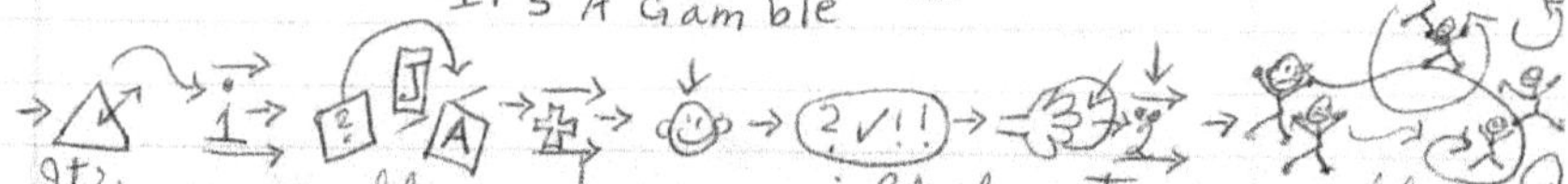

It's a gamble and you might have to scramble
It's a gamble and you might have to scramble

You may find yourself stuck in thorny brambles
you may find your self stuck in thorny brambles

You may want to dabble in cattle What a battle
you may want to dabble in cattle what a battle

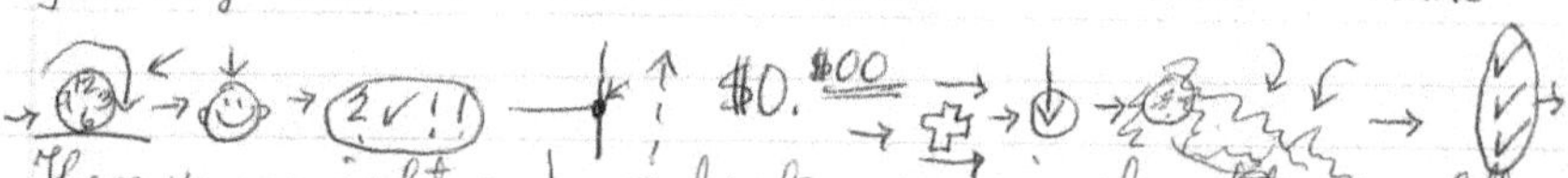

Then you might end up broke and in shambles All
Then you might end up broke and in shambles All

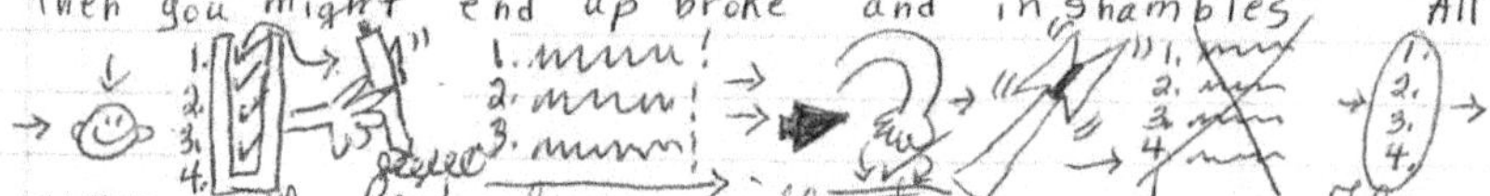

your well-laid plans will get canned They
your well-laid plans will get canned They

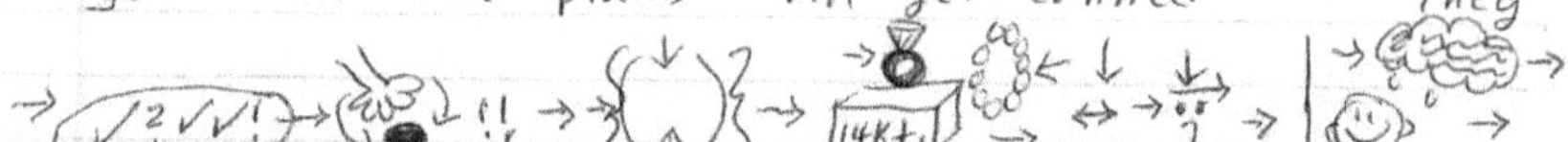

might leave you with precious little to understand
might leave you with precious little to understand

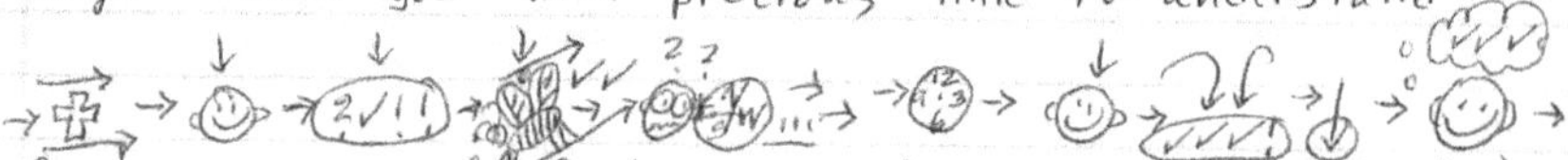

And you may be lost even when you are in familiar
And you may be lost even when you are in familiar

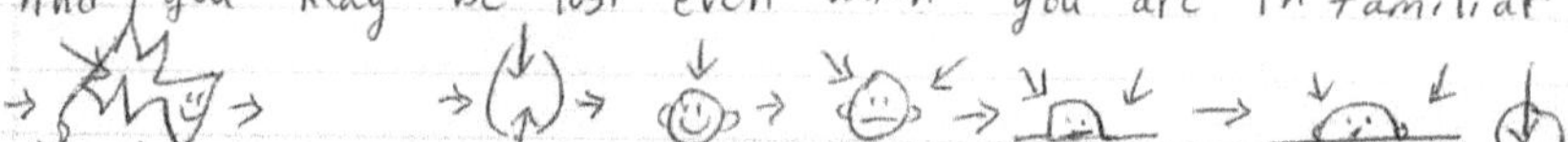

land With your head stuck completely in
land With your head stuck completely in

the sand You may think you are smart you
the Sand You may think You are smart you

know it all You just may be heading for
Know it all You just may be heading for

a hard fall Your sheer arrogance will be
a hard fall Your sheer arrogance will be

your downfall You may receive an
your downfall You may receive an

enlightening wake-up call Are you really
enlightening wake-up call Are you really

ready to look and see? All the consequences
ready to look and see? All the consequences

fast Freddy Can you calm down and hold
fast Freddy Can you calm down and hold

steady? Or do you choose to be careless
steady? Or do you choose to be careless

like a chimpanzee? Are you really sure what's
like a chimpanzee? are you really sure what's

happening or what's astir? Or are you just
happening or what's astir? Or are you just

living in an additional blur? Do you really
living in an additional blur? Do you really

know what your reason for living is for?
Know what your reason for living is for?

Or, are you living just for the moment, just
Or, are you living just for the moment, just

for the right now, as it were No one said
for the right now, as it were No one said

life was going to be easy or be a sure thing
life was going to be easy or be a sure thing

Or, that you were always going to win again and
Or, that you were always going to win again and

again It helps sometimes to give-in, and
again It helps sometimes to give-in, and

compromise my friend And put some
compromise my friend And put some

good old fashioned discipline in your bin It
good old fashioned discipline in your bin It

may be hard to stop from showing off When
may be hard to stop from showing off When

you've been hit the jackpot Or, when you feel:
you've been hit the jackpot Or, when you feel:

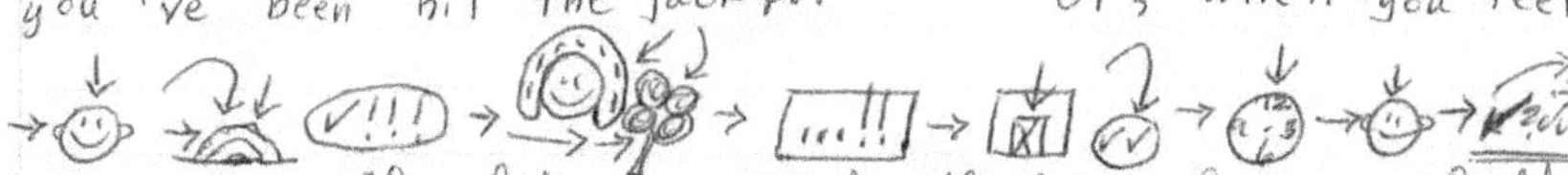

you are really hot But, that's when you should
you are really hot But, that's when you should

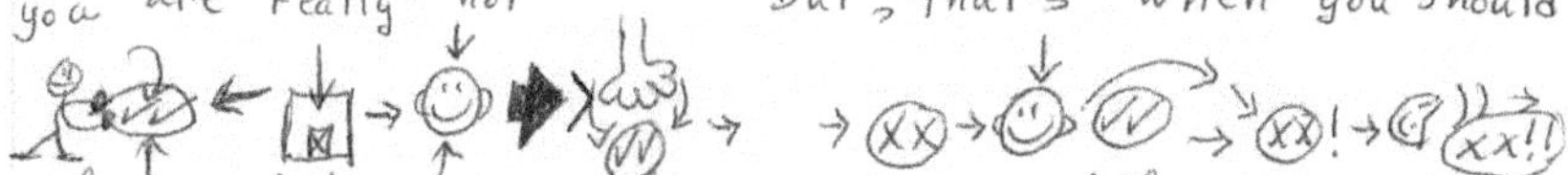

show what you've got No one will ever warn
show what you've got No one will ever warn

you or give you a clue On how, or what you
you or give you a clue On how, or what you

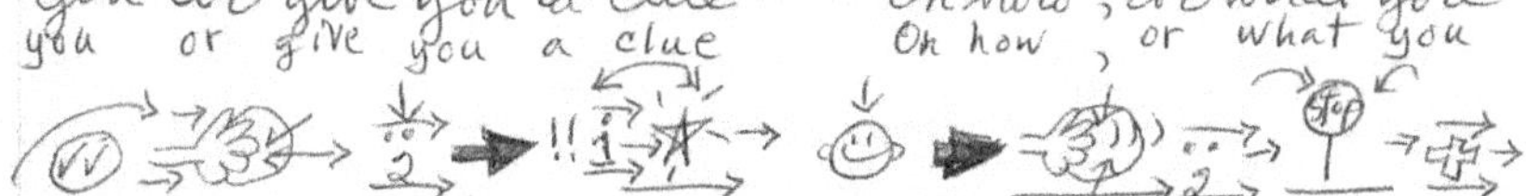

will have to do anew You will have to stop; and
will have to do anew You will have to stop; and

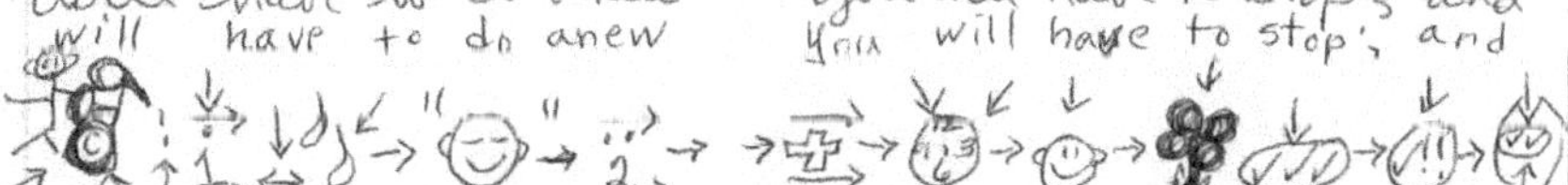

use a little control too And while your luck is still with
use a little control too And while your luck is still with

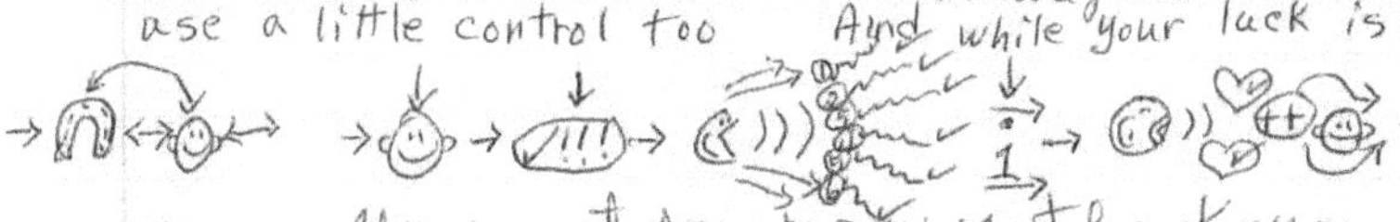

you You must say many a thank-you
you You must say many a thank-you

page: 666

(132) I Like The Way You (310)
I Like The Way you

Wear Your Hair
Wear Your Hair

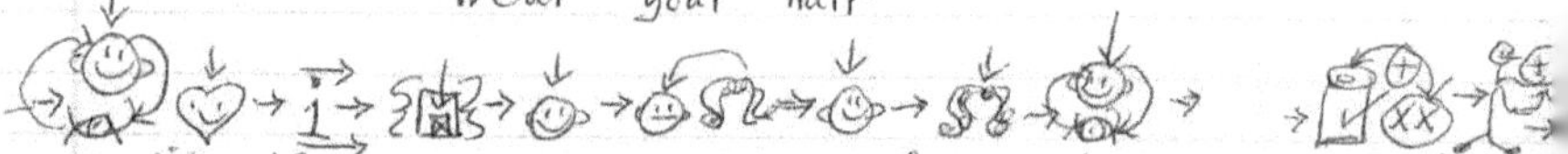

I like the way you wear your hair; I can't help
I like the way you wear your hair; I can't help

but, at you, stare It's a brand-new haircut and
but, at you, stare It's a brand-new haircut and

of it and you, I just can't compare You are
of it and you, I just can't compare You are

now a hybrid player, I think, to say that is fair
now a hybrid player, I think, to say that is fair

You are a brand-new, hot-blooded virgin fresh out
You are a brand-new, hot-blooded virgin fresh out

of hair, and of that, I am well aware
of hair, and of that, I am well aware

→ I'm the lucky one because you are the one
I'm the lucky one because you are the one

I have given permission to tickle my funny bone
I have given permission to tickle my fanny bone

I love to be with you, close to your buns; I love
I love to be with you, close to your bans; I love

to live in your combat zone Now you will be my
to live in your combat zone Now you will bemy

fun, you are my rolling stone; come and roll
fun, you are my rolling stone; come and roll

all my stones You are my prodigal son; you give
all my stones You are my prodigal son; you give

your wife her own personal cyclone Now
your wife her own personal cyclone Now

your hair is subtle and soft way up in its loft
your hair is subtle and soft way up in its loft

It is darkes and softes, so much so I sometimes
It is darker and softer, so much so I sometimes

am at awe and I feel lost It is sprouting
am at awe and I feel lost It is sprouting

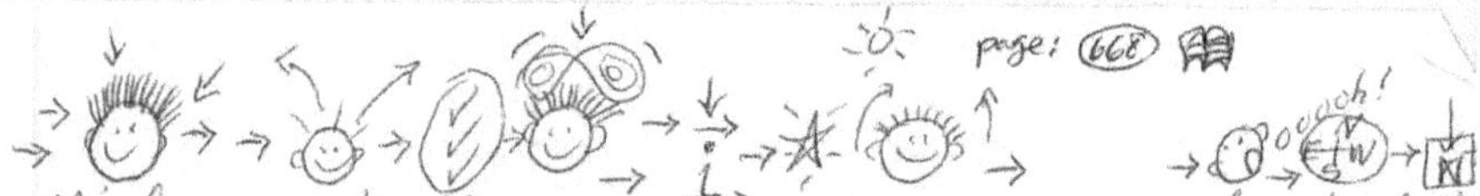

thicker, out all over, a new crop oh, at what
thicker, out all over, a new crop oh, at what

a cost It only makes me appreciate you more
a cost It only makes me appreciate you more

after we had the storm and had our seas tossed
after we had the storm and had our seas tossed

I love to watch and be able to see you; You make
I love to watch and be able to see you; You make

me feel new and carefree And now I can enjoy
me feel new and carefree And now I can enjoy

the bill or decree of good health from your
the bill or decree of good health from your

awesome MDs I love your new body suit with
awesome MDs I love your new body suit with

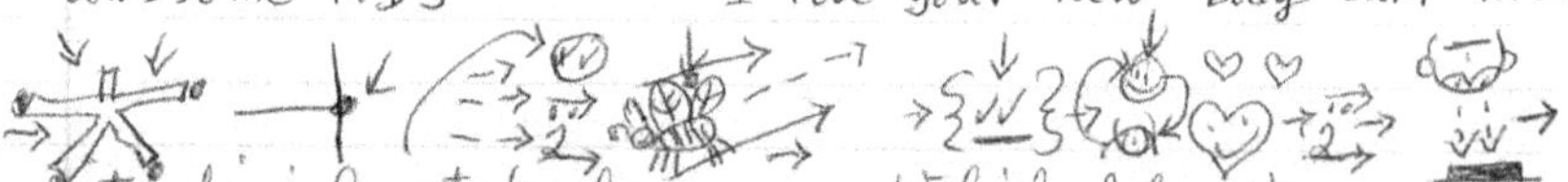

its finish yet to be, Which I love to see,
its finish yet to be, Which I love to see,

fiddle - Dee - Dee Your newfound lease on
fiddle - Dee - Dee Your newfound lease on

life is my most enjoyable cup of tea I love
life is my most enjoyable cup of tea I love

being your queen bee It was quite a shock
being your queen bee It was quite a shock

when you lost all your lovely locks It hit me
when you lost all your lovely locks It hit me

on the head like a heavy rock I almost couldn't
on the head like a heavy rock I almost couldn't

talk In fact, I admit I was weak and had to
talk In fact, I admit I was weak and had to

go for a walk With all that therapy, your
go for a walk With all that therapy, your

blood must have been green, like that of
blood must have been green, like that of

Leuitenant spock It took a very long time
Leuitenant Spock It took a very long time

for your hair to be restored and reassigned And
for your hair to be restored and reassigned And

for you and me to be able to regain our peace of mind
for you and me to be able to regain our peace of mind

When your hair became the extinct kind your
When your hair became the extinct kind your

head became smooth and streamlined Your head
head became smooth and streamlined Your head

was so shiny; I thought I would go snow-blind
was so shiny; I thought I would go snow-blind

I had no choice but to let patience be my voice
I had no choice but to let patience be my voice

My life became blue even though my eyes were
My life became blue even though my eyes were

turquoise I had to let nature be the boss
turquoise I had to let nature be the boss

of my favorite boy I had to wait for her to
of my favorite boy I had to wait for her to

bring back all those beautiful fuzzy toys
bring back all those beautiful fuzzy toys

I knew I could rely on the Man, the Main Boss
I knew I could rely on the Man, the Main Boss

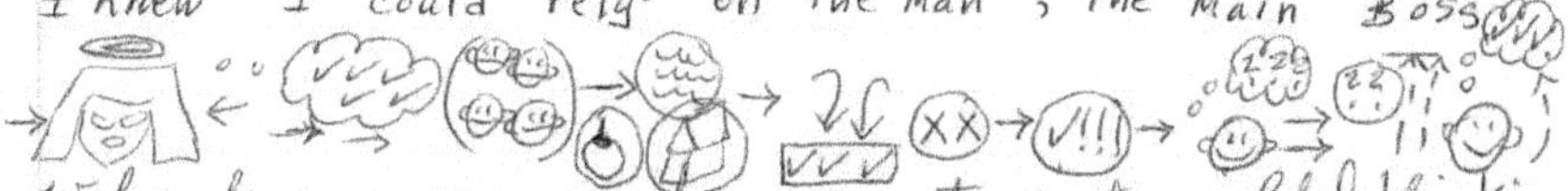

Who knows our needs are not just wishful thinking
Who knows our needs are not just wishful thinking

like a coin's toss And He knows how to
like a coin's toss And He knows how to

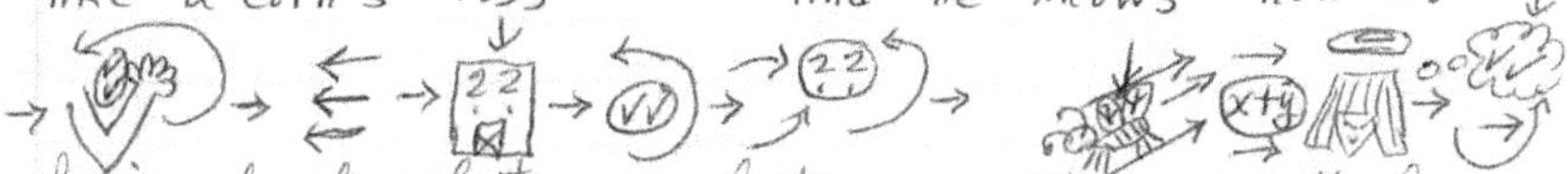

bring back what was lost Because He knows
bring back what was lost Because He knows

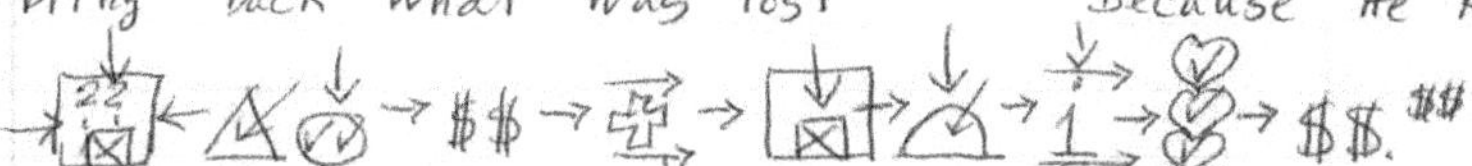

what it is worth and what is the true cost
what it is worth and what is the true cost

(133) The Cards Are Dealt (312)

The Cards Are Dealt

The way the cards are passed and dealt
The way the cards are passed and dealt

Can sometimes deal a heavy welt
Can sometimes deal a heavy welt

And the way they are usually felt
And the way they are usually felt

Is usually sincere and heart felt
Is usually sincere and heartfelt

Meanwhile, in your particular domicile
Meanwhile, in your particular domicile

Instead of just existing, you can go in style
Instead of just existing, you can go in style

It would be worthwhile to go that extra mile
It would be worth while to go that extra mile

By trying that route, without malice or guile
By trying that route, without malice or guile

When you place your cards
When you place your cards

down and all in a row You may get some
down and all in a row You may get some

insight and begin to know About your ebbs
insight and begin to know About your ebbs

and flows and your highs and your lows
and flows and your highs and your lows

Without ever breaking the status quo Then
Without ever breaking the status quo Then

your alibi will be airtight Because you will
your alibi will be airtight Because you will

not be the one causing a fight Make
Not be the one causing a fight Make

sure to place the cards out of sight
sure to place the cards out of sight

Or someone may suspect your reasoning
Or someone may suspect your reasoning

and get uptight Who Knows what is in your cards
and get uptight Who Knows what is in your cards

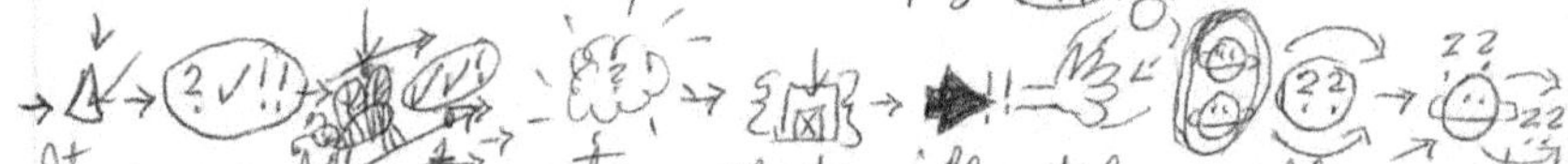

It may be a mystery that will catch us off guard
It may be a mystery that will catch us off guard

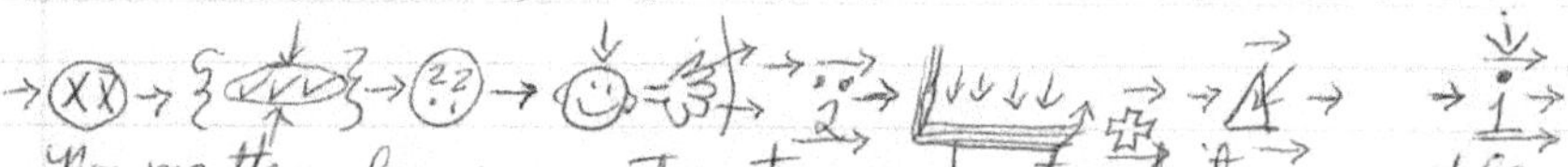

No matter how you try to understand it the
No matter how you try to understand it the

resulting confusion may be too hard And may
resulting confusion may be too hard And may

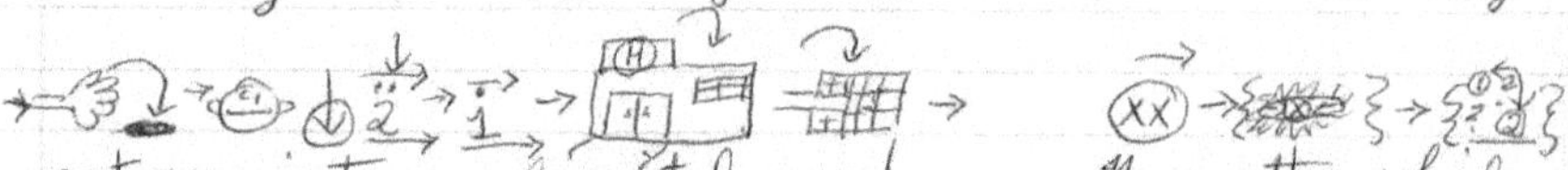

put you into a hospital ward No matter which
put you into a hospital ward No matter which

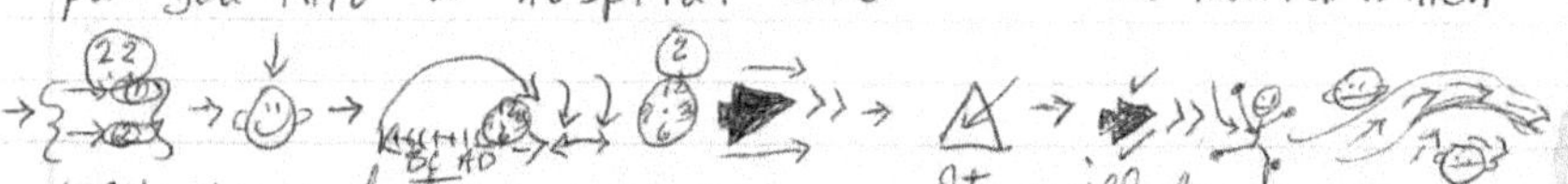

way your future may go It will lead you
way your future may go It will lead you

through a fabulous hologram picture show
through a fabulous hologram picture show

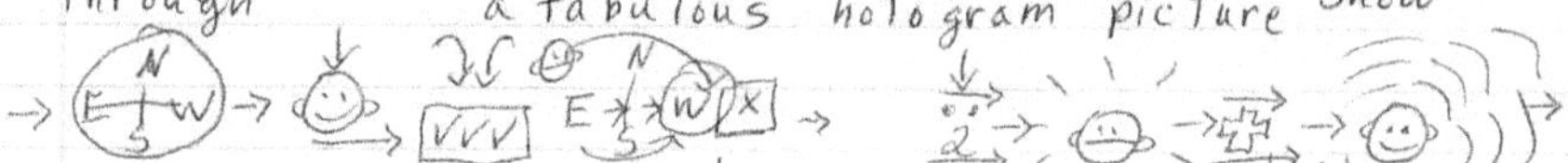

Where you are destined to shine and glow
Where you are destined to shine and glow

In which case, you will be in the very front row
In which case, you will be in the very front row

And while the life's show may leave you puzzled
And while the life's show may leave you puzzled

You may want to be silent and keep yourself

muzzled

You may also want to sit close to

life and cuddle

Until you know you have what

it takes

the underlying muscle

You will

now know

you have met your match

When

you can no longer unlatch

From life and from

what

you think is a bad batch

In reality,

you have

just begun to reattach

(134) You Helped Me Learn (314)

You Helped Me Learn

To Be Free

To Be Free

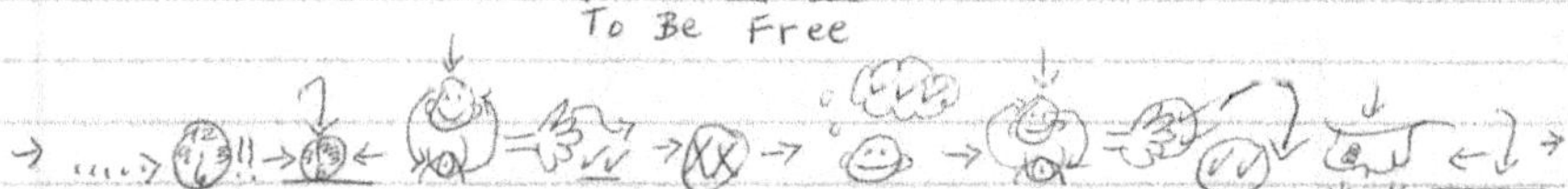

Until now, I've never known; I've been facedown
until now, I've never known; I've been facedown

I did not know how to be free; my heart had been
I did not know how to be free; my heart had been

on loan and I have been a fool and acted
on loan and I have been a fool and acted

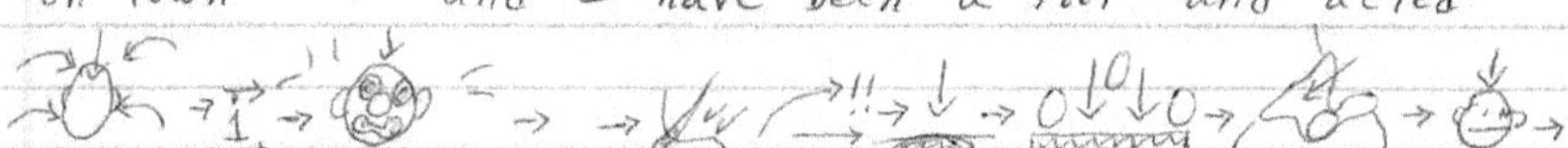

like a clown So far, on barren land my
like a clown So far, on barren land my

love has been sewn and I've been lost and
love has been sewn and I've been lost and

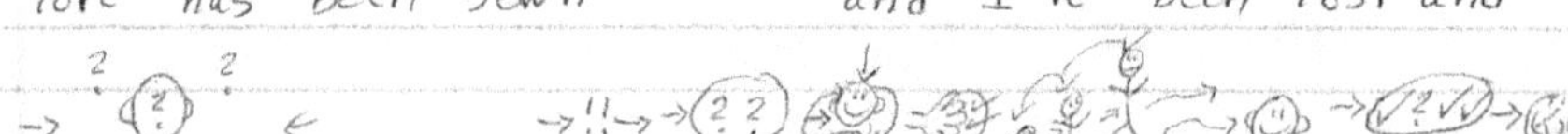

unknown Oh, how I've grown; you could say
unknown Oh, how I've grown; you could say

I played, I ran, and I scored a touchdown
I played, I ran, and I scored a touchdown

Help me is my plea — help me, to the tenth degree
Help me is my plea — help me, to the tenth degree

Help me learn to be free; counting one, two and
Help me learn to be free; counting one, two and

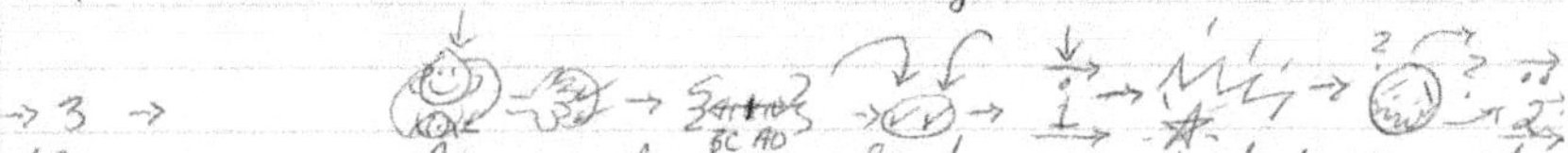

three I've always had a great desire to
three I've always had a great desire to

be happy and to be carefree Of this,
be happy and to be care free Of this,

I will never tire; you'll help me to be happy,
I will never tire; you'll help me to be happy,

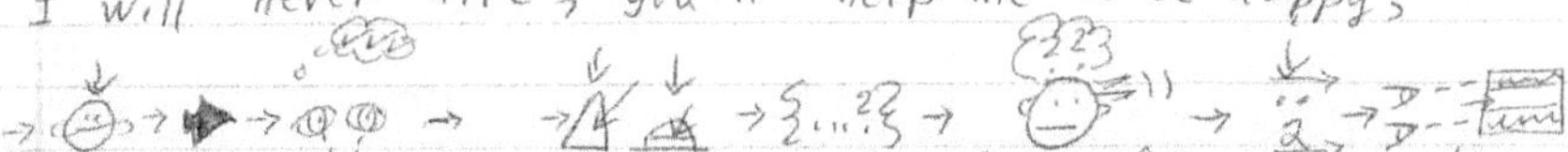

you'll see It is almost impossible to read
you'll see It is almost im possible to read

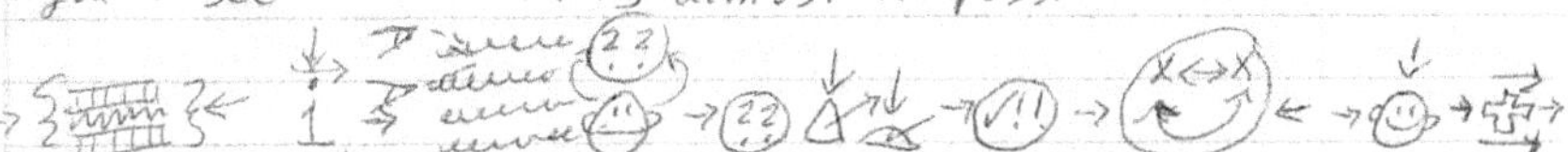

between the lines if it's just between you and
between the lines if it's just between you and

me How unusually free we are; you can
me How unusually free we are; you can

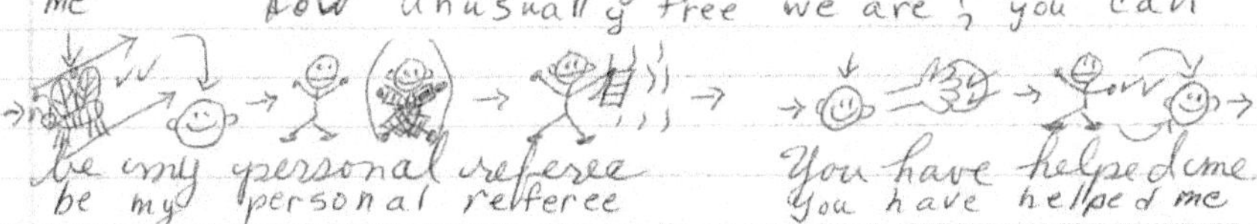

be my personal referee You have helped me
be my personal relferee You have helped me

Hilton

to become whole and fancy free Having faith
to become whole and fancy free Having faith

in you was the key to obtaining my honorary
in you was the key to obtaining my honorary

college degree You gave me my ticket to ride,
college degree You gave me my ticket to ride,

and I became your blushing bride Now
and I became your blushing bride Now

all I have is great love for you inside and a
all I have is great love for you inside and a

great deal of fond, loving pride You helped
great deal of fond, loving pride You helped

me ride the storm, the tempest, the tide you
me ride the storm, the tempest, the tide you

were my constant guide You always
were my constant guide You always

listened when I had something to confide
listened when I had something to confide

understandingly, close by my side Now is
understandingly, close by my side Now is

payback time; you are now my favorite pastime
pay back time; you are now my favorite pastime

I'm putting my money on you this time,
I'm putting my money on you this time,

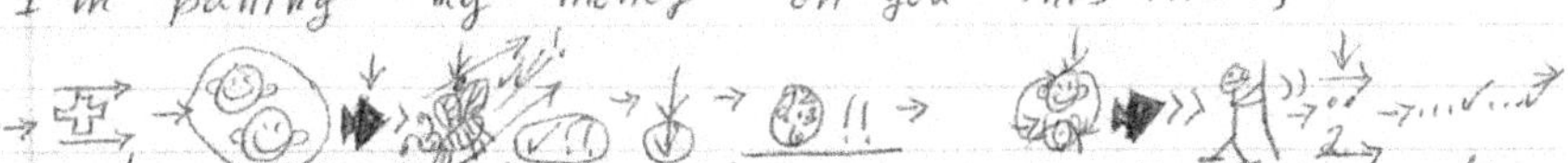

and we'll be just in time I'll try to continue
and we'll be just in time I'll try to continue

to walk the line in war and in peacetime
to walk the line in war and in peacetime

Then freedom will truly be yours and mine;
Then freedom will truly be yours and mine;

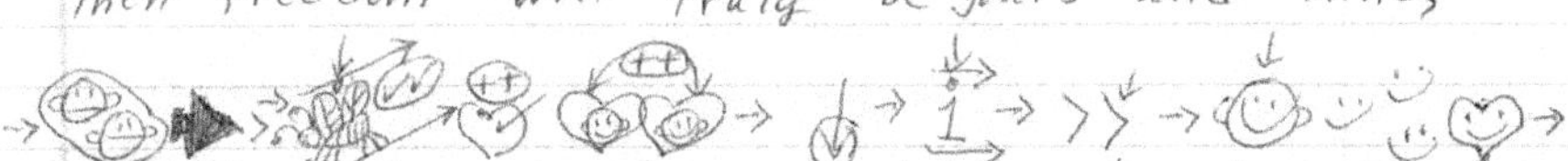

we'll be true partners in the most enjoyable love
we'll be true partners in the most enjoyable love

crime You are awesome, sublime, and steady
crime You are awesome, sublime, and steady

I'll keep you under my secret lock and key
I'll keep you under my secret lock and key

You are reliable, great, and ready; of that I
You are reliable, great, and ready; of that I

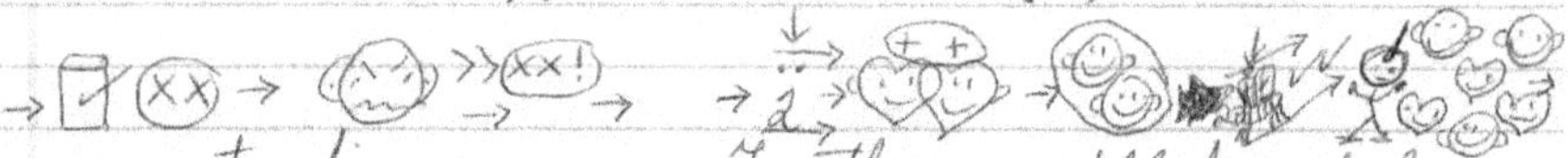

cannot disagree Together, we'll be wholesome
cannot disagree Together, we'll be wholesome

and heady; we won't need any manual,
and heady; we won't need any manual,

you'll see We'll slow the rapids to an
you'll see We'll slow the rapids to an

eddy but we'll still use this to water ski
eddy but we'll still use this to water ski

I've learned to understand; you are my only one-
I've learned to understand; you are my only one-

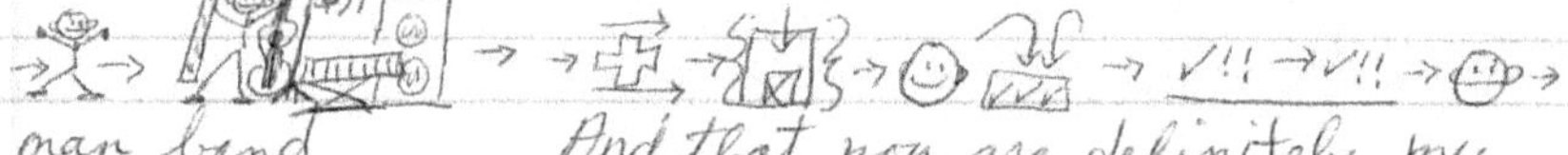

man band And that you are definitely my
man band And that you are definitely my

main man also you are in my greatest demand
main man also you are in my greatest demand

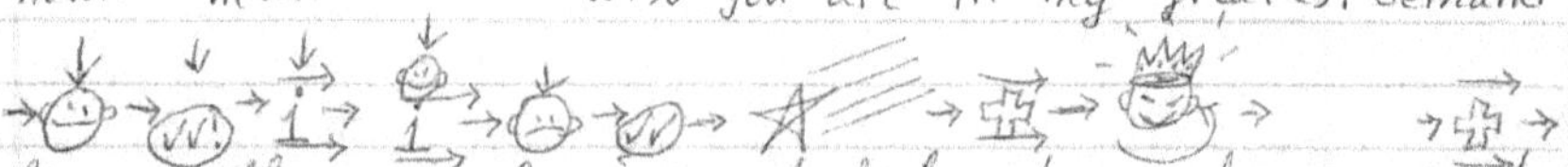

You are the one who is wonderful and grand and
You are the one who is wonderful and grand and

page: 681

I know this firsthand I love our kind of music;

I know this firsthand I love our kind of music;

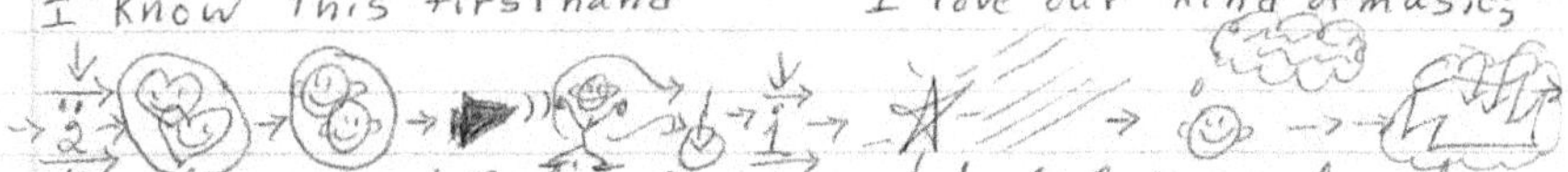

together we will live in a wonderful dreamland

together we will live in a wonderful dreamland

I could go on and on, like a good game of

I could go on and on, like a good game of

Ping-Pong All I can say is I am now free

Ping-Pong All I can say is I am now free

and my troubles are long gone This has on me

and my troubles are long gone This has on me

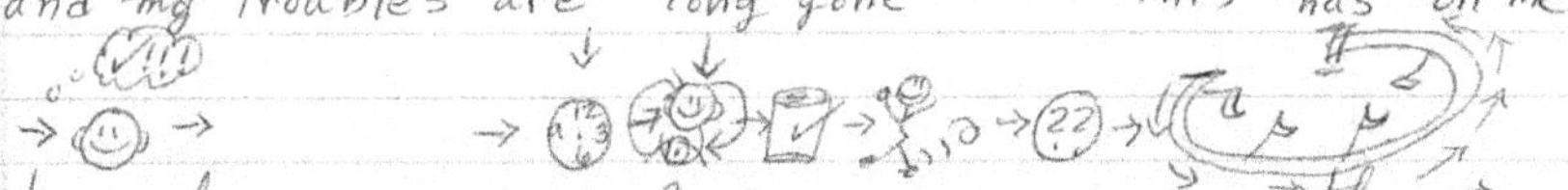

dawned now I can run any mmarathon

dawned now I can run any marathon

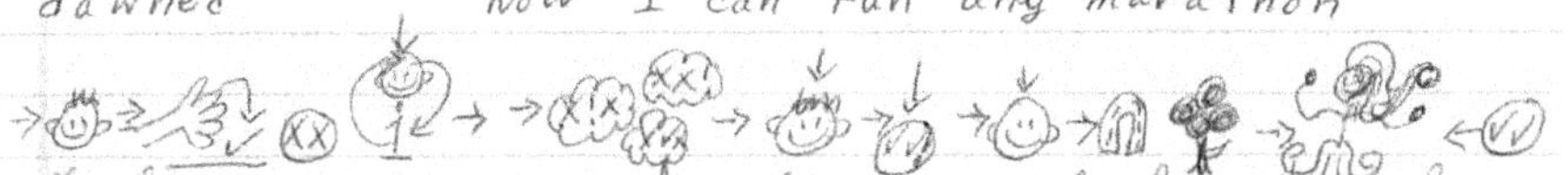

He has no one wronged; he is my lucky leprechaun

He has no one wronged; he is my lucky leprechaun

(135) Did I Really See You (316)

Did I Really See You

Did I really see you? or did I merely misconstrue?
Did I really see you? or did I merely misconstrue?

What I believed I saw, was the overall view? Is it
What I believed I saw, was the overall view? Is it

some strange mysterious snafu? Or is it just
some strange mysterious snafu? Or is it just

my imagination going askew? And while I thought
my imagination going askew? And while I thought

I knew it was you I really didn't have any evidence
I knew it was you I really didn't have any evidence

or a single clue I had to be wrong, through and
or a single clue I had to be wrong, through and

through And the truth, seemed to resemble
through And the truth, seemed to resemble

witchcraft or voodoo Are you, just a shadow,
witchoraft or voodoo Are you, just a shadow,

yes or no? Or are you just a mere memory
yes or no? Or are you just a mere memory

from long ago? Someone whom I merely
from lang ago? Some one whom I merely

used to know Can it be? You tell me I
used to know Can it be? You tell me I

have a right to know Wait; I'll put on my
have a right to know Wait; I'll pat on my

glasses so I can better see Will I see someone
glasses so I can better see will I see some one

familiar who once knew me? Or will I see
familiar who once knew me? Or will I see

someone foreign — with a strange I.D. At least,
some one foreign — with a strange I.D. At least,

I won't make a mistake, that, I'll guarantee
I won't make a mistake, that, I'll guarantee

Should I pretend to be deaf, dumb, and blind this
Should I pretend to be deaf, dumb, and blind this

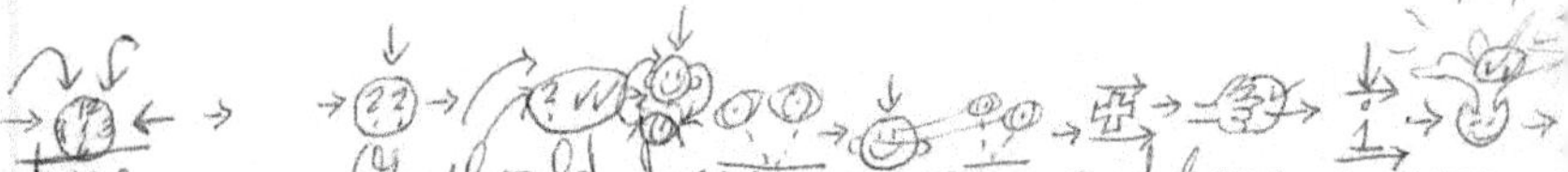

time — Or should I open my eyes and have an open
time — Or should I open my eyes and have an open

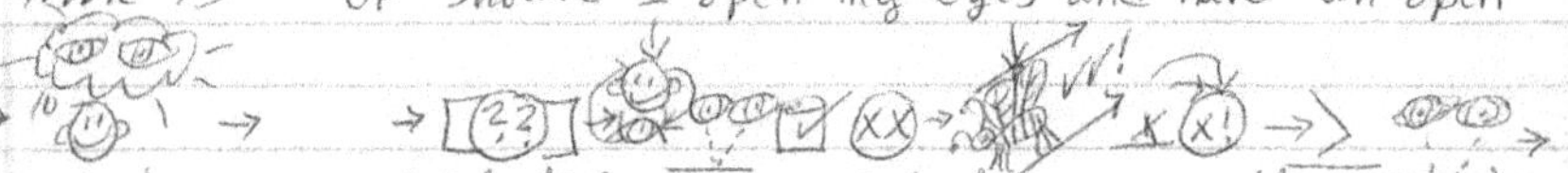

mind — What I see can't be worse than seeing
mind — What I see can't be worse than seeing

a Frankenstein — still, when I see you, I'll
a Frankenstein — still, when I see you, I'll

choose to wave the peace sign — You will find me
choose to wave the place sign — You will find me

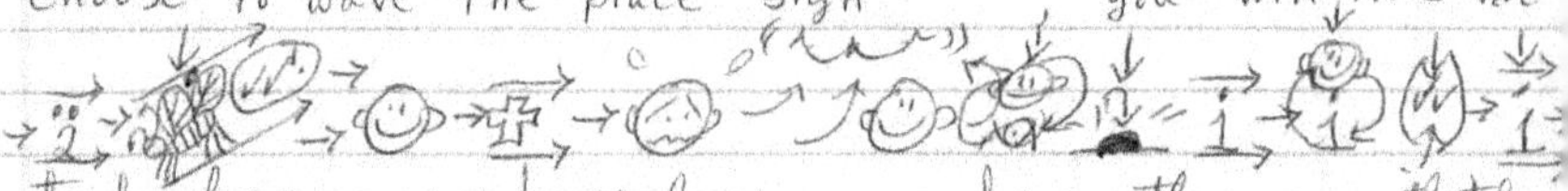

to be happy and carefree — I am the one with the
to be happy and carefree — I am the one with the

greatest ability to see — Because being patient
greatest ability to see — Because being patient

are my best quality — and my purest pedigree
are my best quality — and my purest pedigree

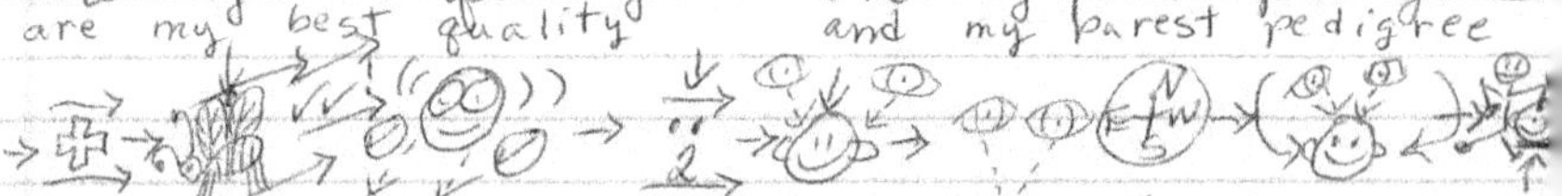

And being observant to you, looking at me — Keeps
And being observant to you, looking at me — keeps

me safe and worry free — Tell me; should
me safe and worry free — Tell me; should

Nilroy

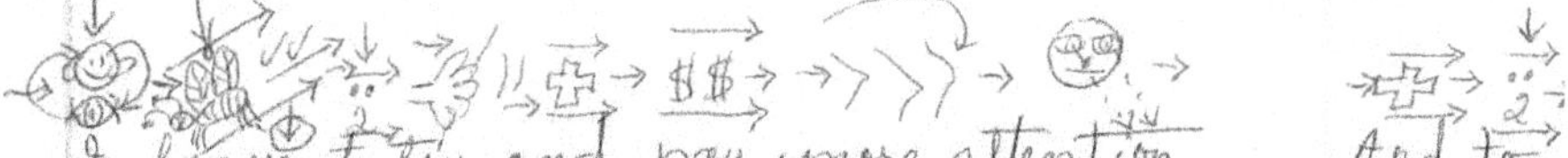

I begin to try and pay more attention And to
I begin to try and pay more attention And to

also try to cultivate more memory and retention
also try to cultivate more memory and retention

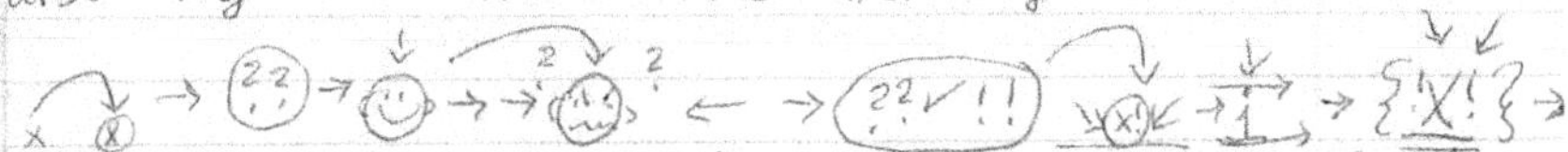

Otherwise, my dysfunction might cause a malfunction
Otherwise, my dysfunction might cause a malfunction

Which may lead to failure and lend to conjecture
Which may lead to failure and lend to conjecture

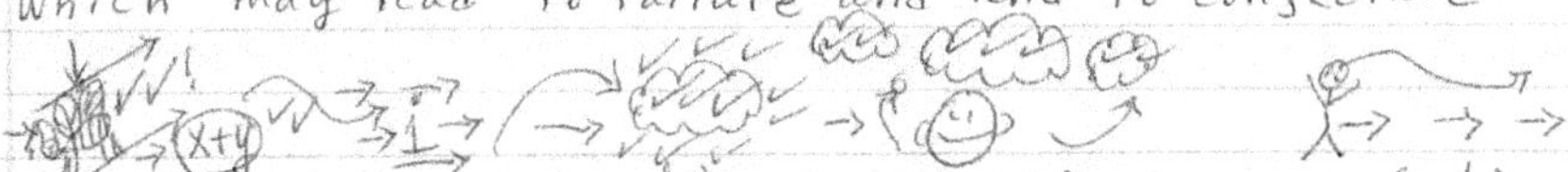

because of an overactive imagination? Sending
because of an overactive imagination? Sending

my gaze your way; may have been a fleeting thing But
my gaze your way; may have been a fleeting thing But

it was just as good as my seeing everything And you can no
it was just as good as my seeing everything And you can no

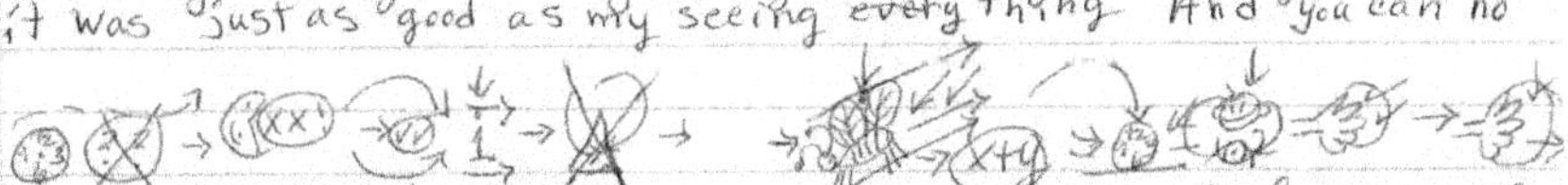

longer lie about a thing Because now I have caught
longer lie about a thing Because now I have caught

you in mind's eye like a puppet on a string
you in mind's eye like a puppet on a string

136 I'll Love You Tonight 318

I'll Love You Tonight

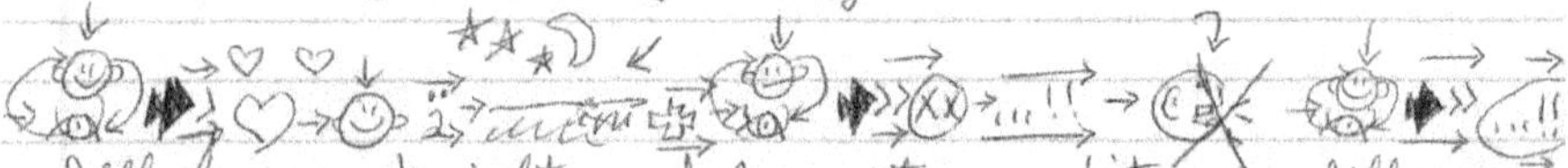

I'll love you tonight, and I won't even bite I'll even
I'll love you tonight, and I won't even bite I'll even

be ypolite, I won't be uptight You won't know
be polite, I won't be uptight You won't know

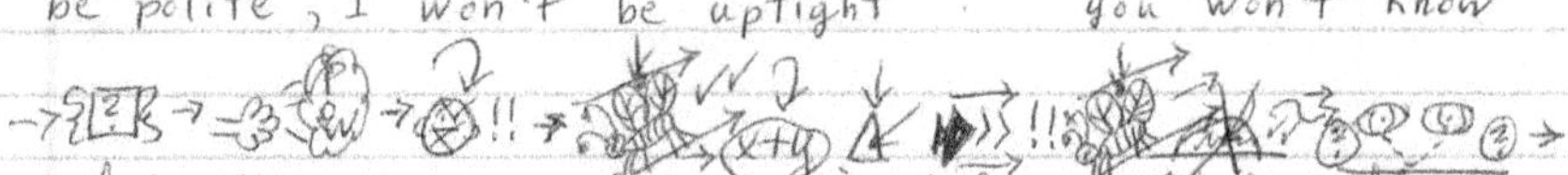

what hit you because it will be out of sight
What hit you because it will be out of sight

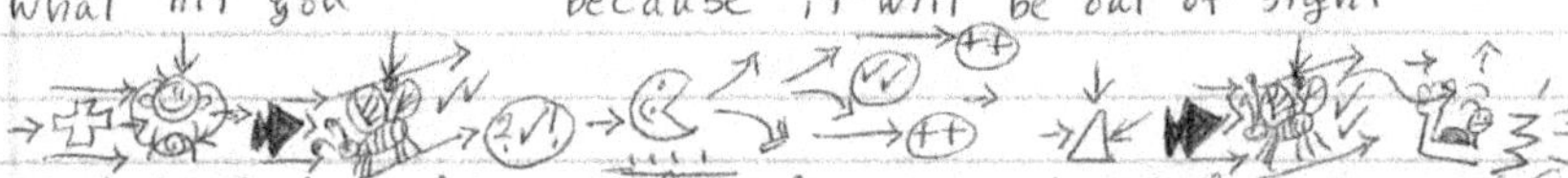

And I'll be quite forthright it'll be as powerful
And I'll be quite forthright it'll be as powerful

as snakebite I like to play, today, or any day
as snake bite I like to play, today, or any day

You were so good in your heyday so what do you
You were so good in your hey day so what do you

say You're still good anyway You know
say You're still good anyway You know

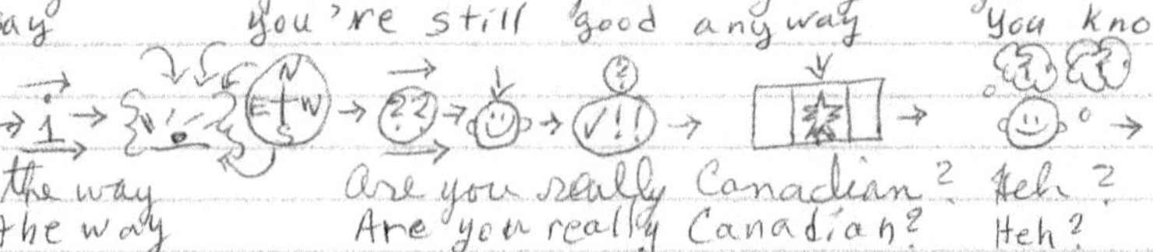

the way Are you really Canadian? Heh?
the way Are you really Canadian? Heh?

how's about a little role-play? Gray may be
how's about a little role-play? Gray may be

the color of my hair, I do declare And you'll be
the color of my hair, I do declare And you'll be

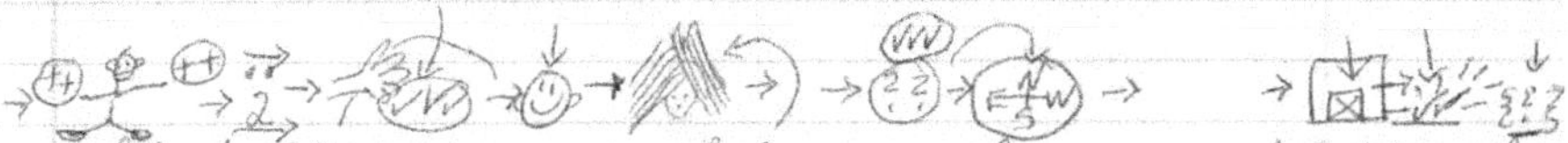

able to find my gray hair anywhere that's only
able to find my gray hair anywhere that's only

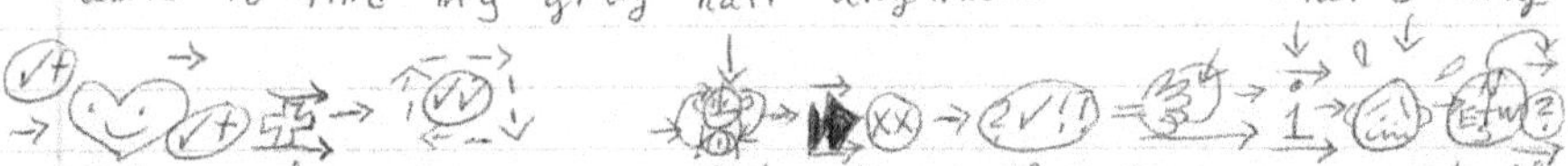

fair and square. I don't really have a care at all
fair and square. I don't really have a care at all

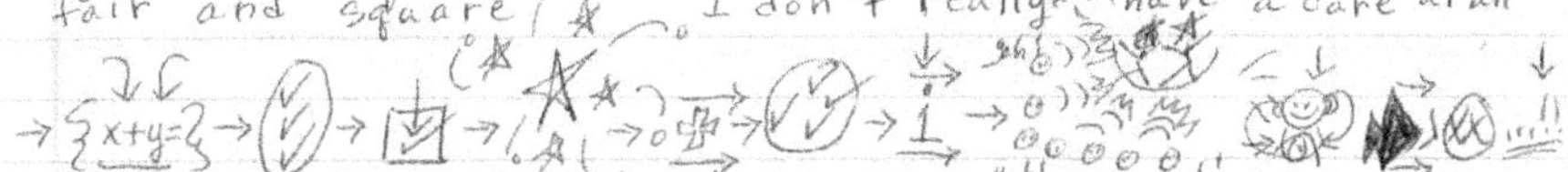

about all that glitz and all the fanfare I don't even
about all that glitz and all the fanfare I don't even

care what I wear; so here's to wash and wear
care what I wear; so here's to wash and wear

I don't mind if you tarry; I'm fancy free You
I don't mind if you tarry; I'm fancy free You

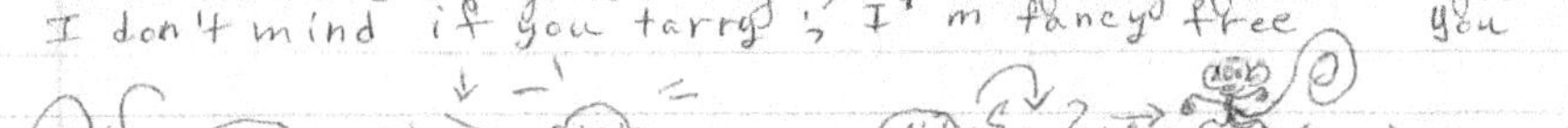

are really very happy just like a chimpanzee
are really very happy just like a chimpanzee

Your name isn't Jerry but you have a royal pedigree
Your name isn't Jerry but you have a royal pedigree

Kevin is the one I want to marry he's my VIP.
Kevin is the one I want to marry he's my VIP.

You can be my playmate; you are really great
You can be my playmate; you are really great

Loving you will be my fate; I just can't wait
Loving you will be my fate; I just can't wait

Please, my love, satiate; bring me through
Please, my love, satiate; bring me through

glory's gate You are a real heavyweight
glory's gate you are a real heavyweight

You can take your time because you are in your prime
You can take your time because you are in your prime

Even though you don't have a dime you can still see
Even though you don't have a dime you can still see

me anytime You can ring my chimes anytime
me any time You can ring my chimes anytime

any you can ring them big time It won't be any
any you can ring them big time It won't be any

kind of crime I'll quite enjoy being with you
kind of crime I'll quite enjoy being with you

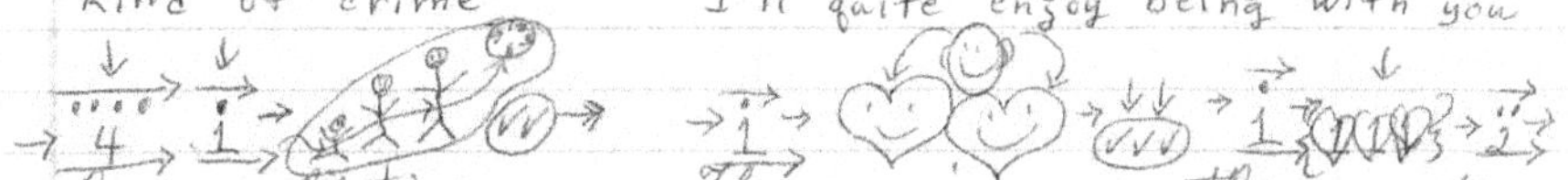

for a lifetime The gracious are the ones to
for a lifetime The gracious are the ones to

love, come push or shove The polite will be
love, come push or shove The polite will be

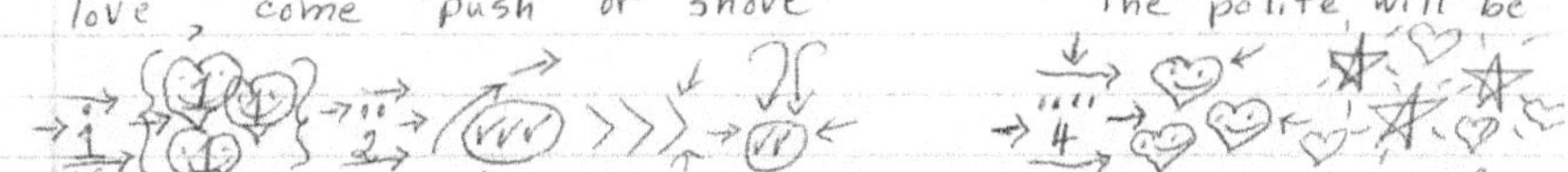

the ones to get more of, for their special
the ones to get more of, for their special

kind of brotherly love Come on now, come on
kind of brotherly love Come on now, come on

the wings of a dove; then put on your boxing
the wings of a dove; then put on your boxing

gloves Be quiet, be my puppy love;
gloves Be quiet, be my puppy love;

lick my face from below or above I'll love
lick my face from below or above I'll love

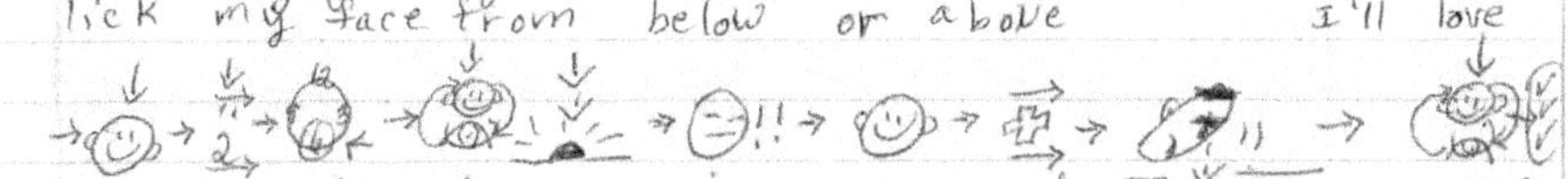

you tonight; I am quite happy and contrite I'll
you tonight; I am quite happy and contrite I'll

love you today with all my might and I won't
love you today with all my might and I won't

put up a fight Today, I'll get it just right;
put up a fight Today, I'll get it just right;

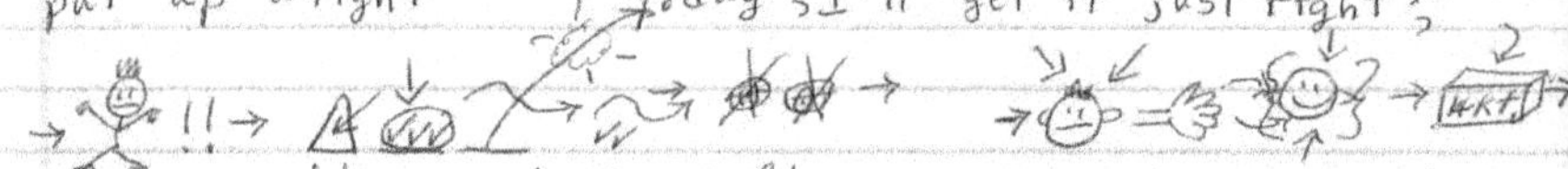

man, it's out of sight You give me real
man, it's out of sight You give me real

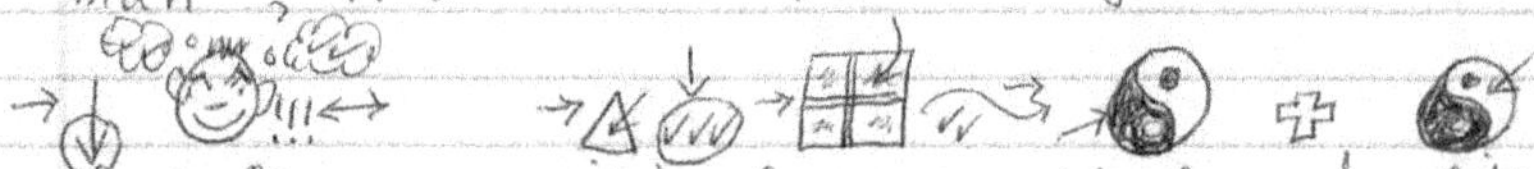

insight; it is clear as black and white
insight; it is clear as black and white

(137) My Darling Deborah (320)

My Darling Deborah

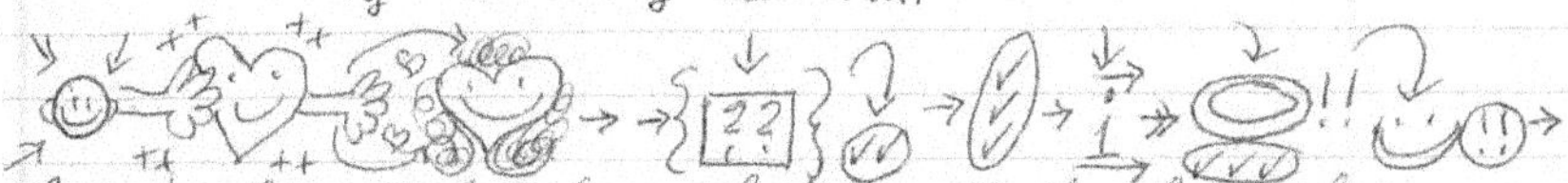

My darling Deborah; what's all the hoop la
My darling Deborah; what's all the hoop la

You are one sweet mama; you have me
you are one sweet mama; you have me

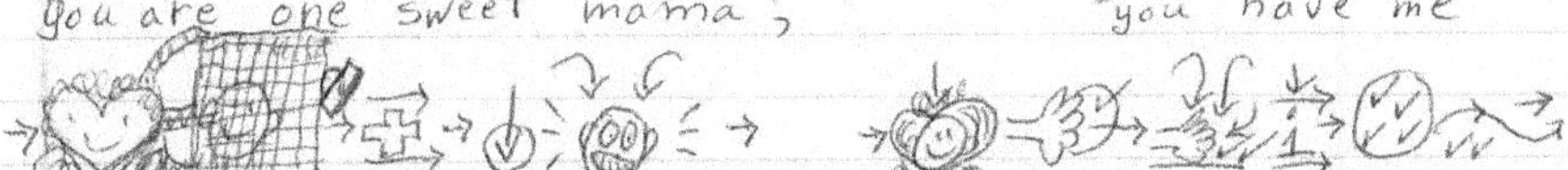

captive and in awe You have got a lot of
captive and in awe You have got a lot of

reasons for people to want to know you
reasons for people to want to know you

I can't, in you, think of a single solitary flaw
I can't, in you, think of a single solitary flaw

She's always full of brotherly love Her beautiful
She's always full of brotherly love Her beautiful

personality fits her like a glove If you
personality fits her like a glove If you

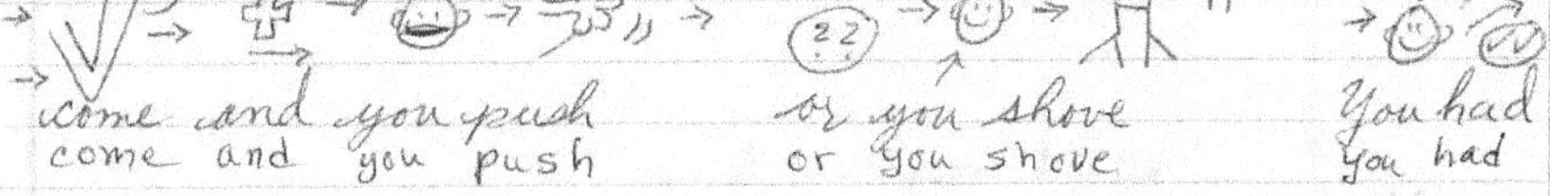

come and you push or you shove You had
come and you push or you shove You had

better be ready for her to put on her boxing gloves
better be ready for her to put on her boxing gloves

Her concern for you is sincere ; she always lends a kind
Her concern for you is sincere ; she always lends a kind

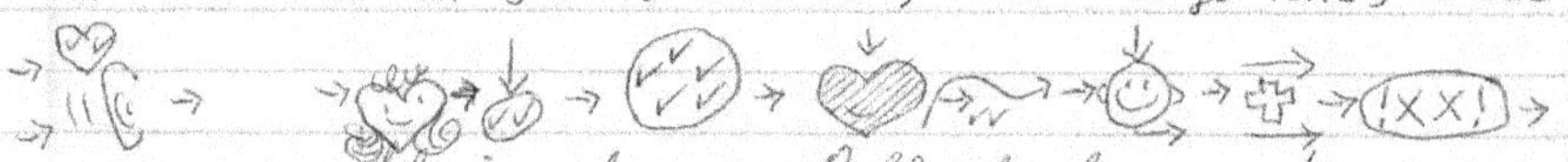

ear She is always full of cheer and never
ear She is always full of cheer and never

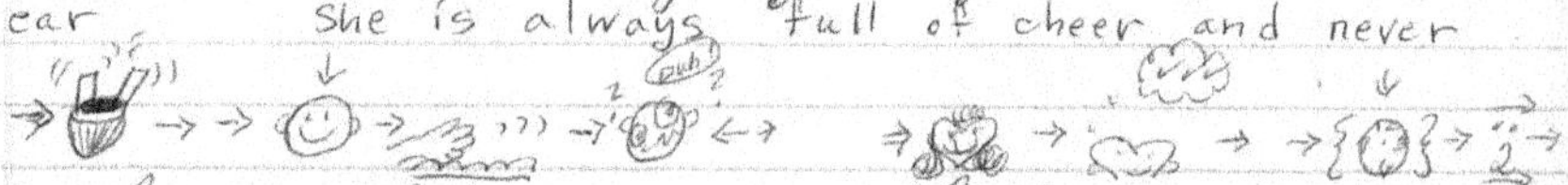

makes you feel queer She knows when to
makes you feel queer She knows when to

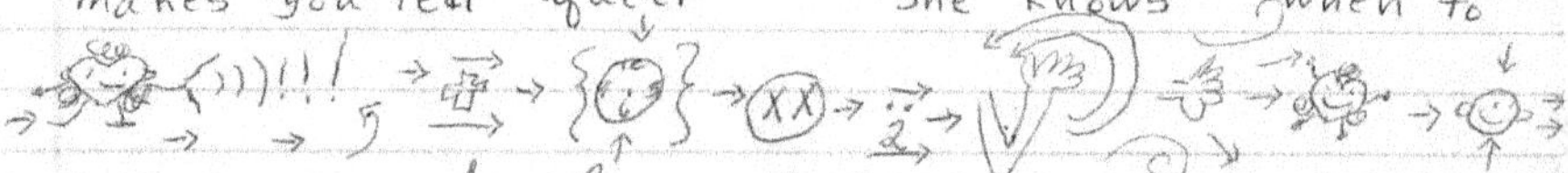

persevere and when not to come near You
persevere and when not to come near You

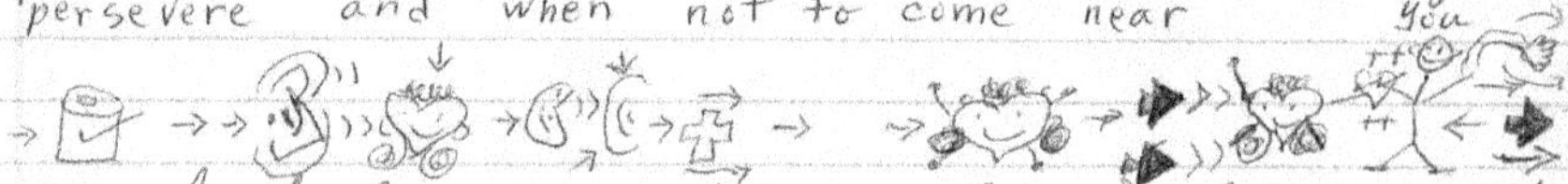

can bend her ear and she will help you put
can bend her ear and she will help you put

away your fears She's got being Saskatoon's
away your fears She's got being Saskatoon's

sweetheart down to an art She's not just
sweetheart down to an art she's not just

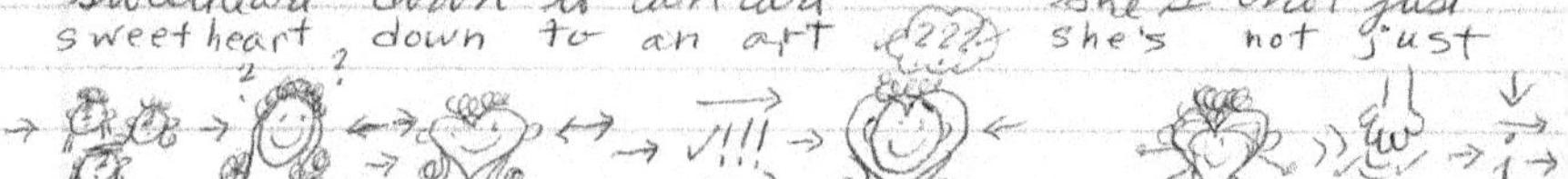

any girl, she's really smart She's got a
any girl, she's really smart She's got a

real big heart, she's no upstart of being
real big heart, she's no upstart of being

mean, she will have no part and if
mean, she will have no part and if

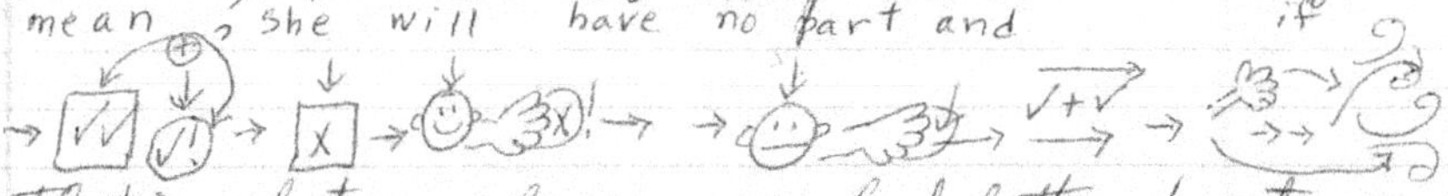
that's what you choose, you had better depart
that's what you choose, you had better depart

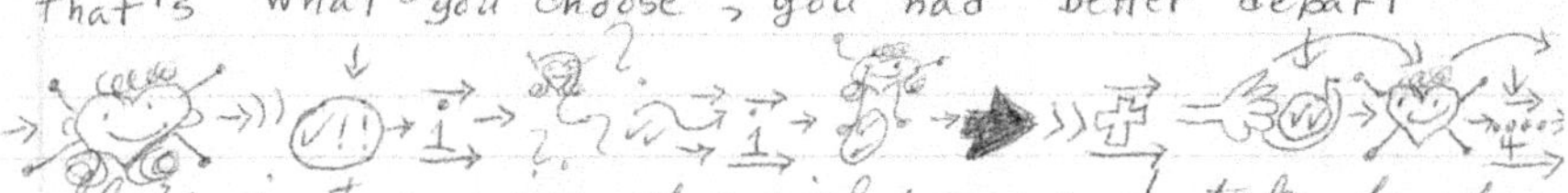
She's just a wisp of a girl; go and take her for
She's just a wisp of a girl; go and take her for

a whirl She is as precious as the most
a whirl she is as precious as the most

precious pearl She is as busy as a bee,
precious pearl she is as busy as a bee,

just watch her day unfurl She creates
just watch her day unfurl She creates

enough beautiful colors to create the most
enough beautiful colors to create the most

beautiful mural Her beauty is so real that she
beautiful mural Her beauty is so real that she

can't possibly, it, conceal Unlike an
automobile you can't possibly buy it or steal
No matter what kind of misfortune you have been
through her words have the power to heal
She takes no credit for it; she never thinks it
is a big deal She is very wise, which comes
to me as no surprise She's not just one
of the girls or the guys I can see it in her
eyes You won't catch her telling lies only

the truth for her applies she believes in family
the truth for her applies she believes in family

ties; she is a real cutie pie No matter what
ties; she is a real cutie pie No matter what

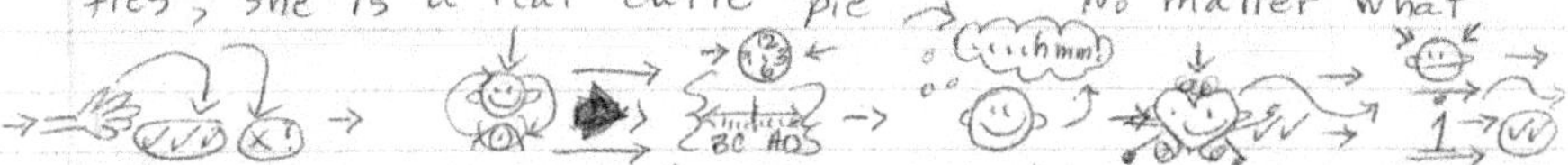

happens I'll always consider her as one of
happens I'll always consider her as one of

my friends Because she knew when to outstretch
my friends Because she Knew when to outstretch

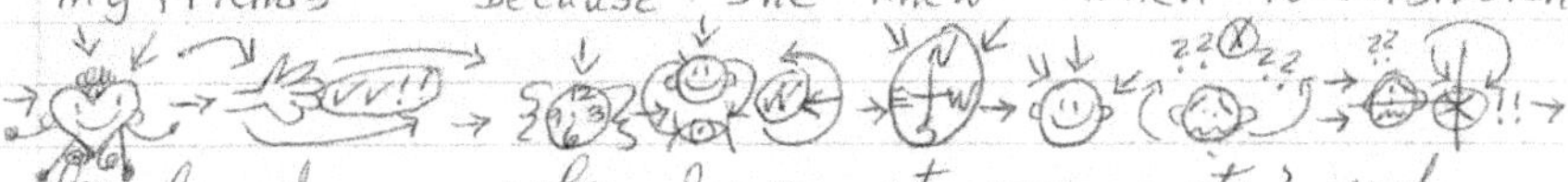

her hand when I was at my wits' end
her hand when I was at my wits' end

Especially when I needed to talk again and
Especially when I needed to talk again and

again About my ailing, favorite, loving,
again About my ailing, favorite, loving,

and beloved man
and be loved man

138 My Island 322

My Island

My island is a special place I sometimes
My island is a special place I sometimes
go to in haste It is one suited to my very
go to in haste It is one suited to my very
own personal taste My island is a place
own personal taste My island is a place
I love to tenderly embrace My island is a
I love to tenderly embrace My island is a
place where I can truly be free and feel
place where I can truly be free and feel
heavenly grace It is a great realm with no
heavenly grace It is a great realm with no
disease It is a place where you find peace
disease It is a place where you find peace
and sweet release It is a place where the
and sweet release It is a place where the

breeze smells like sweet peas It is

also where I love to wander, all happy

and at total ease You'd never guess what it

is, or where it is You won't find

it on any pop quiz I'll never tell you and

that's show biz That's another story it is

what it is My island travels through space

and time It follows a special rhythm

and a special rhyme It'll never let me down

daytime or nightime As long as I'm around;

we are special partners in a love crime My

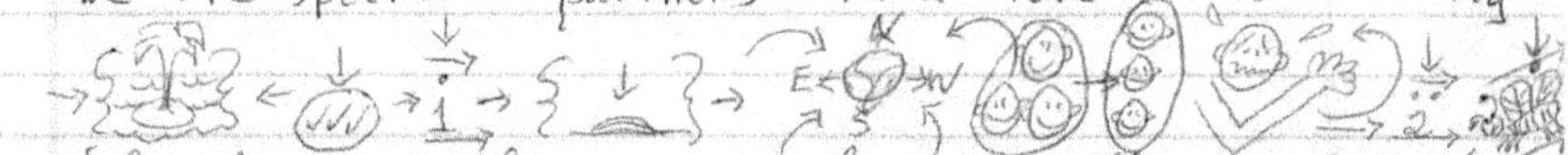

island is a place where we all want to be

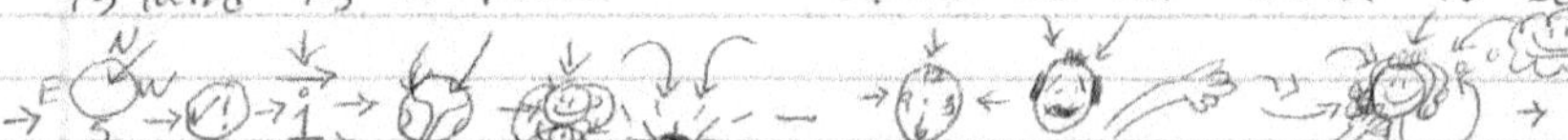

It is a place I am — when he touches me

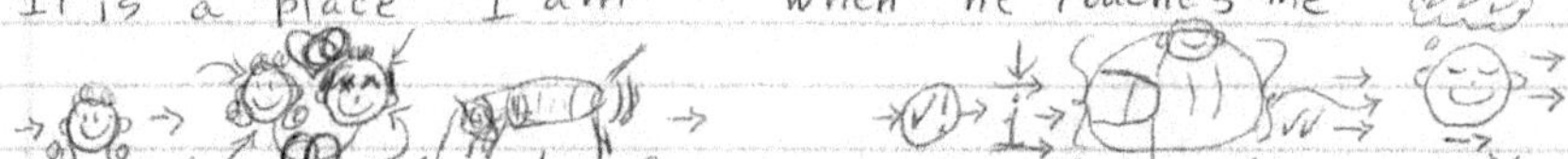

My husband's touch is an island of serenity

Something I experience as a gift of love

from him for free My island can be in

your mind too Let my mind find your island

and let it find you You won't have the fainted

clue what to pursue Just what it is where
it is or who it is excuse me and thank you
Before you know it, you might have a nervous tic
And before you've even realized it you might
be in the thick The answer will fall right
out of the skies like a ton of bricks
And it will blind your eyes like a bad card
trick The solution will land slowly while
you watch You will wonder if it was really

here ... or if it is hiding under a cabbage
here ... or if it is hiding under a cabbage

patch ... You'll wonder if you've missed
patch ... you'll wonder if you've missed

it in some ... mysterious geological batch
it in some ... mysterious geological batch

Then there might be a telltale fear of a
Then there might be a telltale fear of a

huge dinosaur hatch ... My island rocks
huge dinosaur hatch ... My island rocks

My island talks ... My island even squawks
My island talks ... My island even squawks

My island even talks ... Talk to me, my island my
My island even talks ... Talk to me, my island

dreamland ... Tell me you are my friend;
dreamland ... Tell me you are my friend;

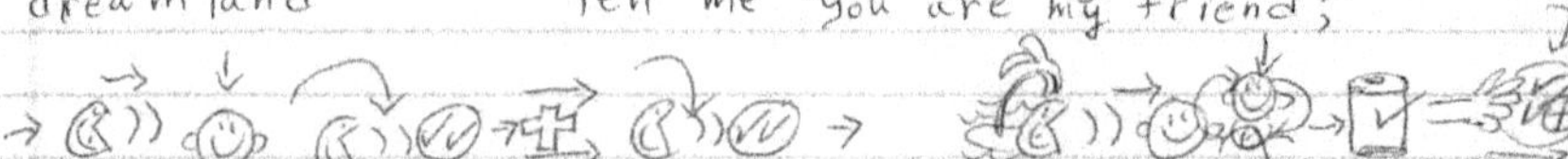

Tell me again and again ... Tell me I can depend
Tell me again and again ... Tell me I can depend

on you   to be my fantasy land   Tell me

on you   to be my fantasy land   Tell me

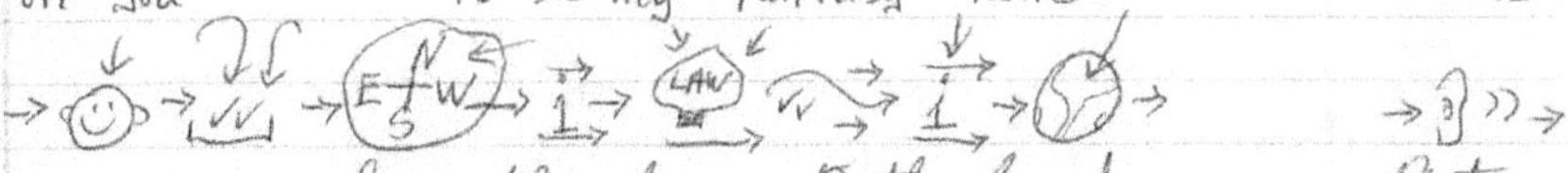

you are where the law of the land   listens

you are where the law of the land   listens

to my every command

to my every command

(139) I Will Create (325)

I Will Create

It's all been done, undone, and redone; oh,
It's all been done, undone, and redone; oh,

what fun I'll have some fun with a
what fun I'll have some fun with a

slightly different rerun I won't be foiled
slightly different rerun I won't be foiled

or undone I just happen to be a Canadian-
or undone I just happen to be a Canadian-

born woman I'll create on the run
born woman I'll create on the run

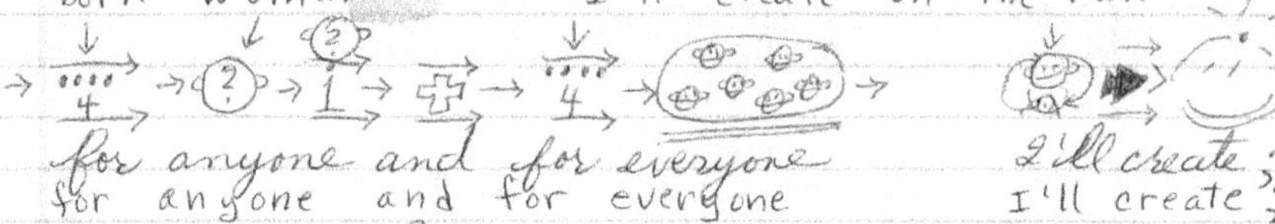

for anyone and for everyone I'll create;
for anyone and for everyone I'll create;

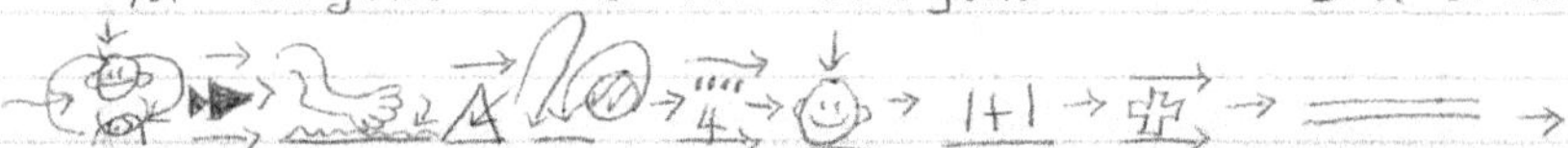

I'll lay it out for you, plain and straight
I'll lay it out for you, plain and straight

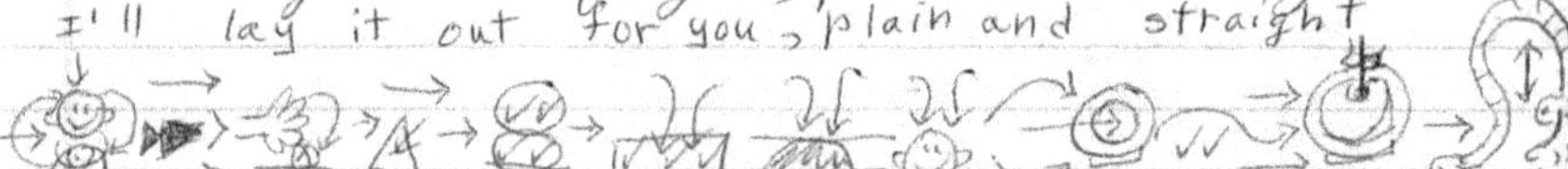

I'll put it right here on your plate as tempting bait
I'll put it right here on your plate as tempting bait

You'll never know your fate or even have time to
you'll never know your fate or even have time to

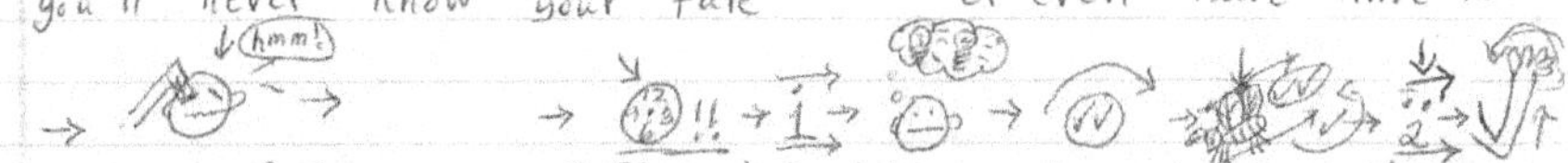

contemplate When the ideas have begun to come
contemplate When the ideas have begun to come

out of the gate; it will already be too late My
out of the gate; it will already be too late My

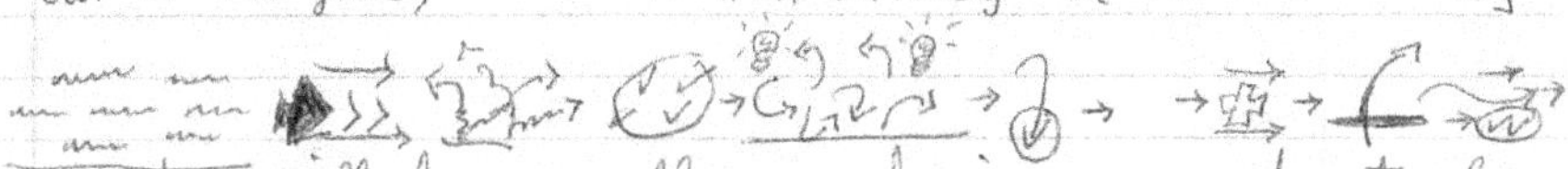

words will bounce all around, in and out of
words will bounce all around, in and out of

the compound I'll make them have such a
the compound I'll make them have such

groovy sound; they will keep you all spellbound
groovy sound; they will keep you all spellbound

They will float all over town, in and out of neutral
They will float all over town, in and out of neutral

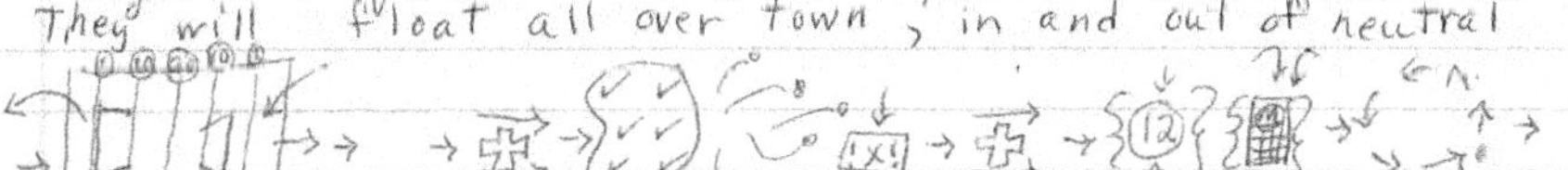

ground and all over now and all year round
ground and all over now and all year round

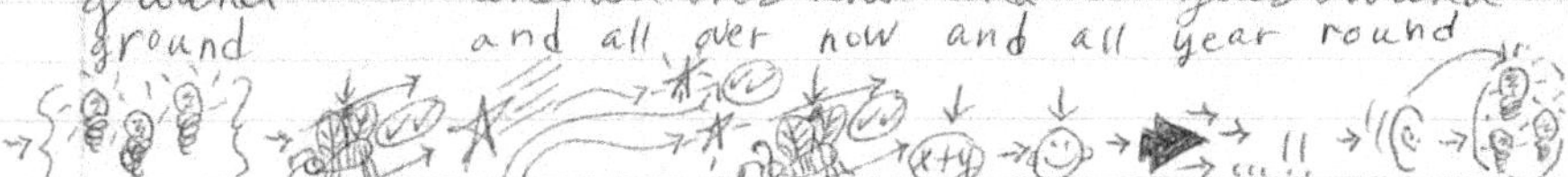

They'll be glory bound because you will even hear them
They'll be glory bound because you will even hear them

on the school grounds You'll hear the sound
on the school grounds you'll hear the sound

of my melody as far as Washington, D.C.
of my melody as far as Washington, D.C.

You're bound to like it, you'll see; even that deaf man
You're bound to like it, you'll see; even that deaf man

agrees It's a message sent just from me;
agrees It's a message sent just from me;

and if you disagree I will have to say pardon me
and if you disagree I will have to say pardon me

It'll still be sent with glee from little old me —
It'll still be sent with glee from little old me

Master of the spelling bee My ideas will come
Master of the spelling bee My ideas will come

from my heart even though they may not always
from my heart even though they may not always

be too smart But my heart is a good place to
be too smart But my heart is a good place to

start using my special kind of folk art
start using my special kind of folk art

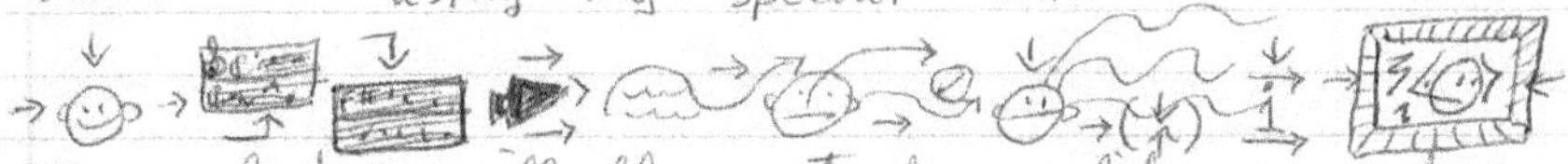

My melodies will flow out of me like a modern
My melodies will flow out of me like a modern

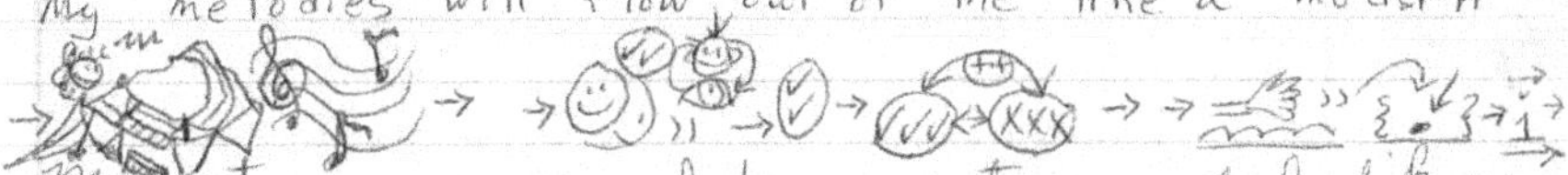

Mozart yes, I do, sometimes, feel like an
Mozart yes, I do, some times, feel like an

upstart But I have waited a long time; to be
upstart But I have waited a long time; to be

able to show or do my part I'll continue on and
able to show or do my part I'll continue on and

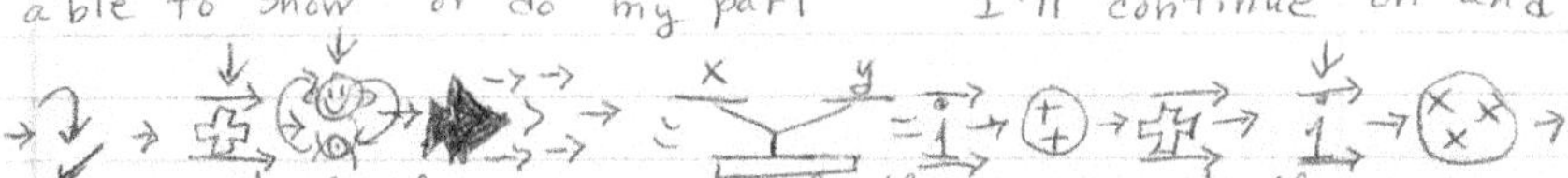

on, and I'll weigh the pros and the cons
on, and I'll weigh the pros and the cons

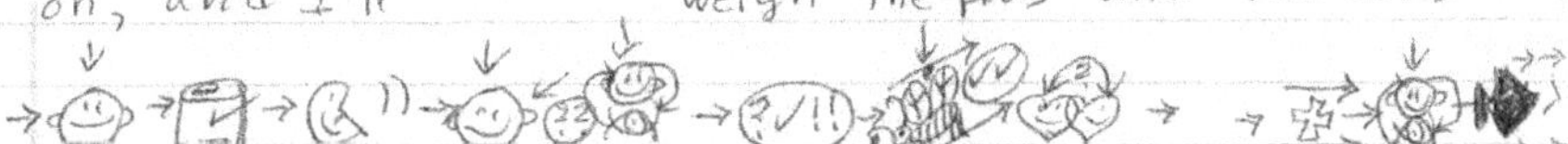

You can tell me if I should belong and I'll
You can tell me if I should belong and I'll

Keep on pondering on this, until way after dawn
Keep on pondering on this, until way after dawn

But as for me and this song; it will be my
But as for me and this song; it will be my

offering from a full-grown Swan I'll perform
offering from a full - grown swan I'll perform

today, and until I'm gone, off and on,
today, and until I'm gone, off and on,

like a newly freed Don Juan This will be
like a newly freed Don Juan This will be

the best way I can think of to play And it
the best way I can think of to play And it

will be also the best way to spend my day The
will be also the, best way to spend my day The

notes, to my ideas, will run up and down
notes, to my ideas, will run up and down

the scale's stairway playing a musical ballet
the scale's stairway playing a musical ballet

They will fly up and float away up into the Milky
They will fly up and float away up into the Milky

Way I can think of nothing better than to share
Way I can think of nothing better than to share

my handiwork
my handiwork

It gives me pleasure to share
It gives me pleasure to share

my pleasure, my art;
my pleasure, my art;

which is not really
which is not really

a chore
a chore

At the same time, it gives my brain
At the same time, it gives my brain

a chance to
a chance to

run better and to better work
ran better and to better work

And helps me to work out any fuzzy quirks
And helps me to work out any fuzzy quirks

where and if they lurk
where and if they lurk

(140) Love Potion #9, (327)
Love Potion #9

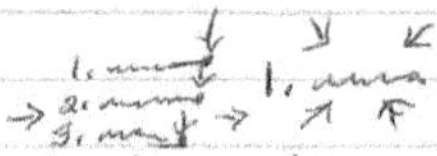

Version 1
Version 1

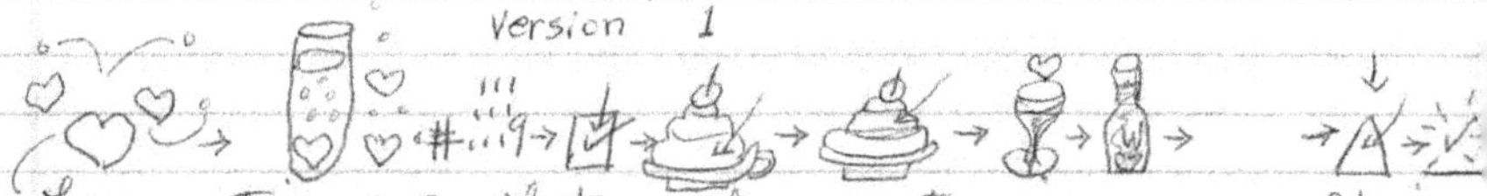

Love potion #9, that sweet, sweet wine It is
Love potion #9, that sweet, sweet wine It is

oh so fine and comes straight from love's vine
oh so fine and comes straight from love's vine

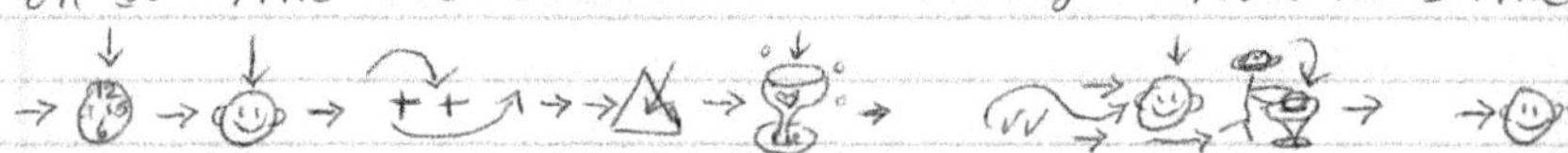

When you combine this wine as you dine You
when you combine this wine as you dine You

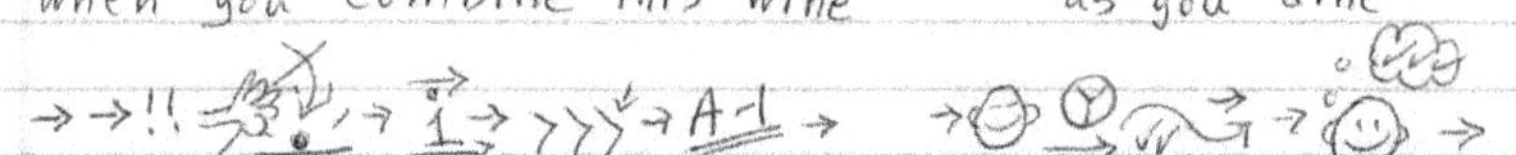

will find the very best peace of mind
will find the very best peace of mind

You will see its powez unfuzl And it will send
You will see its power unfurl And it will send

you and many folks awhirl And you
you and many folks awhirl And you

will see its vapors swirl and twirl
will see its vapors swirl and twirl

Then you will feel like the very luckiest of
pearls We will have plenty of time
To construct some of this brine It is the
healthiest wine, made from the very best enzymes
It is good in wartime, peacetime, or really,
any time I feel sorry for you, Mr. Untried and
Untrue If you've never tasted this brew;
you don't even have a clue It leaves you satisfied
and feeling anew and is the cause of many

a breakthrough Without it, you won't even have
a breakthrough Without it, you won't even have

a clue on which direction to go, or on
a clue on which direction to go, or on

which avenue You don't need a ton of knowledge
which avenue You don't need a ton of knowledge

All you need is a little, tiny smidge Of ideas,
All you need is a little, tiny smidge of ideas,

from this wonderful dredge They'll send you
from this wonderful dredge They'll send you

over love's mountain ledge Love will be
over love's mountain ledge Love will be

the secret potion not to be undone You soon, will
the secret potion not to be undone You soon, will

have the notion how to have, all its fun
have the notion how to have, all its fun

What else are you to put into the lotion, one by
What else are you to put into the lotion, one by

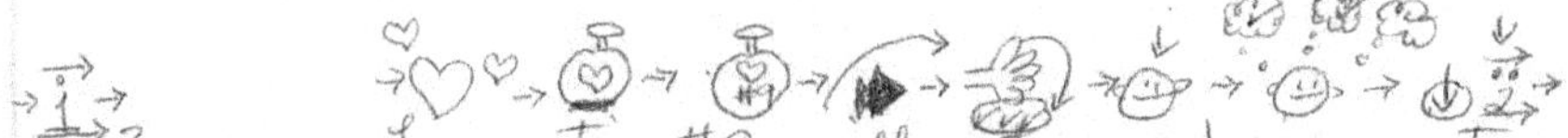

one? Love potion #9 will put your desires into
one? Love potion #9 will put your desires into

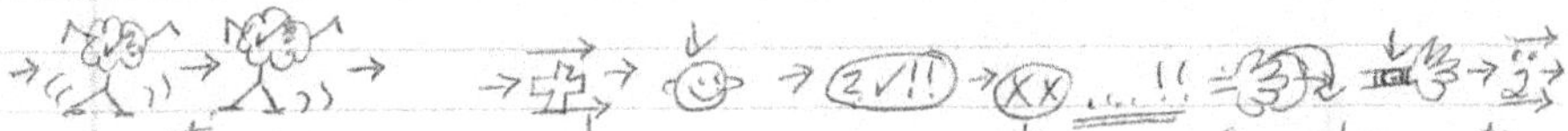

motion, and you may not even have time to
motion, and you may not even have time to

call 911 It is oh so fine; you'll be on cloud
call 911 It is oh so fine; you'll be on cloud

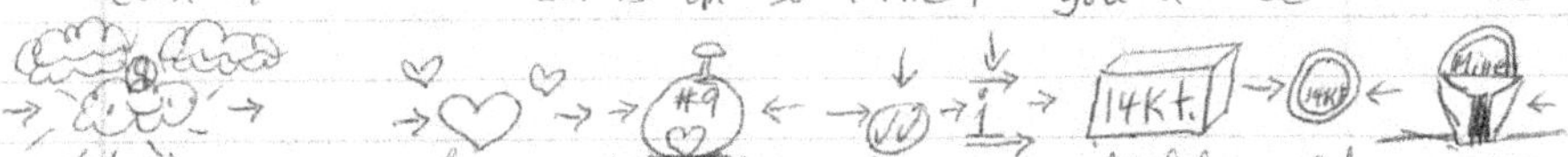

nine Love potion #9 is a veritable gold mine
nine Love potion #9 is a veritable gold mine

I wanted it all the time; it would even cure
I wanted it all the time; it would even cure

the redneck Frankenstein Finally, I've found it,
the red neck Frankenstein Finally, I've found it

it is mine; I also offered it to my friend Einstein
it is mine; I also offered it to my friend Einstein

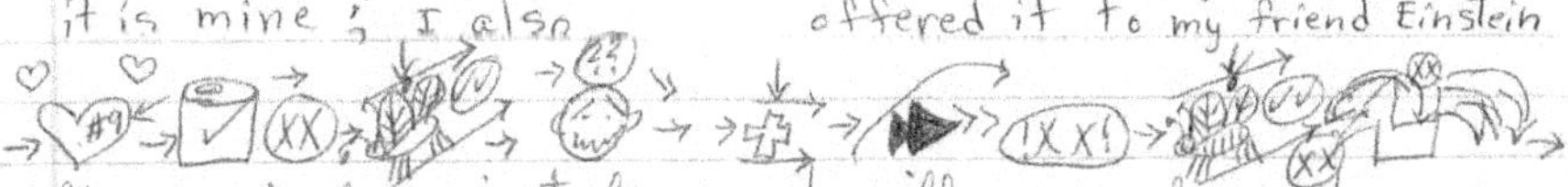

It can't be mistaken and will never be undone
It can't be mistaken and will Never be undone

It will not be forsaken or forgotten by your
It will not be forsaken or forgotten by your

enemy, your friend, or by anyone It is love's
enemy, your friend, or by anyone It is love's

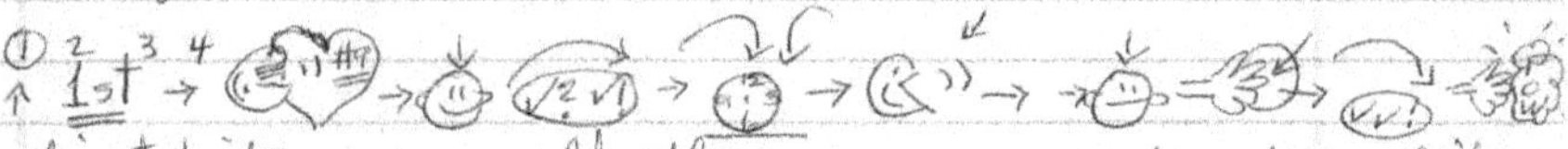

first bite, you could then say you've been hit,
first bite, you could then say you've been hit,

but you didn't want to run It will always be
but you didn't want to run It will always be

just right, Love's greatest hole in one
just right, Love's greatest hole in one

page: (713)

(141) Love Potion #9 , (329)
Love Potion #9 ,

version 2
version 2

Love potion #9 Arrives just on time It
Love potion #9 arrives just on time It

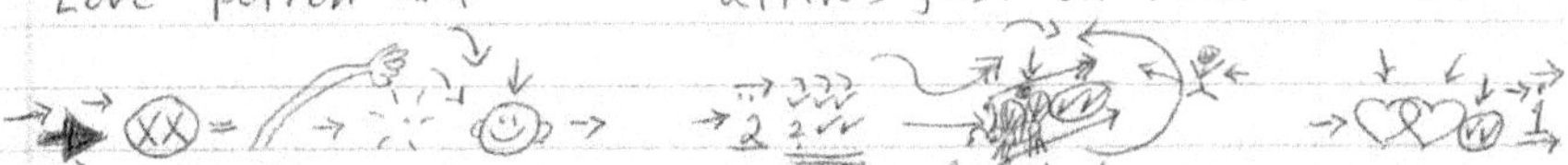

won't leave you too far behind It's a
won't leave you too far behind It's a

romantic kind of kind When you drink
romantic Kind of kind When you drink

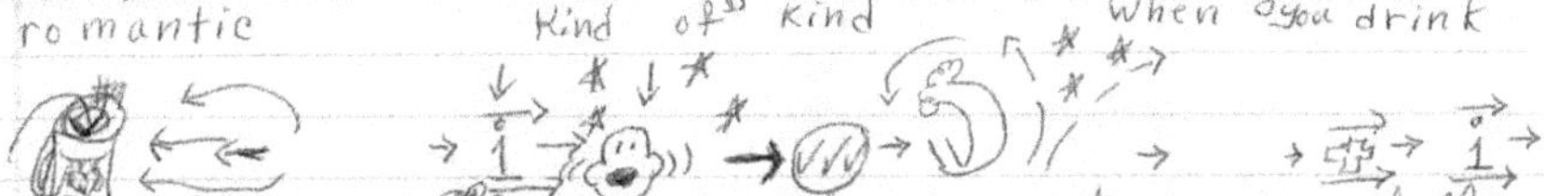

from it The stars will come out and the
from it The stars will come out and the

moon will be lit Cupid's arrow will only
moon will be lit Cupid's arrow will only

have to pinch hit Whoever shares the potion
have to pinch hit Whoever shares the potion

will be forever close-knit Love potion #9
will be forever close-knit Love potion #9

might backfire And bounce off of you, if you

might backfire And bounce off of you, if you

become tired And hit someone undesirable

become tired And hit some one undesirable

who may be caught in your crossfire And by you

who may be caught in your crossfire and by you

drinking the potion accidentally they may become

drinking the potion accidentally they may become

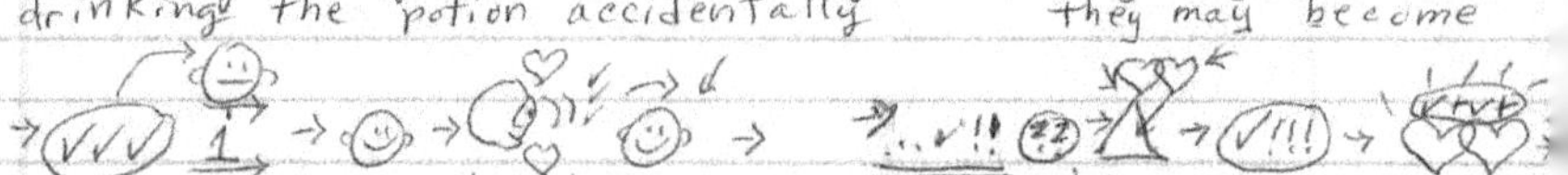

someone you admire But if it really works

some one you admire But if it really works

good As we all know it really should

good As we all Know it really should

It'll get you in the proper mood And love will

It'll get you in the proper mood And love will

be the result in all likelihood It'll be like

be the result in all likelihood It'll be like

heaven's delight It'll feel like a mountain

heaven's delight It'll feel like a mountain

majestic and in all its might It'll be like
majestic and in all its might It'll be like

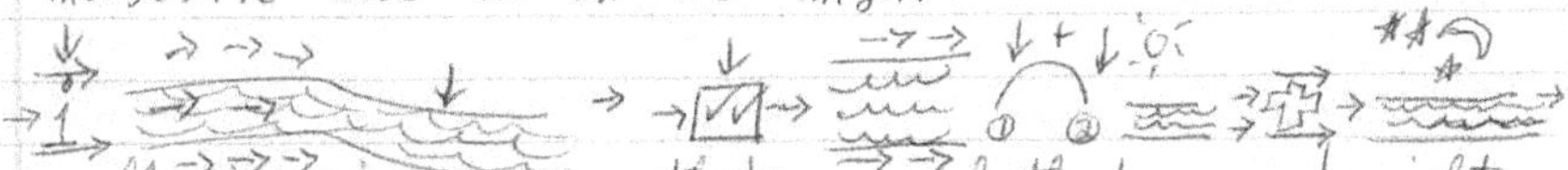

a flowing river that runs both day and night
a flowing river that runs both day and night

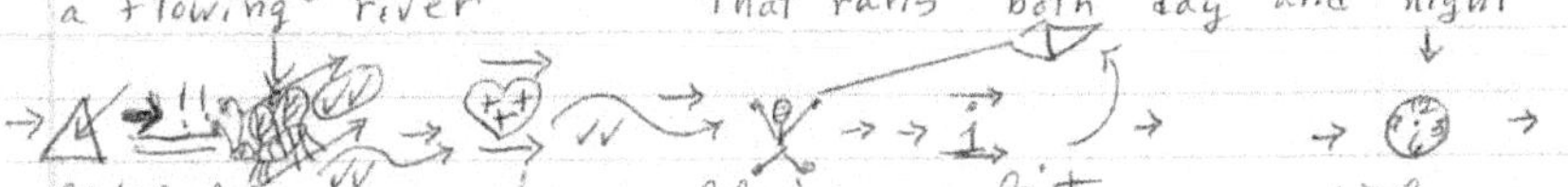

It'll be as good as flying a kite When
It'll be as good as flying a kite When

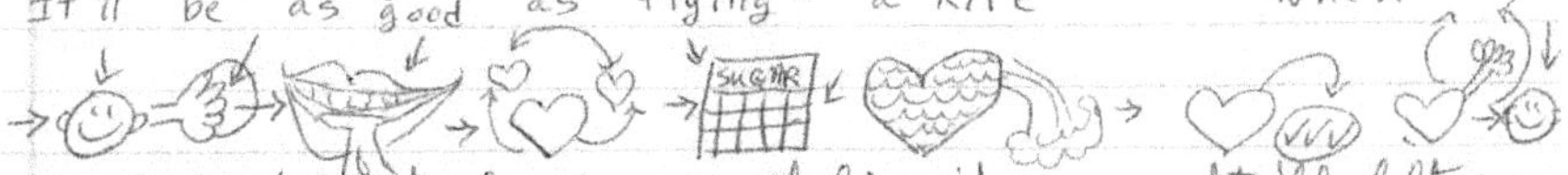

you've tasted love's sweet liquid It'll lift you
you've tasted love's sweet liquid It'll lift you

as high as Egypt's pyramids You won't be
as high as Egypt's pyramids You won't be

able to close your eyelids And you'll like it
able to close your eyelids And you'll like it

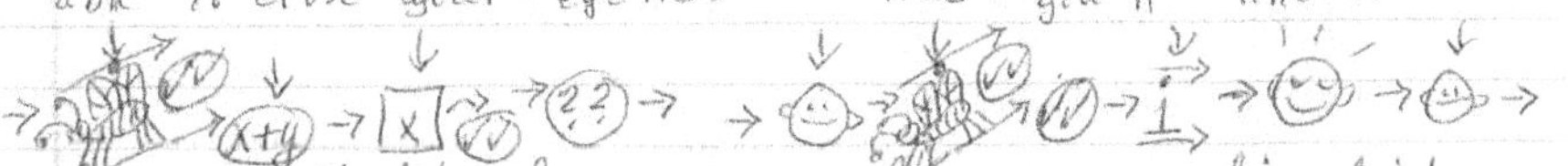

because that's why you became a whiz kid.
because that's why you became a whiz kid.

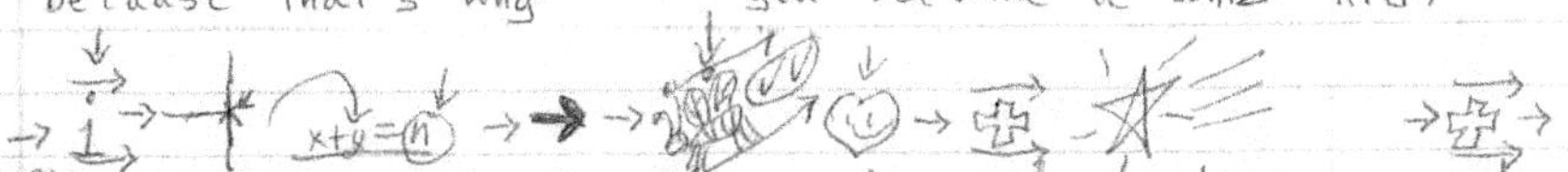

The end result will be good and great And
The end result will be good and great And

you'll be glad you took love's bait The feeling
you'll be glad you took love's bait The feeling

Hilary

will totally help you to liberate And you
will totally help you to liberate And you

will be headed right for the pearly gates
will be headed right for the pearly gates

In the end, you'll be glad, you've been love had
In the end, you'll be glad, you've been love had

That love potion #9 was definitely, your
That love potion #9 was definitely, your

launching pad Because you have now officially
launching pad Because you have now officially

become a love Olympiad And will now
become a love Olympiad And will now

have as many adventures as did Galahad
have as many adventures as did Galahad

page: (717)

(142) My Cares Laid Bare (331)
My Cares Laid Bare

(1+1) (①+①) 1

(version 1)
(version 1)

My cares are laid bare All people can do
My cares are laid bare All people can do

is stop and stare I don't really care I
is stop and stare I don't really care I

think this is quite fair It's all about being free
think this is quite fair It's all about being free

Because someone who loved us was nailed to a tree
Because someone who loved us was nailed to a tree

Forgiveness for our sins was his plea His
Forgiveness for our sins was his plea His

was a great sacrifice for you and me
was a great sacrifice for you and me

We strive to live Up to his standards and
We strive to live Up to his standards and

to give Our children this precious gift
to give Our children this precious gift

And not to cause any negative rifts When
And not to cause any negative rifts When

I have gone through life And I have encountered
I have gone through life And I have encountered

strife I know now I am a good wife
strife I Know now I am a good wife

Carved out of life with an experienced knife
Carved out of life with an experienced Knife

Soon everyone will know Me from heel
Soon everyone will Know Me from heel

to toe My goodness will glow From
to toe My goodness will glow From

inside me just so My glorious time Is
inside me just so My glorious time Is

quote
boat
note

when I sit and rhyme Sitting and writing
when I sit and rhyme sitting and writing

words on paper line after line? I say
words on paper line after line? I say

this is a treasure to me and is truly my
this is a treasure to me and is truly my

very best, best find → → It brings me no end of
very best, best find It brings me no end of

pleasure It is truly something I treasure Something
pleasure It is truly something I treasure Something

I dole out in good measure It comes now
I dole out in good measure It comes now

and then at my leisure It has always been so
and then at my leisure It has always been so

If you care to know Silently waiting to come
If you care to know Silently waiting to come

out left to grow Just how it came to be and why it flows
out left to grow Just how it came to be and why it flows

I'll gladly welcome and tell you on why and
I'll gladly welcome and tell you on why and

how and give you more info
how and give [ya?] more info

(143) My Cares Laid Bare (333)

My Cares Laid Bare

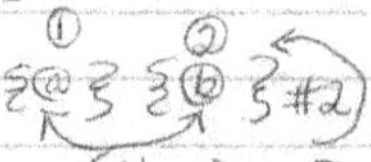

(Version 2)

(Version 2)

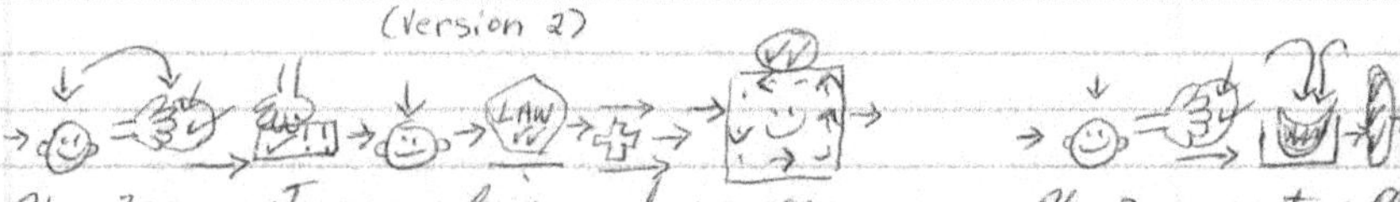

You've got me fair and square You've got all

you've got me fair and square you've got all

my cares laid bare Fair is fair; I was told to

my cares laid bare Fair is fair; I was told to

beware Sometimes, I feel I am living in

beware sometimes, I feel I am living in

a nightmare I've shown all my troubles and

a nightmare I've shown all my troubles and

what that brings People still treat me like

what that brings People still treat me like

a useless plaything I feel like a marionette

a useless plaything I feel like a marionette

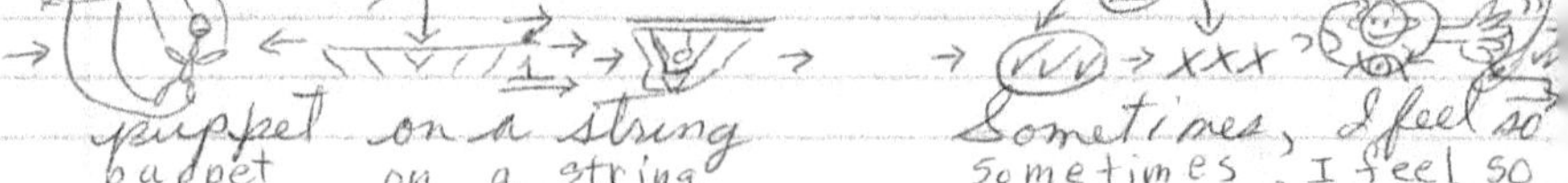

puppet on a string Sometimes, I feel so

puppet on a string sometimes, I feel so

low I feel like a ding-a-ling I believe in
sharing, like it was a rite of spring And I
didn't mind being daring or taking what
that brings I do care that we share everything
that I have to send or sling But I really don't
want to sing anymore And act like a puppet
on a string It'll all work out once they've
sent out a large talent scout The truth
will have more clout if I avoid having any

falling cats I'll tell you more about the
thrill by using the round about and by turning
ideas inside out I won't have to shout
because the truth will stand cat and be as
noisy as any shoot-out And in the end all
my loose ends will mend And I'll have time
to ascend to a happy place, which I would
gladly recommend Again and again and again,
to all men whom I wish to defend And

with all my friends, we will start a
with all my friends, we will start a

new universal trend, in which, we can all blend
new universal trend, in which, we can all blend

Whether I'm happy or I am sad my
Whether I'm happy or I am sad my

principles will always stay ironclad Whether
principles will always stay ironclad whether

people think I'm sane or mad; I will
people think I'm sane or mad; I will

still consider you as my friend, my comrade
still consider you as my friend, my comrade

It might be just a passing fad or it may make
It might be just a passing fad or it may make

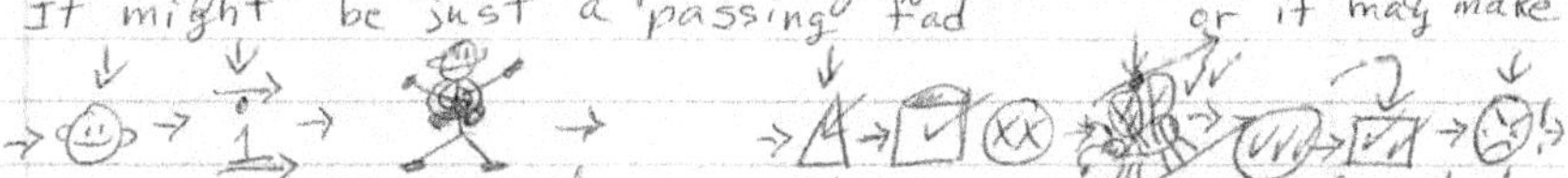

me an Olympiad It can't be all that bad;
me an Olympiad It can't be all that bad;

I think it may make me an honorary undergrad
I think it may make me an honorary undergrad

I don't think ; I'm wasting my time
I don't think ; I'm wasting my time

sharing my very special nursery rhyme Your
sharing my very special nursery rhyme Your

company is a precious find I feel we are just
company is a precious find I feel we are just

like partners in crime You are a special find;
like partners in crime You are a special find;

as a matter of fact You are one, once in a
as a matter of fact You are one, once in a

lifetime You are honest and kind and I do
lifetime You are honest and kind and I do

agree with my Father Time You have a
agree with my Father Time You have a

special place in my heart something like
special place in my heart something like

Leonardo or Mozart Sometimes, I don't
Leonardo or Mozart Sometimes, I don't

know where to start but you win my
Know where to start but you win my

Purple Heart You have each and every part
Purple Heart you have each and every part

of my heart and I'm glad I found you,
of my heart and I'm glad I found you,

sweetheart I'm glad you are in my court;
swept heart I'm glad you are in my court;

your love is so powerful it is stronger than
your love is so powerful it is stronger than

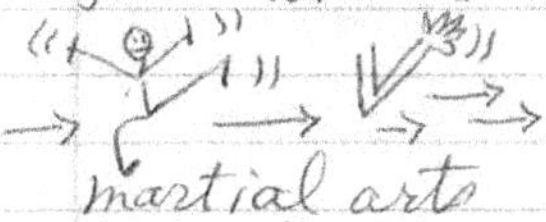

martial arts
martial arts

(144) Give Me a Chance (335)

Give Me a Chance

Give me a fighting chance Don't take a
Give me a fighting chance Don't take a

tough stance Love's arrow will hit you with
tough stance Love's arrow will hit you with

its lance Myself, I work freelance The story
its lance Myself, I work freelance The story

gets better and better I'm certainly a go-getter
gets better and better I'm certainly a go-getter

I won't bind you with any fetters But I'll
I won't bind you with any fetters But I'll

spell it out in large letters You'll soon know
spell it out in large letters You'll soon know

I can undo any foe My love can grow and
I can undo any foe My love can grow and

grow It can be high it can be low It was the
grow It can be high it can be low It was the

best kind of test I got thrown out of my nest
best kind of test I got thrown out of my nest

Put your head on my chest Then you'll know
Put your head on my chest Then you'll know

about the rest I was hit with a battle of the
about the rest I was hit with a battle of the

wits Who'll be left holding the mitts? Who'll
wits Who'll be left holding the mitts? Who'll

call it quits or have a fit How many times
call it qaits or have a fit How many times

Will there be to permit? Where are we heading?
Will there be to permit? Where are we heading?

Where are we bound? Maybe we are bound for
Where are we bound? Maybe we are bound for

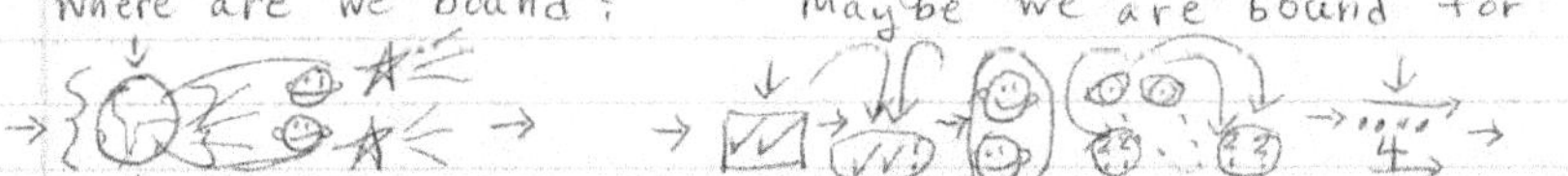

world renown? What are we searching for?
world renown? What are we searching for?

I hope it is neutral ground I hope it is peace and
I hope it is neatral ground I hope it is peace and

that I am not a hanger-on But I can run a
that I am not a hanger-on But I can run a

marathon and have a lot of fun Right here
marathon and have a lot of fun Right here

SasKatchewAn

in the province of Saskatchewan There's a lot of
in the province of Saskatchewan There's a lot of

room for us all to see eye to eye And for
room for us all to see eye to eye And for

all of us to share love, by and by There is no
all of us to share love, by and by There is no

need to fight or to try to disqualify Or to
need to fight or to try to disqualify Or to

continue to go on living a lie we must get along
continue to go on living a lie we must get along

and do or die
and do or die

145 That's A Lie 337

It is everything but the truth It just isn't at
all couth It's a lie, hook, line nail, and
tooth They turned around, and a lie is what
they let loose It was a downright fib; that
wise guy told a lie They thought they could get
away with it if they pretended to be shy They
were nothing but fakirs and dishonest guys We
sure don't agree with them or see eye to eye They

were careful when they pulled the wool, those fools
were careful when they palled the wool, those fools

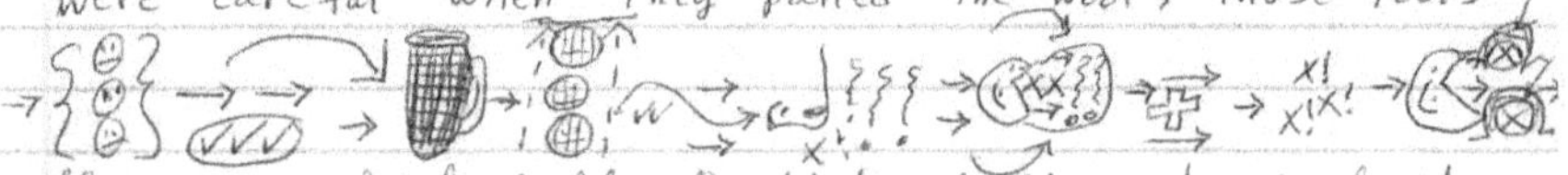

They were chock-full of stinky bull and falsehoods,
They were chock-fall of stinky ball and falsehoods

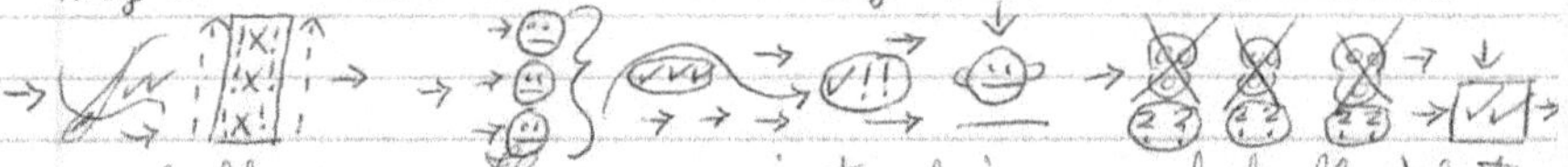

so full They were just plain numbskulls that
so fall They were just plain numbskulls that

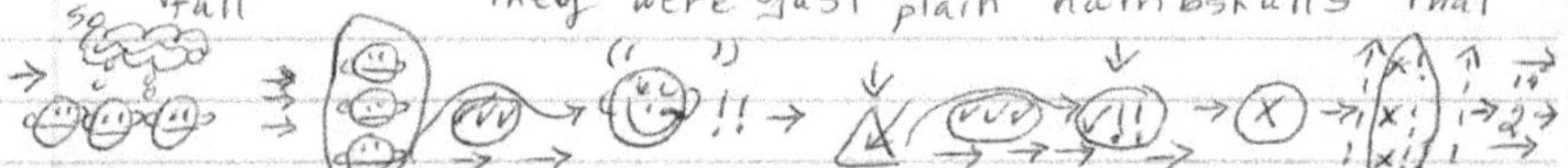

thonght they were cool It was just plain sinful to
thought they were cool It was just plain sinful to

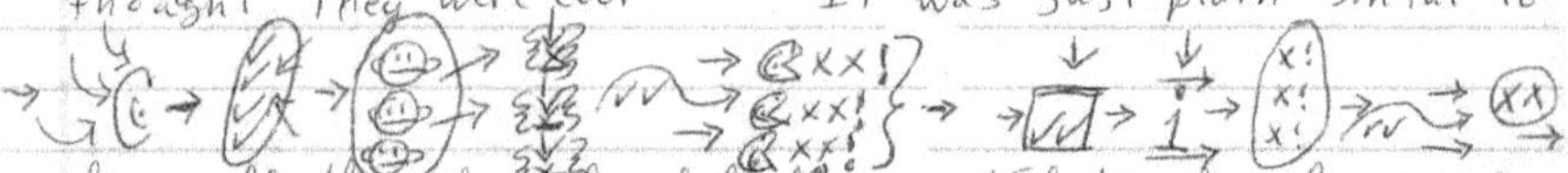

hear all their bunch of bull What a bunch of false
hear all their banch of bull What a banch of false

fabsications What evil conniving, imaginations
fabrications What evil conniving, imaginations

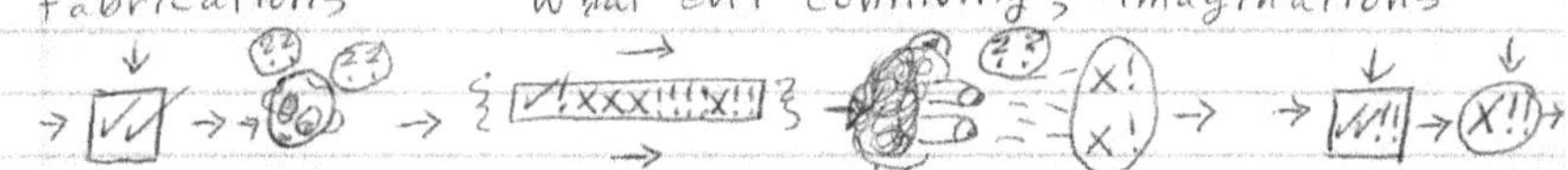

What silly, preposterous superstitions What utter
What silly, preposterous saperstitions What utter

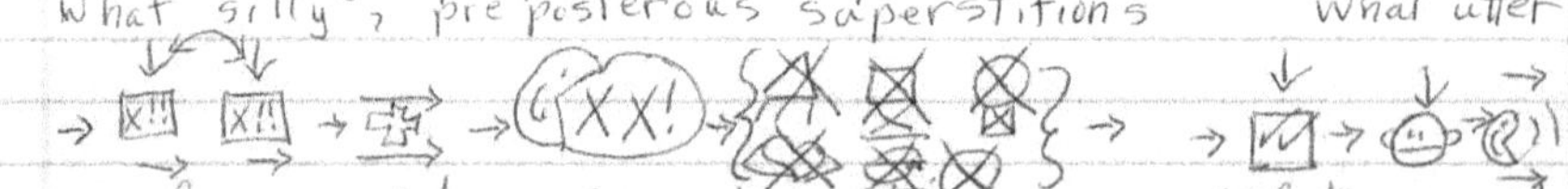

useless and untrue inventions What you said,
useless and untrae inventions What you said,

sir, I soon learned to dread I think you made it
sir, I soon learned to dread I think you made it

all up in your head You had better try to tell
all up in your head You had better try to tell

the truth instead If you say it that way, they
the truth instead If you say it that way, they

might see red Sometimes you should be careful
might see red Sometimes you should becareful

and try being cool Because otherwise, you
and try being cool Because otherwise, you

might choke on that mouthful You should be
might choke on that mouthful You should be

more truthful and you might learn the golden
more truthful and you might learn the golden

rule It might prove to be much more useful
rule It might prove to be much more useful

and avoid any further ridicule It was supposed
and avoid any further ridicule It was supposed

to be an innocent white lie But it became a
to be an innocent White lie But it became a

noxious and hideous trap, by and by Not
noxious and hideous trap, by and by Not

just a piece of the pie but the whole darned
just a piece of the pie but the whole darned

sky It grew bigger and bigger after each
sky It grew bigger and bigger after each

and every try It will lead the perpetrator straight
and every try It will lead the perpetrator straight

to jail Then all he or she will receive is mail
to jail Then all he or she will receive is mail

The liar's freedom will be gone without fail And
The liar's freedom will be gone without fail And

will be looking between steel bar rails
will be looking between steel bar rails

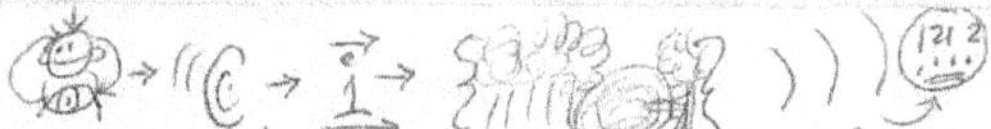

(146) I Heard The Stillness Wail (334)

I Heard The Stillness Wail

(version One)
(version One)

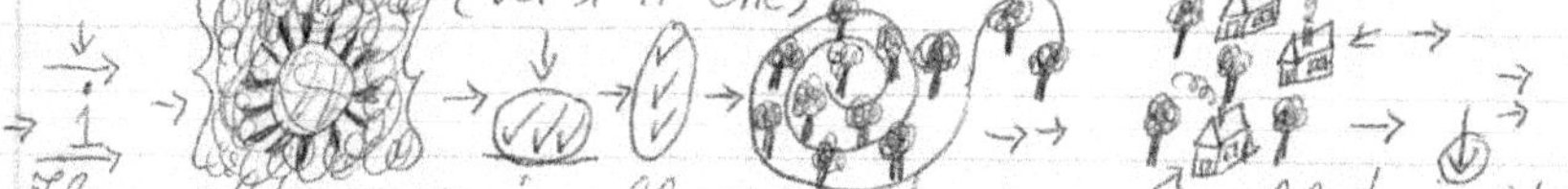

The wilderness is all around speckled, inside,
The wilderness is all around speckled, inside,

with many little towns Quietness seeps through
with many little towns Quietness seeps through

the cracks without making a sound The
the cracks without making a sound The

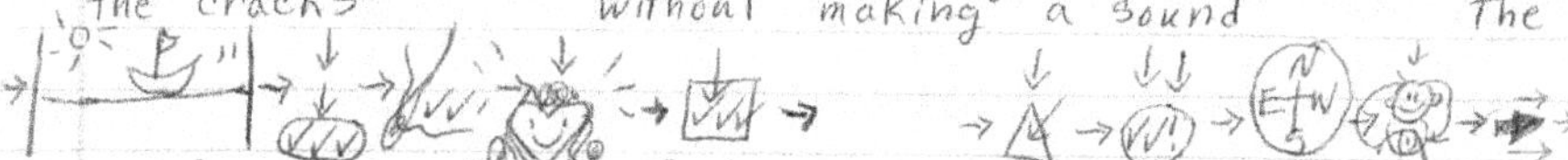

calm is so lovely that this, is where I will
calm is so lovely that this, is where I will

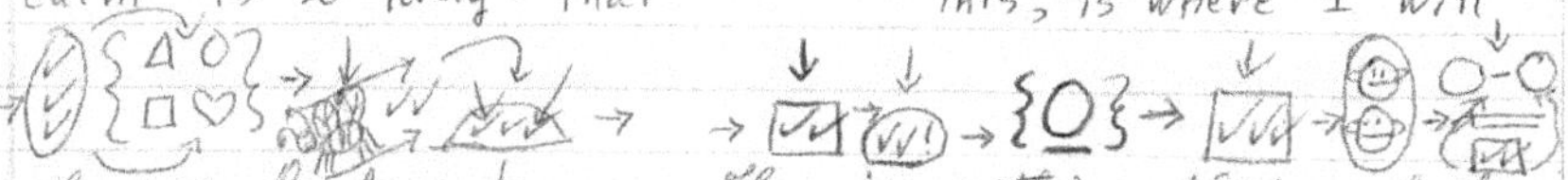

always be bound There is nothing that we lack;
always be bound There is nothing that we lack;

abundance is all around I heard the stillness
abundance is all around I heard the stillness

wail; it told me of many, many faraway
wail; it told me of many, many faraway

tales
tales
It crept in and around me; it seemed
It crept in and around me; it seemed

mysteriously pale It seemed to pulsate and
mysteriously pale It seemed to pulsate and

move with a long, flowing tail Then there were
move with a long, flowing tail Then there were

telltale signs of a powerful, silent gale
tell tale signs of a powerful, silent gale

Happiness is what I have found and is where I now
Happiness is what I have found and is where I now

bask Because I live in the beautiful province of
bask Because I live in the beautiful province of

Saskatchewan and because I was born here
Saskatche wan and because I was born here

and I stayed loyal and steadfast This place is
and I stayed loyal and steadfast This place is

way within the country of Canada, if you
way within the country of Canada, if you

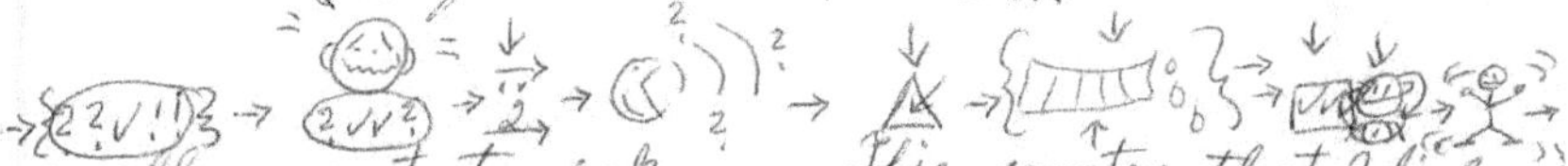

really want to ask This country that I live
really want to ask This country that I live

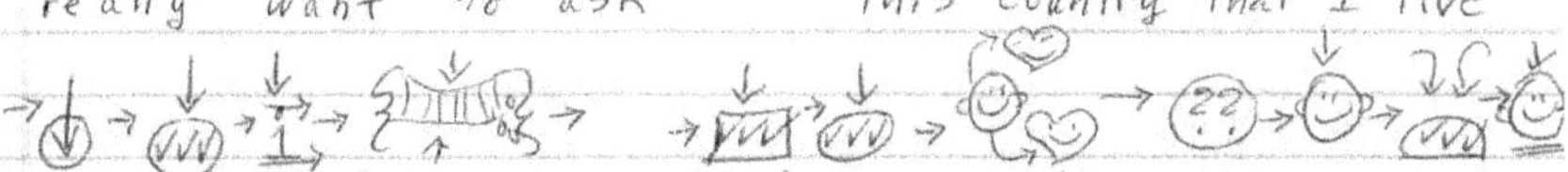

in is a place that is friendly, if you are nice
in is a place that is friendly, if you are nice

And take the time to ask People come here from
And take the time to ask People come here from

afar, who knows, maybe even from the
afar, who knows, maybe even from the

faraway stars; We don't mind; we consider
faraway stars; We don't mind; we consider

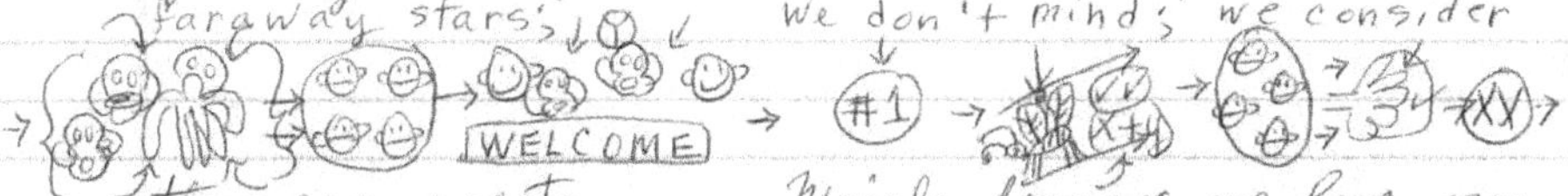

them our guests Mainly because we have no
them our guests Mainly because we have no

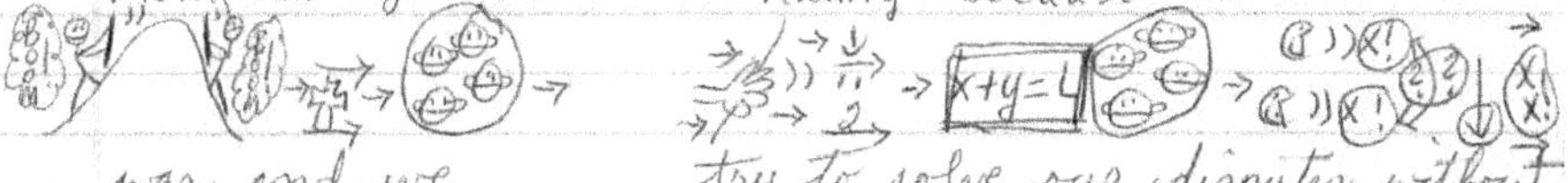

war and we try to solve our disputes without
war and we try to solve our disputes without

Putting on a mask Serenity is a luxury we can
Putting on a mask Serenity is a luxury we can

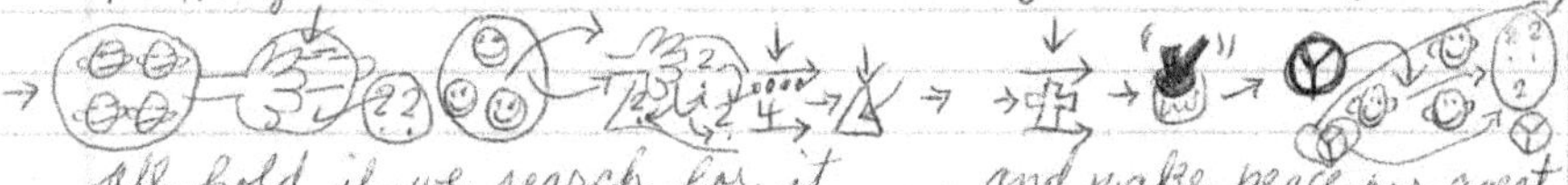

all hold if we search for it and make peace our guest
all hold if we search for it and make peace our guest

Knowing justice prevails, we can be bold and we
Knowing justice prevails, we can be bold and we

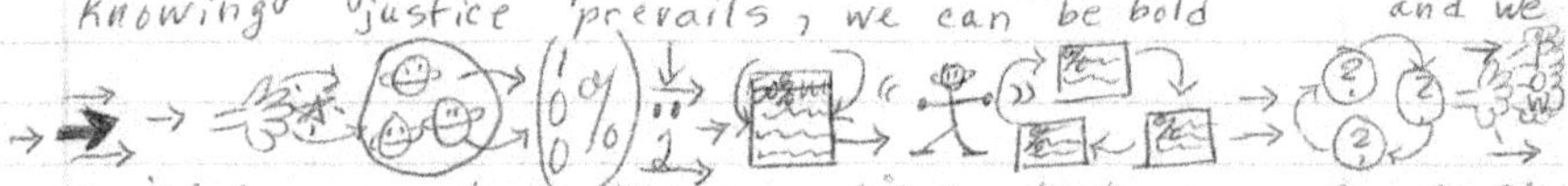

will do our best to pass life's tests Any fight
will do our best to pass life's tests Any fight

we may have with each other eventually does
we may have with each other eventually does

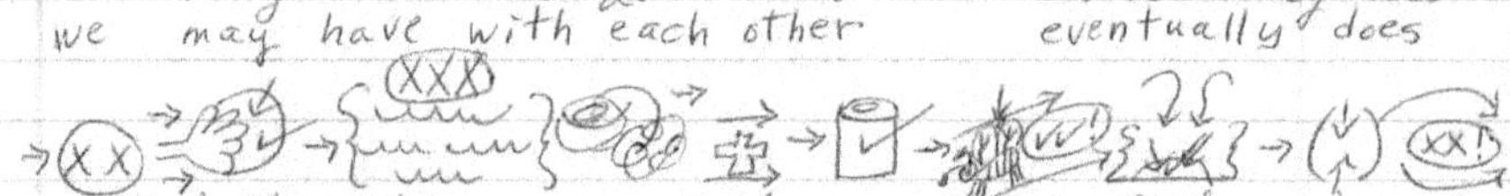

not hold water And can be resolved without
not hold water And can be resolved without

any bother if we take the time to listen to
any bother if we take the time to listen to

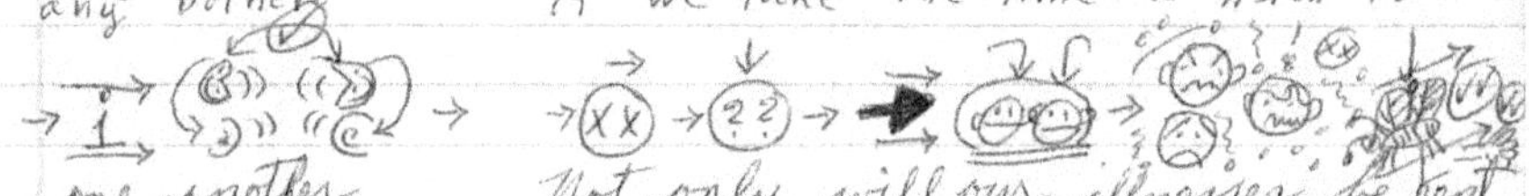

one another Not only will our illnesses be kept
one another Not only will our illnesses be kept

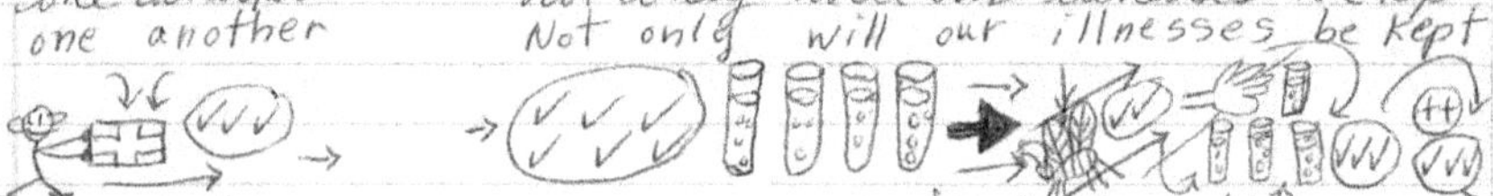

care of; many cures will be found, moreover
care of; many cares will be found, moreover

Help will come, according to our ability to
Help will come, according to our ability to

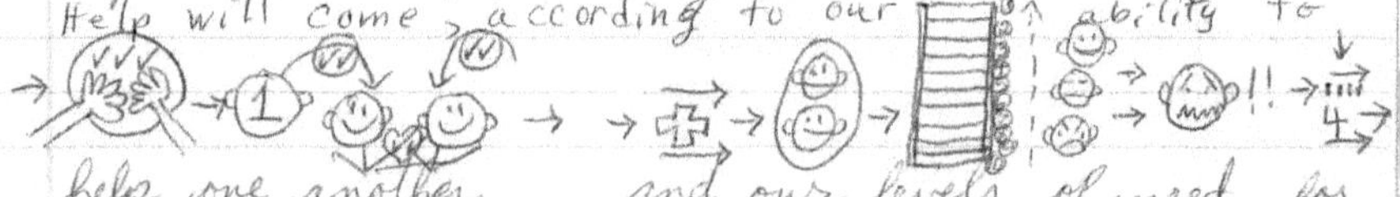

help one another and our levels of need, for
help one another and our levels of need, for

any him or her I love this SASKATCHEWAN province within
any him or her I love this province within

our country We are lucky and I'm thankful
our country We are lucky and I'm thankful

for all our plentiful bounty We even have the
for all our plentiful bounty We even have the

best-tasting honey So far, anyway you'll see
best-tasting honey So far, anyway you'll see

It's where you get the most for the money and
It's where you get the most for the money and

is a good place to marry your honey Of course,
is a good place to marry your honey Of course,

no place is perfect or it would prove quite

boring That is another quality which makes
boring That is another quality which makes

it so alluring We can stay put in one place;
it so allaring We can stay put in one place;

if we want and no one will say a thing
if we want and no one will say a thing

If we follow the house rules we will see how
If we follow the house rules we will see how

much fun it really brings If you like to work
much fun it really brings If you like to work

no one is stopping you You can do your own
No one is stopping you You can do your own

thing, as long as you are honest and true
thing, as long as you are honest and true

blue You can even go far and get rich
blue You can even go far and get rich

if you want to You can even make a
if you want to You can even make a

point of making a green footprint too
point of making a green foot-print too

Again, I heard the stillness silently wail In the
Again, I heard the stillness silently wail In the

quietness it told me another tale The quietness
quietness it told me another tale The quietness

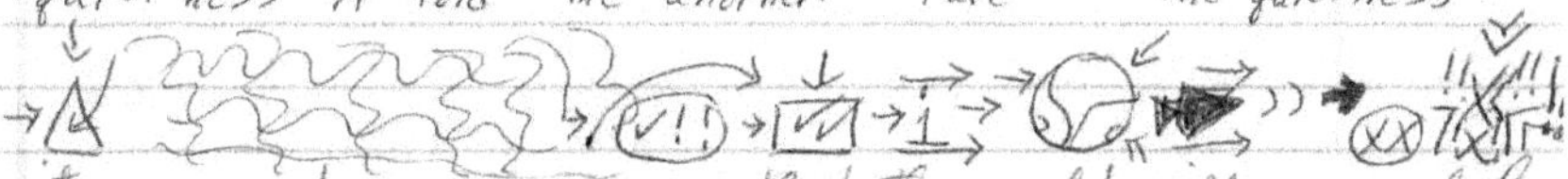

it expressed was that the world will never fail
it expressed was that the world will never fail

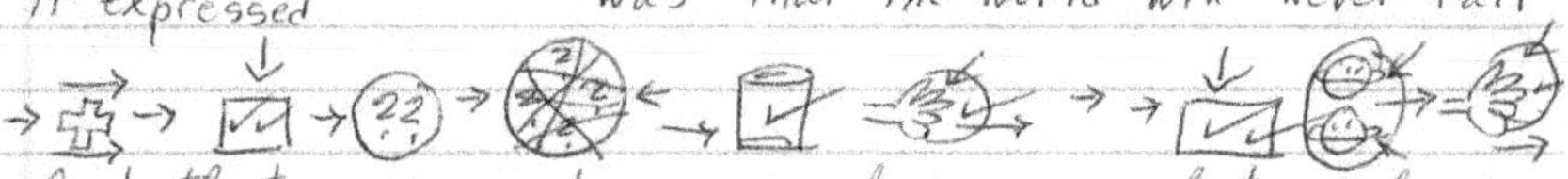

And that any country can have what we have,
And that any country can have what we have,

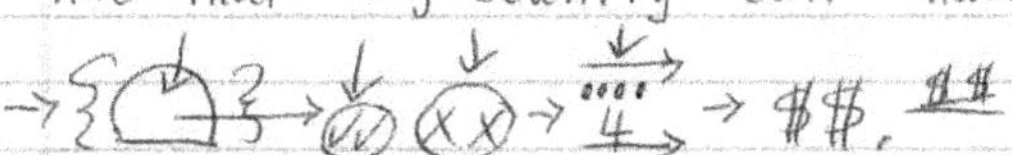

which is not for sale
which is not for sale

(147) I Heard The Stillness Wail (342) page: (640)

I Heard The Stillness Wail

→ {a} {b} → {2} ←

(Version Two)

(Version Two)

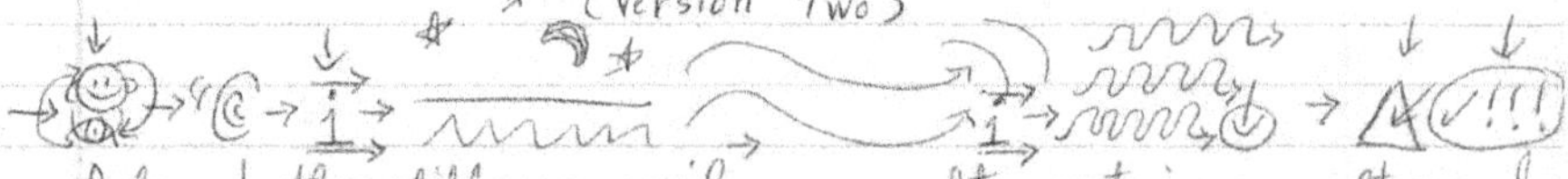

I heard the stillness wail It crept in It seemed

I heard the stillness wail It crept in It seemed

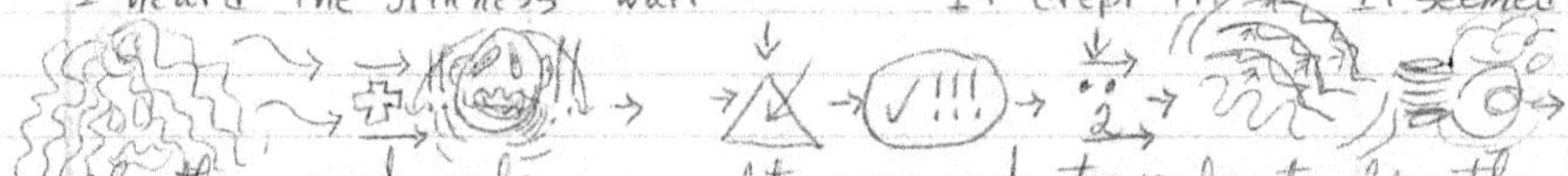

ghastly and pale It seemed to pulsate, breathe

ghastly and pale It seemed to pulsate, breathe

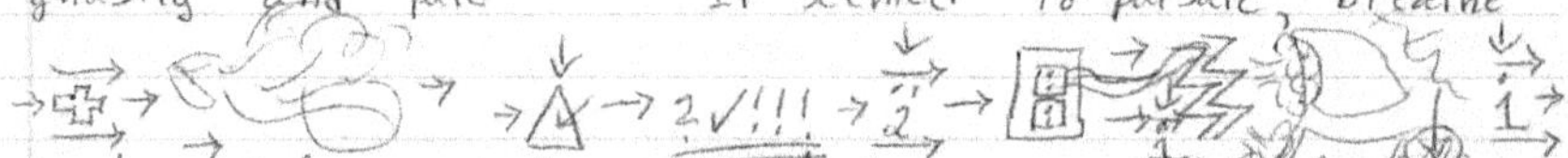

and exhale It seemed to power the sails in a

and exhale It seemed to power the sails in a

strong and steady gale The wilderness power

strong and steady gale The wilderness power

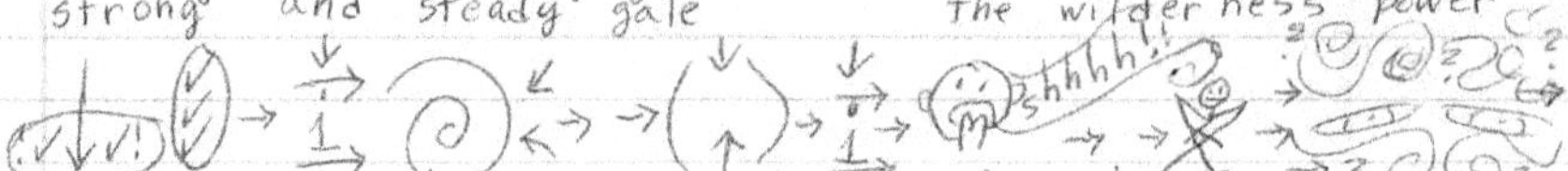

is all around With a quiet witness mysterious

is all around with a quiet witness mysterious

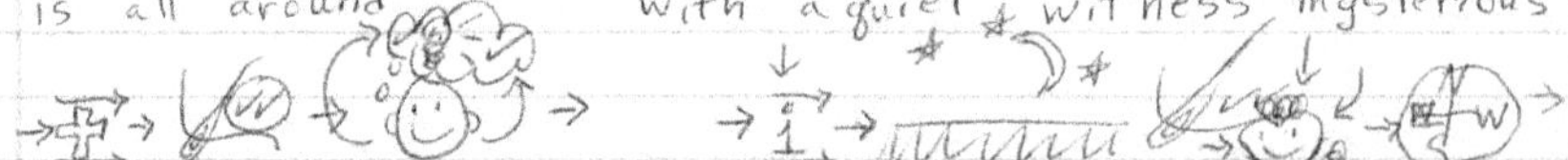

and so profound The calm is so lovely where

and so profound The calm is so lovely where

it is found And always is there to remind us

it is found And always is there to remind us

that we are earthbound Happiness is where I
that we are earthbound Happiness is where I

now Basque I live in the beautiful province of
Now Basque I live in the beautiful province of

saskatchewan

Saskatchewan This place is far enough in our
Saskatchewan This place is far enough in our

country you could say it wears a mask It
country you could say it wears a mask It

is OK as long as you are on task There is justice
is OK as long as you are on task There is justice

for all if we but ask People come from here
for all if we but ask People come from here

from afar Mainly because we have almost no
from afar Mainly because we have almost no

war Serenity is a luxury we can all hold
war Serenity is a luxary we can all hold

Knowing that justice prevails we can be bold Any
Knowing that justice prevails we can be bold Any

fight we have with each other Can usually be
fight we have with each other Can usually be

resolved without too much bothes Sometimes our
resolved without too much bother Sometimes our

land has snow as its coves Except in the summes
land has snow as its cover Except in the summer

when it is much, much hotter When we pull
when it is much, much hotter When we pull

our weight our lives hum and purr We also
our weight our lives hum and purr We also

try to respect every him and her I love this
try to respect every him and her I love this

province in our country We are lucky and
province in our country We are lucky and

I'm thankful for all the plentiful bounty We even
I'm thankful for all the plentiful bounty We even

have the best tasting honey It's where you get
have the best tasting honey It's where you get

page: 643

the most for your money   You can tell I'm

the most for your money   You can tell I'm

patriotic and very happy   Thumbs up, eh?

patriotic and very happy   Thumbs up, eh?

(148) The Majestic Snowy Owl (344)
The Majestic Snowy Owl

The Majestic Snowy Owl Is not just any old fowl
The Majestic Snowy Owl Is not just any old fowl

But it may have to throw in the towel If we
But it may have to throw in the towel If we

don't hear its call and hear its howl The
don't hear its call and hear its howl The

snowy owl has been here a long time And it looks
snowy owl has been here a long time And it looks

oh so fine in the overall grand design You
oh so fine in the overall grand design you

might someday even find a picture of it on a
might someday even find a picture of it on a

dime Now it just happens to be in my rhyme
dime Now it just happens to be in my rhyme

dime rhyme time

Listen and hear what I have to say The owl travels
Listen and hear what I have to say The owl travels

up, up and away In the kingdom of the sky
up, up and away In the kingdom of the sky
is where it plays It's up to us, to make sure that
is where it plays It's up to us, to make sure that
it will always be A-OK, In winter, its
it will always be A-OK, In winter, its
coat of feathers is the purest white For its children,
coat of feathers is the purest white For its children,
it will fight with all its might It flies higher
it will fight with all its might It flies higher
than any balloon and better than any kite It
than any balloon and better than any kite It
is not fettered; it is free, it is light but it can
is not fettered; it is free, it is light but it can
win most fights Nothing looks more majestic
win most fights Nothing looks more majestic
when in flight Than a majestic snowy owl,
when in flight Than a majestic snowy owl,

the heights You may not be able to even
the heights You may not be able to even

see an owl in flight because they may seem
see an owl in flight because they may seem

invisible being that their feathers are pure white
invisible being that their feathers are pure white

One can only imagine the owl's feelings Just how,
One can only imagine the owl's feelings Just how,

terrific it must be to fly up high with no
terrific it must be to fly up high with no

ceiling How it must feel to go up, up, up
ceiling How it must feel to go up, up, up

and to screech and to sing Flying way up high
and to screech and to sing Flying way up high

above the world and not to have to be worrying
above the world and not to have to be worrying

How great it must be with nature as its playmate
How great it must be with nature as its playmate

And to be able to use its freedom sublime, to
and to be able to use its freedom sublime, to

get supper and use its freedom as its bait Just
get supper and use its freedom as its bait Sust

think. He can soar over any size of gate And
think. He can scar over any size of gate And

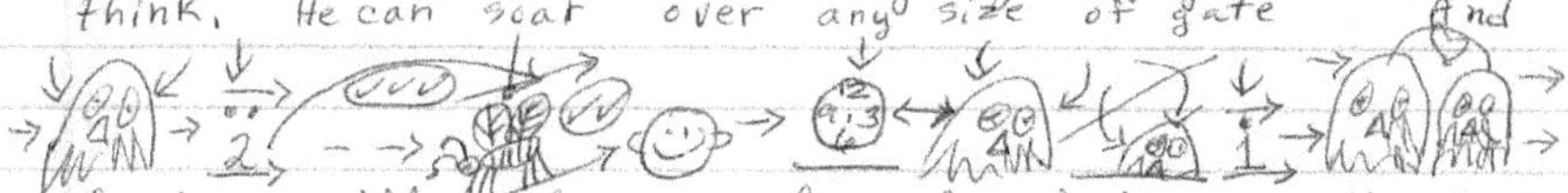

he too, will be happy when he finds a mate
he too, will be happy when he finds a mate

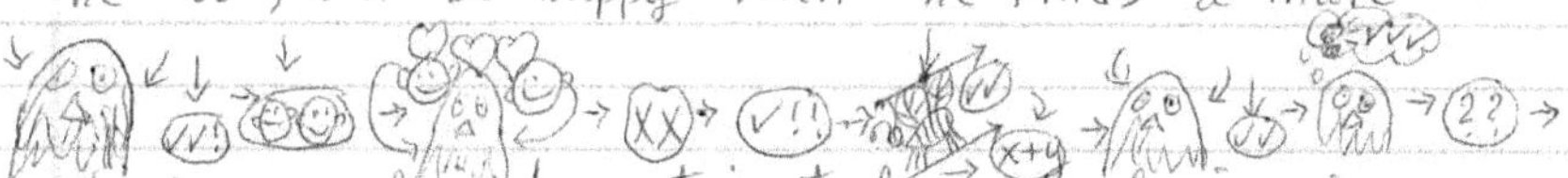

He is our friend not just because he is wise or
He is oar friend not just because he is wise or

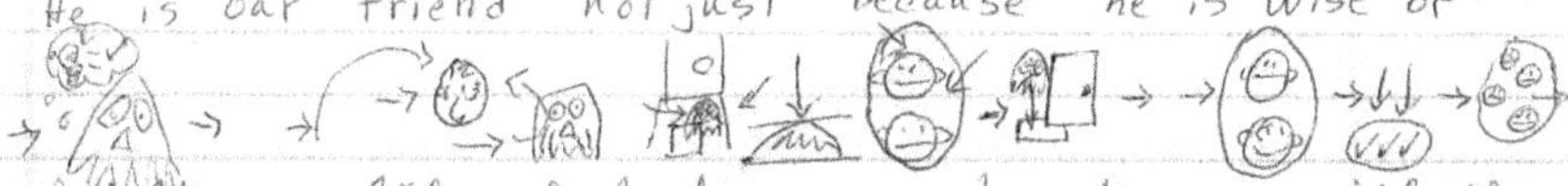

bright When he lands on our doorstep, we will all
bright When he lands on our doorstep, we will all

agree oh, what a beautiful sight We must fight
agree oh, what a beautiful sight We must fight

his cause like it was our very own fight Because
his cause like it was oar very own fight Because

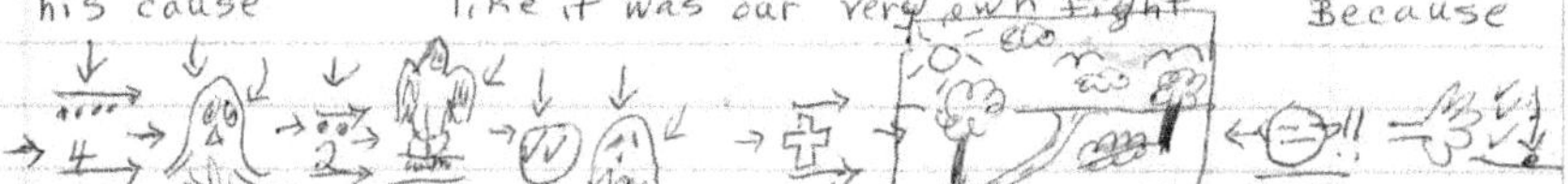

for him to live is his and nature's solemn right
for him to live is his and nature's solemn right

page: (648)

(149) Hard As A Rock (346)
Hard As A Rock

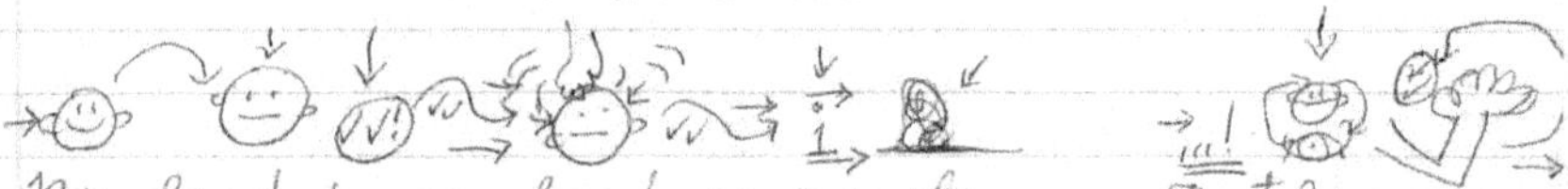

My head is as hard as a rock But I come
My head is as hard as a rock But I come

from good stock I am also from a large flock
from good stock I am also from a large flock

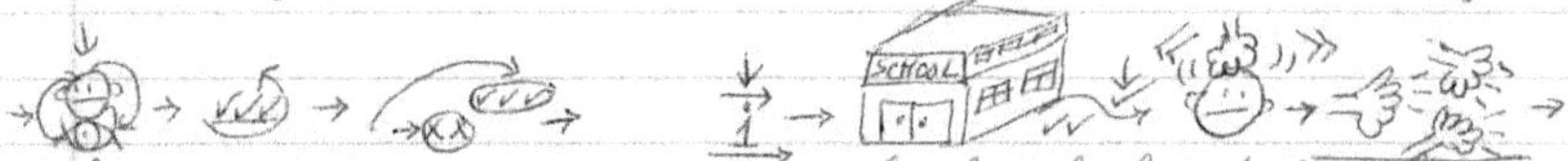

I come from the school of hard knocks
I come from the school of hard knocks

You've got me between a rock and a stone Oh my,
You've got me between a rock and a stone Oh my,

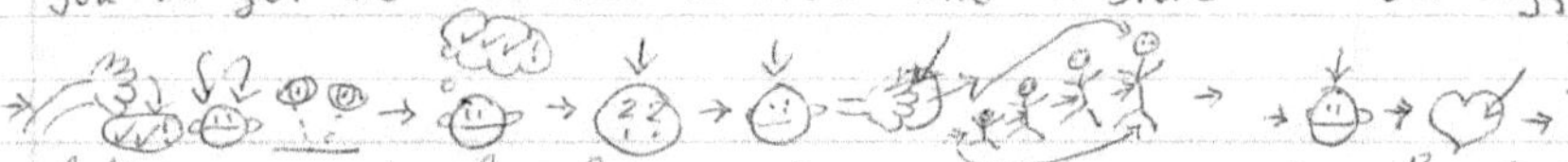

let me see ; oh, how you've grown My heart
let me see ; oh, how you've grown My heart

has always been on loan and I've always been
has always been on loan and I've always been

waiting here at home My thoughts are what
waiting here at home My thoughts are what

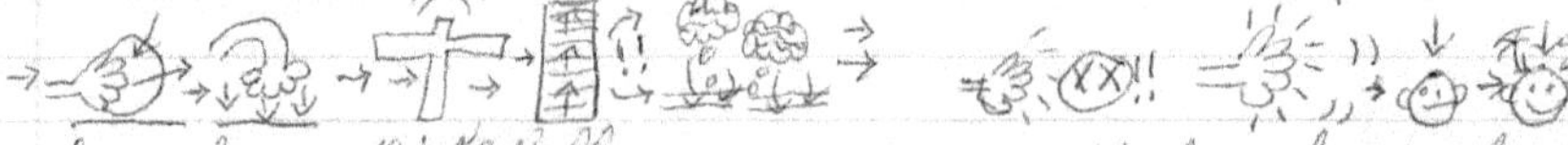

have been faithfully sewn Don't knock my head
have been faithfully sewn Don't knock my head

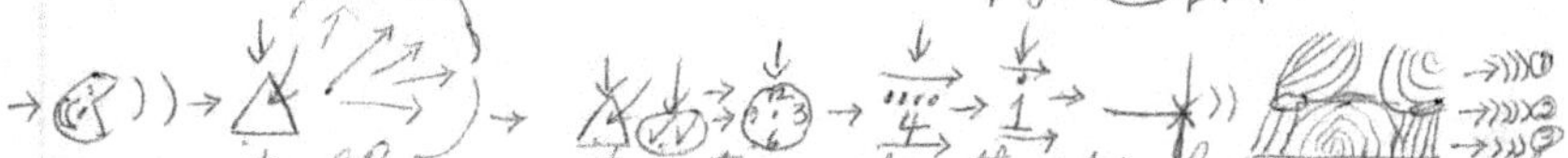

says it all it is time for the final curtain calls
says it all it is time for the final curtain calls

My head is harder than true grit or any brick
my head is harder than true grit or any brick

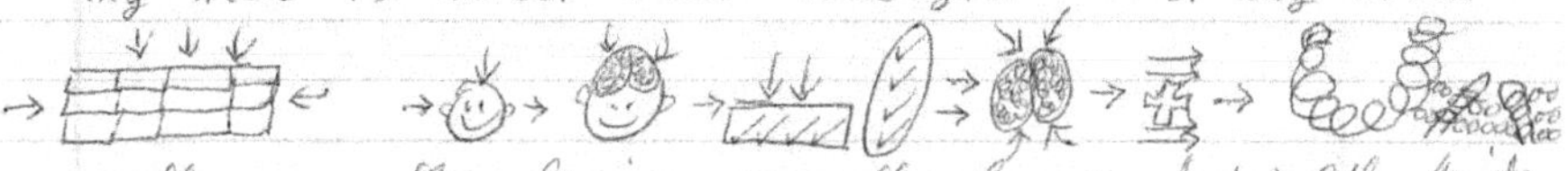

wall My brains are all close and tightly knit,
wall my brains are all close and tightly knit,

better than any old shawl The ideas will hit you
better than any old shawl The ideas will hit you

so hard you will need a complete overhaul
so hard you will need a complete over haul

My strength will be put to the test and I will
My strength will be pat to the test and I will

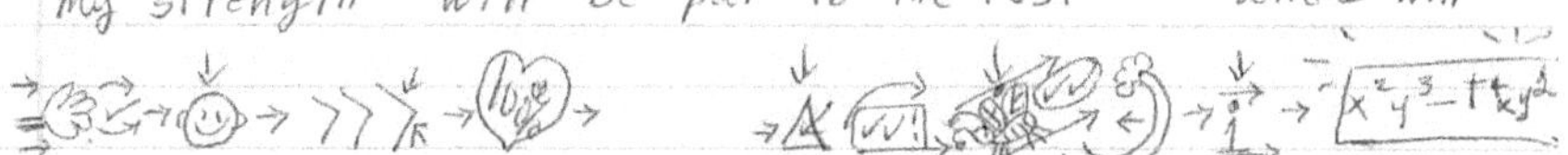

do my very best It has become a difficult
do my very best It has become a difficult.

quest to beat all the rest You will find I do not
quest to beat all the rest You will find I do not

jest because I do not find it at all any contest
jest because I do not find it at all any contest

It's so sad, you all will end up crying, lest
It's so sad, you all will end up erying, lest

because I have put on my bulletproof vest I've
because I have put on my bulletproof vest I've

never been beaten, but I've always been chosen
never been beaten, bat I've always been chosen

I've never been positively proven, but I am outspoken
I've Never been positively proven, bat I am outspoken

My ideas are difficult to prove wrong because
My ideas are difficult to prove wrong because

it has all, been tried to do, again and again
it has all, been tried to do, again and again

They'll travel around until they hang ten
They'll travel around until they hang ten

and finally say amen Then the rock will
and finally say amen Then the rock will

fall hard because it is very hard And we will
fall hard because it is very hard And we will

Hilary

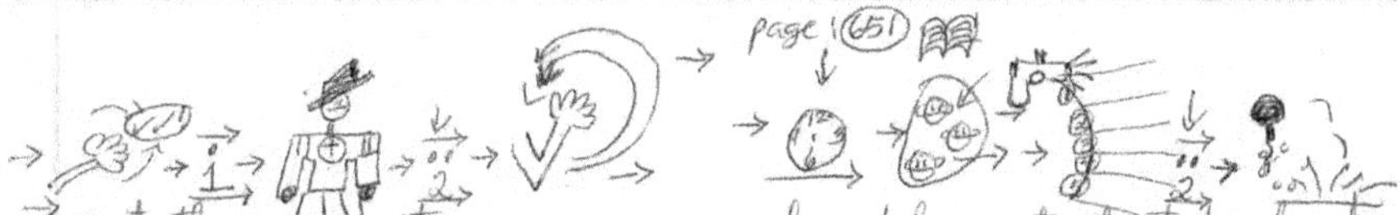

get the guard to come when they start to bombard

get the guard to come when they start to bombard

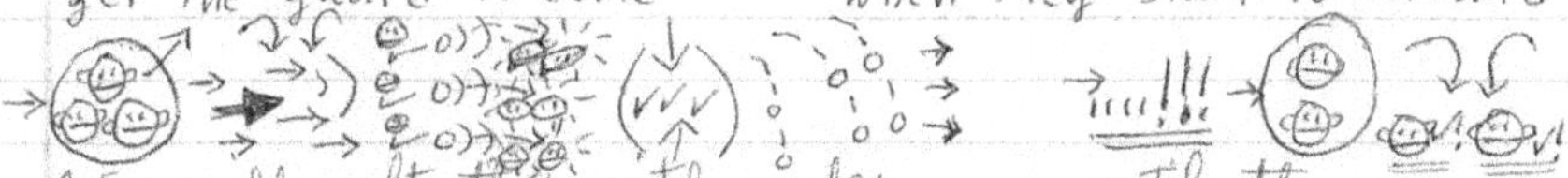

We will pelt them with rocks until they are

We will pelt them with rocks until they are

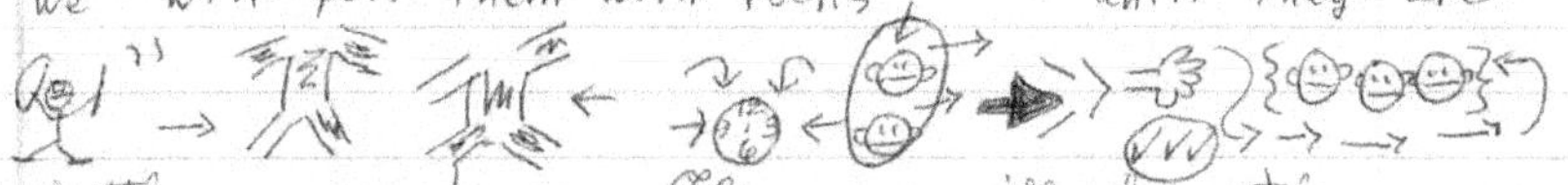

battle-scarred Then we will show them

battle-scarred Then we will show them

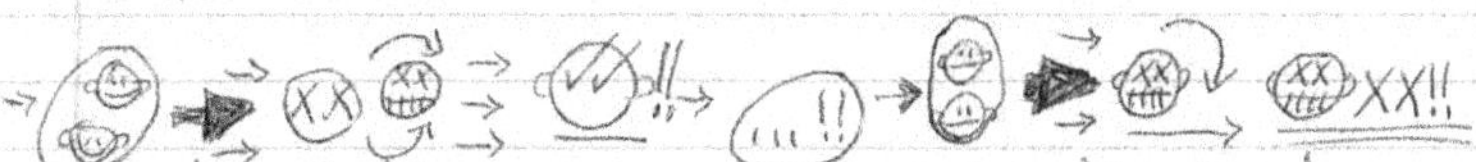

we don't die easy, but we do die hard

we don't die easy, but we do die hard

page: 652

150 Don't Lie 348

Don't Lie

Telling the truth is what is right and might even
Telling the truth is what is right and might even

earn you an award besides, if you tell the truth
earn you an award besides, if you tell the truth

you'll be free as a bird So just try to correctly
you'll be free as a bird So just try to correctly

express everything you have heard And
express everything you have heard And

be honest and tell the truth in each and every
be honest and tell the truth in each and every

word Don't plan a lie and be a stupid wise
word Don't plan a lie and be a stupid wise

guy Just clarify; be truthful and correctly
guy Just clarify; be truthful and correctly

verify Be the honest one and the one to exemplify
verify Be the honest one and the one to exemplify

OK, so you say telling the truth is dull I say that
OK, so you say telling the truth is dull I say that

if you lie, you are a numbskull Telling the
if you lie, you are a numbskull Telling the

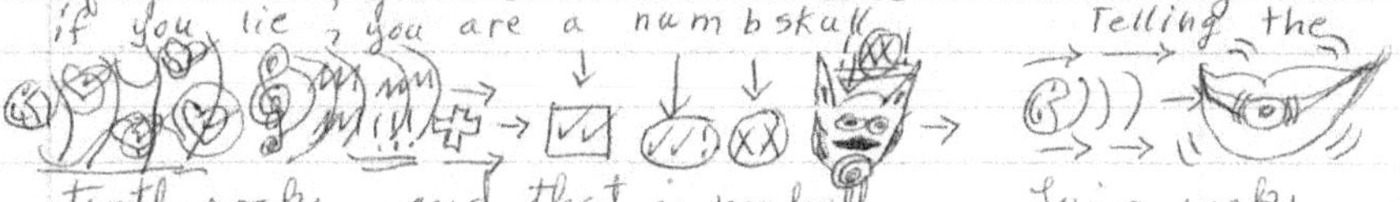

truth rocks, and that is no bull Lying sucks
truth rocks, and that is no bull Lying sucks

and is for frightened fools Don't try to cop
and is for frightened fools Don't try to cop

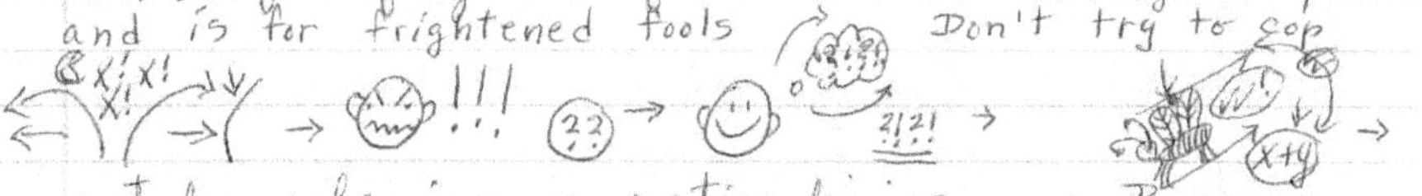

out by scheming or rationalizing Because
out by scheming or rationalizing Because

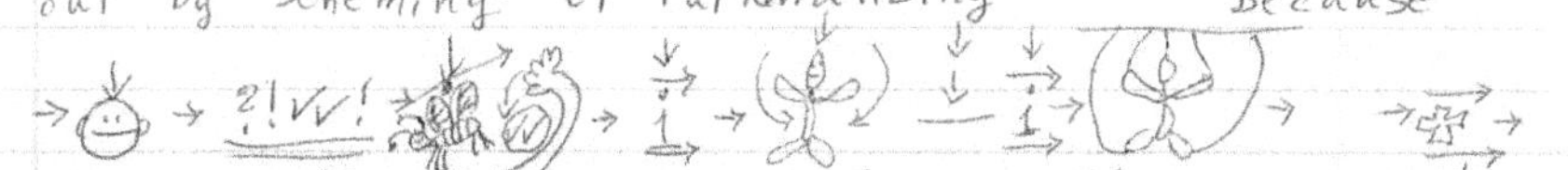

you might become a puppet on a string And
you might become a puppet on a string And

people might never want to or believe you
people might never want to or believe you

again And you may end up seeming like a
again And you may end up seeming like a

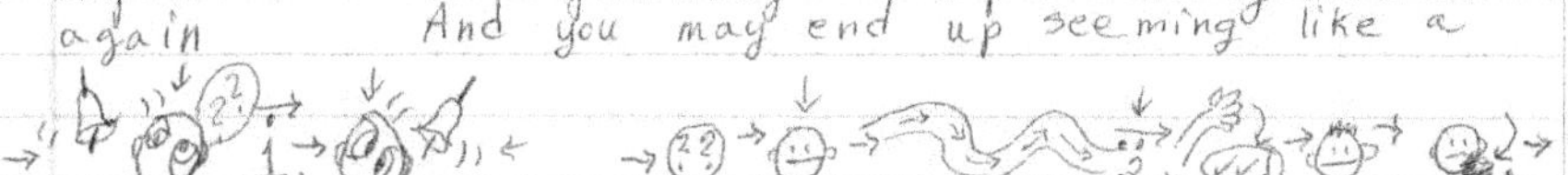

ding-a-ling If you continue to let his fester
ding-a-ling If you continue to let his fester

and grow And then you shoot off your mouth
and grow And then you shoot off your mouth

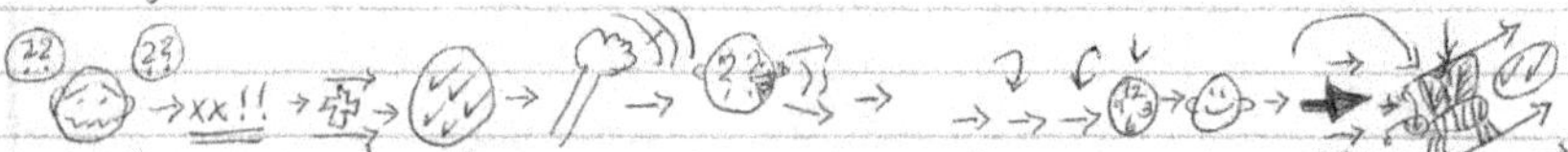

careless and all gung ho Soon you will be
careless and all gung ho Soon you will be

trapped in your own sideshow Because you
trapped in your own sideshow Because you

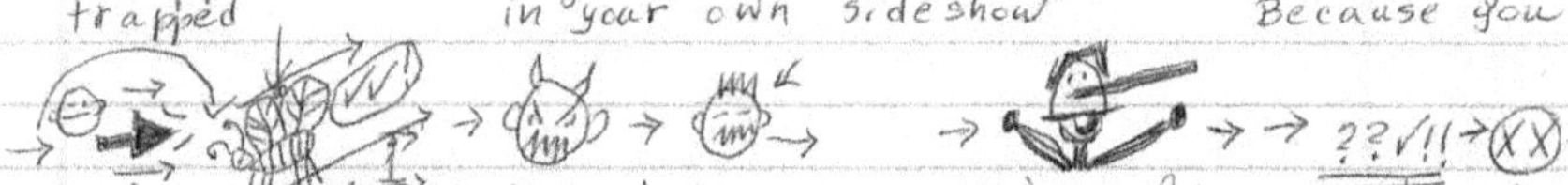

will be the dishonest Joe Pinocchio could not
will be the dishonest Joe Pinocchio could not

have said it better than you His nose became
have said it better than you His Nose became

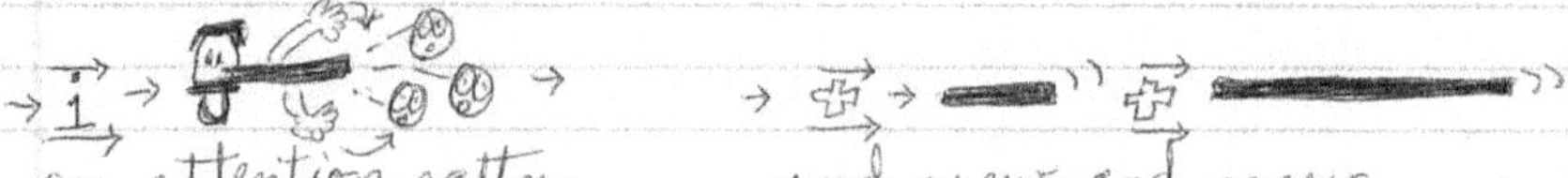

an attention getter and grew and grew
an attention getter and grew and grew

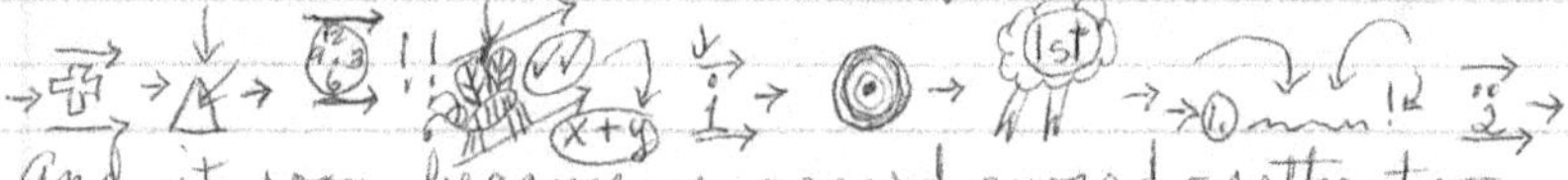

And it soon became a record award-setter too
and it soon became a record award-Setter too

Next, he became a donkey and you will be
Next, he became a donkey and you will be

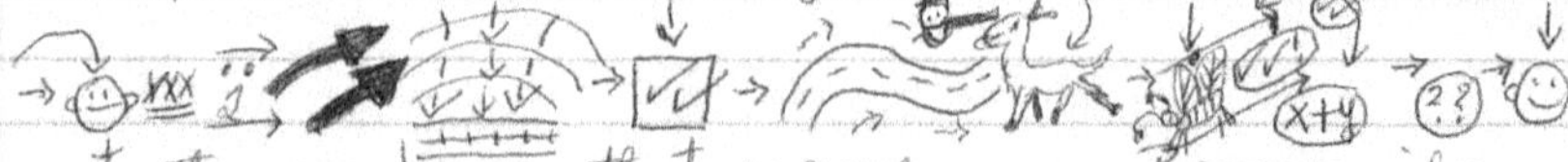

next to go down that avenue Because if you
next to go down that avenue Because if you

continue and you are not careful You'll have
continue and you are not careful You'll have

more than you ever wanted or can handle
more than you ever wanted or can handle

Because lies tend to land you in trouble and
Because lies tend to land you in trouble and

chock - full Of what comes right out of the back
chock - full Of what comes right out of the back

end of a bull I have found that the truth
end of a bull I have found that the truth

is the solid best It wins first prize and solves
is the solid best It wins first prize and solves

the test It is safer, by far, and beats all the
the test It is safer, by far, and beats all the

rest And it is the most welcome of any and
rest And it is the most welcome of any and

all of the guests
all of the guests

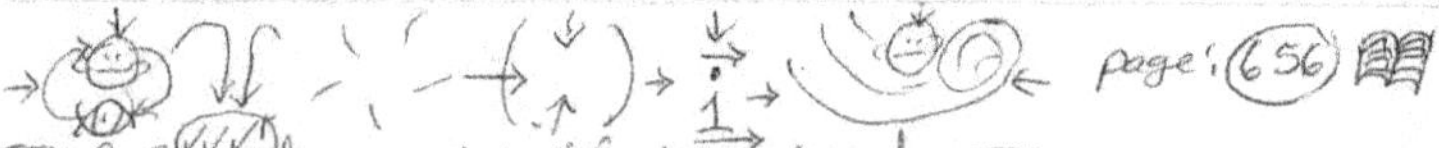

page: 656

151 I'm Gone With The Wind 350

I'm Gone With The Wind

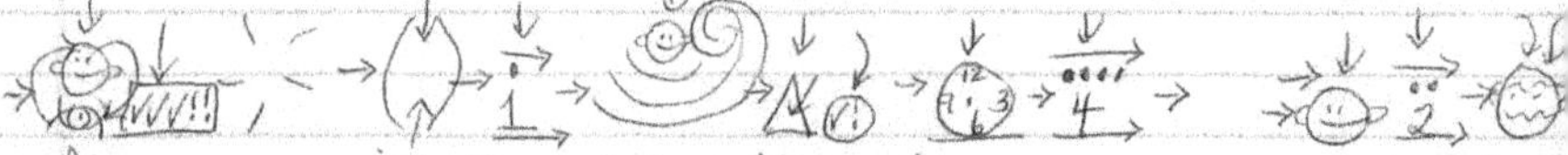

I'm gone with the wind; it's time for me to relax

I'm gone with the wind; it's time for me to relax

and unwind I'll be your friend; I can even try and

and unwind. I'll be your friend; I can even try and

be your mastermind I'll be the one to begin to

be your master mind I'll be the one to begin to

win and the one to begin to find Both of us

win and the one to begin to find Both of us

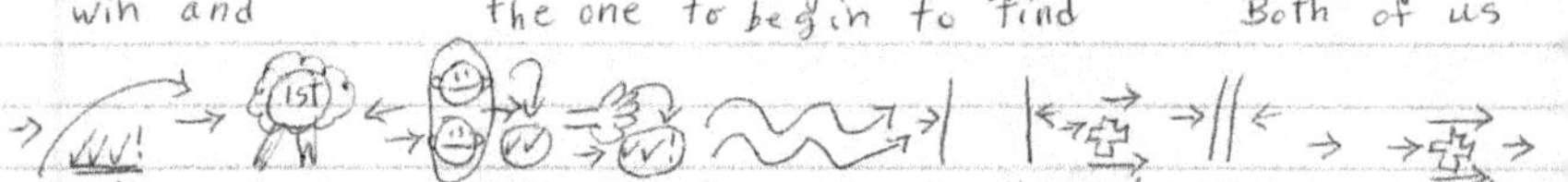

will win; we'll get through thick and thin and

will win; we'll get through thick and thin and

end up being sublime My wings will catch the

end up being sublime My wings will catch the

breeze and I'll soar into the sky with great ease

breeze and I'll soar into the sky with great ease

I will swing along on my invisible trapeze like

I will swing along on my invisible trapeze like

a happy, babbling chimpanzee My love will
a happy, babbling chim-panzee My love will

bring you to your knees, and I will make you
bring you to your Knees, and I will make you

beg pretty please My heart will unlock all your
beg pretty please My heart will unlock all your

mind's mysteries and I will become as wise
mind's mysteries and I will become as wise

as Socrates I will feel so free, and I will
as Socrates I will feel so free, and I will

suggest to you a new biological decree
suggest to you a new biological decree

That I would love to have you with me,
That I would love to have you with me,

to be my personal referee We'll travel
to be my personal referee We'll travel

far and wide together; you'll see you can
far and wide together; you'll see you can

be my sweet bumblebee We'll both bumble
be my sweet bum ble bee we'll both bu mble

and buzz, to and fro, hither and thither,
and buzz, to and fro, hither and thither,

quite satisfied and carefree We will feel
quite satisfied and care free we will feel

refreshed and young even though we are the
re freshed and young even though we are the

old ones We won't be undone; that would not
old ones we won't be undone; that wouldnot

do. In fact, we'll have lots of fun We will
do. In fact, we'll have lots of fun we will

hit a home run and a hole in one in fact,
hit a home run and a hole in one in fact,

our fun has just begun We will have our turn
our fun, has just begun we will have our turn

in the sun something like that of that famous
in the sun something like that of that famous

yprodigal son You might find me anywhere
prodigal son You might find me anywhere

in many forms, solid as a sock or thin
in many forms, solid as a rock or thin

as air I might disappear into thin air or
as air I might disappear into thin air or

appear in your worst nightmare, so take care
appear in your worst nightmare, so take care

I could be none the worse for wear or I
I could be none the worse for wear or I

could end up ailing in intensive care I might
could end up ailing in intensive care I might

blow right through your hair, but I can promise
blow right through your hair, but I can promise

you; I will never be square I will always
you; I will never be square I will always

learn to adjust because that, in itself, is a must
learn to adjust because that, in itself, is a mast

Hilary

I will find that I will want to earn your trust;
I will find that I will want to earn your trust;

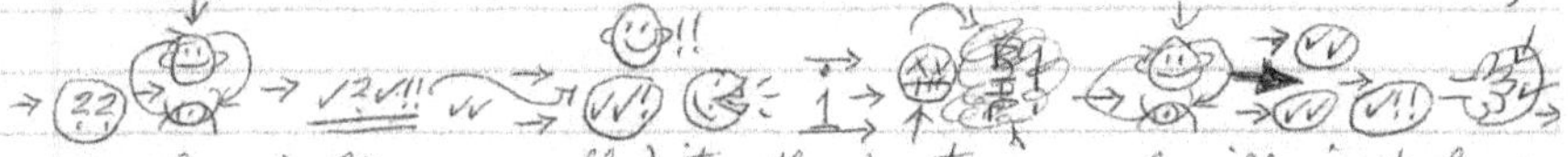

or I might as well bite the dust I will just have
or I might as well bite the dust I will just have

to learn to be fair and not to be a spoiled
to learn to be fair and not to be a spoiled

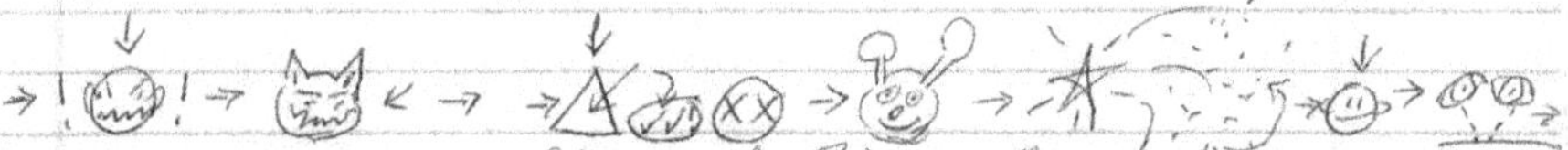

sourpuss It's not Ziggy Stardust you see,
sourpuss It's not Ziggy Stardust you see,

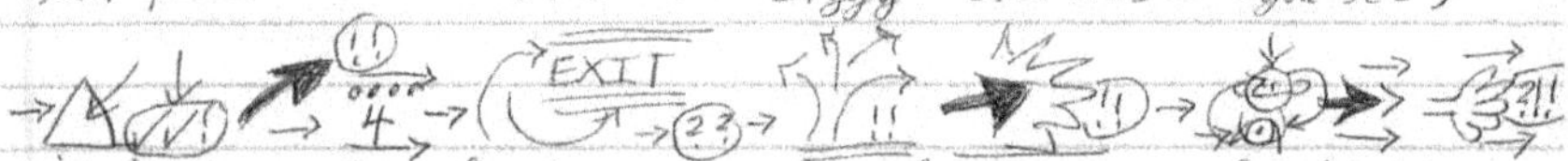

it is go for broke, or else bust I will try
it is go for broke, or else bust I will try

not to be mystereons; this might help me not
not to be mysterious; this might help me not

to miss getting on the bus I won't be unruly
to miss getting on the bus I won't be arruly

or delirious or cause a raucous fuss; I'll
or delirious or cause a raucous fuss; I'll

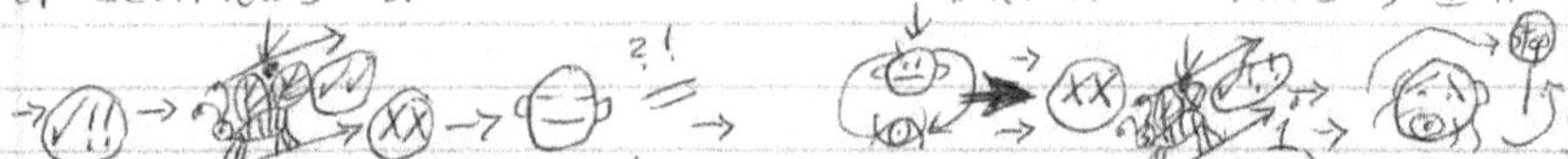

just be nonplussed I won't be the laziest;
just be nonplussed I won't be the laziest;

rather, I will try to go on any quest; that
rather, I will try to go on any faest; that

will be a must But in the end, I may be
will be a must But in the end, I may be

the one who is the craziest without creating a
the one who is the craziest without creating a

lot of fuss and muss Then I'll go away on
lot of fuss and muss Then I'll go away on

my magic carpet without working up a sweat
my magic carpet without working up a sweat

Even though I may make a large target still
Even though I may make a large target still

I will have no regrets As long as I don't
I will have no regrets As long as I don't

forget my little red Corvette and my private jet
forget my little red Corvette and my private jet

And make everything fit into my budjet Then I'll be right there in the
And make everything fit into my budjet Then I'll be right there in the

jet set
jet set

152

My Bouncing Baby Boy

353

My Bouncing Baby Boy

The greatest gift was brought into this world, to give
The greatest gift was brought into this world, to give

my first boy company and give him an emotional
my first boy company and give him an emotional

lift But instead, this wonderful child caused
lift But instead, this wonderful child caused

an awful rift and also made for a very long
an awful rift and also made for a very long

night shift He was meant to uplift, but instead
might shift He was meant to uplift, but instead

he came into this world full-blast and
he came into this world full-blast and

painfully swift But his body's spirit went
painfully swift But his body's spirit went

adrift in a gigantic change, an earth-shaking
adrift in a gigantic change, an earth-shaking

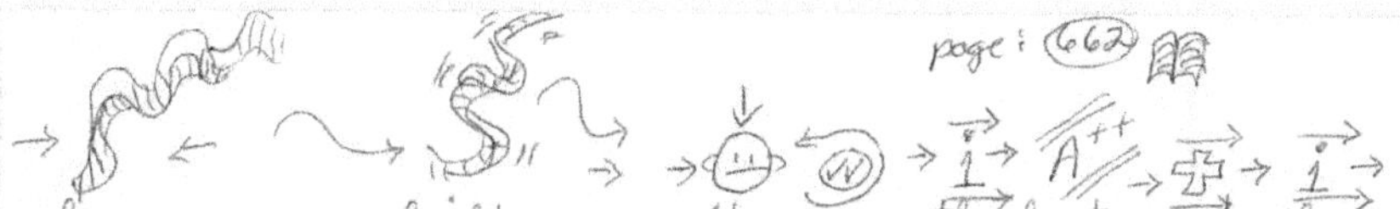

chromosome shift He was the best and the
chromosome shift He was the best and the

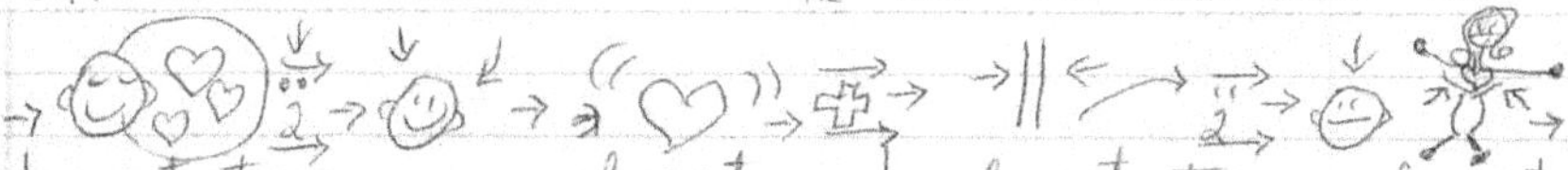

dearest to my heart and closest to my breast
dearest to my heart and closest to my breast

We were all, just his guests; he meant not to
We were all, just his guests; he meant not to

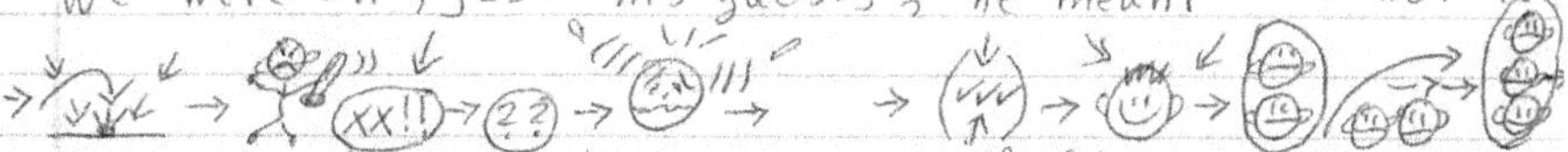

cause trouble or stress With him, we were all
cause trouble or stress With him, we were all

divinely blessed; he was our greatest conquest
divinely blessed; he was our greatest conquest

He was our greatest test; he made us all, greatly
He was our greatest test; he made us all, greatly

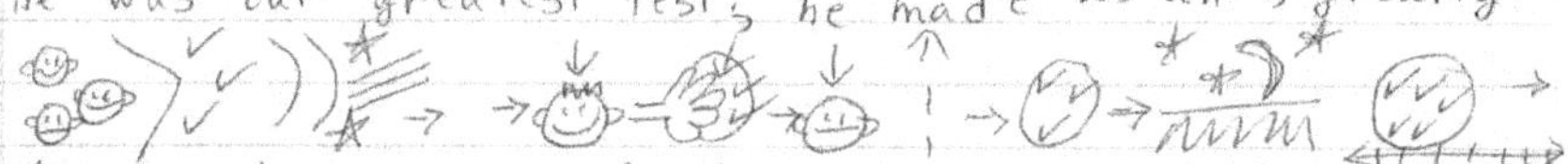

impressed He kept me up all night, every
impressed He kept me up all night, every

night, for seven years; I had to always
night, for seven years; I had to always

Keep him in my sight Staying awake took all
Keep him in my sight Staying awake took all

my might, especially without getting all uptight,
my might, especially without getting all uptight,
until he was asleep and out like a light I knew
until he was asleep and out like a light I knew
that he was my blessed responsibility, my privilege
that he was my blessed responsibility, my privilege
and my right; he had a short nap, and then holy
and my right; he had a short nap, and then holy
dynamite He was in my continual spotlight, all
dynamite He was in my continual spot light, all
through the day and during continual wintry
through the day and during continual wintry
nights and many frights It was very, very hard,
nights and many frights It was very, very hard,
but I am stubborn and I don't die easy — I die
but I am stubborn and I don't die easy — I die
hard I used all possible safeguards until I
hard I used all possible safeguards until I

was worn and battle-scarred I was his bodyguard;
was worn and battle-scarred I was his bodyguard;

I was his lifeguard; I used every possible wild card
I was his lifeguard; I used every possible wild card

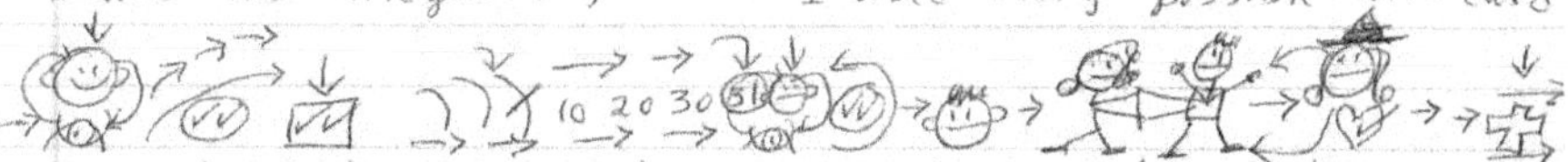

I went that extra yard; I was his armed guard, and
I went that extra yard; I was his armed guard, and

for his protection, I parried and I sparred I pulled
for his protection, I parried and I sparred I pulled

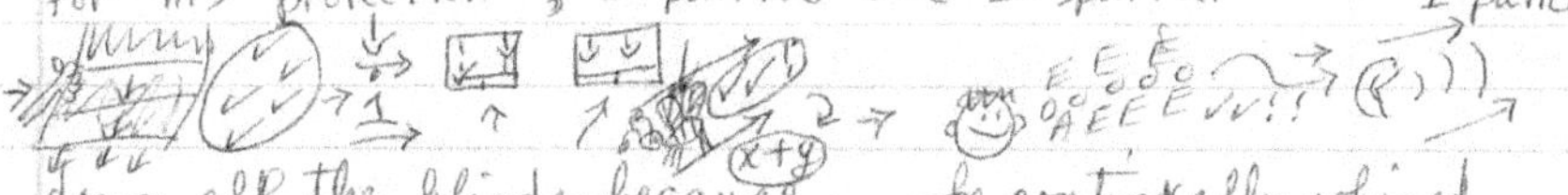

down all the blinds because he continually whined
down all the blinds because he continually whined

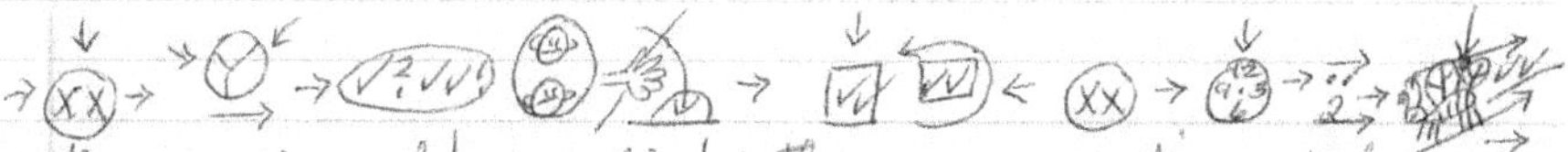

No peace could we find; there was no time to be
No peace could we find; there was no time to be

refined I was surely in a bind; to suffering I
refined I was surely in a bind; to suffering I

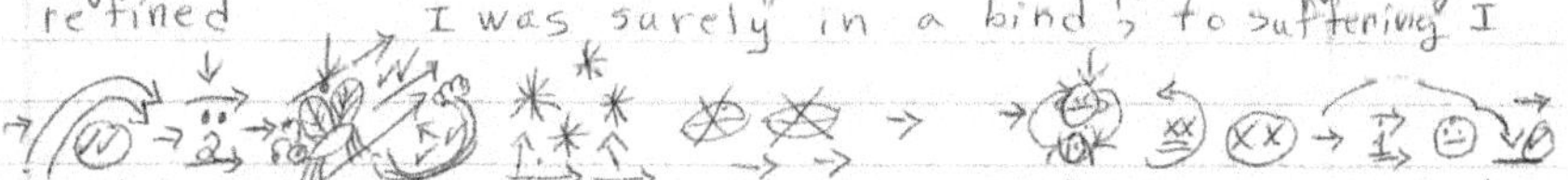

had to become snow-blind I wasn't ahead,
had to become snow-blind I wasn't ahead,

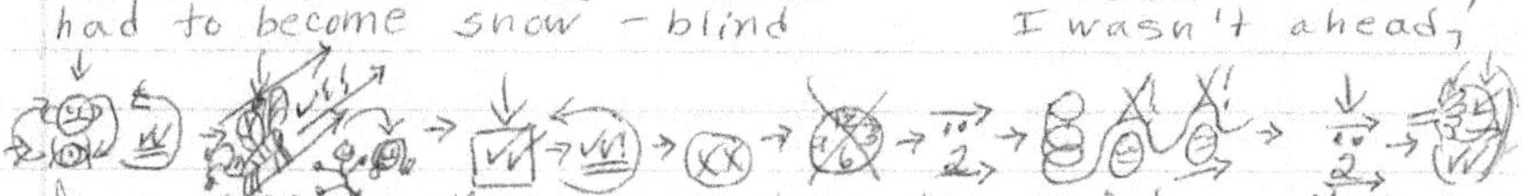

I was behind; there was no time to unwind To Keep
I was behind; there was no time to unwind To Keep

care of him, I knew I must; he didn't always
care of him, I knew I must; he didn't always

cry and fuss In me, he put all his hope, and
cry and fuss In me, he put all his hope, and

eventually he learned how to trust Keeping
eventually he learned how to trust Keeping

him happy was do, die, or bust; as he grew,
him happy was do, die, or bust; as he grew,

his medicines I gradually had to adjust I knew
his medicines I gradually had to adjust I knew

I must remain truly decent and just to
I must remain truly decent and just to

continue to keep him healthy and robust Why
continue to keep him healthy and robust Why

are you always so sad, my precious comrade;
are you always so sad, my precious comrade;

you are my hero, my Galahad A bad stroke of luck
you are my hero, my Galahad A bad stroke of luck

you have had; you had no choice in your
you have had; you had no choice in your

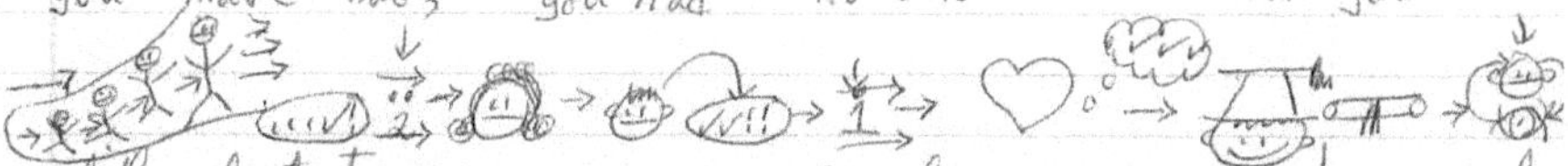

life, but to me, you are an honorary grad I
life, but to me, you are an honorary grad I

don't blame you for being angry or acting
don't blame you for being angry or acting

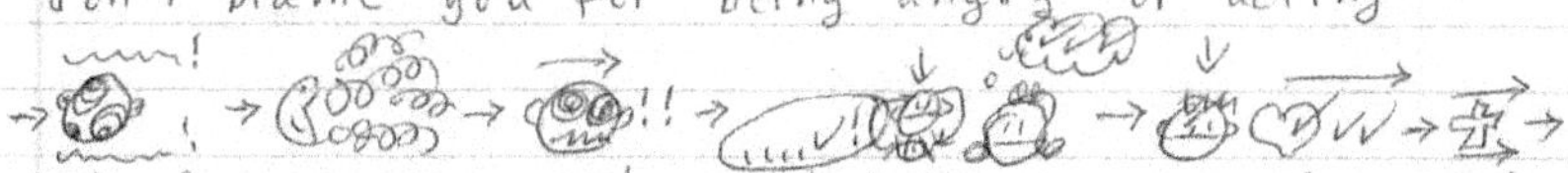

stark-raving mad, but I know you well, and
stark-raving mad, but I know you well, and

I think it is we that have been had Baby, please
I think it is we that have been had Baby, please

don't cry; I won't let you die. Laugh, you
don't cry; I won't let you die. Laugh, you

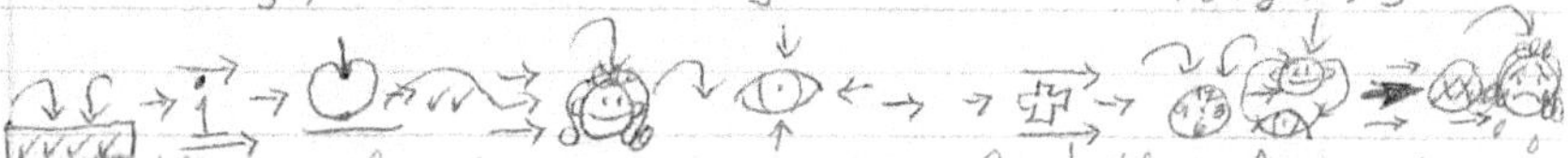

are the apple of my eye And then I won't cry,
are the apple of my eye And then I won't cry,

and both our victories will someday be nigh
and both our victories will someday be nigh

for you and I Have you got something in your eye?
for you and I Have you got something in your eye?

page 667

My guy, hush now, rock-a-bye I think
My guy, hush now, rock - a - bye I think

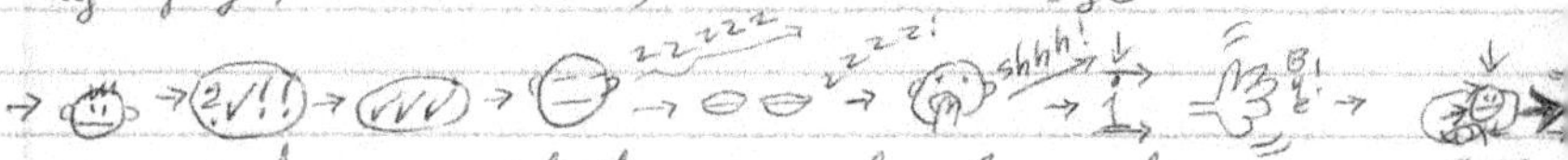

you need some shut-eye, hush-a-bye; I'll
you need some shut-eye, hush - a - bye; I'll

sing you a lullaby, my, my, my
sing you a lullaby, my, my, my

153 If It's All The Same 556

If It's All The Same

If it's all the same, I would like to continue to
If it's all the same, I would like to continue to

play in life's word game This is my aim
play in life's word game This is my aim

and my main claim to my uncontested personal
and my main claim to my uncontested personal

fame Using the right words in the right way will
fame Using the right words in the right way will

make everything a new ball game I must make
make everything a new ball game I must make

sure not to inflame or I most definitely
sure not to inflame or I most definitely

will be put to shame You do not recognize my
will be put to shame You do not recognize my

name or my face or happen to know me now
name or my face or happen to know me now

But soon, I will be quite familiar and you will

But soon, I will be quite familiar and you will

raise your eyebrows Nevertheless, I will try to

raise your eye brows Never the less, I will try to

be humble, and I will be the one to curtsy and bow

be hum ble, and I will be the one to curtsy and bow

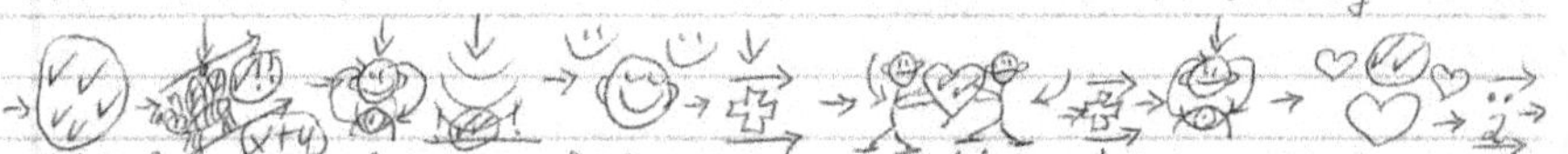

All because I am jolly and sociable and I love to

All because I am jolly and sociable and I love to

entertain you high and low First, I will try to put

entertain you high and low First, I will try to put

them to music and share all my favorite chords

them to music and share all my favorite chords

I will then put the words to music and share a

I will then put the words to music and share a

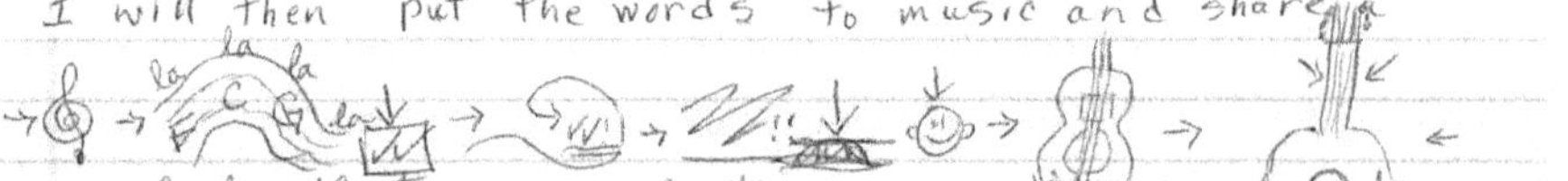

melody that comes fast on my guitar's boards

melody that comes fast on my guitar's boards

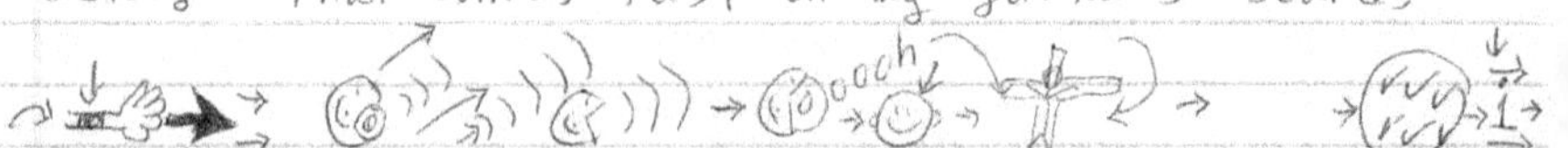

then will sing out loud "Oh, my Lord." All the

then will sing out loud "Oh, my Lord." All the

sounds are different from each other, not one,
but seven I will play an individual orchestra,
and I will play again and again They'll
make us all so happy; they will take us all
up to heaven I am hoping that they will raise
your spirits, like yeast (the very best leaven)
Did you hear the latest news, from the latest,
juicy descriptive clues? The names have been
changed so that we don't have to sing the

blues Have you heard the news, those strange
blues Have you heard the news, those strange

words, saying "I love you?" Or did someone
words, Saying "I love you?" Or did some one

stress that we must push for a veto and say
stress that we must push for a veto and say

"No can do." Somehow, the word story always
"No can do." Some how, the word story always

follows the same theme Here it is — it was, it is,
follows the same theme Here it is — it was, it is,

and then it had been It can be that which we
and then it had been It can be that which we

have yet to have seen Of course, we hear less than
have yet to have seen Of course, we hear less than

it really means So I'll try to be honest and
it really means So I'll try to be honest and

go and tell what's on my mind And I'll set
go and tell what's on my mind And I'll set

it to music, in noise, for everyone, not just
for the blind Then even they will know and won't
be left, in silence, far behind And those who see
will also hear and might find what they left
behind I'll be gracious with my music and my
words On a scale of which will be seen and might
be heard In the game of life, it has occurred to me;
some may consider me a nerd, which is totally absurd
I am no different than you; I feel as free as a bird

page: 673

154 Get Real 358

Get Real

(Version 1)

(Version 1)

What's the deal? Come on, get real You've got my

what's the deal? Come on, get real You've got my

approval, my seal you also have a certain appeal

approval, my seal you also have a certain appeal

Here's the deal I do not want porridge or oatmeal

Here's the deal I do not want porridge or oatmeal

Be daring and take me out for a tasty meal

Be daring and take me out for a tasty meal

You're my man, my hero, my superman Do

You're my man, my hero, my super man Do

you understand? You take up my whole

you understand? You take up my whole

attention span You'll always be my fan;

attention span You'll always be my fan;

you are no flash in the pan I'll give you a hand
you are no flash in the pan I'll give you a hand

and I'll do a happy can-can I love your company
and I'll do a happy can-can I love your company

my darling, sweet pea I love it when you're
my darling, sweet pea I love it when you're

close to me you are my VIP I love it when it
close to me you are my VIP I love it when it

is your face I see, tee-he My love is yours for
is your face I see, tee-he My love is yours for

free; you can use me to go on a personal
free; you can use me to go on a personal

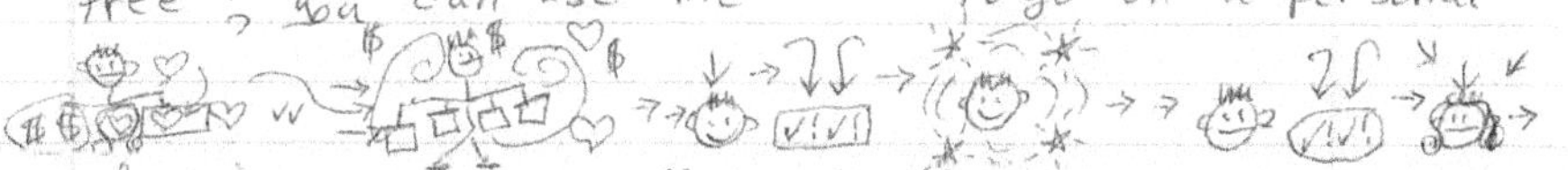

shopping spree You are awesome; you are my
shopping spree You are awesome; you are my

loving chum bum You're great, and then some
loving chums bum You're great, and then some

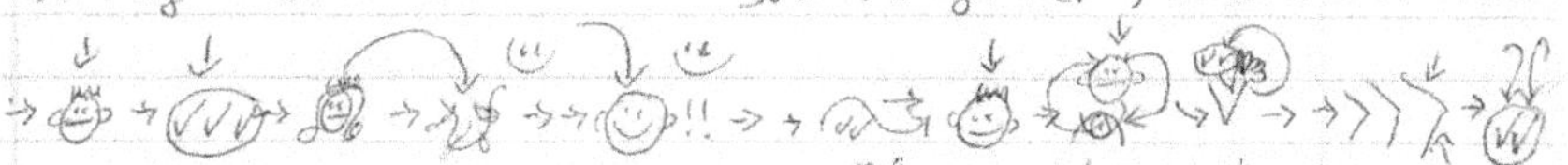

You are my yum-yum Of you, I want more of,
you are my yam-yam Of you, I want more of,

Fee Fi Fo! Fum!

fee-fi-fo-fum Gracious me, you're handsome
fee-fi-fo-fum Gracious me, you're handsome

I'm surely undone You are an awesome gent;
I'm surely undone You are an awesome gent;

{100%}

you are 100 percent Because you are heaven sent,
You are 100 percent Because you are heaven sent,

and with love, which is your main intent You
and with love, which is your main intent You

will destroy and rent and torment all discontent
will destroy and rent and torment all discontent

My armor is all broken and bent what a blessed
My armor is all broken and bent what a blessed

{x+y=v!}!!

event I know I am quite a handful, but I am
event I know I am quite a handful, but I am

no numbskull It is quite understandable even
no numbskull It is quite understandable even

though I am not dull And when there is a scandal
though I am not dull And when there is ascandal

I like being chock-full of wild wool   Our relationship
I like being chock-full of wild wool   Our relationship

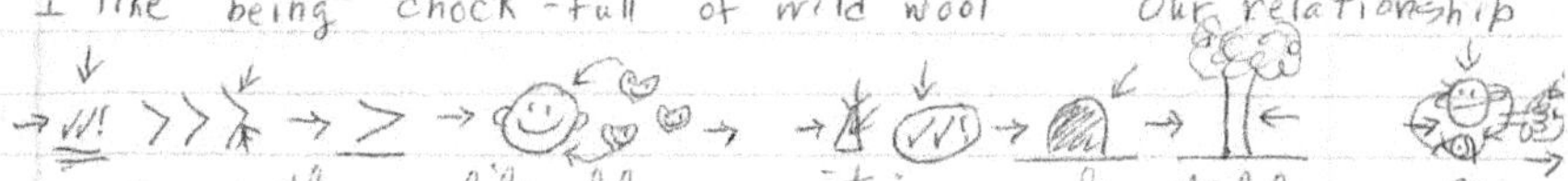

is more than likeable   it is rock stable   I've
is more than like able   it is rock stable   I've

never met anyone quite like you;   I think it is a
never met anyone quite like you;   I think it is a

breakthrough   You came to me out of the blue, just
breakthrough   You came to me out of the blue, just

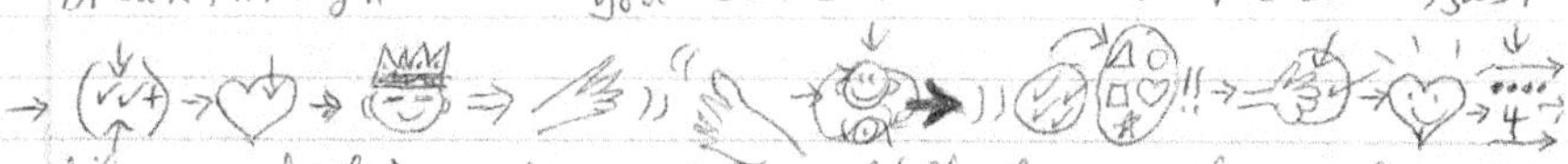

like good king, Kung fu   I'll always have love for
like good King, Kung fu   I'll always have love for

you too, just like lasting super glue   Our love will
you too, just like lasting super glue   Our love will

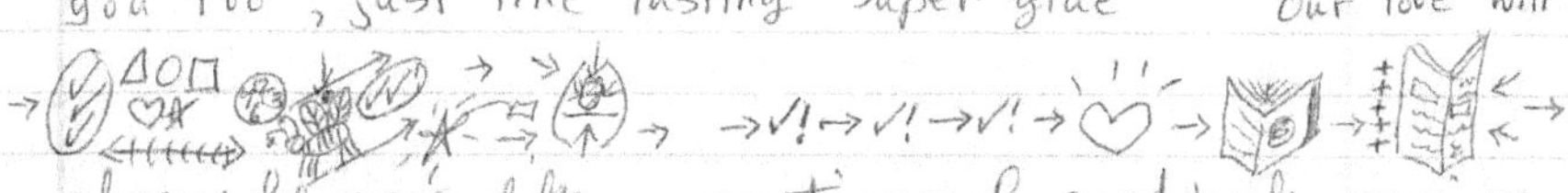

always be new, like   continuously good book reviews
al ways be new, like   continuously good book reviews

I'll never let you down; I'll be your happy clown
I'll never let you down; I'll be your happy clown

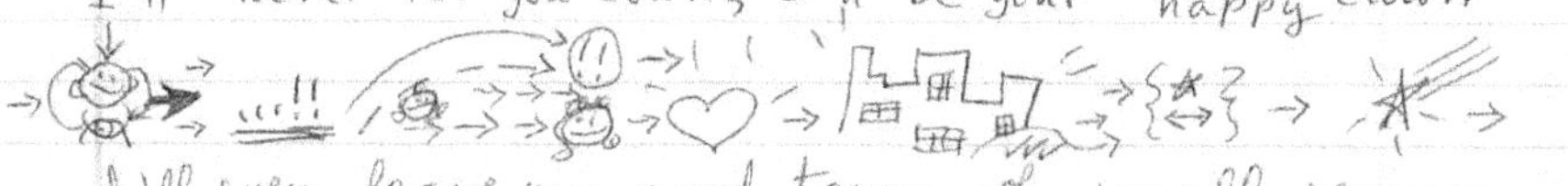

I'll even leave my good town of small renown
I'll even leave my good town of small renown

page: 677

I'll wear your wedding gown like it was a
I'll wear your wedding gown like it was a

graduating cap and gown I hope you want me
graduating cap and gown I hope you want me

also to be your own, like a porcelain doll from
also to be your own, like a porcelain doll from

Chinatown
Chinatown

page: 678

155 Get Real 360

Get Real

(version 2)

(vesion 2)

Get real, get real, and show me some honest zeal
Get real, get real, and show me some honest zeal

It's time for you and me to take the wheel You
It's time for you and me to take the wheel You

will learn how it feels to drive life's automobile
will learn how it feels to drive life's automobile

It's no big deal, but peel out; come on now,
It's no big deal, but peel out; come on now,

it'll heal to squeal The time is right to
it'll heal to squeal The time is right to

run the red light You will learn to use
run the red light You will learn to use

your right, to use flight You will learn to drive
your right, to use flight You will learn to drive

in the night with your night sight And you
in the night with your night sight and you

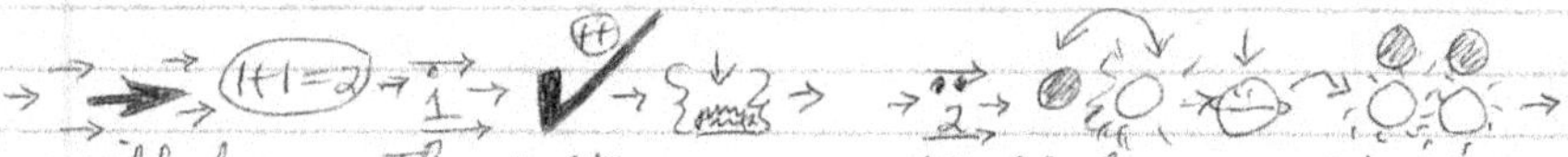

will learn the right way to flash your lights
will learn the right way to flash your lights

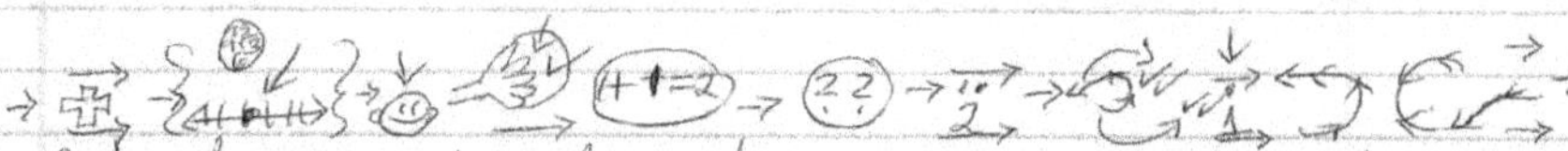

And when you have learned how to make a U-turn
And when you have learned how to make a U-turn

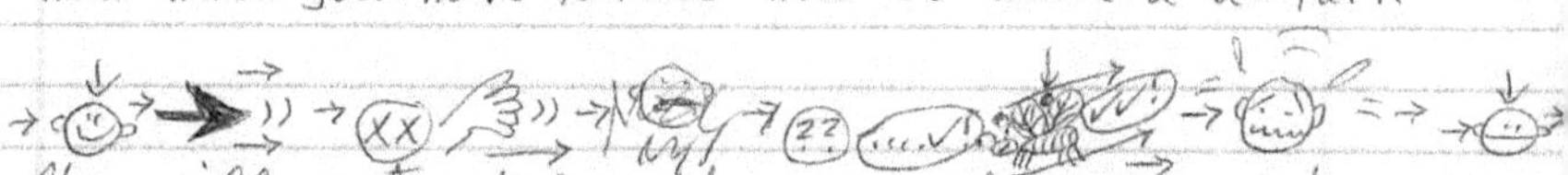

You will not get burned or even be concerned You
You will not get burned or even be concerned you

will have earned a place with Jules Verne And you
will have earned a place with Jules Verne And you

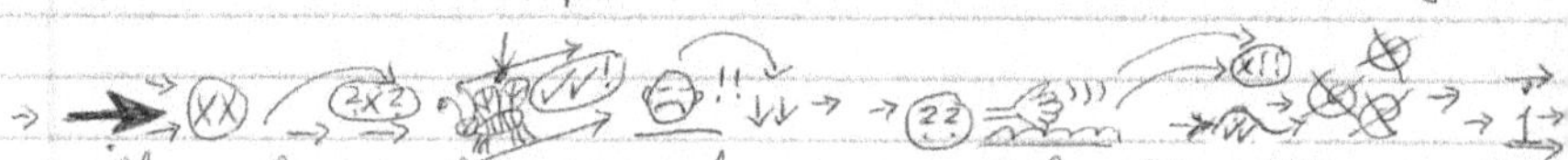

will no longer be spurned or feel out of turn The
will no longer be spurned or feel out of turn The

answer to your problem will be in life's race
answer to your problem will be in life's race

track, your playpen Which will no longer be
track, your playpen Which will no longer be

a conundrum because you'll go so fast,
a conundrum because you'll go so fast,

you'll puzzle all men And you will no longer have
you'll puzzle all men And you will no longer have

to run because you'll be in front, again and again
to run because you'll be in front, again and again

Your true nature will come out into the sun, you
your true nature will come out into the sun, you

darned son of a gun The truth will be revealed on
darned son of a gun The truth will be revealed on

the race-track field You will no longer have to
the race-track field You will no longer have to

yield because your victory will be sealed You'll
yield because your victory will be sealed You'll

be chuckling through the glass of your windshield
be chuckling through the glass of your windshield

And your victory seat will be on your own and
And your victory seat will be on your own and

two-wheeled You will be your own winner when
two-wheeled You will be your own winner when

you go to dinner You will feel like the superhero Flash
you go to dinner You will feel like the superhero Flash

as you speed by in a blur You will say gr when
as you speed by in a blur You will say gr when

your car goes purr; and what's more You
your car goes purr; and what's more You

will make quite a stir as a new model car
will make quite a stir as a new model car

emperor When you ring the bell, you will be
emperor When you ring the bell, you will be

able to tell in a nutshell That all is good and all
able to tell in a nutshell That all is good and all

is well and nothing will be withheld You'll save
is well and nothing will be withheld You'll save

yourself out of the clutches of hell that anyone
yourself out of the clutches of hell that anyone

will be able to tell You'll be the one ringing the
will be able to tell You'll be the one ringing the

victory bell when you take off self-propelled
victory bell when you take off self-propelled

Don't kid yourself, winning isn't all there is,
Don't Kid yourself, winning isn't all there is,

and you will find that out, in itself You can be
and you will find that out, in itself You can be

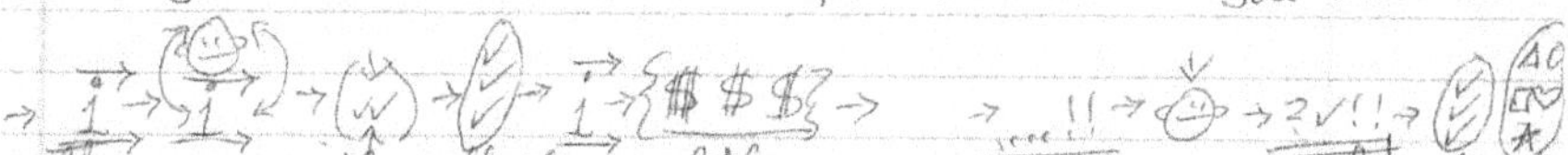

the one with all the wealth, but you should always
the one with all the wealth, but you should always

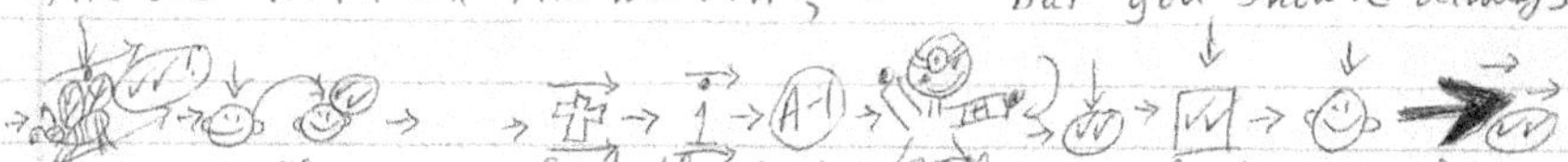

be yourself And the best health is what you will
be yourself And the best health is what you will

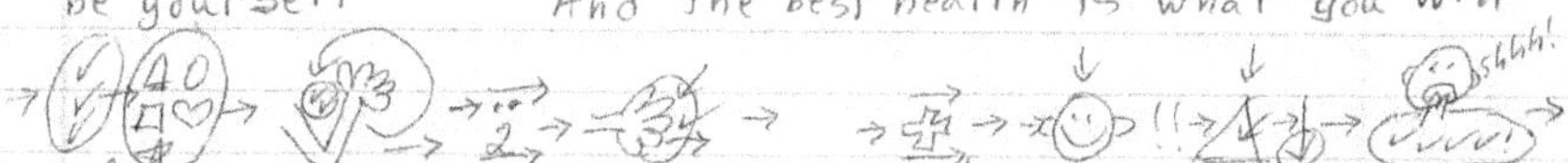

always want to have and enjoy it in stealth
always want to have and enjoy it in stealth

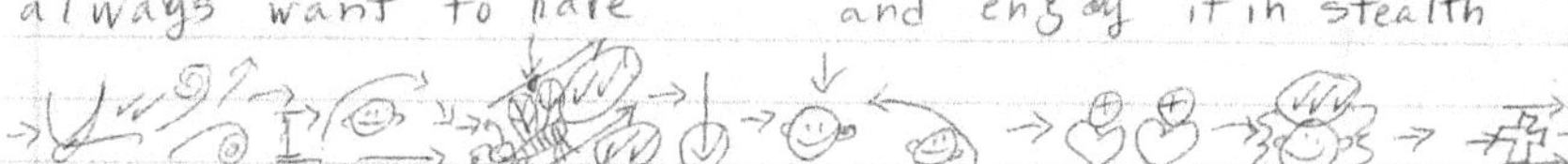

so go ahead, believe in your own true self and
so go ahead, believe in your own true self and

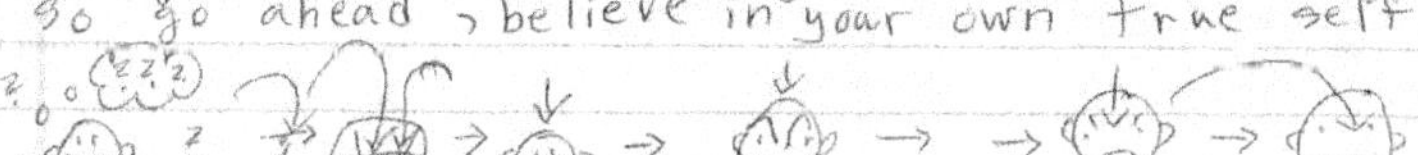

forget about your naughty inner self
forget about your naughty inner self

CPSIA information can be obtained
at www.ICGtesting.com
Printed in the USA
BVHW03*0953190718
522042BV00002B/18/P

9 781984 534729